EVA RAE THOMAS
THE
MYSTERY SERIES

MILLION-COPY BESTSELLING AUTHOR
WILLOW ROSE

Copyright Willow Rose 2019
Published by BUOY MEDIA LLC
All rights reserved.

No part of this book may be used or reproduced by any means, graphic, electronic, or mechanical, including photocopying, recording, taping or by any information storage retrieval system without the written permission of the author except in the case of brief quotations embodied in critical articles and reviews.

This is a work of fiction. Any resemblance of characters to actual persons, living or dead is purely coincidental. The Author holds exclusive rights to this work. Unauthorized duplication is prohibited.

Cover design by Juan Villar Padron,
https://www.juanjpadron.com

Special thanks to my editor Janell Parque
http://janellparque.blogspot.com/

To be the first to hear about new releases and bargains from Willow Rose, sign up below to be on the VIP List. (I promise not to share your email with anyone else, and I won't clutter your inbox.)

- GO HERE TO SIGN UP TO BE ON THE VIP LIST :
http://readerlinks.com/l/415254

Tired of too many emails? Text the word: "willowrose" to 31996 to sign up to Willow's VIP text List to get a text alert with news about New Releases, Giveaways, Bargains and Free books from Willow.

FOLLOW WILLOW ROSE ON BOOKBUB:
https://www.bookbub.com/authors/willow-rose

Connect with Willow online:

https://www.amazon.com/Willow-Rose/e/B004X2WHBQ
https://www.facebook.com/willowredrose/
https://twitter.com/madamwillowrose
http://www.goodreads.com/author/show/4804769.Willow_Rose
Http://www.willow-rose.net
madamewillowrose@gmail.com

DON'T LIE TO ME

EVA RAE THOMAS MYSTERY, BOOK 1

The secret of change is to focus all of your energy, not on fighting the old, but on building the new.

                                                            Socrates

Prologue
CAMP SEMINOLE SPRINGS, FLORIDA

"MOM. I don't want to stay at the camp for two weeks. I want to go home."

Sophie Williams choked back a sob as a tear left her right eye and rolled down her cheek. She had promised herself she wouldn't cry. She had promised herself she would complete this. But hearing her mother's voice on the phone had made her lose it. She couldn't hold it back anymore.

"I know, sweetie," her mother said. "I miss you too, baby. But it's only for two weeks. You'll be fine."

It was the first time Sophie had been away from her mother for this long. She was the one who had wanted to go when their scout leader had told them about the camp. Sophie had immediately known that she wanted to do this. But the other girls had been so mean on the bus ride there, and she had ended up sitting all alone without anyone to talk to. Now she felt lonely and, even though they weren't allowed to call home, she had snuck outside while they were eating dinner and walked back to her tent and found her phone in her backpack. She wanted to hear her mother's voice, just for a few seconds. But once she did, the tears piled up, and she felt so homesick it almost hurt.

"You'll be fine," her mother repeated. "It'll be over before you know it, and then you'll want to go again next year. I went through the same thing when I was your age."

"I'd much rather be at home and go surfing all summer," Sophie said.

"I know, baby, but you need to do other stuff too. You need to socialize with other children. Besides, you were the one who told me you wanted this, remember? You wanted to go to this camp with your new friends."

"But they're not my friends anymore," Sophie sighed.

"Really?" her mother said sounding tired. "That was fast."

Sophie knew her mother was disappointed. Sophie had never been good at making friends. That was why her mother suggested she join Girl Scouts. Sophie was homeschooled so she could focus on her competitive surfing on a daily basis and attend contests all over the country on the weekends. It was practically all she did in her life, and she loved it, but you didn't make any friends at surf contests. She would chat with other kids while waiting for her heat to start, yes, but in the end, they were competitors, and there was no room for friends. It was a lonely world for a twelve-year-old, especially since she was so young, yet better than most who were much older. Being a Girl Scout would be good for her, her mother had said. Plus, it would teach Sophie skills that would be beneficial later in life.

And Sophie had made friends. Marley and Grace had been her friends right from the beginning. But not anymore. Now they had turned their backs on her, for no apparent reason, and she was—once again—all alone.

"This is good for you," her mother said, and Sophie could tell she wanted to end the call. "Besides, it's only the first day. Sleep on it and then see if you don't feel different tomorrow when all the fun starts, okay?"

Sophie sighed. "Okay."

They hung up with an *I love you*, and Sophie put the phone back in her backpack. She glanced at her sleeping bag, then killed a mosquito that was sucking blood from her arm. Her legs were already covered in bug bites.

SOPHIE RETURNED to the main building and found the others in the common area. Marley and Grace stuck their heads together as she walked past them and whispered, not even bothering to keep it so low that she couldn't hear every word they said.

"Where do you think she's been?"

"Probably out signing with a new sponsor."

"You think her underwear is sponsored?"

"Of course, it is. She can't even eat anything unless it's sponsored by the right company. When she poops, it comes out wearing that sponsor's name."

They laughed. Sophie gave them a look, then went to sit with someone else. She tried smiling at a girl named Britney, thinking maybe she could be her friend, but Britney rolled her eyes at her and turned her head away. Sophie exhaled and looked down at the floor while one of their leaders, Miss Michaela, explained what they were going to do for the next couple of days. The camp was right next to a spring and tomorrow they were supposed to go canoeing. Sophie had been looking forward to that part, but there had to be two girls in each canoe, and she knew none of them would choose her.

"They're just jealous," her mother had told her over and over again all through her childhood when things like this happened. It didn't make things any better that she was chosen as surfer of the year by Ron Jon's Surf Shop and they had her displayed on their billboards all over town. All the adults thought it was so cool, but the kids not so much. The neighborhood's girls had mocked her and told her she looked fat in the picture and that their parents would never allow them to be on display like that for child-abductors to see and get crazy ideas.

"Does your mom *want* you to be kidnapped?" A girl named Victoria who lived on her street had asked.

"Of course not," another girl named Alison had said. "She's planning on living off her money for the rest of her life. Sophie is her golden goose, remember?"

"That's right," Victoria had answered. "Now that your dad left, she's counting on you to provide for her. That's why she's pushing you so hard. At least that's what my mom says."

Sophie felt anger rise inside of her when thinking about those girls. What did they know about her life anyway?

"All right, next up is a bonfire," the leader said and clapped her hands.

"Yay," the girls exclaimed. "S'mores!"

"And scary stories!" Miss Michaela said, then looked at Sophie, who didn't get up when the others did. She walked to her and reached out her hand toward her.

"You can sit by me," she said with a wink.

Sophie felt relieved. She hated to constantly sit alone. She grabbed Miss Michaela's hand in hers, then got up.

"To tell you the truth. I don't really like scary stories either," she said smiling. "But don't tell anyone."

Sophie didn't mind the stories, but she was happy that someone had finally spoken to her, so she simply nodded and held the hand tightly in hers.

At the bonfire, she stayed close to Miss Michaela, trying hard not to pay any attention to the other girls. As they sang songs and roasted marshmallows for s'mores, she thought about her mom and how she was going to call her in the morning and tell her she had made up her mind. Coming here had been a mistake. She wanted to go home. But she would at least finish the night. One night here could hardly hurt her.

THEY HAD BARELY FINISHED their s'mores when a loud thunderclap surprised them, sounding almost like the sky cracked above them. Seconds later, the rain came down hard and soaked their clothes.

"Quick. Everyone go to your tents," Miss Michaela yelled.

Sophie ran to hers and rushed inside, then closed it up. The sound of the rain on top of it was comforting. She had slept in tents many times in her life when going to surf contests where they had to stay the weekend. It was the cheapest way for them to stay the night, and usually, they would find a local camp and set up the tent. None of her friends knew this about her, how much she had to go through to get to where she was, even sleep in tents on frozen ground in the winter time when they attended contests up north. But back then, her mother couldn't afford a hotel room like many of the other contestants, not when it was almost every weekend that they went somewhere. In the beginning, when she had started to surf, they had only done the local contests in central Florida, but as she got better, she was soon invited to bigger contests out of state, sometimes all the way in California, and that soon became very expensive for her mother. Yes, she would win money, if she won, but that wasn't a given. Especially not in the beginning when she was so young and new to it.

It wasn't until she made the big leagues that the money started to come. That was when she got commercial contracts too, modeling for surf products and swimwear. That was where the money was.

Sophie grabbed her sleeping bag and opened it, then slid inside of it, thinking about her mother. They were really close since she was usually always with her wherever she went. Being away from her was a lot tougher than she had expected.

Sophie zipped up the sleeping bag and got comfortable while another tear escaped the corner of her eye. She wiped it away, then lay completely still, hoping for sleep to come quickly. She wanted this night to be over, so she could go home.

Some of the other girls were sharing tents, and she could hear them chattering and giggling as she tried to sleep. Seconds later, Miss Michaela shushed them, and they went quiet. Thinking she would finally be able to sleep, Sophie closed her eyes again and did a few of the breathing exercises that Coach Thomas had taught her to calm her down before a heat. She would always get a nervous stomach by the time they were about to enter the water, and it could throw her completely off balance. She loved surfing and the ocean, but not so much the fact that she had to constantly perform.

She enjoyed training for a competition way more than actually competing in it. But her mom was so proud of her for making it so far and for seeing her name and pictures in all the magazines and the local paper, that she never dared to say anything to her. But, if she was to be completely honest, all Sophie wanted was to surf for her own sake. Because it was fun. She didn't need the magazines or the fame or even to win. She liked it when she did but could be sick for days afterward if she didn't make it past the first round. Heck, even a quarterfinal wasn't enough to satisfy her mom anymore. She had to win, or it was the same as a failure.

"That's how real champions think," she always said.

Sleep, come on, sleep.

A hooting owl startled her, and her eyes popped wide open. Sophie stared into the ceiling of the tent, her heart pounding in her chest, then scolded herself for being such a wimp.

It was, after all, just an owl. She was out in nature, and there would be nature sounds. Sophie calmed herself down again using her breathing techniques, and soon her heart was beating normally again. She was about to close her eyes when the beam of a flashlight landed on the side of her tent.

Sophie gasped while her heartbeat ran amok. Seconds later, the beam disappeared.

Thinking it was probably just one of the leaders walking around to check on them, Sophie calmed herself down again. But now it was hard to fall asleep. Even harder than earlier. Sophie couldn't stop thinking that she had made a mistake in letting her mom talk her into staying the night. She should have insisted on going home tonight instead.

Sophie had barely managed to close her eyes again before she heard footsteps outside her tent. She laid completely still while listening to them come closer, then stared at the tent door, when the steps stopped right outside and lingered for a few seconds.

Maybe if you lay completely still, whoever is out there will go away.

But they didn't. The person outside bent down, zipped her tent open, then peeked inside. Before Sophie could even scream, this person grabbed her, then zipped up her sleeping bag until it covered her face completely. Sophie tried to scream and kick but was lifted off the ground and was soon moving swiftly through the night.

Chapter 1

THREE MONTHS LATER

"I'M CALLING DAD. He knows how to do it."

"No."

I stared at my twelve-year-old daughter, Christine. She was still holding her laptop in her arms. It had gotten a virus, and I had no idea how to fix it. The look in my eyes made her freeze.

"What do you mean, *no?*" Christine asked.

"Just what I said."

"But...?"

I shook my head while biting my lip. We'd had this conversation a lot lately, and it got to me every time.

"Dad's on his honeymoon, remember?" Alex, my six-year-old son, said from the other end of the kitchen counter. He was eating cereal with no milk because we had run out and I hadn't had time to buy more with all the unpacking I had to do. For some reason, my kids were like sponges when it came to milk, and no matter how much I bought, it was never enough. I couldn't believe how often I had to shop in order to keep up. After only a month as a full-time single mom, I was already quite overwhelmed.

It was Chad who had taken care of these things while the kids were growing up. He had the privilege of being able to work from home for his insurance company, and so he was the one who had taken care of most of the housework for years. Needless to say, I was quite in over my head ever since he decided to leave me for a younger model and become a full-blown midlife crisis cliché. Kimmie had legs to up above her ears and hair blonder than platinum, not to mention a waist so slim it looked to be the size of my thigh. She also had a teenage son, and now Chad wanted to start a family with her. A new family. He had told me that a month ago, exactly to the date. I was still recovering from the enormous shock that had destroyed my world, not to mention our children's.

"It's not a honeymoon, sweetie," I said. "That would require them being married, which they are not."

"Yet," my fourteen-year-old daughter, Olivia, grumbled from the doorway.

"Hi, honey, are you hungry?" I asked, hoping to take the conversation elsewhere. She shook her head. I was worried about her since she hadn't talked much to any of us since her dad told us he was going to live at Kimmie's apartment from now on.

I still couldn't believe he would do this to us…throw fifteen years of marriage down the drain just like that. No…*I am sorry*, or *I hate to do this to you all*. There were simply five devastating words—said over the phone—that still rung in my head:

I am not coming home.

"But, Mo-om, what do I do about my computer?" Christine asked.

I stared at her, then at the boxes behind her. The moving truck had brought it all two days earlier, and I still hadn't unpacked half of them.

"I don't know," I said with a deep sigh. "Maybe I can take it to an Apple store next week?"

"Next week?" she whined. "Next week? I can't wait that long. I have math I need to do."

"Use my computer," I said. "You can access Google classroom from anywhere."

Christine made an annoyed almost gasping sound. I could tell by the look on her face that the thought of being without her computer for more than an hour was too much for her to handle, let alone several days. I knew the computer was her entire life, next to her phone, naturally, but she was on that darn thing all day when she wasn't in school. I had no idea what she did on it, but so far, I hadn't given it much thought either. I was in way over my head here, and what she was doing on her computer was the least of my problems.

"I won't do it," she said with an air of finality like there was nothing I could do or say that would make her accept the fact. This computer had to be fixed, now. That was the only solution she would take. But I just didn't have time for it right now. I was planning on unpacking all day and then hopefully getting some work done before going to bed.

"I am sorry, sweetie," I said. "But it's the best I got. I can do it first thing Monday morning, okay?"

My daughter grumbled loudly, then placed the computer on the counter.

"This would never have happened if dad was here," she said, then walked out the door.

I swallowed with the sensation of guilt fluttering in my stomach. I could have told her off; I could have said something back to make her behave, but I didn't.

Because—let's face it—she was right.

Chapter 2

I HAD JUST HUNG up with the local pizza place when the doorbell rang. I opened the door and found my mom and dad on the other side. My mom held up a casserole for me.

"It's vegan," she said.

"Yum," I said without meaning it.

My mother looked at me victoriously. "I told your dad you didn't have time to cook."

I shrugged as they walked inside, and I closed the door behind them. "I ordered pizza. Does that count as cooking?"

My mom snorted. "Most certainly not. That's not food, Eva Rae Thomas. You really should start to think about what you eat."

She gave me a disapproving look, and I felt guilty once again. Yes, I had let myself go after the third child. And it hadn't been easy to eat healthy over the past few weeks with everything that had been going on. I did enjoy my comfort food. But so far, eating healthy wasn't exactly at the top of my long list of things to do. Right now, I was just surviving. I didn't care much what I looked like. I was just happy I wasn't in my PJs all day, crying over my failed marriage. That had to count for something, right?

"It's good to see you, Squirt," my dad said and kissed my cheek. *Squirt* had been his nickname for me since I was a child because I was the shortest in my family.

"The place looks better every time we come over."

I sighed comfortably. My dad. My private cheerleader and biggest fan. In his eyes, I could do nothing wrong, much to my mother's regret. She, on the other hand, believed I did everything wrong. I guess, between the two of them, you could say they landed on a healthy middle road. Maybe my dad just wanted to make up for what he saw my mom didn't give me. No matter what, I had spent most of my life trying to impress her, trying to get her to notice me and approve of me. Maybe even love me. Over the years, I had learned it was probably never going to happen.

"I was just finishing up another box in the kitchen," I said and guided them out there. My mother looked like she wasn't sure she could sit on the chairs and not get dirty.

"Sit down," I said, and they did, my mother brushing her seat off first.

"Can I get you something? A glass of wine?" I asked. "Beer?"

"I could do with a beer," my dad said.

He received a look from my mom, but I still served him one, knowing he wasn't allowed to have any at home. Not since my mom got on her health kick, ever since my dad was hospitalized with a colon disease that they had initially thought was cancer but turned out to be just an infection. Other than that, he was as strong as an ox and ran on the beach three times a week. But my mom only saw the disease and, over the past two years, she had been almost hysterical about what he ate or drank. I figured she had been terrified of losing him and scared of the loss of control she had suddenly felt, and therefore thought, if only she controlled what he ate, she could somehow get some stability in the chaos she felt inside. Emotions weren't easy for my mother and, over the years, I had learned to read between the lines to figure out how she really felt. I guess I never really felt like I knew her very well, but it had gotten better. I wanted it to. I wanted to be closer to them both, and that was why I had decided to move back to Cocoa Beach, where I was born and raised.

My dad drank from the beer with a satisfied expression on his face while my mom looked like I had served her lemon juice.

"We should probably eat that casserole while it's hot," she grumbled and got to her feet. "I'll set the table. Where are your plates?"

"In one of the brown boxes over there," I said and pointed at a stack of boxes leaning against the wall.

"You haven't even unpacked your plates?" she said. "You've been here a week?"

"I haven't gotten to it yet. Besides, the boxes only came two days ago."

"But still…? You certainly…you must have plates. What have you been eating from?" she asked, appalled.

"Pizza boxes, using napkins," I said with a shrug.

"Why, I have never. Why would you do that? You have children, Eva Rae Thomas. They need plates. They need things to be like they used to be. They need stability."

I bit my lip, knowing she wasn't actually talking about plates anymore. This was about something else. I knew she blamed me for Chad leaving us. Of course, she did. Why wouldn't she? She had never approved of me working and having a career.

"Yeah, well, you can't really control everything in life, can you? Sometimes you have to improvise, work with what you've got," I said, then walked to the counter and poured myself a glass of wine.

Chapter 3

DINNER WENT DECENT. My mom tried hard not to criticize me too much in front of the kids, which I could tell took quite an effort. Meanwhile, my dad hung out with Alex, and they talked about fire trucks, which was Alex's favorite subject to discuss. During the conversation, Alex got really loud and was almost yelling. My mom sent me a look.

"Alex, sweetie, remember to use your inside voice," I said, then added, "Grandma has a hangover and doesn't like loud noises."

"What's a hangover, Grandma?" Alex asked while my mom hissed at me.

"Eva Rae Thomas..." she turned and looked at my dad. "Jon, did you hear what she said?"

My dad and I locked eyes, and he struggled not to laugh. I chuckled, then grabbed another piece of pepperoni pizza. My mom gave me a disapproving look, but I ignored her. No one had touched her casserole except for herself. Even my dad had thrown himself at the pizza, and I was just happy that I had ordered the family size, so there was enough for everyone.

Alex grabbed my dad by the hand and pulled him up to his room to show him all his books on fire trucks. I loved seeing the two of them together. It was great for Alex to have a male role model these days, and not many understood him. I had enrolled him in my old elementary school, Theodore Roosevelt Elementary School, as soon as we got here, but almost every day he had come home with notes from the teacher about his bad behavior. He was loud and refused to sit still, she said. It was never a problem before, so I told her it was probably all the new things going on in his life, plus the fact that his dad wasn't with him anymore. But as I said that to his teacher, I realized I actually didn't even know if it had been an issue earlier in his life. Chad and I had drifted apart over the past several years and hadn't talked much about those things. And the last thing I wanted was to call him in Greece and ask. I was determined to do this myself without his help. He was the one who had decided to pick up and leave. I was these children's mother. Of course, I could take care of them, even if it had to be alone.

"He's very loud, isn't he?" my mom said in almost a whisper. "And wild. Keep an eye on him all the time. You heard about that girl who was kidnapped recently, right?"

I had. How could I not? It was everywhere. It was all over the news constantly; they had put up posters downtown, and it was on the lips of everyone I met. A young girl, twelve years old, and a local surf-idol, the new Kelly Slater, if there ever was one, had gone missing from a Girl Scout camp three months ago. They had made several arrests but not found who took her yet, nor had they found her. As every day passed, it became less and less likely they'd find her alive. From my experience, it was very improbable that she would show up alive after so long. Still, the locals kept up their hope. Some even believed her father had taken her since there had been a dispute between the parents during their divorce. But her dad had been questioned, and there had been no sign that he might have taken her. Personally, I thought the local police seemed to have let him off a little easy since I would have gone harder on him, knowing kidnappings were most often done by family members, but it wasn't my case, and I was done with that part of my life.

"You need to keep him home till it's safe to go out," my mom continued. "Till they catch this guy. Especially with that wild nature of his. He might get himself in trouble, you know. He's trouble waiting to happen. I see it in his eyes. He's got that crazy look. I don't see it in other children. Lord knows, I never saw it in mine."

I shrugged. My mom never had boys; how would she know if he was wilder than others?

"He's a boy," I said. "They get wild sometimes. There's nothing wrong with him. He's just been through a lot lately."

"He sure has," she said and gave me another look.

"Okay, just say it, will you?" I said, sensing I had to stop with the wine now before I said something I would regret later on.

But my mom didn't. She never said anything directly to me. It was all between the lines and in her looks. I felt like screaming at her to just speak out. Just be honest.

"Say what?" she asked.

"You blame me for Chad leaving, don't you?" I swallowed the lump that was growing in my throat. "Because, of course, it's my fault, just like everything else in life. Ever since…that day. Was it also my fault dad got an infected colon, huh?"

She shook her head, then looked away.

I felt tears pressing behind my eyes and couldn't really hold them back anymore. A couple rolled down my cheeks. I felt so helpless, so lost. I had rented this strange house and had no idea if I would be able to afford to live in it. I didn't even know how to buy enough milk for my kids.

I stared at my mother, secretly praying she would stretch out her arms and just hold me. But she didn't. She spotted the tears, then sat there like she was paralyzed and looked at me before she finally rose to her feet.

"It's late. We should probably get home. Your dad needs his rest. Eight hours every night, per doctor's orders."

I can't even remember the last time you touched me, Mom. Can't you just give me a hug? Can't you just put your arm around me and tell me it'll be all right? That I am going to make it?

I looked after my mom as she walked up to Alex's room to get my dad. Seconds later, they had both left, and I was once again alone with my thoughts, the smell of vegan casserole lingering in my nostrils.

I wiped away my tears and finished my glass of wine, reminding myself I had decided not to feel sorry for myself in this, when Alex climbed into my lap and attacked me with a toy fire truck, making me laugh. I rustled his hair and kissed his forehead with a sniffle.

"We're going to be fine, aren't we?" I asked the child like he understood.

He gave me one of his endearing smiles. "I like it better here, Mom. You're home a lot more, and you don't yell as loud as Dad. Besides, you smell better."

"I sure do," I said, chuckling, hugging my son closer.

Chapter 4

THE LIGHT IS BRIGHT, almost too bright, and it hurts my eyes as I look up to the ceiling. I can't find my mom. Sydney is standing a few steps to my right, looking at a doll. Mom went down another aisle, and I don't know which one. Panic is about to erupt, but I don't dare to cry. My sister will only think I am a wimp.

"Are you lost, little girl?"

I look up. The man has no face in the light coming from behind him. He's wearing a green sweater. It's winter in Florida.

"No."

"Tsk. Tsk. Don't lie to me, little girl."

I shake my head. "I am not. Mommy's right over there."

He looks but can't see her. Neither can I, but I won't admit it. I don't want him to know that I don't know where my mom is. I feel scared. Sydney doesn't see anything. She keeps pulling Barbie dolls down from the shelves.

"Let me take you to her," the man says.

The faceless man grabs my arm and pulls. I freeze up. A lady passes with her cart, pushing it in front of her. The man smiles at her, then explains that his daughter is upset because he wouldn't get her a toy. The woman tells him her son just threw a fit because she wouldn't give him candy, then continues, smiling at me. I want to scream, but I don't. Why don't I?

I WOKE UP WITH A START, bathed in sweat, gasping for air, heart thumping in my chest. It was still dark out, and my phone told me it was three in the morning. I couldn't sleep, so I got up, then walked down to the kitchen and grabbed a glass of water. In the dark window, I spotted my own reflection, then thought I saw the faceless man standing behind me, I gasped and pulled away. I closed my eyes for a few seconds, reminding myself it was nothing but a dream, then took in a few deep breaths before I once again opened my eyes and the man was gone.

    I drank some more water while trying to get the dream out of my mind, but it didn't help. I then decided to go for a run. I found my running clothes and left the house, then ran down my street, where all the dark houses stared back at me.

    With music blasting loudly in my ears, I ran through my new neighborhood where the houses had canals on both sides of them and boats in their backyards. Since I had grown up in Cocoa Beach, I still knew my way around town, and soon I was running down Minutemen Causeway toward downtown, panting loudly. It wasn't a very big town, and one that lived mostly off tourism and the notorious snowbirds that came down from up north and stayed the winter in their condos on the beach.

    I ran past City Hall that also housed the police station, and the newly built fire station next to it that I had promised Alex we'd visit one day. I continued down to the beach and turned left, running toward the pier. As my feet hit the sand by the restaurant, Coconuts on the Beach, I began to run faster, trying to get rid of that grisly feeling the dream had left me with, trying to shake every emotion it had stirred up inside of me. You might say I was trying to run from it, but I wasn't doing a very good job. No matter how fast I went, no matter how much I pushed myself to my maximum, I couldn't get rid of it. Soon, I ran out of energy and had to stop, realizing I was very far from the shape I used to be in. The past few years had been a lot of desk work and, even though I tried my best to keep in shape, I had to admit I hadn't been doing enough. It was one of my promises to myself when I decided to leave my job and come down here, to get back in shape. Three children, too many pastries, and no exercise hadn't done much good for my body. To think I had once been the fastest in our unit.

    You're forty-one, Eva Rae. You're not dead yet. You can still get it back.

    I sat in the sand by the pier and stared out at the ocean so calm and beautiful. The moonlight was glittering on the surface, and I suddenly remembered all the evenings I had hung out here with my friends, drinking beer under the pier when we weren't allowed to yet, listening to Michael Jackson on cassette tapes, sitting around bonfires till the police chief came by and told us to get out of there, confiscating our beers. We knew he wouldn't tell our parents if we let him take the beers for him and his colleagues. That was how things worked back then. I wondered if kids still hung out under the pier at night. Cocoa Beach was the kind of town that didn't really change much, and right now, that was exactly what I needed. I'd had change enough for a lifetime over these past couple of weeks.

Chapter 5

I STAYED under the pier for a few more minutes, thinking about Chad and our life together, then cursed him for ruining everything, before once again ending up blaming myself because I hadn't taken proper care of what I had. It was the same circle of thoughts that would rush through me every night and even during the daytime.

Then I decided it was time to get back. Alex had suffered from nightmares a lot since his dad left, and I couldn't risk he would wake up and come to my room and not find me there. Luckily, his two older sisters were there in case it happened, and to my regret, he more often than not crept into Christine's bed instead of mine. I guess it had become a habit of his over the past several years since I had been away a lot on the job, and was often gone at night when they needed my assistance somewhere in the country.

I liked to tell myself I was saving lives, that I was doing something good, but I wasn't sure it had been worth it. Was it worth losing my marriage?

I got up, then brushed the sand off my behind, glanced once more across the ocean, then turned around and ran back, this time running a little slower, so I didn't exhaust myself quite as much. It took a little longer, but I felt better. When I walked up past the restaurant area by the beach, I thought I saw something and paused. A car was parked in the alley between Coconuts and Fat Kahunas, really close to the Hunkerdown Hideaway Bar. But all the restaurants and bars were closed now. A figure was by the car, just standing there, motionless. I stopped running and walked toward downtown, through the small square that had recently been renovated and closed to cars. I watched this figure in the alley as I walked by and felt like the figure was watching me as well, even though I couldn't see a face. I shivered even though it was eighty degrees out, thinking about the faceless man and almost felt the grab on my arm again. I walked faster, my eyes fixated on the figure that wasn't moving.

Are you lost, little girl?

I could still hear the faceless man's voice in my mind. My heart was pounding in my chest while I rushed past the alley, and soon I was running again. I was certain I heard footsteps behind me, but as I turned to look, no one was there. I ran as fast as I could down Minutemen Causeway and into my house, where I, wheezing and panting, threw myself on the floor after closing and locking the door thoroughly behind me.

You've gotta relax, Eva Rae. It was probably just someone going home after a night on the town. It was probably just some drunk.

I coughed while trying to calm my poor beating heart down. Meanwhile, I kept seeing the faceless man and feeling him grab my arm.

Don't lie to me, little girl. I noticed you were all alone.

When I caught my breath, I showered, then as my head hit the pillow once again, I finally managed to doze off. I got two hours of deep dreamless sleep before the door to my room slammed open, and Alex stormed inside, dressed in his full-blown fireman outfit that I had bought for Halloween, screaming FIRE, then pretending to rescue me.

"Alex, it's Sunday; please let me sleep, will you?" I moaned tiredly.

But it was too late. The boy yelled STOP, DROP, and ROLL, then started to pull my arm, trying to get me out of bed, then continued screaming DANGER, DANGER, swinging his plastic toy ax around, knocking down my lamp.

I sighed, then realized I might as well get up. I stumbled down the stairs, dreaming of coffee when I realized we were completely out. I looked at my phone. It was six o'clock. I wondered if anything in this sleepy town was open at this time, then decided something had to be. The gas station or Publix maybe?

Alex was screaming loudly and jumping on the furniture—the little I had since Chad had taken half of it—while saving imaginary people from an imaginary fire, and my head began to hurt. I knew I had to find coffee somehow. I grabbed my car keys and looked at my screaming son, realizing I couldn't leave him here. He would tear the place apart before I made it back, and both his sisters were still sound asleep.

"Alex, we're going for a drive. Come."

"Yay, a drive! In the fire truck?" he exclaimed.

I smiled and nodded. "Yes. The big one. With the ladder. There's a fire downtown we need to put out."

"Then, we must hurry," he said, as he swung his ax and stormed out the front door, holding onto his fire helmet with one hand. "Come on, Mom!"

I trotted after him, feeling soreness in my legs from the run. What was I thinking? Going for a run in the middle of the night? It wasn't very like me. It had been a long time since I had last run like that, and I knew it was going to make me sore for days.

Getting in shape was harder than I had expected.

I strapped Alex into the back of my minivan, and we drove toward downtown, him wailing like a siren the entire way.

Chapter 6

AUBREY SIMMS YAWNED LOUDLY. She could barely see out of her eyes as she staggered around the corner, her two-year-old daughter pulling her arm while pointing and yelling behind her pacifier.

"Beach! Beach!"

Aubrey yawned again and followed her young, energetic daughter while dreaming about her bed. It was way too early to go to the beach if you asked her. The sun had barely risen yet. The sky was changing colors like it was preparing for its arrival, but it was still pretty dark out.

Going on a vacation with her daughter wasn't exactly how she had thought it would be. Naively, she had dreamt of long days at the beach, where she would lie in a chair working on a tan while her daughter played happily for hours in the shallow water or she would be swimming in the cool ocean while her daughter built sandcastles.

Boy, had she been wrong.

Just packing for a toddler had turned out to be quite an ordeal. Just the diapers alone had filled an entire suitcase, along with washcloths. And she had almost forgotten her special zip-up blanket that makes sure she isn't strangled at night. Not to mention the organic sunscreen and mosquito repellant, just to mention a few things.

But that wasn't the worst part. No, the packing she had done pretty fast. It was more the throwing up on the airplane, the diaper leaking accident in the Uber, and then there was the part about her getting up at five-thirty every morning begging to go to the beach. It would have been fine had the child only been able to entertain herself once they got down there, but, oh, no. Aubrey had to constantly observe her since otherwise she would run into the water on her own, or simply take off down the beach, running after birds or talking to people she didn't know. Aubrey usually wasn't overly protective, but she knew she had to keep an eye on the girl constantly, and it exhausted her immensely. There was no time for her to simply sit in a chair and work on her tan or even bathe comfortably in the ocean. There was a lot of crying and a lot of constant running from early morning to late at night. And if she didn't put her down for a nap during the day? Forget it. The rest of the day was completely destroyed with crying inconsolably and even screaming and throwing herself on the ground in a fit of rage when she didn't get her way.

It was true. She would never tell anyone, but Aubrey couldn't wait for this so-called vacation to be over, so she could go back to New York.

Now, they turned the corner toward the beach entrance next to the restaurant, where Aubrey had bought French fries for her daughter every day for lunch all week. She had done it even though it filled her with such a deep sense of guilt—just to make her sit still and be quiet for even just a few minutes so Aubrey could breathe.

As they turned the corner, Ani's hand slid out of her mother's, and she began to run.

"Beach! Beach!"

Realizing her daughter's hand was no longer in hers, Aubrey rushed to catch up with her. Aubrey yanked her daughter's arm and pulled her back and was about to scold her for running away when she spotted something odd in the middle of the pavement. They had recently renovated the area and made it look nice.

"What's *dad*, mommy?" Ani said and pointed.

Aubrey shrugged. "Probably a homeless person," she said, knowing her daughter had no idea what a homeless person was. She stared at the sleeping bag that was zipped completely shut, but there was definitely someone inside of it.

"That's odd. Who sleeps in the middle of a street like that?"

Even for a drunk, this was an odd place to sleep. Yes, the area was closed to traffic, but still. There could be trucks coming to unload food or drinks for the restaurants or the bar next to them. They didn't open till ten o'clock, but people working there would most surely arrive soon. And in a few hours, the place would be crawling with tourists walking to the beach or the restaurants. Whoever it was could get hurt.

"Someone ought to do something," she mumbled, biting her lip and hoping it wouldn't have to be her. She looked around to see if anyone else was out, but the area was completely void of people. Even the Hunkerdown Hideaway on the corner was closed, and the drunks had left.

Aubrey looked down at her daughter, then shrugged. "Guess there's just us, then."

She walked to the sleeping bag, then knelt down next to it. Her daughter imitated her every move and sat next to her in the exact same manner, chewing on her pacifier, waiting to see what her mother was up to next, probably thinking it was all some fun game Mommy had come up with.

"Hello?" Aubrey said. "You can't sleep here."

The sleeping bag didn't move. It remained eerily still, and there was something about it that made the hairs rise on Aubrey's neck. There was a stench that made her stomach churn.

Heart in her throat, Aubrey poked the person inside the sleeping bag. Still, no movement.

"Hello?"

Her daughter chewed her pacifier very pensively, then imitated her mother and poked the person too.

"Hello?"

Her daughter shook her head and threw out her arms.

"No one's home?"

Aubrey locked eyes with her daughter, then decided she'd have to take action. This person was in danger. If he was passed out drunk, there was no other way. She'd have to wake him up or move him to the side of the street. She grabbed the zipper and pulled it down.

With a gasp, she recoiled, and seeing her, Ani did the same. Next, Aubrey grabbed her daughter in her arms and ran down the street, both of them screaming.

Chapter 7

THANK GOD FOR GOOD BRAKES. I almost hit them with my car as they rushed into the street without looking where they were going. I stepped on the brakes, and the car skidded sideways and finally came to a halt.

Heart in my chest and panting in fear, I jumped out of the car.

"What the heck are you doing?"

The young mother and her young child in her arms both had terrified looks in their eyes. She tried to speak but didn't make much sense. She was gasping between the words.

"There...there's a...up there," the mother said, pointing. Her daughter was crying helplessly.

Thinking someone had tried to hurt them, I turned to look up the closed-off street, but they were all alone except for something lying on the pavement. The mother whimpered slightly, then caught her breath and spoke.

"There. Over there."

I stared at what she was pointing at. It looked like a sleeping bag.

"Stay here with my son, will you?" I asked. "I'm gonna have a look."

The woman nodded, then walked closer to my car that had ended up on the side of the road. Meanwhile, I approached the sleeping bag, bracing myself for whatever could be inside of it.

Was it some homeless person? Maybe he had died in his sleep? Maybe that was why she was so upset?

I decided that had to be it, then walked even closer, but as I did, my heart began to thump harder in my chest. As I moved closer, a face was being revealed from inside the sleeping bag that had been zipped down just enough for me to see it.

I clasped my mouth and gasped as the realization sank in. This was no homeless man who had drunk too much or even died in his sleep. No, this was a young girl, and I knew exactly who she was.

"Oh, dear God," I said, pressing back my tears.

Fumbling, I reached inside my pocket and found my phone. Then I dialed a number. It wasn't 911. Instead, I called the guy I knew would want to know about this first. The man I had watched on TV talk about the young surfer girl's disappearance over and over again. His name was Matt Miller, and he was a detective with the Cocoa Beach Police Department. He was also an old friend.

"Hello, Matt?"

"Who's this?" he asked, sounding sleepy and confused.

"It's Eva Rae."

A long pause.

"Eva Rae Thomas?" He suddenly sounded less tired. "Really?"

I bit my lip and looked at the dead girl in front of me. In the background, the woman and her child were still crying.

"Yes, really. I need you to come downtown. By Coconuts. I...I've found your girl."

He went quiet for a few seconds, then sighed profoundly.

"I'll be right there."

Chapter 8

IT TOOK him less than five minutes before he drove up and parked behind me. He rushed out and ran toward me. As I spotted him, my heart skipped a beat. I hadn't seen Matt in maybe twenty years, but he still looked the same. Older, yes, but that didn't make him any worse. Like many other men, he had gotten even more attractive with age. I didn't know how they did it.

His eyes locked with mine and he ran a hand through his thick hair that was brown but had been lightened by the sun and looked almost blond in places. It was a side effect of surfing and something a lot of the locals walked around with around here. Everyone surfed. Even the mayor and the city commissioners you would meet in the line-up in the water. I used to surf too as a child and teenager but hadn't been out there in many years. I often wondered if I still remembered how. I was a lot heavier now than I had been back then.

"You sure it's her?" he said, wrinkling his forehead.

"I have no doubt," I said.

He nodded heavily. "Okay."

He knelt next to the girl. I did the same. "The woman over there thought it was a homeless person and was worried he would get hit by a truck or something, then went to take a look. She zipped it down and spotted the girl, then ran into the street, where I almost hit her with my car. I took one glance at her, then called you."

He swallowed. "Thank you."

Matt then grabbed the side of the bag and pulled it down to get a better look. As her face came completely into the light, I could tell his hand began to shake. Sobs emerged from his throat and, even though he tried to choke them back, he didn't succeed. Sobbing and gasping for breath, he pulled the zipper further down, so the girl's small body came into the light.

Then, he lost it. He sobbed and bent forward, crying, touching her long blonde hair between his fingers. "Oh, dear God, Sophie. What have they done to you?"

Knowing Cocoa Beach, I realized that Matt, of course, knew this girl very well and probably her parents too. I fought my tears as I wondered just how hard this was going to hit this small community, losing one of their own.

"Maybe we should not touch anything," I said, trying to remain professional. I wondered if this was the first time Matt had been called out to a dead child before. I had a feeling it was. I, on the other hand, had seen my fair share. I remembered each and every one of them and knew their faces. I knew what it was like. I knew it would never let you go again. I knew this one would never let Matt go either. She would haunt him for the rest of his days.

Matt didn't listen to me; instead, he zipped the zipper all the way down, so we could see the entire body, and that was when it got really creepy. It was so nasty that I almost threw up. Sophie's dead body wasn't complete. She had been dismembered.

With his face pale, Matt rose to his feet, took two steps to the side, then threw up on the pavement. The sound of him throwing up made me gag too, but I managed to remain in control, keeping all my emotions bottled up inside as life had taught me to.

Chapter 9

THEN

"WE NEED TO HAVE A TALK. Sit down, please."

The boy looked up at his father as he pointed to the couch. His sister was next to him and just as confused as he was.

"What's going on, Dad?" he asked.

"Just sit down, will you? Your mom is coming too."

The boy swallowed and did as his dad told him. He looked at his toys that were in a pile in the middle of the living room. He had forgotten to put them away when he was done playing. Was that why they needed to talk? They were mad at him, weren't they? Would they kick him out of the house? Or would they just yell? The boy didn't like the sensation deep in his stomach.

There had been a lot of yelling lately. Mostly by them, the adults, but also by him and his sister. None of them seemed to be getting along. It wasn't that he didn't love his sister, he really did. The day they brought her home from the hospital was the best day of his young life. He had wanted a sister for so long, longing for someone to play with. But lately, she had been so annoying he had to yell at her, just like his parents yelled at him. Otherwise, she would never learn, would she?

His mom entered the room. She looked so pale, it was scary. The boy wondered if she was sick. Tommy from down the street's mom had been pale too for a long time, and then one day she hadn't gotten out of bed anymore. She was sick, his dad had told Tommy. And now he had to be quiet and let her sleep. And so she did. She slept and slept, Tommy said. Till one day when she didn't wake up anymore.

Was that what was what happening? Was Mommy sick? Was there a mommy sickness going around?

"We have something important to talk to you about," his mother said.

The boy's eyes grew wider. He could hear his own heartbeat and was about to cry, but knew he wasn't allowed to. Big boys like him didn't cry, they always told him. So, he had to keep it inside if he felt the need to. These days, it was only his baby sister who was allowed to cry. And she cried a lot. The boy was nothing like her. He could keep it in if he had to.

His dad took in a deep breath. The boy could tell he was angry by the way he was clenching his jaw. He could see it moving under the tight skin.

"Your mom and I…" he said, then looked briefly at the boy's momma before continuing. "We're…"

Then he stopped like he forgot the words, but luckily, the boy's mommy could remember them for him, so she took over.

"We're getting a divorce."

The word seemed so strange to him. Divorce? The boy had heard it before. Irene from his pre-school class had parents that were divorced, but he wasn't quite sure he knew what it meant. Apparently, it was something they had decided to get, so it wasn't a sickness. Because who would choose to get a sickness? The boy certainly wouldn't. He could still remember the time they had taken him to the hospital because he had a high fever. That wasn't very fun.

The boy's sister looked up at them, sucking her pacifier. The boy knew she certainly didn't understand what they were talking about. And neither did he. All he knew was that Irene sometimes came to class wearing the same clothes as the day before because her mom forgot to pack enough clothes. The boy didn't exactly understand why she had to pack any clothes for school but never dared to ask. Did this mean he had to wear the same clothes to school two days in a row? He didn't mind that much.

"Do you understand what we're telling you?" his mother asked.

The boy looked at his sister, who luckily shook her head, so he didn't have to admit he didn't.

"It means mommy and daddy won't live together anymore," she added, then looked at his dad, who had his head turned away while rubbing his hands against each other. The boy saw him clench his fist, then return to rubbing again before he turned his head back to look at them, his eyes almost glowing red.

"But...?" the boy asked, still confused. If they didn't live together, how would Daddy get food? They always ate Mommy's food at the round table together at six o'clock.

"It won't be too bad, kiddos," his dad said with a sniffle. "You'll be five days with your mom, then five days here with me."

"We've decided to split you evenly between us," his mom said. "That way you'll get just as much time with me as you get with your dad."

His father chuckled and poked the boy on the shoulder. "It'll be almost the same. Heck, you'll hardly even notice the difference."

The boy stared at his parents, wrinkling his forehead while wondering why it was so important for them to have this talk if it wasn't that big of a deal.

Chapter 10

I TOOK Alex home and woke up Olivia, then told her to keep an eye on him. She grumbled something about her wanting to sleep more, but I didn't listen. Alex jumped onto her bed and started to blabber on about the body they had found downtown.

"Wait, Mom?" she said and sat up on the bed. "You're working again?"

I shook my head. "Not really. Just helping out."

She looked confused. Her hair was standing out in all directions. She had cut it short a few months ago, and I thought it was cute on her. She had one of those thin fairy-like faces that made a haircut like that look good. She got most of her features from her father. Not like her sister. When her younger sister wanted the same haircut, I had to explain to her that it probably wouldn't have the same effect on her since she had my rounder face shape. It hadn't come out right, and she had ended up getting angry with me.

"Oh, okay," Olivia said.

"I'll be back again soon."

"Don't forget to bring back coffee," she yelled after me as I rushed out the door and into to my minivan.

I drove back to the scene where a flock of spectators had now gathered. I spotted Matt fighting to keep people back. Photographers from local newspapers were there too now, and reporters were yelling their questions at them.

Matt looked like he could scream.

Our eyes locked and he let me come back in under the tape. "Boy, am I glad to have you back," he muttered.

"How does it look?" I asked.

He shrugged. "Still waiting for the techs. They should be here any minute now."

"Have you alerted the parents?" I asked.

He shook his head and scratched his stubble. "That was my next move."

"You might want to hurry up," I said and glanced at the crowd behind us. "It won't be long before the word is spread. The last thing you want is for them to be alerted through others."

Matt bit his lip. I remembered he used to do that as a child too when dealing with something difficult. A fond memory of him helping me learn how to ride a bike rushed through my mind.

"You could send someone else," I said. "If you don't want to leave the scene."

"No…it's not that. It needs to come from me. I've been on the case since the beginning and…I feel like I owe them."

"There's something I feel like I have to tell you," I said. "Last night, I went running down on the beach, and I passed by right here. I saw someone. A figure in the alley and a car. I can't help thinking that maybe…"

"Did you see who it was?"

I shook my head. "I couldn't see anything except that it was a white car. I couldn't see what type it was, but it was a four-door."

"SUV?"

"I don't think so, but I could be wrong. It was the middle of the night. It was after three o'clock, and it was very dark."

"But you saw someone here in the middle of the night? After the restaurants and bars had closed?"

I nodded. "It could have been anyone. At least that's what I thought. But now, I kind of think it might have been…whoever did this, whoever placed Sophie Williams here."

Matt nodded. "It might have been."

"Dang it," I said. "I knew I should have checked up on it instead of running away. I just…well, I wasn't armed or anything. I had this dream about…well, it doesn't really matter, but I couldn't get rid of this feeling. It brought me right back."

Matt nodded. "That's only natural. I'll need to…"

He didn't get to finish the sentence before there was a loud scream coming from the back of the crowd. We both turned to look simultaneously. A woman elbowed her way through. Her screams made the crowd disperse and create a path for her. As I saw her face and heard her shrieks of horror, I recognized her from TV.

Sophie's mother.

"SOPHIE!"

Matt approached her. "Ma'am…"

But she didn't listen. She pushed him aside, then ran to the sleeping bag, wailing.

"Sophie! No! Sophie, no!"

Matt glanced at me, and I knew he needed my assistance, so I followed him toward the woman.

"Mrs. Williams, Jenna…"

But the woman didn't budge. She stood like she was paralyzed and stared at the dead body, her torso shaking.

"Please," she said and fell to her knees. "Please…God…no!"

It was hard to hold my tears back. I took a couple of deep breaths while Matt looked at me for help. I signaled for him to stay back and let the woman grieve.

Jenna Williams did. She cried and sobbed and then, as she had no more tears, she turned to face Matt.

"You knew about this. Why didn't you tell me?" she hissed, tears streaming across her cheeks.

"Jenna, I…I…" Matt said.

"Who?" Jenna said. "Who did this? Why? Why, Matt?"

"I…We don't know," Matt said.

"You don't know? You don't know?" Jenna Williams said, her voice shrill and high-pitched. She looked at Matt for an explanation, but none came. He had no words.

"Yet," I said stepping forward. I could tell Matt was in over his head, so I reached out my hand. "Hello, Mrs. Williams. Eva Rae Thomas, FBI. If you come with me, I'll try and answer your questions to the best of my knowledge."

Chapter 11

"I OWE YOU. BIG TIME."

It was past noon when Matt came up to me. His hair was standing out in all directions, and I swear I could see a couple of grays I hadn't seen earlier. I had been talking to Jenna Williams for about an hour, explaining to her what would happen next, that they would take her body in for an autopsy and then we would know more. I also assured her that Matt and his colleagues would do everything in their power to find whoever had hurt her daughter and make sure that justice was done. Then, after trying to answer her many questions as best I could, I hugged her, then sent her off with a couple of officers who wanted to take her statement.

I smiled at Matt. "You sure do."

He handed me a cup of coffee, and we sat on a bench that leaned up against the oyster bar.

"You're gonna need to do more than just bring me coffee," I said, "but I'll take it. For now."

He chuckled, and we sipped our coffees for a few seconds, not saying anything. The place was crawling with crime scene techs, and Matt had called in all his colleagues to ensure that the scene remained clear of people. The local NEWS13 was doing a live segment a few yards away, the reporter trying to explain what had happened. Matt had given them a statement, and that seemed to satisfy the vultures for a little while at least. There were still so many unanswered questions, and I knew from experience that they would be back.

"So…I heard from Melissa that you were back," he said. "I ran into her outside of Publix two days ago."

Melissa was another of my old friends. I had known her and Dawn since we went to pre-school. I hadn't seen any of them yet. I had planned to but kept postponing it, telling myself I wanted to be unpacked first. But the fact was, I was scared to see them again. Were they still my friends after all these years? I hadn't exactly been good at keeping in contact with them.

"So, what do you make of it?" Matt asked and nodded toward the scene where the techs were still securing evidence.

I shrugged. "Hard to say before we have anything from them."

"I've never seen anything like this," he said.

"You don't say?"

He gave me a look. I shook my head. "Sorry, sarcasm is my thing now. Comes with the job…and growing up with my mother, I guess. So…how long have you been working homicide?" I asked.

"Couple of years."

"And homicide also works kidnappings?" I asked.

He shrugged. "We do everything, I guess. We've never really had any kidnappings around here before…or at least not since…you know…"

I felt a knot in my throat. "Of course."

He sent me a sympathetic look, then stared down at his coffee as he sensed I didn't want to talk about it.

"You know how it is in this town and with the Cocoa Beach Police Department. Everyone pitches in. We do a little of everything. We help tourists who had their phones or wallets stolen, we drive home drunks, remove gators if they get too close to people, take care of traffic issues downtown, and keep an eye on the citizens during Friday-fest. We did have this guy recently who was conning old ladies by selling them stuff for their pools that wasn't actually his. I got him nailed down. But that's about it. Oh, yeah and then there was that bar fight last year where a man was stabbed. I got that guy too."

"Looks like you've got quite the track record here."

"I'm their shining star," he grinned.

I bobbed my head, realizing that nothing had truly changed in twenty years around here. A few new restaurants had popped up while others were gone, but that was about it.

"So…" he said. "What brings you back here? The Hoover building not big enough for you anymore?"

I chuckled and sipped my coffee. "Something like that."

"Where's Chad?" he asked, saying his name like he was annoyed by just the mere sound of it. "That's his name, right? The guy you ran off with?"

"I didn't run off with him," I said. "I met him in college, and we got married."

He sipped his coffee. "So, where is he now?"

"Greece," I said. "Last I heard."

He widened his eyes. "Oh."

"Yeah, you can say that again," I said. "With some girl named Kimmie."

Matt nodded. "I see. And the kids?"

"They're here with me." I gave him a look. "Hey, you already knew all this, didn't you? Nothing gets past you in this town."

He chuckled and nodded. "Just wanted to hear it from your own lips."

Chapter 12

IT WAS early afternoon before I finally made it back home, holding a package of coffee from Wahoo Coffee in my hand and a gallon of milk from Publix in the other. I could hear their loud voices as soon as I opened the door to the car. I rushed to the front door and walked inside.

"What is going on here?"

Christine looked at me, and so did Alex. She had her arm wrapped around him in a tight grip.

"Mo-om," she said and let go of him. He pushed himself free, then turned around and kicked her shin.

"Ouch, you little…" she said and ran after him.

"STOP!" I yelled. They both froze in place.

I slammed the door shut behind me. I stared at Christine. "Why are you hurting your brother?"

She made an annoyed sound, making sure I understood how unfair this was. "He…he started it."

"That's not what I asked," I said.

Christine gave me a look. I could tell she was looking for the right words to say.

"I can't believe you," I said. "When I'm not home, I expect you and your sister to look after your brother, and this is what I come home to?"

"But…but he…"

"You're the big sister, Christine. This was an emergency situation today, and I had to be somewhere else. I need to know that I can count on you in emergency situations. Now, where's your sister?"

"Upstairs," Christine said. "Doing her homework."

"Okay, then when she's not available, you need to be the responsible one, okay?"

Christine stared at me, her nostrils flaring. "But..."

"I can't do this right now," I said, exhausted. "Just for once, say, okay, Mom, will you?"

Christine bobbed her head. "Okay."

"Thank you." I looked at Alex and held up the milk. "Now, who wants cereal?"

He beamed with happiness. "Me, me! I'm starving."

I chuckled and looked at Christine. "How about you? You want a little late breakfast?"

Christine shook her head, turned around, and stormed up the stairs. I looked after her for a few seconds, then reminded myself that she was a pre-teen and it would pass. I returned to the kitchen and poured Alex some Cheerios with milk. He ate greedily and told me all the games he was planning on playing for the rest of the day, and I got exhausted just listening to it.

I glanced at the living room. It looked like a bomb had gone off in there. Toys were everywhere. The house was a mess. I looked at the clock, then sighed. I had hoped I would be able to work a little today, but I also had to unpack more boxes.

Gosh, I loathed moving.

Chapter 13

I WAS DOING GREAT. I really was. Two more boxes had been emptied, and their contents had found their place in my new small house. It was beginning to look like a real home.

Then I found the box with our photo albums. That's when everything broke down.

I knelt next to it and pulled them out. Most people didn't do albums anymore. I hadn't been one of them. As the kids grew up, I had made sure to have books made with all our photos, and now I was staring at myself sitting on a beach in Italy on our honeymoon. The sight of my happy and tanned self next to Chad brought tears to my eyes, and I put the album aside. But only to pull out the one from our vacation in New Orleans with our two girls, before Alex was even a thought. I couldn't help myself; I had to look through them. I couldn't believe how happy we all seemed back then…how much I was smiling. The girls were only three and five years old and the cutest things ever. In each and every picture, I beamed with pride and glanced lovingly at Chad by my side.

Had life ever been that happy? I could hardly remember feeling that way.

It wasn't just albums in the box; it was also all the photos that we had hanging on the wall by the staircase in our old house back in D.C., the children's childhood home. All those wonderful photos I had looked at every day when coming home late at night or sneaking out early in the morning to go off to work. Or at least I ought to have stopped and looked at them, but I never recalled doing so. I was so busy rushing on with my career that I had hardly noticed them in the end; the photos and those in them.

I sunk to the carpet in the living room. Leaning my back against the wall, I stared at this weird room I was in now, not knowing what I was even doing there.

"STRANGER DANGER!"

My heart literally skipped a beat. Alex jumped out in front of me, holding a lightsaber, screaming the words he had learned in school recently and that he couldn't stop yelling at me every chance he got to scare me. I had explained to him that Stranger Danger was something you yelled if a stranger came up to you and tried to grab you, not something you yelled at people to scare them and give them a heart attack. It was a silly saying, I had always thought. It only told the kids to fear strangers, that all people they knew were safe, when, in fact, most abductions were made by people the child knew.

"Alex!" I said. "You can't do this to me. It has to stop."

The boy gave me a confused look, then swung the lightsaber at me like he was killing me. I pretended to die and made gurgling sounds. The boy laughed victoriously, turned around and left. A few seconds later, I heard him yell the words once again, and one of his sisters screamed at me from upstairs.

"MO-O-OM!"

I exhaled. I wondered if I had any more wine, then cursed myself for not buying more while I was at Publix. I wasn't very good at planning ahead. I walked to the kitchen and found the empty bottle from the night before, then sighed.

Alex yelled something from upstairs, and I turned around with the intention of going up there and yelling at them when there was a knock at my front door. I walked to open it.

Outside stood Melissa and Dawn. Melissa smiled and held up a bottle in her hand.

"We brought wine."

"And a pie," Dawn said. "To welcome you back."

Chapter 14

"I MEANT TO CALL; I really did," I said as we sat down in the kitchen. Melissa found three glasses and started to pour the wine.

"We know," Dawn said and found the plastic forks and plates. She cut out a piece of the key lime pie for each of us and handed me a plate.

"I feel terrible," I said.

Dawn grabbed my arm. She looked me in the eyes. "Stop it. It's okay. You've been through hell. You're here now. And so are we. The rest is water under the bridge."

I swallowed, remembering how much I had missed those two. Back in high school, we had been inseparable. We had shared everything. Then I went off to college, and we lost contact, even though we tried to keep it.

Both Melissa and Dawn had attended local colleges and stayed in town like most people did. Meanwhile, I had run away as fast as I could.

Melissa handed me a glass of wine, then smiled.

"Now, you tell us everything. From the beginning."

I took in a deep breath, then sipped my wine. I told them everything. Beginning with the day a month ago when I had come home from work and found the kids home alone.

"At first, I thought he had probably just popped out for pizza or maybe some wine," I said. "So, I walked to my bedroom and got into some more comfortable clothes and, when I opened the walk-in closet, half of it was empty. His side was nothing but empty hangers. That's when panic set in. I ran to the kids' rooms, and they were just hanging out. They had no idea where their dad was. He had been there a few hours earlier, Christine told me. She thought he had passed out in front of the TV.

"So, he didn't even say goodbye?" Dawn asked, almost dropping the piece of pie on her fork.

I shook my head. "He had just left. I called him, but he didn't pick up. Needless to say, I didn't sleep at all that night. The next morning, he finally picked up. He was at Kimmie's, he said. He lived there now. I didn't even know who Kimmie was. Apparently, he had been seeing her for quite some time now. More than a year. They had met at Olivia's school play, where they were both volunteering, doing the props together. Her son went to Olivia's school. He was done, he said. With me, with our life together, with everything."

"Oh, the bastard," Melissa said and sipped her wine, fuming. "And to think that you supported him all that time. He never worked, did he?"

"I made enough money, so he didn't need to work at all, but he wanted to. So, he started selling health insurance out of the house. But in the beginning, we had a deal. I was to work, and he would stay at home, at least while the kids were young. He was the one who suggested it be that way, and now, that was why he was leaving me. He didn't feel appreciated, he said. Kimmie appreciated him."

"But you got to keep the kids?" Melissa asked, her big brown eyes staring at me.

I shrugged. "Nothing's settled yet. So far, he and Kimmie went on a trip to Greece. I'm guessing we'll deal with it when he comes back. I told him I wanted the kids, that he was the one who left, so he wasn't getting them."

"But…you moved down here?" Dawn asked. "Why?"

"I needed to get away. I couldn't stay at that house; I couldn't stay in the job. I tried for the first few weeks, but it didn't work. I was too much of a mess. The kids and I were constantly fighting, and I couldn't handle both them and my job. It was too much. I wanted to come back to be close to my family, to start over, fresh. Chad said it was okay. I get the feeling that he doesn't really want the kids anymore. I don't know how you can just turn it off like that, but it feels like he has. I fear that he's going to start a new family with that Kimmie character and forget all about us, forget about his children."

"Oh, the bastard," Melissa repeated.

"So, you don't work for the FBI anymore?" Dawn asked, sounding almost disappointed.

"Nope. I quit," I said and sipped more wine. "I needed a break."

"But why? You had this big career and everything? We were so proud of you," Dawn said.

That made me smile. "I don't know if there really is much to be proud of."

"Nothing to be proud of?" Melissa gaped. "What are you talking about? You made a difference in that job. Remember when you solved that case with that guy who had kept children in his house for years and raped them and made those awful videos? I think you made quite a difference to them."

"And to all the other children he will never touch in the future," Dawn added. "Don't think we didn't hear about your accomplishments down here."

I felt mushy. Maybe it was the wine. I stared at them and their pride-filled eyes looking back at me. They seriously saw me as some hero? The case they mentioned was so many years ago. How could I tell them I had screwed up? That I had messed up a case and lost a child in the process?

I decided not to.

"Aw, you guys."

"So, what are you going to do now?" Dawn asked. "You can't just be a full-time mom, can you?"

"Hey," Melissa complained, "I'm a full-time mom."

Dawn pointed at me. "Her. I'm talking about her. It's Eva Rae Thomas. She couldn't sit still if her life depended on it."

"She's right. I am not going to be a full-time mom," I said. "Or, that is, I am, but I am also doing something else. I'm writing another book."

"Uhhh, that sounds awesome. What's it about?" Melissa said.

"Serial killers. I signed a contract with a big publishing house to write about the minds of some of the most notorious serial killers in US history. You know, seen from a profiler's perspective."

"Nice," Dawn said.

I shrugged and looked at the boxes still surrounding us. "If I can ever get to it. Between unpacking and taking care of the kids, I don't really have much time."

"It'll come," Melissa said. "Speaking of gruesome murders, did you hear about Jenna's daughter?"

I nodded. Dawn did too. "Awful," she said. "Can you imagine? Going through a divorce and then this? She must be devastated. That girl was her entire life. She homeschooled her and everything, so she could focus on her surfing. Jenna took her to competitions every freakin' weekend."

"And she was good. We haven't seen anyone like her since Kelly," Melissa said. "At least that's what they say. I have never surfed myself, so I really don't know much about it."

"It's truly awful," Dawn said. "I mean, who would want to harm Sophie Williams? We all freakin' loved her. She could draw quite the crowd when she surfed by the pier—such a talent. It's a shame. It's going to crush so many around here."

"I feel for her mother," Melissa said. "Can you imagine losing your daughter like that? I hope they catch the bastard and do the same to him. But until then, I, for one, am keeping a close eye on my children. I bet the dad did it, though."

"Why do you say that?" I asked.

"They went through a custody battle. But not because of the girl. He wanted part of her money. You know her sponsorships, her prize money and so on. That girl was made of pure gold. She's made a ton of commercials and has modeled for all kinds of stuff, like those expensive watches and sports drinks. They say the girl is good for almost five hundred thousand already, and they predicted she would go on to make millions once she got a little older. He wasn't going to let all that money go without a fight. It got ugly and was in all the papers. The media loved the stuff. They were all over it."

"But why would he kill her if he wanted the money?" I asked. "She's not going to make him anything now."

"To get back at his ex? So she wouldn't get anything either. I don't know. You're the expert here. You tell me."

"You were there, weren't you?" Dawn asked. "When she was found. Mrs. Hannigan from down my street said she saw you…and Matt."

Melissa gave me a look. "You were hanging out with Matt?"

I shook my head. "Not exactly hanging out. I happened to be in the area when the woman who found her came running into the street.

I actually almost hit her with my car. Then I called Matt. I knew he was on the case. That's all there is to that story."

"I bet you and Matt are going to solve the case together," Dawn said.

"And then live happily ever after," Melissa added. They laughed and clinked glasses.

"Dream on," I said. "I am not exactly looking to hook up with anyone right now. I'm in the middle of a divorce, in case you didn't notice. Kind of brokenhearted right now."

"It's always been you two," Melissa said, completely ignoring what I had said. "Remember how he used to run after you in pre-school? He got himself in so much trouble because he kissed you once. The teachers had to have his parents come in and everything."

"I don't remember that," I said.

"Well, you were four," Melissa said. "I just have a freakishly good memory. At least when it comes to stuff like this. He also gave you a ring once, I recall. On the playground at the school."

"That, I remember," I said. "I also remember giving it back to him in fifth grade because I thought he had grown to be rude and annoying."

"But you dated in high school. You can't have forgotten that," Dawn said.

I sighed and leaned back in my chair. "Only a few times. We were best friends. I didn't want to ruin that."

"I think he saved himself for you. Waited for you to come back," Melissa said.

"You're such a romantic," Dawn said. "He just couldn't find anyone as good as her. You ruined him."

"Either way, he's single and has loved you forever. It doesn't get any more romantic than that," Melissa said, her eyes swimming.

I threw a spoonful of the whipped cream at her, and she ducked. Then we laughed. Her smile created dimples in her round cheeks. Hearing them both laugh like that made me remember how much I loved hanging out with them. Being back with them felt more like home than D.C. ever did for fifteen years.

Chapter 15

WE TALKED FOR HOURS. I called for pizza, and we ate with the children while laughing loudly and sharing fond memories and catching me up on everyone in town. I quickly learned that Melissa's husband, Steve, had been diagnosed with MS a couple of years ago, and was fighting the symptoms that grew more and more persistent each day. Meanwhile, Dawn still hadn't settled down with anyone yet.

There was a honk from a car outside, and Dawn's face lit up. "That's Phillip."

"Phillip?" I asked.

"Her latest boyfriend," Melissa said with a deep sigh.

"What?" Dawn asked. "He's cute."

"He's a firefighter," Melissa said as Dawn rushed to the door and waved for him to come in.

"He's more than that," Dawn said. "He's the captain. Here he comes."

Melissa rolled her eyes. Phillip came to the door, and Dawn grabbed his hand. "I want you to meet someone," she said.

Phillip smiled and approached me, holding out his hand. "You must be Eva Rae Thomas."

"I am."

"I live right down the street from you. Two houses down. I've heard a lot about you," he said.

"Oh, really?"

"Yeah, well, people talk; you know."

"They sure do," I said.

"Phillip came to town two years ago from Daytona Beach," Dawn said, still holding his hand in hers.

"I see, and how do you find it here?" I asked.

He smiled. "Hot and humid. Listen, we should get going. It's late, and I have to be at the station early tomorrow."

Dawn gave me a hug and told me how happy she was that I was back before they left. Melissa shook her head.

"What? You don't like him?" I asked.

"He's too perfect; you know?"

I chuckled. "How can anyone be too perfect?"

"He just is. You should see his house. Everything is so neat. And clean. Dawn says he cleans all the time when he's not working."

"Does he have any children?" I asked and grabbed another piece of the pie that Dawn had left behind.

"A daughter," she said. "Recently divorced. According to Dawn, he is perfect. But a guy like him is bound to have a few skeletons in his closet, am I right? Nobody is that perfect. I mean, did you see his body? You can practically count the muscles through his shirt. It's too much."

"I take it you're not a fan of them dating," I said and poured us some more wine. The kids were too quiet upstairs, and I had to get Alex to bed soon but hanging out with my friends made me feel better than I had in a very long time. Even before Chad told me he was leaving me. I was beginning to realize I hadn't been happy for years. It wasn't just the divorce; this had started way earlier.

"I don't know," Melissa said. "I'm happy for her, but I just hope he treats her right, you know? She has a way of picking them."

I bit my lip, remembering her with Tim who she had dated right after high school. I also remembered the bruises she was trying covering up with heavy make-up when I met up with her when coming back for winter break from college. My guess was he wasn't the only one she had found who had been abusive to her. Just like her dad had been when we were growing up.

"She had cancer, you know?"

I shook my head, almost choking on my wine. "No. I didn't."

"Ovaries," she said. "Had it all removed down there. Can never have children."

I sighed and leaned back in my chair. My friends had been through so much while I had been gone, and I had no idea. They had needed me, and I hadn't been there for them. Just like I hadn't been there for my family. I had been busy saving others, yes, but at what cost?

As I said goodbye to Melissa, who needed to get home to the kids and Steve, I couldn't stop thinking about that poor girl Sophie and her mother, Jenna. I wondered if Matt would get any sleep at all tonight. I, for one, knew the images of the poor girl lying in that sleeping bag were going to haunt me for a very long time.

Chapter 16

"I DON'T WANT to wear that!"

Alex growled and pulled off his pants that I had just helped him put on.

"No, Alex," I said, then looked at the clock on the stove. We only had ten minutes before the bus would be here. We had overslept, and I hadn't made lunches yet.

Olivia came rushing down the stairs, then grabbed the milk and poured some on a bowl of cereal. She had headphones in her ears, and they were playing very loudly while she ate and put on shoes at the same time.

"Why are you up already?" I asked. She stared at me like she didn't understand. I signaled for her to pull out the headphones, then repeated the question.

"I have A-OK club today before school," she growled at me. "I told you Friday that I joined this club for volunteer hours. You should know this by now, Mom."

I stared at her but didn't want to ask what A-OK club was since I had a feeling I had asked before.

"Okay," I said. "And what time are you out today?"

Olivia sighed deeply, then grabbed her backpack. "I have volleyball practice. It's Monday, Mom. You know this."

"Volleyball, check. I got it."

Olivia stared at me.

"What?"

"Lunch?" she said.

"Shoot!" I replied. "I'll give you money."

Olivia rolled her eyes and walked away. "Never mind. I already have money."

Then she left. My eyes fell on Alex standing by the fridge. He had no pants on. They were lying on the floor in front of him.

"Alex!"

"It's Monday," his sister said coming down the stairs. She picked up his pants and folded them. "On Mondays, he always wears his *Star Wars* pants."

"What?" I asked.

Christine shrugged. "It's been like that since Kindergarten. You really should know this, Mom. Dad would always make sure his pants were washed and ready for him."

"And since I haven't done the laundry this weekend, they aren't. I see."

"I want my pants," Alex yelled and stomped his feet. I sighed deeply. "Well, you can't have them. They're dirty."

On that response, Alex threw himself on the floor in a regular fit of rage. I felt so worn out, so exhausted, I didn't know what to do. Christine sighed, then disappeared up the stairs. She came down holding his red *Star Wars* pants featuring Darth Vader on the right leg and Chewbacca on the left.

"Here. Wear them even if they stink," she said and threw the pants at the boy.

Alex grabbed them happily and put them on. I looked at my daughter with gratefulness. She grabbed the milk jug standing on the counter, then shook it.

"Really? We're out of milk…again?"

I stared at her. "What? How is that possible? How are we out of milk already? I just bought this yesterday? How did you kids drink a gallon of milk in less than twenty-four hours?"

Christine sighed. "Really, Mom? It's our fault now? Maybe next time you should buy some more."

I exhaled. The girl was right. I should get better at planning ahead.

"All right. I'll buy two gallons today. Until then, can you just eat it with no milk, please? After that, I'll drive you both to school since I just saw the bus drive past our house."

Chapter 17

I DIDN'T GO BACK HOME after dropping off the kids. Instead, I continued through my neighborhood and stopped at a house two streets down. The Williams were new in town, or at least they hadn't been there back when I used to live here. But I knew they had moved into old Mrs. Robinson's house after she died ten years ago.

I walked up the driveway holding a box of chocolates I had bought at the gas station in my hand. I rang the doorbell.

It took a little while before Jenna opened the door. Her eyes were bulging and red. She looked like she hadn't slept in a year. I smiled compassionately, then handed her the chocolates.

"I thought I had to at least bring something."

"You and everyone else," she said, then opened the door, so I could see all the flowers and covered pans with food in them. "Come on in."

I followed her inside. The house was dark and had a musty smell to it. We walked to her kitchen, and she put the chocolates down. There was hardly room on the counter for all the food.

"I don't know why everyone seems to think lasagna is what you need when you lose your child," she said. "I can't fit it all my fridge. Please, take one home with you."

"How are you?" I asked.

"How am I? Well…I guess…at least, I finally got closure, right? That's what they all tell me. But I didn't want closure. I wanted my daughter back. I want to hold her in my arms. I want to be down on that beach watching her surf. I want to drive her to North Carolina this weekend for the nationals."

I sighed. "It must be tough. I can't even imagine."

Jenna grabbed a photo of Sophie from the fridge and looked at it. "This was her first time surfing. She stood up on her first try. Look at her face. She was so happy. I never could get her out of the water ever since. She lived and breathed for that sport. It was her everything. I wanted her to have that dream come true. To be able to live off of what she loved."

"I can't blame you," I said. "It's great when they find something they're passionate about. You want to encourage them. I think all mothers would."

"Only now, I can't help thinking I made a mistake. I should never have pushed this life on her. It was too early. She could have waited. Maybe the killer wouldn't have targeted her. She was in the public eye, you know? It can be dangerous. Someone stalks her or thinks he's her father or something like that."

"Someone stalked her?" I asked.

Jenna nodded. "Last year. This guy started writing messages on her Facebook profile. She has it for sponsor reasons, but I'm the one who manages it. We found out he was at her contests and had been watching her for a long time. At one of them down in Melbourne Beach, he showed up with flowers that he gave her. The card said something nasty about him not being able to wait until she was his. We had the police on it. Gave him a restraining order."

"Has he been questioned?" I asked.

"I sure hope so. But they don't tell me anything. All I can do is just sit here and wait for more bad news. I'm not sure I can take anymore, you know? I just want to see him be put away, so he won't hurt anyone else."

"Who was he, the stalker?" I asked.

"He lived in Rockledge, I think. The creepiest part was I had seen him at so many of the contests. He was always cheering Sophie on and taking pictures, but I just assumed he was one of the photographers. There are so many of them that hang out down there. I just never realized he was only taking pictures of my daughter. The police said he had his computer filled with them. They also told me it wasn't unusual with a child like her being in the spotlight the way she was. That was when I started getting nervous for her."

I nodded, then spotted a picture of Sophie with her dad holding a surfboard between them.

"What about her father?" I asked. "I understand there was trouble during the divorce?"

Jenna scoffed. "You can say that again. The bastard tried to take me for half of Sophie's money. But the money isn't mine. It's hers. I've put it away for her college education. That was actually part of why I divorced him. He was obsessed with her career and making money off of her. I kept telling him she was our daughter and she was allowed to have a childhood, but he believed she had to perfect her game constantly and he pushed her way too hard. He would come home in the middle of the day and take her surfing if there was the least bump on the ocean, even if she was having friends over or was in the middle of her schoolwork. She loved surfing, so it wouldn't make her mad, but he would stay out there for hours with her, yelling at her till she got one maneuver right. Sometimes she would be so exhausted she couldn't even eat when she came home, and she would wake up at night screaming, having nightmares about losing a final. She was so afraid of disappointing him that it was hurting her. He would always yell at her if she came in from a heat and he didn't think she had done well enough. I couldn't get him to stop and, finally, I threw him out. My parents bought the house for us, so I could stay here while he had to go live in some condo. He never forgave me. And then…well, as soon as I threw the D-word out there, I don't know what happened to him. I didn't recognize him anymore. It was like he became someone completely different. At one point, he even tried to turn Sophie against me, telling her I was crazy, and I was the one trying to push her, so I could make money off of her. It was all a mess."

I nodded again, remembering how Chad had changed overnight, how the man that I loved suddenly had turned into my worst enemy, and I had seen hatred in his eyes where there had once been love. A love that had brought us three wonderful children.

"You think he could hurt Sophie?" I asked. "I know it's hard to imagine about a man you once loved."

She threw out her hands, a tear escaping her eye. "I don't know, to be honest. I feel like I don't even know him anymore."

Chapter 18

SHE WAS late for the bus, again, and just as she ran out of the condominium and into the street, she spotted it passing her.

"Shoot!"

Maddie bit her lip, not knowing what to do now. That bus was her only means of transportation. She looked back up at the window to her condo, wondering if she should just stay home. But she had missed so much school lately that she risked being held back again. Nine days were all they could be absent in a semester if they didn't have a doctor's note. And she never did. Her mom couldn't afford to take her to the doctor.

Maybe I could walk to school?

Maddie looked down the street. It wasn't that far, was it? She would be late, yes, but at least she would be there. A tardy was hardly as bad as a day of absence. She looked down at her shoes, where her big toe was peeking out from a hole in the right one. She wondered if the shoes would last for that long of a walk. Her mom would get so angry with her if she had to buy her new shoes already. They cost a fortune, even though they were from a thrift store. And that was money she could have used on food and rent.

Maddie looked at her T-shirt. It had a big stain on the front, but it was the best she could do. There were no clean ones this morning, and this was the one that looked the best. The other kids were going to laugh at her and point it out, but she didn't care. She had to not care. It was the only way of surviving. Rosa, her pit-bull, was barking from the window, and that made her laugh. Rosa was her best friend and the one who protected her when her mom was working at night. She could sometimes be gone for days, but luckily, Maddie had Rosa to keep her company. They would eat cereal from the box or toast waffles in the toaster and eat them together. The neighbors were often fighting at night and yelling loudly, but then Rosa would jump into Maddie's bed and lie close to her, making her feel safe, and she would be able to fall asleep, even if they threw stuff out the windows, which sometimes happened. During the daytime, the neighbors were nice enough and sometimes the lady, Matilda, would give Maddie a cookie if she sat out on the stairs when Matilda came home from grocery shopping. But once darkness fell, the yelling started all over again. Maddie's mom had once told her it was because that's when they had too much to drink and then they would fight over something stupid. Maddie didn't understand why they just didn't drink all those beers. Then they wouldn't fight, and everyone would get better sleep.

But it wasn't as simple as that, her mom had explained, then added that she would understand once she was older.

Maddie wasn't sure she wanted to grow older if it meant drinking too much and staying up all night yelling at one another. Or if it meant she'd have to work all night like her mother, getting beaten up by strangers because she didn't do her job well enough.

No, Maddie was very happy being a child, she thought to herself as she began to walk down the street in the direction of her school. She had only taken a few steps out of the parking lot before a car stopped by her side and the window was rolled down.

"Hey there, little girl. Where are you going?"

Maddie couldn't really see the face of the person talking to her because of the strong sun coming from behind the car, but she was certain she knew the voice and moved closer.

"To school," she said.

"Are you walking all the way to school from here? You'll be late," the voice said.

Maddie shrugged. "I missed the bus."

"Again? Someone's gotta learn how to get up earlier in the morning. How about I take you there, huh?"

Maddie looked at the face, then hesitated. She stood for a few seconds, contemplating what to do. Then she remembered her teacher's face the last time she had been late. Maddie smiled widely, then ran to the passenger seat and opened the door, yelling, "That would be awesome. Thank you!"

Chapter 19

WHEN LEAVING JENNA'S HOUSE, I should have gone home and continued unpacking. It was my plan to, it really was, but while driving down Jenna's street, I couldn't stop thinking about the dad and what Jenna had told me. Ever since I had heard about Sophie's disappearance, I had been wondering about the father and why they didn't seem to consider him a suspect.

So instead of going home, I grabbed my phone and called my dad. If anyone knew where Sophie's dad lived, it was him. He knew everything around here, and I was right. A second later, I had an address, and I hung up after my dad had reminded me that *I was no longer working for the FBI* and that *it was time for me to rest and lick my wounds.*

I knew he was right, but still, I couldn't just leave this alone. I was curious and needed to know.

So, I went. After all, it was only a few blocks away and would hardly take long. I drove onto his street and parked. I knew these condos very well. When growing up, they had been the place our parents told us to avoid. It was the type of place where the rent was cheap, and the owners didn't do background checks, so anyone could live here, even if they had a record. Growing up, I had been taught to ride my bike on the other side of the street and to never talk to anyone here. All us kids were terrified of the people living there. There would always be these men standing outside on the grass, with big dogs that would growl at you when you passed them.

Now, as I came here as an adult, the place didn't seem so terrifying anymore. More tragic than anything. There was an old man sitting on a chair outside, his old dog lying beneath him. He barely looked up when I walked past him and inside the building.

I rang Todd Williams' doorbell, but there was no answer. After ringing the second time, I decided it was time to go. I had nothing much to do there anyway. This wasn't my case, and I had my plate full as it was. I turned around to walk away, when someone came up the stairs, a golden retriever walking up a few steps ahead of him. I recognized his face from the pictures I had seen in the papers and on Jenna's fridge.

His red eyes spotted me, and his lips started shivering. "Who are you? If you're a reporter, you'd better get the hell out of here."

I shook my head. "No. No. I'm not."

His eyes grew milder. "Oh, okay."

The puppy sniffed my legs, and I reached down to pet him. "He's gorgeous," I said. "How old?"

"Four years. He's a rescue."

I knelt next to the dog and petted him, then let him lick my cheek. "A rescue, huh? Golden retrievers aren't that common as rescues, are they?"

"No, I got lucky."

I giggled as the dog got playful. Todd walked to the door and opened it with his key.

"Say, haven't I seen your face somewhere before?" he asked. "I know where. You're that FBI lady."

I looked at him, startled. "You heard about me?"

"I read one of your books," he said. "I'm a geek when it comes to stuff like that. You know with serial killers and all that. I like the real stuff, not all the fake stuff on TV like CSI this and CSI that, but the real true crime. I read all of it."

"Really?"

"Yes, say, could I get you to sign my book? That would be so cool."

I nodded, thinking this was easier than I had expected. I didn't even have to lie.

"Sure. If you have a pen?"

Todd's face lit up. "Yes, yes, of course. Come on in."

Chapter 20

THEN

THE BOY STOOD by the window. As a car drove onto the street, he winced, thinking it had to be her. But as the car continued past his house, his heart sank again.

He felt a hand on his shoulder and looked up. It was his dad. He smiled at the boy.

"She'll be here, son. Soon."

The boy looked at his backpack on the floor. He had packed it the night before, knowing he was going to spend the next five days at his mom's place. His sister sat on the couch, playing with her dolls. She too had her coat on and her backpack packed, but other than that, she didn't seem to care much about what was going on. Didn't she know that Mommy was late?

"What if she forgot?" the boy asked. "Like last time?"

His dad shook his head. "She won't. Last time was just a misunderstanding, remember? She thought it was next weekend instead. Your mom gets busy, you know. Sometimes, she gets the days mixed up."

The boy nodded. His dad had explained to him that it was just a misunderstanding. It wouldn't happen again. Last time had been horrible. The boy had waited and waited all weekend, but his mother never came, and then the following weekend, his dad had taken him camping, and when they came back, they had found their mother sleeping in her car in the driveway. She had been angry and yelled at his dad for taking the boy away on her weekend, and they had ended up yelling at one another and the boy hadn't been able to spend time with his mom at all since, during all the yelling, his dad had told her to leave because she was crazy and too upset for him to trust her with the children. Then, right before he shut the door, he had called her high. The boy had meant to ask him what that meant, but he hadn't dared.

Another car drove up the street, and the boy turned to look, flocks of butterflies fluttering in his stomach. Maybe this time it would be her; it had to be, right? His dad had told him she would be there at eight o'clock in the morning, and last time he asked his dad for the time, he had said it was ten. The boy didn't know much math or about time in general, but he did know that ten was way past eight. And that meant she was late. Again.

The car drove close to the house, but it passed too. The boy sighed and looked up at his father, who smiled again.

"She'll come, son. Don't worry."

But he was worried. He was very worried that she wouldn't come. Not just for his sake, because he really missed his momma, but also for his little sister. She had cried several times this week because she missed her mom.

"Momma?" she said from the couch, looking up from what she was doing. The boy had told her all morning over breakfast how wonderful it was going to be to see their mom and spend five days with her again, but now he was regretting it.

The boy shook his head. "No Momma. Not yet."

His father sighed and sounded tired. He was worried too, the boy could tell, and grabbed his hand in his.

"Why doesn't Mommy want to be with us, Daddy?" he asked.

His dad let out a heartfelt sigh. "I don't know, son. I just don't think we're good enough for her anymore."

The boy nodded and glanced at his baby sister while biting his lip. Then he shook his head.

"We don't need her, Daddy."

His dad chuckled and ruffled his hair. "You're so right, son. We have each other, and that's all that counts."

Chapter 21

"WE CAME to Cocoa Beach when Sophie was just three years old," Todd said and looked at his daughter's picture. "That's when she tried surfing for the first time...on one of those big soft-top boards that you can rent by the beach. I pushed her into the wave, and she stood up. On the ground, she would stagger around and often fall, but on that thing, she was steady as a rock. She was a natural, and I saw it right away. I had grown up surfing myself, with Kelly and the boys back then, but never made it very far. I could just see that she had a gift, and I signed her up for surf camp that same summer. In the beginning, it was all just fun and games, but she developed her skills so fast we couldn't ignore it. By the time she was five, she surfed better than I did. Her learning curve was amazing."

I nodded and sipped the coffee Todd had served me. I had signed his book and slowly led the conversation onto his daughter and, luckily for me, he was more than willing to talk about her. It was something I had experienced lots of times in my line of work. People who had recently lost someone often needed to talk about them, talk about how amazing they had been.

"This is from her first contest," he said and showed me a picture on his phone. "I was the one to push her into the waves back then. And she won, of course."

I smiled. "You look very proud," I said and studied the picture of him holding the big trophy.

"Proudest moment of my life. Since the birth of Sophie, naturally." A shadow moved over his face as the memory faded and he returned to the harsh reality. "I thought she would make it on the World Tour one day; I really did. I thought she would be the next Kelly. I mean once she was ten and everyone talked about her, all the magazines and so on, they started saying it. Never had this town seen such a big talent since Kelly Slater. Of course, I wanted her to reach her full potential."

"You and your wife had a falling out, I understand?" I asked.

He chuckled. "That's very diplomatically put. She was the one who wanted the divorce, not me. Suddenly, she decided to throw me out and keep me away from Sophie. I never fully understood why. My best guess is she wanted to keep the money for herself. It was all Jenna's mother's doing if you ask me. She never liked me and kept telling Jenna to take the money and run. She thought Jenna did all the hard work because she homeschooled the girl. But I sacrificed myself too, you know. I was a chef, but once Sophie started to really get serious, and we traveled constantly, I couldn't keep it up. They sacked me, and here I am. No job and no daughter. Can you blame me for at least trying to get some of the money? I had worked hard to get Sophie to where she was. I was broke, and I only thought it was fair that I got my cut. Jenna just took everything, and I wasn't even allowed to see the girl. In court, she told the judge that I had molested the child. She even had some blood in Sophie's underwear to prove it, she said. It was so messed up. She would do anything to keep the girl to herself. And then look what happened."

"You say she believed she was molested?" I asked.

Todd sighed and rubbed his forehead. "Yeah, but you can't believe anything that woman says. She's such a liar. I don't even think she knows what's true and what isn't anymore. She told the judge all these lies about me and, of course, he ended up giving her full custody. I didn't even get to say goodbye, and now…she's…well, it's all her fault. If she hadn't told Sophie to go on that Girl Scout trip. What was she even doing there? You can't surf in the middle of the country. She was wasting her time. She should have been training for her next competition." Todd sighed and leaned back in his worn-out leather couch that he told me came with the fully furnished condo he had rented. "Ah, what does it matter anyway? It's all too late now. We'll never know what she could have amounted to."

I nodded, sipping my coffee, wondering about this news, when I realized it was getting late. I had to get back. I rose to my feet, thanked Todd for his time, then walked to the door, where I stopped.

"She had a coach, right?"

"Oh, yes. I couldn't get her to where she was on my own."

"Who was he?"

"Thomas Price. He's a local boy. Was on the World Tour for two years before he was injured. He could have been big too but never made it any further. It was his back. Too bad. It's a story you'll hear a lot around here. Lots of broken dreams walking around this town."

Chapter 22

I MADE it to Publix and, while I pushed my cart through the aisles, pulling down milk—getting two gallons this time—and eggs, I called Matt.

"This is a nice surprise."

I smiled. "I thought I'd check in on you. How are you holding up?"

"Eh."

"That well, huh?"

"This isn't exactly a trip to Disney."

"I spoke to the mother today. I went to check in on her," I said. "See if she was all right. Pay my respects."

"Are you doing police work?" he asked. "I thought you were done with all that?"

"I am. I just…well, I was curious, and then I wanted to make sure…"

"You do realize we've already talked to her? I'm a highly trained detective. I don't have much experience, but I know how to perform an investigation."

"Of course, you have. And, of course, you do. I didn't mean to… imply that…I just asked a little about Sophie and the divorce and all that."

Matt sighed. "I've been over that…"

"Did you know there was a stalker?" I asked, cutting him off.

"Of course," he said. "He was the first person we had in."

"And?"

"He had an alibi for the day she went missing. He was in south Florida visiting his aunt at a nursing home in Ft. Lauderdale. Lots of witnesses saw him at dinner."

"He could have driven back. She was taken late at night," I said.

"He spent the night there. In his aunt's room, sleeping on a sofa."

I nodded, grabbed a pack of sliced American cheese, and put it in the cart. "I'm not completely convinced, but okay. How about the claims that Sophie was molested?"

"Wow, you've been busy," Matt said. "Yes, we talked to her mother about that. She made the claims in court, but no charges were ever made. There was no investigation into the matter. She withdrew the claims while the custody case was still ongoing."

I stopped. "She withdrew it, why?"

Matt sighed. "I don't know, listen…"

"I know. You're tired. You sound awful, Matt. Have you slept at all? I know how cases like these can take a toll on…"

"Eva, stop, will you? I've got this. I can do it. The chief has given me the case and wants me to solve it. As much as I appreciate your involvement—and I do—I need to get back to work."

"Are you working on it alone?" I asked, startled.

"No. I have a partner, but the chief put me in charge."

"Who is your partner?"

"Nosy much, are we?" he said.

I grabbed a pack of freshly baked glazed donuts and put them in the cart, telling myself I'd diet next month.

"I…well, yes. I just thought I might know him, that's all. Is he from around here?"

"As a matter of fact, he is," Matt said. "And you do know him."

"I thought so," I grinned.

"It's Chris Cooper."

I stopped right in front of the candy aisle. "You're kidding me, right? Cooper who used to pick his nose in class? Who couldn't run ten feet without having an asthma attack?"

"The very same. But he's different now. Grew out of the asthma, I guess," Matt said. "Listen. I gotta go. Chief's calling my name."

"She's not. You're just trying to get out of this conversation," I said.

He chuckled. "Okay, yes, I am. I have tons of work to do."

"Before you go. What about the autopsy?" I asked.

"Should be in soon. I'm waiting for it."

"Okay. Well, good luck, and Matt?"

"Yes?"

"I'm rooting for you. Catch that bastard, so we can all sleep safely at night again, will you?"

He chuckled again. "I'm doing my best."

Chapter 23

I LOADED the car with all my groceries, then drove home and unpacked it all. I looked at the filled fridge and Jenna's lasagna on the counter with great satisfaction. I had bought all the kids' favorite things. I had forgotten how much I loved taking care of them and making them happy.

It hadn't been Chad who did all the work constantly. When they were younger, we had split it more evenly. He was at home and did most of it, but every now and then, I would come home early and cook or shop on my way home. I would even read stories for the children before bedtime and tuck them in. But as my workload grew and I traveled more, those precious moments stopped occurring, and Chad took over more and more. Suddenly, I no longer did any of those things, and I guess it was around then that we stopped talking as well. There was so much about my work I could never tell him, and since that was such a big part of my life, I just stopped telling him anything. On weekends, I would try and spend as much time as possible with the children, taking them to soccer or volleyball games, and slowly Chad started to resent me for always coming in from the sidelines and sweeping away the kids with my presence, only doing all the fun stuff. I guess I just thought being with the kids was more important and this was the only way I would get to. I neglected him and our marriage in the process. I guess I assumed he would still be there once the kids had grown up, that they were the ones I needed to cherish because, sooner or later, they would be gone. I had never imagined it would be the other way around.

The door swung open, and Olivia came in, still listening to music on her headphones. I smiled victoriously.

"Hi, hon. You hungry?"

She pulled out her headphones, then shook her head.

"No? I bought donuts. I thought we could make a cup of coffee and talk a little. How was your day?"

My daughter stared at me, eyes wide.

"I just ate. Literally. Me and Brooke just had an acai bowl at Café Surfnista."

"Oh. Really?"

"Yes, really."

"I thought you had volleyball practice this afternoon?" I asked.

"It was canceled. Coach had a thing."

"Oh, okay. So, no donut?"

She shook her head and walked to the stairs. "I have homework."

"Wait," I said.

She stopped at the foot of the stairs.

"Where's your sister? Don't you get out at the same time? If you went to Café Surfnista with a friend, then where is she?"

Olivia shrugged. "You don't know?"

"I know I'm probably supposed to, but no, I don't know. Enlighten me, please."

"She has choir. They're rehearsing for the concert."

"Ah, I see."

Olivia smiled. She was about to walk up to her room, then stopped herself at the foot of the stairs.

"It's okay, Mom. You know that, right?"

"What is?"

"That you can't keep track of our lives. It's normal. All the other moms are clueless too. Don't be too hard on yourself."

I swallowed and sent her a smile. "Okay. I'll remember that. Thanks."

"No problem."

Feeling good about myself for once, I sat down and sunk my teeth into a donut alone, when the door slammed open again, and Christine stormed inside. Her eyes gleamed with excitement. Seeing my daughter happy for once made my heart skip a beat.

"Is it fixed?"

I froze. "Is what fixed?"

"The computer. Did they fix it?"

My heart dropped, and my eyes fell on the laptop on the counter in the same spot where it had been since Saturday when she asked me to get it fixed.

Uh-oh.

Christine's eyes grew wide. "You didn't take it?"

I swallowed, then grabbed the computer under my arm. "You know what? I'll do it right now."

"Aren't you forgetting something?" Christine asked.

I looked at her, then remembered. "Alex! Shoot. It's Monday, and he is doing reading club and has to be picked up." I smiled, looking at my watch. I still had fifteen minutes before he was done.

"You know what? I'll just take him with me. I'll have that computer fixed in no time. Meanwhile, grab yourself a donut, do your homework, and then I'll be back in about an hour or two. Your sister is upstairs."

Christine smiled again. The sight made me relax.

"Thanks, Mom. You're the best."

I smiled and rushed out the door, feeling like I was finally getting the hang of this being a full-time mom thing. It wasn't about being perfect; they never expected that of me, but they did expect that I did the best I could.

Chapter 24

SHE WAS BEING PULLED by her hair and dragged across the floor. Maddie was screaming her heart out. Her scalp was hurting, and every bone in her body was aching from bumping against the stairs. She tasted blood in her mouth from the many punches she had received in the car. Her cheeks felt like they were on fire and her heart was thumping in her chest.

At first, she had cried and asked for it to stop, but the person wouldn't. The punches kept falling on her, and she had covered her face with her hands. Then they had stopped, and the car had started to move. Maddie had cried when they passed the road she knew led to the school and tried desperately to open the door, but it was locked. She had cried and kicked it, then received another punch, one so hard everything had gone black.

When she woke up again, the car had stopped in a strange place she didn't recognize. Then the door was pulled open, and she had been grabbed by the hair and dragged across the hard ground.

Now the pulling of her hair suddenly eased up, and she plopped down on a carpet, crying and spitting out blood.

"Please," she said. "I just wanna go home."

She looked up at the perpetrator, her eyes pleading for mercy. But as their eyes met, she knew there was no pity to receive. There was hardly even humanity. She had seen that look in the eyes of the men her mom sometimes brought home. The ones that left her mom with bruises, even though Maddie could hear her pleading with them not to since she wouldn't be able to work if she was beat up.

"I want my mommy," she said, nevertheless.

For years, Maddie had been alone with her mother. It had been just the two of them, getting by the best they could. She had a dad somewhere, but she could hardly remember him anymore. They used to be together, her parents. The first couple of years of her life, they lived in a house, her mother had told her—not a big one, but one good enough for the three of them. It was a real house with a small backyard. Maddie had always dreamt about living in a house with a backyard she could play in.

"Did we have a swing?" she had asked her mom.

"We could have had one," her answer sounded. "If we had stayed there."

"Why didn't we, Mommy?"

"Because your dad left. I couldn't afford to keep it alone. I didn't have a job. I never had an education. That's why I always tell you to get an education, okay? I worked where I could, but never managed to keep a job very long. Then I met Tommy. And now I'm making a lot more money than I ever did. Enough to take care of you and make sure you get a proper education, okay? So, you work hard now, you hear me? It's hard out there, baby. Life is tough. Always remember that."

Her perpetrator looked down at Maddie with those dark eyes, then tied her hands and her legs together using zip tie strips. He then put a blindfold over her eyes and pressed a dirty, bad-tasting cloth into her mouth. He almost choked her when taping her mouth over so she couldn't move her lips. The feel of the cloth inside of her mouth made her gag. She was left lying on her side with the carpet rubbing against her pounding cheek.

Maddie heard the footsteps of her perpetrator leave and then there was nothing but a deep scary silence.

Chapter 25

ALEX WAS in an excellent mood when I picked him up and, together, we drove the long way to Vieira and the Apple store. The guy behind the counter told me they would take a look at the computer, but they'd have to keep it overnight and then call me with their diagnosis. I texted Christine the news, to make sure she was prepared not to have her computer for yet another day, and she texted back that it was okay.

Then we left the store and drove back. I felt happy and sang along to Bruno Mars, my son screaming his little heart out in the back seat, singing along as well. He wasn't exactly musically talented, and his singing was way out of tune, but boy, he loved to sing. And he loved being allowed to use his voice. I knew he had to keep it down in school all day and that his teachers were constantly on his case to get him to be quiet, so I figured it did him good every now and then to be able just to scream and have no one yell at him.

We drove up A1A and passed the gas station when suddenly I noticed a bunch of police cars passing me and stopping in a driveway a little further down. I drove past slowly and spotted a massive amount of police officers in the same driveway.

"That was odd," I said and looked at Alex in the rearview mirror. He stared at them too, pointing his finger at them. No one loved blinking lights and sirens more than him.

Curious as to what was going on, I parked the car and told Alex to stay there for a few seconds. Then I hurried toward the house, where a few neighbors had already gathered in front of the big beach mansion.

"What's going on?" I asked a random man standing there.

He shook his head. "They say his son is missing. Never came home from school."

"Couldn't he just be with some friends?" I asked.

The man shrugged. "I guess."

"Who lives there?" I asked.

"Senator Pullman."

My eyes grew wide. "So, he's the son of a senator?"

The man nodded. I spotted Matt walking out of the house and rushed up to him. A police officer tried to stop me, but Matt told him I was okay. He could let me in.

"What's going on?" I asked. "Senator Pullman's son is missing?"

Matt wrinkled his forehead. "I...how do you know this already?"

"Does it matter?" I asked. "Do you think he might have been kidnapped?"

Matt exhaled. He nodded. "The senator was sent a video on Facebook."

"Are they asking for a ransom?" I asked.

"It's not like that."

"Then, what is it? What was on the video?"

"I really shouldn't be discussing these things with you," he said. "You handed in your badge. You're like a civilian now."

I lifted both eyebrows. "What was on the video, Matt?"

Matt sighed again. He never could say no to me—not when we were kids, and not now.

"It was a clip. Showing the son sitting in a chair, tied up, crying helplessly."

I stared at him. "And what else? A ransom request?"

He shook his head. "That's it. That was all it was."

"But you are tracing the video, right?"

"I've called for help from the county's IT department, but they're all the way in Rockledge."

"But until then, you need to find the boy before it's too late," I said pensively. "Can I take a look at the video?"

Matt sighed. "I don't know...why?"

"Can it harm anyone that I take a look?" I asked.

He shook his head. "Probably not. Come with me."

I paused. "I kind of have my son in the car. Let me go get him first…"

Matt stared at me, then chuckled. "Of course, you do."

Chapter 26

MATT SHOWED me into the huge mansion. I was holding Alex by the hand, nodding politely at every police officer I saw. Alex stared at them with wide-open eyes and muttered under his breath:

"Cool."

"This is FBI-profiler, Eva Rae Thomas. She's gonna help us find your son, Nathaniel."

Matt presented me to the senator. He was sitting in his massive kitchen with high vaulted ceilings, his wife next to him, her long fingernails tapping nervously on the side of an empty coffee cup.

I reached out my hand and shook the senator's. He looked at me, impressed.

"FBI? That was fast."

"I was in the area," I said.

Alex made a loud noise sounding like a siren, and the senator and his wife stared at him. I sent them both a smile, then looked at Matt.

"Over here," he said and guided me to a laptop.

Alex had his eye on a beautiful Goldendoodle who was wagging his tail and holding a tennis ball in his mouth. Alex whined and started to pull away from me.

Matt was about to start the video when I stopped him. "Can you take Alex, please? Just for a sec?"

Matt looked confused. "Take him?"

"Just entertain him while I watch this. And no matter what you do, don't let him get his hands on that tennis ball in the dog's mouth. He'll throw it, and something will break. Believe me; you don't want that."

Matt held back a chuckle, then stretched out his hands toward Alex. "Hi there, buddy. Say, have you ever seen a real police baton?"

My eyes grew wide. "Don't. He'll break stuff."

Matt smiled. "I'm not going to let him hold it, just show it to him. Now, go watch that clip, and I'll handle him, okay? Don't worry."

I cleared my throat, then walked back to the computer, still keeping one eye on my son. He and Matt were talking for a little while and then Matt took him by the hand, and they started to walk outside to the pool area. I stared in their direction, wondering how long it would take before Alex would begin to yell something or scream, but it didn't happen. The two of them seemed to be deeply engaged in their conversation, and Alex looked up at him with big admiring eyes.

"Well, I'll be…" I mumbled under my breath, then pressed the play button on the computer.

The clip wasn't more than twenty seconds and showed the senator's son sitting in a chair, hands and feet tied to it. The boy was crying. He had to be about fifteen or so, judging from the light hairs growing on his upper lip. The clip was nothing but just him sitting there, and then it was over. I played it again, then again, and once more until I finally stopped it midway.

"You seeing something?"

The voice was familiar, yet so different that I wasn't sure. I turned around and looked into the eyes of Chris Cooper; only this was nothing like the Cooper I had known in high school. Only the eyes gave him away. The rest, well…the rest was quite a different story. He was tall, but he had always been one of the tallest boys in school. What he didn't have back then were those broad shoulders and buff arms. I didn't quite recall that jawline either or those abs.

"Cooper?"

"They told me you were back," Cooper said, then gave me a hug. "I can't believe it. How have you been?"

I grimaced. "Eh."

"Yeah, I heard about your divorce. What an idiot, huh? Leaving a woman like you?"

I blushed just as Matt came back into the room, still holding Alex's hand. He looked at the two of us with an odd expression.

"Anything?" he asked, sounding almost mad.

I nodded and took Alex in my arms. "As a matter of fact, yes."

I turned and showed them both the computer, then pointed. "Look at that. There's a window behind him. Even though the blinds are pulled, you can still see the shape of it, if you look closely. There's only one place in this town that has windows that are diamond-shaped like that."

Both men's eyes grew wide. "She's right," Matt said. "I can't believe I didn't see it. Thank you."

I shrugged. "To be honest, it was almost too easy."

Chapter 27

I FOLLOWED the police cars in my minivan, and we parked in front of the townhouses. I made sure to park on the other side of the street, to keep away if something went bad. It was a row of about six small houses that had been built in a certain style back in the seventies. They were known to be cheap to rent but located right across the street from the beach. Most people thought it was a shame that such ugly houses were situated in such a lucrative spot. Others thought they were worth preserving because of their unique architectural style, with their diamond-shaped windows and draped roofs.

"So, which one do you think it is?" Matt asked as I got out of the car. I left the engine on, and Alex stayed in the car.

I looked up at the sun. "The video. It said in the corner that it was recorded at eleven o'clock…earlier today. There was sunlight coming in through the window behind him, which tells me he was sitting in one of those facing the street," I said and pointed.

"So, one of those two?" he asked.

I nodded. He gave me an unsure smile and put a hand on his weapon. "You better stay here."

I smiled and glanced back at Alex in the car. I had left the music on, blasting out of the speakers, and told him to sing as loud as he could, just in case. I didn't want him to hear anything.

Matt and his colleagues walked to the two front townhouses and knocked on both doors.

"Police. Open up!"

A small wave of excitement rushed through my body and, for just a second, I missed being back in the field. I just hoped they would find the boy alive.

One door was opened, and an elderly woman peeked out. "What's going on here?"

"We need to check your house, ma'am," Cooper said.

The old woman looked afraid. "W-why?"

Meanwhile, no one opened the door to the house next to it, and Matt pulled the handle. The old woman next door saw it.

"No one lives there anymore," she said. "It's been vacant for the past year."

Matt sent me a look, then mouthed, *should I?* I nodded in agreement. Matt knocked his shoulder into the door, and it opened easily. Then he disappeared inside, holding his gun tightly in his hand. I felt my heart rate go up and looked back at Alex, who had no idea what was going on. He was singing his heart out and swinging his toy ax around.

Not a sound came from inside the townhouse, and I felt scared for Matt for a short second. He came back out looking sick to his stomach.

"Matt?"

He closed his eyes for a brief moment. His eyes were brimming with horror. I rushed to him.

"Matt? Are you okay? What happened?"

Cooper stopped talking to the old lady and ran to him.

"I...I found him," he said.

"Who?" Cooper asked. "The senator's son?"

I could hear Matt's ragged breathing. He was fighting his tears. His answer came as a silent nod.

Chapter 28

I HAD PREPARED myself for something bad, but what I saw still pulled all the air out of me, like a punch to my stomach.

I walked inside first, Cooper coming up right behind me. The townhouse was completely empty. No furniture, only an old refrigerator was humming in the corner of the kitchen.

We found the senator's son in the living room in front of the fireplace, the diamond-shaped window behind him just like we had seen in the video. He was still tied to a chair, but unlike in the video, he was no longer fighting or crying. He was sitting completely still with his head slumped to the side. His eyes were still open, staring eerily at us like they were asking us why we were so late, why we were too late.

In his mouth, someone had stuffed hundred-dollar bills. A handful of them had fallen to his lap and the wooden floors beneath him.

"My God," Cooper said and clasped his mouth. He turned away like he couldn't bear to look at it.

I exhaled, fighting to keep calm. The boy was only a few years older than my Olivia. Probably even went to the same school, like all the kids in this town. This was unbearable.

"I called it in," Matt said, returning. His color had come back, but he still looked sick. "Who does this? What kind of a sick pervert kidnaps a kid and kills him, stuffing money down his throat like that?"

I stared at the boy, then shook my head, realizing this wasn't my case and I had a son in my car. Suddenly, I just wanted to get back to be with my children.

"I'll guess I have to go notify the parents," Matt said.

"I should go," I said. "I'm not supposed to be here, and you guys have work to do."

"It was nice to see you again, Eva Rae," Cooper said and gave me a warm hug, holding onto me for a few seconds too long.

"Maybe I'll see you around?"

"We'll have to see about that," I said, and I turned around and walked away. Matt stared at me, then walked out in front of me. His steps were suddenly big and angry. He scoffed loudly.

"What?" I asked, baffled.

He shook his head. "Nothing."

I stopped. "What's going on here? Matt?"

He stopped too, then gave me a look.

"You don't think it's a little early? Not to mention inappropriate, given the circumstances?"

I couldn't believe my ears. "Excuse me?"

"Your divorce isn't even finalized yet, is it?" he asked as we came outside in the sunlight. I could hear the loud music blasting from inside my car. Alex was still at it. I could see his ax swinging through the air. That kid never ran out of energy. Chad used to say he was like that Energizer Bunny. I thought he was exaggerating back then, but now I understood what he meant.

"You thought I was flirting? I can't believe you," I said and grabbed the door handle.

"What?" he asked.

"Jealous much, are we?"

He gave me a look, then shook his head. "Don't flatter yourself. You've gotten really snooty, do you know that? You come here, big and mighty, and think you can tell us how to do everything. Well, we were doing just fine till you got here."

"Wow," I said and opened the door. "I guess I won't flatter myself and think you actually want me here. If you don't want me to help you out on this case, I don't have to. I'll walk away right now."

"Yeah...I think we've got it from here."

"All right," I said and got in. "Good to know."

Chapter 29

I COULDN'T BELIEVE HIM. I drove home, fuming. I felt so angry that I started unpacking right away and, by dinnertime, I had gone through two more boxes. My mom had called and invited us over for dinner, so I put the lasagna back in the fridge, got ready, and walked over there with the kids since they only lived two blocks down. My mom opened the door.

"I guess late is better than never, right?" she said, then looked at me. "What's happened to your hair? Did you do something to it?"

I felt it, then shook my head. "I stopped washing it. I'm going to try for dreadlocks. I think I might look good with them, don't you? Kind of get that Bob Marley thing going that I've wanted for years."

My mom stared at me, eyes wide. Then, realizing I was kidding, she gave me one of her annoyed smiles.

"Get in."

We walked into the living room. My parents lived in a beautiful house on the canal. It was huge, way too big for two people to live in alone, but they loved it there. It was my childhood home, but going there didn't exactly bring back fond memories. I had always hated living in a house where I had to be careful where I sat because the furniture was so expensive. I often joked that the furniture was more important to my mother than me. Except it wasn't a joke. It was often the truth. It got more of her attention than I ever did.

Christine went to sit on a couch, and my mom saw her, then rushed to grab a towel and placed it where she was going to sit.

"There you go," she said. "Jeans can leave a mark."

Christine gave me a look for help, and I nodded to tell her to simply indulge her grandmother. Olivia sat next to her, making sure to sit close enough so she was on the towel as well. I wasn't so worried about the girls as much as I was Alex. He had already finished two rounds of the living room, running with his toy ambulance, making loud noises. I gasped every time he passed the big human-sized sculptured vase that I knew my mom had shipped from Vietnam.

"Squirt!"

My dad came in, gave me a kiss on the cheek, then greeted the girls before catching Alex as he ran past him. He grabbed him around the waist and lifted him into the air, then spun him around till they both laughed.

"Jon!"

My mom came out of the kitchen, holding a tray with some sort of food on it.

My dad put Alex down. "Sorry, darling."

My mom gave him another look, then clapped her hands. "Appetizers, everyone. I made zucchini chips. Let's take them outside, shall we, so we can avoid greasy fingers on the furniture."

I exhaled, relieved. Outside, Alex could roam wild without breaking anything. Relieved, I sat down on the patio furniture while Alex took to the lawn and started somersaulting across the grass.

"So…" my dad said and sat next to me. He never got to say more before my mom came over too, interrupting us.

"Did you hear what happened to that senator's son? It was all over the news," she said, speaking with a low voice so the kids wouldn't hear. Olivia and Christine put on their swimsuits and went in the pool. I couldn't blame them. I wished I had done the same. It was too hot to just sit there.

"Of course, she did," my dad said. "She was there. I was just about to ask."

I turned to face him. "How did you know I was there?"

My dad smiled. "I know everything, remember? I see everything around here."

"Ah, don't listen to him, Eva Rae," my mom said. "Crystal called earlier and told us. I wasn't home, so he picked up."

Crystal was Matt's mother. Of course, Matt had told her I was there. I was beginning to remember why I was in such a rush to get out of this place twenty years ago. It was suffocating how everyone always knew everything you did.

"So, what do you think?" my dad asked.

"About the senator's son?" I shrugged. "I don't know, to be honest. It's all very strange. There was a video leading us to him. It was like the killer wanted us to find him. Like he had put the boy out on display. There was no ransom, no demands of any kind."

"It's horrifying," my mom said. "You hardly dare to go out anymore. Nowhere is safe."

"Do you think it was political?" my dad asked.

"That's what they said on TV," my mom added. "That he was targeted because of his father's job. Something about a bill he recently signed or maybe his stance on gun control. I don't know. It was all a little out there if you ask me."

"Yes and no," I said.

"What kind of an answer is that?" my mom said.

I bit my lip while watching Alex rolling on the grass. "I don't know yet. But I do think that choosing a senator's son has to have some sort of significance. I'm just not sure it's political. I think he might have chosen the senator's son because it would wake the interest of the media."

"You think the cases are connected, don't you?" my dad asked. "The surfer girl and the senator's son?"

I shrugged. "It's not really up to me to conclude anything. I stopped, remember? I am actually trying to stay away from this."

My dad nodded pensively. "You should be taking care of yourself and your children right now. Let someone else deal with this. Besides, you have that book to write. How's that coming along?"

I smiled, feeling guilty. "Eh. Not so much right now."

"Don't blow this one, Eva Rae," my mother said. "They might get angry with you at that publishing house and then where does that leave you? You have no additional income. You're a single mom now; your husband left you…you can't blow this too."

I glanced at my mom, then forced a smile. "Geez. Thanks for reminding me, Mom. I had completely forgotten how awful my life was."

My mom grimaced, then stood to her feet. "Oh, my, the food."

My mother rushed off, clacking along on her high heels. My dad leaned over and spoke with a low voice.

"She made curried quinoa with garbanzos and peppers. It's vegan, plant-based, and gluten-free. Does anyone even know what gluten is and why we're all suddenly allergic to it?"

I chuckled, then placed my arm around my dad's shoulder. "She means well. She wants you to stay healthy and stay with us for many years."

"I'm sixty-two. I'm not dying. Heck, I'm not even retired yet. I don't plan on going anywhere anytime soon. But I might if I don't soon get a big fat juicy steak."

I chuckled. You can always come eat from our fridge, Dad. Anytime you want a real meal, you just come over."

"It's good to have a backup plan," he said, whispering, while my mom yelled from inside the house that dinner was served.

After picking at my mom's food, pretending to eat, the kids and I went back home and played a card game, while eating Jenna's lasagna. We stayed up till ten o'clock, completely forgetting it was a school night. I wanted it to last forever. I couldn't stop thinking about those poor parents, the senator and his wife, who now sat alone in their big beach house without their child.

Chapter 30

THE FACELESS MAN is pulling my arm. It hurts, and I scream, but he grabs me around the mouth and tells me to shut up. His fingers taste like cigarettes. I am scared. I can hear my heart pounding. I can see my mom walking, pushing her cart, but she's too far away. I want to scream again, but I can't. I want to alert her to what is happening, but she's busy taking things from shelves; she doesn't notice; she doesn't even look in my direction.

"What are you doing?"

The voice coming from behind the faceless man is Sydney's. She's holding a doll in each hand and is staring at us. The man turns to look at her, then pauses.

I want to scream at her to get away, to go get Mommy, but I can't. Instead, I bite down on the man's finger so hard, he yelps and lets go of me. Heart pounding in my chest, I push myself out of his grip.

I OPENED MY EYES, still feeling my heart pound in my chest. My mouth was dry, and I looked at the clock, then realized I had overslept.

I sprang to my feet, then ran into Alex's room. He was already awake and sitting on the floor playing with his trucks, letting them crash into one another, making noises with his mouth.

"Alex. We're late. Get dressed."

He didn't react, but I felt certain he had heard me, so I moved on to the girls and woke them up one after the other. Olivia cursed and hurried to get dressed. Christine got sad and began to cry.

"I can't keep going in late, Mom. I'm gonna get in trouble for this."

"I'll write a note," I said. "Just get dressed and come down for breakfast. I'll drive you to school."

Christine sighed. "I hate this place. I miss Dad."

I paused and was about to say something, but then decided not to. It wasn't fair of me to demand that they never think about their father anymore. Fact was, he had abandoned us all, but the blow was especially hard on them since, for the past couple of years, he had been their entire world. He had been the only adult who took care of them. And just like that, he was gone. I cursed him inside my head, thinking I had no idea how to tell the kids that he didn't want them anymore, that now he wanted a new family. It was going to break their hearts. I wondered if I should have a talk with them about it, or simply let them find out on their own. Would they think I was just making it up if I told them? Because I was angry with him?

Probably. They adored their father, and in their eyes, he could do no wrong.

"I do too," I said. "But he's not here, and we have to try and do this on our own, honey."

"I don't want to," she said, crying. "I want him to come home."

I hugged her, not knowing what else to do. She cried for a few seconds, then stopped and wiped her eyes.

"Listen, honey. I know there are a lot of changes right now. But I promise it'll get better, okay? You have to trust me on this."

She didn't say anything but got out of bed and put on her clothes. My heart was still bleeding as I served them cereal, for once having enough milk for them all and for my coffee. But right now, I wasn't sure milk was enough. They needed their father, and I loathed him for what he was doing to them.

Chapter 31

AFTER DROPPING THE KIDS OFF, I drove to the beach, my Yeti containing my coffee still in my hand. I had so much on my mind; I couldn't really face my house and the loneliness inside of it when the kids weren't there.

I felt exhausted. I hadn't slept well in a long time. The kidnapping of two kids since I got back here brought back too many bad memories.

I went for a walk and greeted a nice old couple who were obviously snowbirds. You could always tell by their pale skin and by how much they enjoyed the sunlight hitting their faces.

As I reached the pier, I stopped and watched the surfers. There were a couple of them out there. The waves were big and very glassy. One of the surfers stood out in particular as he shredded the waves and even went for some air. After watching him for a few minutes, he came up, and I realized it was Coach Price.

"Nice air," I said as he exited the water.

He smiled widely. "Thanks."

I sipped my coffee.

"Could you teach my kids to surf that well?"

He shrugged. "I don't really do beginners."

I nodded. "Of course not."

"But there's a really good surf school downtown. You can sign them up for camp and then maybe if they make it big, you can sign me on as coach. I can take them all the way."

"I'll remember that if we ever get that far," I said, chuckling at the idea of my kids surfing. It was mostly Alex I was thinking about. He needed a sport that could take some of the energy out of him. I looked at the coach, who was standing next to me, watching the other surfers out there.

"It doesn't hurt your back, surfing like that?" I asked.

"My back?"

"Yeah, you injured your back, didn't you? That's why you stopped on the tour?"

He nodded. "Ah, yes. No, I can do some stuff, just not all of what I used to be able to, and some days are better than others. Anyway. I should get back. Nice to meet you."

I looked after him, then smiled. "You too."

I stayed in my spot for a few minutes longer, sipping my coffee and watching the surfers, thinking about Sophie and Nathaniel, the senator's son, wondering why the killer—if it was the same one—had chosen those two kids of all the children he could have chosen. They were both very much in the spotlight and killing them had to have some significance. If it was the same guy, he clearly had some sort of message he was trying to get out. These kills weren't random.

I shook my head, once again reminding myself this wasn't my case, then began to walk back, planning my day in my mind. I would unpack a few more boxes and then sit down at my laptop and get some writing done. I needed to get at least the first page on paper today. I had written three books before this one and knew that the first page was mentally very important. Once you got that down, you had actually begun writing it, and then it would start to flow and come naturally. I just had to get past that first darn page. And for some reason, I kept postponing it.

Chapter 32

THEN

THREE YEARS LATER, the boy got a new mommy. She was beautiful, and the boy really liked her. He could tell his dad did too, and that made him even happier. She was very nice, even to his baby sister, and that made the boy happy. Having her at the house brought new joy, and it was like everything changed, especially his father, who no longer sat for hours in the living room, staring into thin air, saying nothing.

They told them to call her, *Mommy*. The boy found it a little strange at first since he already had a mommy. But his new mommy and his daddy had a new name for his old mommy. They called her The Thing. Every time they mentioned her, they would always say *The Thing said this* or *The Thing did that*. They also talked about her being on drugs and how it wasn't very good for the boy and his sister to visit her.

They didn't see each other often anymore. A couple of times a year. She kept getting the dates mixed up or missed the appointments, his dad and new mommy explained to him. It wasn't his fault, they kept saying, but it was hard for the boy not to feel a little guilty, to feel a little like his mommy didn't really want him.

"It's okay to be mad at her," his new mommy said one day when tucking him in. "She has not been treating you very well."

"The kids would sometimes come home with bruises," his dad said, coming in to say goodnight as well. "She hurt them when she was alone with them. And still, I can't say they can never see her again. I can't protect them. She's their mother."

"It's tough," the new mommy said.

And then they kissed.

Later that same night, the phone rang, and the boy hadn't fallen asleep yet, so he could hear his dad pick it up. He could tell it was his mommy or The Thing by the way his dad talked to her. He talked like he did when he was very angry with the boy or his baby sister. Like when they had gone to Michael's house down the street one afternoon without telling him. He talked to The Thing in the exact same way. Like he was mad.

The boy walked out of his room, and his dad saw him just as he hung up.

"What are you doing up, buddy?" he asked. "I thought you were asleep. You should be. It's a school night."

"Who was that on the phone?" he asked.

"That? Oh, it was no one. Wrong number. That's all. Don't you worry about that; just go to sleep."

"Was it Mommy?" he asked, rubbing his eyes.

"No. No, it wasn't. Now, go back to sleep."

The boy looked up at his father, then wrinkled his forehead. He had been so sure it was her, and he wanted to talk to her. He wanted to tell her he got a new bike. It had been so long since she had last called.

"It was no one. Now, get back to bed, buddy. You have school tomorrow."

"But…?"

"Now, I said. Now."

"Can I call her?"

"Can you call who?"

"Mommy. I want to call her."

His father scoffed. "Your mother doesn't want to talk to you. Don't you understand that? She abandoned all of us, and she doesn't want to see you. Now, get back to bed. I don't want to have to say it again."

The boy felt like crying. Still, he didn't. He held the tears back, then ran to his bed, cursing his mother far away, deciding he never wanted to see her again. Never.

Chapter 33

I FOUND ALL the baby pictures of Olivia, and that's when I stalled. Up until then, I had been through several boxes, and the kitchen was beginning to look decent. My mom would be pleased to see that all the plates were finally in place. She would probably find them to be ugly, yes, but at least they were there.

I told myself it was time for a cup of coffee and went through the baby books. I looked through them, lingering especially long on the ones from our trip to California when she was just a year and a half. I remembered the trip as exhausting because I spent most of the time running after her, but as I looked at the pictures, I was suddenly reminded of how simple life had been back then. I was nothing but a young detective with tons of dreams and aspirations of climbing the ranks one day. It had always been my ambition to get to the FBI, but back then, it had been nothing but an idea, a dream that I loved clinging onto.

I placed a finger on Chad's handsome face.

Gosh, I was in love with him back then.

My trip down memory lane was violently interrupted when there was a knock on my front door. It sounded urgent, and I hurried to open it. Outside stood Melissa. The look on her face told me something was very wrong.

"I need your help with something."

"Well, hello to you too. What's going on?" I asked. That was when I realized Melissa hadn't come alone. Behind her stood a woman that I had never seen before.

"This is Patricia," Melissa said. "She's actually the one who needs your help. Can we come in?"

"Sure. Sure," I said and stepped aside to let them in. "The place is still a mess, but what can you do, right?"

Patricia smiled at me feebly as she walked past me, and I closed the door behind them. I guided them into the kitchen and served them coffee.

"I think I still have some of that pie left," I said. "You want some?"

Melissa nodded. "Sure."

I found the plates and served us all some pie. Patricia barely touched hers.

"So, what's going on?" I asked midway through my piece. Unpacking had made me hungry, and I realized I had skipped lunch.

Melissa looked at Patricia, then at me. "Patricia has a request for you."

"Yeah?"

Melissa put her fork down. "Her daughter has gone missing."

I almost choked on my coffee. "Missing? What do you mean missing?" I looked at the woman next to me, then at Melissa for answers.

"She never came home from school yesterday," Patricia said.

My eyes grew wide. "Yesterday? But that's almost twenty-four hours ago?"

She nodded, heavily. "Yes, that's why I'm worried."

I couldn't believe what I was hearing. Knowing how important the first twenty-four hours were when a child went missing, I couldn't believe they were just sitting there.

"But…but surely you filed a missing person's report? Have they had search teams out…to search the canals and the streets?"

Melissa stopped me. "That's the thing. She hasn't told the police."

"You haven't? But…why not?"

"She can't," Melissa said.

"And why is that?"

Patricia sighed. "I'm a prostitute. I work at night and leave my ten-year-old daughter home alone all night. I'm not happy about it, but it's the only way I can survive. I can't afford a babysitter, and I have no family nearby."

"If the police get involved, they'll take her daughter away," Melissa took over. "She can't go to the police; you must understand this, Eva. I told her it would be safe to come to you. We were hoping you could help find Maddie…without the police."

Chapter 34

IT WENT against everything I believed in. Everything I had been trained for and knew as the way to handle things, yet I still agreed to help her. How could I say no? Her daughter was missing.

I told them to take me to her condo, so I could look around. Patricia showed me in, grabbing the big pit-bull who ran for us as the door opened.

"This is Rosa. She won't harm you. She looks fierce but is like a lamb. She keeps Maddie safe at night."

I smiled and petted the dog.

"This is where she sleeps," Patricia said and opened a door.

It was the only bedroom in the condo. The mother slept on the couch.

"I never bring clients home anymore," she said, looking shameful. "I used to when she was younger, but then I realized how bad it was for her because she could hear it when they treated me badly. I was afraid she would begin asking questions. Now I have them take me to motels, or we just handle it in the car. So, I figured I might as well give her my bedroom."

I looked at the small woman in front of me, then felt like hugging her, yet slapping her at the same time. No one should have to live a life like this. Not the child who had no choice, not the mother who suffered abuse every day.

Patricia saw it on my face. She looked shameful.

"I tried getting other jobs, but...when I lost the one I had...well, I have to eat, right? I have my girl to feed. My ex refuses to pay anything."

"No one is judging you," Melissa said and placed a hand on Patricia's shoulder.

I smiled at her to reassure her that I wasn't, even though I had to admit that I had been at first. I was just suddenly so extremely grateful that I had made my own money and could take care of myself. Chad had promised he would pay alimony, but so far, I hadn't received any. He was still having the time of his life in Greece and not thinking about the kids or me. He had inherited a good amount of money when his mom passed recently, and I suspected that he was out burning all that off on his screaming midlife crisis. Luckily, the publishing house had given me a big advance, and I still had royalties coming from my previous books. If I didn't overspend, I'd be fine. And if everything went south, I always had my parents. My mother was cold and emotionally distant, yes, but I knew she and my dad would always bail me out if they needed to. I was one of the fortunate ones; Patricia wasn't.

"So, you say she left for school on Monday morning?" I asked and looked around the girl's room. Patricia had handed me a school photo of her daughter, so I knew what she looked like.

Patricia nodded. "Yes. I spoke to Mrs. Altman downstairs. From her window, she saw her walk to the road wearing her backpack, but she was too late. The bus had already been there. Mrs. Altman saw it pick up another kid from this block. But Maddie came out afterward. Before Mrs. Altman could come out on the porch to tell Maddie that she was too late, a car drove up on her side, and Maddie got in."

The blood in my veins froze. "She got into a car?"

Patricia nodded with a loud sob. "I just learned it this morning when I came down. I thought she was at a friend's house all day yesterday and I went to work in the evening, thinking she would be home later. I was preparing to scold her for being out so late. Then, when I came home this morning and could tell that Maddie hadn't been home all night, I panicked. I ran downstairs and knocked on Mrs. Altman's door to ask her if she had seen her and she told me this."

"I need to talk to this Mrs. Altman," I said. "Now."

Chapter 35

BEFORE WE LEFT Patricia's condo, I texted Olivia and asked her if she could be sure to be home when Alex came home with the bus today since I was out. He was usually about half an hour later than her if she came home directly from school and didn't go into town with her friends. Luckily for me, she texted me back that she had tons of homework, so she was planning on going home straight after school anyway. I was pleased with this. I needed my kids home today.

"Mrs. Altman?" I said as the old lady opened the door, leaning on her walker. A smile appeared on her weathered face.

"Yes?"

"My name is Eva Rae Thomas," I said. "I'm with the police. We're trying to figure out what happened to Patricia's daughter, Madeleine Jones. She told me you saw her get into a car?"

The old woman nodded. "Yes. It's true."

"What can you tell us about the car? Do you remember what it looked like? Maybe the color or the brand? Was there anything particular that stood out about it, like a sticker or anything?"

The old woman became pensive, and her face lit up. "I don't know any of those things since my eyes aren't what they used to be, but I did take a picture of it with my phone. I had a feeling that car was up to no good, and watching little Maddie get into it scared me. I knew something wasn't right. Wait here a sec while I go get my phone."

"You took a picture with your phone?" I asked, surprised.

The old lady returned a few minutes later, holding a phone in her hand. She pressed the screen and navigated through it like it was the easiest thing in the world.

"I love this thing. My daughter bought it for me, and I can't seem to stop using it. This is how I keep track of my grandchildren up north when she posts pictures on Facebook. The kids use Snapchat more, and we have over one hundred streaks. I send them pictures of myself wearing all these different filters; it's loads of fun. Keeps their old grandma on her toes. Here it is," she said. "It's not a very good picture since I took it as the car took off, but you can see some of it. Have a look for yourself."

I took the phone and looked. The car was definitely in motion when the picture was taken, making it a little blurry, but I could see that it was white, and I could see the shape of the driver. Unfortunately, I couldn't see a face, no matter how much I zoomed it in.

"There's more if you swipe sideways," she said.

I did, and to my excitement, there was a perfect picture of the license plate. This was our lucky day.

"Can you send me these two pictures, please?" I asked.

"I can airdrop them to you," Mrs. Altman said, as she touched the screen a couple of times, and then I had the pictures.

"Thank you so much, Mrs. Altman," I said and shook her hand. "You've been a tremendous help."

"You're very welcome. I just hope you find the girl. So much bad stuff is happening these days. Find her and bring her back home, will you?"

"I will do my best, Mrs. Altman. I will do my best."

Chapter 36

I CALLED the station and asked to speak to Cooper. Patricia was sitting on her daughter's bed, biting her nails, while Melissa sat next to her and tried to calm her down. While waiting for Cooper to pick up, I saw Melissa pull out a pack of Kleenex from her purse and hand them to Patricia. The sight made me chuckle since I suddenly remembered how Melissa always took care of all of us back in the day. She always had a shoulder to cry on when you needed it and always had a piece of chocolate in her bag or a pack of Kleenex. It was just who she was. Always taking care of anyone in need.

"Miss me already?" Cooper said as he picked up.

"Very funny. No, I need your help."

"And Matt isn't your go-to guy anymore?" he asked. "That's new. Can't say I'm not flattered…"

I exhaled. What was this? Sixth grade?

"Matt and I aren't exactly…you know what? It doesn't really matter. That's not why I'm calling. This is urgent. I need your help. And I need you to be discreet about it."

"Sure. I guess I can do that," he said, sounding a little hesitant. I knew it was a lot to ask him.

"I need you to run a plate for me," I said.

He breathed, relieved. I don't know what he had feared I would ask him to do, but clearly, he had thought it was something bad. "I can certainly do that. Hit me."

I read the numbers for him, then waited while he put it in the system. I smiled confidently at Patricia to make her feel calmer. I hated seeing that look of despair in her eyes. I didn't even know how I would react if I didn't know where my child was and if I knew she had gotten into a car with some stranger. It would tear me apart with anxiety. It was unbearable to even think about, especially when thinking about what had happened to Sophie Williams and Nathaniel Pullman.

Cooper returned a few minutes later.

"I got it. It belongs to Thomas Price."

My eyes instantly grew wide. "Thomas Price?"

"Yeah, " he said. "Why are you checking up on him?"

I swallowed, thinking about Sophie and her mother.

"I have to go, Cooper. Thanks for helping me. I owe you one."

"But…?"

I hung up before he could ask any more questions. I stared at the name I had written on a piece of paper on Maddie's desk. I had seen this guy this same morning. Had he taken Maddie? If so, what had he done to her? Was she still alive or had he killed her? Was he also responsible for the death of Sophie Williams?

I wondered for a few seconds how to handle this. I knew Patricia was terrified of involving the police. She was absolutely right. If the police found out she had left her daughter alone all night, they would have to involve the DCF, and she would lose her child. I couldn't do that to her. But if this guy had taken Maddie, there was no time to waste. Not if we wanted to find her alive.

Chapter 37

MADDIE COULDN'T CRY ANYMORE. She had been crying so much her blindfold had gotten soaked, but now there were no more tears left in her. Her arms were strapped around her back so tightly they began to hurt, and she tried to sit up straight, but it was impossible when she couldn't use her hands to help. She tried anyway, using her elbow, but just as she just managed to get herself almost up, she fell over and landed flat on her face.

Maddie cried out in pain as her cheek hit the carpet. She sobbed, feeling sorry for herself and so, so very hungry. Her prison guard had been there and poured water down her throat before pushing the bad-tasting cloth back into her mouth, so she felt like she was choking, taping it shut with duct tape. But she had welcomed the refreshing water in her mouth and throat. Now, she was mostly hungry, but so far, she had gotten no food at all while being held like this and she felt like she was about to die. Her stomach hurt so bad.

Maddie had felt this starving feeling before when they had run out of food, and her mother hadn't come home. Sometimes, she would be gone for days, working, she said, then come home with purple bruises all over her body. Maddie hated going hungry for days or waking up to an empty fridge. It was the worst. Actually, if she was honest, that wasn't the worst part about her life. The very worst part was the fact that all her friends knew what her mother did for a living. And they would tease her about it. Just the thought of how the kids in her class looked at her filled her with such deep shame it almost made her cry again.

One time, a boy from her class, Gareth, had held her down and spat in her mouth, telling her to get used to that feeling since she would grow up to be a whore too. That was the most humiliating thing anyone had ever done to her.

It was Gareth's dad who had seen Maddie's mom down by the harbor one night and then told Gareth about it. The next day, Gareth had told everyone else in their school.

What Gareth's dad was doing down there at night was something Maddie had often thought about asking him, to get back at him, but that was only when she thought about it afterward, lying at home in her bed. Once the teasing started, she never knew how to say anything. At least nothing clever. Fact was, she too was embarrassed by her mother's profession. She didn't even want to defend herself. Because if her mother was dirty like they said, then so was she.

Maddie sobbed a little more when she realized that her blindfold had slipped up slightly on the right side and light was coming in. It must have happened when she fell. She managed to push it further up by sliding across the carpet, and soon she could actually see something.

Maddie gasped as she looked around the barren room with nothing but the carpet she was lying on and strange black foam on the walls. There was only one other thing there. A huge wooden box was placed against the end wall. Maddie stared at it, and as she paid attention, she thought she could hear a noise coming from inside of it.

It sounded an awful lot like nails scratching against the wood.

Chapter 38

"WHAT'S THE RUSH?"

Matt got out of the police cruiser. I was standing in my driveway, where I had asked him to meet me.

"You said you owed me, remember?" I asked. "Big time, you said. I'm going to have to cash in on that right now."

It had taken me a couple of deep breaths to call for his help, but the fact was, a girl's life was on the line, and our little quarrel shouldn't be allowed to end up costing her life.

Matt gave me a look. It reminded me of how he used to look at me on the playground at school. It was a look that I never knew if he wanted to hit me or play with me.

He scratched his stubble. "Okay. What is it?"

"It needs to stay between us. You can't tell any of your colleagues."

"I...I don't know, Eva. It sounds like trouble."

"It is trouble, but a girl's life is depending on us," I said.

He wrinkled his forehead. "You're telling me you want me to help you do police work...illegally?"

I threw out my arms. "Not illegally. Just...bend the rules a little. Help me save a young girl."

He rolled his eyes at me. "You're going to be my death, Eva Rae Thomas. I always knew you would be."

I leaned over and smiled. "I'm counting on it. So...do I have your word? That you will keep this between you and me?"

He stared at me, contemplating, weighing the pros and cons, his nostrils flaring lightly.

"All right," he said. "But then we're even, you hear me?"

I exhaled, relieved. "Thank you."

I told him the story of Maddie and Mrs. Altman and the photo, while his eyes grew wider and wider.

"And she never told the police?" he asked with anger in his voice.

"No," I said. "She can't. She's a prostitute. She'll lose her daughter. DCF will take her."

"Darn right, she will. And she should. For leaving her alone at night," Matt argued. "No kid should be home alone all night."

"You and I can agree on that, but we can also agree that sometimes desperate times call for desperate measures, okay? This woman is trying her best. Besides, that's not the point here. The girl is in danger, and we can help her. Let's help a girl and her mother, okay?"

Matt looked at me. He was about to argue again but stopped himself as our eyes locked. I saw the softness in them that I remembered so well. He never could say no to me.

"All right," he said. "You said you know where she is?"

"I know who took her," I said. "And I think maybe he's the same one who took Sophie Williams. I did see a white car parked in the alley that night before she was found. It could be this one. You could end up solving your case. Not half bad, huh?"

"Okay, I'm buying into it. Who is he?"

"Thomas Price. Sophie Williams' coach."

I opened Mrs. Altman's photos on my phone and showed him.

"Here. This is his car that Maddie was picked up by. This is the last time she was seen. I had Cooper run the plate, and it belonged to Thomas Price."

He grabbed the phone and studied the picture, then nodded. "Cooper is involved too?"

"Just for running the plate. He doesn't know anything else."

Matt gave me a look, then sighed. "All right. Let's go have a chat with him."

Chapter 39

MATT HANDED me his Police jacket to put on while we walked up to the house.

"Just to make sure you look official," he said.

I nodded while putting it on. It felt strange to wear one again. Especially in this heat.

Matt smiled when he saw me wearing it.

"What?" I asked.

He shrugged. "It suits you."

"Very funny," I said as I walked up to the door and knocked. It took a few seconds before Thomas Price opened it. He stared at Matt, then at me, a look of confusion on his face.

"Officer Miller?" he asked. "What's going on?"

"We're looking for a girl," he said and showed him the picture of Maddie. "Madeleine Jones. Have you seen her around?"

He took a quick look, then shook his head. "Nope. Never seen her before."

"We have reason to believe she might be hiding somewhere around here," I said. "Could we take a look around inside?"

Thomas Price shrugged. "I don't see why. She's not here."

The tone in his voice got angrier...almost hissing.

"We're not accusing you of anything, Mr. Price," I said. "We just need to take a quick look around."

He gave me a strange look. "Who is she, Matt? Why is she

suddenly everywhere? I thought you had kids to take care of. Or was that just a lie you told me this morning? What is all this? Why are you harassing me?"

"I assure you, sir, I am not..." I said, but we had lost him. He shook his head violently.

"If you don't have a warrant, then you're not coming inside," he said.

"Thomas," Matt pleaded. "It's just a quick look around. If she's not there, we'll be out of here immediately."

"Why would she be here?" he asked aggressively. "You don't think I know what's in my house? You don't think I would know if a girl was inside my house?"

"She could be hiding, maybe under a bed or something," I said, thinking this was getting too far out. He was onto us, and there was no way we were getting inside that house.

"You know what? How about I take a look around myself and then I'll call you if I find a little girl, how about that, huh?" Thomas Price said. As he was about to slam the door shut, I put my foot in it to stop it. It hurt like crazy as he tried to close it anyway, but I didn't care. I pushed it open, pushed him aside, and rushed past him.

"Maddie?" I called, hurrying into the living room.

The TV was on but muted. The News was on, talking again about the senator's son. I turned away, then spotted a door and ran to open it. Thomas Price was yelling behind me, but I hurried, so he couldn't catch me. Matt was yelling at me to come back out too. Meanwhile, I rushed into the bedroom and looked around, but found nothing, not even in the closets that I pulled open. I then ran to another bedroom and looked around, even under the bed, but found nothing.

"Maddie!" I called, hoping she would hear me and answer, but there was nothing.

Thomas Price was now in the doorway, yelling at me to get the hell out of his house. I walked up to him, stared into his eyes, and felt a chill run down my spine as I saw the look in his.

"You can't just come in here," he growled. "I know my rights."

"Where is she?" I asked and showed him the picture of his car from my phone. "She got into your car."

Then Thomas Price started to laugh. "Did you see my car in the driveway?"

"No."

"I don't have a garage, and you assume I have the car somewhere? Where? In my living room?"

"What are you saying?" I asked.

He leaned over. I could smell his breath as he spoke. "I gave my car to my mom three weeks ago. She needs it more than I do since hers broke down. I can walk to the ocean from here. If I need to go further, I just pick it up at her place."

Matt came up behind him. I felt the blood leave my face.

"Embarrassing, huh, Officers?"

"You could still have borrowed it, and the car is part of an ongoing investigation," I said.

Coach Thomas shook his head. "You're crazy, lady. Now, please, get out of my house. I wonder what the chief is going to say when she hears about this. You know she and I go way back, right?"

Chapter 40

I LOOKED AT MATT. We were driving back in his cruiser. It was getting dark out, and bugs were dancing in the headlights. I felt terrible.

"I am so sorry," I said. "I was so certain she was there, you know with his connection to Sophie Williams and everything."

Matt sighed and stopped the cruiser outside my house. "You were only trying to help…I guess."

"I hope I didn't get you in trouble?" I asked.

"We'll see. But maybe…just maybe you should leave the police work to me from now on, okay?" he said, forcing a smile. "I know you used to be a big shot and everything, but maybe you need to focus on yourself and your family right now."

I grabbed the door handle, then opened the door before looking at him again.

"Thank you, Matt. I am glad you were here today. I'm just sad we didn't find the girl."

"Well, I did owe you one. But now we're even, okay?" he said. "I'll go talk to Price's mother before I head home today. Just to make sure the girl isn't over there, but I know her, and she's an old woman. Still, I'll check just to be certain. I'm sure that'll help you sleep better tonight."

I nodded. "Thanks."

I watched his cruiser as it disappeared down the road, then turned with a deep sigh and walked inside. I knew I wasn't supposed to do any more police work, but how could I not? Maddie was still out there somewhere, and her mother had put her confidence in me finding her.

Barely had I set my foot inside of the house before Olivia stood in front of me, hands on her sides, an angry look in her eyes.

Uh-oh.

"Where have you been?" she asked.

"I...I had to be somewhere, why? Is everything all right?" I grabbed my phone and looked at it—eleven calls and seven texts, all from Christine. My first thought was that something had happened to Alex, but as I finished the thought, I heard a loud scream coming from the stairs, and Alex came storming toward me, holding out a sword. I exhaled in relief. The boy was okay. Louder than ever, but okay. Then what was it?

"Is it Christine?" I asked, my heart beginning to race.

"You're darn right it is," Olivia said.

"What happened?" I asked, panic beginning to rush through me.

"You missed it," Olivia said.

"I missed what?" I asked. "Olivia, tell me what is going on right away. You're scaring me."

"Her concert," Alex screamed.

I looked at him then up at Olivia. "What concert?"

"Christine's concert. It was tonight," Olivia added.

"What concert? I never heard anything about a concert?" I asked, still feeling confused.

"Her choir concert," my daughter said. "She even put the note up on the fridge to remind you; look. You really mean to tell me you didn't know?"

I rushed to the fridge. There it was, right in the middle where I couldn't miss it.

How could I not have known this?

"So...where is she now?" I asked.

"She's still there. But it's too late to go," Olivia said. "The concert is over now. She'll be home soon."

"Oh, okay," I said, disappointed. "Guess I'll have to make my famous chili for dinner, huh? Her favorite." I was about to take out some meat when I paused. "Say...how did she get there? Did she bike?"

Olivia shook her head. "Nope. She got a ride from someone."

"She got a ride? From whom?" I asked.

Olivia shrugged. "How am I supposed to know that? Some parent, I guess."

Chapter 41

I WAS ABOUT to explode with anxiety for the next fifteen minutes. It felt like forever; that's how nervous I was. I couldn't stop thinking about Maddie Jones and the white car. What if Christine never came back? Just like Maddie had never come back?

I was terrified.

I called my parents and talked to my dad. My mom said she couldn't deal with this right now and gave the phone to my dad, who calmed me down. I told him about Maddie and how she had gotten into a car with a stranger and how I was so scared the same thing had happened to Christine. I told him how we had been on the trail of finding her, tracing the car, but had run into a dead end.

"I get why you're freaking out," he said. "Believe me; I do. There is nothing worse than not knowing where your kid is. But you have to remain calm. It won't help anything if you lose it. It won't bring her back. Give it time. She might be back."

After exactly fifteen minutes of me watching the driveway from my window, my stomach in knots, biting my nails, a car drove up the street, and I spotted my daughter in the window. The car slowed down to a stop, and she got out, then walked up to the house. I ran to the door, heart beating hard in my chest.

"Christine!"

I was about to take her in my arms, but she pulled away.

"Mom. How could you forget?"

"I am so sorry, baby, I am so, so sorry. I...I hadn't seen the note on the fridge. I know I should have but I didn't...and I was just so...scared."

She wrinkled her forehead. "You were scared? Why?"

"Christine. You went in a car with a complete stranger. What have I told you all your life about strangers?"

Christine stared at me. "You've got to be kidding me? You're making this about you again? Of course, you are. You're trying to make me feel bad when you're the one who screwed up? All the other parents were there. I was the only one whose mother wasn't there. Do you have any idea how that feels? I almost missed the entire concert because you weren't there to take me. I waited forever for you to come home. I called you a million times, but you didn't answer. I was about to go by bike, but I knew I would get there too late, when he came along. Luckily, he could take me, and I made it in time."

"Who?" I asked, my hands still shaking. "Who took you there?"

"His name is Phillip," she said. "He's the captain at the fire station. He was wearing his uniform. He said he knew you."

"And you went with him? In his car? Just like that?" I said, my heart thumping in my chest. After all the years I had spent telling my girls to be careful, I couldn't believe she could be so careless.

"Would you stop it? It's not like that," she said. "He was only trying to be nice. Besides, I'm back, aren't I? Nothing happened."

She was about to walk past me when I grabbed her arm. "This time. Promise me you'll never do it again. Never get into a car with a stranger."

Christine looked at me, then rolled her eyes at me. "Mom, would you cut it out? I know something bad happened to you once. I know some guy tried to grab you in Wal-Mart; I know it happened to you, but it doesn't..."

"My sister was kidnapped, Christine. It wasn't just a little thing. It wasn't just me overreacting. I never saw Sydney again after that day. No one knows what happened to her. Not a day goes by when I don't wonder why the guy took her and not me."

Christine looked into my eyes, then exhaled. "I know this story, Mom. You've told it to me a thousand times. It doesn't mean the rest of us can't live our lives. Now, can I please go? I have homework to do."

I let go of her, and she ran up the stairs. I looked at my trembling hands. I walked into the kitchen and grabbed a bottle of wine, my hands shaking so heavily I could barely hit the glass when pouring it.

Chapter 42

THEN

THE BOY WAS DOWN in the living room when it happened. His dad had brought home a new toy truck for him, and he had woken up early on this Saturday to play with it. His baby sister came down too and brought her dolls with her, and now they were playing on the floor, blocking out the world and forgetting everything around them for just a few hours.

The knock on the door was loud and demanding. The boy gasped and looked at his sister when they both heard it. The boy swallowed, knowing he wasn't allowed to open the door when his dad and new mommy were sleeping. Still, the knocking continued, and the two children got curious.

Together, they walked to the window and peeked outside.

Baby sister gasped. "It's Momma!"

The boy's heart pounded, and he could hear his pulse in his ears. He didn't know what to do. Seeing his mother made him feel warm and happy, yet he knew he couldn't count on her. She could be high and then there was no telling what she might do. That was what his dad had told him. That was why they didn't go visit her anymore. Their dad was afraid of what she might do to them.

"We have to let her in; come," his baby sister said.

Mommy knocked again, hard and angrily. It frightened the boy. Soon, she was yelling too.

"Let me in! I want to see my children! Tommy, I know you're in there! TOMMY!"

His sister looked at him, pleading. "She wants to come in. She wants to see us; come."

His sister rushed to the door and reached for the handle. The boy stood like he was frozen.

"Wait," he said worriedly. "We should wake up Dad first."

"Why? She wants to come in. Let's let her in," baby sister said, tilting her head, not understanding. "It's Momma."

"No," the boy said and walked to her, grabbing her hand. "We can't."

His sister burst into tears. If there was one thing in this world the boy couldn't stand, it was his sister crying. It hurt his heart so badly he couldn't stand it.

"I want to see my momma!"

"Okay, okay," he ended up saying. He grabbed the lock and unlocked the door. His sister stopped crying and grabbed the door handle, then turned it and the door swung open.

Outside stood their mommy and, as he saw her, the boy's heart started to race. She smiled and bent down, holding out her arms.

"My babies!"

Baby sister ran to her and hugged her tightly, while the boy stayed behind scrutinizing his mother. She had gotten skinnier, her cheeks had sunken in, her eyes had deep dark marks beneath them, and she looked different. He didn't like the way she looked.

"Aren't you going to hug your mommy?" she asked.

The boy stared at her, contemplating for a few seconds more, then decided he would love to feel her embrace once more and took off toward her. He had barely reached her when a voice yelled from the stairs behind them.

"What's going on here?"

It was Daddy and New Mommy. They were storming down the stairs, barely dressed, New Mommy wearing a silky robe, daddy in his jammies. They grabbed baby sister and the boy and New Mommy pulled them inside, while Daddy started to yell. The boy heard it all from inside the house, while his sister cried her little heart out.

"You can't just come here like this."

"They're my children too, Tommy. I am entitled to see them."

"Look at you. You can't even look me in the eye. Look at how your hands are shaking, not to mention your slurred speech. You're high again, aren't you?"

"No! Why would you say that? Tommy?" their mommy pleaded. She was crying now, and the boy wasn't sure he could hold his tears back much longer either.

"Get off my property before I call the police. You hear me? I don't want to see you here."

"But…Tommy…they're my children…I want to see them," she cried. "How can you be so cruel?"

"Get out."

"I don't want to go," she said, hissing. "I'm not going till I have seen my children."

"Then I'll just have to call the cops then," their dad said.

"You can't steal them from me."

"Go home."

The boy looked out the door, just as his mother picked up a rock from the flowerbed, the one with the irises that New Mommy loved so much. His old mommy threw it at the window. The window shattered with a loud noise and both children screamed. Glass scattered everywhere in the living room. Outside, their mother was screaming too as their dad tackled her and pulled her into the street.

"Don't you ever come back here, or I'll make sure the police put out a restraining order," he yelled.

The boy grabbed his sister in his arms as their mother walked away, head slumped, still yelling. Meanwhile, their father came back inside, snorted, then slammed the door behind him. He knelt by his children and pulled them into a warm embrace. Both kids were shaking heavily.

"What's wrong with Mommy, Daddy?" the boy asked, tears streaming across his cheeks.

"She's not well, son," he said.

"Can't a doctor make her well?" little sister asked, with a sniffle.

Their dad shook his head. "I'm afraid not."

"Why not?" the girl asked.

"She's a drug addict," the boy answered. "It can't be cured."

"I'm so sorry you had to see her like this," their dad whispered. "That's what drugs do to people. They make them act irrationally. Right now, your mother isn't acting rationally. You can't trust her. But I promise you, it won't happen again. I won't let it. I'll protect you."

Chapter 43

AFTER SAYING goodbye to the kids the next morning, I walked upstairs and opened my safe, then found my gun. When we moved to Cocoa Beach, I had put it away, thinking I wasn't going to get any use of it, but I wasn't feeling safe anymore, not even in my small cozy hometown. Maybe I was just being paranoid like my daughter said; I didn't know. But I knew this feeling a little too well, and I also knew that wearing a concealed gun made me feel safer.

I sighed and looked at my phone. I still wasn't convinced of Coach Thomas' innocence, to be honest, but at the same time, I found it hard to keep looking into him since it would only end up hurting Matt. I would have to tread carefully.

There was something, though, that I had to check. A thought that had entered my mind and I couldn't let go. I grabbed my computer and began a search, then found some old articles that I began to read. I made a few phone calls back to some old colleagues out west in California and made tons of notes on my pad. Then my dad called, and we chatted for about half an hour. As I hung up, there was a knock on my door. I walked to the window and looked down into my driveway.

It was Matt.

"What's he doing here?" I mumbled.

Probably came to yell at you for ruining his career.

I walked down and opened the door, preparing an entire speech of excuses but also ready to defend myself, when I took one glance at his face and realized that wasn't why he was here. This had nothing to do with what had happened the day before.

"We need to talk. Can I come in?"

"Of course," I said and stepped aside. He had his laptop under his arm, which he placed on my kitchen counter. He sat down on a stool with a deep sigh. There were cereal leftovers all over and spilled milk, which I hurried up and wiped away.

"You look like you could use a cup of coffee," I said.

"Yes, please." He tried to smile, but I knew him well enough to know that he was forcing it. He was biting his lip and, from the look of it, he had been at it all morning, maybe even all night.

I poured coffee for the both of us, then found some cookies and put them out, but Matt didn't touch them. Instead, he sipped his coffee, then looked deep into my eyes.

"What's going on, Matt? You're scaring me. Did something happen? Have you gotten in trouble with Chief Annie because of me?"

He rubbed his forehead. "Chief Annie sent me here. Not to scold you, but to beg you. It's time we bury the hatchet and face reality. We can't do this on our own. I've come to ask you to help us out with the case. We're in deep here. Too deep, Eva Rae. We need your help. Do you think you can do that? Chief Annie told me I had to get down on my knees and beg you if I needed to. Do I need to?"

I sat down on a stool next to him, completely taken aback, holding my coffee between my hands.

"I…I have…"

"I know you have this book to write," he interrupted me, "and that you're super busy with other stuff, but we can't do this without you. Things have gone from bad to worse since yesterday, and we simply don't have enough experience to deal with it. Please?"

I put my hand on his arm to stop him talking. "That's not what I was trying to say. I was about to say that I would love to. But I need to have free hands. I need to do this my way."

"Whatever it takes," Matt said. "Chief's orders. And I will behave too."

I chuckled. "Was that an excuse?"

"I guess. I was an idiot the other day. I'm sorry," he said. "You're allowed to flirt. I don't know why I got so mad."

"I get it," I said. "The pressure is on your shoulders. Now, show me what's on that computer. I don't assume you brought it to check your emails."

Chapter 44

"WHERE DO I BEGIN?" Matt said, his voice heavy. He had opened his laptop and was clicking the mouse. "Oh, yes. The autopsy. Let's begin there."

He opened a document, and I moved my stool closer, so I could look over his shoulder. He smelled just like he used to when we were younger. It brought back many fond memories and a sense of comfort to me.

"Sophie Williams died from asphyxiation, they concluded," he said.

"When?" I asked. "When was she strangled? She was taken three months before she was found, but the body wasn't decomposed."

"Oh, yes, well, time of death is set to be somewhere between eight p.m. and eleven p.m. on the night she was found, October 5th."

"Okay, so in other words, he kept her for three months somewhere before killing her and placing her there," I said. "What else? Was she abused sexually?"

He shook his head.

"Okay, so it's not something sexual, which I'm quite surprised about, to be honest. She was dismembered; we saw that," I said. "Do they know with what tool?"

Matt nodded. He swallowed hard. "A sharp object, possibly an ax, it says."

I nodded again and sipped my coffee. "A common household tool. What has me rattled is the fact that he dismembered her but not to dispose of the parts. That's usually the reason for dismembering someone. To get rid of the parts one after another in order not to be discovered, but that's not this killer's motive. It's not the kill itself; it's the displaying of the victim that gets him going."

"Which leads me to the next part, the one that has us all puzzled."

I sipped more coffee, then looked at him. He looked like he needed a moment to prepare himself to be able to say what came next. I braced myself for something nasty.

"The body parts didn't belong to her," he said.

"Excuse me?"

He swallowed again. "The arms and legs weren't hers. The head and torso were."

It took a few seconds before the realization finally sunk in. I blinked a couple of times, then wrinkled my forehead.

"They weren't hers?"

He shook his head.

"Then whose were they?"

He tapped on his computer, and another file came up. A picture appeared of a young boy, looking to be about the same age as Sophie.

"Scott Paxton, also twelve years old, disappeared on Sunday, September 12th while biking home from a friend's house. He's from Titusville. His mom's a drug addict who didn't notify the police till several days had passed and then she told them she believed his dad had taken him. They put out an Amber Alert, but neither the dad nor the boy was ever found. In the end, they just assumed he had run away with him…maybe to another state."

"But he hadn't," I said and ran a hand through my hair while thinking about all this new information. The Cocoa Beach Police had done an excellent job of hiding this from the press. As soon as they found out, they would gobble it all up and spread panic in town. It was a good call to hide it for as long as they could. Especially since it seemed like the killer wanted this out; he wanted this part to be told, the gory details. I wasn't sure why yet, but there was no doubt that this was his goal. Otherwise, he wouldn't have gone to such trouble to do it and display the body the way he did. The more I got to know about this killer, the less I liked.

"There's more," Matt said.

"I had a feeling there was," I said and finished my cup. "Let me just get a refill first. I have a feeling I'm going to need a lot of caffeine for this."

Chapter 45

I REFILLED both of our cups and grabbed a cookie. I know that most people wouldn't be able to eat in the middle of something like this, but I wasn't like most people. I could always eat and, the more troubled I was, the more I did. Or maybe I just couldn't help myself. I needed some comfort in the middle of all this human tragedy and misery.

"So, last night, this came to our attention," Matt said. "Or rather it was sent to me directly, in an email addressed to me."

I leaned over and watched him open an email, then click on a link. The link sent him to YouTube where a video appeared. He started it and leaned back so I could see better.

At first, it showed a video of Sophie Williams from when she was still alive. She was sitting in a room, on the floor, tied up, her mouth duct-taped. She was crying and screaming behind the tape.

"Oh, dear Lord," I said.

"There's more," he said.

Another clip appeared, this time of the senator's son sitting in the room where we found him, money stuffed down his throat, gasping for air behind the bills.

Then there was text sliding across the screen, while the boy was groaning and gasping for air behind it.

DO I HAVE YOUR ATTENTION YET?

I glanced quickly at Matt next to me when he signaled for me to keep watching.

A new text appeared.

FACTS:
Every 36 seconds, there's one divorce in the U.S.
That's 2,400 divorces a day.
16,800 a week.
876,000 a year.
50 % of American children will go through their parents' divorce.
Children of divorce suffer in school.
They have behavioral problems.
They are less likely to graduate from high school.
Kids of divorce are more likely to commit a crime while juvenile.
They are five times more likely to live in poverty.
They suffer from health issues like anxiety and depression.
Their suicide rate is twice as high.
Even God hates divorce, Malachi 2:16

THE TEXT STOPPED, and the camera then zoomed in on the face of a crying Sophie Williams. And then the camera was turned off, and the screen went black.

I leaned back and stared at Matt, who was still very pale. I shook my head and scratched my forehead, then grabbed my phone and found my Bible app and read out loud from Malachi 2:16:

"'*For I hate divorce!*' *says the LORD, the God of Israel. 'To divorce your wife is to overwhelm her with cruelty,' says the LORD of Heaven's Armies. 'So guard your heart; do not be unfaithful to your wife.*'"

I put the phone down, wondering if I should send this passage to Chad. Matt gave me a look.

"You understand now why we need your help?" he asked.

I sipped my coffee while chewing on all this new information. I grabbed another cookie and bit into it. A couple of crumbs fell to the counter. I ate the cookie while thinking some more.

"So…what do you think?" Matt asked cautiously.

I spoke with my mouth full, lost in my thoughts. "First off, he placed the body for us to see, somewhere he knew tourists came, where everyone comes. He wants our attention. That's why he chose Sophie, a girl in the public eye. The same goes for the senator's son. He wants to make sure he's the talk of the town. That the media will talk about this. But not because he gets a thrill out of it; no, this runs deeper. He has some sort of mission with this. Now the part about dismembering the body and putting it together the way he did using parts from another child—also from a home of divorce—it symbolizes something for him. There's a message here for us to read. After seeing this video, there is no doubt. It represents the way children are split in a divorce. There's a split between parents, and sometimes siblings are split as well, torn apart in their loyalty and sometimes physically between two homes, two lives. I must say, it's very carefully created. He's put a lot of thought into this, which tells us he's extremely calculated and deliberate. This is well-planned beyond anything I have seen before."

Matt nodded, growing paler as I spoke. "And the senator's son?"

"The senator's son, and the money in his mouth, I will assume represents poverty. How children often end up in poor conditions after a divorce. Mothers who don't get alimony or just the loss of the extra income often sends children into a life of poverty."

"But the senator's son isn't poor?" Matt said.

"I know. That's what has me wondering a little. Wait a second. The place he was found. The old lady living next door said the place had been empty. Why was it empty?"

Matt sighed. "A colleague told me yesterday that there was a tragedy about three years ago. A woman was shot by her own son. He was sick, mentally ill and had been since his dad left them. She had been pleading for help from the county to handle him because she couldn't afford it for him."

"And so, he shot her. Poverty led to tragedy. Poverty after a divorce," I said, pointing at Matt. "Now…I have a feeling that Maddie Jones fits into this picture as well. As much as I don't want to, I feel like she is about to play her part in this twisted plan."

"How?"

"Her mother," I said. "After her parents divorced, she was forced into prostitution. Not an uncommon result in poorer neighborhoods. Now, Maddie must have felt shameful about her mother's profession."

"So, you're thinking she represents the guilt and shame that children who go through a divorce often suffer?"

I gave him a smile. "Exactly."

He leaned back in his stool. "Wow. So, you're telling me we're looking for a killer who is angry about divorce?"

I grabbed another cookie and dunked it in my coffee. "Yes. It must mean something to him, something profound."

"But…that could be anyone?"

I nodded and bit into the soaked cookie. "I know. He is highly intelligent. He is most likely a very well-functioning person, might have a family and children even. He probably even holds a steady job where he never takes any sick days, and his work is impeccable, and he is very likely part of your local community or has been at some point. Why else would he choose this place?"

"Yak."

"I know. The guy is highly delusional and thinks he's on some sort of mission. He might even think he's doing something good, like he's helping the world to be a better place. Those are some of the most dangerous killers you get. They see the flaws, but they also see the solution, and they're determined to let the world know. They want to fix us all."

"So, he's a…"

"He could also be a woman, just sayin'."

"Okay, so he or *she*…is a delusional psychopath trying to change the world? Working for the greater good? And his—or her—kills are inspired by how divorce affects children? A killer who targets children of divorce?"

I nodded. "And then the worst part."

Matt's eyes grew wide. "There's a worse part?"

I nodded. "I'm afraid so." I handed Matt a cookie for comfort. He took it with worried eyes.

I tilted my head with an exhale. "This is not his last kill."

Matt sighed resignedly. "I was afraid you might say something like that. There will be more?"

"Most likely, yes. I fear that he's just getting started. He has more planned for us. That's why he has taken Maddie."

Matt looked overwhelmed. I couldn't blame him. This was quite a lot to take in.

"So, what do we do next?"

I swallowed the rest of my cookie and looked at him. "First of all, did you get someone to trace the email?"

"The IT department is on it," Matt said. "I don't know how long it will take, though."

"Okay, good. Next, we need to find Maddie before it's too late. We start by making a list of possible suspects. On the top of mine is Coach Thomas Price. It was his car that she was seen getting into. That's where we begin. Can you tell me what his mother said last night? About the car?"

He nodded. "She didn't have it anymore. It was stolen from her driveway a week ago. At first, she thought it was just some kids who had taken it for a joyride. It had happened before several times with her old car. It would come back eventually smelling of weed. But when it didn't come back the first couple of days, she figured her son had taken it back. That he needed it for something. She's old and didn't really want to get involved with the police over an old car that she didn't use much anyway, so she never reported it."

"That sounds a little off to me," I said and made a mental note. "Plus, she's saying that her son still used it even though he gave it to her. If someone was trying to hide what they were up to, that would be a good way to do it. Hiding the car at your mother's, am I right?"

"Sure."

"All right. Is she divorced?"

Matt nodded. "As a matter of fact, she is. She was married twice, and neither of the marriages lasted."

"Could be a traumatic experience for a young boy, couldn't it? I say we take a closer look at him and put a search out for the car."

Matt nodded and grabbed his phone. "Got it."

As Matt walked out on the porch to call Cooper and have him do the search, I grabbed my phone and made a call of my own, following my strong hunch from earlier.

Chapter 46

MADDIE WAS WATCHING the box that was pushed up against the end wall. She had been staring at it for forever, listening to the scratching coming from inside of it. But there was one thing that worried her deeply. As the hours passed, the scratching grew lower, and soon it was very hard to hear.

Maddie wanted so badly to yell, to talk to the box, as she wondered if someone was actually inside of it or if it might be an animal of some sort. She thought at one point that she heard someone moan.

The blindfold was still pulled up on one side of her face, so she was able to gaze out a little bit from underneath it, just enough to take a look around. Not that there was much there to see. There was nothing on the floor except the carpet, and the walls were covered in some thick black stuff. The two windows were blocked by hurricane shutters that had been pulled down, and not much sunlight came in through the cracks. But it was enough for her to know when it was daylight outside and when it was nighttime, so she would know when to sleep. She also believed she heard an engine at some point and wondered if they were close to a road. She hadn't heard any other cars, though, so it had to be a small road.

Maddie lifted her head slightly, then turned around when she saw something she hadn't noticed before. On the wall. Someone had written something. By bending her legs and moving like a worm across the carpet, she squirmed closer and was able to look at it up close. By the bottom of the wall, where the black foam stopped, someone had scratched a word into the wood.

Sydney.

Maddie looked at it, then remembered she had known a girl named Sydney once. She had lived in her building. Had there been someone here who was also named that? Who was she? Had she been a prisoner too?

The thought made Maddie shiver as the realization sunk in. She wasn't the only one, was she? There had been others, others trapped in this room just like her. But what had happened to the other girls?

Maddie began to cry, and she couldn't stop it once she had started. Not till she heard fumbling behind the door and the key was put in the lock. Knowing what this meant, Maddie gasped behind the cloth, then fought to squirm her way back to her corner. She had been able to hide from her captor that she was able to look out beneath her blindfold. If she was found at the other end of the room, her captor would find out.

More fumbling as another lock was unlocked, then a hand on the door handle, and it turned.

Hurry up, Maddie!

Maddie squirmed and squirmed, her eye constantly on the door as it opened, and she slid into her corner just in time for her captor to enter. She whimpered and rolled up into a ball, but her captor didn't seem to care about her. Instead, the dark figure moved across the floor toward the box. Maddie was able to watch as the captor peeked inside the box, lifting the lid. A smile spread across her perpetrator's face, and there was a small whisper from their lips.

"You're ready. Just in time."

Chapter 47

"WE FOUND THE CAR."

"Already? That was fast," I said as I walked back to the kitchen. Matt had been waiting for me to finish my phone call, sitting patiently by his computer, his fingers tapping nervously on the counter.

"They just called from the station and said a state trooper found it on I95 on the side of the road."

"Ditched," I said. "Someone knows we're onto him and is getting rid of evidence."

"I'll have it checked for fingerprints," Matt said.

"Good. But don't expect to find anything, just like I wouldn't expect the IT guys to be able to track the email. This guy is too clever to be tracked. He won't leave any evidence behind."

"Chris is working with YouTube to get them to take the video down," Matt said. "Before anyone else sees it."

"Great. We need to keep it bottled up for as long as possible; if the media gets…"

There was an alarm on my phone, and I looked at the display. I had received a notification on Facebook from Melissa.

Have you seen this? She wrote.

I opened the post and saw the link. Then, my heart sank.

"It's too late. It's out," I said. "It's all over Facebook."

"What is?"

I turned my phone and showed him the video—the exact same one that had been emailed to him. Matt grew pale again.

"Oh, dear God."

I sighed. "It's already been shared more than three hundred times. I'd say you have about ten minutes before you'll have the entire press corps at your station, asking for answers. Even if you manage to get Facebook to remove it, it's still too late. The damage is done."

Matt found his cell again. "I better call the chief."

While Matt called her, my own phone vibrated in my hand, and I looked at the display. It was a call from California. I took it.

"Eva Rae?"

"Yes?"

"My name is Violet Dunn. You've been searching for me?"

I exhaled and walked to the living room, then sat down with my pad and a pen. "Yes, thank you so much for returning my call. I expect you know what this is regarding?"

"Agent Fisher filled me in, yes."

"So, what do you say?"

"I say we nail this bastard. I'm ready to talk."

I clenched my fist in victory.

"Great. Let's get to work. Why don't you tell me the entire story? From the beginning. Assume I don't know anything."

Chapter 48

THEN

THE BOY WAS DRESSED in a nice suit, and his dad was putting his tie on him, then he water-combed his hair.

"There. You look very handsome."

"Thanks, Dad."

His dad gave him a friendly pat on the shoulder. "Now, you remember what to say, right?"

The boy nodded, looking down at his feet. His dad saw it and grabbed him by the chin, then pulled his face up till their eyes met.

"It's okay, son. You're doing the right thing."

The boy nodded and held his dad's hand in his as they walked out to the car and drove through town. Neither the boy nor his sister spoke during the ride there. They stared out the window, wondering what state their mother would be in when they saw her.

Inside the courtroom, a lot of things were said that the boy didn't understand. He did get words like *long-term drug abuse, aggressive behavior, and unfit mother*. The rest seemed like a blur to him. But when it was his turn, and the judge asked him, the boy stood to his feet, cleared his throat, and said:

"That's right, sir. I want to live with my dad. I don't want to see my mother anymore."

The words fell like rocks from the sky. The boy's legs were shaking as he sat down again, feeling his sister's hand in his, squeezing it. Seconds later, it was her turn, and she did as she had been told.

"No, sir. I want to live with my daddy. I don't want to see my mom anymore. She hurts me."

Then, she sat back down, and they held hands again. They kept their eyes focused on their thighs and didn't lift their gaze to look at their mother, who was sitting at the table next to them.

Daddy and New Mommy had been very careful in telling them how to do this and not to cry. They knew it would be tough. They had told them it would, but it was for the best. This way, their dad could take care of them full-time and wouldn't have to send them to her when she was high and incapable of taking care of them.

They had been talking lots and lots about how it would go down in the courtroom, and they felt ready as they left the house, but nothing had prepared them for their mother's reaction.

The crying, the wailing, the screaming. It made the children lift their heads and look at the woman they no longer recognized as their mommy. She was yelling bad words, cursing at their father, screaming at them until someone stopped her and helped her sit back down.

Next to the boy, his sister started to sob, and he squeezed her hand once again to let her know he was there, and he was strong. He wasn't going to crack, even though he sensed how the knot in his stomach was growing so fast it threatened to burst.

Chapter 49

"WHAT ARE WE DOING HERE? You can't keep us here."

The words fell as Matt and I entered the interrogation room at Cocoa Beach Police Station. Thomas Price looked at us, then laughed.

"You two, of course. I should have known."

"What is this about?"

Jenna Williams was sitting next to him, looking more confused than ever.

"We just need to have a chat with you both; that's all," Matt said and held the chair for me so I could sit down. Matt was a gentleman to the bone. It simply was against his nature to let a woman sit down on a chair without holding it for her, just like he would never enter a door without holding it for a woman first. It was so deeply rooted in him that it was impossible for him not to.

Two of Matt's colleagues had brought Thomas Price and Jenna Williams in for us after I had hung up with Violet Dunn and the district attorney's office in Orange County, California. It was late afternoon now, but all the papers had been emailed to us, and now I was looking through them.

"Does Annie know what you two are up to?" Thomas Price asked. He looked at me.

I ignored his remark, then pulled out a picture of a girl and placed it in front of him. "You remember her?"

Thomas Price glanced at the photo with an indifferent attitude. "This is an old story."

"That's not what I asked," I said. "Do you recognize her?"

He shrugged "I don't know. Maybe."

"Well, let me help your memory. Her name is LeighAnn Dunn. She's the daughter of Violet and Peter Dunn. Peter Dunn was a photographer on the World Tour of Surfing at the same time you were a competitor, am I right?"

"Sure. I remember Peter." He looked at his watch. "Listen, could we get to the point here, please? I have a lesson in half an hour."

"You might be late for that," Matt said.

I smiled, then bobbed my head. "Yeah, you might be a little late."

Thomas Price slammed his hand on the table. "What the heck is this? Why are you harassing me at my home and now dragging me down here?"

"How's your back?" I asked.

He shook his head. "It's fine."

"I thought so. What can you tell us about LeighAnn?" I asked and pointed at the girl.

He exhaled and rubbed his forehead. He was getting sweaty now. "As I told you, it was a long time ago. It's not relevant anymore."

"Six years ago," I said and showed him the file. "It says here you were arrested for molesting her in Huntington Beach at a contest there when the girl was eleven."

He sighed again. Jenna let out a light shriek.

"Listen," he said. "The girl was nuts. She lied. The charges were dropped. If you did your research well, you'd know."

"I do know that," I said. "But today, I spoke with several people, and lots of them aren't part of the WSL-tour anymore. And now they're ready to speak up. And they're telling me something funny. You know what they all told me? The same exact story, actually, which is kind of funny. At least I think so; you might not. But they all told me that the charges were dropped, but only because the WSL wanted them to be. They wanted to deal with it themselves. You had friends in high places, didn't you? They pulled the strings you needed. You were their wonder kid. A scandal like that might ruin the illusion. So, they made a deal. They told the Dunns to drop the charges and then you'd agree to drop off the tour. See, that was actually what made me wonder when I heard your story, and I went online to look into it. You were such a promising surfer. A huge talent and, suddenly, you dropped out and were never heard of again. The official story was that you had injured your back, but as I saw you the other day, doing airs and some pretty radical moves, I started to wonder if that was the entire truth. And that was when I started to ask around. A good friend of mine who works out of the FBI's LA office looked into you and found the old charges."

Thomas Price looked at me, then shrugged. "So what? As I said, it's an old story; the charges were dropped. Now, if you'll excuse me, I have to go help a kid achieve her dreams of becoming a professional surfer."

"The thing about child molesters is that they don't just stop," I said. "At least, not in my experience. They can cool down for a few years, being scared of being caught maybe, but the urge is still there. It never goes away. It nags inside them and refuses to let them go until they give in. And then one day, they slip up. They give in, just for a little…just one time."

"And then that time becomes a second time, then a third," Matt said.

I pulled out an evidence bag with Sophie's bloody underwear and put it on the table.

"And then one day it starts over again. Someone discovers what you're up to and the police get involved. You're back to being scared again."

"The blood proves nothing. She's twelve. She could have had her period," Thomas Price said.

"But she didn't," I said. "Jenna thought so too, so she took her to a gynecologist, who alerted her that this wasn't menstrual blood. She also told her that Sophie was training on way too hard of a level to have her period yet, right Jenna? She wasn't developed at all. That's when you got suspicious, right?"

"You thought it was your husband, didn't you?" Matt said, addressed to her. "At first, when the gynecologist told you her concerns. So, you wanted to divorce him. But when you realized it was Thomas, your daughter's esteemed coach, the one whose hands you had put your child's entire future in, you revoked the charges. And then you shut up like a clam."

Jenna started to cry now. She bent her head down. "I confronted him, but he told me if I ever told anyone, he wouldn't train Sophie anymore. She would never amount to anything. I knew he was right.

He's the only trainer around here good enough to take her to the top. It was her future. It was her dream."

"And your dream as well," I said. "You couldn't risk it being shattered over such a small thing, could you?"

"Exactly," she said.

I exhaled and leaned back in the chair. "So, you just decided to close your eyes to the fact that your daughter was being molested. To pretend like it wasn't happening. She trusted you. You were the adult. You were the one who was supposed to protect her. And then, every freaking day, you sent her right back into the arms of the man who molested her, the very one who hurt her. How? How does anyone do that to…your own child?"

I felt Matt's hand on my shoulder.

"I've heard enough," he said.

I nodded and gathered my files. "Me too." I rose to my feet and put my chair back in place, then walked out, Matt holding the door for me.

"What happens next?" he asked.

"The California District Attorney's Office is gathering evidence to reopen the case against Thomas Price," I said. "The parents are ready to come forward and press charges, and they say there are others too. I'm pretty sure Jenna is willing to tell her story as well, so that should be enough to put the bastard down for a long time. FBI's Orange County office will take over now. One of my old colleagues works in that office. The statute of limitations for child molestation in California is ten years after the child turns eighteen, so that shouldn't be a problem."

Matt nodded, and we walked to his desk. They had cleared the desk across from his for me to use while I was working on this case as a consultant. Barely had we sat down before Cooper came in, looking perplexed.

"We didn't find anything. Not in his house or garage or at his mother's place. No sign of Maddie Jones or that any of the others have been there."

"Because he's not our killer," I said. "Thomas Price is just a child molester. This guy we're chasing is a mastermind. He's highly intelligent. Thomas Price is not. Besides, Sophie wasn't sexually abused when we found her. As I said, that is not what turns him on."

"So, what do we do next?" Chris Cooper asked. "All of our leads are gone. The car had no fingerprints, the email couldn't be traced, neither could the Facebook post. People and the press are gathering in the lobby, asking for answers. We don't have any?"

"We get some," I said and opened my laptop that I had brought with me. "And fast. Maddie Jones is still out there and hopefully still alive."

Chapter 50

THEY CALLED from the Apple store, and I drove down there to pick up Christine's computer right before they closed. It cost a fortune to get it fixed, but I knew just how happy my girl was going to be, so I paid up and drove back home.

As I walked inside, I stumbled over a fire truck. I could hear the kids upstairs and, as the door slammed shut, Alex screamed at the top of his lungs, then jumped down the stairs and threw himself into my arms.

"Mommy!"

Christine came down after him, yelling his name. "You clean up the mess you made in my room, immediately!"

She spotted me, then sighed. I had called earlier and had my dad come over and look after the kids while I was gone. I didn't want them to be alone all afternoon.

"Oh, good, you're home," she said.

I held out the computer toward her, and her eyes grew wide. "It's fixed? You fixed it?"

I nodded victoriously, taking full credit as if I had actually fixed it myself. I handed it to my daughter, and her face lit up. She threw her arms around my neck.

"You're the best mom ever."

"You're very welcome," I said and kissed her cheek, smelling her hair. I couldn't stop thinking about that girl LeighAnn and wondering who else Thomas Price had put his nasty fingers on. For once, I felt like I had made an actual difference, and my daughter had just called me the best mom ever. That called for a glass of wine and putting my feet up. In the kitchen, I found pizza and grabbed a piece. I also found my dad at the dining table, working on his laptop.

"I thought I heard your voice," he said.

I hugged him. I liked feeling his strong arms around me. My dad had always been in good shape and still ran several times a week on the beach. I was lucky that my parents were young when they had me, and I had always been grateful for that. I hoped to keep them around for a very long time. Even though my mom often made me want to scream. They were still my parents.

"So, what are you working on?" I asked. "I thought the markets were closed now?"

"There are always deals to be made," he said, "emails to answer."

"An investment banker never sleeps, huh?" I sipped my wine.

"I guess not," he chuckled and looked at me. "So, how was your day? Did you catch your killer?"

I sipped my wine again and took a bite of pizza. "We caught a bad guy, yes. But he wasn't the guy we were looking for."

My dad nodded pensively. "I never liked that Thomas Price. That's who it was, right?"

"I am not at liberty to say," I said. "You know, ongoing investigation and all that."

He laughed. "You don't have to. I met Mrs. Weiner outside of Tiny Turtle earlier. She's Thomas's neighbor. She told me Thomas had been taken in, and Jenna too. She assumed it had to do with the murder of little Sophie."

I scoffed. "Nothing gets past you, huh?"

"Nope. It's all anyone talks about these days. Especially with the video and all that. It creeps them all out."

"It wasn't Thomas, but we'll catch the right guy. Don't worry," I said.

"I'm not worried; well, that's not entirely true. I am worried about you. It's *we* now? You're working the case?"

I nodded. "They can't do this alone. This guy is seriously deranged. And clever."

"Just make sure you take care of yourself," he said with a deep sigh. "A guy this clever can also be dangerous, remember?"

"I'll be fine," I said. "Don't worry so much."

He shook his head, then reached over for a piece of the pizza with a smile. "Don't tell your mom."

"I'm not usually in the habit of sharing secrets with her anyway," I said.

He sighed and sunk his teeth into the cheese. "It's not getting better, is it?"

I shook my head. "Why is she being like that, Dad?"

"You know your mom. It's been tough for her…ever since…you know," he said. "She was never really herself again. It broke her."

"Why can't we even talk about it?" I asked. "We never did. It was like we just decided never to mention Sydney again. Like she never existed."

My dad exhaled and put the pizza down. "It was just easier that way, I guess."

I nodded and drank my wine, thinking about that day at Wal-Mart when that man had grabbed first me then my sister. I could barely remember what she looked like anymore. I had been so young. My mom had always resented me for not being able to remember anything, and for being the one he didn't take. I couldn't blame her. I felt guilty about that too.

"Well, I should get going," my dad said and rose to his feet. He leaned over with his laptop under his arm and kissed my forehead. "Remember to take care of your family first. That's why you came down here. Don't you forget that. Enjoy every second you have with them. They won't be around forever."

Chapter 51

THE DARKNESS at nighttime was the worst part. Maddie hated when she sensed the lights go out of the room and darkness fall upon them. She knew another day had passed, another day she had spent in captivity, another day when she didn't get to see her mother or even the outside again. Oh, how she missed the fresh air.

They must be looking for me by now, right?

She sure hoped and prayed they were. She knew her mother would be, but she didn't know if her mother had returned home yet and discovered that Maddie wasn't there anymore. She could sometimes be gone for days. It could be like that time when she had ended up in the hospital and stayed there for four days before they let her go home. Her mother had told no one that she had a daughter at home, and she had been unconscious for days on end, she later told her, when Maddie was crying and asking where she had been for so long. It could be like that time, so maybe she hadn't found out that Maddie was missing yet.

Maddie had gotten some food. Earlier in the day, her captor had come into the room and had taken the cloth out of her mouth, ripping the tape off first. She had felt water splash into her mouth and bread hit her lips, and she was told to eat. So, she did. Greedily, she chewed on the old bread like it was the finest delicacy in the world. Never had bread tasted better, she thought as her stomach rumbled for more. But no more came. Her captor gave her more water, then put the cloth back in her mouth, Maddie pleading with him not to while he was taping it shut. Then she put her cheek back down on the carpet till her captor was gone again.

Now, as the darkness descended, she started to wiggle toward the box. Experience had told her that the nights were usually quiet. Her captor didn't come around at night, usually only once a day as far as she knew.

Maddie wormed her way to the box, then put her ear against it. There was a light scraping against the wood coming from inside of it. Maddie wiggled herself around so her back faced the box, then leaned her tied up hands against the box, reached out with her fingers as best she could and scratched the wood with her nails.

Then she stopped and listened. A few seconds later, there was a response. More scratching from the other side, this time louder and steadier.

Maddie laughed behind the cloth, then scraped the box again rhythmically. The scratching was repeated from inside the box.

I knew it! It's not an animal. No animal could repeat it exactly like that. This has to be a person. A real person, a human. I am not alone. Someone else is in here with me!

Up until now, Maddie had debated whether it was mice or rats maybe that she heard, but she had a feeling it was more than that, and now it was confirmed. Maddie wasn't alone.

She smiled behind the tape, then scratched the box again to let this person know she was there, and they weren't alone. The person returned her gesture, and they continued like that for a very long time until Maddie felt so exhausted she couldn't keep her eyes open behind the blindfold anymore. Knowing she had to get back to her corner, she wormed her way back across the room, this time with a feeling of hope emerging inside of her. Not only wasn't she alone in this awful place, her chances of someone looking for her—for them—had just doubled.

Chapter 52

THE FACELESS MAN is screaming and yelling because I bit his finger. Sydney is standing in front of us, dolls in her hands, as the man hisses at me. My mom has turned her cart around and sees us now.

"Help!" I scream.

"Hey!" my mom yells, panic in her voice. She runs toward us. The man sees her, then gives me a short glare. I can see that he is panicking. He doesn't know what to do. That's when I notice his eyes for the first time. They're blue.

"Stop!" my mom yells. "What are you doing?"

The faceless man reaches out toward me, and I scream. Confused, he turns around and grabs Sydney instead. He holds her with his hand over her mouth and drags her away. She drops both dolls to the floor. I'm screaming; in the distance, I can hear my mom yelling. My heart is throbbing loudly in my chest as I watch the faceless man drag my sister out toward the entrance, my mom storming after him. I watch as he carries the screaming Sydney out of the store, where a white van waits for him, engine running.

The last thing I hear is my mom's heartbreaking screams, and then the engine roaring as the van takes off.

I WOKE UP WITH A START. It wasn't the dream that woke me up; it was something else. A noise, I realized as I came back to myself. It was my phone; it was glowing in the darkness and vibrating. I looked at it. It was Melissa.

"What's going on?"

"It's Dawn," she said. "She's in the hospital."

I jolted upright. "What happened?"

"He beat her up."

"Oh, no, is she all right?" I asked.

"I...I don't know. I just got the call from her mother, and then I called you."

I sprang to my feet. "I'll pick you up in two minutes. Be ready."

I walked into Olivia's room and woke her up, telling her what had happened and that I needed to be gone for a few hours.

"It's okay, Mom," she said and kissed me. "You do what you have to do."

Neither of us spoke in the car while driving down Minutemen Causeway. As we reached A1A, Melissa sobbed.

"I knew he was bad for her, you know?"

I nodded. "He just seemed so nice."

"They all do," she said. "But she has a talent for finding them in a crowd. It's like she's drawn to them somehow. She only finds the true psychopaths, the ones who have everyone fooled."

I drove up in front of Cape Canaveral Hospital and parked the minivan. My heart was aching for Dawn as we took the elevator up to her room and walked inside. Her mom was sitting by her side when we entered. She stood to her feet. I remembered her from my childhood. A small woman who—just like Dawn—seemed to carry the weight of the world on her shoulders, but she was doing everything in her power to hide it.

"Melissa, and...Eva Rae? Is that you, girl?"

I nodded and hugged Dawn's mother. I could feel the bones in her body and feared I might crush her as I put my arms around her.

"How's she doing?" I asked. I looked at Dawn on the bed. Her face was almost unrecognizable. It was painful to see. Melissa burst into tears when she saw her. It was tough not to follow.

"She's sleeping now," her mother said. "They gave her something. She couldn't find rest."

We went to get some coffee and waited by her side for a couple of hours, sleeping in chairs, curled up uncomfortably. The night there gave me lots of time to think while looking out over the Banana River that the hospital faced. In the distance, I could see the lights from the cruise ships docked in Cape Canaveral while I thought about the case. It had brought so many memories up in my life that I could hardly sleep anyway. I kept thinking about Sydney and what had happened back then. I remembered how devastated I was, especially when I couldn't talk to my parents about what had happened. I just remembered the house suddenly going so quiet. It was like we stopped talking altogether. And laughing. There was no more laughter in my childhood home, where there had been so much before. Sydney had been the funny one, the one who always kept the rest of us happy.

I sipped my coffee in the hospital room, wondering what she would look like now if she were still alive. I remembered thinking I saw her everywhere in the days afterward. So often, I was certain it was her, but of course, it wasn't. It was just my imagination. She was gone and probably dead. Still, I never could stop wondering. What if she was still around? Every now and then, I would still think I saw her in a crowd.

"Mom?"

Dawn woke up. She blinked her eyes, and we went over to her. "Eva? Is that you?"

I grabbed her hand in mine and squeezed it. "We're going to nail that bastard for what he did to you. I'm going to talk to Matt as soon as it is morning, and he'll…"

"Stop," Dawn said and shook her head.

"What?"

"I don't want you to make a big deal about this," she said. "Phillip is a nice guy. He's just…well, I'm the one who…"

"Don't you even dare go there," I protested. "This can never be your fault. Never."

"Eva Rae is right," Melissa said, wiping tears from her eyes. "You shouldn't let him get away with this."

"He's been through so much," Dawn said. "His ex-wife left him just two months ago. Took the kid with her. He just misses his daughter. That's all. It was his night off. I was drunk; we both were and then… we got into a stupid fight. I said something about him probably being the one who pushed his ex away and that was why she left. He couldn't take that. So, he hit me. Please, just leave him alone."

I looked at her, shaking my head. "I can't believe you. He does this to you, and you're…you're making excuses for him?"

"He's not a bad guy, Eva Rae," Dawn said. "I just have to be more careful what I say to him. That's all."

I left the room angrily. Melissa ran out after me. "Eva Rae, don't."

I stopped. I couldn't hold the tears back anymore, and now they were rolling down my cheeks.

"I can't just…I can't just…"

She grabbed my hand. "If she doesn't want to press charges, then that's her choice," she said. "You can't force her. You have to let it go."

"I'm going to freakin' kill that guy," I said.

"She won't press charges," Melissa said. "It's how it always goes. We can't change her, Eva Rae."

"What the heck happened to her? She used to be so strong?" I asked through tears.

"You also remember her dad, right?" Melissa said.

"Of course, how could I forget?"

"So, you remember how he treated her and her mother like dirt. All of Dawn's life while growing up. She would come to school with bruises, always on her body so no one would notice except her closest friends. Now, she's doing it to herself. How many times do you think I've been out here with her like this? It happens all the time. And, every time, she says she will stop seeing the guy, but next thing, she's back with him again. Or she finds someone new just like him. She can't help herself."

I wiped away the tears with my hand. "Maybe she can't stop it. But I can."

"Eva Rae, I don't like that look in your eyes," she said as I turned around and walked away. "What are you going to do, Eva Rae? Eva Rae?"

Chapter 53

I DROVE down my street and continued past my house. Two houses down, I parked and shut off the engine. Wild rage still rushing through my veins, I walked up to his door and knocked.

It took a few minutes before the light was turned on inside and someone came to the door. It was him. His hair was tousled, and his face bore marks from sleeping.

"Eva Rae? What...?"

"You sick bastard," I said, then clenched my fist and placed a punch right on his nose. His nose made a loud cracking noise as it met my knuckles. Phillip screamed and bent forward.

"What the...? What are you doing?" he yelled. He held a hand to his nose, and it came back with blood on it.

"That was for Dawn," I said, then turned on my heel and walked away. I could still hear him yelling at me as I started up the car and backed all the way down to my own house and went inside.

Once inside, I found some ice and applied it to my pounding knuckles, then sat down by the kitchen table with a deep sigh. I knew I wouldn't be able to sleep, so instead, I grabbed my laptop and opened the lid.

I entered the station's database, then opened Sophie Williams' case and went through all the files, going through every little detail of her disappearance from the Girl Scout camp. I wasn't quite sure what I was looking for, but anything that would stand out, anything no one had noticed before.

Except there wasn't anything. The leader, Michaela Strong had been interviewed over and over again about the last hours before the girl disappeared. She was also the one who had found out that Sophie was no longer in her tent when she came to wake her up the next morning. She had started the search in the woods afterward. She had called the police. For a very long time, they believed Sophie had walked out at night and gotten herself into the swamps and drowned. They had searched the river and swamps nearby for days afterward, using helicopters and airboats, but found nothing. The dogs hadn't been able to pick up a trace either. They had found nothing, not even a shoe or a piece of her clothing. Her sleeping bag had been gone with her, and that was what puzzled the investigation team. If she had wandered off, why bring the sleeping bag? If she were kidnapped, why would the perpetrator take it with him? It made no sense to them. Until now.

He placed her there in her sleeping bag for us to unwrap her, like a freakin' Christmas present.

I sighed and leaned back in my chair, running a hand through my hair. My eyes fell on the stacks of books and research files I had left out in the hope that I might one day get a little time to write my book. I wondered if I ever would. I had to, at some point, find the time. It was my bread and butter now. I had a deadline.

I grabbed one of the books and flipped a few pages, wondering about this Phillip character. He rubbed me the wrong way and had from the first time I met him. Why had he given Christine a ride the other day? I had met him once, and then he believed he could just drive around with my daughter? His car had been white too, like the one I saw at night in the alley, and like the one we saw in the picture. I hadn't taken a look at the license plate when he dropped off Christine. I should have paid more attention. That would have told me if it was the same one that picked up Maddie. He could have stolen it from Thomas Price's mother's driveway. It would be easy, and it would drive the suspicions elsewhere. Maybe that's what he wanted all along? To get us to focus on Coach Thomas so he could continue his mission on his own. Was it possible? Could Phillip be the killer? Was he sending me a message by taking my daughter for a ride? To let me know he could get to me at any time he wished? Get to the ones I loved?

He's too perfect, were Melissa's words. Could she be right? He sure fit the profile. He'd just gone through a difficult divorce too.

My eyes returned to the screen while a million thoughts rushed through my mind. Did Phillip Anderson know Sophie Williams from somewhere? I looked through the files and found his name on the search team along with the rest of the firefighters from our local station. They had pitched in and helped where they could, of course they had. Everyone did that around here, so nothing suspicious about that.

My head was spinning out of control. I opened Google and searched for articles about Sophie's disappearance and found hundreds in *Florida Today* alone. I spent the next several hours reading through them all until daybreak came and the sun began to rise outside my window. When the alarm rang on my phone, I laid my eyes on a picture in one of the later articles, an interview with Michaela Strong, the leader. As I stared at the picture, my heart started to pound heavily in my chest.

There it was; staring right back at me from the newspaper clip was what I had been looking for.

Chapter 54

"ARE YOU INSANE?"

Matt stared at me as I entered the police station and walked up to my desk. The place smelled of freshly brewed coffee. I needed that. I had fought with the kids all morning to get them to school on time. Christine had ended up yelling at me that she hated me. So much for best mom ever. Guess that was already forgotten by now.

"And a good morning to you too," I said and put my laptop down. I sat on my chair.

He came closer and leaned in over me. "You punched Phillip Anderson last night?"

"Oh, that, well…yes."

He shook his head and threw out his arms. "Are you crazy?"

"You already asked me that once," I said. "But to answer, no."

"He was in here earlier, blabbing on about how you came to his house in the middle of the night and punched him in the nose. The chief was furious. Why, Eva Rae? Why would you do that?"

"He deserved it."

A furrow appeared between his eyebrows. "I don't get you. He was threatening to press charges and everything. You're lucky you have me. I managed to talk him out of it."

"Let him," I said.

"What?"

"Let him press charges. I'll show the judge the pictures of the woman that he beat senseless last night."

Matt pulled out his own chair and sat down. "What are you talking about? Phillip? He would never do anything like that."

"Oh, I have the pictures to prove otherwise," I said and grabbed my phone. I found a series of pictures I had taken of Dawn while she was sleeping, just in case we needed them for prosecution later. I was still hoping she would change her mind and press charges against this guy.

Matt grabbed my phone and looked through them, swiping with small light gasps emerging from between his lips.

"In case you can't tell, that's Dawn. What's left of her."

"Phillip did this?"

I nodded.

"Oh, the bastard, I have never…" He looked up, and our eyes met. "He's such a nice guy?"

"They're usually the worst," I said, thinking about Chad and how wonderful he had been when we first met. He had never laid a hand on me; that wasn't his style, but he had turned around completely and showed a side to himself I didn't know existed. I could never have imagined he would abandon his children like that and not want to be with them anymore. Just like that. Had anyone told me six months ago, I would have laughed. Those kids were his entire life. I thought I knew him, but apparently, I had no clue.

"Wow, I must say, I am…baffled."

"Yeah, well…I have more," I said. "I've been looking into our little friend Phillip a little and guess what I found?"

"I have a feeling I'm not going to like this," he said.

I pulled out a print of the article and pushed it toward him. Matt looked at it, then back at me.

"So?"

"His ex-wife is Michaela Strong," I said. "And there's more. He was there. At the camp on the day Sophie disappeared."

"Okay, just as you were about to make sense, you go full-blown crazy on me again," Matt said. "What are you suggesting? He was there in the afternoon, yes, to talk about fire safety. His wife had asked him to. He does that all the time. He talks at the school every year too."

"But he was there on the day she disappeared. He stayed the night too. At the camp."

"With his wife and daughter, who was also part of the Girl Scout camp," he said. "It's perfectly normal. We were actually very happy he was there, so he could help with the search from the beginning and take charge of the situation. It could have ended in terrible chaos. He and his wife stayed on top of it from the beginning."

"Okay, but there's more," I said.

"Of course, there is," Matt said. He looked at me with a sly smile, like he was enjoying this. I ignored him and slid another piece of paper toward him.

"Have you been up all night or something?" he asked.

"Something like that," I said. "Read."

"What am I looking at here?" he asked. "Can't you just tell me and save some time?"

"Okay," I said. "I did a little search on Phillip in the newspaper's database, and this came up. This is a picture of Phillip with the senator's son from last year's Christmas parade."

"I can see what it is," Matt said, "but why is it important?"

"They knew each other," I said.

"This is Cocoa Beach; everyone knows each other."

"Okay, but there is one last thing that I found," I said.

"I can't wait to hear what it is," he said. He was starting to annoy me, but I did my best to ignore him.

"Maddie Jones," I said.

"Let me guess, he knew her too?" Matt asked.

"I called her mother this morning after driving the kids to school because Alex missed the bus again. She went to high school with Phillip up in Daytona. Before she was divorced, they lived not far from one another, and their girls used to play together when they were younger."

I looked at Matt. He shrugged. "So what?"

"Don't you see? He's connected to all three children?" I asked.

"So what? It's Cocoa Beach. We're all connected in one way or another. That doesn't prove anything."

"I know it doesn't, but it creates a connection. And that's all I need to get suspicious. The guy fits the profile like a glove. I'm sure if I dig a little deeper, I'll find more, something we can actually use against him."

Matt leaned back and crossed his arms over his chest with a sigh.

"What?"

"Listen, I get it. You want to nail this guy for what he did to Dawn;

heck I want him punished for that too, but that doesn't mean he's our killer."

I nodded, knowing he was right. I couldn't let myself be blinded by my desire to get justice for Dawn.

"True," I said. "But it doesn't mean he didn't do it either. Besides, right now he's our only lead so far, so I say we go with it."

Matt sighed, then rose to his feet. "I'll get us some coffee."

Chapter 55

THEN

AFTER THE COURT had given their dad full custody, they moved to another part of town. The boy liked it there. His father built a playhouse in the treetop, and the boy spent many afternoons up there in that place that he had all to himself because his sister was busy swinging on the new swing set that their dad had put up for them.

New Mommy got a big bump on her stomach, and soon they were blessed with another sister, one who cried a lot at night, but otherwise brought much joy to the family.

As the years passed, the boy almost forgot about his mother, even though he sometimes sat in his tree house and cried about her. But he never told that to anyone. That was his little secret and the treehouse his hideout, where he could think about her and cry if he needed to without anyone seeing it.

He was angry with his mother for choosing the life she had and for not wanting him like his dad said she didn't. Instead, she had chosen a life of drugs and drinking and being a stripper. Hearing him talk about The Thing and how she lived her life made the boy feel ugly and dirty. His mother didn't even call on birthdays and, by the time the boy was a teenager, he resented his mother and he decided she was dead to him. He decided he might as well pretend like she didn't exist.

One day, as they were crossing the street and he was holding his sister's hand on their way home from school, there was a sudden yelling of his name. He recognized the voice, and the boy knew very well that it was her.

He didn't turn and look, but pulled his sister's arm to cross the street, but hesitated for just a second as his mother yelled their names once again. As he paused, the light changed, and he could no longer cross. This meant their mother could catch up to them.

"Hi, baby; hi, sweetie," she said, panting from running.

The boy didn't even look at her. He kept his eyes focused on the light and kept himself ready to rush across the street as soon as it changed. He held his sister close.

"Oh, my God," his mother said, clasping her face with her hands. "You've both grown so much."

She reached out her hands and felt his face. The boy pulled away, still without looking straight at her.

"Oh, my babies," his mother said, sobbing loudly now. "I can't believe it. Do you live nearby? I know your dad moved you. Is it close to here? Oh, it's so wonderful…I am so happy to see you both."

As she spoke, the light changed, and the boy pulled his sister's arm forcefully, saying:

"We're not happy to see you."

With those words he walked away, pulling his sister hard, still maintaining his posture and not letting even one tear escape the corner of his eyes. He wasn't going to give her the pleasure of seeing that.

Chapter 56

EVER SINCE THE BREAK-IN, Mary hadn't been sleeping well. It had happened three weeks ago but still gave her the chills, especially at night when everything was so quiet. It was on nights like these that she wished Don was still there with her. He had left her when the kids were one and three years old. Right when it got really tough, he had simply left and not looked back. Mary knew she too played her part in him leaving. She didn't fool herself and say she was the innocent one. She hadn't been herself since the birth of their second child. A depression her doctor had later told her it was. Postpartum. But at first, she didn't know what it was. It had knocked her out completely. For months, it was like she walked in a haze like she couldn't cope with anything in life, especially not a young child crying all night. And that was when she started taking it out on Don. He was the one who had worked all day to support them and, as soon as he came home, she couldn't help herself. She had to unload. At first, it was because she wanted him to feel sorry for her, to know that she too had a rough day, that she felt inadequate and guilty for not feeling all oozy and happy at the arrival of a new child. But when he hadn't been understanding the way she wanted him to, when he hadn't said the right things, and instead told her she was lucky that she got to stay at home, that was when she started to resent him. Mostly, she probably resented herself for not enjoying staying at home with the children like her mother had when she was a child. It was all Mary had ever dreamt of when growing up.

Like her friends, she didn't dream of some big career. She just simply wanted to be a mother. But once the kids, Rylan and Faith, arrived, it had been nothing like what she wanted, what she thought it would be. Instead of feeling fulfilled, she had felt inadequate. She had this constant feeling of not being enough nagging inside of her, and this voice in her mind telling her she was doing it all wrong, that she was not cut out to be a mother, that she would end up destroying her children.

The yelling was bad, but it wasn't what drove him away. It was when the yelling stopped. Realizing it did her no good, that nothing in this world could make her feel better, Mary simply gave up. She dragged herself out of bed in the mornings and only did what was most necessary until she could crawl back into bed. Soon, she didn't even leave the bed at all.

Don begged her to talk to someone, to go to a doctor, but she didn't want to. She couldn't deal with the guilt that would ram her if she explained to someone from the outside that she couldn't even cope with her children, if she had to tell him how she had neglected her own children. She simply couldn't face that conversation.

So, she stayed in bed, and one day, Don didn't come home from work. He stayed out all night, and after three days, he finally came home...drunk. He told her he couldn't take anymore, that he had taken a job in Louisiana and he and a buddy were going up there the very next day.

Mary hadn't even asked him to stay. She had barely looked at him, and Don had left crying, slamming the door behind him. The divorce papers came with the mail a few days later when Mary had finally managed to get up and take care of her children. She realized she was all alone down here in Florida since all of her family lived up in North Carolina. It was after a phone call from her mother that she finally got herself to a doctor, who gave her the diagnosis and some medicine. Now she was doing a lot better and so were the kids. She didn't even miss Don, to be honest. Or all the fighting. It was actually better now that she was all alone. Don sent a check every month for them, and they lived decently.

The break-in had happened a few weeks ago. It wasn't so much the fact that there had been someone in her apartment; that was bad, yes, but the worst part was that it happened in the middle of the night, while Mary and the kids were asleep.

When they woke up the next day, the window facing the street was open, and there were dirty footprints on the carpet. Luckily, nothing had been taken, and the police told Mary that it was probably just some homeless person looking for shelter, thinking there was no one home, and then when he realized they were there, he had left.

Mary had believed them but still felt uneasy in her own bedroom. So it was again this evening when she had put the children to bed, and she lay in her bed, waiting for sleep to overpower her. She couldn't help hearing all these sounds, and it kept making her open her eyes and look toward the window. She thought she heard something again, then opened her eyes and thought she saw a shadow walk past her window. The shadow continued on, and she knew it was probably just someone walking on the sidewalk outside of her building, then she closed her eyes again.

Sleep, come on, wondrous sleep.

Finally, Mary dozed off, and soon she was snoring lightly. She didn't even hear the window being pulled open from the outside, nor did she hear it when a pair of very dirty shoes landed on her carpet. She did, however, hear her own name being whispered very close to her ear, and she opened her eyes with a gasp, just in time to feel the fingers as they tightened their grip around her neck.

Chapter 57

"FIRE!"

I had barely set foot inside the house before Alex jumped out in front of me, screaming the word. I grabbed my chest.

"Alex! You scared me!"

The boy swung his ax in the air, making noises like he was smashing a window, then ran off.

"Oh, good, you're home," Christine said as I entered the kitchen and put down my computer. She was eating cereal and handed me the empty milk jug. "We're out of milk. Again."

"Awesome," I said and threw the jug in the recycle bin.

"And we're out of clean underwear too. All of us."

I nodded and sat down on a stool next to her by the counter. "I see. And how was your day?"

She shrugged. "Normal."

"And school?"

She shrugged again and looked at her phone. "Usual."

I nodded, then looked at my watch. I could still make it to Publix before dinner and put in a load of laundry.

"Dad called today," she said like it was the most natural thing in the world. My eyes grew wide.

"Excuse me?"

"He called me. From Greece. Said he was coming home in two

days. He wants to see us when he comes back. Can we go up there next weekend?"

"He wants to see you?" I asked, startled.

"That's what I just said," she said, annoyed.

"Well, I just…" I stopped myself. I couldn't really tell her that I had thought he didn't want to see them, but that was silly. I could see that now. Of course, he wanted to see them on weekends and vacations from time to time. He was, after all, their father. They had once been his entire life. What he didn't want anymore was the workload, all the trouble it was to take care of them.

"So, can we go?"

"Sure," I said.

She smiled. "Good. I can't wait to see him and hear about his trip. You think he bought us something?"

I nodded. "I'm sure he did."

She smiled again. "He better."

Christine finished her cereal, then left the kitchen, still playing some game on her phone. I chuckled, then decided to make the trip to Publix when my phone rang. It was from Alex's school. That was never a good sign. I picked it up.

"Eva Rae Thomas."

It was Alex's teacher, Miss Melanie. She sounded serious, and I braced myself for what Alex had gotten himself into now.

"We need to talk," she said. "Can you come in tomorrow? Say, around eleven o'clock?"

I swallowed and felt my hands go clammy. I knew Alex wasn't easy and wondered what he had been up to now.

"Sure," I said. "May I ask what this is about?"

"I prefer we talk about it when you come. See you tomorrow."

I put the phone down, feeling like I had just been called to the principal's office. I sighed, then walked up to Christine and told her to look after her baby brother while I went to Publix. On my way out the door, I texted Olivia and asked her what she was doing, why she hadn't come home from school yet, then received the answer that she had volleyball practice and that I really should know these things by now.

Chapter 58

MADDIE STARED at the letters scratched into the wall.

Sydney.

She couldn't stop wondering about this girl and who she was. Where was she now? Had she gone home to her mom? Was she back with her friends, back in school again, and was everything back to normal again? Maddie would give anything for normal right now. She would love to be able to go to school again, even to be faced with Gareth and his bullies. Even they would be better than what she was facing now.

The person inside the box had grown quiet, and there hadn't been a sound coming from in there all day. She wondered if this person was still in there at all. She had scratched on the outside of the box several times, but there had been no response. It felt devastating to Maddie because she felt like she had just found this person, she had just realized she wasn't alone in this, and yet now she somehow was again.

I miss my mommy. Why can't I just go home to her?

Maddie wondered if this was all her own fault. Maybe it was some sort of punishment? But for what? Could it be for breaking her mother's watch and not telling her about it? Could it be for the bad grades she had on her last report card and because she had signed it for her mommy because she didn't come home in time? And maybe because she didn't want her to see it because she'd only get mad at her because she wanted so badly for her to do better in life than she had?

Or was it because it was all her fault that her dad had left and that her mother had to work as a hooker? That's what Gareth and his friends had told her it was called. A dirty hooker. Did that mean Maddie was dirty too?

Maddie sniffled, then looked out under the blindfold, when suddenly there was a sound coming from outside the door. Maddie knew these sounds by now. The scrambling, the rustling, then the opening of locks, and soon the creaking of the door, followed by the heavy footsteps.

She knew the procedure by heart, and it always filled her with the greatest terror. Maddie gasped and realized she wouldn't be able to get back into her corner, so instead, she crumpled up into a ball by the opposite wall. The footsteps walking across the floor were determined, but they didn't come close to her. Instead, they walked to the box, then stopped. Out of the small crack under her blindfold, she could see a dolly being inserted underneath the box and it being lifted into the air, then rolled across the carpet toward the door. Maddie gasped as she saw it disappear out the door, then the door being slammed shut again behind it and the sound of it being locked.

Maddie sobbed when she realized that now she was actually all alone again. The person in the box was gone. She didn't know what this meant. Did the person get to go back to his or her family? Or was he…or she…?

Maddie didn't dare to finish the thought. Instead, she crumpled up on the floor next to the name on the wall, then cried till she exhausted herself so much that she fell asleep.

Chapter 59

I GRABBED three gallons of milk to make sure we could make it for a few days before I had to shop again, then got the rest of the items on my grocery list, and even added some candy for the kids. To sweeten their lives a little. I knew I was going to end up eating most of it, but I bought it anyway. Halloween was coming up at the end of the month, and you had to have sweets in your house.

I spotted him in aisle three. He was looking at cereal, holding a box of Cinnamon Toast Crunch out and putting it in his cart. I wondered who in his household ate that.

Phillip Anderson spotted me as I came closer and took two boxes of Cheerios.

"What? Are you stalking me now?" he asked. His nose looked swollen and crooked. It was still purple in places.

I looked into his cart. There was a roll of duct tape and zip tie strips. "To put up Halloween decorations," he said.

"I'm just getting cereal for my kids," I said.

"You're lucky I don't press charges; do you know that?" he asked.

"Well, I could say the same about you. How did you convince her not to, huh? Did you tell her you'd beat her even more?"

Phillip looked at me, his teeth gritted. "I wasn't even with her when it happened."

I wrinkled my forehead. "You're lying!"

"You think you know me, huh?" he asked. "You've never even

talked to me properly. You just come down here and start judging me. You have no idea who I am and what I am capable of."

"Wow. That sounded almost like a threat," I said.

He growled. "Argh, it doesn't matter what I say to you. You'll just twist it anyway. Don't you get it? I didn't hurt Dawn. I love her. I don't understand what happened. Yesterday, we were dating and having a wonderful time, and then suddenly today I hear she's in the hospital and everyone thinks I put her there. I've tried to call her, but her mom keeps answering the phone, telling me to stay away from her. I am completely freaking out, and I have my daughter coming this weekend, and I was hoping they'd meet. What if she hears these stories too? About me beating Dawn up?"

I paused. "Well…didn't you?"

"No! That's what I've been trying to say all this time. Even my colleagues at the station won't believe me. Everyone in this stupid town thinks I beat her up."

"Wait…Why should I believe you?" I said.

He threw out his arms. "I wasn't even with her last night. She was going home for dinner with her parents. I had coffee with her at Juice N' Java at three o'clock and then she kissed me and told me we'd see each other tomorrow. She had promised her mom she'd take her dad for a walk. He's in a wheelchair, you know? They like to drive out to Lori Wilson Park, and she helps him get all the way down to the beach. He loves it there. He misses the ocean."

"He was an excellent surfer back in the day," I said, remembering Dawn's dad in the lineup. It was always spectacular to watch him do tricks on his longboard. I chewed on this new information while my eyes locked with Phillip's, wondering what the heck was going on. If Phillip hadn't put Dawn in the hospital, then who had?

I left Phillip in the aisle, then rushed to the checkout, holding the phone between my shoulder and my ear while calling Melissa.

Chapter 60

MELISSA TOLD me Dawn had been discharged from the hospital and that she was staying with her parents, so her mother could take care of her. I drove to their house and parked in the driveway, my heart racing in my chest. What was going on here? I kept wondering.

I grabbed a bag of Reese's Peanut Butter Cups and walked up to her door, then rang the doorbell. Her mother opened it.

"Eva Rae? What a nice surprise." She wiped her hands on a dishtowel, then opened the door for me to enter. "I put her in her old room."

"How is she?" I asked.

Her mother shook her head and looked down. "Not good."

"Can I go see her?"

"Yes, yes, of course. Go ahead. You know your way."

I did. It was strange how being there again brought back so many memories and emotions I had completely forgotten. Inside her parents' house, it was as if time had stood still. Even the smell was the same as it had been back then. The furniture was all in the same place.

I knocked lightly on Dawn's old door, then peeked inside.

"Hey there."

"Eva Rae!"

She sat up in the bed, but I could tell by her strained face that she was in pain.

"I brought you chocolates," I said and handed her the bag.

She smiled. I opened the pack and fed her one. She could barely get it inside her swollen lips and winced in pain from where they were cracked. As she opened her mouth, I could tell that two of her front teeth were chipped.

I stuffed my mouth with two pieces at the same time, trying to suppress my desire to burst into tears. Dawn chewed cautiously, but it seemed to be more pain than pleasure for her.

"You want another one?" I asked.

She shook her head, and I exhaled, then ate another chocolate. I had a knot in my stomach, and a big part of me just wanted to run out of there, but I had to have some answers. I had to know what was going on with her. Something wasn't right.

"I punched Phillip," I said and grabbed her hand in mine.

"No!" she said, her swollen eyes lingering on me.

"Yes," I said with a chuckle. "Hit him right on the nose. I was that mad at him for what he did to you."

She slumped her head, and her eyes looked away.

"Dawn?" I paused. I really didn't want to ask about this, but I had to. "It wasn't him, was it? He didn't do this to you, did he?"

Dawn lifted her head and glared at me from inside the small cracks between her swollen eyelids. I could tell she was contemplating what to say to me. I let her think it over.

"It was never any of them, was it?" I asked and held her hand tightly in mine. "All the times you ended up in the hospital. It was never your boyfriends."

Her eyes lingered on me still; her nostrils were flaring lightly. I could tell she was getting agitated, scared even.

I leaned closer and squeezed her hand tightly. "It's okay, Dawn. You can tell me. I remember how your dad used to beat you when we were children. My guess is the abuse never stopped. Am I right? Is it still him?"

Dawn's nostrils flared violently now, and she shook her head.

"It's okay, Dawn," I said. "You can tell me everything."

Dawn shook her head fiercely now and was breathing heavily. Her eyes were staring at me and fear seemed to be spiraling through her.

"What's wrong?" I asked, then turned to look at what was behind me. I barely managed to duck before the crowbar whooshed through the air and hit me on the shoulder. I screamed and fell to the floor, then looked up at Dawn's mother, who was hovering above me.

"This is my daughter," she almost screamed at me. "You're not going to take my daughter away from me, do you hear me?"

She swung the crowbar again, and it whistled through the air, then hit my arm. I screamed in pain.

"MOM, NO!"

Dawn screamed from behind me as her mother jammed the crowbar down on me once again, barely missing me as I rolled to the side. As I did, I reached down my leg and found my weapon and pulled it out of the ankle holster, then pointed it at her.

"Stop, Vivian," I panted. "It's over."

The woman's wild eyes glared down at me, and I could tell she didn't care. She swung the crowbar once again, and I fired my gun, hitting her in the shoulder. The shock was so great that she dropped the crowbar, then fell backward and landed against the dresser, her eyes struck with deep fear. I rose to my feet, still pointing the gun at her as she sank to the floor, blood gushing out of her wound.

Chapter 61

"SO, it was her the entire time?"

Melissa handed me a bottle of water, and I drank greedily, wishing it was something a little stronger. I was sitting with Dawn, who was still crying heavily. I couldn't get her to stop. I had given my statement to the police, and Dawn's mother had been taken away in an ambulance. The paramedics had also tended to my bruises. They wanted me to go in for an x-ray to see if anything was broken, but I told them I had to go home. I felt okay. I was sore and in pain, but I didn't think anything was broken.

Dawn nodded and looked up at Melissa. "I am so sorry, you guys. I should have...I should have told you. I lied to you."

"I can't believe it," Melissa said.

I nodded. "Me either. All those years, we believed it was your father who had beaten you up and...you were just covering for your mother?"

Dawn looked away. Tears spilled onto her bedcovers, and she wiped them away.

"Over the years, it got worse," she said. "And as I grew older, I began saying it was my boyfriends. I didn't mean to lie or get them in trouble. It was just easier that way."

"And because it was too embarrassing to tell anyone that your mother still beat you," Melissa said.

"Using a crowbar, apparently," I said, feeling my sore shoulder.

"I…I tried to get away from her. I tried to stop visiting, but she was just…she had such a stronghold on me. It was like I was powerless. I don't know how she did it, but she always made me come back. She would guilt trip me or tell me my dad was sick, and then when I came to see him, she beat me. It was actually better if I came often because then she wouldn't touch me for a long time unless I upset her somehow. It was worst when I had boyfriends. She got so jealous and would tell me I was worthless, that he would leave me, that no one would ever marry me. I tried to hide them from her, but somehow, she always found out. A neighbor would tell her that she saw me with someone downtown or she would follow me in her car and see us together. And then she would become this monster, yelling at me that I wanted to leave her, that I was a loser and that I was destroying the family and making my dad upset. It was actually mostly to see him that I ever came home. I felt like I needed to be there for him. He was the one who was really trapped here with her."

"Wait…she put him in the wheelchair?" I asked.

Dawn nodded. "He was about to leave her. After so many years of abuse, he was a broken man, and then one day, he finally found the courage to stand up to her. She pushed him down the stairs, and he landed in the wrong way, getting paralyzed from the waist down."

"That way, she made sure he never could leave her, that he was forever dependent on her. Just like she made sure you were," I said. "If you never had a boyfriend, you'd never leave her. So, she destroyed every relationship you ever had. It was a way for her to control you."

"I still…I can't…It's sick. I can't believe I never saw this," Melissa said. "I just thought…I always thought you found these bad guys. I had no idea what you were going through, Dawn. I feel terrible. Poor you."

"It wasn't your fault," Dawn said, smiling between tears.

I couldn't hold mine back anymore either and, a few seconds later, we all three joined in a hug until Dawn groaned in pain and we had to let go of her.

"No more secrets," I said, wiping my tears away. "You hear me? The three of us, we need each other, and we can't be of help if we're not honest."

"Okay," Melissa said with a deep sniffle. "That's a deal."

"You start by telling us what's going on with Matt. And be honest," she said laughing.

I blew my nose, then threw the tissue at her.

"I do know one thing, though," I said. "I owe Phillip a major apology."

Dawn exhaled deeply. "So do I. If anyone owes him one, it must be me."

Chapter 62

I HAD CALLED my dad and asked him to be with the kids till I got back. It was late, and they were all asleep as I entered the house. Even my dad was napping on my couch in the living room, snoring loudly.

I woke him with a kiss on the forehead. He smiled happily. "You're back?"

I nodded and sat down with a deep sigh. He sat up and folded his hands. "That bad, huh?"

"Worse," I said. "I'll tell you about it another day. Right now, I am beat and just want to go to bed. Thanks for coming over."

"I'm glad I could be of help. Your mom has been out all day anyway."

"Where has she been?" I asked and put my feet up on the coffee table that my mom had bought for me because she said I couldn't have a house without a coffee table. I knew she would have a heart attack if she saw me put my dirty shoes on her expensive table, but I didn't care.

"Winter Park, visiting her girlfriends. They all live there now," he said. "Because of the gated communities and golf courses. And less risk of hurricane damage, they believe."

"Let me guess...she wants to go live there as well?" I asked.

"Well, naturally. The neighborhoods are far more well-trimmed, as she puts it."

"But you don't want that," I said.

"No. Of course not. I like it out here. I like the ocean breeze, and I like the surfers and the laid-back attitude. In there it's so…uptight. It's not for me. I need the ocean close. Makes it less unbearable in the summer too. I wouldn't last a day in there in the summer. Besides, I still have my business to attend to."

"You could do that in there," I said grinning, knowing that had probably been my mom's argument too.

"True. That's a lousy argument. But I am not going. End of discussion. If she wants to go see her friends in Winter Park, then she can do the drive."

"Sounds like something you guys can argue about for the next several years," I said.

My dad chuckled and got up. He leaned over and kissed my forehead. I pulled him into a hug, thinking about Dawn and all that she had been through. He put his arms around me. I closed my eyes and enjoyed being held.

"Don't give in to her," I said as he let go of me. "Ever."

He shook his head. "I won't."

I walked him out and then closed the door behind him, thinking I had been lucky with my parents after all. At least compared to Dawn. My mother was just coldhearted toward me. She had, after all, never laid a hand on me. I turned off the lights in the living room, then noticed something on the light carpet. I knelt and sighed, realizing it was some of Alex's green slime. It was deep into the carpet, and someone had stepped in it. It had left big marks all over the carpet and into the hallway. It was going to take forever to get out.

I sighed and decided that would have to wait till the morning, then walked up the stairs, and checked on the kids in their rooms before turning in. As soon as my head hit the pillow, I was sound asleep.

Chapter 63

"MOMMY. MOMMY! I GOT AN AWARD."

I am running through the house, holding the medal in my hand. The house is so quiet. It has been for months, ever since that day in Wal-Mart when Sydney was taken. It is fall now, four months into Kindergarten. I feel proud of myself.

"Look," I say and run into the kitchen, throwing my backpack on the floor as I go. My mom is standing in there, looking out into the backyard and the canal.

"Mom?" I say hoping to get her attention. "Look! I did the project all by myself."

She doesn't turn to look at me.

"What's wrong?" I say.

My mother shakes her head, then looks down at the potatoes she is peeling. "I was thinking maybe we should grow some petunias out in the yard, huh? I bet that would look nice."

"Sure, Mom, but...I won an award. In school?"

My mother doesn't look at me. She shakes her head while peeling the potatoes. "Pick up your backpack from the floor. It doesn't go there. If you keep throwing it there, someone will trip over it."

"But...Mom?"

"Now," she says.

I stare at her back, thinking I can't remember when I saw her eyes the last time, or when I felt her kiss.

"Sydney has a doll in her room, the American girl doll, can I go play with it?" I ask.

It's the first time I've mentioned her name since that day. I haven't dared to, but I really love that doll. And now it's just in there gathering dust like all her other stuff. Every day, I walk to the door and open it, then look inside, but I never dare to go in there. A doll should be played with and not just sit there.

My mother's back turns curvy as she takes in a deep breath. The response comes promptly.

"NO!"

"But, Mo-om, that doll is brand new, and no one is playing with it."

My mom no longer pays me any attention. She shuts up like a clam and doesn't say a word to me, no matter how much I beg. She just freezes me out and, finally, I give up. I turn around and walk out of the kitchen, picking up my backpack on the way. My mom doesn't speak to me for three days after this, and after that, only with short words without even looking at me. I tug at her dress, I yell her name as loud as I can, but she simply ignores me.

I SAT up in bed and let the tears crawl down my cheeks. My pillow was soaked from me crying in my sleep. I felt so overwhelmed inside; I couldn't stop crying. For years, I had forgotten how my mother had shut me out back then. I knew she had, but I had forgotten how lonely it had made me, how inadequate it had made me feel. I guess I needed to put all that somewhere in the back of my mind in order to move on, in order to make it in life. But now that I was back in Cocoa Beach, it was like it had decided to pour out and completely overpower me. There was nothing I could do.

I went to the bathroom and found a box of tissues, then wiped my nose, remembering how I used to get on my knees in my old room and pray to God to allow me to go back in time so the kidnapper could take me instead of her, crying to him, asking him why it had to be me? Why did I have to survive?

It still made no sense to me.

Sensing how thirsty I was, I walked down the stairs into the kitchen and turned on the light. It was still very dark outside, and the clock showed only midnight. I hadn't been asleep for very long. I wondered if I was going to get any more sleep. The emotions from the dream still lingered with me and made me want to cry more.

I grabbed a glass from the cabinet when I spotted a figure outside my window, and I dropped it.

Chapter 64

"MATT? WHAT THE HECK?"

He pointed at the front door, and I ran to open it.

"What are you doing out there scaring me half to death?"

The look in his eyes startled me, and I knew he wasn't joking around. Something was wrong.

"I came to see you," he said. "Then I spotted you in the window and thought, if I could get your attention, we wouldn't have to wake up the kids. Something's happened. Can I come in?"

"Of course," I said and stepped aside to let him in. He rushed to my kitchen and put down his laptop.

"Matt, you look awful," I said. "Can I get you something? A glass of water?"

He looked at me. "Do you have something stronger?"

"Wine? Whiskey?"

He nodded. "A scotch please."

"That bad, huh?" I asked and poured him a glass. I handed it to him, and he downed it in one gulp. Matt had never been much of a drinker, so I was very surprised to see this. A little frightened too, to be honest.

"Worse," he said and put the glass down with a grimace. The alcohol seemed to give him color back in his cheeks, but only for a few seconds. He opened the laptop and tapped on the keyboard. I walked up behind him, clutching my glass of water in my hand, bracing myself for something terrible.

"What is it, Matt?" I asked. "A new video?"

He nodded. "Yes. I was about to go to bed when I received it. It was sent to me directly. Just like last time. I'm beginning to think this guy has something against me personally."

"Or maybe it's just because he knows you're on the case. You have been on the news quite a few times talking about Sophie Williams' disappearance and the finding of her body. He might just have picked you because of that."

"Okay, but how do you explain this then?" he said and opened a video, then started it. I sat on a stool next to him and watched it with him. It showed a box made from wood. On the side of it, someone had painted the word ALONE.

Next, text appeared on the screen.

Loneliness. Divorce often leads to a profound sense of loneliness for the children involved. As parents move into new homes and custodial parents get caught up in trying to make it through each day, children are often left feeling lonely and all alone. This child will often demand unusual amounts of attention from his or her parents. He or she might smile constantly and try to keep everyone happy, hoping to keep peace between the parents. Others might withdraw from friends and family or express anger in order to get attention. Some turn to goofing around or getting in fights to gain attention. Common to all of these is a feeling of isolation from the world.

The text stopped, and the video clipped to another picture, taken from inside the box. A young child was sitting inside of it, bent over like he was sleeping. The video sped up, and we could see him wake up, then start knocking on the sides of the box, hammering it, crying helplessly. As the video progressed, the child became more and more apathetic, and the hammering turned to knocking and a strained face as he called out. The knocking soon became scratching till the boy barely moved anymore.

Then, Matt stopped it.

"What...what the hell is this, Matt?"

"A boy, isolated from the world, slowly dying from his loneliness, is my guess." He rubbed his forehead. "If you look at the date in the corner, you'll see that this has been recorded over a long period of time. Two months, it looks like."

"Has that boy been in that box for two whole months?" I said. "He must have fed him then."

Matt nodded, biting his nails. I had never seen him do that before. That was new.

"Matt?"

"There's more," he said.

"Okay?"

"The boy. He's…he's my son."

Chapter 65

IT TOOK me a few seconds before the realization slowly sunk in. I kept staring at Matt while the thoughts fluttered in my mind.

"You have a son?"

Matt nodded, still biting his nails. "Elijah. He's eight."

"How…you never mentioned him?"

Matt's eyes were avoiding mine. I saw hurt in them. "I don't see him much. His mom has custody of him. It was all a mess. He was an accident—a one-night-stand. I was never really a part of his life. The last few years, she hasn't been letting me see him much."

"When did you see him last?" I asked.

"In April."

"But that was six months ago?"

Matt rubbed his forehead. "I know. I checked the database; she hasn't reported him missing."

I wrinkled my forehead. "That's odd. Have you called her?"

He nodded. "It was the first thing I did. She doesn't answer."

I looked at the clock on my stove. It was past midnight. I grabbed my phone and put it in my pocket.

"I'll drive."

I woke up Olivia and told her she was in charge for a few hours while I took care of some work. She blinked a few times, then sighed.

"I thought you stopped all that."

"Yeah, you and me both, baby. But this is urgent."

Olivia gave me a look to let me know she understood it was important. Matt and I took off and soon drove out of Cocoa Beach.

His ex lived in Vieira, a town on the mainland about twenty-five minutes from my house. It was one of those newer neighborhoods that had shot up in the past few years. There was a big water fountain at the entrance, and the bushes and trees were nicely trimmed, and everything was clean and pretty, but all the houses looked exactly alike. Just like had they been cut out with the same cookie cutter. To me, it all came out as bland, and I knew I would suffocate if I lived in a neighborhood like this. That's what I liked about Cocoa Beach. No two houses were the same. It was messy and a little rough in places, but it had charm.

We parked the car outside in the well-trimmed driveway and walked up the lawn. I noticed that Matt's hand was shaking as he rang the doorbell. I sent him a comforting smile, but it didn't help.

No one opened the door, and he rang again. When nothing happened still, he opened the screen door and started hammering on the wooden door behind it. He was going to wake up the entire neighborhood, but I had a feeling he didn't care about that right now.

"POLICE. OPEN UP!"

A light was turned on in the house next door. I saw the blinds being pulled aside. There was going to be a lot of talking once morning came. No doubt about that.

It concerned me that no one still opened the door after Matt had been yelling. Since it woke up the neighbors, it had to wake up the woman inside this house too.

"Lisa?" he yelled. "I need to talk to you. Now," Matt yelled.

I gave him a look. "Could she be somewhere else?"

He shook his head. "She doesn't have family around here."

"Friends?"

He swallowed. "Sure. She has a few."

I walked to a window and peeked inside, placing my face close to the glass. I couldn't escape the feeling that something was very much off here. Why hadn't the woman put out a missing person's report for her child? If he really had been in that box for two months, she'd had plenty of time to figure out he was gone. Unless the person making the video was just messing with us, and he hadn't been gone that long after all. Except this guy didn't seem to be messing around at all. Everything else he had done had been very seriously and very well planned out. He hadn't taken any shortcuts and had been planning this in very small detail for months, maybe even years. And so far, all we had been able to do was to play by his rules. It was time to change that up; it was time for us to get ahead, but how? So far, his next move had been impossible to figure out in advance. They had all come as surprise attacks.

"I see something," I said, then looked at Matt, concern in my eyes. My heart started pounding. "I see legs poking out from behind a couch. We need to get inside. Asap."

Chapter 66

I DIDN'T HAVE to say that twice to Matt. He kicked the door open, and we both went into the hallway, holding our weapons out in front of us. The sweet yet nauseating stench that met us made me feel sick to my stomach. I knew that smell a little too well...the sulfurous gas that a putrefying body gives off after having been dead for some time. It was similar to the smell of rotten eggs. I covered my mouth and nose with my sleeve. Matt did the same, gagging as he went along.

"Police!"

"It was in the living room," I said.

Matt entered to the right to clear the kitchen, then came back out and nodded.

"Clear."

We continued into the living room, scanning the room first, making sure no one was hiding in there. And that was when we saw her—a woman lying on the carpet by the couch. I turned on the light, and we walked to her. Matt gasped and clasped his mouth, then knelt next to her.

"Lisa," he whispered.

"Looks like blunt force trauma to the back of her head," I said and pointed at the pool of dried up blood surrounding her head like a halo. Flies and maggots crawled in her ears and eye sockets. Her eyes had been pushed out of their sockets, and her tongue was forced out of her mouth. That was also due to the gas and bloating buildup inside the body as it was decomposing. All the fluids and gas had leaked out of her body; her skin had ruptured and fallen off her bones.

"Nails and hair have fallen out," I said. "Which tells us she's been here for more than a month. My guess is that the decay has been slowed down by the fact that she's been lying inside air-conditioning. A good guess will be that she was killed on the day someone took Elijah, two months ago, but of course, we'll need the medical examiner's report to verify that."

Matt stared at her dead body, shaking his head, eyes wet. "Oh, dear God, Lisa. No."

"I am so sorry, Matt," I said. "I'll call it in."

With the phone against my ear, I walked outside to get out of the stench and be able to talk. A few neighbors had gathered outside their houses now to see what was going on. A couple from across the street was staring at me, holding onto one another, their faces struck with fear. As I hung up, I walked to them, trying to look reassuring.

"What's going on?" the woman asked, her voice shaking.

"Police investigation," I said.

"Did something happen to Lisa?" the woman asked, breathing in small gasps.

"I am afraid so, and I would like to ask you a few questions; can I do that?"

The husband looked briefly at his wife, then nodded. "Of course."

"Have you seen anything suspicious around here, anything out of the ordinary around Lisa's house? A car maybe? People hanging out there whom you haven't seen before?"

They exchanged a look briefly, then looked back at me. "No, not that we can think of," the wife answered. "We did talk the other day about how long ago it was that we had seen the little boy. We used to always see him riding his bike around in the cul-de-sac. But we hadn't seen the mother either, so we just assumed they were out of town or maybe just busy, you know?"

"We did talk about if they might have moved," the husband added.

"You didn't notice a smell?" I asked.

They looked at one another again, then the wife gasped. "The smell? Oh, yes…what that…? Oh, dear Lord."

She clasped her mouth with a whimper. Her husband pulled her closer. "We did talk about a strange smell in the neighborhood a couple of weeks ago but assumed it came from somewhere else. Maybe the sewers or the lake. We could never imagine…it coming from over there?"

I nodded. "We believe the crime may have been committed two months ago…"

"Two months ago..?" the wife said with a shrill voice. "But… but…"

"I need you to try and think back. Two months ago, did anything unusual happen around here? Any cars drive by that you didn't know?" I asked. "Anyone walk up to the house that made you wonder who he or she was?"

The wife pondered while the husband shook his head. "That's a very long time ago. I don't think we…"

"Wait," she said and held a hand up to stop him. "We're talking back in August, right?"

"Yes?"

"That's when Daniel was there."

"Daniel who?" the husband asked.

"From the paper."

"I don't remember any Daniel from the paper," the husband said.

"Well, that's because you're never home; you're always out on that golf course." She looked at me, shaking her head. "Nevertheless, there was this guy, this reporter, from *Florida Today* who wanted to do a story about Elijah," she continued. "Because he was such a great baseball talent. He followed him for a couple of days around for practice and so on. Come to think of it, I never read the story in the paper…"

"Okay," I said and wrote it down on my notepad. "This is very good. So, there was a reporter there; Daniel, you say his name was?"

The woman nodded. "Yes."

"Do you know his last name?"

She shook her head. "I'm afraid not."

"Do you remember anything else about him? What did he look like?" I asked.

"Well, he was tall. Taller than Fred," she said and glanced at her husband. "And he's six foot two, so I'll say about six foot four or so."

I wrote it down. "Okay, good, anything else? Color of hair and eyes? Any special birthmarks or facial hair?"

"Brown hair, brown eyes, and a mustache. Kind of reminded me of Burt Reynolds. I used to love that guy. Too bad he passed. The mustache wasn't as thick as Burt's, though."

"Did he drive a car?"

"Oh, yes, a blue BMW convertible. Flashy little thing." She paused pensively. "Are you trying to locate him? I'm sure if you call the newspaper, they'll help you find him."

Fred sighed and rolled his eyes. "Don't you understand? He was never from the newspaper. That's why the article was never printed."

His wife looked at him, annoyed. "I know that."

"Well, we don't know about that yet, but thank you so much for your help. I'll probably be back for more information later. Did he say anything about where he lived?"

"I never really spoke to him myself," she said. "It was mostly what Lisa told me."

"Okay. Was there anything else, anything that stood out to you about him?"

The small woman sighed, then shook her head. "He seemed like such a nice guy."

I nodded. "They all do, ma'am."

Chapter 67

I STAYED at the crime scene all night while the techs searched Lisa's house. We had explained the situation to them and asked them to secure anything that might give us a clue as to where her son might be.

At five o'clock, we drove back toward Cocoa Beach. I had kids I needed to wake up and get ready for school. I told Matt he could come back to my house and crash on my couch for a little while. I figured it was a bad idea for him to be alone right now.

"You need the rest. If you want to find your son, you need to sleep first," I said when he started to argue.

My kids were exhausted and, somehow, they all three managed to get themselves in a fight during breakfast. But, for once, I managed to get Alex to the bus on time, and both girls rode their bikes to school. It was a small victory, but at this point, I took what I could get. I made some coffee then went to the living room where I thought Matt was sleeping. But, of course, he wasn't. How could he? I knew I wouldn't be able to. Instead, he was sitting with his laptop on his knees, watching the video over and over again.

I handed him a cup of coffee, and he took it.

"Do you think he's still alive?" he asked, staring at the screen, where he had stopped the video of Elijah curled up inside of the box, not moving.

I fought my desire to cry when thinking of that poor boy trapped inside that awful box, then sat down with my coffee between my hands.

DON'T LIE TO ME

Images of Lisa's decomposed body rushed across my mind as I briefly closed my eyes.

"All we can do is hope," I said.

"It seems like such a fragile thing to cling to, doesn't it?" Matt said. "Hope. If this guy wants him dead, then he's probably dead, right?"

"We don't know that."

"I spoke to IT," he said, sipping his coffee. "They're trying to trace it. Both emails were sent from a newly created account using Proton Mail, a secure email based in Switzerland. The named used is fake and so is all the other information."

"And the IP address?" I asked.

"Led us to a Starbucks on 520. According to our IT guys, it is most likely that our guy bought a cheap tablet with cash, took that tablet to the local Starbucks, then logged onto their free Wi-Fi, uploaded the video to YouTube, sent the email, then destroyed the tablet afterward."

"And the tablet couldn't somehow be traced?" I asked.

"Some models do send model numbers or even serial numbers, but even if they were able to identify where it was bought, this guy probably bought it with cash, and that means there's no tracing him. At least that's what they told me last time."

I growled and clenched my fist in anger. This guy was just always one step ahead of us. It annoyed me immensely. It was almost as if he knew as much about how the police worked as we did.

"Could he be an inside guy?" I asked cautiously. This type of accusation wasn't something you'd just throw around lightly in the force.

Matt bit his lip and our eyes locked for a few seconds. I shook my head. "Nah, you can probably find all this information online. There are DIY tutorials for everything these days. I saw one recently for how to break into a hotel room. Nice."

I took another sip of my coffee while staring at Matt's screen. Matt placed a finger on Elijah's face. It was torture to watch. I finished my cup, then put it down. I looked at Matt again.

"Say, aren't we missing something?"

"What do you mean?"

"The killer put the others, Sophie, Scott, and Nathaniel, on display for us to find, right? Why haven't we found Elijah yet? Nathaniel Pullman was also in a video, and we were supposed to find him. The killer knew we would, that's why he chose the place that he did."

"So…you're saying we should be looking for a clue of where to find him?"

I nodded. "Let's watch the video again."

Matt played it again. About halfway through, something happened. There was a brief clip in the footage, and I asked Matt to pause it.

"Look."

"What am I looking at?"

"Can you go like one frame back?"

"I can try," he said, then pulled the cursor backward just enough for a picture to show up.

"The video was fast-forwarded to show us the time Elijah spent in there. In the middle, he inserted a picture that we wouldn't see if we didn't slow it down. See?"

Matt looked at me, then nodded. "But what is it?"

"It's a picture of a sign," I said.

"I can see that, but what does it mean?"

"It's from the port."

"But…but the port is a pretty big place?" he said.

I nodded, then rose to my feet. "Call Chief Annie on our way there. We might need a couple of your colleagues to help us."

Chapter 68

IT WAS STILL DARK out when Maddie opened her eyes. With the little light that was left in the room, she could see that the box was still gone.

She was alone.

Maddie sighed and kicked her legs to be able to turn herself around and look out underneath the blindfold. As she stared in the direction of where the box had been, she spotted something on the floor. Not knowing what it was, she wormed herself closer, then looked at it up close.

A nail.

A nail that had to have fallen out of the box when it was moved. Maddie couldn't believe it. She stared at the small thing, excitement—mixed with a load of fear—emerging in her stomach. Was this her break? Was this her chance?

She used her legs to turn her back to the nail, then moved her fingers to see if she could grab it. Her wrists throbbed painfully from behind the zip tie strips, but still, she managed to get the nail up between her fingers. Happily, she grunted in excitement, but then dropped the nail again. Maddie cursed herself for being clumsy, then felt her way to it again, found it, and once again picked it up between her thumb and pointer finger. Straining in concentration, she now fiddled with it till she got the pointy end placed at the lock of the strip. Using her pointer finger, she pushed it hard against the lock, but it slipped and poked her wrist instead. Sobbing in pain, she dropped the nail again.

Come on, Maddie. Stop being so freakin clumsy! This is your only chance.

Maddie took in another deep breath, then felt her way to the nail once more, grabbed it, and placed it back against the lock, pushed it down, forcefully, and felt how it pierced the plastic. The nail was now stuck in the lock and, with much force, Maddie wiggled it around, and suddenly the strip snapped.

Maddie laughed, a little startled, then pulled her hands up in front of her face and pulled off the blindfold completely. She grabbed the nail, then poked it through the plastic strip tying her feet together. Seconds later, she could move her legs again. Exhausted from the lack of food and drink, she now regained much of her strength just at the mere prospect of getting free and maybe escaping.

Mom, I am coming home.

Maddie rose to her feet, got dizzy from standing up too fast, and had to lean against the wall so she wouldn't fall. Her legs were wobbly, but she walked the few steps toward the window, where she peeked out through the crack in the shutters. Then she gasped. She was higher up than she had expected. She looked at the door, then ran to it and pulled the handle, but as she had expected, it was locked. Maddie returned to the window again. She grabbed the small tab poking out on top and unlocked it, then pulled it open. She couldn't believe the relief she felt when breathing in the fresh air once again. She put her nose close to the screen to take it all in.

She looked down through the cracks. Below her was a yard and a screened pool area. She was in someone's house.

Thinking she heard a sound coming from outside the door, she gasped once again and turned to look. There was a rustling behind it.

Her perpetrator was coming back, and there was no one else in the room other than her. Her captor had to be coming to kill her.

As the door was unlocked, Maddie stared through the crack at what was down below her. The yard ended in a seawall and the canal where all the boats passed by. Those had to be the engines Maddie had heard from time to time.

More rustling behind the door and now the handle was turning.

You've got to do something, Maddie. Now!

As the door opened and Maddie once again locked eyes with her captor, she did something she would never have thought possible.

She kicked her foot through the screen, then kicked the hurricane shutters as hard as she could, again and again, till they got loose and fell out, then pushed her body out the window, through the hole in the screen, and slid down the side of the roof till she reached the end of it and managed to stop when grabbing on to a tile on the roof. Then, as her captor yelled behind her and came to the window, she didn't even look back.

She stood up, ran as fast as she could toward the edge of the roof, closed her eyes, and jumped.

Chapter 69

THEN

SHE CAME to them one day as they were walking home from the school bus. She was waiting in the car at the bus stop and, as they began to walk, she drove after them, then rolled down the window.

"Hi there, sweetie."

The boy refused to look at her, but his sister couldn't hide her enthusiasm. The boy knew it was harder for her to understand how wicked their mother really was and how important it was for them to stay as far away from her as possible. But he did. The boy knew more than her, and it was his job to protect her. He understood what his dad told them and had taken it all to heart. He knew that it didn't matter how sweet she talked or how much she pleaded. It was important to keep her away and not give in to the emotions they might feel. 'Cause that was her trick. That was the way she would try and manipulate them. The boy wasn't quite sure he understood what exactly manipulate meant, but he knew it was bad.

"Hi, Momma!"

The boy shushed his sister, then pulled her arm forcefully to get her to walk a little faster. They weren't that far from their house, and in there, they would be safe. There was no telling what their mother might be on right now.

"Come on," he hissed at her, but his sister didn't want to walk anymore. She stopped and looked at her mommy in the car. She pulled her arm out of his grip, then walked to the open window and peeked inside.

"Hi there, baby. How was school?" their mother said.

"Great," the girl said. "I made a turkey."

His baby sister lifted the turkey that she had made by tracing her hands and feet. The boy rolled his eyes, then rushed to her and pulled her shoulder.

"We have to go. Now."

"No," his sister said.

And that was when the boy accidentally lifted his eyes and looked into those of his mother. And that was when he was betrayed. His emotions did it to him; they overwhelmed him and brought tears to his eyes.

"Hi, baby. How are you?" his mommy said.

The boy stared at her, then swallowed.

"We have to go; come on," he said addressed to his sister.

"I don't want to," his sister said angrily.

"Mom and Dad would be so angry if they knew what we were doing," he said.

"Mom, huh?" his mommy said. "You call her that?"

"She's our new mom," he answered.

The hurt in his mother's eyes was painful to watch, and he looked away. She exhaled.

"How about I take you two out for some ice cream, huh? What do you say?"

"Yay!" his baby sister exclaimed.

The boy shook his head. "We can't. We have to go home, come."

But his sister wouldn't hear of it. She grabbed the door handle, pulled the door open, and jumped inside the car before the boy could stop her. She giggled and strapped herself down, then yelled at him to come too.

"Just for half an hour," his mommy said and held out her hand toward him. "They'll never know. Come."

"Yes, come on!" his baby sister squealed from the back seat. "Don't be a party pooper."

The boy threw a brief glance down the road toward their house, then grabbed his mother's hand and jumped inside too.

Chapter 70

"HOW DO you know where to go?"

We had parked the car at the port, and I was rushing off, Matt running after me. Tall cruise ships towered in front of us, along with several enormous cargo ships.

"I had a good friend in elementary school. Her dad worked at the docks," I said and ran down a dock where a big cargo ship was being loaded.

"And?" Matt asked as I slowed down, searching for what I remembered. "We used to come down here and play. I remember how there used to be...over there," I said and pointed. We ran the last part under a big crane.

"What's his statement?" I asked. "What's he trying to say?"

"Loneliness?" Matt said. "That kids in a divorce are often lonely?"

"Yes, but more than that. It's also that Elijah is one in a crowd, only one out of many."

"Yes...and?"

I stopped and looked in front of me. Matt did too. In front of us was what looked like several hundreds of wooden boxes exactly like the one we had seen in the video. Some of them were being loaded onto the ship in front of us.

"Oh, dear God," Matt said, panting. "How? How are we supposed to find him?"

"We're looking for one with the word ALONE painted on the side of it," I said and looked around anxiously for someone to ask. There was a guy in a forklift, transporting three boxes of the same type as ours onto the ship, then returning. I ran to him, then waved my hands.

"Hey!"

He stopped and looked out. "What?"

"Police," I said. "We're looking for a wooden box."

The man grinned a toothless grin. "I got plenty of those."

"It's got something written on the side. A word. ALONE. Have you seen it?" I asked, yelling through the noise from a huge cargo ship sailing past us, tooting their horn as they passed.

"Sure," he said. "I remember seeing it."

My eyes grew wide. "Great! Where?"

He nodded in the direction of the ship passing us. "I loaded it onto that one there. Earlier this morning."

My heart dropped as I saw the end of the big ship with the words SANTA MONICA on its back sail out of the canal.

Chapter 71

WATER SPLASHED in my face as we raced across the waves. Matt had gotten ahold of the coast guard, and they had taken us on board. The cargo ship had left the harbor completely and was far in the horizon as we rushed toward it, bumping along. Meanwhile, Matt was on the radio, trying to get ahold of the ship's captain to get them to slow down and let them know we were coming on board.

While we shot through the big ocean, my phone rang. It was from Alex's school. I picked it up, barely able to hear the person on the other end.

"Hello, Ms. Thomas? Melanie Lawson here."

Miss Melanie? Alex's teacher? *Oh, no, the meeting!* I had completely forgotten about the meeting I was called into. I looked at my watch. It was almost eleven thirty.

"I am so sorry, Mrs. Lawson, something came up."

"I figured as much," she said, sounding like she was personally offended that I hadn't shown up. I looked at Matt's concerned face as I spoke, reminding myself that right now this was more important. I couldn't allow myself to feel guilty over this. A boy's life was on the line.

"Could I come in later, maybe?" I asked.

I heard her sigh on the other end. "How about three o'clock?" she asked.

"Three o'clock sounds fantastic," I said, then hung up, secretly hoping I would be able to come in at three. There was no telling how long it would take to find that box.

We climbed onboard the ship, and they began opening the containers one after another. Three of Matt's colleagues were with us, among them Chris Cooper. I could tell Matt was out of it as I watched him frantically stare into one container after another. As I looked at how many containers there were on the ship, I realized this might take more than a few hours. This could take days.

"I found something!"

It was Chris. He called from the other end of the mountain range of containers. We rushed to him. He stood in front of an open container filled to the brim with wooden boxes.

"How do we do this?" Matt asked, rubbing his hair frantically. "It could be one of those, but it could also be in one of the other containers. How do we even check them? We have to turn the ship around. We need a forklift to get them out. We might have to go through all of them." The sound of deep despair was seeping through his voice. "And by the time we get to the right one, Elijah might be dead."

"I'll talk to the captain," Chris said and was about to leave when I heard something.

"Wait."

"What?" Matt asked.

I signaled for them all to remain silent, then walked closer to the stacked boxes. I put my ear to one of them when I heard it again.

"I hear something," I said. "It sounds like...a scraping!"

"It could be a rat," Chris said. "Plenty of them on ships like these."

Matt's face lit up. He disappeared for a second, and we heard glass being broken, and he returned with a fire ax between his hands.

"Which one?"

"Matt," I said. "You can't do that. You risk hurting him if he's inside."

"Which one?" he said again. "Where did you hear the noise from?"

I swallowed. "Middle row...the one on the very end, but...Matt."

"Elijah, this is your father. If you can hear me, move away from the sides of the box. Move into the middle. I'm coming in!"

I tried to protest once again, but he wouldn't listen. Matt swung the ax at the bottom of the box, and it cracked. He swung it again, and this time it went through. He then reached up and peeked inside. I could hear him sobbing between agitated pants. He looked inside the box, then reached in and grabbed something.

A second later, he pulled a lifeless body out of the box by the legs. He grabbed him in his arms, then staggered toward us, his face torn in pain and anguish. I rushed to him and helped him put the boy down on the ground.

"Is he…?" he asked.

I felt for a pulse but found nothing.

"He must be alive, right?" Matt asked. "I mean, you heard him; you heard the scraping. He must have been alive then, right? That was just a few minutes ago…?"

He looked at me as if I held all the answers, while I frantically searched for the boy's pulse. I shook my head, then placed my hand on the boy's chest and pushed it down, then blew air into his lungs. I kept repeating this for a minute or so. It felt like an hour. Meanwhile, Matt sat on his knees. He cried and prayed for his boy to be alive. I blew one more time into his lungs, then I put my ear to his chest and heard a heartbeat.

"I got a heartbeat!" I yelled. "I've got a heartbeat!"

I stared at Matt, whose eyes lit up in the middle of the gloom.

"I did," I said. "I heard his heartbeat. I can feel it now. His pulse. He's alive, Matt. He's alive!"

Matt laughed and grabbed the boy in his arms, then held him up. He rocked him back and forth while repeating that he was going to be okay, over and over again.

Chris had the coast guard call for help, and soon a helicopter arrived, taking both Matt and Elijah with them. I looked after them as they were airlifted into the chopper, my heart jumping with joy.

We had won one. This time, the victory belonged to us.

Chapter 72

"MOMMY, WAKE UP. PLEASE?"

Rylan grabbed his mother's cold hand and pulled it. When that didn't help, he kissed her like they did in the story of *Snow White*. He had been reading it to his baby sister, Faith, over and over again for the past few days, not knowing what else to do. Their mommy had to have been very tired since she was still sleeping.

"I'm hungry," Faith whimpered and held her stomach.

Rylan was too. They had eaten all the crackers they had found in the cabinet on the first day. The box was empty, and now their stomachs were growling again. There was a box of Cheerios in there too, and now Rylan grabbed it and started to eat out of the box, then handed it to his sister. The milk in the fridge smelled bad, and they didn't want to drink it. There was some juice left, and he poured them each half a glass, then the jug was empty. Then they drank and ate while looking at their mother in her bed. They hadn't left her side since the first morning they had woken up and realized she hadn't.

"I'm still thirsty," his sister said as she emptied the juice glass.

"There's only water now," he said.

He grabbed a chair and pulled it close to the cabinets, then crawled up and found a new glass for her before pulling the chair to the fridge and crawling up on it, managing to fill the glass with water. He then slid down and handed his sister the glass that she drank from greedily.

When she was done, she gave him one of those smiles that their mother loved so much.

"I miss Mommy," his sister said, almost crying again.

"Me too," Rylan said. "She will wake up soon. She was just really tired."

"Do you think she's sick?" Faith asked, standing in the doorway to the bedroom, looking at their mother.

Rylan shook his head. "She's not warm. She doesn't have a fever. She's very cold."

Faith wrinkled her nose. "She smells funny."

Rylan nodded. He had noticed it too. And the night before when he had crept into her bed and laid close to her, he hadn't been able to hear her heartbeat like he usually did. And she hadn't put her arm around him as she usually did. And this morning, the smell was worse than the day before, and he had to hold his nose when he went to check on her and see if she had finally woken up.

"Mommy needs to take a shower," Faith said and grimaced.

"She will," Rylan said. "As soon as she wakes up. She's just really tired; that's all."

"But she needs to take care of us," Faith complained, the sides of her mouth turning downward. Rylan hated when her mouth did that and rushed to hug her.

"Shh," he said like Mommy used to. He also stroked her hair the same way she used to do it and spoke the same words he believed she would have said:

"Don't worry. I'll take care of you until she wakes up. Don't worry, baby girl."

Faith sobbed a few times, then stopped. Rylan felt awkward trying to act like Mommy. He really wished she would hurry up and wake up soon because he was running out of hugs and nice words to say.

Chapter 73

"YOUR SON HAS BEEN QUITE disruptive in class."

Miss Melanie looked up from her papers. I sunk into the seat, feeling like a child at the principal's office. It was a quarter past three before I made it there, and me being late didn't impress Miss Melanie much. I had been late because I was on the phone with Matt, who called me from the hospital to let me know that Elijah was awake. He was severely dehydrated, and as soon as they got his levels back up, he opened his eyes and looked at Matt, then told him he was hungry for spaghetti and meatballs. He couldn't walk, though, since his legs were still too weak from not being used for two months.

"I've seen the notes," I said. "The ones you have him bring home."

She folded her hands in front of her. "We can't have this type of behavior in class. It's unfair to the other students."

"Listen," I said. "His dad and I are going through a divorce. He hasn't seen his father for several weeks now since his dad has been… well, busy. I know that the divorce must be taking a toll on him, with all the changes and the moving and all. I'm sure that, as soon as it all settles down and we get into a good rhythm, then he will calm down too."

Miss Melanie nodded. "I am aware of your situation, and I know these things can be very traumatizing for a young child, but I still think there is more to it than just that. I believe he is a child that needs a little extra attention, and I suggest we have him tested for…"

Oh, no. Here it comes. She wants him tested for ADHD.

"I am sorry," I interrupted her. "I don't think that's necessary. If we only give him a little time to settle down, I'm sure he will get better. Just give him a little time."

Miss Melanie cleared her throat. "Ms. Thomas, I really think he could benefit from being tested…"

"But I don't. These kids, once they get a diagnosis like that, it will follow them for the rest of their lives. It'll be in all his records, and he'll be stigmatized. I don't believe in labels. And then they'll want to medicate him. I don't want my child to be popping pills at this age. I don't think it's necessary and I believe too many children run around with a diagnosis on them when all they need is a little attention or help to get through a tough situation. I don't think my son has ADHD; I just think he's going through a rough patch right now, as are we all."

Miss Melanie looked at me in a questioning manner. She shook her head lightly.

"Who mentioned anything about ADHD?"

I gaped. "Uh…you did?"

She chuckled. "I most certainly did not. I was asking for your permission to have him tested for our gifted program. We believe your son is very smart and that he isn't getting the challenge he needs in school. We often see kids act out and become very vocal under these circumstances. I think your son could benefit tremendously from our program. With your permission, I'll have him tested, and he can join as soon as possible."

I stared at the woman in front of me, wishing for a small space I could crawl into. Me and my big mouth.

"So…do I have it? Your permission?" she asked.

I nodded, biting my tongue. "Where do I sign?"

Chapter 74

I HAD BARELY ENTERED the house before I could hear the kids screaming and yelling at one another. Alex was shooting his toy police gun at Christine, while she was eating a sandwich, and Christine was yelling at him to stop.

"Hi, guys," I said and entered the kitchen.

"Mommy!" Alex yelled, then threw himself in my arms. I hugged him tightly, reminding myself how fortunate I was that it wasn't my kid that had spent two months locked up in some box. I held him for a little longer than he cared for and, as soon as I let go of him, he stormed into the living room.

Christine was on her phone, grumbling something.

"What's with you?" I asked.

She sighed, then grumbled again. I couldn't hear what she said. I walked to the coffee maker and made a fresh pot. Two nights with barely any sleep made it hard to keep it together. It was going to require a lot of coffee to make it through the day.

"So, I've been thinking," I said. "About next week. How about you take Friday off and then go early to see your dad? Make it a long weekend? I haven't talked to your dad about it yet, but thought I'd call him tonight and plan the details."

"It doesn't matter anymore," she said, not looking at me.

"What do you mean?" I walked closer to her. "Did something happen?"

She stared at her screen, punching it harshly.

"Christine?"

She finally looked up. "He canceled, okay?"

"He canceled?"

"Don't act so surprised," she said. "You never wanted us to go anyway. You probably told him to cancel."

"I did not."

I said the words, but she didn't believe me. She shook her head at me.

"You ruin everything, do you know that? Everything. Dad says so too. He says you ruined your marriage. It was all your fault."

Ouch.

"Listen, honey. I know you're upset, but it isn't my fault your dad canceled. I'm sure something came up, maybe work. He's been gone for quite a while. He needs to make money at some point."

She stared at me, her jaws clenched, her nostrils flaring slightly. "It's all your fault. The divorce, the move, everything. Why did you have to ruin it? We were doing fine in Washington. I was happy there. Why did you have to change it?"

"Honey, when two people decide to…"

"Oh, don't give me that," she said with a sniffle, then slid down from her stool. "You don't care about any of us. You never even asked us if we wanted to move down here; you just decided to do it. You don't care about anyone but yourself. You're so selfish!"

"You think I'm selfish?" I said. "Your dad is the one who left. He just left us all. And now he doesn't want you anymore. He doesn't want to see you. He has moved on. He has a new woman now. He wants to marry her someday. He has a new family now. And you think I'm selfish? At least I'm here; at least I'm not going anywhere."

My daughter stared at me, her eyes wild and angry.

"You're lying! You're nothing but a selfish liar!" she yelled, then ran up the stairs. A second later, I heard the door to her room slam shut and music blasting so loud her sister started to yell for her to turn it down. In the living room, Alex knocked over something big, and it shattered with a loud crash.

I sank into a chair with a deep sigh, then hid my face between my hands, thinking it didn't matter how hard I tried; I simply couldn't win in life.

Chapter 75

AS SHE WHISTLED through the air, eyes closed, prepared to hit the water, Maddie was certain it was the end. She would most definitely die now. But as she plunged through the murky water, she felt very much alive, and soon after, she swam toward the surface.

Maddie gasped for air as she poked through and saw the blue sky above her again. She couldn't believe her luck. But as she looked back at the house behind her, where she had jumped from, she realized it wasn't over yet. Her captor was coming out the back door and rushing toward the canal.

Half in panic, Maddie started swimming. Living in Florida, most kids learned how to swim at a very young age, but Maddie hadn't had that luck. Her mom hadn't taken her to swimming lessons and, therefore, she was fairly old before she learned and wasn't among the best of swimmers. That meant she had to fight to swim fast, and it wasn't easy. Maddie whimpered while pushing her way through the dark water, trying to keep the thoughts of what lurked underneath the surface at bay.

Her captor reached the seawall and was yelling at her. Maddie panted and swam as fast as she could when she heard an engine start behind her and turned to look with a gasp. Her captor had wired his boat down from his dock and was soon rushing toward her. Maddie tried to scream but got water in her mouth and coughed instead. As she saw the boat begin to move toward her, she pushed herself even harder, trying to swim as fast as she could, panic eating at her.

Please, dear God. You've helped me get this far; please, help me get away. Please, God.

Maddie splashed in the water, panting as the boat came closer and closer. The engine roared behind her like some wild animal and Maddie was about to cry helplessly. As it came really close, and the man reached his hands down toward her, Maddie took in a deep breath, then dove down into the dark water and started to swim in the opposite direction, going underneath the boat. She kept swimming with all the strength in her small body, underneath the water, getting as far away as possible from the sound of the boat, pushing herself until she could hardly take it anymore.

Finally, she swam to the surface, then turned to look. The boat had disappeared far down the canal, and her captor hadn't realized what had happened. He was still looking down into the water, searching for her in the wrong place. It would take him a while to turn the boat around and, by then, she could be long gone.

Maddie made sure not to make a sound, then continued to swim down the canal, staying close to the seawalls and the houses. She made it down another canal, then heard an engine approaching from behind her. With a gasp, she swam underneath a dock and held onto the pillars while the boat rushed past her, the engine roaring loudly. She stayed there till it got dark and she finally dared to let go again and plunge herself into the water. As she swam again, she thought she heard a sound coming from the mangrove she had just passed and turned to look, staring straight into the eyes of an animal. Maddie had been living in Florida most of her life and knew exactly what she was looking at.

Gator!

Frantically, Maddie splashed her arms to get away from it, then reached a dock and pulled herself out of the water just in time. She crawled onto the grass, panting in exhaustion, and lay on her stomach for a few minutes, catching her breath before realizing she couldn't stay there in case her captor came back. She had to keep moving.

Chapter 76

MY MOM HAD INVITED us for dinner so, after taking a nap, I told Alex to put on his flip-flops, then walked upstairs to get the girls. I knocked on Olivia's door and peeked inside.

"Hi there. You ready to go?"

She took off her headphones, then groaned. "Do we have to go? I can't stand the food she serves."

I sighed. "Me either, but it means a lot to Grandma and Grandpa that we come over. It was one of the reasons we moved down here. So you kids could get to know them better. Plus, it means I don't have to think about dinner tonight. It's a great help."

Olivia scoffed, then rose from her bed. "It's not like you cook anyway. We could just order pizza again."

I gave her a look. She chuckled. "Okay, okay. I'll go. But I won't eat anything."

I laughed. "That bad, huh?"

"Worse."

Olivia walked down the stairs, and I heard her talking to Alex while looking for her flip-flops. I hurried to Christine's room and knocked. The music had stopped. I hoped that meant she wasn't angry anymore.

"Christine? We're getting ready to leave."

I opened the door, and my heart dropped. She wasn't there.

"Christine?" I asked and looked in her walk-in closet and then her bathroom, but she wasn't there either.

That is odd.

I walked back into the hallway, then to the stairs, where Olivia and Alex were waiting. Their eyes rested on me.

"Are we leaving or what?" Olivia asked.

Alex had grabbed his fire ax and hat. I could tell he couldn't wait to go play with his grandpa.

"Have you seen Christine?" I asked.

Olivia shook her head. "No."

My heart started to beat faster in my chest. "She's not downstairs?"

I walked down toward them, then into the kitchen, then the living room, and finally, I checked the backyard. No sign of my daughter anywhere.

"Could she have gone to a friend's house?" Olivia asked.

"Without telling me? That's not very like her," I said. "She knows how terrified I get when I don't know where you are."

Olivia gave me a look. "Because of what happened to your sister, oh, yes, but think about it. Maybe that's exactly why she didn't say anything. To get back at you. You two were fighting earlier, right?"

"Yes, she got really mad and ran upstairs, and then…you think she snuck out while I was sleeping?" I asked.

Olivia threw out her hands. "What better way to get back at you? That's what I would do."

She was right. Christine knew how scared I got in these situations. If she really wanted me to suffer, this was the way to do it.

I grabbed my phone and called her, but she didn't pick up. "It goes directly to voicemail."

"Because she doesn't want you to find her," Olivia said.

"You try," I said. "You call her."

Olivia gave me a look. "Mo-om. First of all, don't you think she can figure out that you told me to call her? Besides, if she shut off the phone, it doesn't matter who calls."

"Then I'll just have to call everyone in her class and ask if they know where she is."

"You really think that's necessary?" Olivia asked. "Think about it. You'll only embarrass her, and she'll end up resenting you even more."

I exhaled. "Then I don't know what to do."

Olivia put her arm around my shoulder. "Relax, Mom. Let's just go to Grandma and Grandpa's; then she'll probably be here when we get home."

"Yeah," Alex said, holding out his ax in front of him. "Let's go now!"

Chapter 77

WE ALL SEEMED to be getting on each other's nerves. I don't know if it was something in the air or the food, but everyone at my mom's dinner table seemed to be grumpy.

The only one who was completely unaffected was Alex. He played with his ax around the house while my mom kept a watchful eye on him, making sure he didn't tip over any expensive antique vases or slam the toy ax into any furniture and make a dent.

I had told them that Christine was at a friend's house but found it so hard to focus on the conversation we were having while my thoughts kept circling around my daughter and where she could be. With all that had been going on, I simply didn't like not knowing where she was.

"What do you think, Eva Rae?" my mom said.

I hadn't heard what they were talking about, so I answered in confusion. "About what?"

"Dear Lord, Eva Rae, where is your mind these days?" my mom said. "I was talking about the Begonias in the front yard and how beautiful they were when they bloomed. I was wondering if I should remove the Periwinkles and make room for more. What do you think?"

I stared at her, my eyes blinking. I had no idea what to say. I couldn't care less about flowers right now. I never cared about flowers. I liked looking at them, but that was about it.

"Christine is missing," I said instead of answering her. As I said the words, tears finally escaped my eyes, and I couldn't hold it back anymore. "I don't know where she is, and I keep imagining these scenarios with all the kidnapped children lately and with Sydney and all that…I just…"

My mother stared at me, mouth gaping. Her eyes flickered a few times back and forth, and then she rose to her feet and was about to walk away.

"No, Mom," I said and grabbed her hand. "You can't go now. You always leave when…"

But my mom wouldn't hear me out; she pulled her hand away. "I have to check on the bean-flour pie," she said.

I slammed my hand onto the table, and the silverware clattered. "No, Mom! I want you to stay now. I need you to stay here and talk to me. My daughter is missing. You can't just run away from me when I tell you something like this. I need you, dammit. I need you to comfort me, to tell me it'll be all right, that she'll be fine."

My mom froze in place. She stood for a few seconds with her back turned to me, then turned around.

"I can't say that."

"Why, Mom? Why can't you say that? Why can't you, for once, comfort me when I need you to?"

She swallowed. Her nostrils were flaring. "Because…it might not be okay, Eva Rae. It wasn't for us. It never became okay again. Life was never okay again. That's why. So, forgive me if I am not very good at comforting you when things go wrong, but it is not my strong side."

She was about to turn again and leave, but I wasn't ready to let her. "Why did you never want to talk to me anymore. When it happened? Why did you freeze me out? Was it because you blame me for what happened to Sydney? Was it because you wished the kidnapper would have taken me and not her? You blame me for it, don't you? Because, believe me; I do too. Every day, I tell myself I could have done things differently and maybe saved Sydney. Because I didn't call for help early enough. Because I fought myself out of his grip and then he chose her instead. It's all my fault, isn't it, Mom? You've always believed it was. And you could never look at me the same way again. Every time I sought you, you'd turn your back on me."

My mom stood like she was frozen. Her eyes stared into mine, and her hands were shaking. I waited for her to respond. I wanted a response from her, no matter what it was. I needed to know.

She walked to me and stood so close I could smell her perfume.

"Why, Mom? Why did you have to freeze me out when I needed you the most?" I asked.

She swallowed like she needed to clear room for the words that were about to leave her mouth.

"I...I couldn't look you in the eyes, Eva Rae. I simply couldn't face you."

Tears rolled down my cheeks now, and she wiped one away.

"Why, Mom? Why not? All I wanted was a hug or a kind word?"

"Because I couldn't. I couldn't face you because I was too...ashamed."

I wrinkled my forehead. That wasn't the answer I had expected to hear from her.

"Ashamed? What on Earth are you talking about?"

My mom looked briefly at my dad, who nodded in agreement. "It's time," he said.

"Time for what? What is he talking about, Mom?" I asked, unable to stop the tears from rolling down my cheeks.

She gave me another look. Inside her eyes was the warmth I had searched for so long, the care I knew was in there, but she never let out.

"Because I knew who took her."

It felt like she had punched me. She might as well have. I shook my head, dumbfounded.

"I...I don't understand."

"It was her father," my mother said, her voice trembling. "Her real father...your real father."

And there it was—the knockout that blew all the air out of my lungs. I heard a ringing in both my ears, and it felt like my blood had started to boil.

"Excuse me?"

My mom reached out for my hands and grabbed them in hers. Tears were in her eyes now too.

"I am so sorry, baby. I am so, so sorry."

"I...I don't understand. Dad?" I said and looked at him. I wanted him to tell me this wasn't true; I desperately needed him to tell me she was lying, to make things right again.

He nodded. "It's true, Squirt. I will always be your father because I raised you, but I am not biologically."

"We were young," my mother said. "He left. I didn't know he would come back for you. I married your father, and we decided to raise you like he was your real father because he was. You could never get a better father than him. But then he came back. Your real father did. He wanted half of the custody. We fought him in court and won. But then he...he came back, and he tried to take both of you. We saw him later on the surveillance video from the store. There was no doubt it was him. He came for both of you, sweetie, but he only got your sister."

"But...so...so, you knew who did it? All this time, you knew?"

She nodded. "The police searched for him everywhere, but they never found him. They suspected he might have taken her out of the country. He had family in Europe."

"So...so, what you're telling me is...so, she could be alive?" I said, crying. "Sydney could be alive? I thought for sure she was dead?"

My dad nodded. "We don't know if she is, but yes, there's a possibility that she is alive."

"But...how...how could you lie to me like this? I grew up thinking that...that my own mother didn't love me, that she didn't want me. And then...then you were both just...lying?"

"We did what we thought was best for you," my dad said. He said the words, but they made no sense to me.

"I have a sister out there somewhere, and a...a dad? And you thought it would be best for me not to know? What kind of logic is that?"

I stared at the man I had called my dad, suddenly feeling so confused I got dizzy. I leaned on a chair while gathering my thoughts. Everything I believed had been a lie so far. Everything. I had gone into the force because I wanted to make amends for what happened to my sister, for not being able to save her from the faceless man, her kidnapper and who I presumed was her killer. But now...now, it had all changed. And my dad? He wasn't who I believed he was, neither was my mom.

And who the heck was I?

"Eva Rae...I..." my mom said and stepped forward.

I pulled back. I needed to get away, get out of there, out of the house where I had been lied to for thirty-five years. I couldn't trust either of them anymore.

"I need to...I have to go. Come on, kids. We should get home."

Alex sighed disappointedly, while Olivia, who had watched it all play out, sprang to me and held me. I leaned on her most of the walk home, none of us uttering a word, except Alex who was pretending he was saving us all from some feisty bushfire.

Chapter 78

THEN

"COME ON, join us in the fun."

It was the third time the boy's mother urged him to come and play cards with them. But the boy still refused. He didn't think his sister should either. He thought she was being ridiculous, the way she laughed and had fun without thinking about the consequences.

"I think we need to go home now," he said. "Mom and Dad might be worried now."

"Nonsense," their mom said. "They'll be fine. Have some fun instead. You're always so serious."

The boy didn't know how long they had been in their mother's apartment, but as he watched the clock on the wall move, it made him feel more and more anxious.

It had gotten dark outside, and the boy knew his dad would most certainly be home by now. He always came home when it grew dark outside. And he would be mad if he found out where the boy and his sister were. Oh, boy, he would get so mad.

"Come on; we need a third man," his mother said. Her voice sounded strange, and he wondered if she was drunk or high. Was it just a matter of time before she hurt one of them?

Her baby sister drank from her soda and ate some gummy bears. The boy shook his head, staring at her. Didn't their mom know that little sister got too hyper when she ate all that sugar? That it wasn't good for her?

"Don't eat that," he said.

His sister grabbed another one and chewed it, loudly smacking her lips at him. He looked away. The boy walked to the window and looked outside. The darkness had settled now. There was no way he could find his way home on his own from here. Especially not in the darkness. But he had to get back somehow. He simply had to. He couldn't leave his sister here, not with her. He simply didn't dare to, so instead he snuck into the bedroom where there was an old phone on the table. He dialed his dad's number.

"Daddy?"

"Son?"

He sounded angry, and the boy's heart sank.

"Where are you?"

"I'm...I'm..." The boy began to cry. "At Mommy's place."

"What? You're at her place? She kidnapped you, son? Did she?" he asked.

"N-No..."

There was another voice on his father's end, and the boy recognized it as his new mommy's.

"What's going on?" she asked.

"The Thing kidnapped our children," his dad said. "Can you believe her?"

"Oh, dear Lord."

"I'm calling the cops," he said, then returned to the boy. "Stay where you are, son. We'll get help. Stay calm, boy, and keep a close eye on your sister. Help is on the way. Just make sure to keep an eye on your sister, you hear me?"

"Y-yes, Daddy."

Chapter 79

"CHRISTINE? CHRISTINE?"

I ran inside the house and up the stairs, then opened the door to her room. But she wasn't there. I had to control myself in order not to panic. I breathed in deeply a few times, then told myself she was fine, that she would come home soon.

"Is she still not here?" Olivia asked as she came inside her sister's room. For the first time, I now saw concern in my older daughter's eyes.

"I'll try and call her," she said, then left with her phone in hand. She came back a second later. "She's still not answering."

I ran a hand through my hair, trying hard to keep calm and to focus on where she might be.

"I'll have to call her friends now," I said, then rushed downstairs to find the list of phone numbers I had for Christine. She hadn't made a lot of friends so far, so it was quickly done.

None of them had seen her all day. Not since school.

Oh, dear God, no!

"Relax, Mom," my daughter said. "I'm sure she's fine. She might just be hiding, or maybe she went down to the beach? Maybe she just went out because she was mad, and now she doesn't dare to come home."

I sent her a series of text messages, telling her to call me as soon as possible, then opened Mappen, the app I used to track my children,

DON'T LIE TO ME

but, as suspected, it wouldn't show me where she was since it only worked if the phone was turned on. For now, it only showed me her phone's last known location, which was inside the house.

"Okay," I said. "I'll go drive around for a bit and see if I can find her. Can you stay here with Alex?"

I looked at the clock. "You know what? Instead, I think I'll call for someone to come over and be with you two. I don't like you guys being all alone."

I called Melissa, but she was out of town, she told me. She and Steve had taken a couple of days off to go camping for the weekend with the kids. They had taken them out of school. I remembered that she had already told me they were going when I called her the day before. I didn't say a word about my daughter going missing. I don't know why I didn't tell her. I guess I didn't want her to worry. Besides, I kind of still hoped Christine had just run away from home, and I would find her down on the beach or maybe wandering around downtown.

Dawn was out of the question since she was still in too bad of a condition to get out of bed, so I didn't want to bother her. Matt had enough on his plate with Elijah.

That left me with only one option. My dad.

I punched in my parents' number. It was my mom who picked up. "Eva Rae? Is that really you? I am so sorry about earlier; could we just..."

"I need to talk to Dad," I said, cutting her off. I wasn't ready to accept any of her excuses or to forgive her yet. I wasn't sure I ever would be. At least not in the state I was in right now.

"Your dad...well, he's not here right now. He left...I guess he was upset after what happened tonight. He didn't take his cell phone. It's still here on the counter."

I closed my eyes. He was my last resort. Unless...I really didn't want to have to do this; it was the last thing I wanted to...to ask my mom for anything in this world, yet I did.

"Can you maybe help me, Mom? Can you look after the kids while I go search for Christine?"

"S-sure. I'll be right over."

Chapter 80

I LEFT without a word to my mom. I had nothing to say to her. I simply let her in, then kissed Alex and Olivia, and left, thinking that she'd have to figure things out or else Olivia would be there to help her. If it wasn't for all the kidnappings lately, I would have let Olivia babysit Alex any day, but I just didn't like leaving them alone on a day like this.

I jumped into my minivan, then drove off toward downtown. I drove through where all the small shops were, then turned around and drove past Juice N' Java and City Hall, searching all the parking lots outside and calling her name. Still, no sign of my princess. Then I drove to the beach. I parked by First Street, the closest access from where I lived, then ran through the heavy sand toward the deep, dark ocean. I kept cursing myself for not having ended things well with Christine, for fighting with her in the first place. Why did I say those things to her?

It's too late now. You've played the blame and guilt game all your life and look where it got you. Nowhere. It's time to stop.

"Christine!" I called and turned to look up toward the dunes and then back down to the water. I looked all around me, scanning the area, but it didn't help much in this darkness.

"CHRISTINE!"

Nothing but the howling wind answered. A dog barked in the distance, probably from one of the beach houses or a balcony belonging to one of the condos north of me.

"Where are you, baby girl?" I asked into the darkness.

Frustrated, I sank to my knees, then sat down in the heavy sand, head slumped between my shoulder blades. I felt so tired, so exhausted.

"Where are you?" I mumbled as tears rolled down my cheeks. As my eyes got used to the darkness, I spotted a big grey heron that was staggering along on its long skinny legs in the shallow parts of the water, looking for fish to eat.

Like he had heard my cries, Matt suddenly called. I sniffled and picked up.

"Matt?"

"I've been thinking," he said. "You might be right; it could be an inside man. I hate to say this, but while sitting here by Elijah's bedside, I keep thinking about Cooper. He had a huge crush on you back in high school and always resented me for being with you back when we dated because I knew about his crush. What if he wanted to hurt me all along? His parents are divorced; they split just last year, and he surfed with Sophie Williams down by the pier. He also helped build the senator's pool house, he told me. To earn extra money."

I exhaled, wiping tears from my eyes. "Matt...I...Christine is missing." As I said the words, I broke down, sobbing. "I think he might have her, Matt. I'm scared."

"Christine is missing? Why didn't you call me?" he asked, sounding almost angry with me.

"I don't know. I'm not very good at asking for help, I guess. But now I'm doing just that. I need you, Matt. I need your help. Please."

Chapter 81

MATT TOOK charge of the situation. He called in help from all the CBPD officers and had every patrol on the streets within the next half hour. He called Phillip at the fire station and asked them to pitch in. Luckily, Phillip wasn't holding a grudge against me and said they'd organize a search team. They'd take the trucks out and drive around in the streets and look for Christine. They even called in the only K-9 in the department, the German Shepherd, Buster—who went by the nickname *the Major*—to go through the bushy areas, the parks and areas surrounding the canals. Two officers went out on a boat to sail through all the canals in case Christine had fallen in. Patrol cruisers in the neighboring towns of Cape Canaveral and Satellite Beach were on the lookout too.

Seeing Matt work his magic made me calm down, and soon I managed to push all the desire to give up along with all the anger over what I had learned about my parents tonight aside. It had to wait.

"All right," he said and smiled at me. "I have literally everyone searching for her; even the coast guard will send out helicopters, and I've put out an Amber Alert. We'll find her. Don't you worry."

I swallowed and forced a smile. "Thanks, Matt. I mean it."

"Believe me; I want to do this. If anyone knows what you're going through right now, it's me. I want to find your daughter and hopefully also get the bastard who hurt my son and put him behind bars for the rest of his life. This is very personal for me."

I swallowed, thinking about Elijah and how close it had been. I kept imagining Christine alone and scared, crying and calling for me. It broke my heart.

"Let's go," Matt said. "We might as well get out there and look for her too."

He grabbed my hand and pulled me into a deep hug. He held me tight, then kissed the side of my head, while whispering, "We'll find her; don't worry, Eva Rae."

We both got into his police cruiser, then drove off. We drove through town once again, and I stared at all the dark empty shops, wondering if Christine could be wandering around or maybe hiding somewhere. If she really had run away from home, then maybe she was just sitting somewhere, not wanting or maybe daring to go home. But where? Where could a twelve-year-old girl hide at this time of night?

We drove down a couple of residential streets, and Matt drove past the houses slowly, so I could look out the window and see if I could spot anything out of the ordinary. The streets looked so calm, so normal. Inside all those houses, people were asleep; families were dreaming sweet dreams, sleeping heavily, the parents knowing that their kids were safe in their beds.

"I don't even know what I am looking for," I said.

"Let's just continue," Matt said and drove up Minutemen Causeway, the main street that went straight through the entire town, past the schools and ended at the country club's golf course. We drove all the way to the end of it and looked at all the residential houses down there. It was one of the wealthier areas in Cocoa Beach and the houses were bigger here and many of them facing the big river instead of small canals like the houses in my neighborhood.

Having a canal in the backyard seemed very grand, and it was really nice, but most houses in Cocoa Beach had that. River views were the ones that were more expensive, and after that came ocean views. Living on a barrier island made it possible for almost everyone to have some type of water in their backyard.

"She's not here," I said.

I grabbed my phone and held it between my hands. My eyes were fixated on the screen as I was willing it to ring and dreaming of her name appearing on the screen. Under my breath, I began praying for her to call and tell me she was sorry and to come get her.

But, of course, she didn't. The phone remained dark and lifeless.

"How about I take you back?" he said. "You haven't slept much lately and, frankly, you look like crap, no offense."

I nodded. "None taken."

"I'll keep looking, and we have literally everyone out here," he said. "You can take a nap if you want to." He reached over and put his hand on top of mine, then squeezed it. "I am not giving up till…"

I was listening to his kind words when my eyes fell on something—or rather someone—running across the street and into a yard. Matt saw it too and paused.

"What the heck was that?" he asked.

I opened the door to the cruiser. "The question is not what, it's *who*, and if I am not mistaken, the answer is a young girl."

Chapter 82

THE GIRL WAS RUNNING. She was fast, and we could barely keep up with her as we began our pursuit. I was the first one out of the cruiser, Matt coming up behind me.

"Christine?" I yelled as I reached a yard and jumped over the fence. The girl was already at the bottom of it and crawling over another fence to the neighboring house.

"Stop!" I yelled, but she didn't. She slid down into the neighboring yard, then ran across their lawn. A dog barked from inside the house. I followed her.

Why is she running away from me?

"Christine," I yelled again. "Stop. I'm not mad at you."

Christine had reached the other end of the next yard and climbed the wooden fence. She was a lot lighter than me, so she was quickly on the other side, whereas I had to fight to get up there. My hands were filled with splinters as I reached the other side, just in time to see Christine reach the next yard, pushing herself through a row of bushes. I sped up and, panting heavily, I reached the bushes and pushed my way through as well. There was a pool on the other side, and I almost fell in but managed to balance my way out of it and around it before I spotted Christine running up toward the house and trying to go back into the street. As I saw the tall wall in front of me leading to the next yard, I realized she had given up climbing it and taken an easier way out instead.

I managed to almost catch up to her, using all the strength I had, and cursing myself for not having gone on more runs since I got back here like I had promised myself.

"Christine! Stop running," I said, gasping for air. My legs were hurting and the muscles cramping from running, but I ignored it all. I had to catch up to my daughter before I lost her again, no matter the cost.

But Christine was faster than me and soon made it out to the front yard before she ran into the street. And that was when I tripped. Over a stupid sprinkler in the lawn. I fell flat on my face into the grass and, before I managed to get back to my feet, I saw her run around the corner at the end of the street.

"Oh, no, you don't," I said, then spotted a shortcut. If I ran through the yard of the corner house, I might be able to get in front of her. So, I did. I ran as fast as I ever had, through bushes that scratched me up, across a yard with a swing set and a pool, jumped a fence, and then ran into the street, right in front of her.

I held my hand out.

"Stop!"

She stopped. With gasping breath, she stared at me, her eyes blinking, terror glistening in them. Matt came up behind her, panting. I stared at the girl, my heart beating hard.

It wasn't Christine.

I walked closer, and a deep furrow grew between my eyes as I realized who she was.

"Maddie?"

"I'm not going back," she said, crying, then looked at Matt standing behind her. "I'm not."

I reached out my hand and shook my head. "Of course not, sweetie. We're the police. You're safe with us."

She stared at me, her eyes revealing doubt in my words.

"It's okay," I said and bent down to seem less frightening to her. "We've been looking for you. I am so glad to see you, and your mother will be too when we tell her we've found you. She's been really worried."

Maddie's face softened. Her eyes were still skeptical. "You know my mom?"

I nodded. "Her name is Patricia, right? She's been so worried. We all have. Even Mrs. Altman who lives downstairs. She was the one who took a picture of the car that picked you up. If you'll let me. I'll take you to your mother right now."

Maddie stared into my eyes and then it was like the air went out of her completely. She started to cry and threw herself into my arms. I lifted her up and carried her to the cruiser, happy to have found her, but secretly wishing it had been my daughter instead.

Chapter 83

THEN

THE POLICE CAME with sirens and blinking lights on their cars. The boy watched them drive up into the street in front of his mother's condominium. His baby sister and their mother were still playing cards and eating candy, laughing like nothing bad had happened, like what they were doing wasn't wrong. For a second, as the boy watched the policemen running toward the house, guns drawn, he regretted having done what he did, having called his dad, but then he reminded himself that his mother was a bad person, that she was the one who had abandoned him; she was the one who had acted crazy and not come when she was supposed to pick him up. She was the one who had chosen the drugs over him; she was the one who used to hurt him, and she was the one who chose that bad life over him and his sister. She was the one who couldn't be trusted, and they weren't safe here with her.

No, it was the right thing to do, to call his dad. And if Dad thought it was a situation that called for the police, then that was what was best for him and his sister. His mother was a dangerous person who had kidnapped them, and now she was going to pay for that.

There was a knock on the door, and then it was kicked in. That was when the yelling began. The boy watched in determination as the smiles finally froze on his mother's and sister's faces. Finally, they realized the seriousness of the situation.

"POLICE! GET DOWN TO THE GROUND. NOW!"

The boy threw himself to the carpet and turned to look as his mother started to scream, holding both hands to her face, when an officer pulled his baby sister out of her grasp.

"NO! You can't do that! She's my child! You can't take my child! Please…"

Two officers held her down while she screamed and yelled, becoming the crazy mommy that the boy had seen and knew she really was deep inside. She screamed so loudly that the officers pointed their guns at her and suddenly she somehow ripped herself out of their grasp and stormed toward his baby sister, ripped the child out of the hands of the officer, and tried to run with her when the officers yelled at her to stop. They reached out to grab her, but she zigzagged her way away from them. When she didn't stop, one of them fired his gun at her as she rushed for the back door, holding baby sister in her arms. But as he did that, the boy's mother turned around in a scream, and the bullet hit baby sister instead.

The boy couldn't breathe as he watched his mommy tumble to the ground, three officers on top of her, tackling her, baby sister falling out of her grip, and falling lifelessly to the ground, bleeding from the wound in her chest.

"NOOO! MY BABY, NOOO!" Mommy screamed while the boy gasped for air. He then felt hands on his body and was lifted into the air and, while screaming and kicking, he was carried out into a car and strapped in. He stared at the building in front of him, screaming and hammering on the window until he spotted baby sister being rushed into an ambulance and taken away from the scene.

The boy never saw her again. She went into cardiac arrest in the ambulance and died on her way to the hospital, he was later told.

As the boy was finally taken back to his home and to Dad and New Mommy, they hugged him very tightly and told him he had done what he could, but the woman was crazy, and she had killed his baby sister. She was the one to blame. The Thing was to blame, and she would end up spending a long time in jail for what she had done. At least it was over now, and the woman would be gone for many years. He would never have to see her again.

Ever.

Chapter 84

WE DROVE Maddie to her mother's apartment and rang the doorbell. Patricia opened the door, her eyes red-rimmed. As they landed on her daughter, it was hard for me to keep my own tears back.

"Maddie! Is that really you? Oh, heaven have mercy; I can't believe it!"

Patricia almost screamed the words out, then grabbed her daughter in her arms and held onto her and kissed her face while Maddie laughed. I was smiling, joyful over having been able to bring her daughter back, but inside I was screaming in pain, wishing terribly that this was me, that I too would get to hold and kiss my daughter again until she screamed for me to stop.

"Let me look at you, baby," Patricia said and held her daughter's face between her hands. "Are you hurt?"

Maddie shook her head.

"Thank God," her mother exclaimed and hugged her again. She gave me a look and mouthed a *thank you*.

"You're welcome," I whispered back, then raised my voice to normal volume, choking back my own tears. "But more children are missing, and we need to speak to Maddie about where she has been and what she saw."

"Does it have to be right now?" Patricia asked.

"I am afraid so," Matt said. "The sooner we talk to her about these things, the better her recollection will be, and the better our chances are to find the other girl we believe he is holding captive."

"Yes, well, come on in," Patricia said. "I'll make some mac and cheese; are you hungry, Maddie?"

She nodded, and I could tell Maddie was wearied. All the adrenaline from running from her captor was almost gone now, and she would soon be overwhelmed with exhaustion.

We went inside and sat down. Patricia served us some coffee, and I held Maddie's hands in mine. Her skin was smooth and soft like Christine's.

"What can you tell us, Maddie?" I asked. "You told us in the car that you were held captive, but you escaped. What can you tell us about the place you were kept? Were there any other children there?"

She nodded while her mother found a box of mac and cheese and microwaved it.

"There were. Do you know who?" I asked, my heart beating fast.

Maddie shook her head. "I never got to see who it was, but there was someone there. In a box."

"Elijah," Matt said, and our eyes met. This confirmed that Maddie had been held by the same guy that had taken Matt's son, the same guy who said he had killed Sophie Williams, Scott Paxton, and Nathaniel Pullman, the senator's son. We didn't know what his plans with Maddie were, but it looked like they were interrupted by Maddie running away, which was good.

"Who else?" I asked. "Was there another girl there?"

Maddie looked at me, then shook her head. "No."

My heart dropped. "Oh, okay. And you're sure about that?"

She nodded with a sniffle. She was so tired now that her face was turning pale. She wouldn't be able to hold on for much longer. We had to hurry and get all the information out of her that we could.

"What about your kidnapper?" Matt asked. "Did you know him?"

She nodded her head while her mother served her the food. "He used to come here and bring us food."

I looked at her mother for answers. "The church. They send us food from time to time when I sign up for it."

Maddie nodded. "There was one guy who came several times."

"Do you know his name?" I asked.

Her mother shook her head. "There have been so many."

Maddie began to eat, and I realized the girl had probably barely eaten for days.

"I was blindfolded most of the time, but I managed to see a little anyway, that's how I saw the nail that helped me get loose."

"So, you saw his face," I said.

She nodded with her mouth full.

"But you don't know where we can find him?" Matt continued.

She shook her head.

"But you said you jumped into a canal, so that must mean the house was one of the canal houses, and there was a pool, you said?"

She nodded. "Yes. A big one."

"Lots of houses around here have pools and are on the canals," Matt said with a sigh.

"Still, it's getting us closer," I said and looked at the girl. "Try and think back. Was there anything about the place that you remember? Anything that stood out?"

She chewed, then swallowed and nodded. "There was a name. It was scratched into the wall. I was guessing one of the other girls had done it, one that had been there before me."

"A name?" I asked. "What name was that?"

"Sydney," she said and shoveled in another spoonful of mac and cheese while my heart stopped beating. I stared at her.

"S-Sydney?"

She nodded, chewing.

"And you're sure that's what it said?" Matt asked, giving me a concerned look.

Maddie nodded.

"I think I need to get her to bed," her mother said. "She's exhausted and, frankly, so am I. I got a new job at the pharmacy and need to be up early. Can we continue the rest tomorrow?"

Matt nodded and got up. I was staring at the girl, while it felt like a thousand pieces of a puzzle fell into place in my mind. It made no sense, but something was beginning to add up.

"We're done here anyway," Matt said. "Right, Eva Rae?"

I steadied my breath and calmed myself down, then rose to my feet as well. "Yes, we're done."

As we walked to the car, Matt looked at me. "Are you okay?"

I swallowed, pressing the anxiety and fear back. "Yes, yes. I'm fine. Just tired, that's all."

"I meant from hearing your sister's name like that. It must be a shock. Do you think it's the same guy who took your sister back then?"

I walked to the door of the cruiser and grabbed the handle. "I...I have no idea. I just want to go home now. And take that nap we talked about. I can't even see straight anymore."

Matt nodded. "Sure. I'll keep in touch with the search crews and let you know as soon as we find her, and we will find her, you hear me?"

I strapped myself in, nodding. "I heard you. And I believe you. Now, take me home, please."

Chapter 85

HE DROPPED me off in the driveway, and I thanked him, then waved and watched him drive away. As soon as he reached the end of the road, I took one glance at my house, then left, walking down the street. Walking soon became running and, a few minutes later, I was standing in front of a house with a swimming pool and a canal in the backyard. I walked around it, kicked the back door in and walked inside, holding my gun out in front of me.

Quietly, I walked to the stairwell, then rushed up the stairs and down the hallway. I stood in front of the white door, my heart thumping in my chest. I tried to turn the knob, but it was locked. I kicked it open, not caring that I broke it, thinking I'd have to deal with this later.

I walked into the room and found it completely barren—no furniture and nothing on the walls except for black foam. I walked to the end of it and found small splinters on the carpet.

From a wooden box.

Then I spotted the words on the wall and walked closer, reaching out my hand to touch them.

"Sydney," I mumbled. A flood of images from the day she had been taken away from me rushed through my mind. I pushed them back, deciding this wasn't the time for me to get mushy and emotional.

I looked around me, searching for any trace of Christine having been here too, then when I didn't find any, I left the room. I searched the rest of the house but didn't find any trace of her there either. Disappointed, I found a stationary computer inside an office and pressed the spacebar. I searched around on it for a little while and found first the video of Elijah that had been sent to Matt, then the video of Sophie and Nathaniel. I found the original videos of them as well and the program he had used to edit them. Then, I found a document and opened it.

Up came a list of names and plans for how to kill them and place them. I saw Sophie Williams' name on top, then followed the senator's son and then Elijah, then Maddie, who was supposed to have been strangled then placed at the house of a famous politician who lived in Satellite Beach, who had often frequented Maddie's mother. A total humiliation for all involved. Next on the list was the name of a boy I didn't recognize. But there was something else.

An address.

Chapter 86

RYLAN HAD TO PEE. It was the middle of the night, and he and Faith had been sleeping with their mommy.

He held his nose as he sat up straight, feeling woozy from sleeping near the bad smell. He blinked his eyes a few times to make sure he wasn't seeing things. As he looked again, he knew he wasn't. Someone was there, sitting in a chair and watching him.

"W-who are you?" he asked.

The man smiled. Between his hands, he was holding a gun. The sight made Rylan gasp. He hadn't seen one in real life before, only on TV. It looked smaller in real life than on the screen. But just as dangerous.

"I'm here to help you," the man replied.

Rylan looked away, then glanced carefully at his mother and sleeping sister. "Help me with what?"

The man scoffed. "How's your mommy? Huh?"

Rylan swallowed. "She's fine. She'll wake up soon. She just needed to sleep; that's all."

"How's that going for you, huh? Taking care of yourself and your sister while she sleeps, huh?"

Rylan breathed heavily. "Fine."

"It's tough, am I right? Taking care of a sibling. You are all alone."

Rylan bit his lip. "I can do it."

"Can you?" the man said

The boy nodded. He felt like crying but knew he couldn't. Not while the man was looking. He had to be strong now. For Faith and for his mother's sake. Rylan had heard stories about Timmy from third grade who had been taken away from his mother because she couldn't take proper care of him. Rylan knew his mother would take care of him as soon as she woke up. Everything would go back to normal. As soon as she...

"You know she's dead, don't you?" the man suddenly said.

Rylan stared at the man, his upper lip shaking. He was biting his tongue, so he wouldn't cry but had to bite so hard that he soon tasted blood.

"You're lying! She'll wake up soon."

The man winked. "You really believe that?"

The boy breathed, his nostrils flaring. But he didn't answer. Because, deep down, he knew the man was right. As the realization slowly sunk in, Rylan began to cry, finally allowing himself to let it all out. The tears rushed down his cheeks while his young body shook with the effort of trying to hold them back.

"Come on, Rylan. Don't lie to me. You know that she's dead, don't you? She has been for a long time."

The boy tried hard to fight his desire to yell and scream at the man, tell him he was a mean liar and that everything would change when she woke up, and to go away. He didn't dare to because the man was still holding the gun, yet despair was filling Rylan with such overwhelming force, he didn't really know what to do with it, how to make it go away.

"So, now it's just you and Faith, I guess," the man said. "Can you take care of her? For the rest of your life? Are you man enough for that?"

Rylan sobbed and wiped his nose with the back of his hand. The man's words hurt him deeply, and he realized he had no idea how to take care of his sister anymore. They had survived so far, but only because he believed his mommy would wake up soon.

There was no way he could do this any longer.

He shook his head. "N-No."

The man rose to his feet, then said, "I think I can help you avoid that."

He then stretched out his hand holding the gun.

Chapter 87

I SLAMMED my hand into the steering wheel, cursing myself for being so stupid, then parked the car in the parking lot outside of the condominiums in the north part of town. I looked at the number that I had written down, then spotted the entrance and rushed up to the second floor. I knocked but didn't expect anyone to answer. There was a distinct smell in the hallway that made me want to gag. I held my sleeve up in front of my mouth, then grabbed my gun and grabbed the doorknob. The door was locked. I kicked it in, thinking I'd have to explain later how I believed someone had died in there because of the smell and that I believed two young children's lives were in danger.

I was right about both assumptions. As I walked inside, I found the boy standing in the bedroom.

"Police!" I yelled and walked closer.

The boy didn't move. He was staring at something and, as I entered the room, first looking around to make sure the children were alone, I realized he was watching a woman I could only assume was his mother. She was lying in the bed, flies in her dead staring eyes. Next to her lay a young child, a girl, sleeping heavily.

"Are you Rylan?" I asked and turned to face the boy. He whimpered and nodded, and that was when I realized he was holding a gun between his hands.

"What are you doing with that gun, Rylan?" I asked.

The boy answered with sobs. "I can't do it," he said.

DON'T LIE TO ME

"What can't you do?" I asked.

"Take care of her."

I looked at the girl on the bed. She was awake now and staring at us both. "You mean your sister? Her name is Faith, right?"

He nodded. "And you have been taking care of her? Of the both of you. Because your mom died?"

He nodded again, then sobbed and sniffled. Tears ran down his small chubby cheeks. He could be no more than four or five years old, his sister maybe two. I put my gun back in the holster, then knelt in front of him.

"Just hand me the gun, Rylan. You don't want to hurt anyone, do you?"

"You know that many kids who go through a divorce end up taking care of their siblings?" a voice said behind me.

The floor creaked under his heavy feet as he moved closer. I knew the sound of his steps like my own heartbeat.

"It's sad when you think about it. The older child has to become a parent because the parents can no longer take proper care of them. Forces them to grow up too fast."

I heard the gun cock behind my head and raised my hands in the air.

"It happened to you, didn't it?" I asked. "You had to take care of your sister when your parents split?"

"Good detective work," he said.

I turned to look at him. "But she died, didn't she? Your mom killed her. That's what you told me when I was a kid. That was why you never had any contact with her. Because of what happened back then."

My dad nodded. "I thought I had it all figured out. My mom was the bad guy. She was a drug addict, she was crazy, she couldn't take care of us, and she tried to kidnap us. That's what we were told. That's what we believed."

I swallowed. "But that wasn't the entire story, was it?"

He shook his head. "I didn't know till she died last year. I hadn't seen her since the day she was taken away when my sister died. I never wanted to know of her for my entire adult life, not even when I heard she was released from prison. I never wanted to see her again. But then they called from the nursing home she had been living before she died and told me she was gone and that they had a box of her stuff they didn't know what to do with. My initial thought was to leave it there to rot, but then I thought maybe I should burn it all, get rid of every tie

243

to her once and for all. As they gave me the boxes, I couldn't help but go through them. And that was when I found the letters. Letters she had written to me while in prison but gotten back unopened. Letters explaining everything in detail. All my life, I had been told she didn't want me, that she forgot about my sister and me and didn't show up on days when she was supposed to have us, but it was all a lie. My father had deliberately given her wrong dates and then told us she would come on days she wasn't supposed to. So, we would wait for her for hours and stare out the window waiting for her to come. That way, he built up anger in us toward her, and it drove her crazy. So, when she came to see us unannounced, she ended up being angry and aggressive because she was sad and frustrated. She wanted to see us, she wanted us, and all that time, my dad told me that she didn't want us. She had fought for us, but when we went to court, my dad had told us to say we didn't want to be with her. He told the judge my mother was on drugs, but she never was, never touched the stuff. She never hurt me. It all came back to me as I read the letters. My dad would tell us how she would beat us, but I don't remember her hurting my sister or me even a single time. She loved us. She loved me, and I lost all those years. I could have had a mother. My dad and his new wife brainwashed us into thinking she was this terrible person, that she was dangerous for us when she wasn't. It was all a darn lie."

"They alienated you from her, so you didn't even want to see her," I said.

"Don't you get it? It was my fault. I did it," my dad said, a tear escaping the corner of his eye. His next words came out as choked sobs, "I lost her. I was the one who killed my sister. I called the police on my own mother and sent her to jail. Just because of some lie, some freakin lie."

"And now, they're all dead, so you can't even confront them," I said, fighting my own tears. I looked at Rylan, who was staring at the gun between his hands. Right now, all I wanted was to make sure he and his sister made it out of here alive. I had to keep my dad's focus away from the boy.

"So, you came up with this." I stared at my dad, shaking my head. "You're sick, do you know that? Killing all those children. Just to tell the world your story? What kind of a warped mind does that? I guess I should have figured it out sooner; I guess I just refused to face it. The mustache, the blue BMW. Instead, I came up with excuses, thinking lots of people own blue convertible BMWs and have mustaches. But there was also the green paint on my carpet; the same paint used to paint the side of the box that Matt's son was in. I should've guessed it then. It wasn't until Maddie told me about the name by the floorboard. I remembered it from Sydney's old room. You kept them in there. Cleared it all out without mom knowing it, and then made it into a prison. You even soundproofed it with foam on the walls. You knew mom would never go anywhere near that room. And she certainly wouldn't let anyone else. So, you made it ready while mom visited her friends in Winter Park and went golfing with them, and you planned everything without her even suspecting a thing. You have volunteered for years as a leader with the Girl Scouts, so even if you didn't go on the campout yourself, you knew where they went and when to grab her. And what about Scott Paxton, huh? The kid you dismembered and used only his legs and arms?"

"He was just a random kid I picked up in a poor area," he said. "He wasn't important. A prop, if you will. I just needed his body parts. You'll find the rest of him in a dumpster in Titusville."

I shuddered. To think of all the times I had left him alone with my children. All the times I had been to their house, and he had been keeping those children right up there in Sydney's room while we were hanging out downstairs eating dinner. The thought made me sick.

"You and Senator Pullman go way back, and you play poker with him from time to time, at his house where you met his son, am I right?" I continued. "You stole Thomas Price's car from his mother's house to lead us to believe he killed Sophie, then used it while dumping the body of Sophie and for kidnapping Maddie from her bus stop. Patricia told me earlier that she knew you because you had often brought them groceries when they were in need. Through your volunteering job at the church, you bring food to many poor people around here, and you took especially good care of them, didn't you? Got to know them well, so when you drove up to Maddie, she believed she could trust you. But I don't know how you knew Matt had a son?"

My dad smiled. "As I told you, I know everything around here. His mom told me when I met her one day and offered her a coffee. She was devastated because Matt wasn't allowed ever to see him, and she wanted to get to know her grandchild too. It didn't take me long to find him."

"And so, you pretended to be a journalist from *Florida Today* and, being the charmer that you are, Lisa naturally believed you. And what about Rylan and Faith? How did you choose them?" I asked.

"I ran into them coincidentally. I was driving down A1A when I spotted two little children on their own, playing outside this building. I stopped and asked them where their mom was. They told me she was in bed, that she was sick and sad. I asked them where their dad was, and they said he had left. Didn't take me long to decide they would be perfect for my final act."

"And just what is your final act, Dad?" I asked.

"Well, you followed me here, didn't you? So, I guess you get to witness it. You weren't a part of my plan when I began this. I tried to stop you, to tell you to stay out of it, but you had to get yourself involved. So, now you're in it. I led you here on purpose, just like I led you to my other artwork. I never meant for you to get hurt, but you leave me no choice. You know I loved you as if you were my own, don't you? I always saw you and Sydney as mine."

"I know you did, Dad. But, please, you don't have to kill any more people. You've proved your point. Please, just let us go, will you?"

"But I'm not done," my dad said matter-of-factly. He glanced above my head at Rylan.

"You can do it, boy. Put an end to it."

Rylan looked up at him, tears streaming across his cheeks, the gun shaking in his hands.

"Rylan, no," I said. "Please, Dad, don't make him do it. Why are you this way? Why do you have to hurt people? I thought I knew you."

"Do you know how many kids commit suicide because of divorce?" my dad asked me.

I shook my head. "No, Rylan, please, just put down the gun. You don't have to do this. You have a good life ahead of you."

"No, you don't," my dad said, hissing. "Feel the pain inside of you? It'll follow you for the rest of your life. It will never leave you; it will eat at you every day you're alive, and the loneliness will grow bigger and bigger till it explodes and you either kill yourself or somebody else. Just pull the trigger. Get it over with now, Rylan; come on, boy!"

Rylan cried, then placed the tip of the gun on his nose. I stared at him with wide open eyes as his small finger slipped on the trigger and he sobbed.

"Come on, boy! Try again."

"No, Rylan, stop it," I said.

The boy was crying, his small body trembling. I looked up at my dad, who stared at the boy in anticipation. He forgot to keep an eye on me for just a short second, and I saw my chance. With a swift movement, I reached up and grabbed the gun my dad was holding, then wrestled it out of his hands. The gun was sent flying across the room, and soon my dad and I were in a fist battle on the floor.

Unfortunately for me, my dad was a lot heavier and a lot stronger, and soon he managed to throw a punch to my jaw that made my ears ring. I kicked him in the groin, and he moaned in pain when I heard a gun go off.

Chapter 88

RYLAN!

My dad fell flat on top of me. While trying to get him off of me, I turned my face to look and spotted the boy. He was still standing next to us, holding the gun between his hands, staring at something behind me. I turned to the other side and spotted Matt, standing in the doorway, holding the smoking gun between his hands.

He ran to me and helped pull my dad off me. I touched my face and wiped my dad's blood away. Matt had shot him in the back of his head. Matt reached out his hand for me to grab it.

"Are you all right?"

I took in a couple of ragged breaths, trying to get a grasp of everything, letting it all sink in.

"That depends. Physically, I think I'm fine, yes. Emotionally is a completely different conversation. How much did you hear?"

Matt shook his head. "Not much, but enough to know he was trying to kill both you and the boy. Was he…?"

I nodded. "Yes, Daddy Dearest…I guess…was our killer all along." I sighed and rubbed my forehead. So many thoughts were rushing through my mind that I couldn't really focus. The initial shock was wearing off, and soon reality would set in.

"I'll explain everything later," I said. "Right now, I need to do something."

I walked to Rylan, then knelt in front of him once again. He sniffled and looked up at me. I reached out my hand toward him, and he hesitated for just a second, then placed the gun in it. I then reached out my arm and pulled him into a hug, while Matt called for assistance.

Once he was done, he came back to me. "Maybe we should take the children outside to wait?" he said. "This place stinks, and my eyes are watering."

We did. We walked into the hallway, Matt carrying Faith in his arms. She cried as we sat down on the stairs outside, rubbing her eyes, asking what had happened. Rylan grabbed her hand in his and sat with her, holding his arm around her shoulder while explaining to her that their mommy wasn't going to wake up anytime soon.

"He killed her a few days ago," I said, addressed to Matt after a few minutes. "And the children have lived alone all this time, taking care of themselves. Just like my dad had to take care of his own sister after his parents' divorce. His sister ended up dying, though. This was all his way of telling his story, of going through his own childhood pain, killing his way through it in a very disturbed way. I can't believe I...that my...dad would do such a thing. I thought I knew him. But after tonight, I realized I didn't know him at all. I'm sorry for not involving you once I realized it had to be him. I had to be certain before I started accusing him of anything."

"I get it," Matt said. "It was something you felt like you needed to do on your own. It was your family. But, luckily for you, I knew you were up to something. I know you. Better than you think. I know you would never go back and sleep when your daughter was missing. After I dropped you off, I followed you as you ran to your parents' house and then waited outside until you came back out and ran back for your car. I followed you here but didn't want to come in at first. I had no idea what you were doing in there until it took too long, and I finally decided to go after you, thinking something had to be wrong. I'm glad I did."

I smiled up at him, and he put his arm around me.

"So am I."

I sighed deeply, trying to shake tonight's events when my thoughts once again landed on Christine. She hadn't been in Sydney's old room. She hadn't been on his list of victims, and he hadn't mentioned her.

If my dad hadn't taken her, then where was she?

Chapter 89

THE NIGHT BECAME PAINFULLY long and, as morning broke, I was finally able to leave the site and go home. Rylan and Faith were in the hands of the DCF and would be sent to live with their grandparents in Wisconsin, they told me.

My mom was sound asleep on the couch when I came back inside. She woke up as I sat down on the coffee table she had once given me. She blinked her eyes.

"Eva Rae, we don't sit on the tables," she said. "That's what we have chairs for…"

The look in my eyes made her stop.

"You didn't find her?" she asked and jolted upright.

I shook my head. I grabbed her hands between mine. "Mom. We need to talk."

"Talk? What about? Don't tell me it's about what happened last night; I know it was…"

I shook my head. "That's not what this is about. We'll get to that later. Right now, I need to tell you something that will completely shake your world, but you have to listen to me and let me finish, okay?"

My mom's eyes grew wide. "O-okay. But could we at least get a little coffee to wash this down with…whatever it is?"

"Deal."

I made the coffee, and we talked for hours. It was Saturday, so the kids didn't have school. I had to repeat a lot of it because my mom refused to believe it. But, little by little, it sunk in and soon my mom sat in my kitchen, crying and shaking her head.

"You think you know people…you live with them for years and years, and…it's all a lie?"

There were so many things I could have said at that moment to make her feel terrible about herself and how she had lied to me through all my life, but I decided against it. I realized I was no longer as angry about it as I had been. We were in this together.

"So…what will happen next?" she asked.

"Your house will be a part of the investigation," I said. "It's a crime scene now. Which means you'll have to live here for as long as it'll take them, God help us all."

"I heard that, Eva Rae," my mom said. In her voice, I heard a sort of relief. I wondered if she would ever want to go back to that place. Maybe staying here with me wasn't such a terrible idea after all. We both had to lick our wounds and find a way to move on past this. I knew we would drive each other nuts in the process, but the fact was, we needed each other.

I served my mom some cinnamon buns that I quickly baked, and she ate them without even talking about sugar or fat or cholesterol or asking if they were vegan or gluten-free. It was a relief to just be sitting there with my mom, and just be. Be human.

Barely had I finished my second bun when my phone buzzed.

"Ms. Eva Rae Thomas?" a voice asked from the other end.

"Yes?"

"TSA agent Frances Lopez, from Orlando airport here. I have someone who would like to talk to you."

"Mom?"

"Christine?"

"Oh, Mom, I…" she broke down and cried. I couldn't hold it back myself either.

"Where are you, baby? I'll come get you now. Just tell me where you are, and I'll be there."

"I'm…I'm at the airport," she said.

"Oh, baby girl. Stay where you are. I'll be right there."

I looked at my mom as I hung up. She smiled. "Well, what are you waiting for, Eva Rae? Go. I'll be here when the kids wake up."

I kissed her cheek. "Thanks, Mom."

"Just don't make a habit of it. I'm not a babysitter, you know," she shouted after me, but I was already gone.

Chapter 90

"CHRISTINE?"

I spotted her in the room that the TSA agent led me into while telling me that they had picked her up when she tried to purchase a ticket with my credit card.

Christine looked up at me, her eyes big and swollen from crying. "Oh, Mom, I'm…"

I knelt down and hugged her tightly. "No, baby. I'm the one who's sorry. I never meant to get so angry at you. I never meant to say those things. I am so, so sorry. You were trying to purchase a ticket to go see your dad, weren't you? To go to Washington?"

She nodded, crying. "Yes, but Mom, you were right. I took a shuttle to the airport and called dad and told him I was on my way, but then he said he couldn't have me. That I had to stay with you. That this wasn't a good time. I even told him I had quarreled with you and that I wanted to come live with him, but he said he didn't want that. I decided to go anyway and thought I could just crash at Amy's place instead until I convinced him to take me in. I didn't dare to come back to you. But you were right, Mom. He doesn't want us anymore."

It broke my heart, and I couldn't stop crying. "Oh, dear baby. I am so sorry."

"Why is he being like that, Mom?"

"I…I don't know, honey. Dad's going through something."

"But...can't he do that without hurting us? His children?" she asked.

I pulled her into my arms. "I don't know, sweetie. All I know is that we need to stick together. We have to help each other get through this. And I promise to try and be home a lot more, okay?"

Christine got up and grabbed my hand in hers. "Good," she said with a sniffle. "Because I can't take care of Alex all on my own anymore. He's exhausting."

We walked out the door, and I smiled at the agent before we found the exit. "Well, I might have a solution for that," I said as we walked back into the parking lot.

"Really? What?"

"Grandma is moving in with us. At least for a little while. Isn't that neat?"

My daughter stopped as we reached the car. She stared at me. "Grandma? Does that mean we all have to become vegan?"

"Okay, so we haven't figured out all the details yet, but we'll get to that eventually. Now, let's get home, baby. It's been a long day."

Chapter 91

"CAN WE OPEN OUR EYES YET?"

Olivia sounded annoyed, but I wasn't going to rush it just because of her. I wanted it to be perfect.

I corrected the board one more time, then said, "All right, you can look."

All three kids opened their eyes and stared at the whiteboard in front of them that I had hung up on the wall in the kitchen. Behind them, my mom was whistling as she was preparing another odd dish for us for tonight. I was eternally happy she was there and that she was cooking for us, but I was getting pretty fed up with beans and lentils by now. I just didn't want to tell her how much we all loathed her food. I didn't want to break her heart. It had been broken so much already.

"Is that it?" Alex groaned. "I thought it was something cool."

"What's this?" Christine asked. "What are we looking at?"

"This, my children, is our new organizer board. See how I put all the days here and then all the hours there? This is where you write your activities down. Like Olivia has Volleyball on Tuesdays."

"Mondays and Wednesdays, Mom," Olivia grumbled.

"Yes, okay, Monday and Wednesday," I said and wrote it on the board. "See? Now we all know where Olivia is between three and five o'clock on Mondays and Wednesdays. And if she has a game on Saturday, then she'll write it there, and we'll all know where she is, and where I'll probably be too because I will want to see all her games this season."

Olivia rolled her eyes. "Really, Mom? Do you have to?"

I smiled. "Yes, and I will be cheering from the sidelines. Probably wearing a funny hat or something embarrassing. And maybe Grandma will want to go too?"

"Leave me out of this," my mom said. "I'll only come if sweet Olivia invites me."

"There you go," Olivia said. "Grandma understands how it works."

"Very well, but I plan on coming anyway. And I'll be at all your concerts, Christine, and your surfing contests, Alex, once you get to that level. Are we clear? Activities go on the board, and you remember to text me every now and then and you always, always pick up when I call, okay?"

"This is turning into a prison," Olivia said and walked away, probably rolling her eyes once again.

"What do you think?"

I looked at Christine for some sort of recognition. "It's okay...for you."

"I'll take that as an acknowledgment," I said and turned just in time to see Alex draw a huge fire truck all over my schedule.

"Oh, no, Alex. I spent a long time making this."

My son smiled and admired his artwork. "It looks much better now, Mom," he said, very visibly proud.

I chuckled and put a hand on his shoulder. "I can't argue with that."

LATER THAT SAME EVENING, I was watching TV with my mom when there was a knock on the door. I went to open it.

"Matt?"

He looked at me nervously and, at first, I feared something was wrong.

"So, here's the deal," he said. "My mom can babysit Elijah this Friday."

I looked at him, puzzled.

"And?"

He was obviously looking for words. When he didn't find them, he walked up to me, grabbed me, and pulled me into a kiss.

"You annoy the heck out of me, Eva Rae Thomas," he whispered as our lips parted.

"Odd thing to say after kissing a girl," I said, still confused.

He shook his head, almost angrily. "Don't you get it?"

"I'm not sure I do, no."

He growled something, then turned around, then returned and looked at me. "Can we try? Please? I know it didn't work out the first time, but can we try again?"

I swallowed, and a smile spread across my lips.

"Is that your way of asking me out?"

He threw out his arms. "Yes!"

"This Friday?"

"Yes!"

I shook my head. "Matt…I can't…"

"Oh, okay. Wow," he said and stepped away from me, his voice turning shrill. "But that's okay. That's okay. At least I tried, right?"

He turned around and was about to walk away when I stopped him.

"Matt, I can't…this Friday. I've promised Melissa and Dawn I'll go out with them. Some local band is playing at the Beach Shack. They're all excited to take me there. But if you can get your mom to babysit on Saturday, then I'll be delighted to."

Matt's face lit up. "Really?"

"Really."

"Yes!" he said, walking backward toward his car. "You've got it. I'll pick you up, right here. That's a date. It's a date!"

Matt got into the car and drove off, while I wondered if he was ever going to tell me what time he would pick me up. I shrugged and decided he'd probably text me, then went back inside where my mom was watching CSI Miami. I decided I wasn't in the mood for any more mystery in my life, then went into the kitchen, opened my laptop, and began to write the first page of my book.

Only, as soon as I had written the first line, I suddenly had a new idea. A story was asking to be let out and felt more urgent than the first one I had wanted to write.

The story of a boy turned killer. The story of the man I had once believed was my dad.

THE END

WHAT YOU DID
EVA RAE THOMAS MYSTERY, BOOK 2

Prologue

COCOA BEACH, FL

IT WASN'T easy to run for your life in a prom dress. Carina lifted the hem of what had once been a beautiful oceanic blue mermaid evening gown; the very same one that had, a few hours earlier, been adored by hundreds of her fellow students' eyes as she was called up on the stage to be crowned prom queen. One of her beautiful Manolo Blahniks, of the first pair she had ever owned, had lost a heel on the asphalt before she made the turn onto the golf course. As she had pushed herself through the grass and the other heel had sunk into the moist and swampy Florida ground, she had ripped both shoes off, panting agitatedly as she heard the steps of her follower approaching in the darkness. She had lost her crown near the entrance to the country club as she ran there, shaking the doors, hoping that maybe someone was in there and could help her. But all the doors had been locked, and that was why she ended up running toward the golf course, her pursuer breathing down her neck.

Carina was a track runner, and as she ran across the golf course, she soon sensed that she had lost him. As she reached a small lake followed by a row of trees, she allowed herself to slow down for just a second. She stopped and listened, thinking she could hide between the bushes, at least till she caught her breath. Her lungs felt like they were on fire, and she was wheezing to breathe.

Stupid allergies!

She feared he might hear her heavy breathing and panting since it sounded so loud in her own ears. Unable to see any movement across the open area behind her, she took a few deep breaths, trying to calm herself down. As she managed to breathe easier, Carina fought not to panic. Her heart pounded against her ribs.

What happened to the others? Where are they?

There had been three girls walking home together when they left the school and the prom. They all lived in the neighborhood right behind the school and had decided to make the five-minute walk home together. There were, after all, three of them, and the area was very safe. Nothing ever happened in Cocoa Beach. As long as they stayed together, they would be safe.

Why hadn't they stayed together?

He had come as if out of nowhere. None of them saw him. They were chatting and talking about the night. Ava and Tara were both telling Carina how beautiful she had looked when doing the mandatory slow dance with Kevin, the prom king. Carina had listened and enjoyed the sound of jealousy in their voices when they talked about her, but the fact was, it had been the most awkward moment of Carina's seventeen-year-long life. Kevin was the boyfriend of her best friend Molly, and all the time she had been dancing with him, she had been looking at her friend, wondering if she looked like she enjoyed it too much. Molly had left during the dance and Carina hadn't seen her since. She had texted her as soon as the dance was over, trying to explain that she only danced with him because she had to…because it was expected of them. But Molly hadn't answered, and Carina had grown worried about her and wondered if she was mad at her. She had seen it in her eyes right before she left. The anger and resentment. She knew that look a little too well since they had been best friends since they met in Kindergarten.

I am so sorry, Molly. I didn't mean to hurt you. You have to believe me; I didn't enjoy it at all.

The girls had screamed when the masked man grabbed Ava and held a knife to her throat. Carina had panicked. Both she and Tara had screamed, while Ava whimpered behind the knife. Then Carina had kicked him. She had no idea where her strength and courage had come from, but she had lifted her Manolo Blahnik and placed a kick right where it hurt the most, and the guy had bent forward in pain.

That was when they began to run. He had reached out and grabbed for Tara, but she had managed to get loose from his grip, screaming helplessly. It was one of the last things Carina saw before she lost track of the others. At what point they got split up, she didn't even know. She just knew they had run, and, in the beginning, she had thought the others were right behind her, but as she ran onto the golf course, she realized she couldn't see them or hear them anywhere.

Now, as she stared into the darkness, she wondered if she had, after all, managed to escape her pursuer.

Had he given up?

Sweat ran down her back, and her blonde hair felt soaked. Her knees were still shaking while she tried to figure out what to do next. She couldn't stay there. If he was still out there, he'd find her.

A movement in the bushes made her gasp. A shadow ran across the grass in the moonlight, holding up her dress in the same manner Carina had earlier.

Tara!

Carina stepped out from her hiding place and wondered if she should yell her name, but as she opened her mouth to speak, a shadow stepped out from behind a tree and grabbed Tara. He swung her, screaming, in the air, then slammed his fist into her face. Carina watched while gasping for air as Tara fell to the ground and she couldn't even hear her scream anymore.

Carina felt her bones tremble, and she knew she should run; every part of her screamed for her legs to move, to get her away from there, yet they didn't. It was like they were paralyzed.

Was Tara still alive?

She watched as the man bent over the motionless Tara for a few seconds before he lifted his head and she felt his eyes on her. She couldn't tell if he was actually looking at her or not, but she felt those evil eyes like knives on her skin.

Swiftly, he rose to his feet and bolted toward her. She immediately knew she couldn't outrun him. Yet, she tried. She turned around and set off, but just as in her many nightmares, it was like she barely moved forward at all. Hands reached for her ponytail, and she was pulled forcefully back and into his arms. When she felt his hand on her neck and smelled his warm breath on her skin, she closed her eyes and prayed that she would feel no pain.

Chapter 1

TWO WEEKS LATER

"GREAT NEWS. I FOUND HER."

My eyes grew wide. They stared at the woman in front of me, behind the cluttered desk. Her name was Rhonda, and she was a private eye that I had hired to track down my long-lost sister.

Sydney was kidnapped from a Wal-Mart when I was only five years old and she was seven. I had recently learned that she might still be alive since it was our mutual biological father who had taken her, and it was believed they had left the country back then. It had taken me a few weeks to gather the courage to start the investigation and hire someone to do it for me. Rhonda had been at it for six months, searching for both my dad and my sister. So far, I had barely heard from her in all those months, and I assumed that was because she couldn't find anything. Her words and excited bright eyes staring at me from behind the deeply furrowed face surprised me.

"Really?"

Rhonda nodded. She grabbed a file from the pile next to her and placed it in front of me. She pushed it closer, and I felt my heart begin to pound. I wasn't sure how to react to any of this.

"Take a look for yourself."

I could hardly breathe. I stared at the file, my fingers unable to stop shaking. I bit my lip, then looked up at Rhonda.

"And you're sure it's her?"

Rhonda nodded. "It wasn't an easy case, this one. But with a little help from a colleague in Europe, I traced your father to London."

"And Sydney?"

Rhonda cleared her throat. "He changed her name. She became Mallory Stevens over there. His name is now James Stevens."

"Mallory? So, that's her name now?" I asked, wrinkling my nose. I loved the name Sydney. It was going to take some getting used to, but then again, a lot of this was. It was about to turn everything in my life upside down once again.

Rhonda shook her head. "She changed her name again…when she moved to Florida."

I almost choked. "Florida? You mean to tell me…that…that…she's *here?*"

She nodded and fiddled with her pen. "It's all in the files."

"And she changed her name…again? So, what is she called now?" I asked, almost unable to take in all this information at once. My life had already been turned upside down quite a lot the past year since my ex and the father of my three children, Chad, had decided to leave me for a younger and blonder version called Kimmie. After the break-up, I had moved myself and the children back to my hometown of Cocoa Beach to reconnect with my parents, only to learn that the man I believed was my father wasn't, and that the man I had loved like a father was a vicious killer who had murdered several children. Now, he was dead, and my mom was still living with the children and me, refusing to go back to the house where they had lived together. I couldn't blame her. I wanted to burn that house down and see all the lies go up in flames along with it.

"So, what's her name now?" I asked.

Rhonda leaned forward, grabbed the front of the file, and opened it. Then she pointed at something on the middle of the first page, tapping at it with her long well-manicured purple fingernail.

I stared at the name in front of me, then up at Rhonda, my eyes scrutinizing her.

Was she pulling my leg?

"But…how…that's…"

Rhonda nodded. "I know. I had to check a few extra times myself to make sure, but there's no doubt. It's her. This woman is your sister."

Chapter 2

THEN:

"Artie. Talk to me. What are we dealing with?"

Gary Pierce approached the local sheriff, who was standing by his car. Surrounding him, his deputies looked nervously at Gary. They were standing by the dirt road leading to an old farmhouse in Riverdale, Maryland.

"Tony Velleda, forty-eight, is being held hostage. Kidnappers forced their way into his home yesterday when he was there alone with his eight-year-old son. The kid was then bound on his hands and legs and left in the home when the kidnappers took his father. The boy managed to free himself and alert the neighbors, who called for authorities. The kidnappers took him across state lines, and as far as we have been informed, are keeping him at the farm up there. We know there are four armed men and the hostage. We know that at least one of the kidnappers has gang connections and another is still on parole for assault with a lethal weapon. These guys don't mess around."

"Neither do we."

Gary felt his gun in the holster. He felt the thickness of his vest like he often did before going into action. It was a strange thing to do, he always believed, but he couldn't help himself. It was like he needed to make sure it was thick enough to actually stop a penetrating bullet... like he didn't completely believe it would.

"We're going in," he said and nodded at the sheriff. "Have your men ready."

Minutes later, they were walking up the dirt road, Gary leading them. As he held his M-4 assault rifle out in front of him, preparing himself for what awaited him inside that small house, he thought about his wife Iris and their newborn son, Oliver. He was no more than three weeks old and the most adorable thing in the world. Just this morning, when Gary had left the house to go to work, the boy had smiled for the first time, and Gary had cursed himself for having to go to work on an important day like today.

"Please, let this go down well," he prayed under his breath. "Please, let me see that smile again."

Gary snuck around the house, then found an unlit window that he broke with his rifle. He removed the glass, then crawled inside, pointing the gun through the darkens. His partner, Agent Wilson, came up right behind him, sliding in after him. They found a door where light came out, then walked closer and peeked in through the crack.

Gary spotted three men, armed to the teeth, and another man sitting in the middle of the room, blindfolded and bound to a chair.

Gary signaled Wilson, then grabbed the door and they burst inside, both yelling:

"FBI! GET DOWN!"

The three men in front of them threw down their weapons, then cast themselves on the floor, heads down, arms lifted.

Gary turned around to search for the last guy, when he appeared in the doorway behind them leading to the bedroom, holding a rifle between his hands.

"Throw down your weapons, Officers. NOW."

Gary swallowed, almost panicking, then did as he was told. Wilson followed, but as the weapons landed on the floor, his partner pulled out a handgun, turned it at the kidnapper, and shot. One clean shot that went straight through his head. The kidnapper sunk to the floor with a thud, rag-doll limp.

Chapter 3

"SO, there you have it, Greg. It still remains a huge mystery to the citizens of Cocoa Beach. What happened to the prom queen, Carina Martin, and her two friends, Tara Owens and Ava Morales, on prom night after they left the high school? Maybe this new evidence they found today will help the detectives get closer to an answer."

I turned off the TV and threw the remote on the couch. It was on as I came home from my visit to Rhonda's, file still under my arm, and no one was watching. Before I turned it off, I paused to hear if they had any news in the case of the disappearance of the three teenage girls who went missing after prom night two weeks ago. It was all everyone talked about lately, and I had to say that the reporter on News13 was right; it remained a strange mystery. They had been gone for two entire weeks now, and still, there was no trace of the girls. The theories went from them being kidnapped to them having planned this themselves to escape the pressure of senior year and exams. The last part was way too far out for my taste, but that left us with the first option, and I really didn't like that either. Matt had been on the case from the night they never came home, and their parents anxiously called CBPD to ask them to set up search teams.

Matt and I had been dating for a little more than six months now, and things were going really well. We were enjoying spending time together and hated being apart, something I had never experienced with Chad. The connection Matt and I shared was so much deeper, which was only natural since we had known each other since preschool and his house had been my place to run to when things got tough for me at home as a teenager. But we had been nothing but friends back then, and now we had finally decided to be more than that. Twenty years apart was apparently what we needed in order to figure it out.

My book was coming along well too. Between unpacking and getting settled, I had managed to almost finish it, and I couldn't wait to be done. I was writing about my—not biological—dad, a serial killer who had managed to deceive the people he loved and hide what he was up to in plain sight, committing these atrocities right under my mother's nose. Writing his story had been a process for both my mother and me since I kept coming to her with my questions into his childhood and their lives together. I think it was therapeutic for my mom to talk about him and what had happened, but I sensed that it also drained her emotionally.

Originally, I was supposed to be writing about some of the worst serial killers in the country seen from the perspective of an FBI-profiler, but when my publishing house learned about my new story-line, a true crime story told by one of the implicated, they threw away the contract for the first book and we signed a new one. And they gave me a huge advance on top of what they had already paid me. That's how excited they were. This one was so commercial and had best-selling potential, they told me. I wasn't opposed to it becoming a best-seller. I could use the money to support myself and the kids. Chad hadn't been in the picture much since he left us, and the few times he remembered to pay alimony, it barely covered half of the rent for our house. Having three children and being a single mom was expensive.

"Knock, knock."

Matt peeked inside, holding a bottle of wine in his hand. I smiled when I saw him. I could hear the children rummaging around upstairs, and Alex yelled something at one of his sisters. It was Olivia who yelled back and then slammed her door. She was now fifteen and had no patience for her six-year-old brother, or her twelve-year-old sister, Christine. Or for me, for that matter.

Matt jumped at the sound of the door slamming. I was so used to it, I barely reacted. Instead, I smiled at Matt again and grabbed the wine from his hand.

"What's the occasion?"

He shrugged, then leaned over and kissed me. "It's Friday, and I have the weekend off."

I sent him a look. I knew the wine was for me and not him.

"I'll order some pizza. There's beer in the fridge," I said.

His face lit up. "I was hoping you'd say that."

Chapter 4

"YUM, MEATLOAF!"

We walked into the kitchen, and Matt laid his eyes on the dish on the counter.

"I love meatloaf," he said and approached it. "Did you make this?"

I put the bottle on the counter and shook my head with a wry smile. "Me? Cooking? If that's why you're dating me, I might as well come clean right now. I don't cook, I'm afraid. I thought you knew this by now."

"It looks delicious," he said. "Why don't we just eat that instead of pizza?"

I found the bottle opener and opened the wine. I poured myself a glass, then gave him a look, and he nodded.

"Ah, I see. Your mom made this, right?"

"Yup."

"And there is absolutely no meat in it?"

"Not an ounce. No meat, no dairy, no gluten. Only plant-based ingredients. She cooked for us all earlier because she was going to Winter Garden to play cards with her girlfriends."

Matt sighed with dissatisfaction. "It looks so good, though."

"Be my guest," I said. "But I have been eating vegan for this entire week now, chewing my way through plant-based dishes so much I fear there might be palm trees growing out of my ears. I, for one, am ordering a pizza with loads of meat on it and enjoying the fact that my mom isn't here to disapprove or get hurt by the fact that I can't stand her cooking."

Matt shrugged, then grabbed a plate. "I'm gonna try some. It's good for you."

I sipped my wine and watched as he grabbed a piece, then found my phone and ordered a family-sized pizza, making sure there'd be enough for the kids and Matt in case he changed his mind. Once I was done, I put the phone down and looked at Matt, who seemed to be enjoying the vegan meatloaf.

"This is good," he said. "I don't know why you're complaining about your mom's cooking. I think it's really good."

I sat down on a stool and watched him take another piece and finish it while sipping my wine.

"So, where's Elijah tonight?" I asked.

Matt found a stool and sat down too. He stopped chewing, and his eyes grew weary. Matt had been a single dad ever since the mother of his child was murdered in the fall. He had never had a close relationship with the boy since he hadn't learned of the boy's existence until he was three years old, and the mother finally told him. She and Matt had a one-night-stand some nine years ago, and he thought he'd never see her again. Now, he was taking care of the eight-year-old boy on his own, and it had completely changed his life.

"He's with my mom," he said. "She took him to the movies, giving me the night off."

I leaned over and grabbed his fork, then took a bite of the vegan meatloaf too. I chewed, then made a face. Nope. Just as bad as the rest of her cooking. I sipped my wine, washing away the bad taste. There was a big part of me that wished I could enjoy my mother's cooking; there really was. I could shed a few pounds or fifteen, but I just didn't enjoy it. And if I was honest, all this healthy eating somehow made me snack more between meals, and I found myself gaining weight after my mom moved in, instead of losing it like I wanted to.

"How are things between the two of you?" I asked. "Is it getting any better?"

Matt looked down at the plate, then shook his head. "He hates my guts."

"He does not. You're his dad."

"I'm telling you; he hates me. He won't let me help him with anything, and he most certainly won't talk to me. He won't even let me tuck him in at night. He spends most of his day with my mom after school since I am at work and every day when I come home, I hope that things will be better, that he'll have warmed up to me, but he hasn't so far. I think he blames me for Lisa's death."

I reached over and put my hand on top of his. "He lost his mother, the only parent he really knew since you had him so rarely."

"And whose fault was that?" Matt asked. "It sure wasn't mine. I begged her to let me see him more, but she always came up with all these stupid excuses. It was like she enjoyed disappointing me...like she only told me about him to hurt me."

"But she did tell you, so she must have wanted you involved on some level," I said. "Maybe it was just hard for her."

Matt ate some more from his plate, then shook his head. "Yeah, well..."

"Don't give up on him. You're all he's got. Give him time. His life has changed a lot in the past six months, and he doesn't know where he stands. He probably misses his mom terribly, and you're the only one around he can take it out on. Give it some time. I'm sure he'll come around."

"It's just...it's nothing like I imagined it would be, you know? Being a father, full-time I mean. It's really...hard."

"Welcome to the club."

I chuckled and sipped my wine, sending a loving glance toward my own children upstairs. Mine weren't doing too badly lately. Alex seemed to have found his peace with his new surroundings. Being a part of the gifted program TAG at school meant they were giving him more challenging assignments, and that seemed to have calmed him down a lot. He still yelled often when he spoke, and it was still hard for him to sit still for more than a few minutes at a time, but he seemed happier. The girls seemed to be doing better, too, than when we first got here. They never spoke much about their father anymore, and I didn't really know if that was a good or a bad thing. In the beginning, they went up to Washington to visit him and Kimmie at least once a month, but the past two months, the girls hadn't wanted to go when I asked them. Especially my oldest, Olivia, seemed like she couldn't care less about her father, and that wasn't like her. I wondered if something had happened the last time they were up there. I felt sorry for Alex since he missed his father, but I couldn't really send him up there all alone on a plane. Maybe other six-year-olds would do fine, but not my Alex. It wouldn't end well for any of the passengers on that plane.

"I saw on the news that they found another shoe they believe is

WHAT YOU DID

Carina Martin's?" I said, trying to change the subject. "This time all the way at the east end of the golf course in some bushes?"

Matt walked to the fridge and grabbed a beer. "Yeah, it was the second shoe. We found the heel on the asphalt and the remains of the first shoe on the night she disappeared."

"But that means she went even deeper into the golf course than you thought, right?"

He nodded, opened his beer, and sat down. "Yeah. It was found close to a bushy area where lots of golfers usually lose their balls. It's like a small forest part that is nearly impassable. I thought we had that place completely combed through, but it's just so…big, you know?"

I nodded. "So, do you think she might have been hiding in there?"

"I don't know. She could also have gone in there with some guy. It was prom, you know? People do some pretty crazy things on prom night."

"But you found the crown by the entrance to the country club, right?" I asked.

He nodded and sipped his beer. "We've found broken shoes in multiple locations spread throughout the golf course. We found Tara Owen's purse with her phone in it and part of Ava Morales' dress that was ripped off was floating in one of the small ponds."

"It's almost like Hansel and Gretel following the breadcrumbs," I mumbled.

He looked up. "What was that?"

I shook my head. "Nothing. What about the two other phones? Have you been able to locate them?"

He shook his head.

"Social media accounts? Anything that might give you a lead? Anyone they chatted with?"

"We're still working on that part," he said. "The forensic lab is taking care of it. They're still working on their computers and getting their cell phone histories. Young people today have so many social media accounts, it takes forever, but so far they haven't found anything useful."

"Have any of the girls had issues with other students at the school? Have they received any threats? Trouble at home with parents or relatives? Any mental illnesses?"

"No, no, and no," he said. "The three girls had perfect attendance, and they were straight A or A-B honor roll. They were well-liked and popular, especially Carina Martin."

"What about boyfriends?" I asked, sipping from my glass.

"Ava Morales was dating a guy from the school, but he wasn't at the prom since he was in Orlando to say goodbye to his grandmother who died the night before. The two other girls didn't have boyfriends. Some of the other students say that Carina was with Kevin Bass that night and that she was stealing him from her best friend."

"And this Kevin Bass, have you talked to him?"

"I think we've talked to pretty much everyone who was at the prom. Kevin was on the cleaning committee and left a lot later than the girls. He was cleaning up with a bunch of teachers until about an hour after the party."

"It sounds like they were running," I said, pensively. "The way the shoes were scattered all over the area. I mean, it's not easy to run across a golf course wearing high heels, so it would be natural to take them off to be better able to run."

He swallowed. The look in his eyes told me he knew I was right, but he didn't like to think about it.

"But if they were running, where were they going?" I said, thinking out loud. "There really isn't anywhere to go. The golf course is surrounded by water," I said.

"We've had diving teams in the river for days on end, searching through every area of the river and the canals leading to the residential areas. You know this, Eva Rae," he said. "They haven't found anything."

"I know; I know. I'm just trying to figure out why you'd want to run across a golf course in the middle of the night, wearing your very expensive shoes and dress unless you were being chased."

"Or drunk. Or high and foolish," he said. "According to their friends, the three of them had been drinking before they went to the prom. Carina Martin even smoked marijuana with her friend Molly Carson behind the performing arts building right before she was crowned prom queen."

"That sounds like prom all right. They had an argument; didn't they?" I asked. "Carina and Molly? Over Kevin? I remember you told me so…or did I read it somewhere? Maybe Melissa told me. Molly is her daughter, you know."

"Yes. That's right. They did. We've been looking into her."

"Molly?" I asked, startled. "Melissa's daughter, why?"

"Because of the fight. Maybe it turned bad later on. Maybe she could have chased Carina, and maybe she fell and hurt herself and

Molly hid her body? Molly's father does have a concealed carrier's permit. She might have taken his gun and gone off, or it could have been an accident."

I shook my head. "I hope you're kidding me. Not Molly. Not Melissa's daughter."

Matt took in a deep breath, then ran a hand through his thick brown hair. He hadn't been surfing much lately because of a growing workload, and his hair wasn't as blond as it used to be.

"Did she have an alibi at least?" I asked.

"Yes, but not a very good one, I'm afraid. Molly Carson went home while the prom queen was still dancing with the prom king. Lots of people saw her leave. She called her mother, who picked her up and took her home, and she went to bed after that, Melissa said. And I have to say that after talking to her friends and teachers, it would be very much out of character for Molly to hurt anyone. They all describe her as someone who takes care of everyone else, always has a shoulder to cry on. When I questioned her, I got the feeling she wouldn't be able to hurt a fly."

I drank my wine. "That's not much of an alibi, though. It could be argued that she might have climbed out of the window."

Matt gave me a look. "I know. That's what worries me. Well, that's one of the many things that bothers me about this case. As much as I would like to rule out Molly as a suspect, it's not possible."

"You don't really think a seventeen-year-old girl killed three of her friends over some boy, do you?" I asked.

He sipped his beer, then shrugged. "I've seen stranger things happen, but of course, I don't. As long as we don't have any bodies yet, there is still hope. But then you're looking at a possible kidnapping. And where does that leave us? I just don't understand why there hasn't been any ransom request made."

"Unless it's a sex offender," I said. "You already checked all that live in the area, didn't you?"

Matt nodded while finishing his beer. He put the empty bottle down.

"Yes. And we also spoke to the parents, over and over again. No fights, no reason for the three of them to want to run away."

I sighed. This was a true mystery, one that had me intrigued, yet scared to death. I had two girls of my own. I wanted to figure out what happened to those three girls as much as anyone, even though it annoyed Matt to talk shop when he was off.

He glanced at the file on the counter next to me.

"How did the meeting go with Rhonda?"

I swallowed and looked away.

"Oh, my," he said. "She found something; didn't she? That's why you have the file?"

I shrugged. "Maybe."

"Did she find Sydney?"

I lifted my eyes and looked into his. Then, I nodded.

"Really? That's wonderful, isn't it? Isn't it, Eva Rae? Why do you look like that?"

"Like what?" I asked.

"Like you're upset and not happy. You've been wanting to find your sister all your life, and now you finally have the chance. Why don't you look thrilled?"

I glanced at the closed file on my counter. I wondered what to tell him…if I could tell him the truth. I needed to process it myself first.

"No reason," I said. "I'm just tired; that's all."

"Yeah, right," he said. "Who do you think you're fooling? Not the guy who has known you since you were three years old. Something is up. Spit it out, Eva Rae."

I sighed, then reached over and grabbed the folder between my hands. I stared at it for a few seconds, then opened it and showed him the first page, pointing at the name in the middle of it. He looked at it, then up at me, his eyes growing wide.

"You're kidding me, right?"

I shook my head. "Nope. This is her name now. And she lives here in Florida, apparently."

Chapter 5

THE ROOM they were being kept in was small and stuffy. The air felt moist and tight. Carina's chest heaved up and down as she fought not to hyperventilate. Ava and Tara were still sleeping on their mattresses on the floor next to her. Carina felt dizzy as she had every time she woke up in the tight room with the massive concrete walls surrounding her.

She had lost her sense of time since there were no windows in their prison. But she remembered, still with great terror, when she had woken up after her prom night. She had been on a carpet, a beige carpet, she remembered. Her head had been pounding like crazy, and she felt disoriented. She had called for her mother, then spotted Ava, who had also woken up, lying next to her. Then, to her terror, she had realized she had something around her neck, a chain. Panicking, she had tried to pull it off and then started to scream.

A masked person had approached her, then slammed his fist into her face to make her shut up. It had worked. She had fallen backward and not regained her sight properly until she felt a pull on her chain so hard that she could do nothing but follow along, crawling on all fours. There had been a hallway of some sort and what else? Oh, yeah, a bookshelf. There had been a bookshelf that he unscrewed and removed. Then, the masked man had rolled the carpet away underneath, and a slab of concrete was revealed with a frame around it. The masked man attached a bar with a hook to the slab and began cranking it open. Carina watched, her eyes swimming, and trying to focus as a hole appeared beneath it. Then the masked person spoke.

"Get in."

Carina had tried to focus on the hole and tried to keep her panic at bay, but now she couldn't anymore. She screamed again with the result that he hit her again, then kicked her in the stomach.

"GET IN!"

Whimpering, Carina climbed down into the hole, and soon the man followed her into the darkness. They walked through a small tunnel that led to a tiny door leading to a room the size of a closet with three mattresses on the floor.

The man pulled her by the chain and attached it to a metal bar inside so tight that she couldn't reach the door if she tried. She could get up and walk to the corner, where he had left a bucket for them to pee in and another one with some sort of kibble for them to eat and a bowl of water for them to drink from like animals. The first couple of days, Carina had refused to eat and drink, but then realized that, if she wanted to survive, she had to do what the others did. She had to become the animal this kidnapper treated them like. Still wearing the remains of her ocean blue mermaid dress, she crawled on all fours till she reached the bowl of water and drank greedily before the others woke up, her chain clanking against the metal bar on the wall when she moved. The bowl was changed once a day, so whoever came to it first got the clean and cold water. One day, Ava had mixed up the two buckets and peed on their food instead of in the toilet bucket. For that, she received a beating by the masked man that left her unconscious for two hours.

Now, as Carina was watching the two of them sleep, eating as much as she could before they woke up, she started wondering how long they had been down in that hole. Her nails were growing long, and her teeth were so sticky she could carve stuff off them with her fingernail. Not to mention the bad smell coming from their unwashed bodies. But as much as she would like to know how long she had been there, another question was beginning to press on her, one even more urgent than the first.

How long did he intend to keep them down there, and what would happen to them when he grew bored with them?

Chapter 6

THE PIZZA ARRIVED, and I went to get it, then yelled at the kids to come down and eat. As I returned to Matt in the kitchen, he still wouldn't let it go.

"But this is huge, Eva Rae. This is massive; don't you think?"

"I don't know," I said dismissively while putting the pizza down. It smelled heavenly, and I grabbed a piece directly from the box. Matt looked into the file again and shook his head, then pointed at the picture of my sister.

"I can't believe it. Kelly Stone is your sister? As in Kelly Stone, the actress? She's like famous, like really famous as in Hollywood famous."

"I guess she always seemed kind of familiar," I said. "I watched her in that movie *The Highway* and the one about that time traveler guy."

Matt lifted his eyes and glared at me. "So, what's your problem? Why aren't you ecstatic?

"Because..." I said, and put the pizza down. "First of all, I'm still processing all this, okay? Secondly, I'm disappointed; that's all. Because I can never go visit her."

"Why not?"

"You don't just walk up to some famous Hollywood actress and go *hey, by the way, I'm your sister. Do you remember that you were once kidnapped in a Wal-Mart?*"

"Sure, you can," Matt said. "It would be shocking to anyone; why is it harder just because she's famous?"

I shrugged, then heard the children's steps on the stairs and signaled for Matt to keep quiet.

"PIZZA!" Alex exclaimed loudly as always.

"With lots of meat on it," I smiled and handed him a piece.

Alex's eyes gleamed as he looked up at me. "I won't tell Grandma; don't worry," he said and stormed to the table and sat down in a chair.

"Really, Mom? You're teaching him how to lie now?" Christine said as I handed her a piece.

I smiled wryly. "Eat your food."

"Meat, Mom?" Olivia said as she approached me, earbuds still in. I could hear the music blasting loudly from them as she pulled one out. "Really? I was kind of getting used to being vegan."

I stared at my daughter. "You're kidding me, right? You used to hate your grandma's cooking."

"Who hates Grandma's cooking?" a voice asked from the doorway. I turned to see my mother standing there, car keys in her hand, her purse over her shoulder.

Shoot!

Her smile was frozen as her eyes landed on the pizza, then on Alex's greasy face, strings of cheese hanging from his chin.

"So...I take it you're having a pizza party, huh? I'm sorry if my food is so terrible that you feel like you have to celebrate when I'm out."

I felt like crawling into a hole. She was hurt.

"Mom, I...I..."

"Save it, Eva Rae," she said. "I've had a long day. I'm going to bed."

She turned around and was about to walk away when Matt yelled across the room.

"I tried your vegan meatloaf, Mrs. Thomas, and it was really good."

I shot him a look. Was he seriously kissing up to my mother?

He shrugged. "What? It's true."

My mom looked tiredly at us. "That's wonderful, Matt. I'm going to bed."

"Mom...I..."

But it was too late. She had left. I felt awful. My mom had been so nice to cook for us every night and, no, it wasn't all terrible; some of it was quite good, actually. But I guess I hadn't really shown my appreciation to her. Fact was, I loved having her at the house, at least most of the time when she didn't criticize me. And it was good for the kids. I was finally close to her again and catching up for all the years we had lost. The last thing I wanted was for her to be hurt. She'd been through so much already. As we all had. And I felt like I was hurting her feelings constantly.

Was I doing it deliberately? To punish her for ignoring me all of my childhood? Because there still was so much unsaid between us?

I felt ashamed.

I drank my wine when Matt came up to me, handing me Rhonda's yellow folder.

"Maybe this could cheer her up, huh?" he said. "A little mother-daughter project?"

I stared into his eyes, then leaned over and kissed him. "You're kidding me, right?"

"Not at all. I think this could be good for both of you."

"I just…I don't feel like it's the right time now. I don't know if I'm ready yet."

"There will never be a perfect time to do anything like this. Think about it," he said and kissed me back, the kids making disgusted sounds behind us.

"Get a room; will you?" Olivia said and pretended to be gagging.

"Yeah, and a car," Alex said, imitating his sister.

I ignored them and laughed. It had taken them a little time to get used to their mom dating again, but after that, they had all been so nice to welcome Matt into our lives, and I knew they liked him, especially Alex, who always asked him to play with his firetrucks with him, and who loved anything with sirens and blinking lights. He had come around on the day Matt took him for a drive in his police cruiser. After that, there was no turning back for the two of them. Sometimes, I felt that Matt wished that his own son, Elijah, was more like Alex and that he enjoyed hanging out with him a lot more than with his own son, which was incredibly sad. I wanted Matt to have that connection with his own son that I felt with my children even though I was gone for a lot of the time when they were growing up. Their trust in me was slowly returning, and now my only regret was all the moments I had missed with them. I was hoping to be able to make new memories with them that we could cherish for the rest of our lives

I glanced at the folder in my hand, realizing that my priorities had changed drastically. I was all about family now, and that also included my sister, famous or not.

Chapter 7

"WHERE ARE WE GOING, Eva Rae? Can't you tell me?"

I looked briefly at my mom, then shook my head. We were sitting in my minivan, the sun baking in through the windows, the AC cranked on high and Bruno Mars playing on the radio. It was a gorgeous day out, one of many when living in Florida, and surfers were crossing the roads, riding skateboards while carrying their surfboards under their arms. Beachgoers and snowbirds were carrying their gear, eyes gleaming at the thought of spending an entire day in the white sand.

"I'm not going to tell you, Mom. It's supposed to be a surprise," I said. My voice was trembling slightly in anticipation and nervousness, but I hoped she wouldn't hear it.

My mom snorted and corrected her skirt. "You know I don't like surprises, Eva Rae."

I had been awake almost all night, thinking this through, and by the time the sun rose above the neighbor's house across the canal, I had made my decision. Today was Saturday, so I had the entire day to do this. Matt was right; the right time would never come if I thought about it too much. I would always come up with an excuse to postpone it, and then I'd never know. If I wanted to face this woman whom I believed was my sister, I had to do it. I had to throw myself into it without any safety net.

"Why can't you tell me where we're going," my mom said after a short break and a deep annoyed sigh. We had left Cocoa Beach and driven past the Patrick Air Force Base on our way to Melbourne Beach, where Kelly Stone lived. Matt had told me that it had been in all the papers when she had bought the house a couple of years ago and it was very close to where the rapper Vanilla Ice had bought his house a few years earlier and had it remodeled during his TV show, *The Vanilla Ice Project*.

"Because I don't want to ruin the surprise," I said. "And, because if I told you, then you would never have come with me."

My mom snorted again. "That's not very reassuring, Eva Rae. You're not selling this very well."

I exhaled, trying to choke the butterflies in my stomach. I feared that I was making a mistake and contemplated turning around for a few seconds but then decided against it. This could end in disaster, yes, but it could also not. It could also end well.

I glanced nervously at my mother, then felt my heart sink. A gazillion thoughts rushed through my mind in this instant. It had been thirty-six years. Would we recognize her? Would she recognize us? What was she like?

My mom looked at her watch. "How far are we going? Did you remember to bring water? It's hot out. I don't want to dehydrate. How about sunscreen? And bug spray, did you bring that? If we're going to be outdoors, then I'll need that. You know how I swell up."

"You won't need that where we're going, Mom. And yes, I brought a couple of bottles of water in my purse. You won't dehydrate. Besides, we're almost there."

"Where? There's nothing much out here?"

My GPS told me we had arrived, and I drove up in front of a gate.

"What is this place, Eva Rae? What are we doing here?" my mom asked. "What have you planned? I have a feeling I'm not going to like it."

I sighed and looked at her, then grabbed her hand in mine. She winced nervously.

"What is this, Eva Rae? You're scaring me."

"Mom. Sweet, dear, Mom. You asked what my plan was? To be honest, I have no idea. I don't think I've really thought this through."

My mom shook her head, her eyes scrutinizing me. "What are you talking about? Why are you being like this? What are we doing here, Eva Rae? What's going on? Won't you—for the love of God—just tell me?"

I swallowed. I hadn't really decided when to tell her and thought I could wing it, but now that we were there, in front of her house, ready to ring the intercom, I wasn't sure I could. How would she react?

"Mom…I…"

"What is this place?" my mom asked, looking out the windshield. Behind the wall, the treetops, and the lion statues towered a mansion. "Whose house is this?"

"It's…It belongs to Kelly Stone; you know the actress?"

"I know who she is. But why are we here?"

"Well, the thing is…I called her assistant earlier this morning and told her we were gathering sponsors for a charity surf event for orphaned children and that all the money will go to prevent human trafficking of children. She's agreed to meet with us and talk about it."

My mom gave me a look. "Why? Why would you say such a thing? I don't understand anything you're saying right now. Have you completely lost your mind, Eva Rae Thomas?"

I shrugged. "Maybe, but it was the only way I thought I could get her to meet with us. She doesn't like reporters and hasn't done an interview in years. She likes to keep private, so it's not easy to get to her."

"But why? Why do you want to get to her in the first place?"

I grabbed the folder from the back seat and held it between my hands for a few minutes. What would happen if I told my mother the truth?

"Kidnapped children are an area close to her heart," I said. "She's donated millions to help human trafficking over the years and helped build shelters for homeless children, so they don't have to sleep in the streets, where they can easily be kidnapped."

"Kidnapped children, but…what…why, why are you…lying to her like that?"

I exhaled again, then decided to go with another lie. "Because I'm actually thinking about doing this event and I wanted you to maybe do it with me. Would you like to do that?"

I swallowed and looked at my mom expectantly, biting my lip. Was she buying this?

"Why…well…Why didn't you just ask me that in the first place? You know I love arranging charity events. Why did you have to kidnap me and keep it a secret?"

I smiled and returned the folder to the back seat. "I guess I was scared you'd say no."

"Why would I say no to helping children? It's not like I have better things to do with my life these days. A project like this could be good for me and for us. And for the children, of course."

"So, you're in?" I said and rolled the window down, ready to press the button on the intercom.

She nodded. "Yes, I'm in. As long as you promise not to sneak attack me like this again, ever."

I sent her a forced smile, then turned around and pressed the button, while a loud voice inside of my mind was screaming at me.

What are you doing???

Chapter 8

AS I HAD EXPECTED, Kelly Stone's house was beyond gorgeous. It was truly worthy of a Hollywood starlet. We walked up the stairs to the wooden double doors, where her assistant welcomed us. The house was directly on the beach, and as we walked inside the hallway, we were hit by the striking views from everywhere we turned. The Atlantic Ocean was glistening in the sun and looked very inviting through the Spanish arched window panes.

"Miss Stone will be right down," her assistant said and showed us into a living room that was big enough to fit my entire house. It was beautifully decorated and obviously done by a professional in the light beach style. For a second, I felt a pinch of jealousy of the woman I believed could be my sister. I was never good at decorating, and my homes were always a mess with toys and laundry lingering in the corners. I would never be able to have a home like this.

"This is nice; don't you think?" my mom said and took a quick glance around. "Very stylish."

"Yeah, well, if you have money like that, it's easy to live beautifully," I said, sounding a little more annoyed than I was. I knew my mom didn't approve of the way I lived, and she was constantly trying to clean up after all of us since she moved in, yet it still looked messy. This type of decor and house was more what she had been used to. It also meant I had grown up in a house where you were hardly allowed to touch the furniture. I had always promised myself that my children wouldn't grow up in a home like that. But that also meant I had to live with the mess. I just wasn't a very neat person. I never thought of it as being important. I preferred spending time with my children. Especially back when I was still in the FBI and used to work so much; I was barely home. Whenever I walked inside that house, my focus was fully on the children. There was no time to clean up or think about decorations. But I never could get my mom to understand that. She believed I was neglecting my family by working and not keeping the house.

"This is quite exciting," my mom said with a slight shiver. "We're going to meet a real movie star."

She whispered the last word like it was a secret. I felt a knot grow in my stomach while wondering how on Earth this was ever going to end well. How was I going to react when I saw her? Would she know who we were just by looking at us?

"Hello there," a voice chirped from the other end of the room. A beautiful woman in a light fluttering dress almost floated across the marble tiles toward us. I gaped at her, eyes wide open, stunned by her beauty as our eyes met, and I felt a pinch in my stomach. I didn't know if she felt it too, but I sensed that she did feel something because her smile froze for just a second. Her eyes lingered on me, then on my mom, *our* mom, before she shook her head and put the starlet smile back on.

Back in character.

"Welcome, welcome, I am so sorry for keeping you waiting."

She shook both of our hands, and we introduced ourselves. As Mom said hers, I wondered if this woman knew anything about us, or if she knew our names, but she didn't seem to react when hearing them. It was only when our eyes met that I sensed she paused every now and then, like she was trying to remember something, yet couldn't.

"Do sit down," she said. "I'm from London, so I think it's a little too hot to sit outside at this hour of the day. Can we just take the couch over there by the panorama window?"

We both nodded and smiled. I glanced at my mother as we sat down on the soft sofas with the massive pillows and thought I saw something in her eyes, but then it was gone.

"All right. What can I do for you ladies today?" Kelly Stone said and clapped her perfectly manicured hands. "My assistant said you have some charity event that you needed a sponsor for?"

Chapter 9

I STARED at the woman in front of me as she spoke, telling us all about how big she believed the issue of kidnapped children was all over the world, while her expensive jewelry dangled from her wrists.

"It has always been very close to my heart, and not only the sex trafficking industry, but also the children who are kidnapped by a parent or close relative and taken far away. Many of them never see their families again. Those children grow up so neglected and always looking for that missing part of them. It's truly a cause that needs focus as well."

"And it's terrible for the families left behind too," my mother said, her voice cracking slightly. "To never see their children again and not knowing if they are dead or alive."

Kelly Stone paused after Mom was done. She stared into her eyes, and I wondered for a second if she knew. But then she shook her head lightly and leaned back.

"Where are my manners? You have been here for several minutes, and I haven't even offered you anything to drink. Where I grew up, that is highly impolite, and I must apologize. What can I get you? Coffee? Water? A glass of lemonade?"

My mom stared at her, her eyes following her every movement carefully like she was studying her. My pulse grew quicker.

"I'd love some lemonade," I said. "And my mom would too. If it's not too much trouble."

Kelly Stone turned to look at me. "Not at all."

Our eyes met again, and my heart was racing in my chest. There was no longer any doubt in my mind. This was her. This was Sydney. She looked very different than she had when we were children, and I suspected she had some work done on that face, but looking into her eyes, I knew it was definitely her. The realization filled me with so many emotions; it was hard to hold it back. I had been missing her for so many years, believing she was dead and gone, and here she was, doing awesomely for herself, perfectly alive and more beautiful than ever. I wanted to blurt it out, just tell her the real reason we were here, but I didn't. I was too scared of losing her again, of her getting angry at us.

She called for her assistant and told her to bring us both some lemonade. Then she returned and sat down.

"This is nice," she said with a light exhale. "Mother and daughter doing an event like this together."

"Yeah, well, we're sort of trying to reconnect after many years apart," I said. "I just recently moved back here to the area."

"That's nice," she said, smiling. "Do you have children?"

I nodded while it felt like my throat was swelling up. It was hard to swallow or even breathe.

"Three," I said, my eyes growing wet. I was fighting my tears but losing. "Two girls and a boy."

"How lovely," Kelly Stone said. "I bet they're excited to be close to their grandmother. Sounds like you have a nice family."

"Yeah…well…we do our best, I guess."

"It's not always easy, is it? Families," she said.

"It sure isn't," I said. "But it's so worth it."

Kelly Stone clenched a fist in front of her mouth and closed her eyes briefly, then gathered herself when the lemonade arrived. My mother grabbed her glass and emptied the entire drink in one gulp. I stared at her, startled. She usually never drank anything with sugar in it.

"Boy. I guess I was thirsty," she said, looking surprised at the empty glass in her hand. "Gotta be careful not to dehydrate at my age."

Kelly Stone's eyes grew wet as she looked at our mom putting the glass back down, making sure it landed on a coaster she found.

"It sure is getting hot out," Kelly said. "We all need to drink a lot to stay hydrated. Especially me who isn't used to the Florida heat just yet."

I sipped my lemonade as well, unsure of what to do or say next. I wanted us to stay as long as possible because I wanted to talk to my sister; I wanted to know everything about her now that I had finally found her, and I wanted her to know everything about me. But at the same time, I felt like I had to throw up. I was getting too emotional, and I wasn't sure I could keep it at bay for very long.

"I...I think we...Could I use the bathroom?" I asked.

Kelly Stone smiled and nodded. "Of course. It's right down the hall and to your left."

I got up and rushed down the hallway, then found the door leading to the bathroom. I shut the door behind me, then slid down to the floor, my back leaned against it, finally letting the tears escape.

Chapter 10

AS I RETURNED, my mom had gotten a refill on her lemonade and was taking it slightly easier this time, taking smaller sips. I wondered if the two of them had even spoken a word while I was gone; they were so quiet when I got there. I knew from Google that Kelly Stone didn't have any children, but still, I searched the place for pictures of anyone she might hold dear yet found none.

"Do you live here all alone?" I asked as I sat down.

Kelly shook her head. "My fiancée lives here too."

So, she did have someone in her life. That made me relax a little. I didn't like the thought of her being all alone.

"I'm getting used to him being here. I've always lived on my own. I was alone a lot when growing up," she said, tearing up, yet hiding it very well behind a bright smile. "Didn't have a big family or any… siblings. It was just me and my dad." She sniffled, then looked first at our mom, then me. "I don't know why I'm telling you all this. You must think I'm silly. I'm usually a very private person, and you have no interest in hearing all this about my…"

"Yes, we do," I said, then regretted it. I looked down as I spoke. "I mean. We don't mind at all. It's nice to know there is a human behind the actress, if you know what I mean?"

Kelly nodded. "I got carried away. I apologize. You're probably in a rush to get out of here and get back to the children. It is, after all,

Saturday. Now, let's get into the details of this event, shall we? How much do you need to make this happen?"

I don't know where I got it all from, but I just threw out numbers. I had put together some imaginary plan before we left and showed it to her, not knowing if it looked remotely like anything plausible for a charity event. I didn't even know if Kelly Stone was simply just humoring me, but she went along, and before we knew of it, she had promised to fund the entire thing, as long as we kept her identity a secret. She didn't want it all over the media. That wasn't why she was doing it.

We said our goodbyes and soon after my mom and I were back in the car, and I turned on the engine. My mom was completely quiet as we drove out of the driveway and the gate closed behind us. I could hear my own heartbeat in my ears and wondered what the heck I had done. What had I expected to get out of this today? I knew I wanted to see her for myself before I decided anything. I wanted to make sure it really was her. I guess I thought that, when I saw her, I would know, and I was right. I knew it was her, but I hadn't thought this through enough. What would I do next? Did I have to put on this charity event? Did I come clean and tell her? How would she react if I did?

I rushed onto A1A and sped up toward Cocoa Beach, my mom sitting silently beside me.

Twenty minutes later, as I parked in my own driveway and killed the engine, she finally looked at me. Just as I was about to get out, she placed a hand on my arm. Tears were in her eyes as she looked at me.

"Thank you," she said. "For involving me in this."

"Mom...I..."

She nodded. "I know, sweetie. I know. You don't have to say anything. I think we should all sleep on it and then decide how best to handle this."

She exited the car and left me sitting back, baffled. What exactly did she mean? Did she know and just didn't want to tell me? Or was she actually talking about the event?

There was no way of knowing with my mom.

Chapter 11

THEN:

On the night he returned after the shooting at the farmhouse, Gary Pierce held his baby a little tighter than usual. His wife Iris stood behind him as he held the small bundle in his arms, a tear escaping his eye.

Iris put a hand on his shoulder. She had a concerned look in her eyes. "Did something happen today?"

Gary swallowed and kissed her forehead. He didn't want to tell her about it and have her worry.

"Just work, baby. Just work."

He sighed and pulled his wife into the hug, then held his two beloved ones as tightly as possible while the fear and anxiety slowly faded away. Today had been a close one. Staring down the barrel of that assault rifle had almost made him lose it. He had been certain he would never see his son and wife again. It was amazing how many thoughts could rush through someone's mind when staring death in the face. Most of his had been about Oliver and how he would miss out on all the important stuff in his life. He would never get to see him start to walk; he wouldn't be there when he had his first day of school or when he graduated. He wouldn't get to see what a handsome and smart young man Oliver would become and how he would constantly amaze him with his wits and how caring he was toward others. All those things, Gary dreaded he might miss. It was a constant fear that lingered inside of him every day when he went to work, not knowing what the day might bring.

And it had to be in Iris's mind too when sending him off every morning with a kiss and a coffee in his hand. It had to be tough on her as well.

They had told Gary and Wilson that they were heroes, that they had saved a man from his kidnappers and saved his life, so he could get back to his son. The man had been kidnapped to pressure him for money that they believed he owed them. It was gang-related and wouldn't have ended well for the man or the boy if Gary and Wilson hadn't been there, they were told. There had been a lot of shoulder claps and high fives and kind words, but all Gary could think about was how close it had been. It was the first time in the line of duty that he had been so scared of dying, and it frightened him. He never used to be afraid of anything, especially not on the job. As an FBI agent, you couldn't allow yourself to be afraid. Danger came with the job, and you knew that going in. It had never bothered him before. He barely thought about it. So, what had changed?

Gary stared at his wife and son, his heart pounding.

He had so much to lose now.

Iris stood on her tippy toes and kissed him, then stroked his cheek gently, while Oliver was fussing in Gary's arms, probably getting hungry when smelling his mother's presence. The child seemed so fragile in Gary's arms; it seemed almost impossible that he would ever make it in this cruel world. Yet that was exactly why Gary did what he did. He truly believed he contributed to making the world a safer place for Oliver to grow up in by putting the bad guys away.

If they don't get me first.

"I should take him," Iris said when Oliver's fussing grew to a squeaking that they both knew soon would be crying. After three weeks, they were slowly beginning to know the boy's signals and figure out what he wanted. They usually tried feeding him first, then checked if he needed a clean diaper, and if that didn't work, then he was probably just tired and needed to be put down for a nap. Still supporting his head, Gary handed the boy to his mother, who sat down and started nursing the boy. Oliver grunted, satisfied, as he ate, and his mother stroked him gently across his sparse hair while singing. Gary stared at the two of them, a huge knot growing in his throat, and realized this

WHAT YOU DID

was the happiest moment of his life. There was nothing he wanted in life right now other than to be right there.

How did he get to be so lucky?

Chapter 12

"WHAT DO you think he wants from us?"

Ava spoke with a small hoarse voice that bounced off the walls of the small room. Carina lifted her head to look at her. They had all been thinking about it, but she was the first to say it out loud. When they first got there, they had screamed for hours on end and knocked on the sides of the room, hoping someone might hear them and come to their rescue. But soon they grew tired and could hardly keep their hopes up. It felt like they had been down there forever, and they began to wonder if it would ever end. Were they just going to die down here in this hole?

"You think he wants to rape us?" she continued.

The word made Tara sob loudly and hide her face, curling up on her mattress.

Again, Ava was only saying what they had all been thinking, yet hearing it made Carina very uneasy. She didn't want to think about it, yet she did, constantly. She kept thinking it was only a matter of time.

"I watched this show recently on Netflix about these girls who were abducted and kept at this man's house for eleven years."

Carina closed her eyes to try and calm herself down. The thought was terrifying.

"He raped them, and they even gave birth to his babies. Eleven years," Ava said, then paused. "I'll be twenty-eight by then. All my youth will be gone, wasted."

"Please, stop," Tara said. "Just, stop."

Ava looked at her, then bit her lip. "There are also those men who kidnap girls and then kill them when they get pregnant."

"Please, just stop, will you?" Carina said. "Just stop talking about things like that."

Ava stared at her, the chain around her neck clanking as she lifted her head. That was when Carina realized tears were streaming down Ava's cheeks. The small lightbulb underneath the ceiling gave them just enough light to see their food and where to pee, but it wasn't very bright.

"We need to encourage one another," Carina said and placed a shaking hand on her arm. "So far, he hasn't wanted to touch any of us, so maybe that's not why we're here."

Tara sat up, the chain banging against the bar on the wall where it was attached.

"Of course, that's why we're here. Why else would you kidnap three young girls our age? He wants to rape us till we scream and then he'll kill us. Don't you understand?"

Carina did, and she also knew that the two others were probably right. But more than that, she knew that thinking about all the terrible things that might happen didn't help them one iota. It only made them weak and paralyzed with fear, and that was exactly what this guy wanted them to be. She had seen it in his eyes when he pushed her down the hole. He wanted them to fear him, to know that he was in charge. He had that power trip in his eyes that she had seen once when her dad was harassed by a cop who had pulled them over. Ava's dad was black and used to them treating him that way, and even them thinking Ava couldn't be his since she had fair skin and didn't look anything like him. But she was. Ava just looked more like her mother.

"Aren't you scared at all?" Ava asked her.

"Yes, of course, I am," Carina replied. "I'm just saying that right now we need to keep calm. Panicking will get us nowhere, okay? I want to make it out of here alive, and I think that if we stick together, then maybe we can outsmart this guy somehow."

Tara stared at her, her mouth open. Her entire body was shaking, even though it was very hot in the small room, and the air was sparse. Carina suffered terribly from claustrophobia, and it took all her strength not to panic completely.

"But how?" Tara asked.

"I don't know yet," Carina said. "But I want you both to keep alert.

He comes down here once a day, the way I figure it since he took our phones and watches. But I think it's about once a day. We keep our eyes and ears open when he does, okay? It's all we can do right now. And then—most importantly—we don't panic."

Chapter 13

THE SUN HIT my face through my curtains on Sunday morning. I turned over in bed and put my arm around Matt. He had ended up going to the station after all and had worked late. He had come over right before I was about to turn in. I had stayed up an hour longer, talking with him in the living room, telling him about my meeting with my sister, before we started to kiss intensely and soon—after a couple of glasses of wine—were all over each other. We had ended up upstairs in my bed and then fallen asleep.

It slowly occurred to me what had happened, and that Matt was still here when I opened my eyes.

"Shoot," I said.

Matt woke up with a broad smile on his lips. "Good morning to you, too."

He leaned over to kiss me, but I pulled away.

"You're still here," I said.

He sat up and ruffled his hair. He didn't look less cute in the morning; I had to admit. I stared at his abs. Chad had never had abs like that. Not that he was fat or anything; he wasn't, but he wasn't buff or even well trained like this. I suddenly became very aware of my own chubby thighs and a bulging tire of a stomach that still bore very visible marks of having given birth to three children.

"That I can't argue against," he said, grinning.

"No, no, you don't understand. The kids," I said. "They can't know you're here...that you spent the night."

Matt exhaled and rubbed his head. "I'm sorry, but we fell asleep after..."

"Not so loud, they might be listening," I said. "They can't know."

His eyes landed on me. "You really think they don't know? We've been dating for six months, Eva Rae. I'm always around. I've just never been here all night."

I looked at him, then covered myself up with the sheet. He put his arm around my shoulder and pulled me into a deep kiss. "I like waking up with you," he said in a whisper. "I want to do it more."

"What about Elijah?" I asked.

"What about him? He stayed with my mom last night."

"But are you ready to tell him about us yet?" I asked.

He wrinkled his forehead. "What do you mean? He knows we're dating. He likes you. I think he likes you better than me, to be honest. But I think that he likes anyone better than me these days."

"But do you want him to know you spent the night here?" I asked. "I'm not sure I'm ready to tell my kids that we...that the two of us are..."

He chuckled. "Having sex. Just say it, Eva Rae. It won't hurt you."

"Shh," I said. "My mom is in the house too. She might hear us."

"So, now your mom can't know either? How long do you plan on keeping this a secret?"

I swallowed. "I haven't really thought about that. It's just that my family is...well, old fashioned."

"So, they don't have sex?" he asked. "Your mom must have had sex at some point since she did give birth to both you and your sister."

"Shh," I said.

Matt laughed. "You can't even say the word out loud, can you? Sex. Come on, say it. Sex, sex..."

I leaned over and placed my hand on his lips to make him stop. "I swear," I said, laughing. "If you don't stop, I'm gonna tape your mouth shut."

His eyes were grinning at me, and he broke loose, holding both my wrists, fighting me off, pushing me down on the pillow. Then he stared into my eyes, and I felt myself blushing while staring at his lips, craving them, my body overwhelmed by such deep desire for him. Holding me still, he leaned over and kissed me deeply. My body grew soft, and I gave in to him once again.

Chapter 14

WE TOLD THE KIDS – and my mom – that Matt had come over to take me out for a run. That was why he was here early in the morning on a Sunday. He did have his gym bag with his training clothes in the back of his police cruiser where he always kept it, so he could go to the gym after work. He brought it in, and we both got ready. Me mostly because I wanted to make this little white lie look plausible, even though I could tell my mother saw right through it. Still, she was polite enough not to say anything, only give me a look to make me feel shameful. I'm not sure Olivia bought it either, but Alex did and maybe Christine.

I didn't care, I thought to myself as I got dressed for our run. I needed this little lie to remain for a while. Maybe it wasn't as much for them as it was for me that I lied. I wasn't sure I was ready to move on fully yet, at least not admit that I was. I wasn't sure why, though. Chad was clearly having sex with Kimmie and had been for a year before we were even separated. I was just still trying to figure myself out, and somehow hiding the fact that Matt and I were…intimate…made it easier. It also made it less serious somehow, and I think I needed that.

"You ready?" Matt asked, doing jumping jacks in his sneakers on the kitchen floor. He looked like he could run a marathon without even getting out of breath.

I smiled awkwardly, remembering the last time I had gone out for a run right after I had just moved back. I had been sore for a week afterward, and my knees had been stiff. I used to love to run, but the extra weight made it a lot harder than when I was younger. I used to be the fastest on my team when just starting at FBI's Behavioral Analysis Unit. But that was before the last two children, and before life got so busy that I had no time to keep in shape. I had always thought it would be easy for me to get it back since I had always been in good shape when I was younger.

"I guess," I said with a shrug.

I glanced at my mom, who was making her gluten-free pancakes for Alex. She had barely spoken to me after we went to see Sydney—or Kelly—the day before, and her eyes kept avoiding mine. I wondered what was going on inside of her.

But then again, I had wondered about that my entire life.

Matt and I left the house and ran down my street. By the time we had passed four houses, I was already panting heavily. The air was so moist it made it hard for me to breathe. I had forgotten how the Florida air was so tough to run in, especially when you weren't used to it.

Matt, who was a few feet ahead of me, slowed down so I could catch up and we turned down Minutemen Causeway. I followed him, barely able to keep up with him.

"Come on, Eva Rae. You wanted this to seem legit, right?" he said with a grin, running backward in front of me so he could see me. The look on his face reminded me of when we were younger and would run races to compete at the school's track. Back then, I had always been faster than him. Well, at least before we hit high school. After that, he got stronger and usually beat me, but only barely.

"You need to sweat to make it look like you were actually running."

I stuck my tongue out at him, then pulled myself together and sped up. I ran past him, and he whistled, impressed.

"I see you've still got it."

"Catch me if you can," I said, speeding up, pushing myself so much my knees began to hurt.

Matt laughed behind me, then started to run faster, and soon we were racing down the sidewalk, past the high school, and continued toward the golf course at the end of the causeway. I managed to keep ahead of him almost all the way, right until we reached the beginning of the grass when he sped past me, and I had to stop. Panting, I threw myself in the grass, wheezing for breath, feeling lightheaded, and my heart pounding in my chest.

Matt came up to me, also panting. He sat down next to me. "Not bad, Eva Rae. For a girl."

I chuckled, remembering he always used to say that to me when we were younger, and I hated that. When growing up, I had always gotten so angry when he said that, and he had known it and used it to provoke me.

"You try giving birth to three children, and then we'll talk, all right?" I said.

That made him laugh. "Touché."

He lay down next to me, and we stared at the clear blue sky for a few minutes while catching our breath, or at least I did. Matt was quickly ready for more, whereas I was done. My body was hurting all over and my cheeks so red they must have looked like they were about to explode.

"You want a rematch?" he asked after a few minutes.

"Not in a million years," I said. "I want water, and then I want coffee and food."

He laughed again, then stood to his feet. He reached out his hand toward me when I spotted a group of kids sitting behind a bush not far from us. Four children, not much older than Alex, were playing with something that made my heart freeze the moment I realized what it was.

"Oh, dear God."

Matt's eyebrows shot up. "What is it?"

I didn't have time to explain. I rushed toward the children. The one holding the item hid it behind his back as soon as he saw me approaching. His lips started quivering when I spoke.

"Hey, you. Yes, you kid. What was that you were holding in your hand just now? Yes, I'm talking about the thing you're trying to hide behind your back. Show it to me, please."

The boy's big brown eyes stared up at me. The three other kids looked at him, then up at me.

I reached out my hand. "Hand it over, please. You shouldn't be playing with that. It's dangerous."

The boy swallowed, then finally reached his hand toward me and placed the syringe in my hand. Matt came up behind me and looked down at it.

"What the heck?"

"We were playing doctor," the girl standing next to him said.

"This is no toy, kids. This can be very dangerous to play with. Where did you find this?" I asked.

The boy stared at me, then finally pointed.

"At the golf course?"

"We usually look for golf balls," he said. "In those bushes over there at the end of the course."

"Probably some addict who shot up out here," Matt said.

I bit my lip and stared at the syringe in my hand. It was almost empty, and there was dried blood on the tip of it.

"When did you find it?" I asked.

"Two weeks ago," he said and held out a small wooden box. "I kept it in this box. I keep all my treasures in this."

"He also found a phone," the girl next to him said.

The boy gave her an annoyed look.

"Show them, Evan. He's the police." She said the last part nodding toward Matt.

Evan sucked in air between his teeth, then opened his treasure box and pulled out a phone. With shaking hands, he handed it to Matt, who took it and looked at it, turning it in the light. As his glare fell on the back of it, his eyes went dark. He looked at me, then leaned over and whispered:

"I think it's Carina Martin's. Her mom described a case looking very much like this with the flowers across it."

I stared at him, then looked down at the syringe.

"I think we need to get both of these items to the station and have them sent to the lab. You'll probably need a team out here to go through those bushes over there and have this boy show you exactly where he found them. I have a feeling these are more breadcrumbs to your case."

Chapter 15

I LEFT Matt to do his work and ran home as soon as I had turned the syringe over to the crime scene techs when they arrived.

My kids were done eating breakfast and had returned to their rooms as I entered, except Alex, who was sitting in the living room playing with his firetruck. He barely noticed that I returned and was deep into what he was playing.

"Where on Earth have you been?" my mom said as I walked into the kitchen. "You've been gone for an hour and a half. And don't tell me you went running for all this time."

I looked at Alex to make sure he wouldn't hear, then approached my mom. "Matt and I stumbled across what we believe might be evidence in his case."

My mom's eyes grew wide. "In the disappearance of those girls from the high school?"

I nodded and grabbed a gluten-free pancake that had been left on the counter. It tasted awful, but I ate it anyway, pouring loads of syrup on it. I watched my mom as her eyes grew weary.

"Awful story that one," she said. "Those poor parents."

"Now, we still don't know if they were taken or if they have just run away," I said, pouring more syrup on top of my pancake. "They did find a message for Ava on Instagram from a photographer who wanted to make her a model, but the parents told her she wasn't allowed to meet with him. The message was a couple of months old.

The police are working the theory that all three of them might have just gone somewhere. Matt told me this last night, but it's not something you can tell anyone since it's a very loose theory."

"Eva Rae," my mom said.

I looked at her. "What?"

She nodded toward my plate. I had gone a little overboard on the syrup. "Are you really going to eat that?"

"Of course, I'm going to eat that," I said, pretending like I couldn't see what she meant.

"That is pure sugar, Eva Rae. It's not…good for you. Honestly, you eat like you're a child these days."

I sighed, then cut my pancake. "At least I went running this morning. I burned off some of all those calories already."

She gave me a look, and I sent her one back to make her get off my back. I had enough guilt nagging me as it was over my weight; I didn't need her looks or words to knock me out.

"Suit yourself," she said, then left the kitchen. I took another bite of my pancake, then pushed the plate away, realizing it really didn't taste that good with all that syrup on it. I threw the rest out, then planned to go upstairs to take a shower when something stopped me. As I was about to walk up the first step, I accidentally looked out the window through a crack in the pulled curtains facing my backyard, and that was when I saw it.

I am not lying when saying, my heart literally stopped.

Chapter 16

BOOMER LOOKED at the woman through his binoculars. He was keeping his distance; he was no fool wanting to be caught, but he just had to be there when she found it. He just had to see her face when she spotted his work of art.

He watched her run into the yard, screaming loudly. Eva Rae Thomas approached the girl, then pulled the chains, trying to get her loose, but had no luck. Neighbors in the yards across from her canal soon heard the screams and came out to look. Some were pointing toward her, others clasping their mouths in shock. Meanwhile, the screams continued, and it was like a sweet song in Boomer's ears. The chill went straight into his bones and stayed there.

"Someone, call 911!!" The woman screamed. "NOW!"

Several of the neighbors did. Some were yelling; others just stood there, paralyzed in fear.

Boomer took one last glance in the binoculars at her strained face as she fought to get the girl loose, pulling helplessly at the chains, before he realized it was time for him to leave. His presence would end up being noticed if he stayed longer, even if he kept his distance.

Boomer turned the small boat around and chugged away, taking it slowly, holding his fishing pole up to make sure no one would find him to be out of place. As he reached the end of the canal, he took a left, then continued down into the intracoastal waters, where the mangroves would be his cover. In the distance, he heard the sound of blasting sirens. Boomer grinned and took in a deep satisfied breath as a flock of pelicans swooshed by above his head.

Chapter 17

I WAS SCREAMING and pulling the chains. My mom came running out to me, and as I yelled at her to call 911 and keep the kids inside, she ran back in to find a phone.

My hands were moving frantically back and forth on the poor girl's hands as I tried to liberate them from the swing set, which she had been chained to, and was hanging from. Blood was smeared on her face and seemed to be coming from her eyes, I realized as I tried to look at her. I reached up and felt her neck for a pulse and found one. The girl wasn't conscious, but she was alive.

Oh, dear God, what's wrong with her eyes?

I stared at the girl, who looked like a bug caught in a spider's web, the way she was displayed with her arms and legs stretched out. The chains were attached to each corner of the swing set, stretching the girl's body out. Her head hung slumped down on her chest.

"I called 911; they're coming," my mom yelled behind me. "What else can I do?"

"Get the bolt cutter in the garage. I need to get her down," I yelled.

My mom took off. She came back a few seconds later, holding up her long skirt as she rushed across the lawn, the bolt cutter in her hand, her usually impeccable hair standing out in all directions.

"Here. I hope it's the right one."

"It is," I said and took it. I rushed to the girl's leg, then used all my strength to cut through the chain till it snapped and her leg dangled freely. I hurried to the second leg, then put the bolt cutters on the chain, my hands shaking in shock and terror, then closed it around the chain and cut through. The second leg got loose, and my mom ran to the girl and held both of her legs, trying to lift the girl, so her arms wouldn't be strained so terribly. I sent her a grateful look, then crawled up on the swing and stood on it, while placing the bolt cutters on the chain holding the right arm and cut it loose. My mom shrieked as the body became heavier. She managed to hold her still, while I climbed onto the next swing and reached the second corner, then cut through the chain, sending my mom a look before I finished it to make sure she was ready to grab her. I could hear the neighbors gasp on the other side of the canal as the girl came loose and my mom balanced her, stumbling from the weight. I jumped down and managed to grab the girl in my arms before my mom fell with her. Shaking, I held her tight, pressing back my tears, when I heard Matt's voice coming from behind me.

"I came as soon as I heard your address mentioned over the radio. What's going on? Here...let me help you."

He grabbed the girl's legs, and we managed to put her down on the grass. Matt was sweating and panting as he looked down at her.

"Oh, dear God," he said and clasped his mouth.

I did the same as the hair was removed from her face and I realized who this was. My stomach churned, and I felt like throwing up.

"Oh, dear God, oh, dear Lord, no, no, no."

He looked up, tears springing to his eyes. "What did they do to her; what did they do to Molly?"

I swallowed anxiously as I spotted the paramedics running into the yard, carrying a stretcher, and I backed up to let them have their space to work. I stared at the girl while they assessed her condition, then got her hooked up on oxygen and soon rushed her away. I couldn't stop wondering what the heck was going on. Molly had been the only girl in that group of friends who had made it home, the one we had assumed had been safe.

Chapter 18

I WENT BACK INSIDE to check on the children. Christine was sitting by the counter in the kitchen, Olivia holding her arm around her, while Alex was drawing on the floor, getting crayon smeared all over the tiles.

"Are you all right?" I asked and approached them.

Christine didn't look up. My eyes met Olivia's.

"She saw it," she said. "Through the window upstairs. After you screamed, she looked out; we both did. Alex didn't see anything. We kept him from the windows and closed all the blinds."

I swallowed hard. "I...I am so sorry you had to see that. Come here."

I grabbed both of them and pulled them into a hug. I held them for a few minutes, kissing the top of their heads. Christine was sobbing, her small body shaking.

"I know her," Olivia finally said as she broke out of the hug. She sniffled and wiped her eyes dry. "She's from my school, right? A senior."

I nodded and touched her hair gently. My beautiful daughter, who almost seemed too good for this world.

"Yes. Molly Carson. She's my good friend Melissa's daughter." I choked up as I said her name and stopped talking.

"Is she...is she dead?" Olivia asked, eyes worried. She looked so much like her father in this second, and I was briefly reminded of how deeply I had loved Chad once.

I shook my head, thinking about Melissa and how hard this was going to hit her.

"She was still alive when we took her down. She's on her way to the hospital now. I'm sure they'll take good care of her."

"So, she'll live," Christine said.

I bit my lip not to cry. "I...we don't know yet."

I held my girls tight while Matt entered through the sliding doors. Outside, our yard was crawling with uniforms, and soon the crime scene techs would arrive and would be combing through the yard and probably also the canal looking for evidence.

I let go of the girls and told them to go to the living room, where they wouldn't be able to look out at the window and see what was going on out there. They did, arm in arm, and took Alex with them. Matt pulled me into a hug and held me while I tried hard not to cry.

"How?" I asked him almost in a whisper. "How did someone manage to chain a girl in our backyard without us noticing anything?"

He shrugged. "If he did it at night. It was dark; we were sleeping."

"We were in the house all morning. And we didn't see it?"

"The curtains were closed, so were the blinds upstairs."

"But...If we had found her earlier, then maybe she'd have a better chance. What if she doesn't make it, Matt? This is Melissa's daughter. This is my best friend's daughter. Why? Why her? And why my backyard?"

Matt shook his head slowly, looking pensive.

"You think it's related to the disappeared girls, don't you?" I asked.

He shrugged again. "How can I *not* think that? They were a group of four friends. They were supposed to have walked home together, all four of them together, but one went home earlier."

I sucked in a deep breath between my teeth while thinking like crazy about all of this. One thought kept coming back to me:

Why my yard? Of all the houses this guy could have chosen, he chose my backyard, why?

Matt looked into my eyes. "I have to go," he said. "I have to go tell Melissa and take her to the hospital."

I nodded, feeling a knot in my stomach and throat. "I know. I'm coming with you."

He sighed gratefully. "I had hoped you'd say that."

Chapter 19

MATT PARKED the car on the street in front of Melissa's house and killed the engine. We shared a look, and both took in a deep breath.

At least the girl isn't dead. We're not here to tell her that her daughter is dead.

It wasn't much of a comfort. I had known Melissa since we were in preschool. Matt and I both had. Her husband had recently been diagnosed with MS, and they were fighting bravely to keep their heads above water. Melissa had recently taken a job at Surfnista, a local café to help out with the medical bills that were piling up. With the rate Steve was going, he wouldn't be able to work more than a few years, if even that, and then where would that leave them? Just last week, she was sitting in my kitchen telling me this. And I had told her everything would be okay; they would figure it out, and we would all help as much as we could. I knew Dawn and I would, at least, and Matt, of course. Dawn had no children and was back to dating Phillip, the captain at the fire station who lived on my street. She had also been a part of our friend group since we were children and we looked out for one another when it was needed.

But now, I was coming to her house to tell her this? It was going to break Melissa's heart. It felt like kicking her when she was already down.

I got out of the car, and Matt followed me up to the door. I felt his hand touch mine briefly before I rang the doorbell. Melissa came to the door, still in her PJs, hair tousled, slippers on her feet, and a coffee in her hand.

"Eva Rae? Matt? What are you doing here at this hour on a Sunday? Did I forget something? Were we supposed to meet up? Wait, why do you look so serious, Eva Rae…you're…what's going on here, guys?"

I took a deep breath and pressed back my tears. "It's Molly. You need to come with us to the hospital."

She almost dropped the cup in her hand, but Matt caught it from her. "Molly? What do you mean? She's…she went to a friend's house last night; did…did something happen to her?"

Melissa's voice grew shrill as she spoke, and her face went pale.

"Tell me what happened, Eva Rae; is she… is she okay?"

"We don't know," Matt said. "It's too early to say. She was unconscious when she was found and taken to the hospital in an ambulance. We're here to take you there."

Melissa looked at me like she was waiting for me to tell her it was a joke, that we had been pulling her leg in a cruel prank.

"It's true, sweetie. You have to come with us. Now."

"But…Steve…Steve had an attack last night. He can't get out of bed; he's heavily sedated."

"We can drop the kids off at my place," I said. "They're too young to understand what's going on. My mom and Olivia can look after them. I'll help you get them ready, and then we'll leave."

Melissa nodded, her nostrils flaring. She was keeping it together, but only barely. She made room for me to enter and I rushed inside where three young children, two boys and one girl were scattered across the living room, jumping on the couch, screaming, and two of them fighting over a sword.

Chapter 20

"I ALMOST ENVY STEVE, that he gets to sleep through all of this."

Melissa spoke with a scoff. We were sitting in the waiting room where they had told us to stay until they had news on Molly's condition. I was holding her hand while Matt had gone to find coffee. Dawn had arrived too and was sitting on the other side of Melissa. So far, we hadn't spoken to any doctor and had no idea how Molly was doing. I had told Melissa about how I had found Molly in my backyard and she had listened, shaking her head in disbelief.

The wait and uncertainty made me sick to my stomach. I felt so terrible for Melissa and wanted so badly to do something to help her out, to remove this pain.

"It's mostly all the scenarios that you constantly go through in your mind, you know?" she continued. "What if she doesn't make it out of there. What if she dies? How will I get past this? How will I ever live without my firstborn? How am I supposed to do that, Eva Rae?"

Melissa turned her face to look at me. The despair in her eyes made me want to scream. As a mom, I knew exactly how she felt.

Please, let her live, God. I'll do anything, anything!

I parted my lips and wanted to say something to soothe her pain, but the words I could think of didn't seem sufficient at all. I wanted to tell her it was going to be all right, that I was sure the doctors were doing everything they could, but it was all just clichés and meaninglessness.

Matt returned with our coffees, and we took them. I sent him a grateful glance and saw the sadness in his eyes as well.

"Why don't they tell me anything?" Melissa asked when she had taken her first sip. "We've been here two hours, and we have heard nothing. How come they haven't told us anything, Eva Rae?"

"I don't know."

I took her hand in mine and squeezed it. Melissa exhaled and shook her head while a tear rolled down her cheek.

"I'm sure they're doing everything they can," Dawn said and sipped her cup.

"Can't they just tell me if she's alive or not? Everything else we can deal with as it comes along, but I need to know if she's alive."

"I'm sure they'll be…"

I paused when I saw a doctor come through the door, dressed in green scrubs. My heart ached when seeing the serious look on his face. He rubbed his stubble and looked at Melissa, who rose to her feet, still holding my hand tightly.

"Mrs. Carson?"

Melissa nodded, her skin turning paler by the second. "Yes, that's me. How is she, Doctor?"

"She…I'm afraid that her eyes are gone."

"Gone?" I said. "What do you mean gone?"

"I'm afraid they have been removed."

Removed? How?

Melissa's body began to shake. "She's…she's blind?"

The doctor nodded.

"But she's alive?" Melissa added.

"Yes."

Melissa breathed, her chest heaving up and down rapidly. "But she can't see?"

He shook his head. "No. And I'm afraid we believe she has also been raped."

Chapter 21

AFTER THE LAST SENTENCE, it was obvious that Melissa didn't hear any more of what was being said. Her knees went soft, and I felt her collapsing, so I reached over and grabbed her in my arms. Dawn and I helped her get to a chair and sit down, while Matt finished talking to the doctor. The doctor told him they were taking blood samples to check for diseases and infections that could be transmitted through sexual contact and, of course, for pregnancy.

Melissa was shaking all over, and we just sat there while she gathered herself. As the tears finally started to roll, I pulled her close to me and into a hug. We sat there for quite a while, Melissa's body trembling between my arms until Matt returned and sat down next to her.

"There will be a sexual assault nurse examiner, a SANE, who will make sure to do a forensic exam," he said and looked at Melissa, eyes wet, biting his lips, his nostrils flaring. Matt fought his tears, then spoke through gritted teeth.

"I will get this guy, Melissa, you hear me? He's not getting away with this."

Matt got up and crumpled his empty coffee cup, then threw it in the trash with a loud groan. He then kicked a chair in anger and held a fist up to his mouth. I couldn't blame him. He was just displaying how I felt.

Frustrated, helpless, angry.

Melissa sniffled and wiped her eyes. "Well, at least she's alive, right? I mean, I ought to be happy about that, shouldn't I? Why aren't I?"

"It's a lot to take in right now," I said.

She swallowed and tried to hold it back, but more tears sprang from her eyes, and she broke down again. I reached over and held her in my arms while she sobbed.

"My baby was raped?"

"I am so sorry," I said.

"My baby was attacked, raped, and now she's blind," she said. "My baby will never be able to look me in the eyes again. I will never see hers again, ever. She had the most gorgeous eyes. They were beautiful and would sparkle when she smiled. She won't see her siblings as they grow up, and she'll never see the stars at night anymore. She always loved watching the stars. Why…why would anyone take that from her? What has she ever done to them? Why would they take her sight from her? I don't understand, Eva Rae. Who could be so cruel to do this? Who? And why? Her life is ruined. It's completely destroyed."

"Lots of kids live good lives even when blind," I said, but the words felt so empty. I was so frustrated in this second. I could feel her despair; it was unbearable not to be able to fix this for her. She was my friend, going through the pain of her life. And I just sat there, doing nothing but coming up with empty phrases and clichés that meant nothing.

Then I said what I really wanted to say all along. I lifted her face and looked into her eyes, while I spoke the words that I could put meaning behind. Words that I knew weren't empty and indifferent.

"I will catch this guy, Melissa, do you hear me? I will do everything in my power to get this one. Matt and I will do it together. He will not get away with what he did to Molly. I promise you this here and now. Do you understand what I'm saying?"

Melissa sobbed, then smiled and nodded behind a curtain of tears. "Thank you, Eva Rae, thank you so much."

Chapter 22

"IT'S SO hot in here; I can't stand it!"

Ava squirmed on her mattress, and her chain clanked against the bar behind her.

"I feel so disgusting and clammy, and the air we breathe is so heavy; it feels like I'm suffocating."

Carina looked at the wall next to her. She had scratched a mark in the foam for every time she believed a day had started, right after their captor had been to change their bucket and give them fresh water and food. Fifteen scratches on the wall told her they had been down there for a long time, too long. The stench of their bodies brought tears to their eyes, and Ava was right, the air was almost unbreathable. The chain around Carina's neck was hurting her and had gnawed into her skin, leaving sores that were painful to the touch. She felt like crying every day she opened her eyes inside of this hell, and sometimes she gave into it and let the tears roll down her cheeks while wondering if they would ever make it out of there. But she didn't do it while her friends were looking. She had long ago decided that she was going to be the strong one. In a place like this, they needed one, and she knew she was able to be that. The two others panicked several times a day and screamed and cried, and sometimes even yelled at her for not panicking, but Carina kept her composure.

One of them had to.

"I can't stand it here!" Tara said, lying on her side on her mattress.

"I can't take the smell; I can't take the air, and I can't stand the sight of these brown walls."

"I know," Carina said to both of them, trying to cheer them up. "But today, we'll try the thing we talked about, okay?"

Tara sat up. She was so pale in the dim light from above them. She was the skinniest one of the three, and she had been losing weight since they got there. They all had, but it seemed to be going faster with her. Carina was worried about Tara and how much longer she would last. That was why she had decided that today was going to be the big day.

"Really?" she asked.

Carina nodded. "We've talked about this long enough now. It's time we do something before we go insane."

"But I thought you said the plan wasn't perfect yet," Ava said.

"It isn't, but I have a feeling it never will be," Carina said. "We lose a portion of our strength every day, and I fear that if we wait too long, we might not be able to pull it off."

"I agree," Tara said.

Carina could see her collarbone above her ripped prom dress. It was sticking out more and more each day that passed. Her cheeks had fallen in, and her eyes were big as they landed on Ava.

"Did you hear that, Ava? It's time."

Ava nodded. She was way more robust when they were captured than both Carina and Tara, and she seemed to be holding up a lot better than either of them. Still, her eyes were matte with exhaustion, and she was winded from the lack of oxygen.

"It probably won't be long till he gets here, so I want you to go through the plan with me once again, and then keep yourselves ready."

Both girls nodded excitedly. Carina went over the details again before they all leaned their backs against the wall and stared at the door in front of them, waiting for it to open and that nasty man to show his masked face again.

Chapter 23

THEN:

It was a nice day. The sun was shining from a bright blue sky, and it was finally warming up a bit as spring showed its picturesque face. Winters were long and dark, Iris Pierce believed, and this one had been extraordinary long, even though it had been the best in her life. Having a baby had been the greatest achievement. Most parents probably thought so, but they had waited a long time for this baby. They had tried for five whole years before they had finally succeeded in conceiving. It had almost destroyed both her and Gary, not to mention their marriage. Not being able to get pregnant had been by far the biggest shame in Iris's life. Who was she if she wasn't able to give Gary what he so desired? Not a woman, not a wife. Not in her eyes.

Iris wrapped Oliver in a blanket and walked outside to put him inside his carriage. The sun shone brightly in his face, and she made sure to turn the carriage around, so he wasn't in the direct sun, then pull down the mosquito net. She looked at her son in the carriage and felt her heart melt as their eyes met. He looked so much like his dad already, and that often made her laugh. He was like this miniature version of Gary, a wrinkled and prune-like version of him. But he was also so incredibly gorgeous that her heart could hardly contain it. And neither could Gary. She saw it in his eyes when he came home from work and picked up the boy. She saw the deep pride in them. But she also saw something else lately that had startled her a little. She had seen fear, a deep worrisome fear growing inside of him, and she wondered if it had to do with his job and what he saw there. She sensed his job was getting to him somehow. She wondered if he feared something might happen to him, so he wouldn't be able to see Oliver grow up. To be honest, Iris often feared that too. Especially lately. More than once, she had caught herself waiting anxiously by the door as the clock struck six and she expected him home, unable to shake the worry until he was finally inside, hugging her and Oliver.

"Now, there. It's time for you to go to sleep," she said, smiling from ear to ear at her boy. She couldn't help herself. Everything about him made her so warm and peaceful inside. Her love for him was nothing like she had ever felt for anyone before, not even Gary, whom she loved dearly. This was different; this was deeper and so intoxicating, almost like a drug. She needed to be close to him; she craved his presence in her life and to feel his skin against hers. There was nothing in the world that made her feel like this, nothing.

Iris was going to take him for a walk downtown and maybe buy an ice cream for herself at the park, now that the weather was so nice. She liked to take a walk with the carriage at least once a day, and Oliver slept so well inside of it while she got some much-needed exercise and fresh air. Being cooped up inside with the baby was wonderful, but she was also slightly scared of losing touch with the world around her. She needed to get out.

Iris grabbed the carriage and was about to begin her walk when she realized she didn't have her diaper bag with her. She left the carriage for a second and rushed inside to look for it. She walked into the kitchen and found it on the counter, where she had packed it with clean diapers for the ride, just in case. It was funny, she thought to herself with a chuckle, how her small and elegant purse had been exchanged for this big ugly bag filled with essentials for the baby and not her anymore. It was just like her own life. It had been mostly filled with taking care of her own needs, and now she barely even cared if she got something to eat or showered, as long as the baby was happy.

Iris threw a glance at the mirror in the hallway and chuckled again at her appearance. As long as she didn't meet anyone she knew, she was fine, she thought to herself, then hurried outside, grabbed the carriage by the handle, and placed the bag underneath it.

"All right, Oliver," she said. "Let's go for that walk; shall we?"

She hadn't expected the baby to answer because why would he

when he was only three weeks old? Yet there was still something that caught her off guard, and she lifted the mosquito net to look inside the carriage, to check on her son, or maybe just catch another glimpse of him like she so often did when he was sleeping.

But the carriage was empty.

Chapter 24

WE SET UP A "WAR ROOM" at CBPD by Matt's desk the very next day. As we had been reading through case files and going through a ton of details in the case, Chief Annie approached us.

"I heard you were in the building, Eva Rae," she said and walked closer. She pulled me into a hug. Chief Annie was a heavyset woman with a hug that felt like it would crush you. She also had the kindest deep-set brown eyes that lingered on me, and a smile to make me feel welcome.

"Good to hear that you finally decided to come onboard. I told Matt to ask you as soon as those girls disappeared. I wanted you."

I flushed, feeling flattered. "Thanks."

"Good to see you, Eva Rae," Annie said and squeezed my hand. "You look great."

That made me smile. I had a yard filled with crime-scene techs that had worked all night with lights out there and dogs, not to mention the divers in the canal that were keeping me awake. I had fought with the kids all morning to get them out of the house on time, and still, Alex and Christine had missed the bus. Then, after dropping them off in my PJs, I had been stuck in traffic driving down Minutemen Causeway, and as I came back to my house to get dressed, I had discovered water all over the bathroom floor and realized my toilet had a leak. I had called the plumber and told my mom to make sure she was there when he got there. She had been in the middle of reading the paper and drinking her coffee, then politely told me she was going to visit her friends today and play golf in Winter Park, so I probably shouldn't count on that. This meant I had to wait till the plumber got there to let him in before I could leave with his humungous bill in hand, and it wasn't until I arrived at the police station that I realized—because Matt politely told me so—that I had a huge coffee stain on my shirt, right on my chest where everyone would see it. I also had only brushed my hair in the car and hadn't even put on make-up, simply because I forgot to, so to tell me I looked great had to be a very polite compliment.

"Thank you," I said. "You too, Annie. But you always look great."

"We should do lunch one of these days. Maybe I could get you to come on board as a permanent solution," she said, then looked at her phone in her hand. "Whoops. Gotta be somewhere, like five minutes ago, I'm afraid. We're having our monthly *Coffee with the Mayor* event tonight at city hall next door, and we need to find out who will be guarding it."

She looked deeply into my eyes.

"Find my girls; will you?"

"I'll do my best."

Annie left, and I turned to look at Matt and the whiteboard by the end of the wall. We had hung up photos of all four girls. Carina Martin, Ava Morales, Tara Owens, and Molly Carson. The sight of their high school photos staring back at me made my heart drop. I sat down and rolled my chair toward them. Underneath their picture, Matt had written PROM. I stared at the word.

"They all went to the prom that night," I mumbled. "Could he have been at the dance? I know we talked about this before and that you interviewed all the teachers and chaperones present, but why were they all at the same dance right before three of them disappeared? Could it be that they were all four supposed to disappear that night?"

"And then he came for Molly later?" Matt asked.

"Maybe she knew something or saw something that he wanted to stop her from telling."

"But why not kill her then? Why not bury her somewhere or throw her in the river where the gators would eat her?" he asked.

"You make a good point. The part about her being placed the way she was, in my backyard, makes it feel so personal. Like he wanted me to find her there. Like there was a reason for choosing my yard and not someone else's."

"Because you knew Molly?" he asked.

I bit my lip and stared at Molly's photo. Her gorgeous brown eyes stared back at me, and I felt a pinch in my stomach when realizing I was never going to see them again, and neither was her mom.

"Yes, maybe, but maybe it was something else. There's something that seems kind of disturbing to me," I said and got up from the chair, then studied the picture of Molly that Matt had taken at the hospital, where she was lying with bandages across her eyes. We hadn't been able to interview her yet but kept the photo to remind us why we needed to stop this guy before he hurt any of the other girls if he hadn't already done so.

"What do you mean?" Matt asked.

"It didn't really occur to me earlier, but now I can't stop thinking about it. It's the eyes," I said.

"What about them?"

"I...It's just. There was a case once that I worked on. It was early in my career. We tracked down this guy who poked out the eyes of his victims before he raped them, so he would be the last person they remembered seeing, and so they wouldn't be able to recognize him in a line-up. He left them in the street, blinded and assaulted, helpless, unable to find their way back home. Often, they would run into the street and get hit by cars."

"So, could it be him again?" Matt asked.

"It could if I hadn't shot him in '09 as we raided his house."

"Okay," Matt said, "so he's dead, but maybe it could be someone copying him?"

I nodded. "That is definitely a possibility. But why would he target me in that way?"

"Because you got rid of his hero, the one he idolized, and he wants you to know that he is taking over."

I turned to look at Matt. "Look who's the profiler now."

"I took psychology in college," he said, smiling. It felt good to see him do that since we had both been so gloomy since we found Molly. There hadn't been anything to smile about so far.

"You might be onto something," I said. "This guy wants my attention; that's for sure. And he's got it."

Chapter 25

JANE MARTIN LOOKED at the clock on her stove. It was three-thirty in the afternoon. The realization made her bend over in agony and pain. This was the time she would usually go pick up Carina at the high school. She would drive up into the pick-up line and wait for her to come to the car, blushing in embarrassment since all the other kids her age would get into their own cars and drive off. But Carina hadn't been able to pass her license test yet since she had flunked twice, and so she was pretty much the only kid her age who was still being picked up by her mother, much to her embarrassment. It had also been a nuisance to Jane since she had started working as a campaign manager for a local politician and she had enough on her plate these days.

But not anymore.

Not since Carina went off to the prom and never returned home. Jane hadn't left her house since that night when her daughter disappeared, and she wasn't going to.

"You have to start living soon," her husband, Scott, had told her so many times these past few days as he went off to work himself, pecking her unlovingly on the cheek. "We can't stop living just because our daughter ran away. We still have a son, and he needs us."

Scott was determined that Carina had run off with her friends, that they had taken off on some trip to Las Vegas or maybe just Miami to go clubbing, and that they would be back soon. And the stuff they found at the golf course? Well, they had been drunk and goofed around out there before they decided just to take off. They were young and carefree, was his opinion.

It had been seventeen days now. Who went clubbing for seventeen days? What teenager had that kind of money?

"I think something happened to her," Jane had said over and over again. "I can feel it in my heart. She's in pain. She's hurting. A mother knows these things."

But Scott hadn't wanted to hear it. "I did the same thing when I was her age," he said.

"You went on spring break in Miami," she replied.

"But I lied to my parents and said I was staying with my best friend and his parents."

She shook her head. "How is that the same?"

Jane exhaled and looked out the window at the canal behind her house. A boat chugged past. An elderly couple was sitting behind the wheel, smiling, with their fishing poles stuck on the roof. They were probably coming back from fishing on a nice, beautiful day, maybe having caught themselves a couple of trout for dinner.

Jane and Scott used to go fishing, and it was their plan for retirement once that came along. Just the two of them, out on a boat going off-shore fishing off the coast with not a care in the world. That was the dream, and it was obtainable. Except now she feared it would never be. She would never be carefree again if Carina didn't come back. She wasn't sure she'd survive that. The past seventeen days had been so tough it felt like she would die.

Jane exhaled and made herself a cup of coffee. She stared at a box of Oreos that her son had forgotten to put back in the cabinet. Usually, she'd take a couple, maybe eat the entire pack, but not today. She had lost a lot of weight since Carina had disappeared, and normally that would have been an accomplishment for her, something she'd be thrilled about, but now, it didn't matter. She had no appetite, and she didn't care anything about food anymore. It was so useless anyway. Their neighbors from across the street had been so nice and brought them food to eat, so they didn't have to worry about cooking, and she had tried to have some of the chicken pot pie last night, but it hadn't even tasted good. It was like it was growing in her mouth, and she had kept chewing and chewing at it, unable to swallow it. She had ended up spitting it out in the trash, then going for a glass of Chardonnay instead. The wine kept her calm and helped her sleep. Drinking wasn't a solution; she knew that, and it could become a slippery slope. But right now, it was the only thing she could get down, and she needed it. That and her coffee to get her through the dreadful day.

Her doorbell. Her first thought was that it was Carina, that she had finally come back. Jane almost dropped her cup on the tiles. Then she realized Carina would never ring the doorbell. Or would she? What if she was embarrassed? What if she had come back and was afraid they were angry with her, so she didn't dare to walk right in?

It could be.

Jane put her cup down on the counter, feeling her pulse quicken, and rushed for the front door, images of Carina's beautiful face flashing through her mind. There was nothing she wanted more right now than for her husband to have been right about their daughter.

Jane grabbed the door handle and swung the door open when her hope froze instantly. Outside stood not Carina, but a FedEx guy.

He smiled.

"Mrs. Martin?"

She nodded, disappointed. What had Scott bought now that they didn't need? Another useless tool for his garage that he would never use? Something electronic that would end up gathering dust on his desk? Or was it Frank, their youngest? Had he been on Amazon and bought something silly?

"That's me."

"I have a package for you. I just need you to sign right there."

She grabbed the pen and scribbled an ugly signature on the display, then took the package.

"Have a nice day," he said and tipped his hat.

"Thank you," she said, even though she knew she wouldn't. This day would be just like the sixteen previous, filled with despair and pain, longing for her daughter to come home.

Little did Jane know as she put down the box and opened it, that this day was about to be a lot worse than all the previous ones.

Chapter 26

"WHEN ARE YOU COMING HOME, MOM?"

I looked at the whiteboard by the wall behind Matt to see the girls looking back at me, almost accusingly. We hadn't gotten anywhere all day.

Some help I was.

Guilt ate at me for not being at home with my children like I had promised them I would. Christine had come home from school and found my note written on our activity board in the kitchen, where I wrote I was going to help Matt out on a case today.

"I don't know, sweetie," I told her. "But Grandma is there with you today."

"You know I don't like being alone with her," she said. "She's creepy and weird. She keeps telling me to make better choices when I grab a snack, and then she looks at my ripped jeans and makes jokes asking me if *I paid full price for them 'cause then I would need my money back.* Stuff like that. It's annoying."

"She's just from another generation," I said, remembering my old ripped jeans back in the nineties that my mom would look at with a grunt.

"You mean she's old," Christine said.

"Yes, she's old. And maybe she's a little weird, but give her a chance, please? She's the only family we have right now, and we should cherish her. Who knows how long she'll be around? We'll regret it later on in life if we don't make the best of what we have with her."

"Did you read that off Facebook or something? Besides, we do have other family. We have Dad, and his mother is our grandmother too. And she's not so weird."

That shut me up. I had always loved Chad's mother and had to admit that I missed her terribly now that I wasn't with her son anymore. I had more than once wanted to pick up the phone and call her and ask her for advice these past six months when my life was in ruins, but then stopped myself, realizing that she wasn't my mother-in-law anymore, that we weren't family anymore. The thought almost made me tear up.

"Yeah, well, they're all in Washington," I said, trying to sound diplomatic and not blame Chad any more than necessary. I had long ago decided I wasn't going to be that kind of an ex. I wasn't going to say bad stuff about him to the children. He was their father, and they adored him, and I wanted them to keep liking him. But it was a fine line that was easily crossed, I had learned. Especially since I was still so angry at him for leaving me like that, without even a warning, and for cheating on me, of course. "They're not around right now. So, try and make the most of Grandma, okay? Play a board game with her or maybe cards? And try to include Alex. He doesn't have many friends yet, and I worry about him being lonely."

"You worry about him being lonely? What about me?" Christine said, almost whining. "I hate all the girls in my school. There's no one I like here. I miss all my old friends, and I miss Dad."

Ouch.

"I know you do, sweetie. I know you must miss him a lot," I said as Chris Cooper approached Matt's desk. Chris Cooper was another detective at CBPD and also an old friend from school. He looked serious first at me, then Matt. I held up a finger to let him know I'd be right there.

"Do you want to go up there soon?" I asked. "I can call him and ask?"

She went quiet.

"Christine? Why don't you want to go up there lately? Did something happen?" I asked. "You haven't been up there in almost three months. Don't you want to see your father?"

"I want to see him, Mom. I miss him; it's just…" she said.

"Listen, I'll call him today and ask, okay?" I said, trying to end the call. "I'll call and ask him when you can go see him again."

"Okay," she said, almost in a whisper. I could tell she was sad and needed to chat more, but I didn't have the time right now. It broke my heart. I wanted to know what was going on.

"We'll talk more when I come home, Christine, okay?"

"Okay," she said again and hung up.

I did too, then lifted my eyes and met those of Cooper. He handed us a note. "You need to go to Jane Martin's house. Her husband called. It was urgent."

Chapter 27

THE MARTINS LIVED in a beautiful newly-built riverfront house at the end of our island by the golf course. The husband was a partner in a big local law firm, and I recognized his face from one of the billboards on 520 leading to Orlando, even though he wasn't smiling the way I was used to. Today, his face was heavyset, and his eyes were burning in anger as he greeted us in the doorway.

"I don't know who is behind this, but if it is some kind of joke, then I'm gonna..."

"What's going on, Scott?" Matt said.

"You better see for yourself," he said. "Come on in."

"This is my partner, Eva Rae Thomas," Matt said. "She's FBI and working the case with me."

Scott gave me a look, then moved aside so we could come into the big hall. Inside, the house opened up to the most spectacular views of the intracoastal Banana River and the Thousand Islands in the background. Boats were anchored in the distance, probably fishing or going swimming, maybe diving from the rooftops. I remembered my own youth when we always went out to Ski Island and partied with the others from our high school, bringing our coolers with beer and shots. The only life on the islands were snakes and tortoises, and most importantly, there were no police to check for underage drinkers.

We walked to the kitchen where a blonde woman sat on a stool by the counter, crying. In front of her sat a brown package.

"Jane?" Matt said and approached her. She lifted her eyes and spotted him. "What's going on? Did something happen?"

Jane sniffled and wiped her nose on a Kleenex, then nodded. "I… There was a man at the door, a FedEx guy; he brought me this package. At first, I just thought it was something Scott ordered off of Amazon, or maybe our son did, but my name was on it, so I…opened it."

Matt nodded. "And what was in it?"

Jane sobbed, then pulled herself together. She reached inside the box and pulled out something. It looked like fabric of some sort. It was red and silky. She held it up so we could see. The golden letters said:

PROM QUEEN 2019

My heart dropped, and I looked at Matt, then back at the mother.

"It's the sash," Matt said.

"The one Carina got right before she…disappeared," Jane said, then broke down again. I walked to her and put my arm around her since the husband didn't seem to want to. He just stood there like he was paralyzed and stared at the sash on the granite countertop.

"I've seen the pictures," Jane continued. "On Instagram. I've been going through them over and over again from that night. All her friends posted pictures from that night. She wore this on the stage when she was crowned, and I never got to see her in it. I would have been so proud. She really wanted to be prom queen since I was prom queen back in the day too. She knew I was going to be so happy for her."

"If this is someone's idea of a joke, then I am going to kill them," Scott said, fuming.

"I don't think it is a joke, Mr. Martin," I said, still holding his crying wife. "I think this is very serious. Was there any card with the package?" I asked Jane. She shook her head, and Matt peeked inside the box.

"Nothing in here."

"And there have been no text messages or emails demanding a ransom or anything like that?" I asked her, then looked up at her husband.

They both shook their heads.

"Nothing," Jane said and clenched her fists. "What do these people want from us? Why have they taken our poor baby? Why?"

With no ransom request or any demands at all, I had no answer for that. It didn't fit the MO of a sex offender either. I couldn't stop thinking about Molly and how on Earth these cases were connected because I was certain they had to be. Four teenagers from the same group of friends couldn't be a coincidence. But what was this person's goal?

What did he want?

Looking at the sash at the counter and the tearing up mother, I had a feeling we would find out soon, and it wasn't going to be pleasant.

Chapter 28

BOOMER WHISTLED while he drove down Minutemen Causeway, the town's small main street. He saw the many police cruisers as they passed him on their way and knew exactly where they were going. Meanwhile, he stopped at a red light at the end of the road, where it met A1A, and he spotted city hall and the police station on the corner.

While he waited, he took a sip of his soda and emptied it, throwing the empty can out the window while thinking about Eva Rae Thomas. He grabbed his phone and looked at the app, tracking her exact whereabouts. Yes, she was there. She was at the address where he had just delivered the sash. Boomer pulled his lips slowly upwards into a smile. It was all going the way he wanted. They were all playing along like the good little dolls they were. But things were moving slowly, he thought. Too slow. It was about time that he speeded up the events.

Shake things up a little.

That was exactly what he was about to do, he thought to himself as the light turned green and he turned right into the intersection, then hit the brakes and stopped the truck, placing it sideways, so it blocked the entire street. The car behind him honked loudly. Another came around the corner behind it and honked aggressively, but Boomer didn't listen. He got out of the truck, making sure the cap covered his face for the surveillance cameras, then walked onto the sidewalk. Swiftly, he turned a corner and fell into a crowd of tourists waiting to cross the street. He took off the cap, then followed them, hiding in the crowd as they moved across the street toward the beach, hearing the aggressively honking cars behind him as the traffic was getting completely blocked.

Chapter 29

"I JUST GOT OFF WITH FEDEX," I said and looked at Matt. He had called for the Sheriff Office's Crime Scene Unit, and they took the package to the lab to see if they could extract any evidence from it. They were right now working the kitchen and securing the package and the sash.

"They're trying to track the driver down, but according to their headquarters, there were no deliveries on this street yet today. Not even in the entire area. This address is last on their route and wasn't scheduled until a few hours from now. But get this. They did, however, have a truck stolen a couple of days ago from their office in Viera on the mainland. Could that have any connection?"

Matt looked at me and exhaled. "I should say so. I just talked to Cooper. You won't believe this. They found a FedEx truck parked in the middle of A1A in an intersection, right in front of the police station. Someone left it there. It's blocking traffic. The driver was gone."

"Don't let them touch anything," I said, my eyes growing wide. Things were moving a little too fast for my liking. I felt like I was losing control of the case...like someone was pulling the strings.

"You think it's our kidnapper, don't you?" Matt asked. "You think he came here, delivered the package, and then left the truck for us to find; am I right?"

I nodded. "I think he was here. I think he wanted to look at her face when she got the package. He wanted to look her in the eyes."

"Wow," Matt said. "That's sick."

I swallowed. "I don't think there is anything well about this guy. Why do you think he left the truck in front of the police station? Because he's telling us he is in control. There won't be any fingerprints on it, but he wants us to look for them. He's toying with us. I don't have a good feeling about this guy."

"I'll call them back and make sure the truck is taken through forensics," he said. "When I spoke to Cooper, he was still waiting for the tow truck."

"Okay," I said pensively, then looked at Carina's parents, who were sitting on the couch in their living room, barely looking at one another. I approached them, then sat next to Jane. She was staring at her fingers, fiddling with the tissue between them.

"Did you have a good look at the man from FedEx when he was here?" I asked. "Did you see his face?"

She nodded. "Sure."

"How would you describe him?"

She sighed. "I don't see why…"

"Just humor me," I said. "We need to find him."

"You think it was him; don't you? You think it was the guy who kidnapped our daughter?" Jane spoke with a quivering voice. Her eyes grew wet, and soon the tears rolled down her cheeks. "You mean to tell me he was…here? He was here at our…our doorstep? The man who took Carina? Our Carina, our daughter?"

"We don't know if…"

"He was here?" Scott Martin began while rising to his feet "He was here?" he turned to look at his wife. "And you…you did…you did nothing? You just signed and took the package?"

"Please, Mr. Martin," I tried. "There was no way your wife could have known…"

"No, he's right. I could have stopped him," Jane continued. "I could have called the police, and maybe he would lead us to her; am I right? But I didn't. I just signed the darn thing, took my package, and shut the door. I looked him straight in the eyes and then went on with my day. I looked into the eyes of my child's kidnapper and…did nothing!"

"You need to calm down, Mrs. Martin," I said. "We don't know if it was the same man or not. It could also be someone he paid to give you the package. No matter what, we need to find him. The package you received wasn't sent via a normal FedEx office. There's no return address and the guy who brought it wasn't a FedEx deliverer. What he was, we don't know, but the truck was most likely stolen, and the guy was someone pretending to be from FedEx. Whether it's the man we're looking for or just an accomplice, we don't know, but we have to find him. He's our only lead right now. So, please, tell me, what did he look like?"

Jane Martin stared at me, blinking her tears away. Her nostrils were flaring. She glanced briefly at her husband, who was sitting with his head bent to his knees, holding his head like he was afraid it would explode.

"I guess he was…tall, like Matt, about six feet two or so," Jane said, her voice trembling as she spoke. "He was pretty buff, you know? Maybe from carrying all those packages all day. His hair was blond."

"Did you look at his eyes?"

As I said the words, a loud blast sounded from outside, and the windows shook slightly. I looked at Matt as the shaking stopped.

"Was there a rocket launch scheduled today?" I asked, remembering those days as a kid when we went outside to watch them be sent off from Kennedy Space Center. Rocket launches were part of our daily life when growing up on the Space Coast.

The couple didn't seem alarmed either, and Jane continued.

"They were steel grey. And he had very straight teeth. And a beard. Not a big one like a homeless person, or the hipsters, but a small well-trimmed goatee."

"Anything else? Any tattoos?"

She shook her head. "No. At least none that I could see. He was in uniform. He seemed friendly. Like he knew me."

"Did you know him? Had you seen him before?"

She shook her head. "I don't think so. Even though there was something familiar about him."

Matt approached me. "I need to talk to you."

As I looked up at him, I realized something was wrong. He was pale, and his eyes were black. I excused myself quickly, then got up and walked with him.

"What's going on?"

"The truck," he said, his voice shivering.

"What about it?"

He swallowed. His hands were shaking, and I grabbed one of them. "What's going on, Matt? Did something happen? Matt? Talk to me. What's going on?"

Chapter 30

"YOU'VE GOT to get that finger further down."

Carina sat on the mattress next to Ava as she plunged her pointer finger deeper into her throat.

"Hurry up. He'll be here soon. You've got to make it look real," she urged her. "Try with two fingers if it doesn't work."

Ava tried again, this time using two fingers, pressing them into her throat, whimpering as she gagged.

"There you go. It's working."

"You can do it, Ava," Tara said.

Ava gagged, and soon after, yellow bile came out of her, mixed with mostly water. They had let her drink most of what was in the bucket to fill her stomach up enough so she would have something to throw up. They didn't get much food down here, and the little she usually had wouldn't yield much. They needed her to throw up more than once.

As Ava gagged again and threw up on the mattress, the stench quickly filled the small room and made the two others feel sick to their stomachs as well.

As steps approached behind the door, they all exchanged a look.

"Here he comes," Carina whispered. "Just do as we planned. It will work. It has to."

Ava whimpered and nodded, then as they heard the bolt on the door open, she closed her eyes and pressed the two fingers down her throat again, and as the masked man entered, she bent forward and threw up once more.

"What the heck...?" he yelled as it landed on the floor in front of him. He sniffed and then held his nose. "What's that stench?"

"Ava is sick," Tara said.

"She's been throwing up all night," Carina added.

"And she's been shaking all over. She's sick," Tara continued. "I think she's really sick."

"She might infect us as well," Carina said. "Then we'll all get sick."

"We might die," Tara said.

"She needs to see a doctor," Carina said.

Ava gagged again and threw up, throwing herself forward, so a bunch of it landed right at his feet.

The masked man stared down at Ava, a gun clenched in his hand. He bent down and knelt in front of her, holding his hand up against the surgery mask like he wanted to make sure it was still there to protect him in case she was infectious.

"Are you really sick, little girl?"

Ava gagged, but nothing came up this time. Then she nodded with a sniffle, snot running from her nose.

"She needs to see a doctor," Carina repeated. "Please, sir. She might die down here if she doesn't get help."

"And then we'll die too."

Tara looked at Carina like was she asking *Too far?* But Carina didn't think it was too much.

"All right," the man said. "I'll take you upstairs."

He leaned over and grabbed Ava's chain on the bar, then unlocked it with his key. Ava sobbed and cried as he led her out the door, like was she a small dog he was taking out for a walk. As the door slammed shut behind them, both of the remaining girls sat back, sweat springing from their foreheads, silently asking themselves:

Did it work?

Chapter 31

THEN:

"Iris? Iris?"

Gary parked the car outside their house and rushed up the driveway, stumbling over his own feet as he hurried toward his wife. She was sitting on the porch, her head bent. He had been at the office when she called, and luckily not out on assignment. It had taken him fifteen minutes to get home, a drive that usually took thirty.

Gary knelt next to her, and Iris finally looked up, her eyes red-rimmed. All she had said on the phone was that Oliver wasn't in his carriage. She had been screaming it hysterically, and Gary had told her he'd come right away.

"I got here as fast as I could," he said. "What's going on?"

"Oliver is gone," she said.

"I don't understand; what do you mean…gone?" he said, heart pounding in his chest. How did a baby just disappear? Had his wife lost it? Had she put him somewhere and couldn't remember? Was it some sort of postpartum depression? Gary had heard about women who suddenly couldn't figure out even the simplest tasks after giving birth, who got so depressed they couldn't take proper care of their child. He had even heard from a colleague that sometimes they tried to kill their own children since he had once been called out to a case like that. Worst thing in the world, he had said. A mother killing her own child. It doesn't get any worse than that.

Iris shook her head. Gary felt like shaking her, trying to get her to explain this to him, to tell him where their son was.

"I came out here…and then he wasn't…he wasn't in his carriage anymore. I just went in there to get my bag. I was gone for one minute, tops, and then he was…gone."

Gary rose to his feet. He walked to the carriage and looked inside. Oliver wasn't in there. Gary looked on the tiles and the grass surrounding it, in case the child had fallen out.

"How could he suddenly be gone?" Gary asked. "I mean…he can't…he can't even hold his own head up, let alone crawl out of the carriage on his own. He's too small."

Iris looked at him, despair in her eyes. "I…I don't know. He was just…gone."

"And you're sure you put him in the carriage? I mean, maybe you didn't. You haven't been sleeping much lately, sweetie, maybe you left him inside and just thought you put him in the carriage."

She swallowed. "No, I put him in there, and then I went inside. Besides, I've looked everywhere inside too. Oh, God, Gary, please tell me I'm just losing my mind, that he is still here somewhere. I'm panicking; please, do something."

"I'll search the house," he said and stormed into the hallway, heart racing. He ran upstairs first and looked through all the rooms and closets, thinking that if she was as confused and worn out as he suspected, then maybe she had left the child somewhere in there. And if the baby was asleep, they wouldn't be able to hear him.

A baby doesn't just disappear like that.

Unless she hurt him. Unless she did something bad and just blocked it out.

The thought was so terrifying that he couldn't finish it. Gary shook it and continued into the nursery, looking at the changing table and in the bathroom, desperately lifting any blanket or towel he could find to make sure the child wasn't underneath it. He also checked the bathtub and even the garbage bin, just in case. But there was no sign of his baby boy anywhere.

Gary ran a hand through his hair, desperately trying to think straight, but the panic that was spreading like wildfire inside of him made it impossible. It was getting harder to keep the anxiety at bay, and soon there was nothing but chaos inside of him.

He ran downstairs and found Iris standing bent over the carriage, looking inside of it, like she thought the child might still be there; she just couldn't see him.

"Iris?" he said.

Iris didn't answer. She stood like she was frozen and stared into the carriage and, as he came closer, she pulled out something that made his blood freeze.

A hand-written note.

Chapter 32

THE FLAMES and charcoal-gray smoke licked at the sky as we approached the intersection in front of city hall and the police station. The firefighters, who lived and worked in the building next to city hall, had pulled out their engine and were spraying water on it, Dawn's boyfriend Phillip leading them the in action. Meanwhile, paramedics put someone into an ambulance and rushed off, the siren blaring in the air as we exited Matt's cruiser.

We ran toward Chief Annie, who was standing with two of Matt's colleagues, a safe distance from the fire. Spectators had gathered on the corner, and a couple of uniforms were keeping them back. It looked mostly like tourists in their bikinis and trunks with beach chairs slung over their shoulders.

"What happened?" Matt asked, panting and agitated.

Annie looked at both of us. I could tell she was emotional. "It just exploded. The FedEx truck blew up. Cooper had...Cooper was just..."

She paused to gather herself. My heart knocked against my ribcage. This was bad. This was really bad.

"Cooper?" Matt said, his voice growing shrill. "Something happened to Cooper?"

Annie nodded. It was hard for her to speak, and her lips shook as she tried anyway.

"We were waiting for the tow truck, and the FedEx truck was blocking the entire street. This is our most high-traffic area in the entire town, so it was becoming a problem. I asked him if he could check and see if there might still be keys in it, so we could move it. He went to take a look inside the truck, and that's…that's when it went up in flames. He was flung out and landed on the asphalt, flames engulfing him."

Annie's eyes teared up as she said the words. She clenched her fist and placed it in front of her lips, pressing down hard to keep herself from breaking down. Chief Annie was tough and not one to get emotional usually, but this had her at the end of her rope.

I had known Cooper since we were kids too, not well, since he wasn't a close friend of mine, but still. I felt Annie's despair from where she was standing. She had to be blaming herself for telling him to go in there; she had to feel an enormous weight of guilt.

"Was he…?"

She nodded heavily. "He was still alive when they took him away. But severely burned on big parts of his body. It's hard to say if he'll survive being burned like that."

"Dear Lord," Matt said. He worked closely with Cooper, and I could tell he was tearing up. I went to hug him. I held him tight while we stared at the burning delivery truck in the middle of the street, all of us wondering what kind of sick bastard would do this. Who in their right mind would boobytrap the truck and blow it up right when he knew someone would be inside of it? One thing was certain. This was getting very personal, and now he'd have the entire police force breathing down his neck, not to mention the entire town, who always stood behind our men in uniform.

Chapter 33

A BOMB SQUAD arrived from the county's sheriff's office, and the area was combed through in the search for more explosives, using dogs. The schools were put on lockdown, and all of downtown was blocked off. A forensics team arrived to gather bomb debris for analysis. About an hour later, the area was declared clear, and we could go back inside the station.

We had just walked in through the glass doors when Lisa, who managed the front desk, stopped us.

"Detective Miller?"

Matt stopped in his tracks and looked at her. Lisa seemed perplexed. A lot more than usual.

"I know it's terrible timing right now, but…"

"What is it, Lisa?" he asked.

"Well, the Turners are here with their daughter. They said you asked them to come in?"

Matt rubbed his stubble. "I completely forgot."

The Turners were the family that Melissa thought her daughter Molly was having a sleepover with on the night she was blinded and raped. Lisa nodded in their direction, and I turned to look. Three people were sitting in the row of chairs leaned against the wall. One of them was a younger girl wearing a crop top and jean-shorts so short it looked like she wasn't wearing any pants at all when sitting down.

"Mr. and Mrs. Turner?" Matt said and approached them.

They stood to their feet, faces strained.

"What happened out there?" Mrs. Turner asked. "We had just gotten here and sat down when we heard the explosion, and we were told to evacuate the building and go out the back. They just let us back inside. Was anyone injured?"

Matt nodded heavily. "A colleague got hurt. He's been taken in for emergency treatment."

"How awful," Mrs. Turner said and looked briefly at her husband like it was his fault, then returned to face Matt again. "I am so sorry."

Matt nodded. "As are we all, Mrs. Turner. If you'll follow me, I think we'll take this in the interrogation room."

"The interrogation room?" Mr. Turner said. "But…"

He received a look from his wife and stopped. The Turners followed us through the police station, their daughter chewing bubble gum and blowing bubbles as we showed them inside of interrogation room one. Matt found a couple of extra chairs. He brought them in, and we all sat down. Matt exhaled, and I could tell he was struggling to keep it together. He opened Molly's file.

"If you don't mind me asking, why are we here?" Mr. Turner said nervously. He was a small man in brown cargo shorts and a light blue shirt from Salt Life. He had a nice tan. My guess was he was a boater or a fisherman, or maybe both.

"It's regarding Molly Carson," I said.

They looked surprised at one another, then at their daughter. "Molly? What has she done?"

"She didn't do anything," I said and swallowed to remove the knot growing in my throat when thinking about Melissa's poor daughter. "It was more what was done to her."

"Something happened to Molly?" Mrs. Turner said, her eyes growing wide. She looked at her daughter, who suddenly sat very still and wasn't chewing her gum anymore.

"What happened to her?" Mr. Turner said. "We haven't heard anything; have you, Leanne?"

His daughter shook her head. She was beginning to look flushed, and I sensed she was scared.

"We were hoping you could help us clear that up," Matt said.

"Us? But…how?" Mr. Turner said, looking at his wife, then at us. He folded his hands in his lap and leaned forward. I sensed a nervousness, but that wasn't uncommon in people who weren't used to dealing with the police.

"She was at your house for a sleepover the night before last," I said, scrutinizing them.

"A sleepover at our house?" Mrs. Turner said. "But…we've been out of town all weekend. We went to North Carolina just outside of Charlotte. We're looking at houses since we're moving up there this summer."

I wrote it down on my pad. "And you have witnesses that can confirm that?" I asked.

Mr. Turner nodded. "Of course, plenty of people saw us up there, including the real estate agent who took us around town all weekend. Witnesses, huh? Are we being accused of anything because, if so, I'd like to have my lawyer present."

"No one is accusing you of anything," I said, "We're in the middle of an investigation, and it doesn't hurt to have an alibi."

"But…" Mrs. Turner said, looking pensive. "Is…it bad, is…Molly dead?"

I shook my head and looked briefly at Leanne, who hadn't moved an inch and was barely blinking.

"She's not dead."

"Oh, thank God," Mrs. Turner said and clasped a hand to her chest.

"But something terrible was done to her, and we're trying to find the person who did it. So, what we can establish is that Molly lied when stating she was spending the night at your house, right?"

Mrs. Turner nodded, fighting to keep her composure. It was obvious they knew Molly very well, and she had probably been friends with their daughter for many years. Mrs. Turner was visibly affected by the news. I was happy they had a solid alibi and that there was a reasonable explanation for them not being at their house when we sent a patrol out to pick them up right after we had found Molly and taken Melissa to the hospital. The fact that they weren't home had made them seem suspicious at first, but now it was perfectly normal. They seemed like a nice family, and I would hate for anything to destroy that picture. With everything I had been through over the past six months, I needed to know that there were still nice families out there who didn't lie to one another for thirty years or hurt children.

"We didn't know anything about this," she said. "Usually, the girls have sleepovers all the time, but this weekend we were gone, so…"

"And Molly probably knew that," I said. "Do you have any idea why she felt the need to lie to her parents about this?"

Mrs. Turner shook her head. "I don't really see why…"

She stopped then and looked at her daughter. We were all looking at Leanne, knowing she was the only one who could possibly know why Molly was lying, and who she was meeting when her parents thought she was having a sleepover at her friend's house.

Leanne shrugged. "I don't know. It's not like she's my best friend or anything; we just hang out sometimes."

"So, you're not part of her friend group with Carina, Ava, and Tara?" I asked.

Leanne shook her head. "No."

"Leanne doesn't go to the high school," her mother interrupted. "We do Florida Virtual school."

"So, she's homeschooled?" I asked.

"Yes. With all the temptations to vape, do drugs, and drink, we believed it was best for our daughter to keep her out of all that."

I stared at the woman, trying to imagine myself homeschooling my children. The thought was absurd. I loved my children dearly, but I also liked it when they were out of the house. We would only end up fighting non-stop, if not with me, then with each other. It just wasn't for me.

I turned to face the girl, sensing she knew more than she was letting on.

"Leanne, if you know anything about what Molly was up to, then you have to tell us. Was she meeting someone? Had she met someone online maybe?"

Leanne gasped lightly, and her eyes grew wide.

"Okay, she did," I said. "Who? Was it a man? Come on, Leanne. You might as well tell us. We will find out eventually when we go through her computer and social media accounts."

"Leanne, if you know anything, tell the police right now," her father said. He received another look from the mother, and I guessed she wasn't exactly used to being told what to do.

"I don't know, okay?" Leanne said and threw out her arms.

I gave her the look I usually gave my kids when I knew they were lying through their teeth and not getting away with it.

"Leanne?" I said.

"Okay, okay. She was supposed to meet this photographer. He had contacted her on Amino, I think it was, and he told her she was pretty and asked if she had considered becoming a model. He had seen her pictures and would like to take some professional ones. She could make a ton of money, he said. She asked me if she should do it. She said she'd ask her parents about it first, but I told her not to."

"Leanne!" her father said.

"Her parents would never understand," she continued. "They would never allow her to go. Not until they saw the pictures, then they'd see that it was real. If they saw her looking like some supermodel, then they'd realize that she could do this, and that this photographer wasn't some phony."

"So, you told her to lie to her parents," I said. "And to meet with him."

"Well, yes. I said I'd be gone all weekend, so she could tell them she was sleeping over at my house. They'd never know."

"And where was she planning on spending the night then?" I asked.

"She was supposed to meet this guy at dusk at a park so he could take the photos while the sun was about to set. It was the best lighting, he said. He was going to take her to Orlando, and they'd stay the night there, and she would meet some agents in the morning. They were going to stay in a hotel, he said. At the Hilton, that's where the meeting would take place. He knew all the big names in the business, he said, and it was important that she meet with them if they were going to sign her. Molly had always dreamt of becoming a model, ever since she was little. This was her big break."

"Except it wasn't," I said. "Instead, it destroyed her life."

"You sound like you think it's Leanne's fault," her mother said. "It's not like she could have known that this guy wasn't legit; she couldn't possibly know what would happen."

I stared at the woman, wondering about an article I had read recently about the parents of today. They weren't called helicopter parents anymore; no, today they were called snowplow parents. A snowplow parent will "plow" down any person or obstacle standing in their child's way. They were constantly paving the way for their children, removing every obstacle or disappointment that might appear, enabling them never to make responsible decisions or take responsibility for their actions.

I couldn't legally charge Leanne for encouraging her friend to lie to her parents, but boy, I wished I could at this moment.

Chapter 34

I MANAGED to make it home in time for dinner. I rushed inside, threw my purse on the table, and turned to see all of them seated around my dining room table.

Alex saw me first.

"MOMMY!"

He was about to jump down from his seat when my mom stopped him.

"Your mom will come here. You eat now."

I smiled widely at the sight of my family, then rushed to Alex and kissed him. He reached up his small arms and grabbed me, wanting me to kiss him again.

"I missed you, Mommy," he said. "Where were you?"

"Yeah, Mom, where have you been?" Olivia asked.

I sat down in my seat, while my mom got me some food and handed me the plate. I stared at the green stuff, then wondered if there was such a thing as a kale-allergy and whether my mom would believe me if I said I suffered from it.

"I'm helping Matt on the case," I said. "They need me. And, frankly, after finding Molly out there…in our backyard, I feel obligated to help. Melissa is, after all, my best friend."

"There was an EXPLOSION downtown," Alex exclaimed very loudly, yelling the word out. "Were you there, Mommy? Was there a FIRE? And firetrucks, huh?"

"Please, use your inside voice, Alex," my mom said.

I smiled at him. "Alex is correct. There was a truck that exploded right in front of city hall today. And, yes, I was there, and yes, there was fire and firetrucks and firefighters who put the fire out."

Olivia stared at me with big eyes. "I heard about it at school. We were on lockdown for hours. Then they told us all to go out on the football field while dogs searched the school. They say it was a bomb; is that true?"

"I heard someone was hurt," Christine said.

I took a deep breath, then nodded, sticking my fork into the green mass on my plate, dreaming about it being pizza or steak.

I might as well tell the kids the truth, I thought. *They'll only hear rumors from their friends, and that will be worse.*

"You're all correct. It looks like there might have been a bomb placed in that truck and someone did get hurt. An officer. One of our colleagues and Matt's friend."

Olivia gave me a look of concern. I knew that look a little too well. All my children had it right now, even Alex.

"I'm going to be fine," I said. "I was nowhere near the truck when it exploded. I don't want you to worry about me; do you hear me? I'm being very careful."

"Now, enough with the long faces," my mom said. "Eat your dinner before it gets cold."

We ate in silence, and it was nagging at me. The last thing I wanted was for my children to have to worry about their mother too. They had enough concerns in their lives as it was. This wasn't good for them. I hated the fact that they had seen Molly hanging in that swing set and knew so much about what was going on.

After dinner, I cleaned up while my mom went to the living room to relax. She turned on the TV and watched the news until Alex came and sat with her and she turned it onto *Peppa Pig* instead.

Christine and Olivia helped me clean up and, as I was loading the dishwasher, Christine came up to me.

"What did Dad say?"

"Dad? About what?"

I looked at her a little confused; then I remembered.

Oh, shoot. I was supposed to have called him! I promised her.

"You didn't call him; did you?" she said disappointedly. "I should have known."

Christine started to walk away. I stared after her, wondering what I could say or do, but nothing came to mind. Instead, I grabbed my phone and walked out on the back porch, then called him. It was dark out, and I could hear fish jumping in the canal. They did that a lot, especially as it got warmer. No one really knew why, but some people said they were catching bugs; others said they were running away from bigger fish like dolphins or sharks. I had never seen a shark in my canal, but there were plenty of dolphins.

"Chad, it's me."

"Eva Rae?" he said, surprised. "What's wrong? Is something up with the kids?"

"The kids, well…actually, yes, something is wrong. They miss you, Chad. They miss their dad, and you don't seem ever to have time for them anymore. They're asking when they're going to visit you again."

I knew I was putting it on a little thick since, technically, I was the one who was pressing for this to happen, but I sensed it was the only way to Chad's heart.

"Visit? Ah, well…It's just there's a lot right now. I've recently started a new job at a new insurance company, and I no longer work from home, so it's a little difficult to find the time, right now at least…I mean, as soon as things settle down a little, I'm sure…"

I sighed. "What the heck is going on, Chad? You used to be all about the children."

"I just…It's hard to find the time right now. I'm sure it'll get better when…"

"Don't give me that," I said. "This is not you, Chad. After fifteen years of marriage, you don't think I know you? This is not you. This is her; isn't it? She's the one who doesn't want them there; am I right?"

He exhaled, and I knew then that I was right. Tears sprang to my eyes. My poor babies. They had to know by now; didn't they? They had to have realized by now that their dad had chosen his new girlfriend over them. That was why they didn't ask to go. It wasn't that they didn't miss their dad. They sensed he didn't want them there.

"It's just…well, three children are a little much. I can't blame her. We only live in a condo and don't have space for them. It gets very crowded when they're here, and it's a little too much for her."

I closed my eyes and bit my lip. I wanted to yell at him so badly but had to restrain myself.

"So, what are you saying, Chad? You can't see your children because they take up too much space; is that it?"

"No, no, of course not. Darn it, Eva Rae, you know how much I love them."

"Then why won't you see them? Why can't you make room to be with your own children, Chad? Explain this to me because I simply don't understand it. I don't even know who you are anymore."

"We're trying to figure it out, okay?" he said, annoyed. "I'll make it work somehow. I miss them too, okay? But it's...well, it's not that easy."

"I really want to believe you, Chad; I really do, but you're making it hard. You've got to find a way to spend time with your children. You're breaking their hearts. I see it in their eyes. You're not with them every day; you don't see the hurt in them like I do. You can't do this to them. I won't let you."

"You won't let me? What's that supposed to mean?" he said, suddenly sounding like I had offended him. "You're no better yourself, you know? Do I have to mention how little you were home when they were younger? Who took care of all the tantrums, all the homework, all the laundry, all the crying when tucking them in at night, huh? You're no saint in that area either. Don't you tell me how to be a good father when you've only been a mother for like ten minutes of their lives."

Ouch.

"I know I'm not..." I started but realized that the line had gone dead. Chad had hung up on me. Startled at this, I sat down on the porch swing, tears escaping my eyes. Inside, I could hear Alex scream something at one of his sisters, and soon someone was crying. I leaned back, closing my eyes for just a second before the door opened and Olivia peeked her head out.

"Mom? Alex pulled Christine's hair. I think you better come."

I swallowed the knot of tears stuck in my throat and nodded.

"I'll be right there, baby. Just give me a sec; will you?"

Chapter 35

SHE WAS SITTING on the porch swing underneath the porch light. Boomer couldn't stop staring at her. She looked tired and sad, yet so vulnerable and beautiful.

He liked to watch her and did it a lot. Earlier in the day, he had been in the crowd downtown watching too. He had seen the officer walk into the truck right when it blew up. People around him had screamed and run for cover when it happened. Boomer had watched when Eva Rae Thomas had arrived in the cruiser with her partner, the guy she was also dating, Matt Miller. Covered by the crowd on the corner in front of Heidi's Jazz Club, he had watched her closely until a police officer had told them to get out of there, that it was too dangerous for them to stand so close.

Boomer had moved away, still covered by the crowd. He had continued down A1A until he reached Juice N' Java, where he had bought himself a coffee and chatted briefly with the woman behind the counter whose name was Deborah about the horrifying blast they had heard.

"We all ran out there, but our boss told us to get back inside," she said, slightly excited but trying to hide it. "A car exploded, someone told me afterward. Something like that. Did you hear it too?"

"I sure did," Boomer said and paid with cash, making sure not to leave a trail.

"I guess everyone did," Deborah replied. "Good thing it was all the way down there and not right here that it happened. Must have been something wrong with that car or somethin', to go up in flames like that, causing an explosion. The cash register shook and everything. People were screaming in here. For a moment, I feared it was terrorists or something like you hear about in Europe and those places in the Middle East. Terrible world we live in. But Marty in the kitchen said it was just an accident. His brother is a cop, and he texted him and asked."

"Good thing it wasn't anything worse," Boomer said and received his coffee.

He tipped Deborah extra before returning to watch the scene from a distance. A news chopper was lingering in the air above the intersection, and reporter vans had arrived. Styled women in short skirts and high heels were elbowing their way up the career ladder and doing live reporting from the scene. The police had blocked off the entire intersection and big portions of A1A, while dogs sniffed the trash cans and drains. People around him were shocked and talking with fear in their voices, yet not afraid enough to not want to have a look for themselves.

When Eva Rae Thomas had walked back into the police station, it wasn't fun anymore, and he had decided to leave. He knew it wouldn't take long before the police would start questioning the spectators and looking for anyone who stood out, knowing that criminals often returned to the scene of the crime to watch their work.

Boomer had rushed up through the town and taken his pick-up truck, which he had parked behind the Chinese restaurant Yen Yen. He drove to Cape Canaveral, then walked down to the beach, where he sat in the white sand, looking at the pictures he had taken with his phone, pictures right during and after the bomb went off. He kept staring at the pictures, going through them again and again, his heart beating faster each time. Then he opened and looked at the ones he had taken of her, zooming in as much as he could on her face as she received the news from the chief of police. One of her colleagues had gotten hurt. One she cared about.

It hurts; doesn't it?

Boomer then opened the app he was using to trace her phone. He had been surprised that she had accepted him when he had asked for her friendship in the app, using a fake profile with the name of one of her old friends. He figured she had seen no harm in accepting this friendship, thinking it was someone she knew. It was almost too easy.

And now he could follow her everywhere she went, constantly staying one step ahead.

Now, as she rose to her feet to walk back inside, as soon as the door slammed shut, Boomer started up the small boat and chugged away, cruising down the canal. He docked the boat further down in his usual spot by the ramp, then grabbed all his fishing stuff and put it in the pick-up truck and drove it home, listening to Taylor Swift on the radio. As he walked into the house after putting his stuff in the garage, he looked at himself briefly in the mirror in the hallway, then ran a hand through his hair and smelled his sweaty armpit before yelling:

"Honey! I'm home!"

Chapter 36

"WE FOUND the guy who wrote to Molly, the one who claimed to be a photographer."

Matt was at my door the next morning, looking like he hadn't slept at all.

"Come on in," I said. "I have coffee."

"Sounds heavenly," he said and walked inside with me. We entered the kitchen just as Alex turned his spoon with milk and cheerios at his sister and was about to sling it at her.

"ALEX!"

He stopped and turned to look at me, spoon still balancing in his hand.

"Don't you dare do that," I said. "Are you kidding me?"

"But she started it," he whined, letting the spoon fall into the milk. "She's *me-an*."

"Am not," Christine said.

Alex answered by sticking his tongue out.

"That's it," I said. "Both of you go upstairs and brush your teeth. Bus will be here any minute. GO!"

"You're so unfair, Mom," Alex said, then ran up the stairs, Christine right behind him, rolling her eyes at me.

I turned to look at Matt, then smiled.

"Coffee?"

He nodded, startled, then sat on a stool, wiping away a few lost cheerios from the counter.

"What was that all about?"

"That? I don't know. The usual, I guess," I said and poured him a cup. "Who knows what they fight about? I'm not sure they even do anymore."

I poured myself another cup. It was my third this morning. I hadn't slept much myself either and felt the exhaustion in every bone of my body.

"Does it frighten you?" I asked and nodded toward the stairs. "Seeing this?"

He shrugged. "I'm just not used to all this conflict, I guess. But that's probably what makes it so hard with Elijah, you know? Me trying constantly to avoid conflict."

"Ah, yes, conflict comes with the job, and a lot of it. You just can't let it get to you. They can hate you at one second, then turn around and love you dearly the next."

Matt sighed. "I'm afraid he hates me pretty much all of the time."

I put my hand on top of his, then leaned over and kissed him. "It'll get better. I promise," I said as our lips parted. "Now, what was that about you finding the guy who contacted Molly?"

Matt nodded. "Computer Forensics has her laptop, and they found him easily. He wrote messages to her on the social media app called Amino. They managed to pull the entire conversation."

"Never heard of it," I said. "I feel like every time I just learn about social media, another one pops up, and I'm lost again."

"I know," he said. "Our parents had it easy."

Our eyes met, and he immediately regretted his remark.

"Well, my parents had it easy," he said. "Anyway, this is like a social media platform for art lovers, so it seems very safe, but in reality, it's just like all the others. You post pictures of yourself and creeps find you. Molly was no different, she posted many artistic self-portraits as her art, and he saw the photos and thought she was beautiful enough to become a model. This guy has been writing to Molly for several months, and I guess that was why she chose to trust him. I can't blame her. When you read their conversation, he comes off as extremely nice. He's not even trying to push her into it. He cautiously warned her about bad seeds in the business and seems to know what he's talking about. Like he gave her all these references, numbers she could call if her parents wanted to check up on him, he said. Numbers that were fake, naturally. He even told her she could bring her parents if she wished or a friend. He didn't want her to think he was some creep that wanted to exploit her. She ended up being the one pushing for him to help her because she wanted this so badly. He kept telling her she should talk to her parents about it and said that he didn't want her to do the photos without her parents knowing about it."

"Yet, she did it anyway. He probably knew she would. He's clever, this one," I said and sipped my coffee. "Using reverse psychology. Making her think it was her idea and not his."

"Exactly," Matt said.

"So, when can we talk to this guy?" I asked.

Matt smiled. "How about right now?" He pulled a note out from his pocket with an address on it. "Forensics gave me his address. It's ten minutes away."

"Let's go," I said and was about to grab my purse when I heard the school bus sigh outside my door and peeked out just in time to see it take off. I turned to look at Matt.

"Right after I drive them to school."

I heard my kids' footsteps on the stairs. Olivia didn't have classes till later but was awake now too, and I could hear the shower being turned on. She would ride her bike to school, so I didn't need to worry about her, only the young ones.

"How about we all go in my police cruiser?" Matt asked.

Alex heard that and rushed down the stairs.

"YAAAY!"

"Really?" Christine asked less enthusiastically. "You want me to sit in the back seat like some criminal? Everyone will stare at us. They'll all talk. I'm not doing it."

"I will; I will," Alex said, jumping up and down. He rushed to the front door while I sent Christine a reassuring smile.

"Nonsense, honey. It'll be fun. I'm just gonna run upstairs real quick and tell Olivia we're leaving, and then we'll go. Go ahead and get in the car. I don't want us to be late. Don't be so grumpy, Christine."

"I hate my life," Christine said, moaning, then followed Matt reluctantly.

I knocked on the door to the bathroom, then yelled at Olivia that I was leaving and received an *Okay* for an answer. I rushed down the stairs, past my mom, who opened her mouth to say something, then I pecked her on the cheek before she could and stormed out to the driveway where Matt already had the engine fired up and music blasting out the windows. Alex stuck his head out the window, looking like he was about to explode with excitement while his sister hid her face behind her hands.

Chapter 37

"I THOUGHT you'd let me see a doctor? I'm not feeling well."

Ava stared at the man wearing the surgical mask. He had entered the room where she had been kept for hours, alone. After taking her out of the room with the other girls, he had taken her into a bedroom and chained her to a pipe, then told her to lie on the bed, and then gagged her. It had been light out and then dark again before the light came once more, and the darkness came back while she had waited for him to take her to a doctor as she had asked. But he hadn't shown his masked face at all. Now, the room she was in had gone dark. She had prepared herself for another night alone in the bed when the door had opened, and light had hit her face again. The man had flipped the switch by the door, and a lamp had turned on, almost blinding Ava.

"Why are you keeping me in here?" she said, worried as he finally pulled the gag out. "I'm sick. Please, take me to see a doctor."

The masked man sat next to her on the bed, holding a knife in his hand. Ava saw it and felt her pulse quicken.

"You girls think I'm an idiot; don't you? Like I didn't know you were trying to fool me, pretending to be sick. Did you really think I would take you to see a doctor so you could tell him I was keeping you prisoner, huh? Do you think I'm that stupid?"

"N-no," she said, anxiety rising inside of her. He had known all along that it was a trick. The realization caused panic to spread inside of her. "I don't think you're stupid at all."

The masked man tilted his head. "Oh, look at you, trying to make sure I don't get mad, telling me what I want to hear. But the thing is, I am angry. I am a very angry man. You took me for a fool, and now you have to pay the price."

Ava whimpered and pulled back on the bed. She tried to pull loose from the chains but couldn't. She tried to scream, but after throwing up the little she had in her stomach and not having any food or anything to drink for almost twenty-four hours, she didn't have the strength to scream very loud, let alone fight back.

"Please, sir. I...I didn't mean to...I'm not..." Ava tried, but she was so exhausted she could barely think. Whatever kept her awake was fueled solely by her fear.

The masked man approached her, knife still in his hand.

"Now, the thing is, you weren't supposed to die till last, but now that you pulled this trick, I decided to take you first instead. How about that, huh?"

"N-no, please, mister, I am...I don't want to..."

"You don't want to what?" he asked, coming very close to her face. "You don't want to *die*; is that it?"

"Y-yes. Please. I don't want to die," she pleaded, crying now. "I just want to go home."

The man's face was close to hers now, and she could hear him breathing. Looking into his eyes, Ava suddenly recognized them and gasped loudly. Even though he was wearing a surgical mask, she could still tell that he was smiling.

Chapter 38

"SO WHERE ARE we on finding our bomber?" I asked as Matt drove out from the middle school's parking lot, where we had just dropped off Christine. She had blushed and put on her jacket, hiding her face in the hoodie as she got out. The entire crowd of kids that was rushing to school had stopped and stared at the kid arriving in a police cruiser. I had to admit; I felt a little bad for her. Middle schoolers were merciless.

"I'm guessing the lab isn't done with their analysis yet, but have we had any luck with the surveillance cameras from City Hall?"

Matt shook his head. "I had two of my men going through the footage all night. So far, all they've seen is the truck arriving, being parked in the middle of the intersection, and a guy running away from it."

"Any face? ID?"

Matt shook his head. "I'm afraid not. We could only see him from the back. It's almost like he knew where the cameras were. He was wearing a black baseball cap too. It's no use."

"Okay, we'll find him without it, even though it would be nice to put a face to him. Maybe Jane's description of the delivery guy to the artist later today will give us something. I feel pretty convinced he's the same guy who hurt Molly and who took Carina, Ava, and Tara. Say, wasn't there a photographer who contacted Ava as well about becoming a model? I remember you saying something about it at the beginning of your investigation."

Matt looked at me. "Yes, I checked him out. It's the same guy. Or rather, it's the same profile. It's called Space Coast Photography."

"So, he's hiding behind a company name to make it look legit. Easiest trick in the book, but also something young gullible girls might fall for."

"It was the same profile that contacted Ava on Instagram and told her he would like to take pictures of her, but her parents wouldn't let her go. They didn't believe it was real."

"So, he was a suspect earlier on. Did you ever talk to him?"

Matt shook his head. "He was gone when we went for him, and we never found him. A neighbor said they rarely saw the owner of the house, that they believed they had had family up north and maybe was out of town."

"Had he seen the girls?"

"He said he often saw young girls come and go at the house, but he couldn't recall seeing our three girls specifically. Our hunch wasn't enough for a warrant, the chief said, since this was months ago, or we would have raided the house. We had a patrol stationed there for a few days, but there was no activity to report."

"I see," I said. "And what is this guy's name?"

"The house belongs to a Jordan Daniels."

Matt parked the cruiser in front of a small townhouse in South Cocoa Beach and killed the engine. I took off my seatbelt and felt my gun in the holster. This was the moment I hated the most about the job. You never knew what awaited you on the other side of that door. It could be anything from a nice old woman or neglected children to someone willing to end your life.

Chapter 39

THEN:

"He says he wants money. Let's just give it to him."

Iris stared at Gary. He had called it in, and now the house was crawling with uniforms and the forensic team going through every corner of their home. As an FBI agent, Gary had been at dozens of crime scenes, but he had never ever imagined it would one day be his own home.

"It's not that simple, Iris," he said. He was trying not to hiss at her, but it was hard. He couldn't help himself. He tried not to be cross with her, he really did, but the fact was, he was blaming her for not keeping a proper eye on their son.

Why would she leave him out of her sight like that?

"We don't believe he has been inside the house," his supervisor, Agent Peterson, said coming up to him. Behind him stood Gary's partner, Agent Wilson, along with most of his other colleagues. Seeing all of them in his house wearing FBI jackets and gloves made Gary's heart drop.

"There are no footprints or fingerprints anywhere, no sign of anyone breaking and entering," Peterson continued. "Personally, I think he walked up from the street. He might have just passed by out there, then seen Iris as she put the baby in the carriage and thought there was his chance at making some easy money. My guess is that he is some drug addict or someone in deep gambling debt."

"So, you think that if we give him the money, then he might bring Oliver back?" Iris asked.

"I didn't say that," Peterson said with an exhale. "With someone like that, you never really know what their next move will be."

"But it's worth a try; isn't it?" Iris said. "In the note, it says he wants twenty thousand dollars. I have that in my savings from when my mother died. I can go to the bank right now and get the cash. It says in the note that he will bring back the boy *safe and happy* if we do as he says."

"It also says that he will kill the baby if we make *a wrong move*," Gary said. "God knows what a wrong move is in his book. Calling all my FBI colleagues probably isn't a *right* move to him."

Iris's expression changed. Her eyes were red-rimmed from crying, and her shoulders slumped. The hope in her eyes died out for a minute.

"So, what are you saying?" she asked. "Are you saying he might already have killed him?"

"Let's not jump to conclusions," Peterson said. "We have literally everyone looking for the boy right now. Besides, why would he kill him if he wants money? Then he has nothing to bargain with."

Iris nodded, head bowed. "Peterson is right. I say we give him the money and get our boy back. It's all I want."

She lifted her glance, and her eyes met Gary's. It was hard for him to even look at her right now, but as their eyes met, he felt himself grow softer. Maybe she couldn't have helped it. It didn't have to be anyone's fault. Bad things happened to good people sometimes. Accidents happened. At least that was what he always told relatives when he went to their houses to tell them about their loved ones having passed away.

We can't control everything in life. There was nothing you could have done to prevent this from happening. You must forgive yourself.

Iris's lips shaped half a smile as their eyes remained locked. "What do you say, Gary?"

He nodded, biting his lip nervously. "I say we do it. Let's give him the money and get Oliver back."

Peterson placed a hand on Gary's shoulder. "I'll set things in motion. We won't let him get away, Gary. You know we won't."

Chapter 40

"YES?"

I stared at the small skinny woman in front of me standing in the doorway. She was wearing a long black skirt and a green tank top and had her dreadlocks wrapped in a very colorful scarf. In her hand, she was holding what looked like a very expensive and professional camera.

"We're looking for Jordan Daniels," Matt said and showed her his badge.

"That's me," she said indifferently. She was wearing heavy eyeliner and had a tattoo of an octopus licking up her shoulder.

"*You're* Jordan Daniels?" I asked.

She gave me a look. "It can be a girl's name too, you know."

I glanced briefly at Matt, then back at the woman. "Yes, of course, it can."

"So, what can I do for you?" she asked.

"We have a few questions for you if you don't mind?" I asked, sensing she would respond better to a female approaching her than Matt.

She looked at me, then nodded. "Sure. Come on in."

She let us inside her small dark house where all the blinds were pulled in each and every room. In the living room, she had set up a regular studio with lamps facing the backdrop to give the right light.

"I take it you work from home?" I said as we walked inside and she put her camera on the tripod. It was a cluttered place with many magazines spread out and photographs of young girls lying everywhere, yet it still came off as stylish with high-tech minimalistic furniture.

"I sure do," she said. "This is my studio. This is where I do most of my shoots if I'm not called out on a shoot somewhere."

Matt looked at the photographs on the long white desk leaned against the barren wall.

"You photograph a lot of young girls, I take it?"

"Those are the ones who are most in demand, yes," she said with a sly smile.

Matt showed her a picture of Carina Martin. "Ever seen her before?"

Jordan studied the picture, then shook her head. "Nope."

"So, she hasn't been here?"

"No. I would have remembered that. She's very pretty but not exactly a model."

"How about this one," Matt said and showed her a school picture of Molly Carson.

Seeing her picture again made my stomach churn. The previous night, before I went back home to dinner with my family, I had stopped by the hospital and sat down with Melissa over a cup of coffee. She was still in deep shock and had a heaviness to her face I had never seen before. She was barely keeping it all together with the kids at home and being at the hospital most of the day. Luckily, Steve had tried some new medicine and was up and running again now, so he could help her out, but he also needed to take care of his job, so he didn't lose it and with it their whole income. Molly was doing better and was out of the ICU, and she was awake, they said, but she hadn't said a word to anyone yet. We were still waiting for her to start talking so we could ask her about the pig who did this to her. The doctors didn't really know if she was unable to talk or if she just chose not to. Only time would tell, they said. They were hoping it was still just the shock that was blocking her, and as it wore off, she would begin to speak.

I prayed that they were right.

Jordan grabbed the photo and peeked at it. I studied her closely to look for any reaction. Jordan shook her head.

"Nope. Never seen her either."

"Are you sure?" I said. "Maybe take another look. Take your time."

She sat down, the photo still between her hands. She looked again and shook her head.

"Those eyes. I would definitely have remembered those."

Yeah, well that was all any of us could do now. Her mother would never see them again.

"I am sorry; I haven't seen her before. Why?"

"Are you the only one who handles your social media presence?" I asked. "Or do you have someone else doing it?"

Jordan smiled. "Look around you. Do I look like I could afford people working for me?"

"You could have an intern working for you maybe," I said.

"Well, I don't."

I grabbed a photo of a random young girl from her desk and held it up. "How do you find girls? Do you contact them?" I asked.

Jordan looked away as I asked the question, and I took note of her reaction.

"They come to me," she said. "They call me up, or they write to me because they want to become models. I tell them I can't promise them anything, but I can take some professional pictures of them that they can send to an agency. I sometimes help them find the right agencies to send them to as well. It's not illegal what I do."

"No one said it was," Matt said, still looking through the pictures of girls on the desk. He picked one up and looked at it closely, then put it down. I took out the photos of all four girls and put them in front of Jordan. "Could you look at all these girls and tell me if you recognize any of them?"

Jordan was getting annoyed with us now. I could tell by her agitated body language.

"What is this about?"

"Just do it for me; will you?" I asked.

She exhaled and looked at all of them, shaking her head. "I haven't seen any of them before. I am sorry."

"Try again."

"Seriously? It's not like it's gonna change. I told you I don't know any of these girls."

I smiled, trying to hide how much she was annoying me right now. "Just humor me. I want to be one hundred percent certain."

"Are you for real?"

I nodded. "I am very real, thank you. Now, take your time. Don't rush it. We have all day."

"Geez, you'd think you people had better things to do."

As she studied them, I turned to look at Matt, who showed me a picture he had found in the pile. I nodded to let him know I had seen it. Jordan lifted her head and looked directly at me.

"There. I have looked at them three times now, and I don't recognize any of the girls at all."

"And you're sure?" Matt said and approached us, still holding the photograph in his hand.

"I am sure."

Matt turned the photo and placed it on the table in front of Jordan, then slid it across it till it was right in front of her.

"Because this photo kind of looks a lot like this girl; doesn't it?" he said and pointed at Ava Morales's photograph.

"I think we need to have you come in for further questioning," I said.

"But…but I can't…I'm going out on a photo shoot this afternoon."

My eyes met Matt's, and I nodded.

"Let's take her in."

Hearing this, Jordan sprang to her feet and bolted for the door.

Shoot.

"We have a runner!"

I was quickly up and running after her, while Matt was slower to react. Jordan made it past him and opened the door. She leaped out into the driveway, then sprinted down across the lawn and into the street, Matt and I following her closely behind, hands on our weapons, ready to draw should it become necessary.

Agile Jordan sprang down the street toward the river, sprinting like she was some darn track runner. Who would have thought such a small girl had such force in her? I, on the other hand, panted agitatedly as I tried to follow her, cursing myself for not being in better shape like I had promised myself. I guess I hadn't exactly expected to be running after criminals anytime soon since I had actually quit my job.

Matt was doing a lot better and was soon ahead of me, almost within arm's reach of Jordan, ready to grab her. But just as he reached out his arm, she took a swift left turn and sprinted down Brevard Avenue instead. Matt lost speed and was soon left behind, while Jordan made it toward the river.

Oh, no, you don't.

Angrily, I sped up, pressing myself to the utmost, then as I was about to lose her, I threw myself at her, reached out my arm, and wrapped it around her neck, then pulled her backward using all my weight and stopping her in her tracks.

The next second, Matt pulled her to the ground. He was on top of her, turning her around, pressing his knee down on her back, and Mirandizing her.

Chapter 41

WE LET Jordan Daniels sweat for a while, then returned to our desks and sat down. The station was buzzing with activity as Chief Annie had called in help from the county's sheriff's office to find our bomber. I still believed it was the same guy we were searching for that had taken Molly and the three other girls, but Chief Annie wasn't fully convinced. It couldn't hurt to work several angles, she said.

I could hardly argue with that.

Matt brought both of us coffee while the adrenalin left our bodies. My legs were sore from running, and I think I pulled a muscle. I massaged my thighs as he handed me the plastic cup. I took a sip, then his phone rang.

Matt took the call while I read a text from Christine. She was upset because everyone was talking about her in school, and she had no one to sit with at lunch. I shivered, thinking about my own middle school years. They really were the worst.

I texted her back,

I AM SORRY, BABY. I AM SURE IT'LL BE BETTER SOON.

"That was the lab," Matt said when he hung up.

"Any news?"

"The syringe that the kids found. They've analyzed it and believe it contained ketamine."

"A date rape drug?" I asked.

He nodded. "They also found traces of Carina Martin's blood on it. It matched the blood sample we had from Carina Martin's doctor that was taken a few days before she disappeared while she was in for a checkup."

"So, this was what he used to drug her, and probably the others too, when abducting them," I said, then glanced toward the interrogation room where Jordan Daniels was still waiting. "Or maybe she."

"The phone was also Carina's, as I suspected," Matt said.

"Okay, so now we can safely say that the three girls have been taken, am I right?" I asked and looked at the board behind Matt. "The theory of them having run away seems to be shrinking."

"I think it is safe to say," he said.

"Good. Did they have anything else?" I asked. "Any news on the bomb?"

He shook his head. "Not yet. But they got the results of the tests run on Molly Carson."

I sat up straight. "And?"

He shook his head. "Nothing. The rapist left no DNA. There was condom lubrication and no semen present. No DNA elsewhere on her either. Probably wore gloves when touching her."

"Of course, he did," I said and sipped my coffee. It suddenly tasted bitter. I glanced up at Molly's picture and felt guilty. I had promised Melissa I would catch this guy, but of course it wasn't going to be that easy. God forbid I had even one good lead to go on.

Matt sighed and finished his cup. He put it down heavily. "So, now what, Agent Thomas? What's our theory here? We have a woman in custody, but do we really think she raped and blinded Molly?"

"Maybe not. But I do think she might know who did," I said and finished my cup as well. I crushed it and threw it in the trash can in the corner.

Chapter 42

THEY HEARD FOOTSTEPS. Carina was the first to hear them and open her eyes. Next to her slept Tara, who was now so skinny she was barely awake at all anymore.

"What was that?" Carina said and sat up.

Carina had lost track of time and barely knew if it was night or day anymore, but she did know that Ava had been gone a very long time. Carina worried about her and whether she had managed to get to a doctor's office. It was the plan that she should pretend to be sick and then alert the doctor once she got there. Since the day Carina had seen the masked man take her away, she had been waiting and waiting for someone to come. She had tried to stay awake for as long as she could, but the lack of food made her exhausted and, eventually, she had fallen asleep. Once she woke up, she had expected the police to come crashing down the door at any minute, but it hadn't happened.

Where are you now, Ava?

The wait was painful. Still, she kept her hopes up. The man hadn't been there since he came and took Ava. They had no more clean water and no more food. Carina felt her ribs and realized they were poking out now, and her stomach was in pain because of hunger. The worst part was the thirst.

Now, as she listened for more footsteps and didn't hear any, she thought that maybe it had just been another dream.

Carina crawled to the water bucket and poked her head into it.

There was a little left on the bottom, and she lifted the bucket in the air, emptying it completely. Then she glanced at Tara, wondering if she should have left some for her in case she woke up. But maybe she wouldn't wake up at all, and then it would just be a waste. They would both die. At least Carina now knew she could get by for a little while longer, even though the dryness of her mouth and throat was painful.

Carina crawled to Tara and felt her neck. At first, she didn't feel her pulse, and she feared she had died, but by pressing harder into the paper-thin skin, she finally felt it.

She was still alive.

"Come on, Ava," she said. "Have you told them yet?"

Please, say they're on their way. Please, tell me they're coming. I don't know how much more of this I can take.

Carina sat down on her mattress and leaned her head against the back wall, a position she found herself sitting in constantly. She cried weakly and closed her eyes, dreaming about being on the beach with her friends, running around playing ball, eating chips, and swimming in the ocean. She had just drifted away when she heard more footsteps coming from above her head. Carina's eyes shot open.

"I heard it again," she said into the room. "Someone is up there. Someone is here!"

She tried to wake up Tara but had no luck. Now, she heard voices too, muffled voices, and more footsteps. Carina rose to her feet and started hammering on the walls. The foam was soft and made barely any sound, and soon she realized it was no use. Carina took a deep breath, then opened her mouth and started to scream.

"HEEEELP!!! HEEELP!"

There were steps outside of their door now, and she looked at it in anticipation, almost laughing.

"Tara. Tara! Wake up. They've found us. They're coming for us. Help is coming now."

But Tara didn't wake up. Carina stared at the door as the deadbolts were pushed aside.

"HEEELP!" she screamed. "We're in here!"

The door opened slowly, and a face appeared behind it. Carina almost cried with happiness until she realized it was the masked man. And he was alone.

He rushed toward her, then slammed his fist into her face. Carina felt the blow and sunk to her mattress, the room spinning around her.

"Don't you think I know what you've been up to? You think I would fall for your little trick, huh?"

Carina looked up at him, not sure she completely understood.

"A-Ava?" she asked.

As a grin spread behind the mask, she started to cry. "What have you done to her, you creep? What did you do to Ava?"

The man stared down at her but didn't answer. Instead, he walked to the door, found the light switch, and flipped it, turning off the small lamp beneath the ceiling, the source of all their light. Then he slammed the door shut, leaving Carina and Tara in complete darkness.

Chapter 43

"DID YOU CALL DAD?"

Christine had barely entered the house before she asked me. Her sweet eyes stared up at me in anticipation, and it broke my heart.

"You didn't, did you?" she said, disappointed. "I knew you wouldn't."

I exhaled and wiped my hands on a dishtowel. I had been cleaning up the kitchen since I got home. My mom hadn't been home all day since she was out with a friend shopping at the mall, so I decided to clean up from breakfast before the kids came home from school.

"As a matter of fact, I did," I said.

I had been thinking about this so intensely since I spoke to Chad, wondering what to tell the kids when they asked, and I had to admit that I hadn't come up with anything that wouldn't at some point end up hurting them.

"And? What did he say?"

Her eyes gleamed with excitement while I pondered what to do, what to say. I could hardly tell her the truth, that the woman her dad lived with now didn't want them there. She would only end up hurt and then hating Kimmie, and that wouldn't make their visits with their father any easier.

"You know what? Right now, he's a little overwhelmed with his new job, and he has to work a lot, but he promised that as soon as it slows down a little, he'll have you come visit, okay?"

Christine stared at me, her smile frozen in place. I bit my lip, wondering what was going on inside of her. Did she buy it? It wasn't a complete lie. But it wasn't exactly the truth either.

"So…so…he didn't say when?" Christine asked. "Because summer break is coming up, and we could go up there for a longer time, maybe a week?"

"I…sweetie, I don't think…"

Alex came out into the kitchen and looked at both of us while standing behind his sister. I didn't want him to hear any of this and wanted to finish this conversation now.

"Hey, buddy," I said addressed to him. "Are you hungry? How about I make us some cinnamon rolls, huh?"

"Yay," Alex said, his eyes lighting up. He grabbed a stool and sat down at the counter with his firetruck in his hand. He looked at his sister, then at me. I forced a smile.

Christine's shoulders slumped, and I knew she didn't buy my excuse. We had been through this before, back in the fall when her dad had told her not to come, and she almost went anyway on her own but was stopped at the airport. It pained me that nothing seemed to have changed much. For a little while, I had believed things had changed since they actually went to visit him every month, and we seemed to have gotten into some sort of routine. It somehow felt even worse that he was now pulling out once again. The kids were going to feel like it was their fault. They were going to wonder if they did something wrong on their last visit.

"It's her, isn't it?" she asked. "She doesn't want us there."

"Who?" Alex asked.

"Kimmie," Christine said. "She doesn't like us. Remember the last time we were up there? Remember how she and Dad had that big fight in the kitchen when we were in the living room, and they thought we couldn't hear them, but we could?"

Alex nodded, bowing his head.

So, that's what happened. That's why the girls didn't ask to visit him anymore for several months. They didn't feel welcome. They knew they were the cause of their fight. They were in their way.

"I'm sorry, baby…I…"

Christine nodded. "I get it. Dad doesn't want us to come because she doesn't want us there."

"Daddy?" Alex asked. "He doesn't want us?"

"Of course, your dad wants you to visit. He's just trying to figure out a way to make it happen because they don't have so much room in the condo, okay? He promised me he'd make it happen somehow. Don't worry, okay?"

But none of the eyes looking back at me believed a word I had just said. Especially not Christine. She grabbed her phone and started tapping on it, disappearing into that world of her own that I couldn't reach her in, while Alex slid down from the stool, saying, "I'm not hungry."

"Me either," Christine said and turned around without even looking up from her screen.

I opened my mouth to try and say something but couldn't really find the right words. A knock on the door grabbed my attention, and as I walked to open it, both my children disappeared upstairs.

Chapter 44

THE WOMAN STANDING outside my door was dressed in a long gorgeous gown that reached the ground. To her side, standing a little behind her, was a younger man, dressed in a Hugo Boss polo shirt and what looked like very expensive Cartier sunglasses.

"Kelly Stone?" I said. "What are you doing here?"

"This is where you live, isn't it?" she asked.

"Yes, it is, but…"

I stared at the man near her shoulder. "This is Noah. He's my fiancée."

"Nice to meet you," I said, still flabbergasted. It wasn't every day that a Hollywood movie star knocked on your door.

"Can we come in?" she asked with her heavy British accent. I couldn't stop staring at her. I had been thinking so much about her since I had seen her at her house that day. Especially every time I saw her face in the check-out line at Publix, where she was often on the covers of many of the magazines.

"Yes, yes of course," I said and stepped aside. They walked past me, and I closed the door. I picked up some shoes and toys and threw them all inside a cabinet and closed the door.

"I'm sorry for the mess."

Kelly Stone stopped in front of Alex's teddy bear that was lying on the Spanish tiles. She picked it up.

"How old are they?" she said and looked toward the stairs.

I swallowed, still holding one of Alex's firetrucks under my arm. "Alex is six, Christine twelve, and Olivia fourteen, no sorry fifteen; she just turned fifteen. It's hard to keep track, you know?"

Kelly Stone looked at me. She had taken off her sunglasses and held them in her hand.

"Is it? I wouldn't know."

Remembering that my sister was two years older than me, and that meant she was now forty-three, I realized it was probably too late for her to have children. It wasn't impossible, but it had to be something that she wondered about as well. Had she chosen career over family? There was so much I wanted to ask her but didn't dare to.

"Are they here?" she asked, still looking toward the stairs. "The children?"

"The two youngest are," I said. "Olivia has a volleyball game this afternoon, so she won't be home until later."

Kelly Stone smiled, then looked down at the teddy bear.

Just tell her, you fool. Tell her you know who she is and that you're her sister.

"Can I get you anything? Coffee?" I asked.

She looked at me and smiled again. "We won't stay long. We have to get to the airport. I'm shooting a new movie in Canada."

"Canada, huh? Sounds cold," I said. "How long will you be gone? You know, in case we need to get ahold of you for…you know…the event."

Our eyes met, and I felt such a warmth spread in my stomach. God, how I wanted to tell her the truth right there, but for some reason, I didn't. I guess I was scared of how she might react.

"I'll fly back in a couple of days," she said.

"Okay, okay, that's good. I bet you have your own plane and everything, huh? Not that it matters. You're busy and have to leave soon. What can I do for you? Is it about the event? Because my mom and I are working out the details as we speak, and we should have a program for you any day now."

"I know who you are."

I looked up, and our eyes met again. My stomach lurched.

"I…I'm sorry?"

"I know who you are and why you came to me."

I swallowed hard.

"I…I…"

"Why now? Why did you come to find me now?" she asked, still fiddling with the teddy bear between her hands. "After all these years, why now all of a sudden?"

My heart was racing in my chest, and I took in a deep breath to calm myself.

"I just recently learned about you, that you were still alive," I said, my voice quivering. "Up until then, I thought you were dead. My entire life, I thought you had been killed."

Kelly Stone looked at our mother's picture on the wall, then nodded toward it.

"What about her? Did she think I was dead too?"

I shrugged. "I don't know, to be honest. She never talked to me about it. We still don't talk much about any of it."

"You know, you were the reason I came here," she said. "To the Space Coast. I don't remember much about my childhood, but I did remember having a sister. My dad would never talk about any of you, so I had to figure it out on my own. But all I remembered was you on the beach, playing, and then watching rockets and shuttles being sent off into space. That's how I figured that you might be here, but I couldn't find you. I didn't know your name. My dad wouldn't help me, and we lost contact because of it. But now I do. Eva Rae Thomas."

"And you're Sydney Thomas," I said, tears welling up in my eyes. "That was your name back then."

Kelly Stone reached out her hand and stroked my cheek gently, a tear running down her cheek. I fought hard to hold mine back. My lips were quivering.

"I might have been that once, but I'm not her anymore," she said as something changed in her eyes. A hardness settled in them. She put the teddy bear down in the recliner before she faced me once more. "And seeing you again causes me too much pain. I can't do this anymore. I need you never to contact me again."

What?

My eyes grew wide. Startled, I stood back and stared at my sister as she turned around and rushed out of the house, clicking along on her high heels on the tiles, her boyfriend giving me an apologetic smile, then hurrying after her. I stood in the doorway as they got back into the limousine and drove off, feeling like someone had just ripped a part of my heart out.

Chapter 45

BOOMER WATCHED the screen on his computer. In the right corner, he saw Eva Rae's young son, Alex, as he ran through the living room, screaming loudly, arms above his head, wearing only pajama pants. Seconds later, he saw Eva Rae come into the picture, then yell something at the boy, trying to grab him, but he jumped away from her, laughing. Eva Rae Thomas then placed her hands on her hips and, seconds later, the boy stopped, and she grabbed him, then tickled him till he screamed for her to stop. Then they disappeared out of the camera's sight. A few minutes later, they reappeared in the left bottom corner of his screen as they entered the boy's bedroom, and she was finally able to get him to lay down. He was still only wearing pants when she put the covers over him, and they prayed together before she turned out the light. Boomer had been in her house while she was at the police station to set up the small cameras under the ceiling. They were wireless, smaller than a pea, and looked like a screw in the wall. He got them off eBay for only twenty dollars per camera. Easiest thing in the world. He had placed enough of them in her house to be able to follow her every move. He could use his phone if he didn't have his computer nearby.

Easiest thing in the world.

Boomer grabbed a beer from the fridge and opened it. He stood still and listened to see if he could hear the girls, but there was no sound coming from under the house. Either he had soundproofed it well, or they were both dead. Right now, he didn't care either way. He was so angry at them for trying to trick him that he wanted them to die. He only wished he could have shown them what he did to their little friend. Then they would learn never to try anything like that again; they'd know he wasn't someone you took for a fool. Boomer was no ordinary kidnapper or sexual predator. No, what he wanted was different and so much more devious than what any of those fools could come up with. But so far, he didn't feel like he had really been able to show the world what he was capable of. It was about time he turned up the heat a little.

It was time for the next act.

Boomer brought another beer with him back to the computer, so he didn't have to get up again anytime soon. He was in for a long night of watching his favorite show.

He sipped his beer and leaned back in the couch as he watched Eva Rae Thomas walk into her bedroom and start to get undressed. Boomer smiled to himself and put a hand on his crotch as she took off her bra and he got a really good look at her naked. His obsession with her had grown unhealthy; he knew it a little too well. He also knew he had to tread carefully, but it was hard for him not to give in to it. He wanted to possess her; he wanted her to know he was in charge of her, of her life. And he wanted to hurt her. Not in a traditional way or even a physical way. No, he wanted her heart to bleed so terribly she wouldn't want to live anymore. Even if it meant taking it out on someone she loved.

Only then would he be fully satisfied. Only then would he have achieved his goal.

Chapter 46

I WAS TOSSING and turning in my bed. There was a full moon outside, and it shone brightly behind my thin curtains, lighting up my room, making it even harder for me to get some much-needed shut-eye. I couldn't stop thinking about my sister and the strange meeting with her earlier in the afternoon. I couldn't shake the feeling that there was something I could have said or done to make her change her mind, to make her want to see me again. But it didn't matter how many clever things I came up with to say; it was too late. She had left, and she had told me she never wanted to see me again.

I just didn't quite understand why.

Was it because I had lied to her? Had I destroyed everything and ruined all my chances of getting my sister back? Was it because I had pretended to be doing that event and I hadn't been honest and told her who I was? Or was it something deeper?

Was I ever going to find out?

I turned to the other side, to face the door instead of the window, then closed my eyes again to try and fall asleep. The bed felt suddenly strangely uncomfortable, and I twisted back and forth a few times to try and get into a better position. I closed my eyes again and tried to empty my mind of worries. Yet, as soon as I had pushed my sister out of my head, in popped my children. Their sweet faces were staring up at me, their eyes big and sad, asking about their father.

I was getting sick of this and of him ruining everything. Why couldn't he just take the kids every other weekend or at least once or twice a month? It wasn't that much, was it? They missed him so much. How did he suddenly become so heartless? Why couldn't I talk to him at all?

I turned back to the other side, pushing the kids and Chad out of my mind, trying to think about something that made me happy, something joyful. Matt came to my mind immediately, and I opened my eyes, then placed a hand on the empty side of my bed, suddenly missing him terribly. He was at his own place and had spent the evening with Elijah. I wondered how they were holding up and if they were finally able to bond. It was tough trying to get to know your son after eight years and then finding out he blames you for the death of his mother. No, Matt didn't have it easy either.

As I stared at the moonlight coming in through my window, I thought about the case and those three girls who we still had no idea of their location. And then I thought about poor Molly and Cooper at the hospital. Cooper had suffered third-degree burns on two-thirds of his body and had to have skin transplants, Matt had told me earlier. He also said that he probably would lose his right leg. I felt awful for him.

I took a deep breath, then wrinkled my nose. All day, there had been this smell in the house, and I couldn't figure out where it was coming from. My mom had noticed it too, and the kids. I suspected it was the opossum in the attic that had bothered us for months. I had tried everything to chase it away, even had a professional guy out here to set up a trap, but somehow it was too cunning and avoided getting caught. Since then, I had given up, but it had gone silent a few weeks ago, and I figured that maybe it had died. I'd have to find out how to get up and into the attic to see if that was what it was.

Again, I turned around, then looked at my phone to see what time it was.

Three a.m. I only had a few hours before I needed to get up and get the kids to school.

Come sleep, come on.

Finally, I dozed off, and then my phone rang.

Chapter 47

THE NUMBER on my display was unknown, so I picked it up, thinking it could be important.

"Hello?"

Silence. I was about to hang up when I heard someone breathing on the other end.

"Hello? Is someone there?"

"Agent Eva Rae Thomas?"

The voice was deep. It didn't sound like anyone I knew. It sounded distorted like it was using one of those voice changing apps.

"Who is this? Identify yourself, please."

"I'm the one you've been looking for."

I shot up in the bed, eyes wide open. "What do you mean, *you're the one I've been looking for?*"

Silence followed before he answered.

It is a male voice, isn't it? It's hard to tell.

"You know what I mean."

I swallowed, my pulse quickening. If this was the guy who had kidnapped the girls, I had to play my cards right. I couldn't mess this up.

"Where are they?" I asked. "All I want is to bring them home to their families. They're scared, and I think you are too."

"I am not scared."

"Why are you doing this?"

"You'll see. You'll understand. Soon."

"What will it take to get the girls home safely. Money?" I asked.

"There isn't enough money in the world."

"Okay. But what do you need? There must be something you want. Otherwise, the girls would already be dead."

"Who says they aren't dead?" the voice said.

My heart sank. "Are they? Are they…dead?"

"As I said, you'll find out. Soon. Now, sleep tight; tomorrow, we'll know if you're a real princess."

The line went dead. I stared at my phone, my heart pounding in my chest. Had this just happened? Had he really called, or had I dreamt it?

No, he was real enough, and I was very much awake.

We need to trace this call.

I grabbed my phone again and turned the lights on to call Matt, the smell of the dead opossum filling my nostrils. I tried to shake it, then found his name in my address book when it hit me.

Tomorrow, we'll know if you're a real princess!

I stopped in my tracks, a strong unease spreading throughout my body. There was something off about that sentence.

Tomorrow, we'll know if you're a real princess.

Those had been his words. As a mother, I knew it was a line from the fairy tale, *The Princess and the Pea*. They were said by the old queen mother who put the pea underneath the princess's many mattresses because only a real princess would be able to feel it through all those mattresses and say she had slept terribly.

Why had the caller said that?

I smelled the air, uncomfortably, then got out of the bed and took a few steps away from it. My heart hammered in my chest as I found the courage to finally take a look. I grabbed the side of the mattress, then lifted it.

I took one glance at what was beneath it, then turned around and threw up on my brand-new carpet.

Chapter 48

THEN:

"Are you okay, Gary? You feeling okay?"

Peterson was speaking to Gary in his earpiece. They were staying far away, behind the row of trees, ready to jump out as soon as the kidnapper showed himself.

The drop-off area was a small park with picnic tables in the center of town. The kidnapper had called two days ago and told them exactly where to place the money. If any police showed up, Oliver was dead, he said. If they tried to trace his call, Oliver was dead. All they needed to do was to have Gary bring the money to the park, wrapped in a newspaper, and leave it there on the third picnic table. If the money was there, the child would be returned to them unharmed.

It was as easy as that.

"We'll get him, Gary; don't you worry," Peterson said like he had said so many times over the past seven days that Oliver had been missing. Every time he said it, Gary felt less and less convinced of the truth behind those words. He had hardly slept in almost seven nights, and he felt so exhausted. Iris was close to losing it, completely torn to pieces while they waited for the kidnapper to contact them. It tormented him to see her like this, but at the same time, a gap had grown between them. He felt like he should comfort her, but he didn't really want to. He hardly wanted to touch her anymore and could barely look at her.

"Okay, G, this is the spot. You place the money on the table, and then you leave. We'll take care of the rest."

Gary stopped at the third table, then looked down at the newspaper between his hands. He knew he was surrounded by FBI agents and that there would be no way for the kidnapper to escape from the park once he got there, but he wasn't so sure it was a clever move. Didn't he need to get back to Oliver in order to bring him back to them? If they took him down, would they ever find the child? Peterson believed so. There was no criminal that he hadn't been able to crack so far, he always said.

He knows what he's doing. You know he does.

Gary's partner, Agent Wilson, and several of his other colleagues were guarding his home and his wife. They had it all covered.

So why did it feel like they didn't? Why did it feel like everything was about to go wrong?

Gary shook the thought and focused on the task ahead. He took a glance around him, then sat down at the picnic table. Carefully, he placed the newspaper on the table, his fingers shaking when letting go of it.

"Okay, and now you go," Peterson said in his ear. "Just get up and walk away, leaving the package behind like you don't need it anymore."

Gary stood to his feet, abandoning the newspaper on the table like he was told. He looked around him and spotted a woman jogging by with her dog, panting rhythmically as she went. A man was sitting on a bench further down, reading a book. A younger man was drinking from his water bottle, sitting at another of the tables, looking at his cell phone. He glanced briefly at Gary, and their eyes met.

Is that him? Is that our guy?

The young man smiled, then looked back at his phone before he finished his water bottle, then rose to his feet and left, carrying his backpack over one shoulder.

Gary turned around to look in another direction. Two dogs were playing on the lawn. A mom walked with her kid by the hand, pushing a stroller with a sleeping baby. For a second, Gary thought he saw Oliver inside the stroller, but as the mom passed him, pulling her second kid along, he could see it wasn't his child.

"Gary. You need to leave now. Just walk away nice and slow like nothing happened. We'll keep an eye on the package. Come on, G. You gotta do your part."

"I'm walking away now," Gary said, his eyes letting go of the stroller. He turned around and let his eyes fall to the ground, focusing on his steps instead, trying to not look for suspects in the park. He took three steps toward the entrance when someone approached him, running up to him. Gary didn't see her till it was too late and she was standing right in front of him, high heels, short red skirt, and a jacket, holding out a microphone, a cameraman right behind her.

"Mr. Pierce. Have you placed the ransom? When do you expect to see your son again?"

Gary stared at the beautiful woman in front of him, then noticed more movement from behind her, more high heels, skirts, and more microphones. Before he could even protest, a crowd had gathered around him, questions being slung through the air from all sides.

Chapter 49

OLIVIA WAS the first to react. She stormed into my bedroom.

"What's wrong? Why are you screaming, Mom?"

"There's...don't come in here, baby."

She glanced at the vomit on the carpet, then at the bed. I could hear her whimper slightly.

"Call Matt, will you? Please? Use my phone. Tell him to come quickly. And keep the young ones out of here. I don't want them to see this."

Olivia stared at me, her eyes tormented. Then she nodded. "Okay."

I rushed to the bathroom and threw up again, then washed my face, taking in deep breaths to calm myself. A few seconds later, I heard Matt's steps on the stairs. I felt so relieved that he lived close to me. He had been my go-to guy ever since we were very young children and his house was the place I ran to when things got tough at home. His mom always had room for me and, even though we had been apart for twenty years, I had found that nothing had changed between us as soon as I moved back home. He was there for me, and always would be. I don't know why it had taken me so many years to realize he was the one for me, that he had been all along.

"What happened? What's going on?" Matt said as he stormed into my bedroom. "Olivia called?"

I turned to look at the bed. I had pulled the top mattress off, and

WHAT YOU DID

Matt spotted the body inside the cut-open box spring below. He clasped his mouth, and his startled eyes landed on me. I swallowed.

"Oh, no," he said. "Is it…?"

"I believe it's Ava Morales," I said. "But she's so badly beaten up, it's hard to tell."

"And she's…?"

"Dead? I'm afraid so. Rigor Mortis has set in, and you can see the blood has gathered on the bottom part of her body. She's been dead a while. There's something else."

"Yes?"

"He called. He called me and told me, not in so many words, but he told me something that led me to her. If he hadn't, I might have slept on top of her all night."

The thought made me gag again. Maybe it was the smell, but I was feeling sick in every bone of my body. I could hear Olivia talking with Alex in the hallway outside the door. He wanted to see Mommy, *now*, but she wouldn't let him.

"Not now, Alex," I heard her yell, and then Alex burst into tears. Matt met my eyes.

"Go. Go take care of them. I'll call this in, and then we'll have someone trace that call. You should have called right away."

I exhaled. "I was about to when I found…her." I glanced once again at the young girl lying inside my mattress and felt tears pile up in my eyes. Her face was bruised terribly, as was her naked body.

"MOMMY!"

I swallowed the knot in my throat, grabbed the door handle, and walked out into the hallway while hearing Matt call it in as I closed the door behind me so my children wouldn't see anything. I wanted to protect them as much as I could against this. They had seen enough.

In the hallway, I grabbed my son in my arms and lifted him up. He was crying uncontrollably as I held him tight.

"I'm scared, Mommy; I'm so scared," he said, sniffling and rubbing his eyes. "I heard you scream."

"I'm scared too, buddy," I said and looked at Christine who was hiding in her doorway. I grabbed her hand in mine and pulled her into a hug as well, cursing this bastard far away. Who the heck did he think he was? Scaring my family like this? It almost brought me to tears to think about, tears of frustration and anger. I was going to get him for this. No one messed with my family.

No one.

I took all my kids downstairs where my mom was waiting, wearing a robe over her nightgown, a deeply concerned look in her eyes.

"What's going on, Eva Rae?" she asked. "I heard screaming? Is Matt here? I saw his cruiser in the driveway."

My eyes filled as they locked with hers, and she could see it. She could tell it was bad. Alex squirmed and wanted to get down, so I put him on the tiles, and he ran into the living room where he found his favorite teddy bear that Sydney had placed in the recliner. Christine sat down on the couch and looked at her phone.

"There was another one," I said to my mom, trying to whisper so the kids wouldn't hear. I didn't know how much Alex and Christine knew about what I had found, what Olivia had told them. "Here in the house. I found her body inside my box spring under my mattress."

"Oh, dear Lord," my mom said and clasped her chest. "How? Why? I don't understand? Someone has been in here? Inside the house? Why is this person doing this, Eva Rae?"

"I understand as little as you do," I said, tearing up. It was the honest truth. Why was I being targeted like this?

Why me?

"The sheriff's crime scene unit will be here any minute. I don't know what to do with the kids. They're scared. They need rest."

My mom nodded, a serious look in her eyes. "They shouldn't be here. I have an idea. I'll take them all to a hotel downtown. Just let me grab my purse and get dressed."

Olivia packed a bag for each of them with clothes and stuff they couldn't live without, like Alex's teddy bear and at least one of his firetrucks and Christine's favorite pillow. Soon after, they left in my mom's car, and I watched them as they disappeared down the street. It was a relief to get them all out of the house.

I didn't feel like any of us were safe there anymore.

Chapter 50

A TENSE NIGHT FOLLOWED. The sheriff's crime scene unit arrived and parked their mobile lab in our driveway. They sent dogs out into the area and dusted for fingerprints all over my house. Matt sat with me in the living room while they combed through my house and yard, putting all the evidence in small bags as he took my statement for the report.

I went through it all with him, my afternoon with the kids and then the strange call in the middle of the night that led me to look under my mattress. When we were done, Matt then drove me to the hotel where I joined my family for the night, and the next day, I drove the kids to school. My mom asked if it wasn't better for them to stay home, but I felt like it was best for them to go. I wanted them to have as much normality as they could through this, and I sensed they felt relieved when I dropped them off. Tough as it was, I couldn't let this bastard destroy everything for us. I wasn't going to let him. He was in way too much control in all this so far, and I didn't like it one bit. This was also my way of showing him that he wasn't getting to me.

Afterward, I drove down to the station and rushed to my desk. Matt joined me about half an hour later when I was on my second coffee and had gone through the latest news from the lab.

When we realized we were alone, he leaned over and kissed me gently.

"That felt nice," I said.

He smiled and stroked my cheek, looking deeply into my eyes. "Are you okay?"

I exhaled. "Not really. I think I might need another one."

Matt chuckled and kissed me again; then Chief Annie approached us. Matt cleared his throat and went to his chair and sat down, blushing. Chief Annie chortled.

"It's not like it's a secret with you two."

She threw a file on Matt's desk, while Matt sent me a secretive smile.

"The forensics on the bomb are in. Apparently, it was a very simple pipe-bomb comprised of three devices, detonated with a timer, but only the main component exploded. The other two were found wired together in the back of the truck. The device was designed to be powerful enough that it could have caused serious injuries to a lot more people. The FBI's joint terrorism task force wants their fingers on it. I told them it's related to a murder case and that we already have one of their agents on it. So now, you better prove to be right. You catch this sick bastard before we have this entire town crawling with feds muddying the investigation."

I nodded, and Matt grabbed the file. "Thanks, Annie," I said. "I mean it. If they start screaming terrorism, then we will not be allowed anywhere near it. Then we'll never catch him."

"I put all my trust in you right now. Don't make me regret this, Eva Rae," she said and left.

I sure hope I won't.

Matt flipped through the file, then leaned back in his chair. "What are we looking at here? Who is this guy? Three teenage girls have been kidnapped; a fourth was strapped to a swing set, raped and blinded. A pipe bomb exploded and hurt a colleague, and now one of the girls has been found beaten to death. I don't get him. It makes no sense. I mean…think about it. He kidnaps three girls, he molests and rapes another, then he blows off a bomb before he beats another girl to death. There is absolutely no pattern. So, what is all this? Why is his MO changing constantly?"

I put down my coffee cup. I knew Matt was turning to me because of my background as an FBI profiler. I had years of experience with coming up with backgrounds, possible interests, and characterizations of suspects believed to be responsible in serial murders. I had written books on forensic psychology. But I had to admit, I was as dumbfounded as he was.

"I have to say I'm falling a little short here as well," I said. "Just when I think I have him figured out, he turns around and does something completely different. Up until now, I would have said with almost certainty that he was a white male, probably in his thirties, maybe forties, a loner, with military training as his background. But it doesn't fit with his profile of someone killing a young girl in affect, beating her to death. I just got off the phone with the medical examiner, Jamila, who told me they don't think he used a weapon to beat Ava Morales up; he did it with only his hands. They worked on her all morning because they knew we needed quick answers. But the thing is, someone capable of such a thing is an entirely different type of monster than one who sets up a bomb and blows it wanting to hurt a police officer. Is he targeting the police? Yes and no. Because he did place Molly in my backyard, and he did severely injure Cooper. But none of these girls that he has taken has anything to do with the police. Is he a sexual predator? Yes, in part since Molly was raped, but Ava wasn't. Is he a violent sadist who is turned on by torturing young, innocent girls? Yes, because he removed Molly's eyes with a scalpel."

"With a scalpel?" Matt asked, growing pale. He held hand up to his mouth, his eyes tormented.

I nodded. "Results from the ME's office were in this morning. I forgot to tell you," I said. "They're pretty sure the tool used to gauge her eyes out was a scalpel. The cuts were very professional, they said. We are possibly looking for someone with surgical experience, maybe even a surgeon, which is totally deviant from his profile so far…"

"Geez, that's awful."

"I know. It made me almost lose my morning coffee. The only comforting aspect is that they also believe she was sedated while he did it. They found large amounts of ketamine in her blood. With any luck, she didn't feel anything at all, maybe not even the rape," I said and exhaled, thinking about poor Melissa and Molly. Anger welled up inside me once again as I thought about this bastard. There was no telling what I might do to him once I got my hands on him.

"But my point is, he doesn't fit any profile."

"What do you mean?" Matt asked. "How can he not fit a profile? It makes no sense?"

I looked up at him, and our eyes met.

"He doesn't fit one profile," I said. "He fits them all."

Chapter 51

"IT DOESN'T LOOK good for you, Jordan."

Matt glared at the woman in front of us. She seemed to have become even smaller than the last time I saw her. Spending the night locked up could do that to you. She looked desperate and ready to chat.

Matt opened the file containing Ava Morales' case and pulled out the pictures of the girl that we had found under my mattress. Seeing them again made my stomach churn once more.

"Take a good look," he said. "We found her last night."

Jordan peeked at the pictures, at first seeming indifferent, but then as she realized who she was looking at, her face went pale.

"Ava Morales," I said. "The same girl we found pictures of in your house. The same girl you claimed you didn't know. Care to explain?"

"I didn't do that to her," she said, her eyes growing wider and wider. "I didn't. I swear."

I leaned forward. "Then, maybe you could tell us who did."

She shook her head. "How? How am I supposed to know?"

"Tell us how you got in contact with her," Matt said. "Did you write to her like you wrote to the others?"

Jordan looked at him, her nostrils flaring. "I wrote to her, yes. But only her, not the others."

"Okay. Let's start with that. So, you wrote to Ava; why?"

Jordan was scratching her arms. It was obviously a nervous reaction and something she had been doing all night. Her right arm was red and scratched up. She was ready to crack. This girl was hiding something, and I was going to get it out of her no matter how long we had to sit there till she broke down.

"She was pretty. I thought she could make some money. I told her she should consider having her pictures taken, but I was honest up front and said it cost money. I'm not a scammer like that. I gave her my number and then one day she called. She came to my studio, and we took her pictures, and that was it. She paid me, and I never saw her again."

"How much did she pay you for her pictures?" I asked.

"Two hundred bucks. I'm cheap. That's why so many girls come to me. I give them a good product for the money. Normally, they'd have to pay up to a thousand bucks, easily."

"And do they become models?" I asked. "After you've taken their pictures?"

She shrugged. "I don't know. That's not exactly my job here. I just take the pictures and give them a product they can send out to the agencies."

I flipped a few papers in Molly's file and found something.

"To Molly Carson, you said that you had contacts at agencies that she should meet with in Orlando. That was why she was supposed to spend the night at a hotel there with you."

"Can I see that?" Jordan asked.

I turned the paper so she could see the printout of the entire conversation from Amino. She shook her head.

"I never wrote that. I told you. The only one I contacted was Ava on Instagram. I only use Instagram. I never used that other site; what's its name?"

"Amino," I said. "It's a social media platform where you meet people who share the same interests as you, like arts and crafts, sports, anime, or even vegan food."

"Yeah, I don't even know that one. I'm telling you I didn't write any of that."

I exhaled, getting tired of this when there was a knock on the door to the interrogation room. Peter from the Sheriff's Forensic Computer Department peeked his head inside.

"Could I talk to one of you real quick?"

Chapter 52

THEN:

They waited for twenty-four hours, but the kidnapper never showed. The package with the fake ransom remained on the picnic table, but no one came to get it.

"It's the darn media," Peterson said back at the house. He lifted the curtain, and they could see their vans parked outside on the street.

They had kept quiet about the kidnapping so far, but somehow, the media had heard about the drop-off being made at the park, and now there was no stopping them.

"They scared him off."

"So, what do we do now?" Gary asked.

"We wait," Peterson said. "Hopefully, he'll call again with a new drop-off site."

"If he isn't so scared that he got rid of the kid," Gary mumbled.

"Don't say that," Iris said.

Gary peeked out behind the curtain and was blinded by the flashing lights.

"There he is. That's the father," someone yelled, and a photographer took pictures of him. One photographer ran into the yard but was stopped by Gary's partner and thrown back behind the fence.

"Get away from that window," Peterson said and pulled Gary by the shoulder. "You're giving them exactly what they want."

"I hate them," he said. "I freakin' hate those vultures!"

"I know; I know," Peterson said. "But they have every right to be there, unfortunately. We need to focus on getting Oliver back, okay? Now, I want you to get something to eat. You've barely had anything for days, and to be honest, you're looking like you could pass out. We can't have that. We need you to be at your best. Agent Wilson ordered pizza, and there's still a lot left in the kitchen. Go grab a piece, and then we'll talk, okay?"

Gary wasn't hungry at all, but he was feeling weak and feeble. He didn't like the sensation of being out of control. He walked to the kitchen and grabbed a piece of the pizza, then sunk his teeth into it. As he chewed through it, he realized Peterson was right. He did feel a lot better as soon as he got some food in his stomach. They had set up an office at his house, and a bunch of agents were working the case, chatting on phones, tapping on their computers. A couple of handwriting experts had come down from the FBI laboratory to examine the ransom note left in the carriage. They had given the special agents a course in handwriting analysis, and now they were going over specimens maintained by the DMV, the federal and state probation officers, prisons, and other municipalities, trying to figure out if this guy with this particular handwriting was in the system somewhere. It seemed like an impossible task.

Barely had Gary finished his piece and taken up a second one when his phone rang in the living room.

"Everyone, quiet now," Peterson said as Gary walked back inside and stared at the vibrating phone on the table.

"What do I do?"

"Pick it up," Peterson said.

He did, his hand shaking. "H-Hello?"

"The corner where Washington Boulevard meets Sycamore Street at one o'clock sharp. There's a trash can. Put the package in there. No police or your son dies. No journalists or your son dies."

"So…you still have him? Is he all right?" Gary asked.

"Just be there, and I'll tell you where to find your son."

Chapter 53

THE DARKNESS WAS WORSE than anything. Carina fought not to panic. Tara hadn't been awake at all while she had been sitting there, and every now and then, Carina would reach over a hand to touch her skin to make sure she still felt warm. Sometimes, she'd even reach for her neck and feel for a pulse, just to be sure. Now and then, Carina would crawl to Tara and curl up close to her just to feel a human being close to her, just to feel something. All this nothingness surrounding her made her anxious, especially since she had no idea how long it was going to last. The masked man hadn't been down there since he turned the light off, and Carina had no idea how much time had passed, nor did she know if she would live to see daylight again. There was no more water in the bucket and no more food. Carina felt her tongue stick to the roof of her mouth, and her lips were cracked. With no light and no one to talk to, there was nothing for Carina to do but to wait, wait for him to return or wait for death to come.

Carina drifted away, thinking once again about the night she had been crowned prom queen at the school. It had been her dream ever since she started middle school to one day be up there on the stage, with everyone in the school looking at her, admiring her.

Carina's mother had been prom queen at Cocoa Beach High back in the nineties, and she spoke about it often while Carina was growing up. Carina remembered playing with her mother's crown and sash in her bedroom as a child, when her mother didn't see it, dressing up in her high heels and putting them on, pretending to be crowned, holding pretend speeches and twirling in front of the mirror.

It hadn't exactly been in the cards for Carina to become prom queen. Growing up, she had been chubby…some would even call her fat. Her mom didn't know, but Carina saw the looks her mom would give her when getting her ready for her bath or when trying on new clothes and they almost never fit. Carina's mother was skinny and beautiful, whereas Carina was none of those things while growing up. Her mother kept telling her she would outgrow it, but as she hit middle school, she was still fat, and the more the other kids stared at her or teased her, the more she ate.

It wasn't until eighth grade when Tommy Cheatham asked her to the middle school dance that things changed. She was wearing a beautiful green dress that her mother had bought for her, sized XXL. When Tommy asked her to dance, she reluctantly accepted, but as he swung her around to the tunes from *Panic! at the Disco*, her dress ripped in the back, and she was suddenly standing in the middle of the dance floor, half naked. To this day, she still shivered when remembering that terrifying moment. She could recall everything. Every face, all the eyes staring at her, the pointing fingers, and sometimes she could even still hear them laughing.

It was at that moment that she decided enough was enough.

Carina started running the very next day, even if she only managed to walk in the beginning. She stopped eating completely for a few weeks, and after that, only ate vegetables and a little fruit and only meat once a week. It was a strict diet, and tough as heck, but it did the trick. A year after, she was suddenly a size medium, and the year after that, she could fit a size small. The eyes staring at her now weren't teasing or judging her; they were now admiring her. And she had kept it that way ever since. She had even kept the dress in her closet, and every now and then, she would take it out to remind her of how fat she had been back then, and that would keep her off the sweets.

Ironically, Carina could now feel the bones poking out on her shoulders and chest. She was skinnier than ever before, and it was threatening to kill her.

Carina closed her eyes and felt the hunger as it ate at her insides when she heard the familiar sound of the key being put in the metal door and the deadbolts being slid aside. Carina held her breath, listening, while anxiety rushed up inside of her. A moment later, the door was opened, and light flooded the room. It blinded her momentarily.

Once her vision returned, she saw first his boots, then his doctor's scrubs as he was slowly making his way toward her.

"Please," she said, as the stabbing light hurt her eyes. She searched his hands for food or fresh water, but his hands were empty, except for a key in one of them.

"You're coming with me," he said. "It's your lucky day."

The masked man leaned over and freed her shackles from the wall. The man pulled the chain on Carina's neck, and she struggled to her feet. Rising from the mattress was difficult; standing was even worse, and she had to lean on the wall next to her. He pulled the chain again, and Carina was forcefully pulled forward toward the door. She staggered out the door, then glanced back at the sleeping Tara, wondering if she would ever see her again, and then questioning which one of them was the lucky one.

Chapter 54

I RETURNED to the interrogation room. Jordan looked up as I walked to the table and threw a new file on the table. I had been talking to Peter from Computer Forensics for about fifteen minutes and, as I came back inside, both Matt and Jordan looked exhausted. My guess was they hadn't gotten anywhere while I was gone.

I had a pretty good hunch why.

"They're done combing through your house," I said and sat down. "They didn't find any evidence that suggested that any of the other girls have been there."

"I told you," Jordan said.

"But they did find something else," I said. "On your computer."

I opened the file that Peter had given me while Jordan went pale. I pulled out some photographs that Peter had printed out for me and placed them in front of Jordan.

"I think it is reasonable to say that these pictures are fairly different than the other ones we found at your place," I said. "What kind of agencies do you expect your clients to send these pictures to?"

Jordan stared at the naked girls but didn't say a word.

"So, here's how I think it played out. Feel free to correct me afterward if I'm wrong," I said. "You contacted these girls on Instagram, and don't tell me you didn't 'cause we found a lot of history of you doing this on your profile once we dug into it. We found hundreds of girls that you have been contacting, telling them they were gorgeous and that they should consider becoming models. A lot of them bit into it and contacted you, and then you set up a photo shoot at your house, giving them a fair price for a set of photographs, making it a lot cheaper than any other photographers around. Nothing wrong with that. The girls came to you and paid you to do a service. That's not illegal. But these pictures are." I placed a finger on one of the naked girls who shyly looked back at us. "These girls are underage, Jordan. And they trusted you. They came to you with their dreams and money, and they thought you were okay because you were a woman. And you exploited that fact to make them go further than they were comfortable. You told them to take off one piece of clothing then another till they were finally completely naked. And then you took a series of photographs of them completely naked while they thought it was okay because a woman wouldn't touch them and you said it was just for them to feel more comfortable in front of a camera, that it would help them loosen up, that no one would ever see these photos. But then you—and this is the part where it gets a little ugly—then you sold them to pornographic sites online. You sold these pictures to nasty pedophiles out there who would pay a lot of money to see young underage girls naked. Now, please tell me if I'm wrong because I have to say, I really want to be."

Jordan stared at the pictures, her hand shaking. Not a word left her mouth till she finally looked up and said, "I'd like to speak to my lawyer now."

I nodded and closed the files. "You're gonna need one. This is not looking good for you."

Matt held the door for me, and we walked back into the hallway where Chief Annie was waiting. I had asked her to listen in on the conversation from the observation room overlooking the interrogation room. She smiled and nodded.

"Good job, Detectives," she said. "I'll have Jamieson take her from here. You need to focus on your own case."

"So, just to get this straight," Matt said, "she had nothing to do with what happened to Ava Morales or any of the other girls?"

I shook my head. "Nope."

"But she sent those messages to Molly?"

"It wasn't her. Peter from Computer Forensics told me her account was hacked a few weeks ago. The messages weren't sent from her IP address and, when he tried to track them, the trail ended somewhere in Africa."

"So, we're looking for a skilled hacker and not a surgeon?"

"Possibly," I said. "Maybe he's both. One thing is certain; he's someone who knows a lot about how law enforcement works."

"The drawing is done," Chief Annie said and approached me holding out a hand-drawn picture. "This is what the man who delivered the package looked like, according to Jane Martin. This is your guy."

I stared at the picture of the man with the goatee in front of me, looking into his eyes. I couldn't escape the feeling that there was something familiar about him; I just didn't know what.

Chapter 55

WHEN HE ARRIVED at the hospital, Boomer looked at his face in the rearview mirror of the car. He touched the fake goatee and made sure it was on straight and wouldn't fall off. He had sedated the girl and put her in the back seat, where she looked like she was sleeping underneath the blanket. His truck was big and the windows dark, so no one would be able to accidentally peek inside while he was gone and wonder about her. He had given her a dose of Ketamine. She was so skinny now that she didn't need much to knock her out cold.

Boomer smiled at his own reflection, then grabbed his ID badge and got out of the car. He approached the back entrance and let himself in, then walked to the elevator and pushed the button. A couple of nurses greeted him as they passed him with a nod before continuing down the hallway. Boomer smiled and greeted them back and, when the elevator arrived, he got inside.

A doctor was in the elevator already, and he nodded in greeting.

"In for the night shift today?" he asked.

Boomer nodded. "Yeah, it's gonna be a long one all right. And you?"

"Just coming off my shift in fifteen minutes. Then home to spend the night with the wifey. The kids are with their grandmother, so we'll finally get some time alone. It's been awhile."

"That's what this job will do to you," Boomer said.

"I guess we knew what we got ourselves into when we signed up."

"I guess so."

The elevator dinged, and Boomer smiled. "This is my stop."

"See you around," the doctor said as the doors closed.

A nurse smiled at Boomer as he passed her, and he turned right and entered a room with the sign *Acute Renal Dialysis*. Seven patients with acute kidney failure were sitting in there, dialysis lines inserted into their veins. Some were reading, others napping.

"Hello there," he said, smiling from ear to ear. "And how are we feeling today?"

Chapter 56

CARINA'S HEAD WAS POUNDING. She blinked her eyes to be able to see better, but the light was blinding.

Where am I?

She was shaking, her hands unable to remain still, her legs shivering, yet she wasn't cold.

What happened?

She felt confused, disoriented. She tried hard to remember but couldn't. The last thing she did recall was the door opening to the room and the masked man's eyes as he looked at her over the surgical mask.

Light hit her face, and she realized it wasn't from a lamp. It was real sunlight coming from outside. Carina blinked a few times, trying to get her eyes to cooperate, then sat up and stared out the window.

What the…am I…in a parking lot?

Expecting to see the masked man somewhere, she turned around with a gasp as she heard footsteps outside the car, but it wasn't him. It was an elderly couple getting into the car next to the one she was in.

Carina breathed. She looked around and spotted a canned soda by the front seat. It was open and someone – probably the masked man – had already been drinking from it, but it didn't matter. Right now was all about survival. Carina reached between the seats and grabbed the can, then downed the entire Fanta. Never had anything tasted better.

She finished the can and waited for even the last few drops to get the most out of it, then tossed it onto the passenger seat. She looked at herself under the blanket, then realized she was naked. Covering herself up with the blanket, she grabbed the door handle and opened it, then slid out into the parking lot on her bare feet, the black asphalt burning the bottom of her soles. Holding her breath, constantly checking around her, Carina tiptoed across the parking lot, fear rushing through her veins when a voice spoke from behind her.

The sound of it made her shiver in terror.

"Where do you think you're going?"

Chapter 57

"ANY NEWS?"

I looked up from my computer screen. I could barely see Matt behind all the files and paperwork. I was tired and had run out of coffee. We had been going back to the beginning, looking through all the files on the three missing girls, then going through Molly's case files to see if there was anything that stood out, any detail we had missed that might be important. Earlier, we had also been to the hospital and talked to the Medical Director there, asking him questions about the procedure of removing eyes and how skilled a doctor should be to perform such a task. He had basically told us any type of surgeon could perform an enucleation, as it was called, to remove a damaged or diseased eyeball. It was a very common procedure that wasn't very difficult to perform. So that didn't get us any closer to finding our guy. There were hundreds of surgeons in Brevard County, and we didn't have time to visit them all. I had generated a list of the three surgeons living in Cocoa Beach and sent a couple of detectives to check them out. I instructed them to ask them about their whereabouts on the night when the girls disappeared and the night when Molly was taken, and also when Ava reappeared. I had also given them a copy of Jane Martin's drawing to take with them.

Now, I stared at the drawing of our guy on the whiteboard behind Matt, wondering who the heck he was and what his deal was.

"I can't help thinking," I said while Matt fetched me another cup of coffee. I stared at the girls and then at Molly and thought about the way she was found and Ava the way she was found.

Matt sipped his coffee. "Yes? Eva Rae?"

"What?"

"You drifted off just then," he continued. "Where did you go?"

I blinked and sipped my coffee. "I'm sorry. There's just something I can't let go. Remember how I told you that I once worked a case on a guy who removed the eyes of his victims? And how I couldn't believe he was back because he was dead?"

"Yeah, the guy who poked out the eyes of his victims before he raped them, so they wouldn't be able to recognize him in a line-up? I remember that. What about it?"

I stood to my feet and stared at Ava Morales. "There's something else."

I paused while a million thoughts rushed through my mind at once.

"Yes, Eva Rae? Eva Rae?"

My eyes were flickering across the board now, as my mind wouldn't keep still. Pictures of my old case and the victims with their missing eyes ran like an inner movie in my mind.

We'll see tomorrow if you're a real princess.

When the dime finally dropped, I turned to look at Matt, fear struck in my eyes.

"What's going on, Eva Rae? Are you okay? You look like you're about to get sick."

I grabbed my phone, badge, and jacket, then looked at Matt.

"We need to go. Right now."

"Where are we going?" Matt asked. "Could I get a hint, at least?"

But I was already out the door, running toward the cruisers parked in the back.

Chapter 58

HE HAD FELT tired for quite some time but kept thinking it was just his busy schedule and social life. At the age of twenty-nine, Brad Williams was at the prime of his life, and his business selling solar panels was booming. But then came the headaches, migraines so deep and invading they completely destroyed his life, making it impossible for him to be out of bed for more than a few hours at a time. But even then, Brad believed it was just a phase and that it would pass soon.

"Allergies," his mom told him over lunch at Grills Riverside one day. "It's been a terrible season for allergies. It used to knock you out constantly when you were younger too."

So, Brad took a Claritin and went about his life, thinking it would all get better once this allergy season was over. As he realized the allergy pill didn't work, Brad went to his GP to ask for steroid injections like his neighbor had gotten, and *puff*, gone were his allergies. Just like that. It was no biggie, just one shot, and it would all be over.

At the GP office, after Brad was weighed, they took his blood pressure. Brad was joking and flirting with the nurse, ignoring the pounding headache and the itching skin that he had gotten used to. After all, they were nothing but allergy symptoms, and he wasn't going to let those stop him from enjoying his life.

As the nurse took his blood pressure, she went pale, and the flirting stopped abruptly.

"I need to get the doctor in here," she said and, seconds later,

Brad's GP entered, a serious look on her face. She took his blood pressure once more, then looked at him.

"This is not good, Brad. We need you to get you to the hospital right away. I am going to call an ambulance."

And so, she left, leaving Brad back in the room, scared senseless.

Now, as he sat in his wheelchair and a nurse hooked him up for his acute dialysis, he still remembered how it felt, the panic settling in when you see your own doctor get worried and then being rushed away on a stretcher, not knowing what is happening.

At the hospital, they took tests, and his potassium levels were so high he was about to have a heart attack, they said. He came in at the right time. A few hours more like that and it would have been too late.

His kidneys had failed completely, *Acute Renal Kidney Failure*, they called it, and he needed acute dialysis. He would have to prepare himself for living a life on dialysis.

Brad wasn't prepared for that at all. As he sat in his wheelchair, he wondered about how his life had been so normal and so on track just a few days ago, and now he was here, everything changed forever.

"Are you comfortable?" the nurse asked.

Brad stared at her. Comfortable? Comfortable? How could he be comfortable when his life was never going to be the same again?

Some annoyingly cheerful doctor entered and asked them how they were all doing today. Two other patients smiled and said they were just glad to be alive. Brad stared at them, feeling all kinds of anger and resentment. How could they sit there and be so happy to be alive? What kind of life was this anyway? Spending hours attached to a dialysis line three times a week?

It was only the second time Brad was in dialysis, and he had been told it would take some getting used to. So far, Brad had found it to be painful, and he dreaded the treatment. As the liquid ran into his veins and through his body, Brad leaned his head backward and dreamt of the ocean, of running on the beach as a child, feeling the freedom. He took a deep breath and was almost certain he could smell it. It brought him such calm.

About half an hour into the treatment, Brad suddenly opened his eyes with a gasp. A wave of agonizing pain shot forcefully through his chest and, seconds later, he went into cardiac arrest.

Chapter 59

CARINA'S HEART was pounding so loud she could barely hear the sound of the feet running behind her. She was crossing the parking lot, the man right behind her. A couple drove past her and stared at her through their window.

"Help!" she screamed, but they didn't do anything.

Why don't they help me? Why don't they react? Why are they only staring at me?

Carina took a left turn and ran toward the hospital in front of her, forcing her skinny legs to carry her as fast as possible while scanning the area for anyone who could help her. Why couldn't there be a cop? Don't they usually hang out around hospitals? Why couldn't there be an ambulance or just someone for that matter, anyone who wasn't too scared to help? Someone who wouldn't just stay inside of their car, paralyzed in fear?

"You come back here," the man yelled behind her. "I'm gonna kill you when I get my hands on you."

Carina saw the entrance to the ER and managed to speed up, hope fueling the adrenalin pumping in her veins, providing her with the strength she needed right now to outrun this guy.

Please, don't let him get to me, God, please. I'm so close now. Just a few yards more. Just a few.

"Oh, no, you don't," the man yelled as he realized what her plan was. He sped up, and soon Carina sensed that he was right behind her, reaching out his hand to grab her.

Just a few feet, please.

Carina felt his fingers grasping for her hair and shrieked in fear.

I am not giving up. I refuse to give up.

The fingers grabbed her hair and pulled, but then her perpetrator suddenly screamed out in pain, and the hand in her hair disappeared. Carina didn't stop to look what had happened but continued toward the hospital's ER entrance.

Just as she was about to enter, she turned briefly to look anyway, like Lot's wife. And just like the woman she heard about in Bible camp, she was frozen in place. Not turning to a pillar of salt, and not paralyzed, but still, she stood there looking at the man who was screaming in pain as he lifted his foot, blood gushing from the wound where a metal spike had cut through his shoe and into his foot.

Carina now realized she had won, and she sent him a victorious smile, then walked toward the sliding doors.

But to her surprise, they didn't open.

An alarm sounded from the inside, and Carina tried the doors again, but they didn't budge. Desperate, she glanced at the man again and didn't see the gun in his hand till it was too late and the shot was fired.

Chapter 60

"ACUTE DIALYSIS?" I asked the woman at the front desk, showing her my badge.

I had parked the police cruiser outside of the front entrance of the hospital after running it through town with blaring lights and blasting sirens. I hadn't had time to explain to Matt in detail what my suspicion was since I was too focused on my driving, but I had told him what he needed to know, and most importantly that I feared many people might die if we didn't make it in time.

Matt had called it in, and officers from all surrounding areas had arrived to help. I had also tried to call the hospital to get them to stop the dialysis treatment, but they told me it was too late. Four out of seven patients had gone into cardiac arrest just a few minutes ago and were being treated elsewhere in the hospital.

"I need all the entrances blocked," I had told them. "No one leaves the building."

Chief Annie came up behind us, her eyes worried.

"I have men on all the exits. You think he's still in the building?" she asked.

"There's a chance he might still be here," I said.

Matt and I took the elevator up to the third floor, then rushed out. A nurse met us, her eyes bewildered.

"I don't know what happened," she said, crying. "I set them up as usual; nothing was different."

"Was anyone in here?" I asked, looking around the room where the patients had been. "Did anyone touch the dialysis lines?"

"No one who wasn't supposed to."

"But maybe someone who wouldn't cause suspicion. Like a surgeon or a doctor?"

She shook her head. "Only Clark."

My eyes grew wide, and my heart dropped. "Clark?"

She nodded. "Yes, he was here briefly, helping out. He's new around here, so I didn't really know him till he told me today."

"What was his name more than Clark?"

"I don't remember. I didn't get a good look at his ID badge. His last name was something with a T."

"Was he alone with the patients?" I asked. "Did you leave at any point?"

She shrugged. "I went out to get some more magazines for them. Some patients like to read while they wait for the treatment to be over. It's a long time that they sit there. There isn't much to do."

I turned around and scanned the area, then spotted the jug leaned up against the wall in the back, a syringe next to it. I literally felt the blood as it left my face.

"What's going on?" Matt asked.

I hurried to the jug and knelt next to it.

"Bleach?" Matt said. "Care to explain?"

"He injected it into the dialysis lines. That's what caused them to go into cardiac arrest."

"He did what?" he said. "But why?"

"Because he knew I would find out. He even left the jug of bleach like she did."

Matt gave me a look. "Like who did? I think this is the time when you fill me in."

"Back in two thousand and eight, there were nineteen deaths at a dialysis clinic in Texas in just four months. Most of them suffered cardiac arrest while still in dialysis. Two witnesses told the police they had seen a nurse inject bleach into the lines of those patients and an investigation was started, running across several state lines. This nurse had worked many places in the country over the previous ten years, and at all of them, there had been a spike in deaths while she was there."

"I think I heard about that," he said. "The killer nurse. She was sentenced to life with no parole; wasn't she?"

"She was only convicted of five deaths and five serious injuries, but we believed she had killed many more than that. I had at least ten cases that we just didn't have evidence enough to run with."

"So, the case was yours?" he asked.

"Yes, and the woman's name was Nancy Clark."

Matt stared at me. "Clark?"

"A fake name, I assume, but it's a message, as is all this. Our killer is trying to tell me something."

"How do you figure?" he asked.

"Well, there is the old case of the guy removing the girls' eyes, like Molly."

"Yes. We established that."

"And then Ave Morales was found in my mattress, beaten to death."

"Yes," he said. "And?"

"There was another case I worked on back early in my career. A woman had been attacked in her own home by someone ringing her doorbell, pretending to be from the local water company, there to check on her faucets. She let him in, and he attacked her, wanting probably to rape her, but she was strong. She knocked him out with a meat pounder. To her surprise, he was dead when she went to check on him. This woman panicked, thinking she was going to jail and hid the body inside of her mattress so her husband wouldn't find him. I know, it's crazy, but reality out there is often a lot crazier than you think. Anyway, the smell naturally stunk the house up, and she was discovered. But the point is that the finding of Ava Morales felt very familiar to me; it was also like a case I once worked. My first case was the kidnapping of three girls in Cleveland. You see a pattern yet?"

"I see what you're saying. The three girls, Molly, Ava Morales, the dialysis patients. This guy is making you relive all your old cases?" Matt asked. "He reenacts them."

I nodded. "And not only that. He's also using my theories. It's all from my book, the first one I wrote. This guy is toying with me and my knowledge of serial killers. He's following my theories and years of study leading to my book where I was examining the association among four serial killer typologies: lust, anger, power, and financial gain. Molly was raped; that's the first one. Ava Morales was beaten to death in anger; that's the second. And the third one is this here, the patients succumbing to a man with high authority and who holds the power of life and death, as doctors do. He is speaking to me through his choice of victims and how they're killed. Now, we haven't seen financial gain, but that would be his next move."

"So, you're saying that this guy read your book, and he's using it to send you a message?" Matt asked.

"Not only did he read the book. He knows me very, very well."

Chapter 61

THEN:

"I'm terrified. What if he doesn't show?"

Gary stared at his boss. Peterson was holding the package with the fake money inside the newspaper. This was their fourth try at handing the kidnapper the money. He hadn't shown up at any of the drop-off points so far. Every time, he had called afterward and given them new instructions. Gary and Iris's home had been turned into a war room, and they had a handful of agents constantly sitting in their living room. Some were sleeping on the couch, others tapping away on their computers, talking loudly on phones, eating their food in the kitchen, and drinking their coffee. All while trying to find the guy who had taken their son.

Meanwhile, Gary and Iris were barely sleeping or eating. Their son had been gone for fifteen days now, and they had no idea if they would ever see him again. Peterson kept reassuring them that they would, that all this guy wanted was the money, but Gary couldn't—for the life of him—figure out why it had to take so long. Why didn't the guy just show up and take the money so they could get this over with? All he wanted was for life to return to normal, or at least as close to normal as humanly possible. He wanted to spend Saturday mornings with the baby on his stomach, trying to give Iris some much-needed rest from being up all night breastfeeding. He wanted to be tired because he had been woken up by the baby's sounds and crying all night. He wanted to be annoyed because he was falling apart from having to take care of a family and a demanding job at the same time. He wanted all those things back. He didn't want to be exhausted because he didn't know where his child was. This was supposed to be the happiest time of his life. This was supposed to be the time that people told you to cherish because it would never come back.

It wasn't supposed to be like this.

"He will," Peterson said. "He needs money. That's why he took Oliver in the first place."

"But he didn't show up those other times."

"He's scared. He sees the press or even suspects that there might be police or reporters there, and he wets himself. You know these types."

Peterson was still insisting on this guy being some addict who accidentally passed on the street and saw an opportunity when Iris went in for her bag and left the baby alone. But Gary wasn't so sure anymore. Something told him that this guy was smarter than they gave him credit for. But what he couldn't quite figure out was why he had chosen to take the child of an FBI agent, if he was so bright.

"You've got this," Peterson said and put his hand on Gary's shoulder when someone entered the room.

"Peterson, you need to take a look at this."

"Give me a sec," he said to Gary. "I'll be right back. You just keep practicing how to hold your son 'cause you will in a very short while; you hear me?"

Gary exhaled tiredly as Peterson left. He sat down in his recliner and studied a picture of his son on his phone, trying hard to remember what he smelled like. He had loved that smell more than anything in the world.

Soon, Peterson came back in and closed the door, a serious look on his face.

"We have an ID on our guy. It was the handwriting that helped us. The handwriting on the ransom note is very similar to that of a guy in a probation file."

Peterson's eyes lit up as he looked at Gary.

"We've got him."

Chapter 62

"WE'VE SEARCHED the entire area. No sign of our guy."

Chief Annie gave me a disappointed look that mirrored exactly how I felt. I had a feeling he wouldn't be there, that he would have taken off from the hospital grounds, but a girl is allowed to hope, right? I desperately wanted us to find him and get this over with. But of course, it wasn't going to be that easy.

"We should keep the hospital on lockdown for a little while longer, just in case he's hiding somewhere in the building," I said.

"How about surveillance cameras?" Matt asked.

"I have a couple of officers going through them in the basement," Annie said. "But there is something else that you need to take a look at. A nurse came to me and said they had taken in a girl at the ER. She claims to be one of the three that were kidnapped. It might just be a hoax since it has been all over the news, and you know how weird people get, but could you check it out?"

"Sure."

Matt and I took the elevator down to the first floor that held the ER ward and then found the front desk.

"Detectives Thomas and Miller here to see about a girl who claims to have been kidnapped?"

"One minute," the woman said and grabbed the phone. She spoke in it for a few seconds and then looked at us.

"The nurse who spoke to her will be right out."

WHAT YOU DID

A few minutes later, a small woman in scrubs came out to us. She looked terrified.

"What can you tell us about the girl, ma'am?" I asked.

"She was outside when the alarm went off. The doors were locked, and the alarm was blasting so loud that I think I was the only one who heard it."

"Heard what?"

"The shot being fired. I'm pretty sure she was shot right out there on our front step. I didn't see her till it was too late, but I heard the shot. I talked to my colleagues, and they say they didn't hear anything, but I went there to look, and then I saw her. She was in a pool of blood. I know I'm not supposed to since we were on lockdown, but I opened the sliding doors and rushed to her. I dragged her inside and locked the doors once again. I know I'm not supposed to do that, but I could hardly leave a poor girl out there bleeding to death."

"Did you see anything?" I asked. "Anyone run away from the scene?"

She shook her head. "I focused on the girl and getting her inside. Then I called for assistance, and they came with the stretcher. Right before she was rushed down the hallway, she told me to call the police and said that she was one of the kidnapped girls."

"Where is she now?" I asked. "Can we talk to her?"

"She's in surgery. She was shot in the stomach. She'll be lucky if she survives."

"Did she tell you her name?" I asked.

"Carina I believe she said her name was. Carina Martin, yes, that was it."

Chapter 63

"ANYTHING ON THE SURVEILLANCE CAMERAS?"

I walked up behind the two colleagues sitting by the computers in the security room of the hospital. The hospital's own guard was helping them. Chief Annie was sitting with them. She nodded.

"We found the girl," she said and pointed at the screen. "There she is running toward the back ramp behind the ER where the ambulances usually come in. You can see she is running up the ramp and there is someone behind her. There, can you stop it, please?"

The officer clicked the mouse, and the footage stopped. I stared at the screen, getting really close, but it was so grainy and murky I couldn't make out a face.

We can get video of the birth of a star in outer space, but see if we can make a decent surveillance photo that isn't grainy? It makes no sense.

"Is this the best you've got?" I asked.

Chief Annie ran a hand through her bangs. It was hot in the security room with all the electronic gear, and the AC seemed to have trouble keeping up. "He does come a little closer if we run it for a frame or two more."

The officer did, and the man moved closer, but still not much. Now the girl was trying to get inside, walking up to the sliding doors. But they didn't open. My heart dropped as I saw this. Next thing, the girl turned to look at the man again, and that was when the shot was fired, and the girl fell to the ground, rag-doll limp.

"Geez," I said and turned away, clasping my mouth. "She tried to get in but couldn't. Because of the lockdown."

I lifted my glance and met Matt's eyes. He pulled me into a hug. "You can't beat yourself up over this."

"Why not?" I said. "I ordered the lockdown, didn't I?"

"Thinking you were protecting more people from getting hurt by stopping a killer. Don't be so hard on yourself."

"It's all my fault," I said, pressing back tears. "All of it. Don't you see? He's doing this to get back at me. He's hurting all these people to get to me."

"Because he knows you're the type of person who would give her life if it meant saving someone else," Matt said and looked into my eyes. He touched my cheek gently. "He knows this will hurt you terribly. But you can't let him win, Eva Rae. It can never be your fault that he's a sick bastard. Just like it can't be your fault that someone gets cancer and dies."

I sent him a smile, knowing he was talking from personal experience. Matt's dad had died from cancer when we were teenagers. It had taken him years to realize there was nothing he could have done to change it. He kept telling me he knew his dad wasn't well, that he knew it was too long before he even went to the doctor and that if only he had encouraged him to see a doctor sooner, then maybe they would have caught it and maybe his chances would have been better.

"Why didn't people react?" Chief Annie asked, staring at the screen. "A naked girl wrapped in a blanket runs across the parking lot, chased by a man. It's a pretty well-trafficked parking lot. Someone ought to have seen them. Why didn't anyone call for help or run inside to get the guard?"

Matt let go of me, and I approached the screen. "For the same reason that no one reacted when he walked into the dialysis room and injected the lines with bleach. He's wearing a scrubs and a doctor's coat. He looks like he is the one who belongs here. It's the power of the role he is playing. But you are onto something," I said. "There have to have been witnesses. Someone must have seen him. Maybe we could find them. We also need to have a list of newly hired doctors, especially surgeons at this hospital."

There was a knock on the door, and an officer entered. He spoke quietly with Chief Annie for a few minutes, then left. Annie approached us.

"I have news," she said. "They believe he came in through the back entrance, the one that the employees use, and on the list of people that have entered through there today is a name that we know."

"Who?" Matt asked.

"Charles Turner."

"Mr. Turner? Leanne's dad?" I asked. "But he's not a doctor? I checked everyone in the families of the kids involved, including Leanne's family. No one had a doctor's degree."

Chief Annie shook her head and put both hands on her hips. "Nope, but he does work here as a Registered Nurse. And according to this, he entered the hospital today at ten forty-five a.m. using his ID card."

"Well, I'll be…Let's bring him in," I said addressed to Matt. He nodded in agreement.

"How are the patients?" I asked Annie as we were about to leave, and she walked with us toward the exit.

"One has died," she said. "A Brad Williams, age twenty-nine. The three others, they were able to revive. Two more have fallen ill, but not gone into cardiac arrest."

"And Cooper? How's he holding up?"

"He's hanging in there," she said. "He had the skin transplant, so now we're just waiting. It's gonna take some time. He's also looking at having his leg amputated from the knee down. I don't know when."

I swallowed the guilt and anger that were rising up in me, seeing the trail of death and destruction this guy was leaving behind, all because of me. What I just couldn't figure out yet was the reason why.

I hoped Charles Turner would be able to give me some clarification on that.

Chapter 64

CHARLES TURNER WAS in the back, working on his boat when we pulled up. Besides Matt and I, we had brought two other patrol cars just in case this situation escalated. We walked around the house and approached him, hands on our weapons. He was sitting in his boat on the canal and looked up as he spotted us.

"Mr. Turner?" I said.

It is often stated that cops have instincts, that we somehow know that people are up to no good or that something is off when we enter a situation. This was one of those times. I can't explain what it was; it might have been in his eyes, but I just knew this guy would make a run for it.

And I was right.

Charles Turner gave us one quick glance, then made his decision. His eyes scanned the area for possible ways out, and then fired the engine up and took off.

"Darn it," Matt said and pulled his weapon.

As Charles roared down the canal, he pointed it at him. "Get back here, Mr. Turner," he yelled. "Or I'll have to shoot."

But Charles Turner didn't. He was already long gone, exiting the canal and driving the boat into the intracoastal waters.

"He's getting away!" I yelled. The two other officers we had brought with us came running down to the canal.

"I can barely see him anymore. We need boats in the water," Matt said. "And choppers in the air."

"I'll call it in," one of the officers said.

"Is he armed?" the other asked.

I shook my head. "We didn't see any weapons."

"He could have a gun on the boat," Matt said.

My heart pounding, I looked toward the area where Charles Turner had disappeared. I then laid eyes on the neighbor's boat that was docked there, then looked back at Matt.

"That one has two three-fifty outboard engines. That's a lot more horsepower than his. We could catch up to him easily," I said.

Matt knew where I was going and nodded. We ran into the neighboring yard and got the boat lowered into the water, then jumped in. Like most people in Cocoa Beach, this boat owner had left the key in the boat, in a small compartment next to the steering wheel. I grabbed it and dangled it in front of Matt.

"Nothing really changes around here, does it?" he said with an exhale. "We've told people at town hall meetings so many times to never leave their boat keys and car keys in their vehicles if they don't want them stolen. Yet, they still do."

I put the key in the ignition, and the engines roared to life. As I drove the boat out of the canal, and as soon as we were out of the manatee zone, where we could accelerate to top speed, I said:

"I, for one, am thrilled that nothing changes around here. Now, let's get this bastard before he leaves the county."

Chapter 65

THEN:

The most important part was to make sure that Oliver's life wasn't endangered when they raided the house. Peterson had made sure to determine where all the suspect's family members lived, and they were going to hit all of the houses simultaneously. On October 22nd, six weeks after Oliver had disappeared from his home, teams of fifty-five FBI agents and detectives took up positions outside Diego Sánchez's home in Brentwood, one of the tough neighborhoods in the D.C. area. Sánchez was on probation for drug possession and was known by the police as part of one of the well-known Mexican gangs in Washington.

They struck the moment Sánchez came home with his wife, driving into the street and up their driveway, with their two children in the back seat. They had been visiting his parents on the outskirts of town. A patrol car had followed them as they drove home, and Gary watched with his heart in his throat as they parked in the driveway.

"The package is in. Let's rock and roll," Peterson said on the radio. He gave Gary one short glance of reassurance, then left the car.

They had agreed that Gary would stay behind since he was too emotionally wrapped up in this and they couldn't risk him ruining the mission, which was to get the kidnapper and bring back his son safely. One wrong move or emotional decision could put his child's life in danger. This man was dangerous, and there was no saying what he might do under pressure.

Gary held his breath as he watched the team approach from all sides, guns ready. A big part of him regretted having listened to Peterson. He really wanted to be one of them—to be the one to press that gun to the kidnapper's head and ask Sánchez where the child was. Sitting out there all alone in the car made him feel so helpless, so frustrated. Yet he knew Peterson was right. He would only end up killing Sánchez if he got the chance.

Still, it was hard just to sit there and watch, wondering about all the things that might go wrong. Was Oliver with them in the car? Was he in the house? Or had they left him with one of the relatives? If so, then one of the other teams would find him, wouldn't they? Or would they be able to get away with him?

Gary sighed deeply as he watched out the window how Sánchez was pressed up against the front of his car and patted down, his legs spread out, his hands behind his back, then cuffed. There was a lot of yelling, and his wife screamed and took her children in her arms. But the children were taken from her, and she too was put in handcuffs, while she was screaming, and her children taken away in another car. They would be put in the hands of the DCF and probably be taken to another family member to be taken care of while it was determined who was involved in this kidnapping and who wasn't…whether they were in it together. It was probably going to be a mess to figure out, but Gary couldn't really think about that right now. He was staring at Peterson and the agents searching the car and then going into the house, his hands beginning to shake.

Would the child be in there all alone? Had they left Oliver in there while they went out? Was there someone to take care of him? Would they find him alive? Had they fed him?

An agent came out holding something in his hand, and Peterson immediately turned around to face Gary in the car, a serious look on his face. He signaled Gary to approach, while Sánchez and his wife were being held down, the woman crying helplessly for her children.

Gary got out and rushed toward the agent holding the light blue teddy bear in his hand, Oliver's favorite bear, the one he got from his grandmother when he was just born. It was the same one that always made him calm down when he woke up in the middle of the night crying helplessly.

"The boy is not inside," the agent holding the bear said. "He's not in the car either. And Sánchez won't speak."

"You recognize this?" Peterson asked.

WHAT YOU DID

Gary swallowed and tried not to look at Sánchez, who was still pressed down on the front of his car while being searched. Still, Gary couldn't help himself; his eyes met Sánchez's, and he sensed he was about to lose it. He clenched his fists and tried to calm himself, but he couldn't. Instead, it was like everything exploded inside him. Weeks of frustration and helplessness erupted inside of him, and he rushed toward Sánchez before anyone could stop him. He placed his face close to his and pressed his gun against the man's head, yelling: "Where is my son? Where is he?"

Chapter 66

IT REALLY WAS A FAST BOAT. As soon as Matt and I entered the Banana River and I pushed it to its max, we spotted Charles Turner on the horizon. He was flying down the river toward Satellite Beach south of us, but we were going a lot faster. It didn't take us long to gain on him. Meanwhile, Matt was on the phone, talking to the sheriff's office. They had gotten the chopper in the air, and he was keeping them updated on where the suspect was and where he was heading.

"We're catching up to him," I yelled through the loud noise. "Almost there."

Charles Turner realized how close we were and turned to look at us. Then—as we were almost to the side of his boat—he pulled something out and pointed it at us.

"It's a gun," Matt said. He immediately went in front of me to protect me. Then he spoke into the radio. "He's got a weapon. I repeat suspect is armed and dangerous."

Matt pulled his gun too and, as I steered closer, he held it up so Charles Turner could see it.

"Stop the boat," Matt yelled, "and put down your weapon. Put down your weapon now!"

We could hear more boats approaching from the sides, and the chopper was soon hovering not far from us.

"Stop the boat!" Matt repeated.

In return, Charles Turner fired a shot at him.

"Get down," Matt yelled and jumped on top of me, pulling me to the bottom of the boat. I landed on my back, Matt on top of me. I felt something wet hit my face, and I wiped it away, only to realize it was blood.

Matt's blood.

The blood of the man I loved.

"Matt?" I screamed hysterically. "Matt? You're bleeding. You're hurt. You've been hit!"

Crying, I pushed him away from me and sat up. I then turned the unconscious Matt around, searching for an exit wound. The blood seemed to be coming from the back of his head.

Oh, dear God. He's been shot in the head!

Frantically, I grabbed the radio on his shoulder and pressed the button. It was hard for me to get the words across my lips as everything inside of me was screaming.

Not Matt. Not Matt of all the people in the world.

"Officer down. I repeat. Officer down!"

I didn't wait for the response as I realized the bastard was getting away. I rushed to the steering wheel and got the boat back on track and pressed it to its maximum. Crying in anger, I screamed at Turner to stop. Turner sped up and looked back at me when a police boat coming from the other side made him make a sudden turn and, as he did, my boat rammed into the side of his. I felt the impact the moment it happened, but that is all I remember.

Chapter 67

"EVA RAE? EVA RAE?"

I blinked my eyes and slowly regained consciousness. In front of me, bent down over me, stood Matt. His beautiful blue eyes gleamed as he saw that I had opened mine.

"She's waking up. She's awake," he said with a relieved exhale. "God, you had me worried there, Eva Rae."

I stared at him, blinking. "I had *you* worried? What the heck do you mean? You were shot?"

He shook his head. "No. I hurt the back of my head as I jumped to protect you. Some metal pipe that stuck out, I didn't see it myself. But I have a wound in the back of my head from it."

"You weren't shot? But I was so sure…?"

"I'm fine. I'm still bleeding, though," he said and held a towel to the back of his head. That was when I realized we were still on a boat, but a different one. An officer in uniform was steering it.

"Turner?" I asked and sat up, then got dizzy.

"Whoa, whoa," Matt said and put me back on the deck. "You've been out for a little while there, Eva Rae. Too early to start sitting up."

I felt my head. It was pounding. The blue sky above me was moving slowly. The boat wasn't going very fast.

"What happened?"

"Our boat slammed into his, and you were slung through the air.

You landed in the water, where a police boat pulled you out. Same thing happened to me. I woke up the moment my face hit the water."

"Detective Miller is being modest," a man in a uniform from the sheriff's office said. "He was the one who swam to your rescue and made sure to keep you out of the water till we could pick you up."

"I'm just glad you're okay," Matt said. "I feared that I might lose you for a second there."

"Same," I said and looked into his eyes. Then reality hit me again as another wave of pain rushed through my head. Matt handed me a bottle of water, and I drank greedily.

"What happened to Turner?" I asked when the bottle was empty, and my headache eased up on me.

Matt's eyes grew serious. "He was killed in the crash, I'm afraid."

That made me ignore all the pain and dizziness and sit up straight. "No!"

"They airlifted him to the hospital, but he died in the chopper. That was the latest I heard right before you woke up."

"But…how are we supposed to find the last girl? How are we going to find Tara Owens?"

Matt put his hand on my chest and helped me lay down again. "We'll worry about that later. Right now, we need to get you to the shore and have the paramedics check you. You might have suffered a concussion from the crash."

I sighed. "I'm fine. I promise, Matt. Don't worry about me."

He gave me a look. "I'm not taking any chances here. Not with the woman I love."

That shut me up.

The woman he loves? Matt loves me?

I guess I knew this, deep down, and also that I loved him. We just hadn't said it to one another yet. He picked a heck of a time to do so, but I wasn't complaining. But I didn't say anything back. The moment had passed, and it wasn't the right time for me to tell him I loved him yet. It was a little early for me still.

I hoped he understood.

Chapter 68

THREE DAYS LATER, we still hadn't found Tara Owens or any sign of her. We had raided Turner's house and, together with the techs, we had combed through it over and over again, looking for secret attics or basements or just small rooms. We had torn up all the carpet in the house and dug up most of the yard.

Still nothing.

Matt and I were sitting at our desk, staring at the whiteboard after going through the latest in the case.

"And we're sure that Turner is our man?" I asked.

"I'm pretty convinced," he said. "He worked at the hospital. He entered the hospital that morning, even though he wasn't scheduled for work that day."

"The nurse at the dialysis area wasn't sure it was him," I said. "She said she didn't know Turner since he worked in another department, but when we showed her the picture of Turner, she wasn't completely sure it was him she had seen that day."

"He has the goatee," Matt said. "He looks like the drawing, and when we showed the picture to Jane Martin, she said it looked like the guy who had given her the package with the sash in it. Plus, he tried to shoot me when we approached him. He had guilty written all over him. You don't run from the police unless you have something to hide."

"But he's not a surgeon," I said. "And Jamila at the ME's office specifically said the eyes had been surgically removed. Enucleation, she called it."

Matt sighed tiredly and sipped his coffee cup. "True. But he could have seen it done or maybe read about it somewhere. Heck, I bet there might even be tutorials online on how to do this stuff."

Matt was right. I did one quick search on Google and found both an article in the American Academy of Ophthalmology that described every step of an enucleation in gut-wrenching detail, and several videos showing exactly how it is done.

I stood to my feet. I had gotten a clean bill of health from the doctors at the hospital. After that, I had gone back to my house, removed the crime scene tape, and cleaned out all the signs of there having been crime scene techs, especially the fingerprint powder that seemed to be everywhere. The techs had found several cameras the size of a screw installed in my house, and the thought of this perp watching me gave me the creeps. Still, I loved my house, and I wasn't going to let this guy ruin it for me. When I was finally done after an entire day of cleaning, I had let my children and mother come back inside. We were all happy to be home again, especially the girls were glad to be able to hide in their rooms, able to close the door against Alex, who—according to them—ruined everything.

My mother was happy to be back in the kitchen and cooking again, and for once, no one said anything about her Coconut Chickpea Curry dish. We all ate it with delight and told her it tasted great, even though I found it terrible.

Now that I was back to work, Matt wanted me to accept the fact that we had gotten our guy, but just not found the girl yet, and that was our task. I agreed that Tara was our task right now, but I wasn't as convinced that Turner was our man, and it annoyed Matt. He wanted this to be over soon, so everything could go back to normal. I couldn't agree with him more on that part, but I wasn't sure we were going to achieve that if we kept looking at Turner as our main suspect.

I sighed and rubbed my face.

"What's with you today?" Matt asked.

"He had no motive," I said. "For doing the things he did. There, I said it. I know that you and Chief Annie are all excited because we found our man, but we can't answer why he did it, and that, to me, isn't solving anything. Why did he do the things he did? Why did he recreate all my old cases, huh? Why did he target me?"

"We found your book at his house," Matt said. "The one you spoke about with the many serial killer typologies. Isn't that enough? He was obsessed with your work."

"But it still doesn't answer my question. Why? This killer went to such extremes to get my attention; why did he do that, Matt? This guy didn't even know me."

Matt sighed again. I was waiting for him to roll his eyes at me too, just like my kids.

"Maybe he read about you in the paper. There was a story about you when you solved the last case, remember? They did this entire piece just about you and who you are. He could have seen it, then read your book. It doesn't take a genius to find out what cases you solved while working at the FBI, and some of them were mentioned in the article as well."

I sat back down with an exhale, then finished my coffee.

"Maybe you're right," I said, putting the empty cup down. "It just doesn't feel like it's good enough. It doesn't feel right."

I stared at Matt, feeling hopeless, thinking about Tara Owens and how to find her when the phone rang, and Matt picked it up. He spoke for a few seconds, then put it down, smiling.

"What?"

"That was the hospital. Carina Martin is awake and ready to talk."

Chapter 69

BOOMER PACED THE LIVING ROOM. Back and forth he went, biting his nails while watching the news. They were telling the story of the girl who had returned from being kidnapped, a reporter standing outside of Cape Canaveral Hospital, reporting live from the parking lot.

"Well, Greg, we just spoke to one of the doctors here, and he told us that the girl, Carina Martin, has just woken up, but hasn't spoken to the police yet," the reporter said. "They hope, naturally, that she will be able to confirm that her kidnapper was, in fact, Charles Turner, the man who died while trying to run away from the police in his boat. It is believed that he was the one responsible for kidnapping the three girls weeks ago, but also for having kidnapped a fourth girl, one of their friends, blinded her, and raped her. Earlier in the week, the police released this sketch of the kidnapper along with a very grainy picture taken by a surveillance camera outside of the hospital, allegedly showing Charles Turner. The police say they are also working the theory that he was the same man who booby-trapped a FedEx truck and blew it up in the main intersection of Cocoa Beach last week, injuring a local police officer. This is what they hope that Carina Martin will confirm later today when she speaks to the police. Back to you, Greg."

The camera cut to the studio and Boomer turned off the TV.

Things weren't going the way he had planned them, but all wasn't lost yet. Even if he had to abandon his initial ideas, there was still a way to end this in a manner that would satisfy him. There was still the last girl, and she would get to serve her purpose.

Boomer still had a couple of aces up his sleeve.

Chapter 70

THEN:

"I'll tell you where the baby is if you release me."

Gary stared at Sánchez through the glass overlooking the interrogation room, clenching his fists. They had been at it for more than forty hours now, and still, the man hadn't said a word that could lead them to Gary's son.

It almost tore him to pieces.

Who was feeding Oliver? Who was changing his diaper? Who took care of him?

They had kept both Sánchez and his wife María and were questioning them both in each of their rooms. Still nothing. Not even a hint.

The agents had raided all of their relatives' houses but found no baby there either and no sign of him. All they had was the teddy bear. That was the only clue they had that the boy had been at their house at one point.

But where was he now?

The boy had been gone for longer than he had been alive when he disappeared now. They had known more time without him than with him. It was unbearable to think about.

"You're not being released. You kidnapped a baby, Sánchez," Peterson said. "You're the one in trouble here, buddy. You don't get to make demands. And you definitely don't get to go free. You tell us where the baby is, and then maybe we'll feed you, how about that? Maybe we won't stick your head into the toilet bowl."

Sánchez looked up at Peterson. His eyes were exhausted. He hadn't slept, shaved, or showered in forty hours. They had given him water to drink but nothing else.

"Where's the kid, Sánchez?" Peterson repeated.

"Let me and María go, and I'll show you to him," he said like he had said maybe a hundred times earlier. If Gary had to hear that answer once more, he would throw up.

They were getting nowhere, and in the meantime, Oliver was somewhere, alone and scared. He was nothing but an infant, for crying out loud. Completely helpless, completely dependent on his surroundings.

Peterson got up, his chair screeching across the floor. He came out to Gary. Gary ran a hand across his sweaty forehead.

"I can't take it anymore," he said. "Why won't the bastard speak? Not even when I pressed that darn gun to his face did he say anything."

"He's a tough one; I admit to that," Peterson said. "But I still haven't met the criminal that I couldn't break. He's gonna spill. Look at his eyes; he's getting close now, just you wait and see. Give it time."

Gary scoffed. "I don't have time. That's the one thing I don't have to give."

Peterson nodded, then looked briefly at his shoes. "I might have an idea," he said. "Actually, it was Agent Wilson who told me it might work."

"Anything at this point. You know that," Gary said. "What is it?"

"The wife," Peterson said. "We bring her into the interrogation room. See if she can get him to talk."

Chapter 71

"CAN you describe the man who kidnapped you?"

Carina looked at the two detectives that had entered her room. She had explained everything she remembered from the night she was attacked to them and told them as much as she remembered from their time in the room underground. Talking about it made her tear up, even though she tried to stifle it. She was still feeling dizzy and couldn't find rest. Everything felt so confusing to her, almost surreal.

The doctor, a small woman with blonde hair, had told her she had been lucky, that they had performed surgery on her for almost twelve hours to save her life. She had also told her she was malnourished and that all her levels were alarmingly low. Furthermore, they had found traces of a date rape drug in her blood. It could affect her memory, she had been told. And now that the female detective, a small chubby-cheeked redhead with her hair in a ponytail, asked her for details about the man who had tormented her and kept her prisoner, it was hard for her to picture him.

"He was…h-he…"

"Take your time," the redhead, said, sounding sympathetic. "Make sure the details are correct."

"He wore a mask when he came to the room where we were kept —a surgical mask. I can remember the eyes; they were grey. Maybe it was the light or the lack of light in the small room, but they looked grey. Could have been bluer."

"And the hair?" the male detective said. He was quite handsome and looked like he enjoyed surfing, judging from the blond strands of hair in between the brown ones.

"I wanna say blond," she said. "But I'm not completely sure. It could have been a light brown."

The female detective showed her a sketch.

"Is this him?"

She looked at it, then nodded. "Could be."

She showed her a grainy surveillance photo. "And this is the same guy?"

Carina nodded and remembered vaguely running across the parking lot, her heart racing in her chest, fear fueling her, giving her almost superhuman strength. She couldn't believe she had made it out, that she had actually escaped.

The female detective showed her another picture.

"This man," she said. "Do you recognize him?"

Carina looked at the photo. "I think so. He's…he's Leanne's dad, isn't he? She lives not that far from me?"

"Is that the man who kidnapped you?" the female asked.

Carina looked at the picture, then shook her head. "No."

The two detectives exchanged a glance. The female addressed her again, leaning closer with the picture.

"Look at it again, Carina, please. Are you sure this is not the same man?"

Carina looked at Leanne's dad again, then nodded. "Positive. The goatee is fake. I saw him put it on in the car while he thought I was out. He thought he had sedated me, but the syringe fell out while he did it back at the house and the contents were emptied inside my dress instead. I felt it happen but pretended it didn't. I felt the sedation at first, but it was quickly out of my system, so I just laid there while he undressed me and carried me to the car. Then I waited for him to leave the car. But I saw him put on the fake goatee and glue it to his face."

"Are you sure about this?" the male detective said. "He was wearing a mask for most of the time you saw him."

"I am certain. This is not the same guy. I would have known. I used to play with Leanne when we were younger before we drifted apart, and I know her dad very well. I would have recognized his eyes. It's not him."

Chapter 72

"SO, HE IS STILL OUT THERE," I said and looked at Matt, feeling the adrenalin begin to rush through my body. We had killed the wrong man. I know Matt would say we didn't exactly kill him and that he did shoot at the police, so he knew how it would end, but still. A man, a father was dead, and he wasn't even our guy.

This didn't feel right.

I leaned over and whispered to Matt. "We need a guard by her door twenty-four-seven. He's gonna come for her."

"I'll take care of that," he said and left.

I turned to face Carina again, suddenly worried about her and if she would be safe. This guy knew his way around this hospital, and we didn't even know his name.

"Did you know this man from anywhere else?" I asked.

Carina closed her eyes and nodded.

"You did?" I asked hopefully.

"He's a friend of my dad's. Not a very close friend since he only moved here a little while ago, I think."

"Okay, now we're getting somewhere. So, your dad knows him too, where from?"

"He's...He's..." Carina spoke through tears now. "He lives down the street. He kept us at his house in a bunker underground in his yard."

I could barely breathe. "He's someone from the neighborhood? You were kept that close all this time?"

She nodded, biting her lip. "I know this because we helped him build the bunker."

What?

"Excuse me? I'm not sure I understand?" I said.

Tears were running quickly down her cheeks now, and I could tell she was bravely trying to focus and not break down. She knew as well as I did how important it was that she told us everything. Even if it meant she had to force herself to speak.

"I'm sorry if I'm a little all over the place. I should have told you this first when you came in, but I was just…well, I can't seem to focus properly."

"The doctor said this could happen," her mom, Jane Martin said. She was sitting by her bedside, holding Carina's hand. "She's been drugged, and it can affect her memory."

I nodded. "Okay, Carina. So, he lives in the neighborhood, and you helped him build the bunker? Can you explain that?"

"His house is kind of set back on the lot and covered by sea grapes and trees, so you can't really see it that well. One time, some months ago, he paid all the kids in the neighborhood to come and help dig out his back yard. He said it was for a pool, and we believed him. It wasn't until I was sitting down in that hell-hole that I realized I had helped dig my own grave."

Jane Martin clasped her mouth and was about to break into tears. She held her daughter's hand tightly.

"Maybe we should stop for now," she said. "Carina is tired."

"No, Mom," Carina said between sobs. "I want this guy caught; don't you understand? I want him in prison like he put me in prison. And I want them to find Tara before it's too late. When I was taken out, she was still down there. There's an opening under the carpet in the hallway that leads down to it. You need to remove a bookshelf on top first, then you'll see it. Please, hurry. Tara wasn't well when I was taken out. Please, get her out of there before it's too late."

Chapter 73

THERE WAS no time to waste. We couldn't wait for the sheriff's office to get there with a team from the mainland. Every minute counted, so we decided to go in on our own. Matt drove the cruiser up in front of the house on Country Club Road and parked it on the front lawn. Two patrols came up behind us, on Chief Annie's orders after I spoke to her on the phone, letting her in on what Carina had told us.

Matt and I both put on our vests and drew our weapons.

"We're looking for a female, sixteen years of age, light brown shoulder-length hair and green eyes," I told Sgt. Mason as he approached us, the other officers following closely behind him. I had only known Mason for a short while, but Matt told me he was the man you'd want having your back.

"Got it," Mason said and nodded.

"The suspect might be in the house, so be careful," I said. "Suspect is extremely dangerous."

I met the eyes of Sgt. Mason and felt a connection. It was important in situations like these that we operated on the same page.

I cocked my weapon and nodded.

Matt was the one who knocked on the door. "COCOA BEACH POLICE DEPARTMENT. OPEN UP, OR WE'RE COMING IN."

No response. That was expected.

I nodded again, and Matt grabbed the door handle. It was locked. This was also expected.

I signaled for him to walk with me into the back. The fence leading to the yard wasn't locked, and we walked inside, then up to the porch. I looked at the grass area wondering if the bunker was beneath it, then shivered at the thought.

It's open, Matt mouthed as he grabbed the sliding doors. I nodded, and we rushed inside the living room, holding our guns up in front of us, heart hammering in my chest.

I moved along the wall of the living room. It was sparsely furnished with only a recliner in front of an old TV and nothing else. The carpet was old and had stains from where the previous owner had furniture.

I moved into the kitchen.

It was empty. Extremely empty. Only a big bag of dog food on the counter. That was it.

I moved down the hallway to the first bedroom. Empty. Second bedroom, also empty, not even carpet on the floors. The third bedroom actually had a bed in it. Chains were hanging from a pipe under the ceiling. There was blood on the bed.

Whose blood is that? Molly's? Carina's? Ava's? Or Tara's?

"Clear," I said.

I returned to the hallway and met Matt's glare. We both saw it at the same time…the bookshelf in the middle of the hallway. It looked awkward and out of place. Seemed to be the only bookshelf in the entire house.

Matt grabbed the top while I pulled at the bottom, and soon, the bookshelf was removed. The carpet was loose underneath just like Carina had told us. As we pulled it off, a concrete block was revealed underneath. Sgt. Mason came up behind us. He was a big guy.

"Let's get that for you," he said.

Sgt. Mason ran for a crowbar, then cranked it open, lifting the block so we could pull it aside.

I stared into the black hole as it was revealed underneath, my heart crying for those poor girls who had been hidden down here all this time, while the entire town searched for them.

In the neighbor's house of all places.

In plain sight.

Chapter 74

USING flashlights to lead the way, we walked through a small tunnel that led to a metal door with deadbolts on it. Pressing back my tears, I opened them and entered a room the size of a closet with three mattresses on the floor. On top of one of those mattresses laid a girl. She was on her side, curled up in the fetal position.

Tara.

I went inside and was met by a wall of bad smell that almost made me throw up. I held a sleeve to my mouth and knelt next to her. Flies were swarming the room, and I worried that the girl had died. I put a hand on her shoulder, then pulled gently till her body turned to its back. I gasped, startled, and turned my head away for a second. Tara's lips were white and cracked, her eyes were sunken, and her skin dried up, making it look paper-thin.

"She's alive," I said as I put my finger on her throat and felt the weak pulse. "But not responsive."

Matt was right next to me.

"Do you think he forgot her?"

I scanned the room. By the door, I spotted three buckets. Two were empty; the last one was filled with old human excrement, and flies were swarming it. How flies always found a way, even into a room with no windows and a door that thick that hadn't been opened in a while, remained a mystery to me.

"It's hard to say," I said. "There's no fresh water or food."

"We need to get her to the hospital right away," Matt said and rose to his feet.

I sniffled, looking at the poor girl who was barely alive. I took her in my arms and lifted her with no effort whatsoever. She couldn't weigh more than eighty or ninety pounds. As I looked down at Tara in my arms, spotting a big wound on her abdomen that had been recently stitched together, I suddenly remembered something. It was like I had been here before.

In a situation just like it.

"Matt. Stop."

He turned around and shone his light at my face. "What's wrong? Eva Rae? What's going on?"

I lifted my glance and met his eyes. "I don't know. There's something… something familiar about this."

Matt wrinkled his forehead. "What do you mean, familiar?"

"There was a case I worked. Four bodies were found in a basement in Chicago. All illegal immigrants. The FBI was sent there to assist, but as we retrieved the bodies…"

I stopped and looked at Matt, fear rippling through every cell in my body.

"We need to get out of here. Now!"

"But…"

"Matt, get out of here."

"I'm not leaving you here if that's what you mean."

"Matt, if I'm right, then you have to save yourself."

"Save myself? What do you mean? Explain, Eva Rae."

I swallowed, sweat prickling on my forehead. "The bomb is inside of her. If I'm right, the bomb is inside of Tara. Bombs were in the bodies in Chicago. All four of them had bombs surgically inserted into their bodies."

Chapter 75

I HELD Tara close while crying helplessly.

"I don't know what to do, Matt. I can't just leave her here. I can't; I simply refuse to!"

"You have to, Eva Rae. You must. If she explodes, she'll take all of us with her. You have to leave her, and then we'll send down a bomb squad. We need to get away from here. Now!"

"They'll be too late. He wants her to explode with us close to her like it happened back then. We lost fifteen forensic techs, Matt. My partner and I were outside in the yard when it happened. The bombs went off simultaneously, and the house crashed on top of them. They all died. Each and every one of them!"

"You can't save her, Eva Rae. You can save yourself, but you can't save her if it explodes anyway."

I stared at the stitches on Tara's abdomen. "She's someone's daughter, Matt. Somewhere, her mother is waiting for her to come home. I have to save her. I simply have to!"

"You can't. Don't you understand, Eva Rae?"

I held the girl closer still, sobbing helplessly, then made my decision. I was about to put her down but then ran for the door instead.

"Eva Rae!"

I didn't listen. I carried the girl through the metal door, crying like crazy, Matt following behind me.

"COMING THROUGH!" I yelled up toward the entrance to the

bunker, then climbed up the steps, holding her tightly, shaking violently in fear.

Please, don't explode. Please, don't go off now. Not now.

I reached the last step and could hear Matt panting agitatedly behind me. Sgt. Mason reached down to help me, to grab the girl from my arms, but I yelled at him to get away.

"STAND BACK!"

Sgt. Mason obeyed and got out of my way while I reached the main floor, then ran through the house, the girl tightly clutched in my arms. I was screaming violently in fear and to get people to move out of my way. I stormed into the yard and, just as I was about to put her down on the grass, I heard a sound come from inside of her abdomen.

In that second, I knew it was too late.

Chapter 76

I WOKE up to the delightful sound of my children fighting. Usually, it wouldn't make me smile, but on this day, it did.

"You're such a moron, Alex."

"You're a moron."

"Stop copying me."

"Stop copying me."

"Grandma? Alex is being annoying…again."

I blinked my eyes to make sure I was seeing things right. I was. Christine and Alex were standing right next to my bed, engaged in a heated quarrel.

"I think Mom's awake," I heard Olivia say. Then she approached me, and I saw her pretty face. "Mom? Are you awake? Mom?"

I smiled, but it hurt, so I stopped. "Where am I?"

The children surrounded me, their beautiful faces staring at me. My mother came up behind them.

"Ah, thank God, Eva Rae. We were so worried. The doctor said you'd wake up, but it took forever."

Is she seriously blaming me for being unconscious too long?

"I'm so glad you're awake, Mommy," Alex said.

"Me too," Christine said as the two of them fought about the space and who stood in front. Alex elbowed his way in front of her, and she pushed him back. Olivia rolled her eyes at them.

"Could you two lay off it for at least one second so Mom can wake up? She almost died. Geez."

"Where's Matt?" I asked, slowly remembering what had happened. Anxiety spread quickly through my veins. "Why isn't he here?"

My mom came closer. Her eyes looked sad and, in the few seconds before she spoke, I imagined a thousand scenarios, and none of them had Matt being alive.

"Mom?"

"Easy there," she said when I tried to sit up. "Don't get agitated. Christ, you were in an explosion, for crying out loud."

"Where is Matt? Please, tell me."

"Matt is fine. He just went out for coffee. He's been here the past twenty-four hours while you were out."

"And, of course, you wake up the moment I leave my post to get some coffee."

Matt's soft voice filled the room, and I felt myself relax again. He handed my mom a cup and kept the other one to himself, then sat on the edge of my bed. Christine and Alex started fighting again, and my mom told them that she'd take them to the vending machines to get some of that *junk-food you seem to enjoy so much*. The kids forgot their quarrels, cheered, and left with her.

Matt smiled and held my hand in his, then kissed the top of it. "Boy, am I glad to see those eyes again. How are you feeling?"

"My vision is a little blurry, and I have this ringing in my ears," I said. "I'm not in any pain, though, but I assume that has to do with the number of painkillers I'm on right now, am I right?"

Matt nodded. "The doctor said your vision and hearing might be affected for a little while, but it should normalize. You also have a concussion and burn marks on your legs and abdomen. Because of the blast and the pressure that your body endured, you might experience chest pain, and it might have damaged your lungs and central nervous system, but it's too early to tell, they say."

I smiled, then grew serious again. "What happened, Matt?"

"It went off. The bomb went off inside of her," he said. "Luckily, it seemed that the fact that it was inside of the girl sheltered you a little, but you were pretty terribly hurt; luckily, it was mostly superficial. It was an improvised bomb and a low-order explosive, they say. It would have been a lot worse if it had gone off inside the small bunker, though, and we would probably both have been dead. I was right behind you when it happened and I just…saw you be slung through the air. There was blood and tissue everywhere; I'll spare you the details, but luckily, it was mostly hers."

"So…she died?"

Matt nodded. He sent me a caring smile as I felt the tears fill up my eyes again. I couldn't hold them back, and soon they ran down my cheeks so fast I began to hyperventilate.

This was just too cruel.

Matt squeezed my hand tightly, stifling tears of his own. "You did your best. I know you wanted to save her; we both did, but it was impossible. You must understand this, Eva Rae. There was nothing you could have done differently. She would have died anyway. I spoke to a doctor about it, and he said she wouldn't have survived even if it hadn't gone off."

"I had her, Matt. I had her in my arms. We made it outside. We were so close."

"There was nothing you could have done differently," he said again and touched my hair gently. "Nothing."

"This is just too much."

He sighed. "I know; I know."

"Are we at least anywhere closer to finding this guy?" I asked, pressing back tears while beginning to feel tired, but staying awake due to the anger rising in me. I hated this guy. I truly hated this person. I wanted him dead for what he had done. I wanted him to be in pain just like I was in such deep pain right now.

"As a matter of fact, yes. The house is registered in the name of an Anthony Piatkowski. We haven't been able to locate him and believe he is in hiding. But we are pulling his driver's license from the DMV and are going to send the picture out to the press as soon as we have it. We found all his explosives in the garage, where we assume he made the bombs."

"Piatkowski, huh? I feel like I've heard that name before."

"He's new to the area. Bought the house five months ago. But get this, he's military. Two trips to Camp Marmal, Afghanistan. Enlisted in the navy right after high school and became an EOD. He was one of the most skilled recruits they ever had, they said when we spoke to them at Eglin Air Force Base, which hosts the Naval Explosive Ordnance Disposal School. His engineering skills were out of this world, they said."

"EOD, huh? An Explosive Ordnance Disposal technician," I said. "The people trained to safely disable explosive ordnance, improvised explosives, and weapons of mass destruction. That makes sense. He knows everything there is to know about explosives. But that name, though. It's not an ordinary name."

"Do you make a connection?" Matt said.

"I thought I did, but then I lost it. I can't think," I said. "I'm too tired and too sedated."

I closed my eyes, thinking about Tara's poor mother and what she had to go through now when my kids returned, and I bit back my tears.

"It is," Olivia said, addressed to Christine.

"Is not," Christine said.

They were holding candy bars from the vending machine. Alex had already opened his and had chocolate smeared on all his fingers and cheeks. Olivia had chosen a granola bar.

"Isn't it true that a granola bar is healthier than a chocolate bar?" Olivia asked me. "Christine says it is the same."

I felt so tired; I could only muster a weak smile. I didn't care that they were constantly fighting. These kids were mine, and they were all still alive. That was all that counted right now.

"It is not. There is just as much sugar in a granola bar as in a chocolate bar. Look for yourself. Tell her, Mom," Christine said.

"I don't know anything about it. Why is this so important right now?" I asked, almost dozing off, but fighting it. I wanted to be with my loved ones for a little while longer.

"Because Olivia wants to be skinny, so she can be a model," Christine said, dragging the word out in the end.

"Okay," I said, my eyelids growing heavier still.

"But, *Mo-om*, she's not even tall enough. Tell her she isn't tall enough. You have to be like five-ten at least."

"That's not true," Olivia complained. "Ugh, why do you keep saying that? Why do you even care, you little twit?"

I wasn't listening anymore; I was simply dozing off to the sweet sound of my beloved family, and soon, I was completely lost in the land of my dreams.

THEN:

"What is she doing here?"

Sánchez looked at his wife, María, a surprised look on his face as she entered the interrogation room, followed by Gary's supervisor, Peterson.

"Why did you bring her in here?"

María sat down and reached her hands across the metal table. Sánchez's handcuffs clanked against the tabletop where they were strapped down.

"Honey, sweetie," María said, tilting her head with a sniffle.

Sánchez became stiff. The smile on his face froze.

"Why is she here?" he repeated, even angrier than the first time.

"Diego," she said. "Look at me."

He did as she told him to.

"Did you kidnap that baby?"

He pulled his hands out of hers.

"Why do you ask me this?"

María sobbed, then wiped her eyes on her sleeve before she continued. "If you took the baby, you need to tell them where he is. This is an infant who needs to be with his mother. He needs to be fed; he needs care all hours of the day and night. You are a father; you know this. Think if it was Miguel or Juana this happened to."

Sánchez stared at her, his eyes flickering back and forth.

"Get her out of here," he said. "I don't want her here."

"Please, Diego. You have to tell them where he is."

"I don't know what you're talking about."

"Please."

Sánchez slammed his fists onto the metal table. "Shut up. Just shut up, will you?"

"There's a mother out there, Diego. And she is missing her child. If you did this and I was the mother, I would want to know where that child was. Please, tell them."

It was working. They could tell it was. His wife María could get to him like no one else. For the first time, he felt pushed up against the wall; for the first time, he seemed stressed out. Just the way you want him to be, just the way they usually are right before they break down and spill.

Sánchez's nostrils were flaring. He was getting upset now. This was a good sign.

"Diego, please."

"GET HER OUT!"

He rose to his feet, the chains restraining him, growling in anger.

María started to cry, and Peterson put a hand on her shoulder. And that was when it happened.

Sánchez finally broke down.

"I'll tell. I'll tell you everything. I'll even take you to find the boy. But get her out of here. I don't want her to hear. Get her OUT!"

Chapter 77

IT WAS in the late afternoon the next day. I opened my eyes with a loud gasp. The room was empty; everyone was gone, the blinds closed, leaving the room in darkness.

"Olivia," I said, feeling out of breath.

I lay still in the darkness, staring at the ceiling above, a million thoughts rushing through my head. Was it something I had dreamt? Where did this sensation come from? This feeling that something was terribly wrong?

It was something she said.

I sat up, thinking about what the girls had talked about when visiting. Olivia spoke about becoming a model. She had never talked about that before, ever.

Why now?

I grabbed my phone and called her.

She didn't pick up.

I put the phone down on the table next to me with a sigh.

She's busy—probably volleyball practice or maybe hanging out with her friends. Not everything is a disaster waiting to happen.

Yet, that was how I felt. Like a catastrophe was right around the corner, just waiting for me to discover it.

I couldn't leave it alone. The feeling was eating me up. I grabbed my phone again and called Matt. I got his voicemail. Angry, I put the phone down again, then lay still in my bed, wondering.

Why now suddenly? Why all the talk about becoming a model?

I exhaled, telling myself I needed to relax, that I couldn't do anything about it now, that Olivia was fine. She had probably been in school all day, and now she was hanging out with her friends. This was perfectly normal.

I grabbed the phone again, then looked at Mappen, the tracking app I used to keep an eye on my kids. The map showed that she was at Marylin's, the new diner downtown that served milkshakes and burgers. There was nothing odd about that. That was a usual hangout for the teenagers of Cocoa Beach.

But today is Thursday. She has FSA-testing tomorrow and should be at home studying.

The thought made me sit up and sling my legs over the side of the bed. I stared at the map for a few more seconds and realized it wasn't moving at all.

Had she gone there with some friends? Were they eating and maybe studying together?

Yes, that had to be it. Olivia was very determined to do well in school. She would never put her friends above an important test.

I lay my head back down and relaxed. Olivia was fine. I closed my eyes, trying to get some more sleep, but after fifteen minutes or so, I sat back up and tried to call her again.

Still, no answer.

I tried once more, and suddenly someone picked up.

Oh, thank God.

"Olivia? Olivia?"

"Who's this?" an unknown voice said.

My heart dropped.

"Who is this?" I asked.

"I'm Martha. I found this phone. I work at the diner and was taking out the trash when I heard it ring."

My eyes grew wide, and my heart started to pound. "The trash?"

"Yeah, the dumpster behind Marylin's. It was right on top. Is it your phone?"

"It's my daughter's. Please, hold onto it. I'll send someone to pick it up."

Chapter 78

BOOMER LOOKED at the girl on the bed. She was completely out, heavily sedated, and wouldn't move a muscle for the next several hours. He felt satisfied with this. Taking her had been one of the easiest tasks he had ever performed. She was the one who had contacted him. He didn't even have to write to her like he did those other girls using the photographer's account. He had told her to meet him after school in the parking lot by the new diner, Marylin's, and to bring six sets of clothes for the photoshoot. That last part was just to make it sound legit. As soon as she had approached him in the parking lot behind the diner and hugged him, he had told her to get into the car, and he'd drive her to the photographer that he knew, who would take the photos. Believing him—*yes, she was that gullible*—she had gotten in, and he had placed the syringe in her thigh and emptied its contents while holding her mouth so she couldn't scream. Minutes later, she was out, and he could grab her phone and throw it in the trash, knowing how easy those things were to track, just like he was very good at hiding his tracks online.

Boomer was self-taught at hacking but had been helped on his way when hanging out with one of his buddies in Afghanistan. The many long hours at the camp, waiting for a job, they had spent on computers, learning how to hack into any secure system and how to hide their tracks. It was a skill he believed he would get a lot of use out of later, and he had been right.

He had gotten the name Boomer because of the mushrooms he liked to eat that were also called boomers while hanging out under the trees at the camp. They helped him endure those long hours of nothing to do while waiting to be called out to disarming the next IED. It was a job not just anyone could do.

In a combat zone such as Afghanistan, EODs are everyone's friend. They were the ones to call when an explosive threat was found, and Boomer was an expert at eliminating that danger.

But some guys that Boomer went to school with got hurt while out there. And that hit him hard. It was tough not to think, *That could have been me. I could have been that person out there.* Doing what he did kept him constantly close to that threat. It didn't make for an easy return to the civilized world.

He had dreamt of becoming an EOD since he was just a child because his father had been one too. Once he joined the Navy, that was all that was on his mind—making his dad proud.

Chapter 79

MATT STILL DIDN'T PICK up the phone, and I was getting more and more anxious. I even called the station and told them to have Matt or Chief Annie call me back as soon as possible.

Then I decided I couldn't just lie there in my bed and do nothing. Something was wrong with my daughter, and I had to act. Now.

So, I rushed out of my room without being seen and asked for an Uber to pick me up at the hospital entrance. I asked the driver to take me home and ran up to the entrance and walked inside.

"Olivia?"

My mom came out of the kitchen, wearing an apron, wiping her hands on it.

"Eva Rae? What on Earth...?"

"Mom, where's Olivia?"

My mother looked confused. "She said she was going out with her friends after school. They were going to Marilyn's, that new place. I told her I hoped she wouldn't eat any of the greasy food they have there, but..."

"Mom, I think something terrible happened to her."

"Why...why...I took her to school. She's been absent for two days, so I figured it was best she at least showed her face today. Finals are coming up and..."

"Someone threw her phone in the trash behind Marylin's," I said. "When I called it, a woman who worked there picked up."

"But…surely…Are you sure she's not…I mean…listen, Eva Rae. You're on a lot of drugs right now; you're not thinking clearly. Maybe you're hallucinating. Could it have been a dream?"

"No, Mom. I am not hallucinating. I know something happened to my daughter," I said and rushed up the stairs to her room.

I rushed inside, calling her name, but as expected, her room was empty. I sat at her computer and opened her social media accounts, beginning with Instagram, which she used the most. Not finding anything, I went through her Snapchat account, then WhatsApp, Amino, Twitter, and even her Facebook, which I knew she never used.

Nothing. I found nothing suspicious. No creepy photographer, no strangers contacting her.

How did she get this idea into her head?

Frantically, I kept going through all her emails, all her messages on Instagram, when my phone rang. I looked at the display. Since the killer had called me the last time and told me where to find Ave Morales, the sheriff's office had been monitoring my calls. The first one they had only been able to locate within a ten miles radius of Cocoa Beach, which didn't give us much to go after. The phone was a burner. As I saw the *unknown caller* on the display again, my heart literally stopped.

What if it was him? What if he was calling me to let me know that he had my daughter?

My hand shook as I pressed the button.

"H-hello?"

Chapter 80

IT WAS CHAD. I gasped for air while trying to calm my poor hammering heart.

"Always had impeccable timing, Chad," I said and sat down on Olivia's bed.

"Is this a bad time?" he asked. "I can call again later. I was actually looking for Olivia, but she's not picking up her phone. I wanted to know if she received the money."

Money?

"You gave her money, Chad? How much?"

"A thousand dollars. It was for some photo shoot."

"A photo shoot? You gave her money for that? Did she mention when or where she was going for it?" I asked.

"No. She just said she needed the money and that it was a big deal for her, that it was her dream coming true. Are you telling me that you didn't know about this, about her asking me for it? I thought she ran this by you and figured you just didn't want anything to do with me after last time we spoke. You made me feel really awful. I thought giving her the money was a way for me to make it up to her. I wired it to her this morning."

No. No. No!

I rubbed my forehead. "Of course, you did. Listen…Olivia…"

For a second, I was about to tell him that I believed Olivia was in trouble but then decided against it. There was still a chance she was just out with her friends and that she had forgotten her phone at the diner before they left to go somewhere else. Or someone might have stolen it and thrown it in the trash when they realized they couldn't open it. If she was, in fact, missing, I'd have to tell him when I was certain.

"I gotta go."

"Wait; there was something else," he said.

Of course, there was.

"What? I'm kind of in a rush here, Chad, could you get to the point a little faster?"

"I eh...figured out how to be with the kids more."

"Yeah? That's great, Chad," I sighed while my mind worked overtime trying to figure out where my daughter could be. "How so?"

"Well. The thing is, Kimmie left. Or rather, she threw me out. We're splitting up. She gave me two weeks to find something else. I could get a new job closer to you guys. I was actually thinking about coming to Cocoa Beach. Maybe coming...home?" he paused, probably waiting for my reaction, but I had no words yet. It was a lot to take in right now.

"It's always been you and me, Eva Rae," he continued. "I realized this recently. I don't know what I was thinking when I left you. We're a family."

Are you freaking kidding me?

"You wanna come...home?" I asked, not quite grasping this. Things were moving a little too fast for my liking right now.

"So...what do you say?" he asked.

What do I say? What do I say? I say you cheated on me and left the children and me without a word. I say I will never be able to trust you again. I say I am deeply, madly in love with someone else and we're doing fine without you. That's what I say.

But, of course, those weren't the words leaving my lips. Instead, I said, right before I hung up: "Like I said. You have impeccable timing. I can't deal with this right now. I gotta go."

Chapter 81

"WHO WAS THAT?"

My mom stood in the doorway of Olivia's room.

I rubbed my forehead. "That was Chad," I said.

"What did he want? It sounded like he wanted to come home?" she said and stepped closer.

I put my hands up. "Not now, Mom. I don't have time for this. I need to find my daughter, remember?"

"Don't shut him out just because of what he did. He is still the children's father. You didn't even tell him you didn't know where Olivia was. Why didn't you tell him? He deserves to know."

I lifted my eyes and met hers, then sent her a look to make her back off. "I don't owe Chad anything. He left us. Besides, I don't see how this is any of your business. I need to find my daughter now. So, Mom, please forget about Chad for a little while, even if you love him, and try to help me think. Now, Olivia never spoke about becoming a model before, how did she get this idea in her head? Could she have spoken to someone? I checked online, and there doesn't seem to be anything there. Could she have met someone at the diner? At school maybe?"

My mom shook her head. "I...I don't know, Eva Rae. She seemed perfectly normal to me this morning. Are you sure she's not just out with her friends and forgot her phone at the diner?"

Was it me? Was I overreacting? Maybe because of the drugs? I thought it over, then felt this pinch in the bottom of my stomach again.

No, something is wrong. I just know it is. Call it a mother's instinct; call it a cop's instinct, or maybe both. You can call it what you want. I just know this.

I rose from the chair and stood in my daughter's room, looking at the magazines next to her bed. There were all the big ones, *Elle, Cosmo,* and *Vogue*. I flipped the top one and stared at the super skinny models featuring strange clothes that I couldn't believe anyone would ever wear.

Maybe Olivia had been into this for longer than I thought?

"I need to find the list of numbers for her best friends," I said. "I keep it in the kitchen. I'm gonna start calling them."

My mom sighed as I walked past her, then followed me down the stairs.

"I'll help."

I found the list in my drawer, then stared at the whiteboard I had put up to organize our lives. Alex had a TAG—Talented and Gifted—trip today where they went to Kennedy Space Center, so he wouldn't be home till late, and Christine was at Orchestra. She had recently begun playing the double bass at school and rehearsed with the orchestra twice a week. Both of them were out, and that was good. I didn't want them to know what was going on or to worry about their older sister. They had enough with me being in the hospital and everything else that had been going on the past several days.

"I'll take the first one," my mom said. "Vivian, is that her name?"

I nodded. Vivian was one of Olivia's best friends that she had made since she moved here. I wouldn't say she had made any really close friends yet, but she had found a couple of girls from the volleyball team that she liked to hang out with after school from time to time. Vivian was the one she liked best.

"I'll try Shelly," I said.

As I said the words, my eyes fell on something on the floor by the front door. I walked to pick it up, then turned the object in the light, recognizing it.

"What's this?" I asked

My mom approached me, squinting her eyes to see better. "Let me see," she said and took it out of my hand.

"This doesn't belong to anyone who lives in this house," I said. "Someone was here, Mom. While I was in the hospital. Who was it? Who was here, Mom?"

Chapter 82

THE GATE WAS open when I drove up. The entrance was packed with cars, big limos, Teslas, and Maseratis. A young man in a suit asked me if I wanted to use valet parking, so I got out and let him park my car in the garage underneath the house.

It was Friday night, and they were having a party.

Someone held the front door open for the couple in front of me, who slid inside, the woman wearing a long blue sparkling dress. Me, I was in shorts and flip flops. Still, I managed to sneak in with the couple, and soon I entered the big hall where people were mingling. I recognized a couple of local politicians, some Hollywood starlets, a famous rapper that I only knew of because of my children, and I was pretty sure I spotted Tom Hanks by one of the big windows leading to the yard and ocean behind it. But I could be wrong. I never was good with famous people and recognizing them, much to my children's annoyance.

There was champagne in every partygoer's hand, along with caviar, and lobster canapés. I realized I hadn't eaten at all today. Not since the mushy breakfast at the hospital that contained pineapple juice, an orange, and something I couldn't identify but probably was supposed to be an omelet. I had barely eaten any of it, and now my stomach was grumbling angrily at me.

But there was no time.

I spotted Sydney—or Kelly Stone—standing between two well-dressed men, a glass of champagne held lightly between her fingers. Her eyes met mine, and she excused herself to them, then approached me.

"Eva Rae?" She looked nervously around her. "I thought you were in the hospital?"

"Save it. Where is she?"

She gave me a strange look. "What are you talking about? Listen, this isn't such a great time. I'm having a small party. You're welcome to stay, but..."

I held up her bracelet. "I found this in my house. Explain, please."

"I...I'm not sure I follow you here, Eva Rae."

"Cut the crap, Sydney."

"Maybe we should take this elsewhere," she said and looked nervously around her. A woman passed her, and she smiled politely at her while escorting me through a door into what looked like a big library. Thousands of books decorated the walls from top to bottom.

Sydney closed the door.

"Please don't call me that name," she said as she faced me again. "That is not my name."

"Okay, Mallory Stevens or Kelly Stone or whatever the heck your name is. Where is my daughter? I know you came to my house and spoke to her. My mom told me."

My sister sent me a wry smile.

"*Our* mother, if I recall," she said. "And, yes, that's true. When I heard what happened to you on the news, I went to your house. I was there to bring a peace offering. I spoke to our mother. I realized I was angry at her because I had been told my entire life that she didn't want me. That was why I told you I couldn't see you anymore. But as the days passed...and then you were hurt, well, I soon realized that I risked losing you again and that I had been silly. This was my family, and if you were reaching out to me, then I at least owed it to myself to take the chance. That was why I came back here in the first place. To find my family, that my dad—our dad—told me didn't want me. I wanted to find my roots, but gave up, thinking you would have looked for me if you wanted to see me again. But now, Mom told me everything. She told me about how I was taken, and that they didn't know where I was, how you all thought I was dead and gone for all these years. I never knew this. My dad, well our dad, told me she had thrown us out, that she never wanted to see either of us again and that was why we moved so far away and had no contact with her...or you. All those years, I thought our mother had chosen you over me, and that made me resent you. As I listened to her story, I began the process of forgiveness. But it's a journey. Wait. Are you mad about that? About me wanting to talk to Mom? To want to get to know you?"

I shook my head, tears springing to my eyes. "No, of course not. That's what I want too; believe me. It's my daughter. It's Olivia. She's been missing since after school today and I…well…"

Sydney looked surprised, angry even. "You thought I had taken her? Me who had recently learned that I was a victim of kidnapping myself?"

"I don't know what I thought. Maybe I hoped she was here and not taken by some sicko. You were at my house, and I was desperate. I thought maybe she had come to you." I turned around and found a leather chair, then sank into it, feeling hopeless. We called everyone that Olivia knew, and no one had seen her since school ended. She hadn't told anyone where she was going or who she was meeting. I even called the diner, and they hadn't seen her either. I had felt so certain it had something to do with my sister and the fact that she had been at my house two days earlier.

"I wish I could be of more help, Eva Rae," she said. "I really do."

"Yeah, me too, well…I should be…" I rose to my feet when my phone vibrated in my pocket, and I pulled it out. It was a text from Matt.

GOT YOUR MESSAGE. PICKED UP HER PHONE AT THE DINER. HAVE ALERTED ALL PATROLS AND WILL ISSUE AN AMBER ALERT ASAP.

I exhaled, almost in tears. It was the right thing to do, but it suddenly felt so darn real. My daughter was gone. No one knew where she was.

"I have to go," I said and was about to leave when I stopped. "Didn't you say that your boyfriend Noah recently moved in with you?"

I turned to face her. She nodded.

"Yes, he's my fiancée. We're going to marry this summer. I will invite you and Mother, naturally."

"How much do you know about this guy?" I asked.

As I spoke, I received another text from Matt and opened it. It was a picture with the caption:

JUST RECEIVED THIS FROM DMV. THIS IS OUR GUY.

THIS IS ANTHONY PIATKOWSKI. SENDING IT TO THE MEDIA ASAP.

I looked at the picture, then felt my heart drop. I showed it to Sydney.

"That's Noah; why?"

I swallowed. "This is our suspect. This is the guy we believe kidnapped three teenage girls from the school on prom night. This is the guy we believe kidnapped Molly Carson after promising to make her a model," I said, cursing myself for not having told Olivia what happened to Molly. I didn't want to scare her, so I had withheld all the details, but now I realized it was the worst thing I could have done. I should have warned her, and now she had fallen victim to the exact same trick.

"He raped and blinded Molly before placing her in my yard, chained to a swing set. He also killed one person at the hospital, severely hurt several others, and shot Carina Martin as she tried to escape. He killed Ava Morales and Tara Owens and put me in the hospital. It is also the guy I suspect has taken my Olivia."

Sydney looked at the picture on the phone, then shook her head. I could tell she was in shock.

"No. That's not the same person. You must have the wrong guy. That's not my Noah."

"Look at the picture, dang it. Is this your fiancée?"

Sydney's nostrils were flaring, and her eyes were flickering back and forth. She fixed her glare on the photo, then nodded with a sniffle.

"Yes...yes, that's him."

Chapter 83

"WHAT DO YOU KNOW ABOUT HIM?" I asked when sensing Sydney still didn't fully believe me. I couldn't blame her. If she had been living with the guy and they were planning to marry soon, then this had to be quite a shock.

"His name is Noah Greenwald."

"Have you met any of his family?"

"No...well, he doesn't get along with them, he said. It's not like he's met mine either."

"I am so sorry for this, but he has been lying to you. His real name is Anthony Piatkowski. Five months ago, he bought a house on Country Club Road where he built a bunker...where he later kept the three girls."

Tears were in her eyes now as she shook her head. "No, Noah is a surgeon. He works at Cape Canaveral Hospital. He is very skilled and has earned many awards. Hasn't he?"

"Give me a sec," I said, then texted Matt back and asked him to look up Noah Greenwald. A few minutes later, he texted me back.

"I am sorry, sweetie," I said. "Noah Greenwald is a surgeon, or rather he was. He died in Afghanistan in 2017."

Sydney clasped her mouth and fought to stay calm. I placed a hand on her shoulder and looked into her eyes.

"Where is he now? Where is Noah?"

She swallowed. "In there," she said. "With the guests."

I felt my badge in my pocket and pulled it out. I had also brought my gun strapped underneath my CBPD jacket.

"You should probably stay in here," I said and grabbed my phone to call Matt.

"O-okay."

"He's here," I said into the phone. "I'm gonna take him in. I can't wait for backup. I'll risk him making a run for it. I don't care that it's dangerous. He has my daughter, Matt. I am not taking any chances."

Chapter 84

I WALKED BACK out into the big living room where the many people were gathered. No one seemed to notice me, so I continued through the crowd until I spotted him. He was standing by the grand piano in a corner of the living room, in deep conversation with a woman that I was certain I had seen before in some movie but didn't recall the name.

As my eyes landed on him, my blood froze. This was him; this was the guy who had been toying with me for weeks, who had been torturing me and this entire town. He had been here all along? Hiding in plain sight in my sister's house?

I couldn't wait to take him in and have him taste some of his own medicine. He was going to be locked away for a very long time. It was satisfying to know, even though I most of all wanted to kill him right there. I felt such deep anger toward this man, and yet, I hardly even knew him. My question was, why he had felt such resentment toward me that he wanted to put me through all of this.

What was his motive?

As he lifted his glance from the woman in front of me and our eyes met across the room that was humming with chitchat, it hit me.

I knew exactly why he was out to get me, and the realization struck me like a punch in the stomach. It almost knocked me out.

Anthony Piatkowski grinned when he saw me, then asked his company to excuse him, and left. He walked toward the backyard, and I followed him, hand on my gun. I wanted him away from all these people, in case I needed to pull the gun, so I let him rush into the yard and followed him just a few steps behind. Outside, he disappeared behind a corner, and I rushed after him. Barely had I reached the corner before a shovel was swung through the air and slammed right into my face, causing me to drop the gun in the grass. I fell backward up against the wall, a ringing in my ears, barely conscious, sliding down the wall, my back against it until I hit the gravel below. Above me, holding the shovel and seconds later my gun, was Anthony Piatkowski.

Chapter 85

"OKAY, you were smarter than I expected," he said through the fog that was my brain right now. I tried to focus on him. He held the gun against my forehead.

"If you're so smart, I take it you also know who I am?"

I tried to nod, but my head was hurting. "Yes. It took me awhile, too long to realize who you were. It was the name that threw me off. You grew up with your mother; that's why you have a different last name than your dad."

Anthony nodded. "Very good, Detective."

"It was never on the news," I said. "It was never revealed to the public that those bodies we found in Chicago were filled with explosives. It was a terrorist nest, and they were experimenting with implanting bombs into bodies, using illegal immigrants that no one would miss as tests subjects. But all of them died in the process before they could be tested. It would be a gamechanger if they had succeeded. We didn't want to give anyone else that same idea, so it was kept quiet. The entire basement exploded when they discovered the bodies, and many died. My partner and I were outside, luckily. But that was how I knew. After you did the same thing to Tara. I knew it had to have been someone close to the investigation back then. I realized that while in the hospital. How did you get the magnetic ID card from Turner? Did you steal it?"

"He sold it to me along with scrubs and surgical masks. I paid him fifty thousand dollars so he could buy the boat he always wanted."

"And that was why he ran," I said. "He thought we were there because of that."

"What a shame," he said.

"Turner's ID card gave you access to the hospital on the day you went in to poison the dialysis patients. You looked like him in the picture if you put on your fake goatee. You pretended like you belonged, but you never worked there. We checked their records. People just assumed you did. But you're no doctor. Noah Greenwald was. And he was in your battalion in Camp Marmal, right? And then he died."

"We were together on that day. I don't remember much except the birds singing and the blue sky above. We were driving toward Mazar-i-Sharif, the largest city close by when the IED went off on the side of the road. I was trapped underneath our car for almost twenty hours while trying to keep Noah alive. When help finally came along, he was no longer breathing."

"And you took his identity?"

"We were as close as brothers, maybe even closer. I was him; he was me. Sometimes, I'm still him. He lives in me."

This guy is crazy.

"Was he the one who taught you to perform enucleation? Like you did to Molly Carson?"

He nodded. "He showed it to me. One of our colleagues was hit by friendly fire, and the bullet went through his eye. Noah performed the surgery and let me watch. He took me through it step-by-step. I remembered everything he taught me while taking her eyes."

"I bet," I grumbled sarcastically while slowly regaining my strength. Piatkowski seemed lost in his memories for a few seconds. The shovel had cracked my lip, and blood was running down my chin. My face pounded like someone was playing drums on it. I was stalling, hoping to keep him talking until Matt got here.

"Where's my daughter?" I asked.

Piatkowski grinned. "Wouldn't you like to know?"

"Why are you doing this?" I asked.

He stared me directly in the eyes, and I felt my blood freeze.

"Because of what you did."

Chapter 86

THEN:

They took a twelve-page-long handwritten confession from Sánchez, each and every one of them bearing the distinctive "m" that looked like a "z," that had led them to him in the first place. He told them how he had seen Gary's wife, Iris, place the child in the carriage and how he had taken the child and left a ransom note.

Then they asked him to take them to the baby. Sánchez agreed to this and Gary was allowed to be in the front seat as they took off. It took all his strength not to point his gun at this man and kill him on the spot. But he kept himself calm, for Oliver's sake. Finally, the bastard was talking, and finally, he was taking them to the boy.

Sánchez wasn't very intelligent, Gary had realized, and he had to admit he didn't trust him much. Not until he actually held his boy in his arms again.

"Take this exit," Sánchez said.

They did as he told them to and they left the highway. On Sánchez's directions, they drove through town and entered a small neighborhood, very close to where Gary and Iris lived.

Has he been this close all this time? Gary thought, terrified, to himself. It was unbearable.

"Take a right here, and then stop by those bushes over there."

Gary looked out the window, his heart beginning to pound.

"But...but...?"

"Right here," Sánchez said. "Stop the car."

He pointed ahead.

"Right over there in those heavy bushes. That's where I placed the child. When I went to the first drop off site—I had the baby in the car. But I was scared away by all the press and police in the area. I drove away, then abandoned the baby close to the house. I figured you'd find him at some point…but I guess…you didn't."

Gary stared at the man in the back seat. Before he got into the car, Peterson had made him hand over his weapon. For this, Gary was very grateful at this moment.

Petersen got out of the car and opened the door for Sánchez in the back seat. He approached the window, and Gary rolled it down.

"Stay here, Gary," Peterson said.

Gary watched Peterson walk to Gary's partner, Agent Wilson, and they talked for a few seconds. Sánchez pointed again, and next thing, they all hurried toward the bramble patch behind Gary's house. Seconds later, Agent Wilson pulled out a piece of clothing before falling to the ground and beginning to sob uncontrollably.

Gary got out of the car and stood like he was paralyzed as they all turned to look at him. It felt like everything inside of him broke.

Dear God, no!

It took him less than a second to make the decision. He ran to one of his uniformed colleagues and, before he could react, pulled his gun out of its holster. Then he turned around and fired a shot at Sánchez before turning it toward himself.

Chapter 87

"IT WASN'T MY FAULT," I said and tried to sit up.

Piatkowski pressed the gun against the skin of my forehead. He was sweating with distress, his white shirt getting soaked.

"Of course, it was. It was all your fault…Agent Wilson. See, you were there all the time. You were the one responsible for keeping an eye out on the house and its surroundings. And you failed to see the baby. You failed to see a small four-week-old infant in the bushes, crying helplessly for his mother. That baby died because you didn't find him. That's the reality."

Being confronted with this made me want to throw up. Even the name, Chad's last name, Wilson, made me sick to my stomach. I had gotten rid of it when he told me he was moving out, and I had taken my maiden name Thomas instead. I had spent years trying to get over this event. The guilt had eaten me up and forced me to work even harder, neglecting my family in the process. I had wanted to make amends; I had tried to work my way out of it, thinking I owed it to Gary, my old partner. Over the years, I had taught myself to let go of the guilt, telling myself it wasn't my fault, that anyone could have missed the baby, but still it nagged inside of me. Of course, it did. It always would. My partner had killed himself afterward, leaving Anthony Piatkowski—his child from a previous marriage—fatherless.

"But that's not all," Piatkowski said. "There's more. Not only did you fail to find the baby, but it was also your fault it was taken in the first place. Iris, his wife, told me everything. She told me how you and Gary, a week or so earlier, had stormed a house and rescued a kidnapped man, a gang member who owed money. When doing so, you shot a man. This man was the brother of Diego Sánchez. That was why he stole the baby in the first place. It wasn't random. He didn't just walk by on coincidence and decide to grab the baby. It was planned. It was revenge for what *you* did. The FBI believed it was coincidental until Sánchez wrote his confession. That was when the real motive came out. He wanted to revenge the death of his brother, and that was why he stole Gary's newborn. To revenge a killing that you, Agent Wilson, had committed. I lost my little brother and my father because of you. That is why I want you to be in pain. I researched you over the years and read all of your books about the many profiles of serial killers. My dad had told me about all the cases you worked together. I was just a teenager back then, but I remember each and every one of them, especially the one about the exploding bodies."

"You laid it all out like breadcrumbs for me to follow," I said, hearing tires screech outside of the house. That had to be Matt and his colleagues. I just had to keep him going a little while longer. And then, somehow, lead them to our whereabouts behind the house. "And now you have led me to you. You have my daughter, and you have me. You've won, Anthony. What do you want? What will it take for this to end? Money?"

That made Piatkowski laugh. "Do I look like I need money? I live here. I'm engaged to a Hollywood star who has no idea where her money goes."

"How did you know she was my sister when I didn't even know?" I asked.

"I've been following you for a long time, Eva Rae. Ever since my dad died and I started to ask questions, I realized it was your fault. I spent hours in Afghanistan preparing for this, letting the anger fuel my planning. I have followed your every move since. Six months ago, you went to a PI and started to ask questions about your sister. I broke into her office at night and went through her files. Back then, she didn't know that your sister lived right here, or that she had changed her name to Kelly Stone, but it didn't take me long to figure that one out. I went to New England while she was filming there and then made sure to be at a charity event she attended while there."

I heard yelling coming from inside of the house and knew it

wouldn't be long before they came out here. Unfortunately, Piatkowski heard it too. He growled, then grabbed me by the arm and pulled me up.

"You're coming with me," he said, then pushed me ahead of him, holding a hand over my mouth, gun pressed against my back.

Chapter 88

HE PULLED me into the underground garage and toward a car. I tried to scream, but nothing but muffled sounds came out of me. Piatkowski opened the passenger door and told me to get in when a voice yelled from behind us.

"Let her go, Piatkowski."

Anthony smiled and turned around. "Ah, the knight in shining armor. Matt Miller, is it?"

"Let her go, Piatkowski," he said, pointing his gun at him.

Piatkowski grinned. "Well, you can hardly kill me now, can you? See, then you'll never know where her daughter is. Besides, if you try anything, I'll shoot her."

Piatkowski stared at Matt for a little while, waiting for his reaction, while I stood pressed up against the open door, holding onto the edges, pressing against it, trying to fight him.

Matt lowered the gun.

"I didn't think so," Piatkowski said.

He turned to face me, grabbed me around the throat, and pressed, grinning. I couldn't breathe and had to let go of the edges of the car. It happened so fast; I'm sure Piatkowski didn't even have time to react. I leaned on my hands on the seat and lifted both my legs into the air, shaping them into a V-shape, wrapping them around his neck. I then twisted them hard, and Piatkowski went down onto the cement floor with a loud thud.

WHAT YOU DID

"Eva Rae!" Matt yelled as he came running toward me. Piatkowski was on the ground as Matt called for backup over the radio. Soon, they stormed inside the garage, while I had my foot planted solidly on Piatkowski. I held his arm twisted behind his back.

"Where's my daughter, you pig? Tell me!"

But no matter how hard I twisted his arm or even when I pressed my gun on him, he didn't care. He just laughed at me, then said. "That's the beauty of it. I don't even know."

"What do you mean you don't know, you sick bastard? What did you do to her?"

He turned his head slightly, lifting it from the floor, and managed to look at me while he said the next thing. It was like he wanted to make sure he saw my reaction when the words fell.

"I sold her. You have no idea how much money some people are willing to pay for a beauty like her on the dark web."

"You did what?" I shrieked. The realization made me let go of his arm. I felt like my throat was closing up…like I couldn't breathe.

He sold her?

Two CBPD officers grabbed Piatkowski and pulled him away from me while I screamed in deep pain, Matt holding me back, grabbing my gun from my hand. As they dragged him away, I looked into his icy eyes and his grin sent chills down my spine, while desperation and hopelessness made me sink into the arms of the man I loved, crying.

"What did he do to her, Matt? Where is she?"

Matt held me tight while I sobbed, missing my baby girl, wanting to wake up from this nightmare.

"I don't know," he whispered. "But we will find her. Trust me."

I let him hold me tight for a very long time and cried till I had no more tears. Then, I finally agreed to go back to the car with him, so he could take me home. I cried all the way back and held my two youngest children tight in my arms all night while I tried to sleep.

Chapter 89

THREE DAYS LATER, I went to visit Molly at the hospital and had a long chat with Melissa. I told her everything that had happened, but most of all, I was happy to be able to tell her that we got the guy, that he was in our custody. I had kept my promise to her, and for that, I was proud.

Molly was doing a lot better and would soon be discharged. She was learning to cope with the fact that she was now blind, and they had ordered a service dog for her, while they were training her how to maneuver by using a support cane—or white cane—at the hospital. She had also begun speaking again, even though what came out of her was sparse. She would, however, soon be able to give her entire testimony and help put another nail in Piatkowski's coffin.

"I am so sorry about Olivia, though," Melissa said and held my hand in hers. "You must feel awful. Let me know if there is anything I can do. I'll do anything for you; you know that."

I told her to take care of her own daughter for now and hold her tight, enjoying that she was still here.

I then checked on Carina Martin, who was with her mother. Carina hugged me and cried when she heard we had caught Piatkowski. She told me she would be willing to testify as soon as we wanted her to, and she would even go back to the house and the bunker if we needed her to. I told her she was a very brave girl. I also told her mother to be proud of her before I left. Tears were springing to my eyes as I hurried down the hallway of Cape Canaveral Hospital, while I wondered if I was ever going to see my daughter again.

After crying in the car, and slamming my fist into the steering wheel, I drove back the station to watch the interrogation of Piatkowski through the glass. They had been at it almost non-stop for three whole days, and he still refused to say where my daughter was, repeating the same thing over and over again.

"That is the beauty of it. I don't know. You can keep asking me till we both die from thirst or even old age, but I will never be able to tell you because I don't know. Girls are sold all the time around this world, and who knows where they end up?"

As he said the last part, he looked at the glass window, like he knew I was behind it, which he probably did.

"To whom?" Matt asked, tired and angry. "Who did you sell her to?"

"I don't know his name. He called himself *The Iron Fist*. He buys girls online—through the dark web—and probably resells them. Some he might keep to himself. What do I know? I took the girl to the airport, where we met some of his associates. They took her. Where, I have no idea. She could be anywhere in the world by now. But they paid me good money, and that was what I wanted…money."

Financial gain, I thought to myself. *The last motive.*

He had covered all four serial killer typologies from my book. Lust, anger, power, and financial gain.

I stared into the icy eyes of Piatkowski, and in that very instant, realized that there was no way we were ever going to get him to tell us anything. If I wanted my daughter back, I'd have to find her myself.

"I am sorry," Matt said as he came out of the room. He leaned forward and kissed me. He ran a hand gently through my hair. "I'll keep trying."

I nodded determinedly. "Do that, Matt. Listen, I'm gonna…I'm gonna go back."

He examined me. Our eyes locked for a few seconds, and that was when he knew. I had made up my mind, and he couldn't stop me. I started to back away from him, biting my lip, until I finally turned around and left him, my heart crying.

"Wait," he said. "I don't like that look in your eyes, Eva Rae. Eva Rae? Where are you going? Eva Rae? Don't do anything stupid; do you hear me?"

That was the one thing I couldn't promise him.

. . .

THE END

NEVER EVER
EVA RAE THOMAS MYSTERY, BOOK 3

Prologue
MIAMI, FLORIDA

Earlington Heights Metrorail Station
Orange Line
Southbound

Chapter 1

HE GOT in through the third door after the train pulled in at 7:58 a.m. as usual. Ryan Scott was holding his Starbucks coffee in one hand and had his backpack slung over his shoulder. Once inside, he spotted a free seat and moved toward it, then sat down. The train departed and rattled along while Ryan sipped his coffee and went through the news headlines on his phone.

Ryan had just landed a summer internship at *The Miami Times* and had to make sure he was updated before today's editorial meeting. The dream was to become a reporter, but the road was long. As a part of his Master of Journalism program at the University of Washington, he was required to do a six-week-long internship. He was still going through training but needed ideas to pitch so he could one day do his own story. Ryan knew he needed to stand out from the crowd, and he had learned that, in order to do so, he needed a good story. The newsroom was always on the hunt for the next big breaking news story, and he needed to pitch some original ideas and demonstrate initiative. He desperately wanted to see his name in the paper.

Of course, he did.

The train came to a stop at Allapattah and some of the passengers left while new ones boarded. A black woman sat next to Ryan, and he moved his backpack to make room for her. The train was getting more crowded now, as usual, as they headed south toward downtown Miami.

Ryan smiled politely at the woman who sat down next to him with a heavy sigh. A poster on the wall across from them asked if they suffered from schizophrenia in both English and Spanish. The woman wore striped pants and sat with her big green purse in her lap. Across from them sat an old man, and next to him, a young teenage girl, holding a bag. Ryan smiled at her as their eyes met, but she didn't smile back.

Santa Clara station came and went, and more people came onboard wearing light clothes and sunglasses. The AC on the train wasn't very good, and it was hot. Ryan felt his hands getting clammy as more people came on board. The train moved along next to the road below, and Ryan looked down at the rows of cars that were stuck in a jam, while the train shot through town nice and smoothly. A man about Ryan's age was reading a book in the corner, while another man was holding his briefcase close like he was afraid that someone might steal it. A Hispanic-looking teenage girl at the other end of the train seemed lost in her own thoughts. The window behind the old man had been tagged with graffiti, blocking the view.

Ryan looked at his phone again when the train approached the Civic Center. Ryan stared at the old texts from Susan and wondered if he would ever see her again. She had been ignoring him for days now, and he feared she was moving on. Ryan had liked Susan and wanted there to be more. But she wasn't answering any of his texts anymore, and the last time he took her for dinner at the Olive Garden, she had been distant and continuously on her phone.

Ryan closed the phone with a deep sigh and looked up as the train's brakes screeched loudly, and they came to a halt. At the Civic Center, a lot of people got up, including the young girl in front of him. Ryan still had two stops left, and he leaned his head back when his eyes landed on something underneath one of the seats. Some liquid of some sort was slowly seeping across the floor. Ryan felt his eyes stinging and rubbed them, then felt an unease in the pit of his stomach.

In a sudden attack of inexplicable panic, he rose to his feet and elbowed his way out through the crowd. The doors were about to close as he jumped out at the last second and into the car behind him, heart beating fast in his chest as the train took off once again.

Chapter 2

AS THE ORANGE Line southbound arrived at Government Station and opened the doors, the crowd waiting to get on board didn't realize at first what was going on. As usual, they approached the doors, waiting for them to open, so people could get out and then they could get in.

Evelyn Edwards was one of those waiting for the train. As always, she took the train from Government to Douglas Road, where she worked at Nordstrom in Merrick Park. Evelyn had her driver's license revoked after a DUI and had found that taking the train was actually a lot easier than being stuck in traffic every day.

On this particular day, Evelyn was lost in her own thoughts, thinking about her grown daughter, who she hadn't seen in four months. She had called her the night before to apologize once again, but she hadn't picked up. Evelyn felt shameful and wanted to tell her just how sorry she was for the things she had said. She also wanted to tell her daughter that the drinking had stopped now and she was doing AA, this time really doing the program with all the steps and not just sitting there because she had to. She wanted to tell her that she was better and that things had changed. Really changed this time. She wanted to tell her all those things, but her daughter wouldn't even answer her darn phone.

Don't you know you're all I've got?

Evelyn was so lost in her thoughts that she didn't even notice the passengers behind the doors. She didn't see their crying and strained faces as they were pressed against the glass, nor did she hear the hammering on the doors or the desperate cries for them to open.

When the doors did slide open simultaneously, and the passengers inside, screaming and gasping for air, tumbled out, Evelyn didn't even look up from her phone. She was looking at her background photo, a picture of her daughter taken on the beach when she was only five, the day she remembered as one of the best in her life.

Before everything turned bad. Before she started to drink. Before Juan died. Before she lost Pablo while eight months pregnant. Before the clouds darkened above them. Before she cried in bed all day. Before the fog of grief made her a prisoner in her own mind and destroyed everything.

Before all that.

We can go back, can't we? Can we find ourselves again?

Evelyn lifted her gaze and realized that the crowd in front of her had dispersed and an entire flock of passengers staggered toward her. Several of them collapsed in front of her feet. One woman came toward her, and Evelyn didn't notice her before it was too late, and she collapsed in Evelyn's arms. Blood was gushing from her nose and eyes, and she was gasping for air, choking and wheezing.

Evelyn shrieked fearfully and pushed her away, just as a man sank to the ground in front of her, his rag-doll-limp body falling to the platform with a thud. Evelyn stood, paralyzed, and watched this, blood smeared on her clothes and hands, while hundreds of people lay gasping on the ground, reminding her of the fish on her father's boat when she was a child.

A man in front of her lifted his head and looked her straight in the eyes, then breathed his last breath with a deep sigh. Seeing this, Evelyn whimpered, then turned around, wanting to get away from there, fast, when she suddenly stood face to face with a soldier. He, and the rest of his troop coming up behind him were wearing gas masks and clothes that to Evelyn looked like spacesuits.

ONE MONTH LATER

Chapter 3

"WE'RE HERE for your annual inspection."

I showed the small woman behind the front desk my identification card from Florida Department of Health, moving it very quickly to make sure she didn't get a proper look at it and realize it wasn't me on the picture, but someone who looked remotely like me. The woman had told me she was the manager of the spa.

"We need full access to the premises, please," I said.

We were me and my sister, Sydney. I called her that even though it wasn't the name she went by these days, and no one had called her that since she was seven years old. She was known publicly as Kelly Stone, the Hollywood actress. Still, I insisted on calling her Sydney, which was her birth name before our biological father stole her in a Wal-Mart and kidnapped her to London, where she grew up apart from me. I, on the other hand, grew up on the Space Coast in Florida with our mother, believing my sister was dead and gone. We had recently found one another after thirty-six years apart. It wasn't easy to reconnect after all this time, especially not after her scumbag of a boyfriend had kidnapped my daughter, Olivia, and sold her to an even worse scumbag on the Internet. Sydney, naturally, felt terrible about it, and that was why she had insisted on helping me find her again. As a former FBI agent, I had told her I was capable of doing this myself, but still, she had shown up at my house, ready to go on the day I had decided to leave. There wasn't anything I could say to talk her out of coming.

So, here we were — two sisters on a road trip through Hell.

We had been on the road for three months now, following my daughter's tracks, searching for the man they call the Iron Fist. Our search had led us to this place, The Orient Spa in Leisure City. The badge, I had stolen from a real health inspector in Palm Bay. It granted me access to places like these, where I could do my search. It wasn't exactly legal, any of it, but I was way beyond playing by the rules. My daughter was missing, and I was getting her back. No matter what it took. There was no way I was going to give up on finding her.

Never. Ever.

Sydney stood behind me, still wearing sunglasses so no one would recognize her. She had dyed her hair black and wore fake colored contacts whenever we went anywhere. I was naturally terrified that she would end up drawing attention to us, but I had to admit, she was doing pretty well at hiding her identity. I guess it came in handy that she was an actress. She even spoke completely different, hiding her British accent with a heavy American one.

The small Asian woman in front of me nodded. I saw her eyes grow weary.

"Yes, yes, of course. Go ahead."

We were pretending to be looking for roaches and rats in a routine inspection, so Sydney and I walked around the lobby and soon spotted a door leading to the back.

"What's behind that door?" I asked.

"Just the office in the back," the woman said, shifting on her feet, clearly feeling uneasy.

I smiled. "We're going to need to check that as well."

Her eyes grew big. "Oh, really? It's messy back there. There's nothing there. Costumer never come there."

"Doesn't matter," I said. "It can still pose a health hazard. We need to check everything."

"But old health inspector never went in there," she said. "He says it not necessary."

I smiled again. "Well, that's probably why he isn't here, but I am. Open the door, ma'am."

Chapter 4

THE MANAGER FUMBLED with the keys as she opened the door. The two other women who were introduced as massage therapists stayed behind, while Sydney stayed with them.

"We are up to date on all licenses," the manager said.

"That's good," I said indifferently and rushed in as soon as she had pulled the door open. The small woman hurried ahead of me. She ran into a room to our right, and I went in after her. As we entered and I spotted the mattresses on the floor, she tried to cover them up with a blanket. I still managed to see clothing and personal hygiene items before she covered it all up. Seeing this made me feel uneasy. The manager was visibly nervous while trying to cover up the items.

I continued down the hall and found another room — same thing. Mattresses spread on the floor, bedding, clothes, stuff for personal hygiene. There was a small refrigerator in the corner. I opened it and found it filled with food and drinks. A trash can had empty personal care items in it, mouthwash and shampoo.

It didn't take a genius to figure out what was going on here.

I rushed out the door back into the hallway, the small woman getting nervous now.

"Where you going, huh?"

Not answering her, I walked down the hall and tried to open a third door. It was locked.

"Open this," I said, my pulse quickening.

The woman stared at me. "I can't. No key."

I didn't think about it twice. I gave the door a violent kick, and it slammed open.

Just as I thought. Behind it, staring back at me sat eight young girls. Their eyes glared at me anxiously; their arms were wrapped around each other. Some were crying. All were dressed in barely any clothes.

The sight made me sick to my stomach. I turned on my heel, walked back in the hallway, and spotted the manager. She was backing up toward the exit when I pulled my gun from the holster and pointed it at her.

"You're not going anywhere. Get back here, now."

Sydney came up behind her, blocking her way out. The manager stared at the gun, then up at me.

"We're going to have a little chat," Sydney said and grabbed her by the neck. "In your office."

Sydney pushed her into the office, and I came in, then grabbed her and pressed my gun to the back of her head, pressing her down onto her desk. My hands were shaking when imagining one of these girls being Olivia. This was the fifth of these types of joints we had hit just in the past month, and everywhere it was the same — girls dressed in nothing, malnourished, confused, and scared. They would tell us stories of being taken and of many men coming to them at night, of being raped by hundreds of them a day, and of being shipped from one spa parlor to another during the day, entertaining more men than you'd want to think about.

It was beyond disgusting.

And one of them, somewhere out there, could be my daughter.

I couldn't finish the thought.

"I have money," the manager began. "I pay, you…"

"Shut up, lady. Shut up and listen to me. The way I see it, this can go two ways. Either I call the cops right now, and all of you end up in jail for many, many years."

"Or…?" the woman asked, her voice filling with hope.

"Or you give me what I want."

Chapter 5

JUST LIKE THE rest of them, she opted for the second solution. Of course, she did. I let go of her neck and let her sit down in a chair. Her hair was a mess as it had come out of her tight bun, and her eyes were anxious. She was broken. Just the way I needed her to be.

"What you want?" she asked.

I sat down in front of her; the gun still lingering in my hand.

"There's a man they call the Iron Fist," I said. "I need to get to him. I need to know where to find him. The last place we busted told us you might know."

The woman's eyes went from anxious to terrified as she looked up at me. She shook her head.

"I don't know no Iron Fist."

"And we're back to lying again," I said with a deep sigh. "You have a tell, do you know that? I'm sort of an expert in people and profiling them, and I can see straight through you. You wanna know how? You roll your lips back when you tell a lie, and you gesture with both hands after you have given me your answer. Both are 'tells.' So, do you want to tell me the truth, or should I call my friends at the sheriff's office?"

The woman's nostrils flared a couple of times, and her eyes lingered on me. I placed a picture of Olivia in front of her.

"I am looking for this girl," I said. "Have you seen her?"

The woman looked at it, then shook her head. "No."

I studied her. There were no signs that she was lying this time.
Dang it!

"All right, back to the Iron Fist. What do you know about him?"

The woman's lips quivered as she opened them to speak. "He buy girls," she said.

I nodded. "And where does he get those girls?"

She shrugged. "Wherever he can. Internet mostly."

"Has he bought any girls from you?"

The woman looked at me, then swallowed. She answered with nearly a whisper.

"Yes."

"And where does he take those girls?"

She shook her head. "I don't know."

"You're doing it again, the lip thing," I said and looked at Sydney. "She's doing it again."

Sydney nodded. "I saw it."

The woman exhaled. "Okay, he take them to Miami. That's all I know."

"Miami, huh? Where in Miami?" I asked, feeling relieved that we were finally getting somewhere.

"I don't know."

I could see no sign that she was lying, unfortunately. Miami was a big city to look for one man. But it was better than nothing. I was closing in, and that, at least, was something. I just hoped the guy still had my girl and hadn't sold her to someone else. With the stories I had heard from most of these girls, I wasn't too confident that she had remained in the same place for all this time. But it was the only lead I had, and I knew from experience that if you kept digging in the same place, at some point, you'd find something.

I rose to my feet and looked at my sister. "I guess we're going to Miami, then."

The Asian woman nodded, probably just happy at the prospect of us leaving. I glared at her, anger rising inside of me as I thought about her and people like her who lived by keeping these girls in slavery. What I had seen in the past three months had broken my heart to pieces.

The woman got up too. "So… no police?"

I stopped in my tracks, then leaned over and slammed my fist into her face so hard I heard her nose break.

"Yeah, about that. Turns out I have a tell too. When I knock out scumbags like you right after telling you that I won't report you to the police, then I'm actually lying. Guess you should have known that."

Chapter 6

WE LEFT the three women in the back office, tied up with strips. As soon as we were in the parking lot, in the mini-van that Sydney had bought for us when we decided to leave my old car because we knew it would be tracked after our first bust, I tapped the number of the local police enforcement.

I told them the address and what they would find when they got there. I also advised them to bring someone from a local shelter. I usually recommended a place called *No More Tears* since they seemed to be doing a good job of taking care of victims of human trafficking. I then threw the burner phone in the trash and got into the car, where Sydney had kept the engine running. I looked at her, then smiled, exhausted, before we took off, tires screeching across the asphalt while leaving the small strip mall.

This was the ninth of these types of spas that we had turned over to the police somewhere in Florida over the past three months. I couldn't believe how easy they were to find. Just a simple Google search had led me to the first one not far from my own home in Cocoa Beach. In a forum on the Internet, the all-male customers discussed vividly what you could expect to get there, what services they provided. They didn't even try to hide it. And so, I went to check it out. In the back, I found about ten girls, ages twelve to seventeen, ready to entertain the men who came as customers. To imagine that this was going on right beneath our noses, was terrifying. These girls came from all over the world, and some even from right here in Florida. And they were being held captive right here, right under our noses.

The only issue was that what I had done made me a criminal in the eyes of the law, and now they had put out a warrant for my arrest. Aggravated assault. I had lost it in the first place we took down and beat the crap out of the owner. If Sydney hadn't stopped me, I was certain I would have killed the guy. Still, I wasn't sorry I had hurt him. I was just sad that a surveillance camera had taken my picture as I left the shop.

Sydney looked briefly at me as she hit I-95 toward Miami. I held back my tears and tried hard to erase the images of those young girls in that room, and their big eyes staring back at me, pleading for my help. Hopefully, they would at least be liberated from their hell now. I could only pray that those who pulled the strings would be prosecuted as well, but I wasn't getting my hopes up. Those sleaze bags had a way of keeping themselves out of jail.

Meanwhile, we were going for one of the big guns. The man they called the Iron Fist. We didn't know much about him, but the little we knew made the hairs stand up on the back of my neck.

"You wanna grab a coffee and something to eat before we continue?" Sydney asked.

I gave her a look. She had been so amazing through all this, constantly taking care of me. I didn't know she had this side to her; I had to admit. This was very far from the entitled drama queen and Hollywood actress that I had taken her for, and I felt so thankful, yet I had no way of showing her. I was still so angry at her because of what had happened to Olivia. I knew it wasn't her fault. There was no way she could have known who her boyfriend was, yet I couldn't help myself. I needed someone to blame; I needed someone to take the fall, and she was the closest.

"I'm not hungry," I said and glanced out the window. "Although, coffee sounds about right."

She nodded. "Okay. I'll stop at the next rest area, and we can take a break."

"We should probably ditch the car too," I said.

"Again?" she asked tiredly. "I thought you said it looked like the strip mall had no cameras?"

I nodded with a sigh. "I could be wrong. Besides, there's always a witness; there's always someone who will have seen it and who will call the cops. We need to get rid of it."

Sydney nodded again. "Okay. We'll do that after we get our coffee."

Chapter 7

MATT STARED AT HIS SCREEN. In front of him smiled Eva Rae in a picture taken four months earlier on the beach. It was a great day, he remembered. They had brought all the kids together, her three and his Elijah. Matt had hoped that Alex and Elijah would bond if they spent the entire day together, but that hadn't happened. Elijah had sat underneath the gazebo all day, grumbling because he wasn't allowed to play on his computer. Matt remembered how hard Eva Rae had tried to get him to play with the other kids. She had even built the biggest sandcastle with Alex and kept asking Elijah if he didn't want to help. It wasn't until she pulled out Alex's kite and put it up, running down the beach holding it, that Elijah had suddenly gotten interested. He had crawled out and played with them, laughing when it fell down, and Eva Rae fell flat on her face in the sand.

Eva Rae was the only one in the world who had made Elijah laugh. Matt didn't know how she did it. But that was just her.

That's how amazing she was.

Gosh, I miss you.

She had been gone for three months now, and he had no idea where she was. It was probably for his own sake that she didn't contact him, but boy, it hurt. Matt had followed the investigation into what happened at The Bridge Spa in Rockledge after she beat a guy half to death in there. And he knew that the two detectives at the sheriff's office who had put out a warrant for her arrest had no idea where she was either. He also knew it was good that he didn't know because that would put him a dilemma if they came to question him. Eva Rae had known that, and that's why she had left without telling him where she went.

He had seen it in her eyes on the day he last saw her. It was at the CBPD station when they were questioning Anthony Piatkowski, the man who had targeted Eva Rae and then kidnapped her daughter, Olivia, who was only fifteen years old. They had grilled him for days on end, but he kept saying that he didn't know where Olivia was, only that he had taken her to the airport where the Iron Fist's men had picked up the girl. After that, he had no idea where she went. It was out of his hands.

Unfortunately, it turned out he was speaking the truth.

After weeks of going through his affairs, all they had found on his computer were the brief coded messages where they had agreed to the details. There was no trace of this Iron Fist or Olivia since.

That was when Eva Rae decided to take matters into her own hands, and once Matt heard about the manager at the spa getting attacked, and then how the police had received a call telling them where to find ten trafficked girls, he immediately knew in his heart that this had Eva Rae written all over it. He also knew there was no going back for her now, and that it would be a long time before he saw her again. If he ever saw her again.

Matt didn't know for certain, but he assumed that her sister had gone along with her since she had been nowhere near her house since. He hoped he was right in his assumption that the two of them were in this together since he didn't like for Eva Rae to be alone. She had to be feeling awful, and he was so frustrated that he wasn't able to be there with her to comfort her and hold her close. It tormented him not to know how she was feeling or to be able to help her. He wanted to fix this so badly.

There had been silent calls to his landline late at night that he suspected might be her. He believed it was her way of letting him know that she was okay and that she was still around.

But now that another month had passed, he was beginning to get anxious. What was her plan? And would she ever be able to come back?

Sgt. Mason pulled him out of his thoughts as he approached his desk.

"Chief wants to see you," he said. "Asap."

Chapter 8

SHE SLEPT on a stained mattress in a room with six other girls. There was no furniture in the house she was kept in and only one toilet.

Every night, she was taken out of the house and put into a van. They then drove for about an hour till they reached a factory, where they cleaned dead chicken and put them into a liquid that killed all bacteria before they were packaged and sent away.

They had given them no gloves to protect their skin, and now Olivia had gotten a rash and was itching all the way up her arm. The night before, she had complained about it to one of the men guarding them, but he had pulled her outside the factory and slapped her till she couldn't stand on her feet anymore, then yelled at her that she wouldn't get any toilet breaks for the rest of the night.

Now, as she lay on her stinky mattress, Olivia kept crying. She was thinking about her mother and her siblings and missed them terribly. It was daytime out, and the other girls were asleep, but Olivia couldn't find any rest. She was so scared, and she felt so hopeless. She hated the house, and she hated the factory even more. It stunk of rotten meat. There were chicken blood and innards all over the floors. But that wasn't the worst part. The worst part was that she never got to see the sun. There were no windows in the factory, nor in the house where they were kept. Armed men guarded the doors, and if they tried to escape, they were beaten. On one of the first days Olivia had been there, there had been a girl, Mya, who had tried to crawl out of the small window under the ceiling in the toilet. The guards had caught her in the yard, and Olivia had heard them as they beat her up all night. They had never seen Mya again.

Some of the girls had been to many other places before this, and they talked about being raped over and over again. They liked it better where they were now because at least they weren't raped. They were beaten again and again, but they'd take that any day over being raped by *so many men you couldn't even count them.*

The thought made Olivia cry even harder. Was that what was in store for her next? Would they sell her to some pimp? Would they move her out of state?

Mom, where are you? Are you looking for me? I am here, Mom. I am right here. I just don't know where here is.

One of the girls lying next to her, Juanita, was crying in her sleep. Olivia looked at her, then placed a hand on her shoulder to calm her down.

It worked. The girl stopped whimpering and continued to sleep. Olivia exhaled and looked at the other girls in the sparse light from the small lightbulb dangling from the ceiling. She wished she could sleep like these girls. She wished she could just disappear into a world of dreams and forget where she was for a few hours. She would dream of a day on the beach with her family. She would even want her dad to be there, even though she was so angry with him for leaving them and finding another woman, one who didn't want his kids around.

Still, she wanted him to be there with her because she missed him. She missed the life she had, with everything it contained, even the problems of high school and going through a divorce. At least that was all normal stuff. What she was living through now wasn't normal.

It was Hell on Earth.

Chapter 9

THEN

THEY HADN'T SEEN each other in five years. Helen Wellington looked at her old friend Angela, who smiled and waved at her from her seat at the restaurant Ariete. Helen waved back, then walked to her, a sense of dread in her stomach.

Was it a mistake for her to come?

"Helen," Angela said and rose to her feet. She reached out her arms and pulled Helen into a hug. "Let me look at you. Dear Lord, it's been forever."

"Not since Kylie's wedding," Helen said and sat down.

Angela was still smiling. "Has it really been that long?"

"You look amazing," Helen said, then looked down at herself. She was underdressed compared to her old friend, who was wearing a gorgeous yellow pencil dress and had impeccably styled hair. Helen used to be like that; she used to be the best dressed anywhere she went, and the one to radiate in a crowd, but not anymore. The past two years had been a struggle.

A waiter arrived, and they ordered lobster, pasta, and white wine.

"So, how have you been?" Angela asked.

Helen sighed. Angela had contacted her on Instagram and told her she was back in town and asked her if she had time for lunch.

"To be honest, I'm going through a rough time right now," she said.

Helen was surprised at her own openness; she hadn't expected to want to be since she wasn't usually, but this was her old best friend. They had known each other since third grade, and there was just something about Angela that made her want to open up.

"Really?" Angela said. "How so?"

Helen bit her cheek. She felt the sadness inside of her. It was like this monster that never slept but was constantly looking for a way to show its ugly face. Helen didn't know how to keep it down anymore.

"I've recently discovered that I can't have children," she said.

"Brian and I tried for years, and then we finally got checked out, and lo and behold, I was infertile. Having children was the biggest dream for Brian, so he left, and so, well… here I am. Probably going to be alone for the rest of my life. To be honest, I feel like I have nothing much left to get out of bed for."

Angela put a hand to her chest. "That's awful, Helen. I am so sorry."

The wine arrived, and Helen took a long deep sip. She still hadn't quite gotten used to telling her story yet, and it was a lot harder than she had thought it would be.

"Yeah, well, that's life, right?" she said.

Angela tilted her head. "It doesn't have to be."

Helen sipped more wine, then looked at her old friend suspiciously and a little offended.

"What is that supposed to mean?"

Angela drank too, then exhaled. "Nothing. It's just… well, I used to be miserable like you — two years of depression and anxiety. I was popping all the pills you can imagine, and nothing helped. I could barely get out of bed. So, let's just say I know how you feel."

Helen scrutinized her friend when the food arrived. She looked down at the seafood but didn't have much appetite. She had lost a lot of weight over the past several months because she didn't feel like eating.

"But you're better now?" she asked as she had swallowed the first bite anyway. "I mean you look great and you seem really happy? How did you get out of it?"

Angela sipped her wine, and a smile spread across her lips as she put the glass down.

"I thought you'd never ask," she said and leaned forward. "If you want to, I can get you what I have. I can help you."

Chapter 10

"SO FAR NO one has claimed responsibility for the July 9th attack on the Metrorail, and the authorities are still asking for help from the public. If anyone has seen anything that might help progress the investigation, then please come forward and call the number on the screen."

I stared at the TV in our hotel room. Sydney had gotten us a room at the Ritz Carlton Hotel in Coconut Grove, Miami. I thought it was silly to stay in these expensive surroundings, but she insisted that she would pay for everything.

"It's the least I can do."

Now, she was in the shower while I watched TV without really listening. They were talking about the July 9th gas attack on the Metrorail in Miami, as they had been for the past month since the attack had happened. According to what the authorities now knew, there had been three bags onboard the Orange Line going southbound in the morning rush hour. Three bags with a liquid gas in them that had killed seven passengers and left around fifty passengers still hospitalized. It was an act of terrorism, they said, but still, no one knew by whom and why. ISIS, most people guessed, but they had yet to claim it, as they usually did. According to experts, it had ISIS written all over it, but I wasn't so sure. ISIS had never used Sarin gas before.

"Sarin is a highly toxic and volatile form of nerve gas developed by Nazi scientists in the 1930s," the anchor on the TV explained. *"It's five hundred times more toxic than cyanide gas, which was used to execute people in gas chambers. It*

can be produced by a trained chemist with chemicals that are available publicly. The packages onboard the train leaked a thick liquid onto the floor, and people in the cars began to feel dizzy and lose their eyesight. Stinging fumes hit their eyes and struck them down in a matter of seconds. It left them choking and vomiting, while some were blinded and even paralyzed."

"Don't you want to watch something a little more uplifting maybe?" Sydney asked as she came out of the bathroom.

"I like to keep myself updated," I said.

She shrugged and dried her hair with a towel. She was so beautiful it was almost unfair. I never thought an actress could be prettier in real life than on the screen, but she was.

"Filling yourself with all the terrible things going on in this world?" she said.

"It makes me forget," I said. "It makes my problems seem less. I look at this and think at least my daughter isn't one of the dead ones on that train. Not that I know of, that is."

Sydney sat down on her bed and began moisturizing her legs with some expensive looking creme. "You sure you shouldn't call home? Ask how the children are doing?"

I exhaled and bit my cheek. Sydney kept asking me this, and it was every bit as painful every time.

"I know they're fine."

"I know you do. Mom is taking good care of them."

"Their dad is with them too. He moved to Cocoa Beach, remember? He knows how to take care of them. He got himself a condo, and he promised me he'd take good care of them all while I was gone, no matter how long it took."

Just get our daughter back, were his words. I could still hear them in my head. I called him on the day I had decided to leave, and he said he had found a condo and that he would come down the next day. I never got to see him face to face, but we made an agreement on the phone that day. He would take care of the kids, make sure they had everything they needed, while I brought back our oldest. Chad trusted the police to be able to get her back just as little as I did. I knew I could do better, even if it might end up costing me my entire career and maybe even jail time. Before I left, I had sat down with my mother and explained everything to her as well before asking her if she could help with the kids while I was gone. She had always loved Chad, even after he cheated on me, so it was not a big deal for her. Together, they would hold down the fort, we agreed.

"I won't be able to contact you. I won't be able to see you or help you out with anything for a very long time," I had explained. "I won't tell you where I'm going, what I'm doing, or when I'll be back. Do you understand? The less you know, the better. They can't get out of you what I didn't put in there in the first place. If they take you in for interrogation, you won't be able to give up my whereabouts."

She had agreed, even though she had been slightly scared.

"The kids might miss you," Sydney said now, slapping more moisturizer on her well-shaped legs. "And you might miss them. What's one little phone call, huh?"

I swallowed and stared at the TV. We had this conversation over and over again.

"They know I'm all right. I told them this was how it was going to be. Before I left, I sat down with them and told them I was going to find their sister, but that it meant I was going to be gone for some time."

I closed my eyes and recalled Alex's and Christine's eyes as they stared up at me. Christine was crying but tried desperately to hide it. Alex had placed his little hand on my shoulder and looked me seriously in the eyes.

"Go, Mom. Go find Olivia. We'll be fine. Just bring our sister back."

Christine had sniffled and nodded. "Alex is right, Mom. We just want Olivia back."

"You can just call them from one of those burner phones you carry around," Sydney said. "I know you're dying to hear their voices."

I was. She was right about that part. Every cell in my body was desperately screaming to see them again or at least hear their voices. I wanted to hug them and kiss them, but I wanted to hold their sister in my arms just as much, and right now she was the one who needed me the most, not them.

"It's too risky," I said. "By now, the police might have tapped all their phones. I can't risk them finding us and having all this been in vain. I almost killed a guy, Sydney. It's not small stuff."

"All right, all right. I hear you. I was there, remember?"

"I do," I said and turned off the TV in the middle of pictures from the gas attack. Right before the TV went out, I thought I saw something that made my heart stop.

What in the...?

Heart pounding in my chest I turned the TV back on, but as I did, they had moved on to another story and were interviewing some politician.

"No, no, no," I said and flipped to another channel, then continued till I was frantically scrolling through all the channels.

"NO!" I screamed and threw the remote toward the wall. It slammed against it, then fell to the carpet, the batteries falling out.

"What's going on?" Sydney asked and picked it up. "Why are you freaking out?"

I stared at her, panting and agitated.

"I...there was...on the TV, she was there!"

"Who was? You're making no sense, Eva Rae."

"OLIVIA!" I yelled, grasping my face. "She was right there. On that clip from the attack, the one they just showed. She was on the platform."

Chapter 11

"I'M TAKING you off the Baxter case."

Chief Annie looked at him from the other side of the desk. Matt wrinkled his forehead. The chief had closed the door behind him as he entered her office. This was serious.

"The bar stabbing case? Why? I have it almost wrapped up?" he said, confused.

What was this? Didn't she think he could handle it?

"Annie, I'm almost…"

She lifted her hand to stop him. "I need you elsewhere, Matt, that's why."

"Elsewhere? What's going on?"

She scratched her forehead, then exhaled. "I am lending you to Miami-Dade County. You're going to work on this case with a detective down there; his name is Charles Carter."

She pushed a file toward Matt, and he took it. He opened it and looked down at it then up at her.

"But this is…?"

She nodded. "I need you on it, Matt."

"But Annie, this is…?"

She leaned forward. "I need you to do this. I want you to keep an eye on the investigation. Report back to me."

"But don't they know that I'm personally involved in this?" he asked.

She shook her head. "No."

Matt nodded pensively, then looked at the file, skimming a couple of pages. It was odd to see the woman he loved described like this.

"She was last seen in Leisure City," Annie said. "A small town down south close to Miami. She struck a spa and a massage parlor down there. Miami-Dade has put out a warrant for her arrest, just as the Brevard County Sheriff has one out for what she did in Rockledge, and Broward County Sheriff's office has one out for what she did in Ft. Lauderdale. She's wanted for fraud, theft, assault and battery. You need to get her home before she digs herself in so deep there is no turning back."

Matt exhaled and felt his pulse quicken as he flipped through the case file.

"Listen, Matt. I need you down there to make sure she comes out of this alive. I care about her too much to simply let her dig her own grave down there in the search for her daughter."

Matt nodded. He grabbed the file, thinking this was going to be tough, but it was what was needed. He wanted Eva Rae home more than anyone.

"Any news on Piatkowski?" he asked, knowing that they were still trying to find Olivia that way.

"Our team is still trying to lure the Iron Fist out through the Dark Web, but so far, he hasn't taken the bait."

Matt cleared his throat, then stood to his feet.

"I'll go home and pack a bag, then leave right away."

Annie pulled into half a smile.

"Bring her home in one piece, will you?"

"I'll do my best. You know I will."

Chapter 12

I REFUSED to go down to the restaurant and eat, so Sydney ordered us room service while I roamed the Internet on the laptop that Sydney had bought me in Palm Bay. I hadn't logged onto any social media on it, nor had I checked my email, knowing they might try and find me that way. But I used it for research, and now I was trying to find the clip I had seen on TV from the local TV station's webpage.

Later on, Sydney went to bed while I continued my search, not coming up with anything. I was beginning to think that maybe Sydney was right, and I was just seeing what I wanted to because I missed my daughter so much. Still, it nagged me. Something deep down inside of me told me it was her. What if she was on that platform when those trains were attacked? The thought worried me deeply. Was she exposed to the gas? Was she in the hospital?

I grabbed my phone and started calling the hospitals nearby that I knew some of the passengers had been sent to, but no one by her name had been treated there, they said.

Maybe she could have been admitted under another name?

I found more footage from the scene shown on the day of the attack and played it. A reporter was reporting live from the station, standing outside of the building, while ambulances were parked behind her.

I leaned back in my chair and listened to her words, my eyes fixated on what went on behind her when suddenly something caught my eye. A guy was standing behind her, looking confused while talking to a paramedic. I stared at him, then stopped the clip and looked at his face.

I know him.

There was no doubt. This was Ryan. Ryan Scott. Jack and Michelle's oldest son. They were a couple we had been friends with back in Washington, back when the kids were younger, and Chad and I were still an item. They had a younger son too, Blake, who was the same age as our Christine and went to the same school. We had hung out often when the kids were younger, until my job took over so much that I had no time for a social life anymore and neither of us really wanted to go to a dinner, pretending to be this perfect couple that we no longer were.

What was Ryan doing in Miami? Had he been on the train? Had he maybe seen my Olivia?

Chances were small, but not impossible.

I tapped my fingernails on the desk, wondering how I could contact his parents and ask for Ryan's info, then closed the lid on the computer, deciding to call them from a burner phone the next day. I stared into thin air, a million thoughts running through my mind, then rose to my feet and stared at Miami from my window. There was no way I could sleep knowing Olivia was out there in this big city somewhere.

I grabbed the car keys, wrote Sydney a note, then left the hotel room. I drove to downtown Miami, cruising through the streets, looking at the nightlife, staring at every girl or young woman I laid my eyes on, thinking it could be her; it could be my Olivia.

And then I spotted her. Standing on a corner by a streetlight, just as a car drove up to her and rolled down the window.

Chapter 13

"OH, NO, YOU DON'T!"

I parked the car on the side of the road, then grabbed my gun from my ankle-holster, and stormed out toward them.

"Freeze!"

The girl, who was wearing a short skirt and way too much make up for her age, pulled out from the window and looked directly at me. The sight made my heart drop.

It wasn't her.

It was a young girl about the same age who looked very much like her. She had a bad bruise on her cheek, and from one look into her eyes, I could tell she was drugged.

I lowered the gun, my heart pounding. The girl took one look at me, then took off running while the car drove off, tires skidding on the asphalt.

I stared in the direction the girl had disappeared, then put the gun away in its holster, knowing it would only be a matter of minutes before her pimp and his friends would come for me.

She's someone's daughter.

I backed up and went back to the Mustang convertible that Sydney had bought for us after we ditched the minivan in Leisure City. I thought it was too flashy, but she had argued that this was what the tourists drove down here, and if we wanted to blend in, this was the way.

NEVER EVER

I had to admit; she had a point. With her big hats and scarves and the car, we did look like most of the tourists in this town. And I was beginning to think that the place we stayed was smart too. The people looking for me would never think to look for me at the big expensive hotels. They'd be searching the motels and creepy places where people thought it was easy to hide. And since we were using Sydney's credit cards, it left no trace back to me, since no one — except the people closest to me — knew that she was my sister.

I got back behind the wheel, then took off into the warm night, continuing through town, even driving through Overtown, the worst part of Miami. I made a lot of heads turn, but no one tried anything. I stared into the face of every girl I saw and couldn't help but see Olivia everywhere. So many young girls working the streets, it was unbearable.

What was she doing on that Metrorail platform? Why was she there? Who was she with?

I decided to drive to Government Center and stood for a long time outside of the train station, staring at the leftover crime scene tape, while wondering where Olivia was and if she was all right. Had she inhaled any of the gas? Was she out there somewhere sick and in need of help? Was anyone taking care of her?

"Please, God, help me find her. Help me figure out if it was really her that I saw. Was I just imagining it like I was with that other girl on the street? Or was it really her?"

A tear escaped the corner of my eye, and I let it roll down my cheek. I didn't even have my pictures of her since I had left my phone on the kitchen counter at my house when I left. I only had this paper school photo with me that I used to show people when asking about her, trying to dig my way through the underground world of trafficking in Florida. It was two years old, and she still had long hair back then.

In a weak moment, I dialed Matt's number on my burner phone.

"Hello?"

He sounded sleepy, and I guessed that I had woken him.

"Hello…? Is anyone there?"

I miss you, Matt. I miss your arms and your smile. I miss being with you.

I closed my eyes and held the phone tight to my ear, thinking about hugging him, smelling him, and feeling his strong arms around me.

"Eva Rae? Is that you?"

Pause. A deep sigh.

"Where are you, Eva Rae?"

I hung up, tears streaming down my cheeks, heart pounding in my chest. I was risking everything by doing what I was doing, but it was what I had to do. I had to do this for my daughter. I just prayed that Matt would understand that.

"I love you, Matt," I said to the dead phone and threw it in the trash.

I had never said the words to his face, and as I got back into the Mustang and it roared to life, I wondered if I was ever going to get the chance.

Chapter 14

"RYAN SCOTT?"

The man in the doorway looked at me skeptically through the crack. I had knocked on the door to his apartment after getting the address from his mother that same morning. Apparently, Ryan was in Miami because he was doing a summer internship at a local paper, she had told me. He had been on his way to work when the attack happened.

"Who are you?" he asked.

"You don't recognize me? I'm Eva Rae Thomas; well, I used to be Wilson back then in Washington. I know your parents, Jack and Michelle?"

He stared at me from behind the chain. "The FBI agent?"

I nodded. Sydney stood behind me, keeping her distance. "Yes, that's me."

"And who is she?"

"My sister. She's with me down here while we… Didn't your mom tell you I would stop by?"

"Maybe. What do you want?"

"I just want to talk to you for a second. Can we come in? Please? It's important."

Ryan stared at me, scrutinizing me, then finally opened the chain on the door and let us inside. The small one-bedroom condo was a mess — pizza boxes everywhere, trash bags that should have been taken out long ago, clothes scattered on the floor and the furniture.

"What's going on here, Ryan?" I asked as we came into the living room. "Have you been out of the condo at all since the attack?"

He ran a hand through his greasy hair. "I'm just having a little trouble getting outside. It's nothing."

"You're scared," I said. "It's only natural. But what about your summer internship?"

He shrugged. "I called it in right when it happened. I gave them the story, so they were the first to break it. But the next day, I couldn't get out of my condo, I was so scared it would happen again, so I called in sick. I haven't been there since. I can't seem to get past the door. I just need a little time; that's all. It'll get better."

I felt sad for him as I found a space on the couch that wasn't covered in old clothes or trash and sat down. This wasn't good.

"But that is actually why we're here," I said. "To talk to you about the attack."

Ryan's nostrils flared slightly, and he stared at me with wide open eyes. He rubbed his hair manically.

"The attack? Huh? W-what about it?"

He went to close the blinds on the window, then turned to look at me.

"You were on the train when the gas was released," I said. "What did you see?"

"I didn't see much," he said, still frantically rubbing his hair. "And if I did, I don't remember much of it."

"But what do you remember? Please?"

"I remember a liquid on the floor. It was coming out of a plastic bag. I remember seeing it, then somehow, I don't know why, maybe it was because I felt it stinging in my eyes, but I just knew I had to get out. So, I did, at Civic Center. I changed cars to the one behind it where there was no gas. I had no way of knowing that, though. It was dumb luck, I guess. They say it saved my life that I changed cars when I did."

"But you saw all the people who got sick, and some even died. That must have been terrifying. Did you see anything else?"

He thought it over for a while, then shook his head. "It was all so chaotic; I don't know."

I bit my cheek, then said. "Do you remember my daughter, Olivia?"

He gave me a look, rubbed his neck, then nodded. "The one with the red hair who played with my brother?"

I shook my head. "No, that's Christine. This is Olivia," I said and pulled out the old school photo. "She has short hair now."

He shook his head. "Maybe, I don't know."

"Look at it again, Ryan, please. I have reason to believe she might have been on the same train as you that day. I think I saw her on a surveillance clip on TV. She's been missing for three months, all summer, and I need to find her. Did you see her?"

He stared at the photo, then shook his head. "Maybe, I don't know. The police have been asking me about so many people, and I don't remember any faces. They say the gas might have affected my memory and maybe even made me paranoid."

I felt tears well up in my eyes but refused to let them overwhelm me. I had been so certain Ryan could help me.

"Look at the picture again, will you? Please?"

He did, then shook his head, fiddling nervously with his shirt. "I... I'm sorry."

I rose to my feet and looked at Sydney, who gave me back a glance of sympathy.

"I am sorry to have disturbed you," I said and went for the door.

"There is something," he suddenly said.

I turned around.

"What?"

"There is something that I keep seeing. I see it in my dreams and sometimes even when awake."

"What is it?" I asked, a little harsher than I wanted to. "Ryan? What is it? Tell me; it might be important."

He rubbed his eyes. Then he scribbled something on a note and handed it to me.

"I keep seeing this…this symbol. I think it was a tattoo or something on an ankle, I think. Maybe a wrist. I keep seeing it. I don't know. It might be nothing. It's just that, the past few days, I keep dreaming about it and seeing it everywhere. Again, it might be nothing."

I forced a smile, then took the note. "We'll keep it in mind. Thanks, Ryan."

Chapter 15

"GET UP!"

A boot hit Olivia in the stomach, and she cried out in pain. Above her lingered a face. A man. She gasped and sat up, covering herself with the thin sheet she was sleeping with.

The man smiled creepily at her, then nodded toward the door.

"You're leaving. Now!"

All six girls stood to their feet and walked outside. It was the middle of the night, but still so hot she could barely breathe. Cicadas sang in the darkness while a dog barked somewhere nearby. She couldn't remember when they had last given her a shower, and she felt clammy and stinky all over. A girl walking next to her whimpered in fear. Olivia put her arm around her shoulder, but a guard saw it and slapped her over the head.

"Keep moving!"

They were taken to a truck and told to get in. A girl from another room fell to her knees and cried. Two guards rushed to her and started beating her up. Punches and kicks landed on her small body, and she couldn't get up. The other girls stared, unable to react out of fear of being next. Olivia saw it, then ran to the girl and grabbed her arm. She helped her get up from the ground. A guard pulled Olivia by the hair forcefully. Olivia screamed and was pushed away from the girl. Meanwhile, the girl had gotten to her feet and was now on her way into the back of the truck. Olivia stopped at the edge of the truck, then looked at the guard.

This is not the usual truck that takes us to the chicken factory. What's going on?

"Where are you taking us?"

The guard grinned, then pointed his rifle at her.

"Ask me again and feel the answer."

Olivia stared into the barrel of the rifle, her heart thumping in her chest.

"I didn't think so," the guard said, then nodded toward the back of the truck. "Now, get a move on. We don't have all day."

Olivia pulled herself up, and soon after the back was closed, and the truck took off. She felt how her hands were shaking and tried to hold them still but couldn't. Many of the other girls had told stories of being shipped from place to place and being raped over and over again. Was that what was going to happen now? Were they being shipped somewhere else? Would there be big sweaty men waiting for them, ready to rape them?

Please, God, no.

Olivia closed her eyes; then she felt something touch her hand. She opened them again and saw the girl from earlier. She could be no more than eleven or twelve years old. Definitely Hispanic. Her big brown eyes stared at Olivia, and she spoke to her in Spanish, but Olivia didn't understand. She just smiled comfortingly at her, then tried to control the deep panic roaming inside of her. That was when her eyes fell on something inside the truck with them, leaning up against the back wall, and her heart dropped.

Chapter 16

THEN

"IT'S LIKE A SECRET SORORITY," Angela said excitedly as they walked up the stairs. She was gesticulating wildly as she spoke yet was almost whispering like it was some big secret. "We help each other out. You're gonna love it; just wait and see."

It had been a week since their last meeting at the restaurant where Angela had explained to Helen that she knew exactly what would help her get out of her depression and find purpose in her life again. She had told her she needed to meet with a group of friends that Angela knew, all consisting of famous actresses, billionaire heiresses like Helen, businesswomen, CEOs, and filmmakers. All had felt the same emptiness and lack of purpose in life, just like her.

As she entered the beautiful old house, a group of women turned their heads and looked at her. At first, Helen felt uneasy because of all the stares, and she wasn't sure she belonged there, but seconds later, they all greeted her warmly with handshakes, smiles, and some even with hugs. Someone handed her a cup of herbal tea, and they all sat on yoga mats in a circle, drinking tea, and soon after they were doing yoga, following Angela's instruction. Helen had always loved doing yoga, and it made them all relax in each other's company.

When they were done, she received another cup of herbal tea, and they sat on the floor, all sweaty and dressed in relaxed yoga outfits while laughing and telling harrowing stories about men and dating.

"Who needs men anyway?" a woman called Laura said. She was an heiress to a well-known cosmetic emporium.

That made them laugh, even Helen, who couldn't remember having laughed like that in months.

"So, how do you do it?" Helen asked. "How do you live without men?"

Laura smiled at her. "If you want to, we can teach you. It's called enlightenment."

"I want to learn," she said. "I don't want to be dependent on a man in my life. I want freedom and to be independent. Like you all are."

That made the others smile. They chuckled and nodded.

"Then, you've come to the right place," Laura said and rose to her feet. She went to her purse and pulled out a small book that she handed to Helen.

"Here. Read this. This is the first step. See if you like what this author writes. It's about finding your way to greater fulfillment. He's really good."

Helen looked at the book, then at the author's name. *Christopher Daniels.* From his picture, he stared back at her with deep blue eyes. She couldn't explain how, but he somehow made her feel better already. At least she felt like she was finally doing something to better her life, and the company of these women seemed like just what she needed right now.

"Thanks," she said and took the book.

Angela placed a hand on her shoulder. "That book saved my life," she said. "And now it will do the same for you."

Helen nodded, tearing up. "I can't thank you enough. All of you."

"It's gonna be quite the journey," Angela said, "but soon you'll be one of us, and then there'll be no more sad days. Ever."

Chapter 17

DETECTIVE CARTER WAS A SHORT, bald man who had sweaty patches underneath his armpits in his white shirt that was tucked inside of his black pants. Matt had only been with him for a few hours, but it was enough to know he was also a very stubborn man who didn't exactly want Matt there.

They were going through the case files together in Carter's office at Miami-Dade Police Department, and Matt was showing him what he had brought down with him, the case of the attack of the spa owner from Rockledge.

Carter had four other files to match it, all with the same MO. And he had the personnel file from the FBI.

"So far, she's wanted for fraud, theft, battery, and assault," he said. "But I assume you know that. It's the same charges you brought."

Matt looked at the small, sweaty man as he spoke. He sensed that he probably wasn't going to get very far by trying to defend Eva Rae. To this guy, a criminal was a criminal, no matter the motive.

Carter found a map and showed it to Matt. "These are the four places she has hit within our county. Now, the last place was in a strip-mall, the Harper Shop Malls, where we have this surveillance photo from a nearby ATM." He pulled out a photo and placed it in front of Matt.

"As you can see, Agent Thomas is clearly in the passenger seat of the mini-van. This fits well with our theory that she is not working alone. We just don't know who she's working with. We also assume that this person is the one paying for the party since Agent Thomas hasn't used her credit card in three months. There have been no transactions made or any withdrawals, but she must pay for lodging somewhere, right?"

Matt nodded. "Unless she stays with people she knows. She might have friends down here that we don't know about."

"True, but she needs to eat too, and she has made her way down south somehow, getting new cars on her way. Now, we know that the minivan they ditched after the last hit was registered to an address in Jupiter, and the owner says it was stolen, but as we looked into his finances, it turns out there was a deposit of twenty-thousand dollars in cash about a week before we found it. We suspect Miss Thomas and her accomplice bought it and told the owner to say it was stolen if we showed up, but we have no evidence to back that up."

Clever, Matt thought to himself, slightly impressed, but also concerned. Eva Rae knew all about how the police worked and could stay under the radar for a very long time, but what would happen once they finally caught up to her? Would she come out of it alive?

"We have eyes on her house and her kids in case she decides to come back to Cocoa Beach," Matt said. "She left her phone at the house, and as you said, her credit cards haven't been used. There's been no sight of her in Cocoa Beach or anywhere near it since she left."

"Dang it," Carter said. "I'd expect a woman like her to at least check in now and then on the kids."

"She probably knows it's too much of a risk. How did the owner of the car explain the money in his bank account?" Matt asked. "When you asked about it?"

Carter shook his head. "He gave us some story about selling a boat long ago and then not getting the money until now. He had no proof of ever owning a boat."

"So, where do you believe our suspect is now?" Matt asked. It felt weird talking about the woman he loved as a suspect, but he had to keep a professional distance. Carter couldn't know he was emotionally involved with her, or they would ask for someone else from his department to assist them. Matt wanted to be there; he needed to be on the front line of this investigation.

Or else he feared for the worst.

"We don't know," he said. "The car was found ditched here."

Carter pointed at the map south of Leisure City limits.

Matt looked up. "Could she have left town? Gone south?"

Carter smacked his lips, then nodded. "It's definitely a possibility. I say we push out her description and have it circulated in the police departments all over south Florida, even the airports and security and customs as well. In case she tries to get out of here. Meanwhile, I say we try and find out who is helping her. If we can locate that person, we might be able to find them by credit card transactions."

Matt nodded, biting his lip. He had a strong feeling he knew exactly who was with her, but he didn't dare tell Detective Carter. He wanted to find Eva Rae on his own and then maybe persuade her to come home with him. She would have to take responsibility for her actions, but both Matt and Eva Rae knew Greg, the DA in their home county, and maybe he would let her off easy if both Matt and Chief Annie testified on her behalf. No matter what, her chances were a lot better up north in her home county than down here. And right now, that was all that mattered… making sure her children still had a mother once this was all over.

Chapter 18

"DANG IT. IT'S NOT THERE."

I leaned back in the chair. I was sitting in the hotel room and had been on my computer all day, while Sydney waited patiently on the bed, reading. She put the book down and gave me a look.

"What are you searching for?"

"The clip. I went through all the files on the attack to see if I could find the surveillance clip somewhere, but I can't find it. I can find tons of other ones, but not the one with my daughter on it. But then again, there are a lot of files, and it's going to take me days to go through it all."

"Is it safe to log into the FBI while on the run from the police?" she asked.

I sighed. It wasn't. If they knew I had been on, they could trace me, but I also knew the FBI wasn't looking for me. I had crossed no state lines. I hadn't given them a reason to take over the investigation. The local police were the ones who had it in for me.

"I don't know. But I had to check, you know? I called the TV station this morning, but they said they had shown so many clips, so if I couldn't tell them exactly which one I was looking for, they couldn't help me. I knew the FBI Joint Terrorism Task Force would be handling the gas attack since it's considered an act of terrorism. I figured they had more footage in their database. Maybe there'd be one with Olivia in it."

"So, what are they saying about it? Who's behind it?" Sydney asked and approached me.

"They don't know yet, but they think ISIS is all over it. They think there was a reason the gas was released at Civic Center while the train went on for two more stops and ended at Government Center. The latter services all the government buildings, the judges, state attorney's office, courthouses, etc. They think they were trying to target people working there. Surviving witnesses say there were bags onboard the train and it is believed that the terrorists were on board the train themselves and then poked a hole in the bags with the liquid nerve gas before getting off, leaving the gas behind to poison the remaining passengers, letting them die a slow and painful death. It makes me sick."

"But can't they just find them from CCTV cameras?" Sydney asked.

I shrugged. "How do you recognize who is a terrorist in a crowd? They've talked to many of the passengers, but there were several hundreds of them on board that train. Right now, they're going through the CCTV footage from the Civic Center station, where they assume the terrorists left the train, but finding each and every passenger will take months, maybe even years."

Sydney placed her hand on my shoulder. "Maybe it wasn't Olivia that you saw after all," she said and sat down in a chair next to me. She grabbed my hands in hers and held them tight. I still couldn't believe I had actually found my sister after thirty-six years. It felt so unreal. Yet I couldn't fully enjoy it. Not when my daughter was out there somewhere, lost, and I felt such anger toward my sister for bringing Piatkowski into our lives. I knew she felt it too. She saw it in my eyes, and she let go of my hands.

"It *was* her," I said, not entirely convinced. I had, after all, just thought I saw Olivia on the street the night before, feeling almost as convinced. Was I just fooling myself?

"Think about it," she said. "Your mind might be playing tricks on you, making you see what you want to see."

I turned away from her. "It was her. I know it was. No one has asked you to be here. If you don't like it, then you're free to leave. I sure don't need you here."

I stared at my screen, sensing Sydney's hurt from across the room. She sighed and rose to her feet, then went into the bathroom and shut the door. I closed my eyes for a second, wondering if I had taken it too far. The fact was, I needed her with me through this, but I couldn't get myself to say that.

Chapter 19

I COULDN'T STOP THINKING about that symbol that Ryan talked about. I felt like I had seen it before but couldn't put my finger on where. I stared at the note where Ryan had drawn the symbol, then tried to figure out what it could be. It looked strange, and I wasn't quite sure what was up and what was down. Could it be some sort of Chinese symbol? Or a Greek letter?

I searched for it on the computer. I didn't even hear the door to the bathroom as it opened, and Sydney came out. I was so immersed in my research that I didn't even notice she was packing her bag either. It wasn't until I had gone through all the Greek letters and had submerged myself into the Chinese alphabet that I realized I was all alone. The door slamming shut behind Sydney had caught my attention, but it was too late.

Darn it!

I stared at the closed door, then noticed that all of Sydney's things were gone. My heart dropped. What was I doing?

I thought about getting up and running after her, but for some reason, I didn't. I felt like I was paralyzed. Did she want me to come after her? Or was it too late already? Had I ruined it?

I can't deal with this right now.

I turned to look at my screen again, then continued to go through the Chinese letters, but my brain wouldn't focus. I kept thinking about my sister. As I reached the end of the first row of letters, I stood to my feet, then ran out into the hallway. I took the elevator down, my heart thumping in my chest, then ran into the lobby. But I was too late. As I came outside, I saw her ride away in a taxi, and seconds later, she was gone.

Shoot.

I stomped my foot and cursed, then realized there was a woman standing next to me, staring at me, eyes wide.

"I'm sorry," I said. "She left with my phone in her purse, and now I can't call her and tell her to bring it back."

"That's awful," the woman said.

"Sure is," I said, then hurried inside again and passed the bar that had a TV running. I had almost passed it when I stopped and walked back. On the screen above the bar, I saw my own face looking back at me. They had used an old photo from my days at the FBI. Underneath was written one word:

WANTED.

"Oh, Lord," I mumbled, then looked around to see if anyone had seen it. Luckily, the bar was almost empty. I bowed my head and rushed back into the elevator, then pressed the button to take me to the fifth floor. I hurried back into my hotel room and slid down on the carpet behind the door, keycard still in my hand, tears rolling down my cheeks. There was no way I could continue my search now. Not with my face plastered all over the screens in this town. I looked up toward the ceiling.

"What do you want me to do now, God? How am I supposed to find Olivia now?"

And that was when I remembered. In that very second, it popped into my head where I had seen the symbol before. I rose to my feet and hurried to the computer, then ran a search. A second later, the symbol came up on my screen, and my heart started to throb in my chest.

Chapter 20

IT WAS the first time since his momma died that Jason wanted to go to church again. At only eleven years old, the boy had lost all his faith in God and His goodness. Jason's Aunt Judi, who never missed Sunday Mass, had asked him every week if he cared to go. And finally, this Sunday morning, he had said yes.

"I have a lot to talk to God about," he said determinedly.

Jason put on his Sunday clothes, took his aunt by the hand, and left the house where his father worked in his office, always on the phone, always busy, and never coming out for anything but to eat or rush off to work.

Judi was pleased that she was able to bring Jason to St. Mary's Cathedral on 2nd Avenue. It had been her home church since she moved to Miami five years ago, and to her, there was no better place on Earth to be — especially since her sister died. This was where she felt the closest to her, and she wanted the boy to experience that too. She wanted him to know that his mother was fine, that she was in a better place now. It was a promise she had made to Michaela as soon as she got sick — to keep taking the boy to church and make sure he was raised in the faith. Michaela knew her husband would never take care of that since he never went to mass and didn't believe in anything but making money and more of it.

"Do you really think Momma will hear me if I pray?" he asked as they parked the car and walked up to the cathedral.

Judi held the boy's hand tightly in hers. She was worried about him and what would become of him now that Michaela wasn't there anymore. Peter, his dad, had his own way of grieving, which mostly consisted of burying himself in work till he dropped. There was no room for the boy or his big grief and many questions. She had often thought about taking him in, asking Peter if the boy wouldn't be better off at her house. She had no kids of her own and could take good care of him.

"That's what I believe," Judi said. "I think she's with God now but that she's also keeping a close eye on you, making sure you behave."

She said the last part while tickling him gently in the side. The boy shrieked, then chuckled. His big eyes looked up at her.

"I miss her," he said as they sat down in the pew.

She kissed the top of his head. "I know, sweetie. I know. I do too — every day. I miss her calling me; I miss drinking coffee with her. What do you miss?"

She had read that it was important to talk to children about their deceased parents. Where most people just stopped talking about them since it hurt too much, children had a natural desire to speak about them and keep the memory of them alive.

"I miss hearing her laugh," he said after a second of thinking it over.

Judi smiled and nodded. "Yes, that's what I miss the most too."

Judi turned and looked behind her. The church was filling up slowly. A young girl sat down in front of them, and a couple came in after her and sat next to her.

What a nice family, Judi thought to herself sadly. She had never managed to have a family of her own, and her sister, who had, wouldn't be around to experience her child growing up. It was indeed a sad world they lived in.

As mass started and she stood to her feet, Judi felt her eyes stinging. She chalked it up to her being an emotional mess. It wasn't till her throat started to feel tight, and she could no longer breathe that she realized something was terribly wrong.

By then, it was too late.

Chapter 21

THEN

ANGELA WAS SITTING on a mahogany stool in her kitchen. Her fifteen-thousand-square-foot, five-million-dollar home was tastefully decorated, overlooking the Intracoastal waters and the pool in the backyard. A series of photos of her with her teenage sons decorated the walls behind her. None of them was with her ex-husband, whom she had cut out of her life completely as soon as she ripped him of half of everything he owned after his affair with a woman from his gym.

A hairless cat sat in a bed, while the women in Angela's kitchen indulged themselves in the vegan and gluten-free dishes sitting on the granite counter island.

Helen knew most of the women by now, after many meetings like these. She had read the book by Christopher Daniels five times and taken several of his self-help classes in the hope that she might improve her life. It was expensive but so worth it. And so far, she was feeling more empowered with every step she took — just like the book had told her she would. She was getting stronger and slowly changing what she believed about herself. She wanted to get rid of all her fears and become as powerful and self-reliant as she was able to.

"I don't know how to explain it," Helen said.

They had been asked to share their fears and phobias as a part of their evolvement. Helen was telling them about her fear of dogs.

"It's like this choking sensation. I can't breathe every time I see a dog. Even if it's behind a fence, I just can't breathe. It's so devastating since I can't go to visit friends who might have a dog in the house. It doesn't matter what size it is or how sweet and friendly it is. I just can't be near a dog."

"It's an emotional trigger," Angela said. "Formed in your childhood. Can you remember ever being bitten by a dog? Or attacked by one?"

Helen shook her head. "No. That's the problem. I don't have any bad experiences with any dogs."

"We need to dig deeper," Angela said. "Explore the meaning of this trigger. It might be something more serious. Once you know what is really behind it, you can reduce the power it holds over you today."

"But how?" Helen asked.

"Hypnosis," Angela said. "Come."

She told Helen to lie down on a mat in the middle of the living room while the rest of the women joined in a circle around her. Angela asked her to close her eyes, and in a stream of intimate questions, spoken in nearly a whisper, she asked her about everything from her first meeting with a dog, to her parents' relationships. When they were done, she told Helen to open her eyes and sit up.

Helen felt dizzy and rubbed her forehead while Angela took her hand in hers.

"Your upbringing is what is causing this fear," she said. "The dog represents your own fear of success, your fear of independence. When you meet an obstacle or hardship in life, you run away; you hide from it, thinking you can't deal with it. Your parents have led you to believe that you can't do anything on your own — that you are incapable of taking care of yourself without a man. Meanwhile, your mother had a terrible life, and you believe she was forced into that life by your father. Your mother was unable to become an independent woman and chose to be a victim in her own life. Do you want that, Helen? Do you want to be a helpless woman? Or do you want to take control of your life? Do you want to be in the driver's seat of your own destiny?"

Helen stared at the woman in front of her, her childhood friend, and then at the women surrounding her. She had never thought about life in such a manner. The way they were teaching her was so different from anything she had ever encountered. Was it really true? Was she able to take control? All the things that had happened to her, the loss of ability to reproduce, the loss of her husband, the depression, was it all something she could get rid of? She had always gone running to her daddy when things went wrong in her life. What if she became the one person she relied on?

Helen closed her eyes and suddenly felt the tightness in her chest, which she usually felt all day, loosen. The anxiety that refused to let go of its tight grip daily was suddenly completely gone.

"How do you feel?" Angela asked.

Helen smiled. "I...I don't know what happened, what you just did to me, but I feel good. I feel better than I have in many years."

Angela smiled, and the surrounding women cheered.

"I think you're ready for the next step," she said, tears shaping in her eyes. "It's time you meet Christopher Daniels. But beware. It's a meeting that will change your life forever. We have all done it and it... well, you have to experience it to know just how life-altering it is. Are you ready for this?"

Helen didn't even have to think about it twice. Reading his book and taking some of his self-help classes, she knew that this man was capable of changing lives for the better. She had felt it over the past few months.

"Are you kidding me? It's my dream," she said, tearing up. "I would do anything to meet him. He's my hero."

Chapter 22

I WOKE up next to the computer, an almost empty bottle of wine next to me. My head was pounding, and my mouth felt dry.

Where am I?

I was still in the hotel room and had fallen asleep with my head on the desk. I had left the hotel the night before to go for a walk and clear my head; then on the way back, I had bought myself a bottle of red wine in a small food mart around the corner. I had wanted to drown my sadness and sedate the screaming voices in my head for at least a few hours, and I had succeeded. But now, they were back at full force, and I could add a thundering headache on top of it all. The anxiety was back, rushing through my veins, making me want to scream. The biggest question right now was how I was going to continue my search for Olivia without Sydney to pay for everything. I knew she had paid for the entire week for the room, so I was probably safe for a few days more, but then what? There really weren't many places I could go now with my picture everywhere. I had been on all the screens in the small homes, with my name associated with the words: *Dangerous fugitive*. I had read each and every article I could find written about me last night.

What am I going to do?

I got up, then felt dizzy and had to hold onto the back of my chair. I then staggered to the bathroom and splashed water on my face. I glanced at my face in the mirror, barely recognizing myself.

You can't do this alone.

I found my toothbrush, then rinsed the sour taste of red wine from my mouth and scrubbed the stains off my teeth. I spat, then looked at myself again, thinking it didn't matter what I did. If I didn't find my daughter, I was dead anyway.

You can't go back, Eva Rae.

I walked back into the room and sat down on my bed, a new burner phone in my hand. I tapped the first few digits of Matt's number, then paused and put the phone down.

No, I couldn't involve him. It was too much to ask. He had a son to care for, and he couldn't risk losing his entire career for me. I knew he would, and that was why I needed to keep him in the dark. I wouldn't be able to live with myself if he lost his job just because of me. I was a criminal, a fugitive on the run, and if he withheld information about my whereabouts or about me contacting him, then he would be in serious trouble. I couldn't do that to him. I refused to.

I put the phone down with a sigh, then thought about my children, praying they were all right. Between my mother and Chad, I was certain they were doing fine; both Alex and Christine were probably in heaven for being with their dad again. I didn't have to worry about them. I knew that much.

I found a painkiller in my bag and swallowed it with water, then laid down with my head on my pillow, waiting for it to kill that throbbing headache, when there was a knock on my door.

Chapter 23

"SYDNEY?"

I stared at my sister, standing in the hallway. She was holding her suitcase in one hand and her purse in the other. She rushed past me inside, and I closed the door behind her.

"What are you doing here?" I asked suspiciously.

"I came back," she said. "I spent the night in another hotel close by, but then I saw your picture everywhere and realized I couldn't just leave you. You need me."

I crossed my arms in front of my chest.

"What I don't need is your pity; thank you very much. I can take care of myself."

She groaned. "Why do you have to be so stubborn?"

"*I'm* stubborn?" I asked.

She shook her head. "You know what? Never mind. I shouldn't have come back. You obviously don't want me here."

Sydney grabbed the handle of her suitcase and was about to leave again when I stopped her.

"Yes, I do."

She gave me a look.

"I need you terribly," I said. "I can't do this on my own."

Sydney exhaled. She let go of the handle on her suitcase. "You have got to stop pushing me away. You do this to everyone you love.

Matt, your mother, me. You have to stop it, Eva Rae. I'm here to help. Yet you treat me like dirt."

"I know," I said. "I'm sorry. I'm just under a lot of pressure right now. It's just... a lot."

She nodded. "I know. I feel awful too for bringing that man into your life. There isn't a day when I don't beat myself up over it, when I don't think back at all the alarm bells that should have gone off, at how blind I was for not seeing him for what he really was. And I am sorry, Eva Rae. I really am. But at some point, you have to forgive me."

I nodded, feeling my eyes fill. "I will. I promise. I know it isn't your fault; I just... well, blaming someone makes it easier to handle somehow. At least I thought it did, but it doesn't anymore. It makes me miserable. Fact is, I can't do this without you, Syd."

She sniffled, then pulled me into a deep hug. "I hate that name."

"I'm sorry. Kelly, then."

She let go of me then looked into my eyes. "No, that seems odd coming from you. I think I like it better when you call me Sydney."

"Really?"

"Yeah, it's kind of growing on me. It feels familiar somehow, homey, almost."

I wiped a tear away with my sleeve. Sydney walked to the second bed and placed her suitcase on top of it.

"So... where are we? Any leads? That's how they say it in the crime shows, right?"

I nodded and approached the laptop, then sat down on the bed with it in my lap.

"I found the symbol, the one that Ryan Scott talked about. I know what it is."

Chapter 24

THE OWNER of the food mart looked at him suspiciously from behind the counter when Matt showed him his badge.

"I'm looking for a woman, early forties, red hair, blue eyes, about five-five, a little on the chubby side, but in a cute way," he said and showed him a photo of Eva Rae. Her eyes stared back at him from the counter, and his heart felt warm. All he wanted was to be with her again.

It was Chief Annie who had called this same morning and told him that Eva Rae had used her credit card the night before. They had someone from IT monitoring her activities, and last night, there had been action for the first time.

"I know she was in here last night," Matt said. "She used her credit card at this terminal at nine forty-two."

The cashier nodded. He was a small Indian man with a speech defect, so it was hard to understand what he said.

"Yes, yes. She was here. Bought a bottle of red wine and some gum."

"Was she alone?" Matt asked. "Or did someone come in with her?"

"She was alone. Just her."

"No one waiting for her at the door or outside, maybe?" he asked.

He shook his head. "I don't think so."

"Did she come by car or walk here?"

"Walk. No car."

"Okay," Matt said and wrote it down on his pad. If she walked there, it could mean that she was staying somewhere close by.

"Did you see which way she went when she left? Did she turn right or left once outside of the door?" he asked.

"I did not see," the man said, shaking his head while smiling in a friendly manner.

Matt lifted his glance and spotted a small camera in the corner under the ceiling.

"Could I take a look at that? From last night?"

"Yes, yes," the man said and made way for Matt to come in behind the counter. He showed him into the back office, where a computer was placed on the desk. He tapped on it, clicked with the mouse, and the surveillance footage appeared.

"Here you go."

"Thanks."

Matt sat down and pushed back the timeline to the night before. He stopped and started the video from when someone entered right before nine forty, wearing a hoodie covering their head. Pretty sure it was her, he then watched Eva Rae as she came in through the door and took a quick glance around before walking to the wine section and picking out a bottle. As she did, she turned to face the camera before walking to the counter where she picked out a pack of gum. Knowing her, he knew it was probably because she didn't want to look like an alcoholic.

Happy to see her again, Matt chuckled to himself and stopped the video right when she looked up at the camera from underneath her cap. He could almost see how she froze in place when realizing that she had been spotted.

"What are you up to now, Eva Rae?" he mumbled in the dark room. "When will this ever end? How is it going to end? You're gonna get caught, and then what? Will you come willingly, or will they have to take you down? What's your plan?"

Matt grabbed his phone, then took a video with his phone of the footage, running it all again, making sure he got everything down to the door closing behind her after she had paid.

Why did you use your credit card, Eva Rae? You know better than that. Was it just a moment of weakness?

"Did you get what you needed?" the man asked, and Matt nodded, then rolled the chair back in place.

"I did. Thank you very much."

Matt left the store and walked into the parking lot, feeling worried. He was closer to her than ever in this search, yet he felt like she was slipping between his hands.

Matt hadn't told Carter what he was doing this morning and, luckily, Carter hadn't asked. He was too busy living through his fifteen seconds of fame, doing interviews with all the local TV stations, telling them about the dangerous fugitive that was on the loose in Miami, to even notice. Matt wasn't going to tell him now either. He couldn't risk Carter finding Eva Rae before he did.

Matt drove to the Miami-Dade Police Department. But as he reached the station, he was met by the sight of maybe fifty uniformed officers running out of the building, storming toward their cruisers, and driving off in a rush, sirens blaring.

A sergeant passed him, and Matt stopped him.

"What's going on?"

He shook his head. "You're not gonna believe it," he said, eyes flickering back and forth, terrified.

"Try me."

The sergeant panted agitatedly. Matt guessed it wasn't from running, but from the fear rushing through him.

"There's been another attack."

Matt wrinkled his forehead, fear and worry spreading like wildfire inside him.

"What do you mean by attack?"

He shrugged. "Terrorists probably, what do I know?"

Matt's eyes grew wide. "Terrorists?"

"Listen, all I know is that we have about two hundred people at St. Mary's Cathedral who have been exposed to some type of gas. Just like it happened on the Metrorail last month."

"You're kidding me?"

"I wish I were, buddy. I wish I were."

Chapter 25

WE LEFT the hotel and drove to downtown Miami. Sydney had bought us each a coffee, and I was slurping mine while looking at the town outside my window. It was Sunday morning, and the streets were nearly empty. High-rises and palm trees surrounded us, and the scorching sun was burning through the windshield. We had put the roof on the convertible to keep the heat out, and I cranked up the AC and made sure the air blew in my face. It was already unbearably hot. Big fluffy clouds were building over land, and in a couple of hours, they would turn black as the day's first thunderstorm approached.

The cars on the four-lane road drove slowly and, as we passed one of them, I realized they were tourists busy taking pictures with their phones through the windows.

We stopped at a red light. A man walking on the side of the road was pushing a rusty shopping cart in front of him. Another was begging for money with a sign around his neck pleading to us passersby:

I AM HUNGRY

We passed a Marriott and took a left when I spotted a police car in the side-view mirror. It was coming up behind us.

"Shoot," Sydney said when she saw it in the rearview mirror. Her hands with the many rings on her fingers began to shake on the wheel. "What do I do? Eva Rae? What do I do?"

I looked at her briefly, then at the police cruiser coming up behind us. It turned on the siren.

"Oh, dear God, he knows it is us; he's coming for us, Eva Rae," Sydney gasped. "We're going to jail."

My pulse was beginning to quicken as I watched the cruiser come closer behind us, siren wailing. The sound made my heart pound. Was this it? Was it over?

There was no way I was giving up now.

I felt my gun in my holster, clutching my hand on the grip. My palms felt sweaty. I really didn't want to have to hurt a colleague, but if he stopped us and came to the door, then there was no telling what might happen. One thing was certain; I wasn't going down today.

"He's right behind us now, Eva Rae; what do I do? What do I do?" Sydney said.

"You slow down, then drive the car to the side of the road and stop. Nice and easy," I said. "And you remain calm."

Sydney whimpered something, then did as I told her. She eased off on the accelerator, then turned the Mustang toward the side and slowed even further till it came to a stop.

The police cruiser behind us came closer still, and we watched it, hearts beating fast, holding our breaths, till it continued past us, sirens blasting loudly as it disappeared down the road.

I exhaled with profound relief. Sydney moaned and leaned on the wheel.

"Oh, my God, that was close," she said.

I chuckled and leaned my head back in the seat, my heart finally beginning to calm down. It was like every cell in my body was pumping.

Sydney held her chest and laughed. "God, I was scared."

As we sat there, catching our breath, another police cruiser rushed past us on the road, and then another one and one more. I stared at them as they made their way through traffic, then looked at Sydney.

"What's going on?" she asked.

"I don't know, but it's something big. I've seen more than fifteen police cars drive by in the past minute or two, and now I can hear firetrucks too."

Chapter 26

WE CONTINUED, going slowly, trying hard not to attract unnecessary attention. As we came further down the road, we saw where all the police cars were going. They had parked in front of a big yellow church building. There were fire trucks and ambulances too, and the area in front of it had been blocked off.

"What the heck is going on here?" Sydney asked. "It looks serious."

There were hundreds of people outside of the church, most of them on the ground. Some were wrenching in pain like they were having seizures, others throwing up. Most of them didn't move at all.

Because they're dead.

I bit my lip, feeling anxious. I had seen pictures of situations just like this, many of them — when I went through the FBI files of the nerve gas attack on the Metrorail last month.

This had to be another one.

The thought was horrifying. One terrorist attack was a terrible thing, but two within this short period of time? It was going to unleash a panic unlike anything we had seen.

But that was, of course, usually the terrorists' purpose. To make people afraid of living their lives the way they used to.

Choppers were above us now, hovering over the area. Police choppers and news choppers were circling our heads.

"We should get going," I said. "Before someone sees us here."

"Isn't that…?"

NEVER EVER

Sydney pointed, and I turned my head to look. Right there, talking to someone in a hazmat suit, was Matt, the man I loved.

What is he doing here?

"What the heck?" I said.

"That's your boyfriend; isn't it?" Sydney asked. "That detective?"

I nodded, blushing slightly. I missed him so terribly. I hated myself for leaving him the way I had, for running off. I just hoped he knew that I only did what I had to do. We had known each other all our lives, and I just hoped he knew me well enough to forgive me.

"What's he doing here?" Sydney asked. "Did you know he was down here?"

I shook my head. "I haven't spoken to him since before I left Cocoa Beach."

I stared at my beloved boyfriend, my heart thumping in my chest, then looked at Sydney.

"We should go before he sees us, or before anyone else does, for that matter. We're kind of suspicious the way we've parked across the street from them."

"Right," Sydney said and put the car back into drive. We drove slowly past the scene, and I caught one last glimpse of Matt. As I did, he turned his head and looked directly at me, and I ducked down.

"Go faster," I said. "He's looking at us."

Sydney pressed her foot down, and the car jolted forward in between the tall buildings. Sydney floored it, and soon we were back to blending in among the tourists.

Chapter 27

IT WAS LIKE A WARZONE. Matt would know since he had actually been to one. As a young recruit, he was sent to Afghanistan, and what he had seen there, he tried to keep in the box of things he didn't like to think about. But seeing all those people on the ground, some fighting for their last breath, others having drawn theirs long ago, brought back some very unpleasant memories and popped that box right back open.

Two firefighters dressed in Level A Protective Personal Equipment, Hazmat suits, and SCBA, self-contained breathing apparatus, carried a woman out of the church and put her at his feet. Matt knelt down and looked at her face. She was alive but fighting to breathe.

"We've got a live one over here," he yelled as loud as he could. "Any available paramedics?"

A paramedic came running to him and took over. Matt backed away, sweat running down his spine and behind the gasmask.

"It's a God darn mess," one of the forensics coming up to him said, while Matt fought to calm himself down. The woman was fighting for her life on a stretcher, while the paramedics put her on respiratory support, giving her atropine in an autoinjector.

Matt was wearing a hazmat suit to protect him against the gas, and he had been inside, helping to carry out the churchgoers, trying to get them to a safe place away from the gas.

"I have never seen anything like it," the forensic said.

"Was it Sarin gas like the first attack?" Matt asked.

NEVER EVER

He nodded. "In the liquid form again. It's easier to transport, and fortunately, a lot less deadly, but still enough to kill all these people. Luckily, they have it all contained inside the church. I can't believe it. What kind of a sick mind tries to kill peaceful people going to church on a Sunday morning?"

Matt watched as more people were rushed away in ambulances, while the paramedics were fighting desperately to save them in time.

"It's like a darn insecticide," he said. "It's colorless and odorless. You won't know you've been exposed to it until it's too late and you feel your throat and eyes burn. Once you've been exposed, you have only a few minutes before it kills you. It's nasty."

Matt felt a shortness of breath himself behind the mask when thinking about it. He nodded heavily.

"When the first responders got here, they thought it was just a couple of churchgoers that had fallen ill," he said. "They sent an ambulance to deal with it, but when the paramedics arrived, suddenly there were twenty people who had fallen ill, and that was when they knew. The first responders were exposed too, though, and have been taken in for treatment."

Matt sighed and walked away from the area when he was told that everyone had been taken out of the church. A group of people who hadn't been exposed and showed no symptoms were gathered on the other side of the church. They were crying and holding each other. Matt took off his mask and helmet, then continued to where they were standing. Carter was taking their statements along with the other detectives. Each and every one of them had to be interviewed. It was vital to do it now when the memory of what had happened was still fresh to them. Maybe one of them had seen the person carrying the gas inside? Maybe they could get a description of the terrorists this time?

They had called in everyone from the surrounding departments, and the place was crawling with uniforms and suits.

"Anyone said anything useful so far?" he asked Carter as he approached him.

Carter took in a deep breath. "A guy saw a plastic bag on the floor and saw liquid inside of it," he said. "He didn't think about it but walked right past it and went to the right front side of the church to sit with his fiancée and her family. When he saw it, the bag wasn't leaking, so we assume there was no hole in it at that point."

"So, you're thinking that someone placed the bags there, then pierced them with something and left."

Carter nodded. "That was how they did it on the train, right? But so far, none of the witnesses remember seeing anyone leave the church."

"The FBI Joint Terrorism Task Force is here and will be taking over now."

Matt nodded toward the big black SUVs as they arrived.

"That's our cue, I guess," Carter said. "They'll be taking over then. Always know how to swoop right in after all the dirty work is done, am I right?"

Matt didn't answer. He was happy to leave it in their hands and get back to searching for Eva Rae. As he turned around, he recognized one of the FBI agents. It was an old colleague of his, Patrick Albertson. Patrick saw Matt too and hurried toward him.

"Matt, my man, what are you doing all the way down here?" he asked, and they shook hands. "Aren't you still up on the Space Coast?"

"I am, but I was working on another case down here when this happened."

Patrick nodded. "Eva Rae Thomas, huh? Yeah, I heard what happened. I can't believe she would go rogue like this."

"You knew her?" Carter asked.

"Not well, but back when she was still an agent, I knew her a little bit. She was so good at her job, though. Never would take her for someone who would go nuts."

She didn't go nuts, you idiot. She's just desperate.

"Well, there's two sides to all stories," Matt said, calming himself down. "Now, if you'll excuse me."

Matt turned around to walk away, but as he did, he spotted a car parked across the road from the church, on the other side of the police barrier, where many spectators were standing, along with the reporters and their cameras. It was a yellow Mustang convertible. He didn't know why, but somehow, he felt like the people in the car were watching him, and he felt strangely drawn to the car.

Who was in there and were they really watching him or was his mind just playing games with him?

Just as Matt stopped to get a better look, the car suddenly took off in a hurry, driving fast back down the street it had come from, and soon disappearing between the high rises.

Could it be... was that... was it you, Eva Rae?

Chapter 28

THEN

"I'M SWEATING LIKE A PIG. Can you tell I'm nervous?"

Helen looked at Angela, who smiled comfortingly. She reached over and stroked her cheek gently.

They were sitting in the waiting area in front of Christopher Daniels' office in his multimillion-dollar estate. It was beautifully decorated with gorgeous art and lots of plants and had a soothing aura to it. The surroundings made Helen feel less nervous, but she still had this sensation deep in her stomach that wouldn't go away. She was about to meet the man whose books she had read cover to cover, whose classes she had taken. To her, he was the smartest and most enlightened person in the world. He had changed her life.

"No. You look great, sweetie. Just relax. Christopher is really nice. There's nothing to be nervous about."

"Exactly what is supposed to happen during this meeting?" Helen asked, trying to keep her hands calm.

"This is how you become a full-blown member of NYX and join the inner circle. It'll blow your mind. You'll see. Just go along with it. All of it."

Just go along with it? What an odd thing to say.

It didn't make Helen feel less nervous, and as the door opened, she hid her shaking hands behind her back, then rose to her feet.

"Go ahead," Angela said and almost pushed her forward. "You can go in."

"You're not coming with me?" Helen asked.

Angela shook her head. "No. This is your time to shine. Go."

Helen took in a deep breath, then walked to the door and went inside. A man stood by the window, looking out. He was dressed in white from top to bottom; his long brown hair was hanging down below his shoulders. He had an air of peacefulness around him, and he smiled gently at her as he turned his head. She recognized him from all the books and papers in class.

It was really him. Being the heiress of a billionaire and growing up in her father's self-built entertainment empire, Helen had met all kinds of important people in this world, even presidents. But none of them had made her feel the way she felt in this instant. It wasn't love, not the way she had loved Brian; it was something else, something bigger.

Infatuation.

From the moment he put his eyes on her, it was like she was put under his spell.

"Close the door behind you," he said, and she did, heart pounding in her chest.

"Come into the light," he then said. "So I can get a good look at you and *really* see you."

She did as she was told, and he came closer, studying her, but it didn't make her feel uncomfortable. On the contrary, she found that she enjoyed it; she liked the way he looked at her with his deep blue eyes.

"There you go. Now, I see you," he said. "Now, I really see you. I see so much beauty in you, and it's time you stop hiding it."

Helen blushed. "Really?"

He came up close behind her, and she felt her stomach flutter. She felt his warm breath on her skin and closed her eyes for a second. When he put his hand on her shoulder, it felt like an explosion inside of her.

Chapter 29

"LORI MOORE?"

The woman in the white shirt with the yellow scarf tied around her neck stopped in her tracks. We had driven to Bal Harbor in Miami Beach, a small wealthy community at the north end of town. There were tons of exclusive shopping malls and high-end restaurants. The cars were Ferraris, Maseratis, and Teslas. This was the type of environment that Sydney felt at home in and was accustomed to. Not me.

The woman in the high heels came walking into the lobby of the Ocean View Hotel, a luxury hotel that she owned.

"Who's asking?" she said while signing something a young woman was holding out for her. The woman then rushed off with the signed paperwork. Lori Moore gave me a suspicious look. I was wearing a baseball cap and had dyed my hair black on Sydney's recommendation. Apparently, my red hair was way too obvious now that I was a wanted person. It was the type of dye that would wash out after a couple of days.

"I want to talk to you about NYX," I said, leaning forward and speaking in almost a whisper.

Our eyes met, and hers grew serious. Lori looked around her, then signaled for us to follow her. We took the elevator to the twelfth floor, and she showed us into her office. It had an incredible view of the ocean on one side and Intracoastal on the other, and then Miami downtown towering in the distance. It was quite breathtaking.

Lori closed the door behind us.

"Please, sit down."

We did, and she sat on the other side of her desk and leaned back with a deep sigh.

"Why are you here?"

"We are investigating NYX," I said. "I know you used to be a member and that you have spoken out against them on your blog. I believe this is their symbol, am I right?"

I showed her the note that Ryan had drawn for me. Lori looked at it, then nodded.

"What do you want to know?"

"Everything. What is NYX? How does it work? What do they do?"

Lori leaned in over her desk, folded her hands, then exhaled. "NYX is a self-help organization. Or that's their cover. It's built around the founder, Christopher Daniels. It's supposed to be a way for you to get a better life. Daniels has written several books, and you can take his self-help classes or workshops with the aim to take power back over your own life."

"But the classes are expensive, right?" I asked. "It's not for just everyone."

"Very. A five-day workshop would cost you between seven and ten thousand dollars. And it does work. It has helped a lot of people. Many who graduated from his classes have managed to stop smoking, to overcome their fear of flying or public speaking, and so on. It empowered them to do things they didn't know they could."

"As far as I have read," I said, "it has attracted a lot of famous and successful people. Billionaire heiresses and businesspeople, even actors and the daughter of Venezuela's former president. But there is more to it than just self-help, am I right?"

"Yes. I was introduced to it through a friend when I went through losing my dad in a car crash. I was going through a rough time dealing with the grief. The courses were mostly self-improvement workshops, based on therapeutic techniques, including hypnosis and Neuro-linguistic Programming, which is basically a behavior modification regimen. But the deeper I got, the more I realized something was off. There was a group within the group, like a sorority that my friend became a member of, but soon things started to change with her. She withdrew from me, became more secretive, and she lost weight, a lot of it. I realized it was all part of the behavior modification technique. She told me she had to lose her identity to gain a new one, that she was starving herself as a part of the therapy because it helped her connect with her inner self, her true self. I think she was just easier to control that way, and that Christopher Daniels just wanted to make sure she didn't resist him. I sensed that something was very wrong and left. I tried to warn my friend and asked her to come with me, but she wouldn't. She seemed scared. It's hard to explain, but I felt like I lost her completely, like they were controlling her. They said it was all about women's empowerment, but what I saw was the exact opposite."

"Wow," Sydney said. "I think I heard about this before. One of my friends talked about joining something like it and explained how taking those classes changed her life. Come to think of it, I haven't seen her in a long time."

"You're Kelly Stone, aren't you?" Lori suddenly asked, smiling. "I thought I recognized you downstairs. I love your work."

Sydney nodded. I didn't mind that Lori recognized her since I had a feeling that made her feel more comfortable with us. She didn't seem to recognize me, which was fortunate. I guessed a woman like her was too busy to keep up with the news of wanted criminals, which worked to my advantage.

"You be careful you don't end up in their claws," Lori said addressed to Sydney. "They'd love to have someone like you in their inner circle. You're just their type. Rich, successful, and famous."

Sydney chuckled. "I'll remember that."

I stared at the woman while thinking about this cult and the leader. I had no idea where I was going with this, but my instinct told me it was important. Ryan had seen the NYX sign at the attack somehow, and my daughter was on the surveillance camera footage. How, or if these things were connected, I had no chance of knowing. But it was all I had, and I was clinging onto it for dear life.

"Have you ever heard of the Iron Fist?" I asked.

Lori shook her head.

It was a long shot; I knew it was. But I had to try.

"Tell me about the founder, Christopher Daniels," I said. "I read that he is quite mysterious and rarely seen in public."

"That is true. I never met him myself, as I said, only the inner circle people get to do that."

"Do you have any idea how to get in contact with him?" I asked.

"Are you sure you want that?" she asked while grabbing a sticky note and writing on it. She ripped it off, then slid it across the table. "This is the NYX estate. He lives there, as far as I know. I know this because I was supposed to meet with him a couple of weeks ago in order to join this so-called inner circle, but I never showed up. I don't want to end up like my friend."

I grabbed the note and looked at it. "Did they get angry with you for not showing up or for speaking up afterward?"

She shrugged. "Their lawyers tried to shut down my blog, but I have lawyers too. They can try all they want. They can't touch me."

Chapter 30

THEY BROUGHT IN NEW GIRLS. Olivia was sitting on her mattress, crying when the door opened, and they came in. A young girl, no more than thirteen or so, landed next to her. Her face was swollen from being beaten. She looked up at Olivia like she expected her to explain to her what would happen now, but how could she? How could Olivia tell her what was about to happen to her?

"What's your name?" the girl asked.

"Olivia," she answered without looking at her. She didn't want to care for her; she didn't want to become friends with her. If there was one thing she couldn't do in this place, it was to care for any of the other girls. So many had come and gone, and that taught Olivia an important lesson. If she was going to survive this, she had to keep to herself and never care about anyone else. It was easy with the girls who came from China or Ukraine as some of them did because she didn't understand their language, at least not most of them. It was easy to keep them at a distance, but this girl was American like Olivia. That made it harder to cut her off.

"I'm Tiffany," she said with a sniffle. "I'm from Chowchilla, California. Do you know where we are?"

Olivia shook her head, trying to not look at the girl. Why was she so talkative? Normally, when new girls arrived, they wouldn't say a word for the first day or so.

"I don't know," Olivia whispered.

"I have been so many places," she continued, crying lightly. "It was my mother's boyfriend who took me. He beat me up at the house where we lived, and when my mother didn't do anything, I ran away. But I had nowhere to go, and he picked me up on the side of the road. Not knowing what else to do, I got in the car, and then he took me to his friend's house. That friend raped me. He kept going for hours and hours till I couldn't scream anymore. Then another of his friends came to his trailer, and they put me in a van and drove off. Since then, I have been so many places; I have no idea where I am or who I'm with."

Olivia exhaled. She had heard similar stories repeatedly over the past few months while being held there. It was so much tragedy; she couldn't bear it. It also frightened her to the core, especially when she heard of the amount of time some of these kids had been kept as slaves.

Was she ever getting out? Would she ever go home?

Olivia looked up toward the ceiling, stifling her tears. She'd had a lot of time to think about how to get out, and so far, come up with only one way. But it was too dangerous, and she wasn't sure she dared to follow through with it.

"Do they rape you here?" Tiffany asked.

Olivia shook her head. "No."

"Really?" Tiffany said, her eyes gleaming with hope.

"Yes, really. But they make you work for them."

"What type of work?"

"Cleaning chickens, mostly. In a factory. But there's other stuff too."

"Like what?" she asked.

Olivia put her head down on the mattress. She didn't want to kill this girl's hope by telling her the truth.

"Just stuff. You'll see. Now, go to sleep. They usually come at night, so you won't get any sleep if you don't sleep during the day."

Chapter 31

I GLANCED at the note from Lori Moore with the address on it. We were back at the hotel, and I had looked it up online and found the mega-mansion located a little south of town with views over Biscayne Bay. It wasn't far from the hotel where we were staying. It was an area that, according to the Internet, Jennifer Lopez also owned a house in and so did one of the Bee Gees, along with some of the wealthiest politicians and TV anchors in the country. I stared at the Google view from the top of the mansion. With its red-tiled roof, pool, and tennis court, it looked like all the other mansions in the area. It was a twenty-seven-thousand-square-foot house with both pool house and guest quarters, according to Zillow.

Sydney brought me coffee from downstairs and placed it in front of me. I sent her a grateful smile and sipped it, leaning back in my chair in the hotel room.

"Anything?" she asked and blew cautiously on her coffee before sipping it.

I exhaled. "I've gone through everything I could. I couldn't even find a driver's license for him in the DMV register. I tried to get information on his financial situation, but according to the IRS, he hasn't made any money in the past ten years. Yet he lives in a mansion in one of the most exclusive neighborhoods in the world. But the house isn't in his name. It's registered to a woman, whose name I also found on the board of NYX."

"Wow."

"He had another company earlier on, under the name Daniels, but that was shut down fifteen years ago because it was accused of being a pyramid scheme. He has a file with the FBI from back then, and it states that he doesn't even have a bank account in his name. He's keeping his name out of everything, so they can't get him for anything. Yet the company owns a jet."

Sydney lifted her eyebrows. "Are you logging into the FBI database? Are you sure that's a good idea?"

"Probably not. I'm using my former partner's login, though, and I don't think he'll notice. But listen to this. I looked through old articles written about the group, and in 2011, a woman disappeared after an NYX session in California. Her car was found abandoned in a parking lot, and on her phone, they found a video she had recorded of herself saying that she was brainwashed, that she didn't realize it, but she was already dead. Then she told whoever found the video to please contact her parents and tell them how sorry she was. Her body was never found."

Sydney almost choked on her coffee. She stared at me, eyes wide. "Did she kill herself; do you think?"

I shrugged. "Who knows? But something is off. Something is very much off here. I can smell it."

Sydney placed a hand on my shoulder. I looked up at her.

"I smell it too, Eva Rae, but what about Olivia? I thought we came down here to try and find her? All we know is that you think you saw her on the platform after the gas attack."

I stared at my sister, feeling a pinch of guilt in my stomach. I knew she was right. I was getting off track here. I feared that too. The fact was, I had no idea if it really was Olivia I saw on that clip, and I had let myself be blinded by the investigation into this strange cult instead.

It was time for me to get back on track — back to what I had come there for in the first place.

To track down the Iron Fist.

Chapter 32

SYDNEY WATCHED TV, flipping through the many news stations and their breaking news about the possible terrorist attack on a local Catholic church in Miami. Meanwhile, I sat by the laptop and, through a downloaded Tor-browser, I accessed the Dark Web, using a VPN for protection.

Now, the Dark Web is pretty easy to get access to, and thereby to all the illegal stuff going on there, but the hard part is finding the right sites. You have to know where you're going once you enter the browser. And I did. Back when I started my search for Olivia, I had found a list of pages where human trafficking was taking place. I knew that the FBI had a team of operators operating on the Dark Web to catch people engaged in criminal activity, and I gained access to their files. After finding a lot on murderers for hire, child pornography, illicit sale of body parts, and weapons for sale, I had found the pages that were known to the FBI to facilitate human trafficking, the buying and selling of people as slaves. Going to those sites got ugly really fast, and it made me sick to my stomach, plus I risked getting all kinds of malware on my computer. But it was on one of those sites that Piatkowski had sold my daughter, so I kept going back to see if the Iron Fist showed his ugly face.

So far, I had no such luck.

Until today.

I had recently entered a hacker forum and found someone willing to track down the Iron Fist for me, for an indecent number of bitcoins, naturally. Now, as I entered the chatroom, he wrote to me that he had found him. He then shared a link with me that would lead me to a chatroom he was in. I stared at the screen, my palms growing sweaty. I knew that if this link led me to child pornography, I was in trouble. I would be doing something illegal. I took in a deep breath, then decided to trust this hacker, and I clicked the link.

I held my breath as the page appeared, and a chat opened. Then I saw his name in the forum. There he was. Right in front of me. The Iron Fist. He was writing in the chat, asking for help. He needed four girls, fast.

I almost threw up.

Why is he asking for more girls? What is he doing with them? Does that mean he doesn't have Olivia anymore? What did he do to her? Did he sell her to someone else? Did he kill her?

Someone answered. He had a shipment coming in, tonight. Port-Miami. Midnight.

I stared at the chat as they agreed on a price, then went silent. I snapped a picture of the entire conversation on my phone. There was no way of tracking people who entered the Dark Web, but this was the best I could do. I stared at it, my hands shaking, my breath caught in my throat. I looked at my watch. There were still four hours until midnight.

I lifted my glance and studied Sydney for a second. She was engrossed in the news broadcast from the church. I wondered what to do about her. I couldn't really bring her. I didn't want her to get too deeply involved in what I was doing. It was too much of a risk for her. She had a career to think about.

I had to do it alone.

Chapter 33

THEN

"AREN'T you going to ask me any questions?"

Helen looked at Christopher, her legs feeling wobbly. He was standing in front of her now, looking into her eyes, moving a lock of hair. It felt like his eyes saw straight through her.

"About myself?"

Christopher chuckled. "I already know everything."

"How so?"

"Just by looking at you, I can tell that you are strong, a lot stronger than you think. You have a defiant air about you. You're a rebel. I know that you showed up to your first workshop in a ripped T-shirt, refusing to look like the others, refusing to show off your wealth and take part in in the upper-class materialistic way of life. I know that you are protesting against the bourgeois environment in which you grew up. I know that you are angry at the world and that you think more highly of animals than humans and that you would rather be with horses than humans. I also know that you have a terrible relationship with your father, who thinks he can buy anything or anyone. I also know that, through my workshops, you have looked deep into your psyche and been able to get rid of fears that have tormented you for years. I know that you can't have children and that you suffered from depression before you came to us for help. I know you married a man who left you when he realized you couldn't have children."

Helen stared at him, out of breath.

"Wow."

He took her face between his hands. "You are no surprise to me, Helen. I know you better than you know yourself. And now it is time for you to submit to me fully."

Helen swallowed. "W-what does that…"

He hushed her, and she stopped talking. He touched her hair gently, then ran a hand down her chest, lingering a few seconds by her breast before continuing down her arm, where he stopped by her wrist. He held it tight in his hand when the doors opened, and two women wearing white dresses entered.

"Who are they?" Helen asked. "What are they doing here?"

He hushed her again, then looked into her eyes. "Do you trust me?"

She swallowed hard, then nodded. "Y-yes."

"Good," he said.

He nodded, and the women approached. One of them held a cauterizing device. Christopher took it in his hand, then looked at Helen. It was sizzling in his hand — one of the women filmed with her phone.

"It is time for you to let go of your past, Helen. You're a part of us now. Your old family is holding you back from becoming all you can be. We're your family, and with this mark, I brand you, so you'll know where you belong always. You belong to me. Say these words after me: I give you, Christopher Daniels, full and complete control over my life."

Helen gasped lightly, but one look from his blue eyes made her feel at peace with this. It was the right thing to do. It was the next step, and she wanted it badly.

"I g-give you, Christopher Daniels, full and complete control of my life."

He then placed the cauterizing pen on her arm and pressed it down on her skin. Helen screamed in pain. Christopher smiled and lifted it again, and a mark was left on the skin, burning like crazy.

Helen looked down at it, then up at the two women, who clapped and cheered.

"Congratulations," one of them said. "You're one tough woman."

"And now you're one of us," the other said. As she spoke, she lifted her arm proudly to show Helen her own branding mark.

Christopher grabbed her by her chin, then turned her head to face him. He then leaned forward and placed a deep kiss on her lips.

"You belong to me now. Come," he said and pulled her by the hand. "Don't resist me. It's your upbringing that makes you think you need to resist me, but you need to liberate yourself from it. Only then can you reach healing."

The two women left, and Christopher slowly undressed Helen. He placed her on a yoga mat in the middle of the room, lit all the candles surrounding her, then climbed on top of her.

Chapter 34

LORI MOORE STARED at her wrist and turned it in the sparse light. Then she felt it. The smooth skin felt nice under her fingertips, she thought with a deep sigh. She was thrilled she had pulled out in time, before she too was branded like her best friend was, like all who became part of the inner circle were — branded for life.

Always reminded of what they had agreed.

Lori sipped her glass of Chardonnay while looking at the lights in Biscayne Bay. Out there, the cargo ships waited to be docked in the port, while cruise ships left for or came back from the Bahamas or the Virgin Islands.

She had left the office early, right after the visit from Kelly Stone and her strange companion. Their visit had stirred something up in her that she didn't care for, and she treated herself to the rest of the day off, something she never did. But today, she needed it.

Lori sipped her wine and felt the warm breeze on her face. The light in the pool lit up the entire back yard while the dark windows from her mansion looking back at her reminded her how alone she was.

Living in an eighteen-thousand-square-foot home could be quite lonely when it was just one person.

Lori had never wanted children and a family. It had been pretty clear to her when she became an adult. She wanted a career. She wanted to make something of herself. Growing up poor, she had never thought she would actually live on the ocean one day, in one of the most exclusive neighborhoods in the state. She never thought she would live in a house like this or that people would talk to her with awe and respect the way they did every day. But that was her life now, and boy, was she proud of it. If only her mom wasn't always high on drugs, she would invite her to see it, to see for herself what her daughter had accomplished, even though she always told her she would never amount to anything in life, that she was so ugly she should *consider herself lucky if she made it as a whore.*

Those had been her words when Lori was a teenager, and they had lingered with her ever since, making her determined to prove her wrong.

And this was where it had brought her — a huge mansion, Chardonnay in hand, and more than a three hundred employees beneath her.

But was it enough? Did it satisfy her?

When Lori had entered NYX, she had thought that the classes would help her deal with this sense of emptiness that was growing inside of her. She had believed this was what she needed to fill that void that she had thought would go away when she reached her goals in life.

And for a little while, the teachings of Christopher Daniels had done just that. But then he had asked to have sex with her when she saw him in his office. Lori had refused. She hadn't told this part to Kelly Stone and her friend since it was too private to share. But the fact was, Lori had run out of his house, and even though several men had tried to stop her, she had managed to make it out, running away and never returning.

Now that she had left NYX, she had also lost everyone she knew. She had become a social outcast since most women in her social circles were members, and a lot of them inner circle members. All her network collapsed at once, and now she was more alone than ever, especially after she started writing her blog about what had happened, excluding the sex part since it was too embarrassing, at least for now.

But the fact was, she couldn't have sex with this man. Not because she refused to; no, she could probably have closed her eyes and gone through with it just because of the benefits and status it would give her later on… becoming part of the inner circle. But the thing was that Lori had once been Lorenz. She looked like a woman, yes, and she felt like one. But there was still one thing left that technically made her a man. She hadn't been able to go through with the full transition and become a full-blown woman, removing the one last part that made her a man at birth.

That was why she could never go all the way with Christopher Daniels or any other man for that matter. Not even if she wanted to.

And she hated him for putting her in that position. She hated that he was the reason she had lost her entire social network, her only friends, because of it. Now she was all alone again, as she had been for most of her life.

Lori sighed and rose to her feet. She swung the glass and almost empty bottle in her hands, then staggered barefoot toward the sliding doors, barely keeping her balance.

As she entered the house and closed the sliding doors behind her, she turned around and stared straight into a set of eyes.

"What the heck are *you* doing here?" she asked, forcing herself to focus and stand still, but couldn't help swaying from side to side.

"What do you want?"

Chapter 35

SYDNEY WAS asleep when I left. I wrote her a note, then snuck out, shoes and purse in my hand, feeling like I was cheating on her or doing something criminal. I just didn't want her to know where I was going. She would only try and convince me not to go, to call the police instead, or she would end up coming with me.

I couldn't risk that happening. I needed to do this alone, without the police, without Sydney. Why? Because it was the only way I could get to the Iron Fist. Chances were slim that he would actually be there himself, but someone else might, someone that might lead me to him. This meeting was my only lead to him and Olivia.

I couldn't risk losing that. I had to find him. I had to track him down so I could get my daughter back home.

I rushed out through a back entrance, trying not to be seen by the front desk of the hotel. We had made sure it was Sydney who spoke to them every time we came back or left — to make sure they didn't recognize me. I was disguised pretty well with dyed dark hair and fake colored contacts and glasses, but still. We couldn't risk anyone calling the cops.

So, I snuck out the back entrance and found the Mustang in the parking lot behind the hotel. I drove it out into the street and hit the accelerator, finding the roads leading to the port.

Port Miami was located on Dodge Island; a slim island squeezed in between Miami Beach and Miami downtown on the mainland. It was both a cargo port and a cruise ship port.

The meet was at the cargo port, between the container ships. I found it easily and parked the car. I then ran toward the container terminal, which was a huge glass building. I rushed past it, running down the port, passing a big whale of a cargo ship that was lying there, empty, having just been unloaded, while hundreds of containers were on the dock next to it.

"SS Attra, that's her," I mumbled and looked at the name on my phone from the chat.

Holding the grip of my gun with one hand, I looked around until I spotted a guy standing by the corner of a container, obviously being the lookout. He was the type to be heavily armed, so I hid between a row of containers, pressing my back up against them.

I could hear voices, people talking. I snuck around the other way and came out on the other side of the containers, then ran across an open space until I could hide behind another container. As I peeked around a corner, I spotted them. A group of people was gathered there. They were chitchatting with one another, one even laughing like it was a typical greeting between old friends.

For a second, I thought I might have been wrong, but as I snuck closer, I spotted the girls. They were sitting in the opening of a container, an entire row of them. They were huddled together, trying to hide from the men surrounding them. They weren't even crying. It was obvious they didn't dare to, or they were too drugged even to try.

Seven young girls, some of them a lot younger than Olivia, about to be sold like slaves into prostitution or hard physical labor.

It was gruesome.

Somewhere, seven mothers are missing their children. Seven mothers are crying themselves to sleep at night.

"Not on my watch," I mumbled, just as a car drove up and someone stepped out.

Chapter 36

IT WAS hard to see from where I was standing, so I snuck closer. As I did, someone spotted me, and soon all hell broke loose.

The armed guards yelled and ran toward me. I lifted my gun, but as they turned the corner, they started to shoot, not asking questions. I fired back, then ran around the corner at the other end. I heard screaming coming from the open area. Shots were fired after me, and I turned around the corner, then fired, hitting first the guy to the right, then the one to the left. Both went down. I then ran forward as fast as I could, stormed into the area where I had seen the girls, just in time to watch them trying to get them into the truck that had arrived just a few seconds ago.

"STOP!" I yelled.

More shots were fired while people scattered. I fired back, hitting another guy, just as he tried to shoot me. They gave up on getting the girls in the truck and shut the door, then took off instead. I stopped and fired a round at the truck. The bullets ricocheted off of it, but it kept moving.

"Oh, no, you don't!" I said, then looked in between the containers. I took off running, knowing if I went fast, I would be able to cut them off on their way since they'd have to take a detour around the containers.

I panted agitatedly as I reached the end of the row of containers, then turned left, and now stood right in front of the truck.

"STOP!" I yelled and pointed my gun at them.

The truck accelerated violently and, as it did, I fired two shots straight through the windshield, hitting the driver. The truck turned sideways, then ran straight into a crane pole.

I stared at the crashed truck, my gun still pointed at it, shaking between my hands, but nothing happened. A few seconds later, the door to the passenger seat opened, and someone jumped out on the other side of the truck. The person took off running. I fired a shot and yelled for him to stop, but he didn't. He was way faster than me and soon gone.

I stared after him, then cursed while wondering if he had been the Iron Fist.

I returned to the truck and opened the driver's door. The driver was hunched over the wheel. I had shot him in the shoulder. His forehead was bleeding from the impact when hitting the crane.

I grabbed his head and pulled him back to see his face. Then I let his limp body plunge back down while cursing again. As I let go of him, I spotted something else. A guy was in the back. He had hurt his head when the car slammed into the pole, and he was dead. But he didn't look like any of the others. This guy was well dressed in a nice suit, a very expensive one. His shoes were of the same caliber. This was no ordinary man.

The Iron Fist?

Unlikely. He wouldn't come to something like this on his own. Someone working for him? More probable.

I stepped inside the truck, then pulled him back to see his face properly. As I did, I saw his wrist as it poked out from beneath the shirt.

A wrist with something branded into the skin. A symbol I knew a little too well.

"NYX," I said, gasping lightly. I fumbled with my phone, then took a picture of it before letting him go. I searched through my phone, then sent all the pictures to a secret email address I had recently created, one that no one knew of except myself.

I got out of the truck with the phone clutched to my ear. I walked back toward the open area and saw the girls. They were huddled up inside of the container again, having gone back to what I assumed had been their home for quite some time, while they were transported across the ocean.

Then, I called the cops.

"I'd like to report a shooting. At the port. You'll find several dead men and some young girls that were supposed to be sold as slaves inside of a container."

I gave them the exact address, then threw the phone in the trash before disappearing, hurrying to my car. I took off into the night while hearing the sound of sirens blaring behind me.

Chapter 37

ESTHER HERMANE PRESSED in the code to the door. Her fingers were shaking, and she had to take in a deep breath in order to calm herself. She tapped in the wrong code, then shook her head.

"Where is your head today, Esther?"

She tried again, and the gate opened. She walked inside, holding her purse close to her body. Inside of it was her phone, and she had to make sure that she could hear it if it rang. She would have to keep it close all day while cooking and cleaning.

Coming from Haiti ten years ago, getting used to things here in America, and especially Miami had taken her a long time. But life was better here. It had been better for her son James to grow up here than back home. After ten years, Esther had thought they were safe here now. She had worked hard over the years to provide a good life for him, but the night before, he had been taken in by border agents.

He had been visiting his aunt in Naples as he had done so many times before, going by bus, as usual, when agents had entered the bus right as they reached Miami.

They had asked for his ID, then asked if he was illegal, and he had said yes. He was eighteen years old and had never been able to tell a lie. They had told him they'd take him with them, and then he'd be deported within the next two weeks. He had gotten the right to call his mother, and he had done so, then told her the entire story. Esther had contacted an old friend, who had gotten them an immigration lawyer who worked with cases like these, and today, James was supposed to appear in court.

It was still early in the morning, and the court appointment wasn't till eleven, so she had time, but Esther was already anxious. She had been up all night worrying, wondering if James was all right in that place they had taken him to and whether they had treated him properly.

Was he being fed?

Just thinking about it made her stomach churn, and Esther tried to shake it. She walked up to the front door and pressed in the next code, thinking about the day she had in front of her. Usually, she cooked breakfast for Mrs. Moore before Mrs. Moore left for work, and Esther had the house for herself the rest of the day, cleaning and making sure everything was perfect for when Mrs. Moore came home, which was usually pretty late. Esther would make a meal for her and place it in the fridge, covered in wrapping, so all Mrs. Moore needed was to put it in the microwave whenever she made it back.

It was a good job, Esther had always thought. She liked Mrs. Moore, even though she found her to be a strange creature. Not really man or woman, in her opinion. The fact that someone could simply decide they were of another gender amazed her, but then again, so many things had surprised her in America. It wasn't the place she had expected it to be or dreamed of when she was younger. And living in constant fear of being found by the border agents wasn't living at all. Esther couldn't stand it, couldn't stand being constantly worried about her son and their future. She didn't understand why this was happening now, after all these years. She had been a hard worker; she had taken the jobs no one else wanted. She had stayed out of trouble, and so had her son. And James was doing great in school. All they were guilty of was trying to earn their way to better, safer lives. She wasn't harming anyone. Neither was James.

Esther shook her head and pushed the big door open and entered the house. The first thing she saw was the broken bottle of white wine that had scattered across the tiles and the wine had run across the floor and seeped into part of the expensive Persian carpet. Esther's heart sank when realizing that Mrs. Moore had been drunk again and cleaning up after her would probably take most of the day.

"Stupid American woman-man, wasting away in this big mansion big enough for my entire village to live in," she hissed, then went with determined steps for the closet with the cleaning supplies. As she put her hand on the handle, she spotted the blood on the white tiles.

Now, while growing up in Haiti, Esther had seen some gruesome things. She had seen people lying murdered in the streets and even witnessed her own father being shot. But what she saw in the kitchen on this day was nothing in comparison.

It made her long to go back for the first time in ten years.

Chapter 38

IT WAS late in the morning, and Matt had just gotten his second coffee when Carter approached him.

Matt had hoped that the day would be quiet for once. Just him responding to possible sightings of Eva Rae. Ever since detective Carter had been on TV, the calls had been coming in non-stop. But so far, none had proved to be true.

Matt was still focused on the area around the food mart, and he had planned to visit a few of the hotels surrounding it later in the day when Carter was too busy to ask questions. He had been focusing merely on small motels and crappy places, but then realized that if Eva Rae was with her sister, then maybe they were, in fact, hiding in plain sight, frequenting the more exclusive hotels, since Kelly Stone — or Sydney — would be paying. Matt had thought about getting a trace on her bank account, but he would have to do it behind Carter's back, and that made it harder. It was also more difficult because she was a celebrity. There would be questions asked, and he wasn't sure a judge would allow it when Matt couldn't prove that she was actually with Eva Rae. She could be traveling or staying here for work. A call to her agent hadn't cleared things up since he had no idea whether Kelly was in Miami or not. He also said that Kelly Stone often took off without saying where she went, not even to him. She did this when she wanted to go on a vacation, or just have time off for herself. Then she would go off the grid until she was ready to resurface again and let the world know she was back. It was all to avoid paparazzi on her vacations. The fewer people who knew where she went, the better the chances were for her actually to get some vacation time.

Matt couldn't blame her. He had always thought it had to be awful to live a life as a celebrity and never be able to go anywhere without having the paparazzi chasing you or people gathering to get your autograph or a silly selfie with you.

It had to be exhausting.

Matt had been minding his own business, going through all the latest so-called sightings, and called back on several of them, when Carter had approached him and told him to grab his badge.

"Something happened."

And now they were standing in front of an expensive white mansion in one of the most exclusive neighborhoods south of Miami… Coconut Grove. Patrol cars blocked the street, and the blue lights lit up the palm trees in the driveway. Carter pointed at the house next door, then mentioned casually that Bruce Willis lived there, according to his sources. Matt nodded, even though he had the feeling that Carter was just showing off. So what if he lived there? Celebrities didn't impress Matt much.

"Why are we here?" Matt asked. "What happened?"

Carter signaled for Matt to follow him, and he did. The house was crawling with crime scene techs, and Matt was soon suited up and had put on gloves. A tech showed them inside, and they followed.

The victim was in the kitchen, naked, tied to a chair. The body was drenched in blood. There were already flies in the eyes and the wound on the slit throat.

Matt clasped his mouth, and for a few seconds, he couldn't hear anything but the rushing of his own pulse in his ears.

Chapter 39

"WHO IS SHE?"

Matt wanted to turn around and look away but managed to keep his cool. Carter stepped closer, grinning as he looked up at Matt.

"I think she was more of a he," he said and pointed down to the crotch. A penis had been split in half down the middle, and Matt almost threw up again, thinking about just how painful it had to have been. A knife had been secured as evidence. There was a trail of blood across the white tiles, where the body had been dragged. Matt wondered if she had been still alive, if the killer had dragged it out, just for the pleasure of it.

"*She*," Carter said, "is the owner of Hotel Ocean View in Miami Beach."

Matt looked away. "Could it be a hate crime?"

Carter shook his head. "You'd think, right? But no. I have another theory. The detectives on the case called once they spoke to her secretary. Mrs. Moore here had a visitor yesterday at her office that might be of interest to us. They pulled the surveillance from the lobby as she entered."

Their eyes met, and Matt's heart sank.

"Eva Rae Thomas?"

Carter clicked his tongue. "Bingo."

"Wait," Matt said. "You don't honestly think that…?"

Carter bit his lip. "Oh, yes, I do. She was the last person to see Mrs. Moore alive. After her visit, Mrs. Moore told her secretary over the intercom that she was going home, then left taking the back door."

Matt could hardly breathe. This wasn't good. This was going from bad to worse.

"Why? Why would Eva Rae Thomas murder this woman?"

Carter lifted his eyebrows. "That's what we need to find out. But so far, she is wanted in connection with the murder. This gives us a lot more elbow room to work. I have asked for roadblocks to be set up around town. Cars will be searched, and that means she won't be able to go anywhere without being discovered. The Miami-Dade chief is giving us extra manpower. He wants her caught yesterday."

"Okay," Matt said and nodded anxiously. It was getting harder for him to hide his worry. Eva Rae was in serious trouble, and he found it difficult to see a way out of this. "I guess we have work to do then."

"It gets better," Carter said, grinning again.

"Really?" Matt asked nervously.

Carter nodded. "There was another woman with her on the surveillance footage. You'll never guess who she is."

Matt swallowed hard. "W-who?"

"Kelly Stone," he said, sounding proud, like he was the one who had made the discovery, when in fact, it was another detective who had contacted him and told him this.

"Yes, the actress. The very one and only and get this. They're sisters."

Matt lifted his eyebrows and tried to act surprised. He was never much of an actor or a liar, and he knew it would come off as awkward. He wanted to yell at this guy and tell him that he had known Eva Rae since he was three years old, and there was no way she would ever hurt another human being like this.

Not Eva Rae.

But, of course, he couldn't say that. He needed to stay close to the investigation, and they wouldn't let him if they knew the truth. So, he continued to play dumb.

"Really?"

Detective Carter nodded pensively. "Makes sense, right? Why we couldn't locate them. She's been living the life in first-class, letting her sister pay for everything. Meanwhile, we've been looking in all the wrong places. But that's over now. We're breathing right down her neck, and it's only a matter of time before she walks into our net. And when she does, I am taking her down. She won't know what hit her. There's only one thing worse than a criminal, and that's a criminal cop. I can't stand that. It's a dishonor to the badge. But I know how to get her now. I know exactly how to sniff her out."

Chapter 40

"DID YOU GO OUT LAST NIGHT?"

Sydney and I had just gotten into the Mustang when she asked me the question. I paused before inserting the key in the ignition.

"What do you mean?"

"I woke up around midnight, and you weren't there."

I shrugged. "I went for a walk," I lied. I didn't want her to know what I had been up to.

"I see," Sydney said and looked out the window.

I turned the engine on, and the Mustang roared to life. I sensed that she didn't believe me, but I couldn't deal with that now. I had seen the cult's symbol branded into the skin of that man in the truck the night before and I hadn't been able to think about anything else since.

I hit the accelerator, and we left the hotel's parking lot, then drove into the street. I wondered about the night before and if the police had found the girls and taken care of them. All morning, I had been flipping through newscasts but hadn't heard anything. I worried about those girls.

"So, where are we going?" she asked and looked up at the sky above us and all the tall palm trees that were rushing by.

"NYX headquarters," I said and pressed the accelerator to make the car jolt forward.

Sydney sat up straight. "Excuse me?"

"I got the address from Lori Moore, remember? Well, I thought we'd pay them a little visit, or at least you would. I'm kind of exposed."

"You want me to walk into NYX's headquarters and do what exactly?" Sydney asked, surprised, and maybe slightly appalled by the idea.

"I want you to pretend like you want to take a course. I want you to ask questions and seem interested. I want you to go as you, as Kelly Stone, the famous actress, and let them know you're interested. I want you to ask to see the founder, Christopher Daniels."

Sydney stared at me, mouth gaping. "Me? Why?"

"You heard what Lori Moore said. They'd love to get their hands on someone like you. You're just the type they want. And you're an actress; you can easily pretend like you're very naïve and gullible."

Sydney nodded. "O-okay, I guess I can do that. But what do I do when I get in? What if I get to see him? What do I do then?"

"I don't know," I said and turned right on red.

Sydney gave me a look. "You don't know?"

I exhaled. "I just know that somehow this Iron Fist is connected to the cult. I know they're also somehow connected to the trafficking of young girls. I just don't know how."

Sydney crossed her arms in front of her chest. "And just exactly how do you know this? Yesterday, you didn't seem so certain. Did you discover this when out *walking* last night?"

"You might say so," I said and drove up another street and into a far more expensive part of the neighborhood. I drove up to the house I had seen on Google maps, then parked the car down the street from the entrance so as not to seem suspicious or get caught on a potential surveillance camera.

"Listen, Sydney. Just trust me on this. This cult, and probably its leader, is hiding something, and that something might have to do with my daughter. You've asked me a ton of times how you can help make things better; well, this is it. If you do this for me, it might help me get Olivia back. So, please."

Sydney looked at me, her eyes growing softer.

"Okay. I'll do anything for you; you know that."

I eased up and fell back in my seat. "Thank you, Syd. It means the world to me."

Chapter 41

THEN

THE SEX WAS INTENSE. Christopher was insatiable, and it felt like he could continue forever. Helen was exhausted by the time he finally got off her, and she felt so embarrassed.

She had wanted this to happen, a big part of her had, and she had let it, but at the same time, she felt like she had no choice. Christopher held that type of deep power over her so that she was incapable of saying no to him.

He rose to his feet, ran a hand through his hair, then looked down at Helen's naked body while getting dressed. The yoga mat underneath her felt sticky. His eyes glaring at her made her feel uneasy.

He smiled like he enjoyed looking at her, and that made her blush. She felt like asking what would come next, what was expected of her, but she didn't dare.

The thing was, she enjoyed him and the way he looked at her. Somehow, she had known that she would from the first time when reading his book and looking at his picture. She had known that she wanted to sleep with him. He had that raw sexual energy in his eyes. But he still scared her slightly as well.

Helen reached for her dress on the floor and was about to put it on when he stopped her.

"Wait."

She paused and looked up at him. He pulled out his phone and took her picture. Helen froze, wondering what he was doing. He took another picture, then crept really close to her, spread her legs, and took a series of pictures of her vagina.

"What are you doing?" Helen shrieked. She reached her hand down to cover herself up, but he laughed and removed it.

"Don't be shy. I'm just taking a few pictures of you."

"W-why?" she asked and grabbed her drees, then held it up to cover her body.

He grinned and showed her a picture on his display of her vagina up close, then swiped so she'd see herself lying naked on the floor. Helen winced at the sight.

"Why?" she asked again. "Why would you take those pictures?"

He leaned over her, pushing her back, then kissed her intensely. As his lips parted hers, he looked into her eyes.

"I call it collateral. Now that I have these, you won't tell anyone what goes on here. I own you, and if you tell anyone about us or about what this group is, or if you refuse to do as we tell you to, then these pictures will be sent to everyone you know, starting with your parents."

Helen stared at him, eyes growing wide. She pulled away, appalled. It took a few seconds before she was able to speak again.

"W-what do you want from me?" she asked while pulling the dress back over her head, her heart pounding in her chest. Never had she been treated in such a manner with so little respect. "Is it my money you're after?"

He smiled and tilted his head as she rose to her feet. He grabbed her by the shoulders, then kissed her again.

"What is this?" she asked.

"This is me taking control of you. You're my slave now, and you do everything I tell you to, do you hear me? Everything."

Chapter 42

THE NEW GIRL, Tiffany, stayed close to Olivia at all times. It was getting slightly annoying to Olivia, and she often tried to lose the girl, to push her away, but Tiffany refused to let go of her side. Often, she clung onto her arm so tight, Olivia couldn't use it.

It got them in trouble at the factory that night, and after that, Olivia ignored Tiffany when they got back to the house. She went to bed, hoping that by giving her the cold shoulder, she might give up and finally leave her alone. Olivia didn't have the energy to take care of anyone else.

"I'm sorry," Tiffany whispered later as they were trying to sleep.

Olivia lay with her back turned to her, eyes open, but pretending to be asleep.

"I'm just so scared," Tiffany continued, her voice quivering. "And you remind me of my sister. I miss my sister so much."

Olivia exhaled. She really didn't want to know more about Tiffany or her family. She didn't want to know any details about this girl because that would mean that she'd have to care about her, and she didn't want to. She couldn't allow herself to do that.

Yet she still sat up and looked at the girl, then smiled. "I have a sister too. And I miss her... a lot, even though she can be very annoying at times. What's your sister's name?"

Tiffany wiped her nose on her arm. The stench from the factory and the dead chicken lingered in Olivia's hair constantly, and she felt so sticky.

"Her name is Ariana. She's two years older than me," Tiffany said. "She used to help me with my homework. She's really good at math."

Olivia felt a knot in her throat. She had forced herself to not think about her family for so long, simply because it hurt too much to do so. She tried hard not to picture her mom because, if she did, she would see how sad and desperate she was, not knowing where Olivia was.

There was nothing worse to Olivia than to see her mother cry. She didn't want to think about it.

"I used to help my sister with math too," Olivia said, then chuckled lightly at the memory of her and Christine struggling over math problems. "She was terrible at it."

Olivia bit her cheek, realizing that she had spoken about her sister in the past tense like she didn't expect ever to see her again. Did that mean that she had given up hope?

Maybe.

She had seen several of the girls die while she had been kept there. Only the toughest made it through to the next day. And so far, Olivia had been among the tough ones. But for how long?

"Do you think we'll ever see them again?" Tiffany asked, her big hope-filled eyes lingering on Olivia's face.

Olivia pictured her sister's face, then her brother's, and finally, her mother's. Then a tear escaped her eyes and rolled down her cheek.

"I'm sure we will," she said. "I'm sure we will."

But they both knew it was a lie.

Chapter 43

MATT WAS STARING at the whiteboard in front of him, his hands shaking lightly. On the board, looking back at him, was the surveillance photo of Eva Rae and her sister, taken in the lobby of the Ocean View Hotel. They had both dyed their hair, and Eva Rae was also wearing a cap and glasses, but he could still see it was her. He'd recognize that sweet face anywhere.

Matt closed his eyes for a brief moment and pinched the bridge of his nose, leaning forward.

What am I going to do? How am I supposed to get her out of this mess?

As he opened his eyes, Carter stood in front of him, a file in his hand, and a smirk on his face. He placed the file in front of Matt.

"Our little friend was busy last night."

"What do you mean?" Matt asked, feeling tense. Could it possibly be more bad news? He wasn't sure he could take any more.

Carter nodded at the file, and Matt opened it, then flipped through the top pages before looking back up at his partner.

"There was a shootout at the harbor last night. Three men were found dead. Others were badly injured. No one is talking, though. Seemed to be gang-related at first. But get this, they found seven young girls in a container. All fresh in from Guatemala."

"Trafficking victims?" Matt asked.

Carter nodded, grabbed a chair, and sat down. "Looks like an Eva Rae Thomas project, doesn't it?"

"But... what time did this happen?" Matt asked. "If we assume she was at Lori Moore's house, she couldn't have been at the harbor too. She can't possibly have been at both places?"

Carter leaned back. "I had a feeling you might say that, but unfortunately, one doesn't exclude the other. The medical examiner says Mrs. Moore was murdered between two and four a.m. The shootout took place right after midnight. It's a twenty-minute drive. She could easily have performed both. No matter what, we're looking at at least three homicides at the harbor, and then a possible homicide in Coconut Grove. We're waiting for ballistics on the shooting victims. But I'd say we have ourselves a serial killer now. This is the big stuff, Matt. This is what can make or break a career."

"Except we have no evidence placing her at any of those scenes," Matt said, his voice shivering in desperation.

"Ha. That's where you're wrong," Carter said. "Turn to the next page."

Matt did, his hand shaking so badly it was hard to hide. A surveillance photo of someone getting out of a yellow Mustang appeared. It was obviously a woman, a woman wearing a cap.

"Taken at the port at exactly five minutes to midnight," Carter said. "Notice, she's wearing the exact same clothes as she was on the surveillance from the hotel earlier in the day, the last time anyone saw Lori Moore alive."

Matt's heart sank. There was no way around this. It was her. It was Eva Rae in that photo, placing her right at the scene of a triple homicide.

What the heck are you thinking, Eva Rae!

Matt stared at the photo. Tears were welling up in his eyes, but he managed to stifle them.

"Say... are you... you're not personally involved with this woman, are you?" Carter asked, scrutinizing Matt.

Matt sniffled and shook his head. "No. Of course not."

"It's just... you seemed a little emotional there."

He closed the file. "Well, I'm not. It's just allergies."

"Allergies, huh? Yeah, they can get pretty bad down here at this time of year." Carter looked at him, and Matt felt uncomfortable, sensing that Carter didn't buy it.

Luckily, his phone rang, and he picked it up, leaving Matt to wipe his eyes on his sleeve. Carter walked away for a few seconds, talking on the phone, while Matt cleared his head, convincing himself to remain professional. If Eva Rae had killed these men, then she had done so for a reason.

Eva Rae was many things, among them a strong and protective mother. But a murderer, she was not. And Matt was going to make sure the world knew it.

Somehow.

Carter returned, looking annoyingly cheerful.

"Kelly Stone has been seen at a hotel downtown," he said and grabbed his car keys and placed his badge on his belt. He lifted his eyebrows.

"We've got them. Let's go."

Chapter 44

"THESE GUYS ARE GOOD."

Sydney got back in the passenger seat. I could tell she was shaken up. She was pale, and her voice trembled when she spoke. She had just come out of the NYX headquarters after spending about an hour inside. Meanwhile, I had been sitting in the car, listening to the radio announcer talking about the shootout at the harbor the night before and that the police wouldn't comment on whether they believed it was gang-related. There was no mention of the girls.

I shut the radio off as soon as Sydney approached the car and got back in. She wiped her sweaty palms on her skirt.

"What do you mean?" I asked.

"You were right. They were all over me as soon as they realized who I was. It was crazy. But they were so nice at the same time. Very friendly and not in my face at all. I felt very comfortable. I hadn't expected to. I spoke to one of the women there, and she told me so many good things about how this could be a journey for me, how I could develop into a much stronger individual, and she even guessed that I had a fear of flying, which I've never told anyone. Because in my line of work, you have to fly places all the time, but the truth is, I loathe it, and now I know why. Because I was taken from my family and put on a plane back then when my dad took me. I was forced on a plane and taken thousands of miles away to a life where I would miss my mother and sister every day until my dad convinced me they were the ones who didn't want me, and I stopped longing to get back. But the fear of flying still lingers inside me. Can you believe it? I was in there for what? An hour? And they already made me realize this? I can't imagine how much more they could do for me if I took one of their workshops."

"Wow," I said.

"Are you sure they're not legit?" she asked. "I mean the people I met sure seemed professional. They knew what they were doing."

"That's probably how they get you hooked," I said. "Did you get to meet Christopher Daniels?" I asked.

She looked at me, then nodded. "I was shown into his office, and they served me herbal tea. Then he came in. He was such a handsome man, so charismatic; you won't believe it. He shook my hand, and we spoke for about ten minutes, mostly him asking me questions about my life and what I expected to get out of his classes, what I wanted to change in my life. I told him I would think about it, then get back to them, then shook his hand again and left. But he was so nice, Eva Rae. I didn't expect him to be. I felt so welcome and even at home there. I have never felt anything like it."

"Did you see anything that could help us? Any young girls in the house or pictures, or did he mention anything?" I asked. "Maybe they're working for them?"

She shook her head. "Not at all. The woman who served me herbal tea was about my age and didn't seem to be in any distress at all. I tried to look into her eyes, and she seemed almost blissfully happy. I have to say, Eva Rae, I'm not sure this has anything to do with your daughter and what happened to her. Why do you even think that it has? Because that Ryan guy saw their symbol during the attack? It's a little far-fetched; don't you think? I mean he might have seen it on a bag or something and then just kept remembering it. It doesn't seem to have any connection to Olivia, whom we don't even know for sure was on that clip on TV. There's a lot of loose ends here, Eva Rae."

I started the car up, disappointed, and took off. I don't know what I had expected she'd find in there, but at least something. Instead, I now doubted everything. Could Sydney be right? Was I just going crazy and clinging onto something I had imagined in my mind?

That guy in the back seat of the truck had the symbol branded into his skin.

No, something was definitely off here, and it had to do with this cult. I might have been a hothead, blinded by my desire to get my daughter back, but I just knew it had to, no matter what Sydney said. No matter how nice and wonderful these people were.

Life had taught me that the line between good and bad people was thinner than you'd think.

Chapter 45

I DROVE up in front of the hotel, then hit the brakes, hard. Sydney was thrown forward and landed with her hands on the dashboard.

"Hey!" she yelled. "What's going on?"

I stared at the entrance to the hotel for a few seconds, my heart pounding in my chest. I watched as Matt came out of the sliding doors with a shorter, slightly overweight bald guy. The entry was packed with police cruisers.

Sydney saw it too, then looked at me.

"What do we do?"

"We need to get out of here," I said as I turned the wheel and slid the car back onto the road, making sure not to go fast and cause suspicion. I drove nice and casually past the hotel and continued down the street, then took a right turn and parked in front of Flanigan's Seafood Bar and Grill.

"Let's go get some coffee," I said, then felt my stomach growl. "And maybe some lunch."

We walked inside and sat down in a booth. We ordered coffee and mahi-mahi burgers. I was starving, yet my stomach was almost too upset to be able to eat. The burger was good, though, and it made its way down. Getting food helped me to think more clearly.

"What do we do now?" Sydney asked. "That place was crawling with cops. They were there for us; weren't they?"

I exhaled. "Yes. There's no doubt in my mind. They found us, so we're not going back there; that's for sure. They'll ask the front desk to alert them as soon as we try."

Sydney breathed heavily. She ate a bite of her fish burger, then chewed and swallowed.

"Maybe we should just turn ourselves in," she said. "Before things get out of hand."

I looked up, and our eyes met. I felt a pinch of guilt. I could hardly tell her that things had already gotten way out of hand. I regretted having brought her with me in the first place. Why had I dragged her into this? She risked losing everything.

I stared at my burner phone on the table, then grabbed it and rose to my feet.

"I need to make a call," I said, then left, dialing a number. I walked outside to the parking lot while waiting for him to pick up.

Come on; come on.

Finally, he did.

"Matt Miller."

"Why are you here?" I asked. "Why are you following me?"

It took a few seconds before he said anything, and I assumed he needed to get somewhere where no one could listen in on our conversation. His response came in a gasp.

"Eva Rae? Where are you?"

"Wouldn't you like to know?" I said. "What are you doing down here, Matt?"

"I'm trying to help you," he said agitatedly. "What on Earth do you think you're doing?"

"I'm looking for my daughter. You know this, Matt."

"Last night was a disaster, Eva Rae," he said with a moan. "You've gone too far."

"They were traffickers. Seven girls' lives were about to be destroyed. I saved them."

He sighed. It didn't sound good. I closed my eyes and missed feeling his breath on my skin, and his lips pressed gently against mine. I thought about the last time we had been together and desperately wanted to feel that again.

But it was impossible.

"Eva Rae, please turn yourself in," he said heavily. "This has gone as far as it can."

"I haven't found Olivia yet, so, no."

"Eva Rae, dammit. You're wanted for murder!"

"It was self-defense. They tried to kill me. I liberated those girls."

"No, no, not that. Well that too, but you're also wanted in connection with the murder of Lori Moore. You were there at the hotel before she went home. Next thing, she's found murdered in her house. You were the last one to see her alive."

My heart dropped. "Lori Moore is dead?"

"Yes. They think you killed her or at least that you had something to do with it. Please, come in and tell your side of the story. I know you didn't kill her, but I can't convince everyone else if you keep running. Running makes you look guilty. You, of all people, should know this, Eva Rae."

My heart was hammering in my chest now. I kept staring out over the street and the palm trees on the side of it. A woman walked by with her small dog, not noticing me at all.

Lori Moore was dead? Right after we had been there to see her?

"They think I did it? But... but they're wrong."

"And that is what you need to come in and tell them. Please, Eva Rae. Stop running. We'll find Olivia together. The right way. Through thorough police work. I know it takes a lot longer than what you care for because you'll need the warrants and surveillance for months before we can strike those joints, but we will. Eventually, we'll find her."

"I don't think so," I said. "Eventually isn't good enough. Months is too long. I want her home now. And I am going to continue chasing them until I find her. There's nothing you can do to stop me."

"I love you," he said, right as I hung up.

I stared at the phone in my hand, a tear escaping my eye. Then I whispered: "*I love you, too.*"

I threw the phone on the ground, then stepped on it, shattering it, and threw the remains in a trash bin with a loud cry.

I then gathered myself and walked back inside the restaurant, my heart feeling completely shattered. I looked at Sydney, who was about to pay with her credit card.

I stopped her.

"Use cash instead. They might be tracking your cards."

She swallowed nervously, then nodded. She found a handful of cash, then left it at the table.

"We need to get out of here," I said. "Things have gone from bad to worse. I'll explain later."

Chapter 46

"I LOVE YOU."

He said the words again, but the line had gone dead. Matt stared at the display, then wondered if she had heard him. He still had never heard her say the words back to him, and it tormented him.

Did she love him?

"Miller!"

Carter waved him back toward the entrance of the hotel, and he rushed to him, his heart feeling heavy in his chest.

Would he ever get to kiss her again? Would he ever smell her skin again or just look into those blue eyes of hers?

"Where were you?" Carter asked. "We need to get back. They're not here. We searched their room and the entire hotel, but they're not here. Dammit. I was so certain we'd get them this time. Who were you talking to?"

"Just my mom. She's taking care of my son back home and needed to know where his cleats were for lacrosse. He has a game tonight."

Dang, I am a good liar.

Carter gave him a look of disinterest, then felt his bald head. "All right. The front desk will alert us once they get back."

"Did you find anything in their room?"

Matt had been up there with them going through the few belongings they had left there. Seeing Eva Rae's clothes again had made him almost lose his cool.

Carter shook his head. "They didn't bring much. We took the laptop on the desk in there. Hopefully, it'll contain something we can use in our case against those two."

"What about the fingerprints on the murder weapon? The knife in Mrs. Moore's house?" he asked, hoping to find anything that might clear Eva Rae as a suspect in that case.

"What fingerprints?" Carter said. "The killer wore gloves, I'm afraid. They left nothing. Still waiting to hear if she left any DNA on the body, though. The ME moved our case up because of its urgency, but they're still very busy with the many deaths from the Sarin gas attacks."

"Naturally," Matt said and walked with Carter back to the cruiser and got in.

Carter turned on the engine, and they took off toward downtown. Soon, they were stuck in heavy traffic. Matt stared at the tall buildings, then at the people walking the streets, and at the many cars. Where was Eva Rae now? Would she try to get out of town? Would she go to a motel somewhere? Would she be safe? While talking to her, he had wanted to reach into the phone and rip her through it to keep her safe. Being out there was dangerous for her now. The cops were terrified of her and would shoot if she gave them any reason.

"I can't believe they were right there all this time," Carter said. "Living in one of the most exclusive hotels in Miami, and we had no idea. Makes you feel kind of stupid, right? But we'll get them. Don't you worry. I have one more card up my sleeve."

Chapter 47

THEN

"I HAVEN'T SEEN you in forever. How are you?"

Helen stared at the woman sitting in front of her in the tea-room at the NYX headquarters. Helen lived there now while going through her healing process. The woman who had come to visit was her sister, Aubrey, and she wore a worried look and a slightly tilted head.

"You've lost weight," she said. "You look thin, Helen."

"Well, I've never felt better," she said. "I'm finally in control of my own life."

Aubrey looked like she didn't believe her. "Really? You don't exactly look fine to me. You've gotten so skinny. It doesn't look very healthy."

Helen cleared her throat. Losing weight was part of her self-development, part of the process she was going through. To deny herself food was a way of regaining control.

"Christopher says that…"

"Christopher? As in Christopher Daniels?" her sister said. "You're on a first-name basis with him?"

Helen nodded and sipped her tea.

"Mom and Dad are worried too," she added. "They haven't seen you in almost a year."

"I've been busy. We're busy here."

"We? It's *we* now?"

Helen nodded. "I'm part of something bigger than myself, so, yes."

"Dad says you've completely given up the horses. You never go to the farm anymore and have stopped riding? That's not like you, Helen. Those horses were your entire life, remember?"

"Christopher says it's part of evolving into an enlightened version of myself. It means giving up what has held me back all these years. Everything from my old me no longer applies. I've cleansed myself of everything from my past and can't go back anymore."

Aubrey sighed and leaned back in the white couch. "You should hear yourself; I can't believe you, Helen. Don't tell me you've given them money too?"

Helen chuckled. "It's always about the money with you people. I'm finally free of all that. Christopher says that money is just energy that needs to flow through us. Giving away your money is never a loss. You'll get empowerment back."

Aubrey gestured, annoyed, and groaned. "Can't you hear it? Listen to your own words, Helen. They've completely brainwashed you. Are you also having sex with this Christopher character, huh?"

"Wow. I didn't believe it when Christopher told me, but now I see it clearly that he was right. You're jealous of me. You're jealous of all that I have become, that I have managed to finally free myself from the world we grew up in, from our parents' claws. Don't you see that they're holding you down with all their money? Your ego is so big, you can't see it. But they're controlling you, telling you what to do, and I don't have to be a part of that. Finally, I have found a group that likes me for who I am, where there is nothing but love and peace, and where there is room for me and just me. All my life, I've had this void inside of me, this empty space, and finally, it's been filled in. Finally, I feel whole. And Mom and Dad can no longer touch me. They hold no power over me."

Aubrey rose to her feet, annoyed. "And what happens when you run out of money, huh? When you can no longer pay for the party? What will they ask you to do then? Where will you go when they throw you out? You can't come home. Dad's been very clear about that."

Helen shook her head with a gentle smile.

"You don't understand, sister. I *am* home. This is my home."

Chapter 48

MY EYES WERE FOCUSED on the road, my hands sweaty and shaking slightly as we drove away from the restaurant, the Ritz-Carlton, and the exclusive neighborhood of Coconut Grove. I approached the end of 27th Avenue when the traffic slowed down.

Sydney gave me a look. "What's going on? Why are we stopping?"

I shrugged. "Traffic, I hope."

I looked ahead of us. The rows of cars were slowly crawling forward toward blue flashing lights.

"Could it be an accident?" Sydney asked.

I spotted the patrol cars, then officers in the road peeking inside of cars.

"It's a roadblock," I said. "They put up a darn roadblock."

"For us?" Sydney shrieked.

"Yes, for us," I said, then looked in the rearview mirror. There was still no one close behind us, so I put the car in reverse and backed up, swirled the car around, then drove the wrong way back down the road until I found a small street and turned, while the oncoming cars honked loudly at me.

We drove through the back streets in a smaller neighborhood, then reached a Home Depot before heading out on Dixie Highway, leading out of town. I pressed the accelerator down, and we roared southbound until the traffic suddenly slowed down once again and we came to a full stop.

"What the heck?" I said.

"Another roadblock?" Sydney asked and looked at me perplexed.

A chopper circled above us and made me nervous. The traffic crawled forward, and I found a small exit, leading us back again.

"Shoot," I said and slammed my hand on the wheel.

I took another turn down toward the Chinese Village but ran into yet another roadblock and had to turn around again and drive back.

"They've blocked all the exits," I said. "We can't get out of here."

I hit the accelerator again, and we rushed back toward Coconut Grove. I found a park and stopped the car, trying to clear my head for a few seconds, and looking at the map.

"We've tried all the exits," I said. "There's no way out. We have to stay here, somehow."

"But, Eva Rae, I don't understand," Sydney said. "Why are they chasing us like this? Is there something I need to know?"

I exhaled and leaned back in the seat. "They think I killed Lori Moore," I said. "I called Matt earlier, and he told me. I didn't want to worry you. That's why I didn't tell you."

Sydney stared at me, barely blinking. "Lori Moore? She's... she's dead? But we saw her yesterday?"

"And that's why they think I killed her. We were the last people to see her alive. She was found murdered in her house this morning."

The panic was visible in Sydney's eyes.

"Murdered? But... but... can't you just tell them you didn't do it?"

"It's not that simple. I'm already wanted for a lot of other stuff. And I don't exactly have an alibi for when she was killed."

"You don't? Oh, wait... it happened last night? You snuck out last night... but... why, Eva Rae? What were you doing?"

I started the car back up with a roar. "I went for a walk, remember?"

I didn't want to tell her what I had done. I was still processing it myself. Three people had been killed, bad people, yes, but still. They weren't supposed to have died. It was an accident. I didn't want Sydney to know; I didn't want to give her more to worry about.

"We need to find somewhere to hide," Sydney said and gave me a look.

"I don't think any hotels will take us," I said. "Even if we found a small motel, they'd recognize our faces."

"Maybe we don't have to," she said. "I have an idea. But you're not gonna like it."

Chapter 49

"YOU'VE GOT to be kidding me."

Sydney had taken over the wheel and driven us back to Coconut Grove and into the south end of the neighborhood, far from the Ritz-Carlton. She parked in front of a big mansion and looked at me.

"Think about it. They'll never look for us here. We'll be right under their noses."

"But... Sydney. This is NYX headquarters?"

She nodded eagerly. "I know. It's perfect."

Sydney got out of the car, and I reluctantly followed her. She grabbed my hand in hers and led me to the entrance, where we rang the doorbell. A tall, gorgeous woman wearing white linen pants and shirt opened.

"Kelly Stone!"

"We need your help," she said. "Can I talk to Christopher again?"

The woman nodded. "Of course. Of course. Come on in."

We walked inside the big hall and were told to sit down on a set of couches. A huge flower arrangement on the table in front of us smelled heavenly. All the walls and furniture were white, and everything was very bright.

Even the man coming toward us was dressed in a white suit, his salt and pepper hair slicked back, his piercing blue eyes lingering on my sister.

"Kelly Stone, twice in one day. How did I get to be so lucky?" he said and gave her a warm hug.

"This is my sister," she said and pointed at me. "Eva Rae, this is Christopher Daniels."

The gorgeous man pulled me into a hug as well. His embrace felt warm and genuine. I had to admit, I enjoyed it, and it brought me great calmness.

He looked into my eyes, still while holding me.

"Wow, you're tense."

He turned to face my sister, finally letting go of me.

"My assistant told me you needed our help?"

Sydney nodded. "Yes. We need shelter for the night. The entire town is looking for us."

Christopher Daniels stared at her, scrutinizing her. "I have a feeling I shouldn't ask why. We don't watch the news here and, to be honest, it doesn't matter why you're running. We all run from stuff in our lives. We are here to help."

"We can pay you," Sydney said.

Christopher put his hand up. "We don't need your money. It'll be our pleasure to host you and your sister for as long as you need. I'll put you up in one of the guest cottages in the back. No one will think about looking for you there."

Sydney exhaled, relieved. I was still tense, maybe even more now as I saw the way he looked at my sister.

"Thank you so much. You have no idea how big of a help this is."

Christopher Daniels placed his palms against one another, then bowed.

"It is my pleasure to help. At NYX, we believe in kindness toward everyone."

He turned to face the woman who had opened the door for us. "Angela here will make sure you have everything you need; won't you, Angela?"

The woman nodded, smiling. As she moved her arm and her sleeve was pulled up, I noticed she too was branded with the symbol, just like the guy I had seen in the car at the port. Seeing it made my blood freeze.

"Of course," she said. "If you'll follow me, I'll get you installed."

Chapter 50

MATT SAT AT HIS DESK, sipping coffee, while people rushed around him, talking on phones and tapping on computers. He stared into the empty screen, not knowing what to do. He could still hear Eva Rae's wonderful voice and missed her so terribly. It was like his entire being was screaming for her to come back. The whole town was looking for her now. He was terrified that she would put up a fight and they'd end up killing her.

Carter had ordered roadblocks all over town, especially tight around Coconut Grove, so they wouldn't be able to leave the neighborhood without being caught.

So far, Matt hadn't heard anything, so that was still good news. But Matt felt nervous beyond anything else. If they did catch her, then there was no telling what might happen. Would she resist arrest? Would she try to run? Would they shoot at her if she did?

He couldn't see any good ending to this, and it tormented him.

Chief Annie had called earlier in the morning and told him she too was worried. What she was hearing from down there made her nervous.

"You and I both know she didn't do it," she said. "She couldn't kill that woman — not that way. In self-defense maybe or trying to do something good, yes, but not a brutal slaughter like this. You have to stop them, Matt."

"How?" he had asked her. "I tried to get her to turn herself in, but she refused to. Not until she finds her daughter."

"So, she must have some intel that puts Olivia in Miami," she said. "Maybe she knows that the Iron Fist is there."

"That's what I've been thinking too. But I've asked around and even searched their files down here. They have nothing on this Iron Fist."

"It's probably just a name he uses online," she said with a deep exhale. "They might know him by another name."

"I've asked to look into their human trafficking files, and hopefully that'll pay off."

"And that guy, Carter? Does he suspect that you know Eva Rae?"

"I'm afraid so. He asked about it earlier, but I think I managed to talk myself out of it."

"He can't know, Matt," she said. "You've got to play along, so we know what's going on. We want Eva Rae home alive."

He sighed. "I'm beginning to think it might be hard. This guy wants her taken down. It's become like an obsession to him."

"That's not good, Matt."

"He still doesn't have anything that places Eva Rae at Lori Moore's house at the time of the murder."

"That's good," she said. "I'll try and pull all the strings I can from up here, but there's a lot of heat on her right now, so I fear it might be tough."

They had hung up, and Matt had felt like screaming but kept his cool. Now, he spotted Carter coming down the hallway, a file under his arm, whistling happily.

I don't like that look on his face.

"Guess what?" he said as he approached Matt's desk.

Matt forced a smile. It became awkward, but Carter didn't seem to notice.

He reached inside of his file, then placed a photo in front of Matt. On it was a necklace with a golden heart at the end of it. Seeing it made Matt feel sick to his stomach.

Matt had given Eva Rae this necklace for Christmas.

"Recognize this?" Carter asked, then showed him a photo of Eva Rae where you could see her wearing the necklace.

"That's right," he added. "It's hers, and guess where it was found? You guessed right. In Lori Moore's house, in the kitchen where her body was found. This places Eva Rae Thomas at the scene of the crime. This is exactly the evidence we've been waiting for."

Chapter 51

THE GUEST HOUSE they gave us was really nice — decorated in white furniture and with flower arrangements on the tables, two bedrooms with queen-sized beds, and a small kitchen. It was all we needed.

I took a shower, then threw myself on the bed and fell asleep right away. I slept heavily until Sydney woke me up and told me it was time to go to dinner. I still felt groggy and exhausted when I followed Sydney into the big dining room.

Many eyes were on us as we found two seats and sat down. The food was nice and reminded me of my mom's. Being vegan and plant-based, it was something she might cook. I ate while thinking about her and the kids, wondering if they were all right. I didn't allow myself to think much about them since it hurt too much if I did, and I had to focus on the task of finding Olivia.

I had been so close to the Iron Fist the night before at the port. And now, I didn't even have a computer to gain access to the Dark Web. It annoyed me greatly that I had finally found him in there, found a chatroom where he was arranging the meets, and now, I couldn't even get back to it.

I had been so close, and yet I blew it.

Not everyone in the dining room had been branded on the arm; I realized when looking around. It seemed to be only a few, and those few seemed to be in charge of the rest. Most were women, but there were also a few men. The founder, Christopher Daniels, sat at the end of the table, smiling and chatting to the people sitting next to him. Sydney fell into talking with several other women sitting next to her, and she seemed like she was enjoying herself. Meanwhile, no one spoke to me. I guess I didn't exactly give out the vibe of wanting to chat.

Gosh, I miss my family. Has Alex lost that loose tooth he was so proud of? Will my mom remember to give him money from the tooth fairy? Is Christine remembering to practice her double bass?

Talking to Matt earlier had almost made me lose it. I wanted him to reach in through the phone and hold me tight. I needed to feel his touch, his warm kisses on my skin. I craved to be close to him again. But instead of telling him how badly I missed him, how deeply I loved him, I had been distant and cold toward him.

Because I had to be.

I just hoped he understood that.

When dinner was over, we helped clean up along with everyone else in the big kitchen. I filled the dishwasher and, once I was done, I walked outside on the porch overlooking the big pool area. Two women were in the pool, swimming.

I realized there were four guest cottages like ours on the property, and one of them was located by the edge of the property, its windows covered with plywood. Somehow, that cottage gave me the creeps, and I couldn't stop looking at it.

"You enjoying the view?"

It was Christopher Daniels. He came out on the porch, an orange in his hand that he began peeling. He smiled at me when I turned around.

"Just enjoying that I still have my freedom," I said, feeling heavy. I knew this was a good hideout, but it wasn't going to last. At some point, I had to face what I had done. I just hoped I found Olivia before it happened.

I added, "For now."

"I sense you are weighed down greatly by your past," he said, his eyes scrutinizing me.

Really? How insightful.

"You know there are ways to let go of all this, right?" he asked. "We have workshops that can help you."

I forced a smile. "I'm good for now. But thanks."

"Suit yourself," he said, then finished peeling the orange and opened it. He handed me a piece. I took it to be polite. He slurped his as he ate it, and the sound made me cringe.

"You know it's not your fault that your sister was kidnapped when you were younger," he said.

I almost choked on my piece of orange. I coughed to breathe. He didn't seem to notice.

"You've carried that weight since you were a child," he continued. "But that's not all of what is weighing you down. And this is becoming a problem between you and your sister. Because, deep down, you also blame your sister for what happened. Because she strayed. That day at the supermarket. She walked away from you; she left you to look at Barbie dolls. The man, your father, grabbed you first but then took her instead. You're secretly angry at your sister for letting it happen when she knew she was supposed to keep an eye on you. And now that she's back in your life, you're angry with her because she got the easy part. She got to grow up with your dad while you were stuck with a mother who was emotionally unavailable. She got to become a beautiful, beloved actress, while you became an FBI agent in the attempt to redeem yourself for not being able to save her. She grew up guilt-free while you carried all this weight around. But you need to forgive her in order to be able to move on. Or else it might end up destroying your entire relationship. You need to let go of this. It's important for both of you."

I stared at the man next to me, eyes wide open, my nostrils flaring. At first, I didn't know what to say.

"Did my sister tell you all this?" I ended up asking.

He shrugged. "Does it matter?"

I was about to say something, but as I turned to look at him again, he had left. I stood alone on the porch, warm wind blowing in my hair, feeling myself blush in anger.

Who did this guy think he was?

Chapter 52

MATT COULDN'T SLEEP. How was he supposed to fall asleep with all that was going on?

He was lying in his hotel room, staring into the ceiling, wondering about Eva Rae and how to help her get through this. He also wondered about the necklace and how on Earth it could have been found in Lori Moore's house if Eva Rae hadn't been there on the night of the murder.

Part of him was beginning to worry that maybe she had been there. Maybe Eva Rae had killed that woman?

What if she did?

No, you fool. It's Eva Rae we're talking about. You've known her since you both were three years old.

Matt closed his eyes while rubbing his forehead. He had a headache coming along, and it had been lurking behind his eyes all evening.

His thoughts returned to Eva Rae. He had gone through the case from the port this very afternoon and looked through all the pictures. Three men were killed. Seven young girls rescued. Matt didn't know what to think. Those guys were obviously criminals of the worst kind, buying and selling young girls. But the thing was, if Eva Rae had killed them, then maybe she had killed Lori Moore too. If she was involved somehow in the trafficking? Could she have been some sort of ringleader?

Two of the men were killed in a car crash. The driver had been shot through the windshield, but that wasn't what killed him. The impact was. One was shot in what looked like self-defense. They didn't have their throats slit in their kitchen. Nor had they been mutilated. No, that kill was of another caliber. That was the work of a vicious murderer.

Matt exhaled and lifted his head from the pillow. His watch said two a.m. He looked at his phone to make sure she hadn't called again. But the last incoming call was from his mother when she called for him to say goodnight to Elijah. As usual, the boy had been completely silent on the other end while Matt spoke. It hadn't exactly helped their relationship that he was gone for so long. Matt had thought about taking the boy to counseling to make things better between them. His mother and Eva Rae had both told him to give the boy time, but Elijah blamed Matt for the death of his mother, and it didn't seem to get any better, no matter how much Matt tried.

"Maybe you're trying too hard," Eva Rae had said back then when Matt had taken the boy in. "Maybe he needs a little space."

It had been eight months now, and Matt saw no improvement at all.

Maybe I'm just not good enough to be a dad.

He sighed and put the phone down. He couldn't stop thinking about Eva Rae and how distant she had been earlier in the day when they had talked on the phone. Matt knew she was under a lot of pressure, more than what most people would be able to sustain, but still.

Didn't she miss him at all?

He wondered where she was hiding. There were roadblocks all over town, and they would continue all night and into the next day. How had she managed to avoid them so far? She couldn't go back to the hotel. She couldn't go to any hotel in the area without them calling Carter. Her face was everywhere, on all the screens in the small homes. How was she still keeping herself under the radar?

Carter had said he had one more card to play, one he believed would smoke them out. He wouldn't share it with Matt in detail, but Matt got the feeling that it was bad news for Eva Rae.

Chapter 53

SYDNEY TOOK a late-night yoga and meditation class, while I stayed in the guesthouse raging over Christopher Daniels and the way he believed he knew me. The fact was, he didn't know me at all.

I kept glaring down to the end of the property toward the cottage that was all boarded up. It had me curious. What was in there and why did it have to be boarded up? There hadn't been a hurricane going through since Irma two years ago. Had they simply just never removed them? Because they didn't use it?

Or was there something in there that they didn't want to see the light of day?

Sydney came back after it had gone dark, looking all blissful and relaxed. She took a shower, then threw herself on the bed next to me with a deep sigh.

"My God, I needed that. You should have come, Eva Rae; it was so good, and so empowering," she said.

I looked at her, thinking about what Christopher Daniels had told me earlier, then forced a smile, trying to push down the feeling of jealousy I felt toward her and always had felt since she came back into my life. I wasn't going to let this control me or let Sydney sense it. I could deal with my guilt and blame on my own. I didn't need their workshops to help me. Christopher Daniels might think he knew me, but he didn't know me at all.

"I just feel so refreshed," Sydney said and dried her hair gently with the towel. "Like I'm brand-new. I really like it here. It's been a while since I felt so good about myself."

"That's great," I said, not meaning it.

"You know what Christopher told me?" she asked.

"No, what?" I said, wanting to roll my eyes, but refraining from doing it. I didn't want her to know how I felt about him and all his so-called insight.

"He said something that really resonated with me deep down. And I am a little embarrassed to admit this, but he told me it would be good for me to tell you. He told me that I was secretly blaming you for being the one who wasn't kidnapped back then at the Wal-Mart. I mean, our dad did grab you first, and then he took me instead. According to Christopher, that has been bothering me all my life, and secretly, I've been blaming you for it. And I'm jealous of you for having grown up with our mother. I grew up lacking one my entire life, thinking she didn't want me. It's tough once you get to that age where you really need her, especially as a teenager, you know? I mean, who was I supposed to talk to about getting my period, huh? Dad? He blushed when I even asked him to buy the pads I needed."

I stared at her. "You think Mom talked to me about periods?"

"Didn't she?"

"Mom barely talked to me at all. I would scream for her attention but never receive it. She could freeze me out for days at a time. She couldn't even look at me because it reminded her of what had happened. After you were gone, it was like I didn't exist to her anymore."

Sydney looked at me with compassion in her eyes. "Oh, dear God, Eva Rae. I didn't know."

I shrugged. "How could you? You weren't there."

I rose to my feet, feeling all kinds of emotions stir up inside of me. I hated to admit it, but Christopher Daniels was right. I was upset about Sydney getting to grow up with our dad and leaving me alone with our distant and cold mother.

Dang it, he was annoying.

Chapter 54

I SAT OUTSIDE of our cottage for a long time, maybe a few hours; I didn't know. All I knew was that I felt angry and sad at the same time and that I was sick of feeling this way. Yet I didn't know how to get rid of it, how to solve it. Maybe I should take one of his workshops?

As I sat there, looking up at the stars and the night settled everywhere, I suddenly saw activity down by the boarded-up house. Two people with flashlights approached it, speaking in low voices.

I looked at my watch and realized it was two a.m. Why were they up and walking around down there?

I rose to my feet, then hurried across the lawn, past the two other cottages, then stopped when I got closer. I watched them from afar as they unlocked the door and opened it. When they had entered, and the door was closed behind them, I ran up to the cottage and stood by the window, leaning my ear against it.

I heard whimpering coming from behind it. Someone was crying. Crying and pleading with them.

"Please, let me out, please."

My eyes grew wide. Someone was being kept in there? Against her will?

"You can't get out," a voice said. "You must finish what you came here for first."

"It's part of the cleansing process," another voice said.

"Please," the woman said.

"Remember what Christopher said," the first voice said. "It's for your own good."

"I know," the woman said. "I know."

"Don't you want to reach enlightenment? Don't you want to get rid of your old persona and become like new?"

"I do. I really do."

"Then you must let go of your old ways. Your excessive pride is holding you back. This is the only way to become free from it."

"I know. I know."

I can't believe these people. They're keeping her in there? Locked up? And then they tell her it's for her own good?

I gasped lightly as someone placed his hands on my shoulders. I stood up straight while he held me tightly between his hands.

"Oh, my, still so tense," he said.

Christopher Daniels!

I froze in place while he leaned over my back. I could feel his body really close to mine as he whispered in my ear and breathed down my neck.

"You really need to learn how to relax. I can teach you."

"Just like you're teaching that woman in there?" I said.

He laughed, then closed his arms around my neck, a little too tight for my liking.

"She's in there voluntarily," he said. "No one forced her."

"How long has she been there?" I asked. "Voluntarily?"

"Does it matter?" he whispered. I felt his lips close to my ear, and it made me very uncomfortable.

"I heard her pleading to be let out, yet they didn't do it. Why is that?"

"Because she doesn't know what is best for her. It's part of the process, to strip her of her pride. But no one said it was going to be easy. It's our job to make sure she doesn't give up in the middle of the process."

Dear God, what is this place? We need to get out of here before it is too late.

His arms were still wrapped around me, and he was holding me tight. I wanted to get out of his grip, but he wasn't letting me go. Instead, he chuckled as I struggled to get loose.

"Your life is just one long struggle, isn't it?" he asked. "It doesn't have to be. It could be so much easier."

"Let me guess, if I give in to you and your ways?" I said. "What else do you keep locked up in this place? Do you have any young girls here too? Kidnapped young girls?"

Finally, he let go of me. I panted and turned around to look at him, breathing agitatedly.

He stared at me. The way he looked at me made me feel uncomfortable, and I backed up. Our eyes locked for just a second, and I took off running back to our cottage.

Chapter 55

"I THINK Christopher Daniels is the Iron Fist."

I had barely slept all night. Once my heart had calmed down enough for me to find a little rest, the many thoughts in my mind wouldn't let me sleep.

"Excuse me?" Sydney said.

She was sitting up in bed when I entered her room and sat down next to her. She looked gorgeous, even when having just woken up. It annoyed me.

"Why would you say something like that?" Sydney continued. "He's been nothing but nice to us."

"He's keeping a girl locked up in the cottage down by the end of the property. I heard her plead for them to let her out, and they wouldn't. Then he came and put his arms around my neck, tightly, like he wanted to hold me down."

"That's a technique he uses," she said. "To make you connect with the Earth again. He did it to me yesterday too."

"The guy is a sleaze bag," I said. "Why are you defending him?"

"Why do you keep accusing him? Need I remind you we're staying here for free while the entire police force is looking for us because of you."

I stared at my sister, biting my lip.

"I still think he's the Iron Fist."

"You're insane," she said, then grabbed her burner phone. I had asked her to get rid of her old phone now that they knew she was with me. It was too easy to track.

"Now, if you'll excuse me," she said. "I have to check my emails. I assume this thing can access the Internet?"

"It can. I only bought those that can, assuming we'd need it. The data is prepaid for by cash. But do you have to check your email now?" I asked. "It's risky."

"Yes, I need to do this every now and then. Since I have been on the run with you, I have been completely off the grid, and I need to check in to make sure there isn't some big offer for the role of a lifetime that I'm missing out on."

"Be careful," I said. "They might send you a link for you to click, but it could give up our whereabouts."

She gave me a look that reminded me of Olivia. It almost made me cry. I hadn't realized until now how much those two actually looked like one another.

"There's an email from my agent," she said and pressed on the display of the LG burner phone. I had bought a ton of them at Wal-Mart before we left, so we could get rid of them as soon as we were done using them. I had purchased the most expensive ones since they would be able to do more, like use navigation and access the Internet, but they were still only thirty bucks per phone.

"Oh, dear God," Sydney said.

I looked at her, and her face turned pale.

"What's wrong?" I asked.

She lifted her eyes, and they met mine.

"They're threatening me to turn you in."

"They're what?" I asked.

Her eyes teared up. "The police have contacted my agent and told him that if I don't turn you in, they'll go to all the newspapers and magazines and tell them I am a suspect in a murder case. So far, they have kept it from the public that they are looking for me too, but now they're willing to leak it if I don't turn you in. It'll ruin my career. Oh, Eva Rae, I don't know what to do."

Chapter 56

"WHAT IS HAPPENING? Where are we going?"

It was in the early morning hours, and Olivia and Tiffany were sitting on the floor of the blue van. The armed guards had woken them up around sunrise and told them to get in.

Sitting next to her, Tiffany whispered the words to Olivia. Olivia didn't look at her. She fiddled with the hem of her jeans that had become ripped from the many hours working at the factory. The jeans were so dirty you could barely see the blue color anymore. Olivia's black Converse were worn out, and her pinky toe was poking out the side.

"Olivia?" Tiffany said. "Where are we going?"

Olivia shrugged, then looked away.

"Please, Olivia?" she said. "What's happening?"

Olivia took in a deep breath, then finally looked at the girl. She reminded her so much of her younger sister; she almost teared up just looking at her.

"Remember that I said that sometimes we do other stuff besides work at the factory? Well, this is it. This is the other stuff."

"But what is it, Olivia? What are we going to do?" Tiffany asked, her lips shaking.

Olivia shrugged. She had grown to care for the girl. Even though she had promised herself she wouldn't, it had happened anyway. And now she was worried about her. It was the last thing she needed right now, to have to worry about someone else besides herself. But spending days with this little girl, having no one else to talk to, she had done what she decided never to do. She had gotten to know her. And now she feared something might happen to her. She wanted to protect her.

"Just follow my lead when we get there," she said. "And don't ask questions."

"But...?"

Olivia sent her a look, and she stopped. Olivia felt her hands begin to shake as she worried about what was ahead.

They soon ran into a roadblock, and they could hear the driver talking to an officer outside, while the guards signaled for the girls to be very quiet. The talk lasted a few minutes, and Olivia had to bite her lip hard to not scream for help. But when looking at the guards' guns, she knew there was no way she dared to do it. They would only kill her.

Someone walked up behind the van, and they heard voices. Hope filled Olivia and made her stare at the door, praying they'd open it and find them all.

We're in here; Please, help us!

But the door never opened, and soon the voices faded out, and the van started back up again. Olivia felt her heart hammering in her chest as she stared at the guards with their guns. Sweat was springing from her forehead as she slowly realized they had passed the roadblock. A tear escaped her eye as her hope dwindled.

When the van came to a halt again, she gasped and looked up toward the door that was opened, and a face appeared. Their leader smiled widely at them.

"It's time, girls."

They rose to their feet and walked in a line out of the van, Olivia making sure that Tiffany was right behind her. Once outside, they were told to stand in a line up against a wall. The area around them was void of people. The guards had new clothes for them to wear along with plastic bags and sharpened pencils.

"Now, some of you have done this before and know what to do," one of them said, staring each and every one of them into the eyes to make sure they understood. "The new ones follow what the rest do. As soon as you're inside, you place the bags, hiding them under a chair or a bench, and then you poke the bag right before you leave and rush back outside, where we will be picking you up at the back entrance."

The bags were handed to them, and Olivia took hers along with the pencil. Tiffany stared at the bag between her hands with the liquid inside of it. Olivia could tell she wanted to ask questions but held it back like Olivia had told her to. The guards and the leader didn't like them asking questions. Olivia had seen them beat a girl until she could barely walk because of that. If you wanted to survive, you just did what they told you. Those were the simple rules to follow.

The leader came up in front of them, then walked down the line and pointed at one girl, then at another.

"This one. And that one. And…?"

The leader stopped in front of Tiffany, then placed a hand on top of her head.

"This one."

Olivia's heart stopped when she saw it.

"No!" she yelled and stepped forward, nostrils flaring. There was no way she could let this happen.

The leader stopped. A furious set of eyes landed on Olivia.

"Do you want to take her place?"

Olivia swallowed, then looked down at Tiffany, who was crying now. Olivia nodded.

"I'll take her place."

"All right," the leader said. "As you wish."

As they had changed and began walking in a straight line, Tiffany tugged at Olivia's shirt.

"What was that? What did you do?"

Olivia exhaled. She felt her hands begin to shake.

"Every time we do this, they choose three girls who will be the ones who go in first. They usually don't make it out alive. Our leader wanted you to be one of them, but I took your place."

Chapter 57

THEY WERE TOLD to merge into the crowd and look like any of the other children there. They had given them uniforms to wear and had even given them backpacks on their backs to make it look like they were just kids going to school. The grown-ups pretended to be teachers and wore skirts and carried briefcases.

Olivia walked with the two other girls toward the crowd entering the school, then blended in with them, and she lost sight of the two others. They were instructed to be the ones to go upstairs and place the bags there. By the time they made it downstairs, the girls down there would already have poked holes in their bags, and it would be too late for them to make it out. Olivia knew the drill. She had done it twice before.

But the other two times, she had been among those to survive. This time was different. She had chosen to sacrifice herself.

Olivia's hands were shaking as she followed the other children inside. She had no idea what had become of Tiffany since she had stayed behind and would enter with the four others, the ones that were going to survive. One of the adults looked at her, and she could tell she was scared too. But there was no way around it. The first time, on the train, one of the girls had tried to run before they got on the train. Two guards grabbed her and took her away. They never saw her again.

What they did was terrible; Olivia was well aware that it was. She knew the bags held a gas in them and that it killed people once it

NEVER EVER

was released. She looked at all the kids hurrying to class, grins on their faces. She saw the girls chatting by the lockers, happily, only worried about the next test or maybe a boy, not knowing what was about to happen. She felt such terrible pain in the pit of her stomach.

How was she supposed to do this to them? They were nothing but kids like herself.

"If you run and we find you — and we *will* find you — you will be killed. If you talk to anyone, you will be killed. If you refuse to do as instructed, you will be killed. Is that understood?"

Those were the words before they sent them off, just as they had been the two other times. Olivia had listened to them, shaking, and she hadn't dared not to do as she was told. She had wanted to survive.

She still wanted to survive. But the guards waited by the entrance and exits of the school. They would catch her and kill her if she tried to escape.

The first time they had sent them into the trains, Olivia hadn't known what was in the bags. She had been instructed to go one stop and then place the bag under her seat, poke a hole in it, then get out of the car and into another one, the only one that wasn't attacked. Then as they rode one more stop, she was told to get out and walk away like nothing happened. *Don't look back*, they had told them. *Just keep walking till you reach the stairs.* But Olivia had stopped and turned to look. That was when she had seen them. Hundreds of people that had fallen out of the car that she had been in first, and crawled across the platform, gasping for air, some screaming in pain, others squirming until they took their final breath. Three of them had been girls she knew from the house. They had been in the first car at the end of the train and didn't make it out in time. Olivia had stopped for just a second and stared at them, then realized that she had done this, that what had been in those bags had caused this. Her stopping had cost her a beating when they got back to the truck because she almost exposed herself, they said. Olivia hadn't cared. She thought she deserved a beating for what she had done.

Now, she was up the stairs and looking down the hallway at all the smiling faces. Olivia realized it was August, and school was back in session. She had been gone all summer, and school had started back up without her. The thought made her tear up.

I am never going back to school. I am never going to be with my friends. I am never going to see my parents or my siblings again. I will die here, squirming on the floor like a worm until I can't breathe anymore — like they did on that train and like they did in that church.

"No, I will not. I will make it out, somehow," she told herself, shaking her head.

She then walked inside a classroom and placed the bag underneath a chair. She was instructed to wait until right before class started. A couple of kids looked at her strangely, probably wondering if she was a new student. She looked down, then placed her foot against the bag to make sure it was still in place. She felt the pencil in her hand. It was amazing how heavy such a little pencil could feel when it held the power of life and death.

Chapter 58

WHAT DOES it matter if I'm dead anyway?

Olivia stared at the pencil in her hand and felt the pointy end of it with her finger. Still more kids were coming into the class and putting their backpacks down. Two boys were goofing around and fighting for fun. Three girls were watching, giggling at their stupidity, hoping one of them would look their way.

Olivia looked at the clock on the wall. There were still ten minutes until class started. She spotted a girl sitting a couple of desks down, on her phone.

Heart hammering in her chest, Olivia made a decision, one she feared she would end up regretting.

"Can I borrow your phone for a second?"

The girl looked up at her. She was wearing black lipstick, and her eyes blazed in anger.

"No. Why would I loan my phone to someone I don't even know?"

Olivia leaned over her desk, then said with a low voice. "Because if you don't, we're all going to die."

Now she had her attention. The girl looked up at her, eyes wide, mouth gaping.

"What did you just say? Is this some kind of joke?"

"Listen to me," Olivia said. "I'm trying to save your life here, but I need you not to panic, okay?"

The girl scrutinized her for a long time. Olivia was certain she could hear the clock on the wall ticking loudly in her head. She had no time to spare. She didn't know what the response time was around here. Would they be able to make it in time?

"Just let me borrow the phone, please," Olivia said with the calmest voice possible. Sweat was springing from her forehead, and her palms felt clammy.

"Please."

The girl swallowed, and Olivia could tell she knew this was serious. She looked down at the phone for a second before finally handing it over to Olivia.

Relieved, Olivia grabbed it, then dialed.

"9-1-1. What's your emergency?"

"There's going to be a gas attack on a school," Olivia said, keeping her voice low, hoping that the other students wouldn't hear her and panic. If they started to run, the girls in the other classrooms would poke their bags prematurely as they had been instructed to. People would die.

"What school are we talking about?" the dispatcher said. Olivia could hear her tapping on a keyboard. Olivia found it difficult to calm her pounding heart.

"I...I don't know..." Olivia said, then looked at the girl with the black lipstick. She seemed to understand and pointed at the emblem on her shirt.

"Our Savior's Catholic school," Olivia said, her voice trembling. "It's the same as what happened on the trains and at the church. The gas is in bags. But you must hurry. It's gonna happen in six, no wait, only five minutes. Please, hurry."

Chapter 59

"WHAT'S GOING ON?"

Matt saw the officers begin to run. Carter looked up from his desk too. A sergeant came to them.

"Sarin gas attack on a school. Someone called it in. Apparently, the attackers are still inside, and it hasn't happened yet."

Matt rose to his feet, then looked at Carter.

"I'll drive," Matt said and grabbed his gun. They stormed to the cruiser and took off, sirens blasting, following the nine other patrol cars that were leaving at the same time.

"We need the entire perimeter sealed off," Matt said. "If the attackers are still inside, then they'll come out at some point, trying to get away, and there will be someone waiting for them. We need to get them."

Over the radio, they learned that firefighters and paramedics were almost there, but they were told to stay back in case the terrorists were armed. If they were to stop this, then they had to play their cards right. They also learned that JTTF were on their way, but coming up behind them, so Miami-Dade police were to intervene if possible once they got there.

"Leaving the tough work to us normal cops," Carter grumbled under his breath. "As usual."

"We're talking ten terrorists, armed with Sarin gas, inside the school," the radio informed. "One of them called dispatch. She's on the top floor. She's just a young girl. She informed dispatch that there were seven young girls who were forced to do this. And three adults."

"They're using young girls?" Matt asked, startled.

It suddenly made sense. He had been going through the files from the two previous attacks and seen that there had been at least three young girls in each place that were unaccounted for. They had been in the age range from ten to seventeen. And so far, no one had looked for them, and they hadn't been able to ID them yet. Some were Hispanic looking while others were assumed to come from Eastern Europe. Only one girl had been ID'ed as being American, and her parents had been notified. They had told the police that she had run away from home two years earlier. How she ended up in a Catholic Church on a Sunday morning in Miami had been a puzzle until now.

"They're using trafficked girls," Matt mumbled.

"What's that?"

"To do their dirty work," he said.

"The terrorists?"

Matt nodded as Carter drove up in front of the school and parked behind the many other patrol cars. They each grabbed a vest and put it on. They were going to be there with the first responders, and Matt felt anxious. It was almost eight o'clock. They had thirty seconds to get in there, identify the terrorists, and stop them before they pierced those bags like they had at the Metrorail and the church.

The responders leading the charge suited up in hazmat suits and put on gas masks. Matt waited outside, gun clutched between his hands, while the men in suits stormed inside and the screaming began.

Chapter 60

AS THE FIRST SCREAM RESOUNDED, all in the classroom turned to look at Olivia. She had explained the situation to them and told them to remain calm, that the police were on their way.

"Why can't we just run?" a girl said, her entire torso shaking in desperation.

"Yeah, I want to get out of here," a boy standing next to her said, his eyes flickering in fear.

"Don't," Olivia said. "The police have just entered the building; that's why they were screaming downstairs. But as they did, the bags were most likely poked, and the gas has started to seep out. If you run out in the hallway or down the stairs, you'll run right into it, and then you'll be exposed."

The kids stared at her, eyes brimming with terror. More screams were coming from downstairs, and it made another wave of fear go through the classroom.

"They'll come for us," Olivia said. "But until they do, we keep the door closed and stay in here."

More screams made a boy rise from his seat. "I can't stand this. I can't stay in here!"

Before Olivia could stop him, he ran for the door, opened it, and stormed out into the hallway. Olivia slammed the door shut behind him, crying helplessly.

Barely had she backed away from the door before it opened, and a man made his way inside. Seeing his face made Olivia's blood freeze. He was one of them; he was one of the men that had brought her there.

He took one glance at Olivia, then at the bag on the floor beneath the chair.

"We've been compromised. You know what to do next," he said. "Poke the bag."

Olivia stared sat him, her hands beginning to shake. In his hand, he was holding a gun, and as the other kids in the class saw that, they screamed and backed up.

Olivia stared at him defiantly, blocking his way to the bag.

"It must be done," he said and lifted the gun to her forehead, then clicked the hammer back. "You know this."

She closed her eyes and shook her head. If he shot her, then so be it. She wasn't going to risk all these children's lives.

"DO IT!"

She opened her eyes and stared into his, determined. Then she opened her mouth and said:

"No."

The man trembled in anger and pressed the barrel of the gun against Olivia's skin. She prepared herself, readied herself to pay the ultimate price.

She didn't see the chair as it flew through the air until it was too late. It slammed into the man's back and knocked him to the floor. Olivia glanced toward where it had come from and spotted the girl with the black lipstick holding it, panting agitatedly.

Next thing she knew, she was on top of him, her hands gripping over his and over the gun. Olivia didn't know where she got her strength, but it just happened. The man let go with one hand, and Olivia pulled the gun out of his grip, but as she almost had it, he gave it a push, so it flew across the room. He then punched Olivia in the stomach and blew out all the air from her lungs. Olivia panted, and the man managed to squirm away. It was too late when Olivia realized that he had a pencil in his hand, and she couldn't stop him before he poked a hole in the bag, and the green liquid slowly seeped out onto the classroom floor.

Chapter 61

OLIVIA LUNGED AT THE MAN, but it was too late. A shot blasted through the air and whizzed above her head. The bullet hit the man in the forehead, and he fell to the floor, instantly dead. Behind her stood the girl with the black lipstick, gun between her hands, shaking. She let it go, and it dropped to the floor.

Screams of panic soon filled the classroom, and Olivia stared at the leaking gas, panting and agitated.

"Get away from it," she yelled at the top of her lungs. "Go to the windows and open them!"

Someone lifted a chair and threw it through the window. The window was pushed out of its frame, and soon the boy crawled out. He stood on a ledge, screaming his heart out.

"Help! Help us!"

A girl crawled out after him but slipped. Her hands gripped for the ledge, and she was now hanging there, screaming. There were two windows in the classroom. Olivia ran to the other, the one that faced the other side of the building and spotted the firefighters below. She pulled the blinds off, then pushed the window open. She yelled at them to come to the other side of the building. They did and entered the school courtyard below. The firefighters spotted the kids on the ledge and soon backed a ladder-truck up in the courtyard. The girl dangling outside the window let go of the ledge with a scream and jumped into the arms of a firefighter on the ladder below who took her to safety. Seeing this, the two others soon followed.

"Hurry," Olivia said and looked back at the gas at the other end of the room. Luckily, the hole in the bag wasn't very big, and it was coming out very slowly. She couldn't even feel it in her eyes yet, and she knew of several other girls who had survived that. As soon as it pinched the eyes, that was when you should run; she had learned from them.

Run, if you can.

Olivia turned to the others, then pointed at the window. "Get out there, and they'll take you down. It's the only way to survive this. If you stay here, you'll die. We can't wait for the police and paramedics to come up here. We need to go now."

One after another, Olivia helped them crawl outside, and they were soon crawling down the ladder. When it was the girl with the black lipstick's turn, she stopped.

"You go first," she said.

"No, no, it's all my fault; I'll go last."

The girl looked into her eyes. "No. You go first."

"I don't want to," Olivia said.

"Listen," the girl said. "Once we get down there, they'll start looking for you. You saved us. I don't want the police to get their hands on you; you hear me? There are only three of us left, and we all agree you should go now, so you'll have time to get away. Please, just go."

Olivia sighed deeply. "Thank you."

"I'm Emma, by the way," the girl said and hugged her.

"I'm Olivia."

Olivia gave Emma one last glance of gratefulness, then slid her body out of the window and stood on the ledge, looking down. The area was now crawling with cops, and her legs were shaking badly. Right before she let the firefighter help her onto the ladder, she spotted a set of eyes belonging to someone standing behind the crowd and looking into them made her scream.

Chapter 62

I STARED at my burner phone when the breaking news sign filled the screen. I had been sitting in our guest cottage on the bed with Sydney ever since she told me that the police were pressuring her to turn me in. Neither of us had a solution to the problem, though, and now we were sitting in silence when the phone vibrated.

BREAKING NEWS: SCHOOL ATTACKED WITH SARIN GAS IN DOWNTOWN MIAMI.

"What the heck?" I asked and looked up at Sydney. "Another one?"

I turned my phone to show her. She had turned hers off completely in anger because of the email. She had told me she wasn't going to do it, that her sister came before her career at any time, but I sensed it was tough for her to make that choice, and I wasn't sure I wanted to put her in that position. I didn't want her to have to make the choice.

You'll never work in the business again, had been her agent's words.

I pressed the link, and it led me to a TV station's live feed from the scene. A chopper flew above the school and filmed as the chaos unfolded beneath. I watched as students came out of the school screaming, some falling to the ground, and the paramedics were rushing to them. My heart cried when I saw the panic and chaos as the chopper continued to the other side of the school building, where kids were standing on the ledge, reminding me of the horrific scenes from nine-eleven.

Luckily, the kids were being rescued by the firefighters. But as the chopper paused above them, lingering as close as it could get, I saw something that just about made my heart stop.

I saw her. I saw Olivia.

I was so surprised; I burst out in almost a shriek.

"Olivia?"

My voice cracked, and Sydney looked at me. "It's her," I said. "It's her; look. She's on the ledge."

Sydney looked over my shoulder and saw her too, just as she was helped down by a firefighter.

"She's going to make it," I almost cried while Olivia crawled down the long ladder. "It's my Olivia, Syd; it's her. We've found her!"

"I can't believe it," Sydney said, tearing up as well. "It really is her."

"But…how? What is she doing at a Catholic high school?" Sydney asked.

"I…I don't know," I said, almost laughing when I saw Olivia put her feet on the ground. She was soon greeted by a flock of students, and I lost track of her as she blended in.

"Where is she? She disappeared," I said.

Then the chopper suddenly took off. It moved away, then took a turn and returned to the main entrance.

I shook the phone in my hand in frustration.

"No! Stay there. Stay on these students. I need to see where she's going!" I yelled at the phone in my hand, but it didn't help. The cameras were now on the front side of the building where more students were carried out. They were lying on the grassy area outside of the school, making it look like a warzone. I gasped and clasped my mouth.

"Do you think she was exposed to the gas?" I asked. "She was in there, just like those other kids."

Sydney grabbed my hand and made me look her in the eyes.

"Eva Rae, no. We saw her. It was her. She was fine. She got down. Eva Rae, listen to me. This is good news. She's alive, and she's here. She's in this town. We found her, okay? We found her."

Chapter 63

MATT RAN AROUND THE BUILDING. The first responders were still working on the inside, trying to get all the victims out, and everything was total chaos. His job was to make sure none of the terrorists escaped and to help the victims as they came out.

Never had he seen anything like it. So many kids came tumbling out of the building, coughing and screaming in panic. The terrorists had let the gas out just as the first responders entered the school building, and after that, it was all turmoil.

Later, he had heard about the kids on the ledge of the second floor and run to help.

Now he was staring up at one of the kids standing on the ledge, and his heart dropped. He couldn't believe who he was looking at.

Olivia.

He walked closer, heart throbbing in his chest. Could it be? Could it really be her? Or was it just someone who looked like her? Was his mind playing a trick on him?

No, it's her. It is definitely her.

Matt hurried closer. Olivia didn't see him. She seemed to be staring at someone else, and Matt discovered it too late. Someone was standing behind the crowd, poking his head out, and as she got onto the ladder, her eyes locked with his. Olivia then screamed before climbing down.

Matt rushed to her, running, but as soon as she had her feet on the ground, she ran fast. She ran toward a flock of kids who were all wearing the exact same uniform as her. They surrounded her, and she blended in so quickly, he lost track of her. He couldn't see her anywhere.

"Olivia?" he yelled. He reached the crowd and stood in the middle of it, surrounded by kids the same age as Olivia. They were all were wearing the same uniforms. Matt was turning around, frantically looking into each and every face, repeating her name, when he finally realized that she wasn't there.

Olivia was gone.

Heart hammering in his chest, he looked toward the man that she had been looking at when she climbed down and realized he too was gone. He was nowhere to be seen.

NO!

He left the flock of kids and ran toward where the man had been standing, then jumped behind the row of bushes and spotted a street behind it — one that was beyond the police barrier. At the end of the street, he saw a blue van disappear.

"Stop that van!" he said and began to run after it, sprinting down the street. The van turned right and, with the tires screeching, it swung into traffic. Seconds later, it had completely vanished out of Matt's sight.

Matt ran to the end of the road, screamed his anger out, then slammed his fist into a light pole next to him in frustration.

"Dammit!!"

Chapter 64

I WAITED until Sydney had her meditation class, then grabbed my purse and put my burner phone in it. I wrote her a note on a small notepad in the room that was supposed to be used for us to write down our thoughts during our *cleansing process* or something. I wasn't listening when the branded woman told us about it when we first got there.

I left the note on Sydney's pillow, then grabbed my purse and left the cottage. Most of the entire group was at the meditation class, so this was a perfect time to get out of there without anyone asking questions.

I knew that Sydney would be upset with me for leaving her like this, without a word, but I also knew that if I told her about it, she would ask to come along. And I wouldn't be able to say no.

It was time for us to split up. I didn't want her to go down with me. She still had a career, and I wanted it to remain that way. I didn't want her to give up everything for my sake. I wouldn't be able to live with myself if she did.

I walked across the lawn to the main house and in through the dining hall, finding it empty as I expected. I peeked inside the kitchen and grabbed a banana and a pack of bread to keep me alive for a little while since I was going out into the world without any money, and I couldn't risk using my credit card again. I had made that mistake once, and I had a feeling that's what led Matt right to me.

I turned around, ready to walk out through the main hall when a voice stopped me.

"Eva Rae Thomas. Running away, are we?"

It was Christopher Daniels. He was standing right in front of me, flanked by two of his goons. There weren't many men here at his cult headquarters, but the few that were here were big and looked like they could take me down without using much effort.

"As a matter of fact, yes," I said. "I'm leaving today because I've gotten news about my daughter and her whereabouts. I need to find her. I thank you for your hospitality; it's much appreciated. As you'll see, my sister will be staying a little while longer."

I tried to walk past him, but he blocked my way.

"How's that song go again?"

"What song?"

"*You can check out anytime you like, but you can never leave.*"

I lifted my glance and looked into his eyes. "What the heck are you talking about?"

"You can't run away now. Not when you have begun the process of becoming a better human being. You are so close, Eva Rae. The world out there will tear you apart, literally. They'll arrest you, and then what? In here, you can reach enlightenment. You don't have to care about what goes on out there. You don't need the world. We'll take good care of you."

"Excuse me? Are you telling me I can't leave this place?"

"I do believe it's a bad idea."

"You can't keep me here against my will," I said. "Is it because I saw that woman in the cottage? And now you're afraid I might tell the police about her? You know what? I don't have to tell anyone. I don't even plan on talking to them, so there you go. You can let me leave."

I was lying so terribly, it had to show; I just knew it did. Of course, I was going to tell the police everything. Are you kidding me? I was the police, or at least I used to be. I tried to reach inside my purse for my gun but didn't manage to grab it.

"I don't think so," Christopher said, then signaled for his goons to approach me. They ripped my purse with my gun away from me, then grabbed me by the arms and lifted me into the air. They then carried me away, kicking and screaming.

Chapter 65

IT WAS GETTING LATE, but none of them were even thinking about going home. The Miami-Dade Police Department was overwhelmed, and Matt and Carter had been asked to help with the interrogations. They walked into the interrogation room and sat down. The woman in front of them stared at them, her eyes big and scared.

"Helen Wellington," Carter said and looked into her file. He looked up at her, expecting her to confirm. She did with a silent nod.

"They made me do it," she said, her voice trembling. "Said they'd kill me and my entire family if I didn't."

"Let's start at the beginning, Helen," Matt said. "You were stopped outside of Our Savior's Catholic School during the attack today. You were coming out of the building when we stopped you. Several witnesses claim to have seen you place one of the bags of Sarin nerve gas in a classroom, poke a hole in it, then leave and close the door behind you."

Her nostrils were flaring, her body shaking. "I had to do it. They forced me. They forced all of us, even the young girls."

"Who?" Matt asked and leaned forward. "Who forced you to do this?"

She turned her head and stared into his eyes. He saw deep fear in them, and it made him feel uneasy.

"They did. NYX."

"And what is NYX?" he asked.

"It's a cult," Carter said. "That's what they call it around here. A cult for rich people. Their founder is known to run these workshops for self-awareness that he charges the rich women tens of thousands of dollars for."

"So, you're telling me that this group, NYX, told you to walk into the school and place the bags of nerve gas for them?"

Helen nodded with a light whimper. "I never wanted to hurt anyone. I'm not evil. You must believe me."

Matt looked at her file. Helen Wellington was the heiress of a billion-dollar entertainment empire that her father had built. He wondered how a woman like her had ended up in a situation like this.

"You don't know how they are," she continued. "They'll convince you that you're worthless without them. That you need to cleanse yourself of your old self, that you need to become a new person, and that you have to do stuff for the group to get rid of your old pride. They starved me for months and even locked me up in a small cottage for two entire months. I didn't get to see any sunlight or eat anything but dry bread and drink the little water they brought to me."

"They held you locked up against your will?" Matt asked.

She sighed. "That's the thing. I never told them no. I went along with it. So, in that way, it wasn't exactly against my will. I thought I wanted it because they told me I did, that I needed it to become a better person, to reach enlightenment. But that's how they work. They push you and push you until they can get you to do anything for them."

"Like placing Sarin gas in a terrorist attack," Carter said with an exhale. "Doing the dirty work."

Helen stared at him, then lowered her eyes and slumped her head down. "You don't know how awful I feel. I don't understand how it got this far."

"The starvation and being locked up made it easier for them to brainwash you," Carter said. "Stories like these have been heard before concerning NYX — accusations of brainwashing of their members."

"But you said that there were also young girls," Matt said, thinking about Olivia on the ledge.

Had she been one of them?

"Where did they come from? Were they members of the cult and brainwashed as well?"

"No, that was even worse," Helen said. "Those are trafficked girls that they buy online to perform these attacks. They use them because they are expendable. No one will miss them if they die. You'll find them among the victims in both the train attack and the church."

Chapter 66

IT WAS BEGINNING TO RAIN, and the sky cracked above her head. Olivia looked up and realized a thunderstorm was approaching, and she had to rush and find shelter.

Since she ran away from the school, she had been wandering the streets of Miami, not daring to stop for even a few minutes in case the armed guards in the blue van came looking for her.

She still couldn't believe she had managed to escape their claws.

It had gotten dark out, and Olivia was beginning to feel unsafe. Tourists had disappeared from the streets, and now groups of shady looking men had taken over. Their eyes lingered on her everywhere she went, and she rushed past them. Now she was running because of the typical Florida rain that came with the thunderstorm, and she spotted a bridge where a group of homeless people had found shelter.

Hoping there could be room for her, she ran toward them, trying to cover her face from the rain.

As she came in under the bridge, all eyes were on her and her school uniform that she realized made her look very out of place. She sat down on a piece of the pavement underneath the bridge, pulling her legs up underneath her, trying to become as unnoticeable as possible. A young girl who couldn't have been more than five or six came up to her and stared at her. Her face was dirty, and her eyes were lacking that healthy spark a young child her age would have.

NEVER EVER

"It's the Blue Lady," she said like Olivia knew who she was talking about. "She's watering her plants."

"Who's she?" Olivia asked. "This Blue Lady?"

"You don't know about her? My mom says the Blue Lady brings us love and protects us from the Bloody Mary, who will take your soul. She once cured my headache. I saw her standing outside the window, her skin pale, her eyes blue, and she looked in through the window at the shelter where we were staying. When she left, the window broke."

Olivia looked behind the girl when she heard two adults arguing. She realized it had to be the girl's parents. They seemed drunk. The woman was trying to stop him from eating their last can of sardines. She yelled at him, and he yelled back. Another man sitting on top of his black garbage bag let out a high-pitched laugh when the man slapped the woman. The girl didn't even turn to look at her parents. Instead, her eyes were fixated on Olivia.

"That's Crazy Jack," she said. "Don't go near him either."

Olivia tried to smile. "I won't. Thanks for the tip."

The girl turned around and left Olivia. Her parents were still fighting and yelling at one another, while Crazy Jack's high-pitched laughter bounced off the walls of the bridge. Olivia exhaled while wondering if she would be able to sleep there at all at night or if it would be safer for her to stay awake. She didn't have anything they could steal, but she was afraid of being raped or beaten. But not as much as she feared being found by the men in the blue van. If only she knew if they were still looking for her or not. She had a feeling they wouldn't give up so quickly and realized she had to keep moving. As soon as the thunderstorm passed, she would have to leave.

Chapter 67

I WAS on the bare ground, lying on concrete, trying to stay cool inside the small cottage they had put me in. The woman from earlier was no longer there, and I assumed they had finally let her out. At least I hoped that was what had happened and that it wasn't because she had died.

At first, I had tried hammering on the doors and boarded up windows, but when nothing happened, I had given up and laid myself down on the concrete floor to try and get a little cooler. No air was moving inside the cottage, and it was so hot I could barely stand it.

As the night approached, I dozed off, dreaming of Olivia and seeing her standing on that ledge of the school building over and over again. Every time she reached the ground below, I woke up with a shriek, sweat dripping from my forehead.

She's so close and yet I can't get to her. I can't stand it!

I lay on the floor, rage roaring inside of me, fueling me despite the heat and lack of food and water. I was going to get out of this place, no matter what. If only I could somehow alert Sydney to what was going on. But I had left that stupid note, telling her I had taken off on my own to find Olivia. So, of course, that was where she thought I was, while she was having the time of her life meditating with that embezzler, Christopher Daniels. I had seen through him from the beginning but was starting to get the feeling that I hadn't seen half of what he was actually capable of. Both him and this place gave me the creeps.

I thought about the branding I had seen on the dead guy's arm in the car at the port. I still couldn't escape the thought that Christopher Daniels could be the Iron Fist. After all, the *Iron Fist* was a TV show about a rich guy growing up in a monastery among warrior monks that taught him how to fight and meditate before returning for what was rightfully his. Maybe he identified with him somehow.

I opened my eyes with a sudden gasp in the darkness.

"She was at both attacks," I mumbled, then sat up. "Olivia was at both the attack at the train and the school. I saw her at both. Maybe she was at the church too?"

A gazillion thoughts rushed through my mind in this instant as a picture began to take shape. It wasn't one that I liked very much, but it made sense.

They were using her and the other trafficked girls to perform the attacks. That's why they kept buying more girls online. That was why there was a member of NYX at the harbor. He was the Iron Fist's representative. He was supposed to bring the girls back here so they could use them. It was a smart trick since no one would come asking for the girls anyway, and their dead bodies couldn't be traced back to the cult. It was actually very clever. But did that mean that NYX was behind the attacks?

Probably.

"Oh, my God," I mumbled while the pieces fell into place. They had used my daughter to carry out terrorist attacks all over town.

The realization caused an even deeper rage to well up inside of me, and I rose to my feet and started pacing back and forth, determined to get them for this.

These people were going down.

Chapter 68

CARTER HAD LEFT for the night to get in *a few hours of sleep before the chaos started all over again in the morning*, as he put it. Matt didn't feel ready to leave just yet. Helen Wellington's dad had posted the bond of one million dollars earlier that night, and she had been picked up in a limousine. They had told her she could expect to be brought in for more questioning in the future, and she had said that she'd be willing to help in any way she could and that she just wanted NYX punished for what they had done. She wanted the truth out about who they really were.

Now, Matt sat at his computer and began researching this alleged cult, NYX. He had found a lot of articles about its founder and many positive accounts from people who believed their lives to be much better after having attended his workshops.

Then he found a blog, and that was when the blood froze in his veins. It was an old blog, about a year old, but it was the person who was behind it that made him curious. It was written by the now-deceased Lori Moore, the woman who Carter believed Eva Rae had murdered in her kitchen. And it wasn't exactly saying nice things about the cult. In long descriptions, Lori Moore wrote about how this leader had made approaches to her and how she had seen a good friend lose weight to an almost dangerous level and seem deprived of any self-will after having become a member of the inner circle of the cult. She also talked about how they were branded and had sex with the leader and told that they now belonged to him. According to Lori Moore, he had a harem of women that obeyed his every wink and never left his side. Meanwhile, he had kept a woman imprisoned for almost six months in a cottage because she had sex with another man when she was only allowed to have sex with the founder, telling her *it was all for her own sake, for the better of her future, so she could reach enlightenment.*

Matt couldn't help but find all these descriptions very familiar. He remembered something about a Japanese cult leader and then Googled it. He found many articles about this doomsday cult and its leader that had been executed just the year before. The cult carried out a deadly Sarin gas attack on the Tokyo subway, along with several smaller gas attacks back in the mid-nineties. The attack on the subway was known as Japan's worst terror incident. Thirteen people were killed, and thousands injured.

Reading through all the articles, Matt suddenly saw many parallels to the NYX cult and its leader, Christopher Daniels. They too promised their followers a more meaningful life and gained tens of thousands of followers in its peak. Their leader was even invited to speak at universities.

Matt quickly figured it couldn't be a coincidence that Lori Moore was killed after criticizing them in her blog. She was a defector. She was dangerous to them. She might have known details about the attacks or their plans, and that was why they got rid of her.

But what was their aim? A new world order?

The Japanese cult leader, Shoko Asahara never explained any motive for the attacks, and the media was left to guess why a man like him would do something like this. Maybe there was no reason at all, some wrote, while others speculated that the followers of the cult believed that the end of the world was coming, that another world war was about to begin, and only the cult's members would survive.

Was this the same madness?

Matt wondered about it while turning off his computer and getting ready to leave the station. As he walked out of the building, he felt a small beat of hope. If only he could prove that NYX was behind the murder of Lori Moore, then there was still hope for Eva Rae.

Chapter 69

I HAD DOZED off when I woke up to the sound of someone outside the door, trying to get in. I opened my eyes with a deep gasp, then rose to my feet.

More scrambling behind the door followed.

I prepared myself for it being Christopher Daniels or one of his goons coming to finish me off. They had no use for me, and no one knew I had ever been here except for Sydney who thought I had left. No one would come looking for me here, and they could just tell Sydney that I had disappeared while trying to find my daughter.

It was the easiest thing in the world, and they would get away with it in a heartbeat.

I scanned the cottage for any type of weapon I could use to defend myself, but I knew there was nothing in here. I had searched every corner for anything to help me break out.

All I had were my fists and my will to live.

The door squeaked open, and I lifted both my fists in the air, ready to go down fighting when a face peeked inside and signaled for me to be quiet. I almost cried.

"Sydney?"

She shushed me, and I let my fists come down as she sneaked inside. "I stole the key from Christopher's office earlier. I pretended to want to get closer to him and asked to have a personal meeting with him. He said he wants me to join the inner circle and that I will need to come in and have another meeting with him. He then kissed me, and I let him because I wanted him to believe I was all in, that I want to go to the next level, but the fact was, I knew something was off the moment I saw your note. There was no way you'd ever leave me like that. Not after all we had been through. It had to be fake. I remembered that you told me about the woman they kept in the cottage by the end of the property line and thought I'd check it out. While Christopher kissed me, I spotted the keys he had in a cabinet behind his desk. I also saw your purse in there and knew I was right about you still being here. As soon as everyone went to sleep, I snuck back there and found both the keys and your purse."

I stared at my sister, mouth gaping. I had to admit I didn't think she'd ever pull off anything like that.

She smiled. "I am so glad I did this."

"I…I'm so sorry you had to kiss that charlatan," I said.

Sydney chuckled. "That's nothing. I am an actress, remember? I kiss nasty guys all the time and pretend to be in love with them. It's what I do."

"I…I don't know how to thank you," I said.

She looked me in the eyes. "You get out of here, and you find Olivia. That is the best reward I can get."

"But what about you?" I asked. "I can't leave you here. What will they do to you when they find out I'm gone?"

"You have to. It needs to look like I had nothing to do with it. Besides, my face is too well known out there, and I will get us arrested if I try to run with you. You're better off without me. For now, at least."

"But…?"

Sydney shook her head. "She's out there somewhere, Eva Rae. Don't think of me. I'll be fine. This is what we came down here for. Go get your daughter and bring her home."

Chapter 70

SHE HAD FALLEN ASLEEP. She never meant to; she really tried to stay awake, but no matter how much she fought her eyelids, they still ended up closing, and soon she was asleep under the bridge while the rain poured down.

Olivia dreamt about her family. She was with them on the beach, and her dad was there too. She was young, only seven or eight, and Alex hadn't been born yet. They were building a sandcastle together, and her mom was laughing.

Olivia opened her eyes with a deep gasp. She could still hear her mother's happy laughter, but there was also something else. The sound of a car — then the tires screeching as it stopped.

Olivia spotted the blue van as it opened its doors, and two men jumped out. One of them pointed at her and then they began to run.

Olivia rose to her feet, her heart hammering in her chest. She stared at the men running toward her, then took off running. She climbed up the slanted side.

On the plateau above, she found around twenty tents. Someone she had been sitting with below had warned her that those were the sex offenders who had no other place to go after being released from jail. He also told her to stay far away from them.

One of them was awake and looked at her. He had blankets and lots of plastic bags, even a rug, and a TV. He gave her an indifferent look as she stormed past him. Hearing the men gaining on her, she ran to the end and climbed the grass area and came to a road above. She jumped over the railing, then ran down the road, her perpetrators coming up right behind her. Olivia sobbed, pushing herself forward, tears forcing their way through her chest and into her throat. Cars passed her on the road, but most didn't see her because of the darkness. One saw her too late and honked loudly. Olivia screamed as she saw the men gaining on her and could hear their footsteps on the asphalt behind her.

Olivia panted agitatedly and turned left down a smaller street. Soon, she was surrounded by brick buildings and not a streetlight was in sight. Olivia didn't know if that was bad, or maybe it would work to her advantage. Maybe the perpetrators gave up when they couldn't see her anymore.

Unfortunately, she had no such luck. As she turned to look, she spotted them coming up right behind her, and she knew they would soon catch up to her. Quickly, she glanced around her and saw nothing but old flat-roofed buildings. A sign above her said *Welcome to Historic Overtown*.

Olivia had learned about this neighborhood and knew it wasn't somewhere you'd want to be walking through alone at night. She looked behind herself, then realized the men were gaining in on her. She continued ahead, then as she ran past an open door leading into a courtyard, a set of arms reached out, grabbed her, and pulled her inside. Olivia started to scream, but as she looked into the face of the one who had grabbed her and saw the black lipstick, she immediately stopped.

"Emma?"

Emma shushed her when the men stopped right outside of her door. Emma then used her fingers to whistle and running out came five big black guys with clubs in their hands. One of them swung his club at one of the men and hit him straight on the shoulder. The man screamed and backed up, and soon both of them were gone, running down the street.

Chapter 71

EMMA SIGNALED for Olivia to follow her inside, where she sat down on a chair with ripped fabric.

"Welcome to my home," Emma said. "Can I get you something to drink? You look hungry; are you hungry?"

Olivia felt bad for asking Emma for anything since it didn't look like she had much but still nodded. She was starving and couldn't remember when she last ate.

"We have some leftover rice," Emma said and heated it in the microwave for Olivia. Olivia threw herself at it and ate it all down to the last grain.

"Thanks," she said when she was finally calming down and the adrenalin beginning to wear off.

"Who were those guys?" Olivia asked.

"My brother and his friends," Emma said. "We live here with my grandmother. My parents were both killed back in Haiti. We have to be quiet, so we won't wake her. My grandmother cleans houses for rich people. She has to get up really early."

"How do you afford your school?" Olivia asked, drinking the water Emma had served her.

"I got lucky. I got a scholarship. My brother isn't so lucky, and I worry about the friends he hangs out with. Lucky for you, I was out here tonight. My grandmother always throws us out when she goes to bed because she needs the house to be quiet. Normally, I'll go to bed with her, but I don't have to get up early tomorrow. School's out for the rest of the week at least because of what happened, so we were just hanging out when I saw you running down the street."

"That was my luck," Olivia said and looked at the plate, wishing there was more rice.

"You can sleep with me tonight," Emma said and grabbed her plate. "Tomorrow, I can take you to a shelter. They have food and a bed for you there. My Grams is going to kill me if she finds you here."

"Can I borrow your phone again? I need to call my mom," Olivia said with a sniffle.

Emma nodded and handed it to her from her pocket. Olivia fumbled with it nervously, then dialed her mother's number. She couldn't wait to hear her voice and speak to her again. It almost brought tears to her eyes.

One ring, two rings went by.

Come on, Mom. Pick up. Come on.

It went to voicemail, and Olivia looked at the screen of Emma's phone, then tried once more.

Voicemail again.

Shoot!

Olivia tried to remember her sister's number but couldn't get the last two numbers right. Maybe she was too tired. Besides, Christine would most definitely be asleep by now. Her phone would be turned off. And she didn't remember her dad's cell phone number, nor her grandmother's.

Emma looked at the clock on the wall. It was almost midnight.

"Maybe your mom is sleeping," she said. "You can try again in the morning."

Olivia nodded disappointedly. "Okay. Or maybe I should just turn myself in to the police."

Emma turned to look at her. "You can't do that. They're searching for everyone involved in the attack. They'll take you to prison, Olivia."

"But... what I did was terrible," she said heavily. She was thinking about all those people on the train and at the church. There had been so many of them, so many faces. "Maybe I deserve to go to jail."

"No. It'll kill you," Emma said. "My brother's best friend went in, and once he came back, he was never the same guy again. Now, he's one of those crackheads you see lying in the streets, constantly looking for that same high they got the first time they shot up. You don't want that life, Olivia. The police aren't going to help you down here. They aren't your friends. You can't trust them."

Olivia didn't understand. She had never met anyone who feared the police before. It was so different from what she had known all her life. "But… but my mom is part of the police? I trust her."

"Do as you wish," Emma said, throwing out her arms. "I'm just trying to warn you. Now, let's get some sleep before Grams wakes up and throws you out."

Chapter 72

"WHAT'S GOING ON?"

It was the next morning, and Matt had come in a little later, missing the morning briefing. He was holding a Starbucks coffee in his hand when he saw Carter coming toward him, face red in agitation.

"They raided the NYX headquarters this morning. A judge gave the warrant in the early morning hours," Carter said. "We need to go. Might wanna finish that coffee in a jiff or bring it with you. We're going out there."

"Why?" Matt asked.

"They found something that is of interest to us."

Matt followed Carter as they walked out to the cruisers in the back, and he got in. Matt took the passenger seat, coffee still in his hand.

"What did they find?" he said.

Carter took off and drove into the street in front of the Miami-Dade Police Department, tires screeching on the asphalt, putting on the siren. Matt held on for dear life while Carter rushed through downtown toward Coconut Grove. Carter wasn't exactly a good driver, and Matt preferred to be the one behind the wheel.

"Kelly Stone," he said. "She was found in one of the cottages."

Matt almost spat out his coffee. "Eva Rae Thomas's sister?"

Carter nodded. "They knew we were searching for her in connection with the murder of Lori Moore, so they called me. They're taking everyone in for questioning, but she'll be ours."

Matt leaned back in the seat as Miami rushed by his windows. Arresting Kelly Stone would definitely be all over the news and put a dent in her career.

"But we don't have anything that places her at the scene of the murder of Lori Moore," he concluded. "So, technically, we can't charge her with anything. We don't have any evidence placing her anywhere near any crime."

"True," Carter said. "But she doesn't know that. We just need to put enough pressure on her for her to give up her sister. It's her sister we want."

Matt felt his heart drop as they reached Coconut Grove and drove toward the blinking blue and red lights. Patrol cars had blocked the entrance. There was already a crowd outside, and a lot of TV crews. Three news choppers circled the area from above.

This was going to become a huge story.

"Lori Moore was a member of the cult too," Matt said as Carter parked the cruiser.

Carter looked at him.

"Defected a year ago. She wrote some pretty nasty articles about the cult afterward on her blog, and they tried to have her shut down, but without luck."

They both got out of the car, and walked up the driveway, showed their badges to the officer at the entrance, then continued underneath the crime scene tape.

"It doesn't add up," Matt said. "Why would Eva Rae Thomas murder Lori Moore? She barely knew her."

Carter stopped in his tracks. "And how do you know that? If her sister was a member of this cult, chances are Eva Rae was too. I think she plays an even bigger role in this than what we have thought up until now. And I intend to prove it."

He nodded toward a Mustang parked in the driveway. The forensic team was all over it, taking samples and removing seats. Matt knew that Stang very well. It was the same that the hotel personnel at the Ritz-Carlton had shown them on the surveillance cameras from their parking lot. It was the one Eva Rae and Sydney had been driving while in Miami. If her sister was still here, then Eva Rae had to be somewhere close.

Chapter 73

I ENTERED a small food mart and bought myself a hotdog, then ate it while still in there, enjoying the AC. Sydney had given me my purse with my gun back, along with a handful of cash to help me get by after I left the headquarters. We hugged each other and cried a little when realizing we had no idea when we would ever see one another again, but secretly praying that everything ended well for us.

Even though we both knew deep down that things weren't exactly shaping that way.

As I ate the hotdog, I watched several police cars rush by the windows, and I even heard a chopper. I walked back outside, realizing something big was going on. I had spent the night sleeping on a bench at a bus stop and felt exhausted still. I didn't dare check into a motel or even a shelter in case anyone turned me in.

I felt my gun strapped to my ankle and felt certain there was no one who could stop me now. Head bowed and my cap on my head, I rushed in the opposite direction of the patrol cars, then got on a bus and rode it to downtown. I got off close to Our Savior's Catholic School, where the attack had taken place the day before, and I approached it cautiously. I kept my distance since there were still several patrol cars present, and a crime scene unit with forensics was working the scene.

I didn't really know what I expected to find since I knew my daughter would no longer be here. But I just needed to go to the place where I knew she had been last.

Where are you now, baby girl?

Had she been taken in by the police? Had they arrested her? It was very likely.

I pulled away from the area, then jumped on another bus taking me a couple of stops and got out by the Miami Police Department's big building on Second Avenue. As the bus left, I stared at the building, my heart beating fast in my chest.

Was my girl in there somewhere? And if so, then how on Earth would I get to her?

I had an idea, but I wasn't sure I dared to follow through with it.

After minutes of contemplating it, going through it in my mind over and over again, I realized that I couldn't risk *not* to do it.

It was time to get radical.

Chapter 74

SHE HAD NEVER THOUGHT she'd find herself standing in line for a soup kitchen. Olivia tried to blend in while among the homeless men, women, and even families surrounding her. She peered down at her Converse and the shirt and ripped jeans that Emma had given her and thought that if she just kept her head down and her back slumped, then she wasn't doing too miserably. She actually looked like a homeless person.

Olivia had tried again that morning to call her mother's number, right when standing outside the soup kitchen where Emma dropped her off. But once again, she received nothing but the voicemail. Olivia had left a message, telling her that she would be at the soup kitchen and to come find her there. She had then hugged Emma and thanked her for taking care of her and for saving her life, then gotten herself in line. She was starving, and Emma didn't have any food at her house that she could spare. Plus, her grandmother couldn't know that Olivia had spent the night there.

Now, she was looking around and wondered just how long she would have to be in this place before her mother would find her. A set of heavyset dark eyes lingered on her and made her feel uncomfortable. They belonged to a Hispanic looking man who was standing further down the line. Olivia lowered her eyes again and kept her head down, then walked closer to the woman in front of her in the line, pretending to be with her, or at least to make sure she didn't look like she was there alone.

A flock of prostitutes stood on the corner and went to talk to the men in cars that drove up to them. One of them decided to get into a dark car, and they took off. Olivia felt her heart sink, thinking that the girl didn't look like she was much older than Olivia herself.

Please, hear my message, Mom. Please, come and find me.

The Hispanic man approached her, then grabbed her shoulder. Olivia gasped and looked up. He smiled and winked, then leaned forward and whispered, "Need money? I can help you get money. What are you? A runaway? Or did your parents throw you out? You know what? You don't have to tell me. I see girls like you come here all the time, and I can help. See those girls over there? They work for me. They make a thousand dollars a day. Do you want to make a thousand dollars a day? You won't have to eat soup anymore. You'll be able to go to real restaurants and have lobster. Do you want lobster, huh, little girl? Of course, you do."

Olivia breathed heavily. She felt his clammy hand on her shoulder and wanted to scream. Her heart was pounding in her chest with fear, and she tried to move away from the guy, but he held onto her tight with his big hands.

"Please, leave me alone," she said, but the words were barely a whisper as they left her lips.

The guy laughed and held onto her even tighter. She had no idea how to escape him when a van drove up on the pavement and made some of the waiting homeless people jump for their lives. The van came to a sudden halt, and the roller door on the side went up. Two men jumped out and ran toward Olivia. One of them swung a gun in the air, and suddenly, people surrounding them scattered without a sound. Even the Hispanic man was gone in a matter of seconds while the men grabbed Olivia by the arms and dragged her into the van, closed the roller door, and took off.

Chapter 75

"I KNEW IT!"

Carter came to Matt's desk, smiling widely. He grabbed a chair and sat down. Matt exhaled and tried to seem excited, even though everything inside of him screamed with anxiety. That look on his face could only have to do with Eva Rae, and if Matt was honest, he could barely take any more bad news.

"What's going on?"

His voice was slightly shrill as he asked the question, and he sipped his coffee while trying to act calm.

"They found traces of the gas in the Mustang," Carter said, looking triumphant. He threw a file on the desk in front of Matt and opened the forensics report.

"See, here and here," he said and pointed. "Sarin gas. The same nerve gas used in all three attacks. All traces were found in the trunk."

Matt wrinkled his forehead. He couldn't believe any of this. "Nerve gas? In the Mustang that Eva Rae Thomas and her sister drove around?"

Carter snapped his fingers.

"Bingo."

Matt shook his head. Part of him wanted to laugh because it seemed so ridiculous, but unfortunately, it was no joke.

"But… this… I mean come on…" Matt said.

"What are you talking about?" Carter protested. "This speaks a very clear language. I think we're getting closer to a really big fish here. She is involved in these attacks somehow. I just haven't figured out her role in it yet. But she's involved with NYX and the attack; there's no doubt about it. She might even be in charge of it all. She's the only one there who fits the profile. My guess is that Lori Moore didn't want to be a part of it, that she wanted out, and that was why Eva Rae Thomas killed her. One of the men killed at the port was also NYX. Maybe all that was just about her getting rid of him, maybe because he wanted to talk as well. Who knows? Maybe it has all been about the attacks? Even the raids on the spas up north? Maybe they're all in it, and she's been cleaning out her ranks."

"Do you really seriously think that Eva Rae Thomas, honored FBI-profiler, mother of three children, is capable of murdering all these people, among them several children, and even using children to perform the task? You think she could do that?"

Carter shrugged. "Why not? She went through a bad divorce almost a year ago, and that's when things went downhill for her. It's been bad for a while; think about it. She feels guilty about not being able to save her partner's child; she is divorced; she quits her job and moves back to her hometown, where she finds out her father is a serial killer, and she loses it. She wants to send the world a message of some sort, so she starts planning these attacks and joins this cult who will believe anything, especially that the world is going under soon. Christopher Daniels and her plan it all together. Here, she can get the hands she needs to fulfill her plans, and the funds since the cult appeals to millionaires. But then her daughter disappears. My guess is the daughter ran away from her crazy mom, or maybe she was taken by some people who wanted to stop her, but Eva Rae uses it as an excuse to go rogue and get rid of anyone who might stand in her way. The first attack has already been done, but now some of them are getting cold feet when they realize what they have been a part of. These spas have been providing girls for her to train and use in the attacks, and they have threatened to reveal her, so she decides to rid herself of them under the pretense that she is searching for her daughter. Then she comes down here and hooks back up with NYX and helps with the last two attacks."

Carter looked at Matt like he expected applause, but Matt had no idea what to say to him. This was so far-fetched that it made him speechless.

NEVER EVER

"I know; I know," Carter said. "I don't have all the details yet, but I will soon. I'm sure I will. And once I crack this baby open, it will make my career. Just you wait and see."

Chapter 76

IT WAS dark before he came out. I waited and kept my distance, while not letting my eyes look away from the entrance to the police department even for a second. I couldn't risk missing him.

As I finally spotted him walking out the glass doors, my heart dropped. He was standing under the streetlight, talking to someone, then they said their goodbyes, and he left.

I stared at the man I loved, feeling a deep punch in my heart as he got into a cab. I rushed to the cab parked right behind his and got in.

"Follow the one in front of you," I said. "But not too closely. Just make sure we get to the same destination."

The driver looked at me in the rearview mirror, then wrinkled his forehead. "Say, haven't I seen you somewhere around here before?"

"I don't know. Maybe," I said and pulled the cap further down my face. "I take taxis all the time."

"Are you famous or something? I feel like I've seen you on TV," he continued.

My eyes were fixated on the cab in front of us, and as they took a left, I feared my driver would lose them.

"They went left. Go left here."

"Easy there, lady. I've got this. You're not the first girlfriend in my cab trying to stalk their cheating boyfriend."

I wanted to tell him that Matt would never cheat on me, that he was the most honorable, most noble and loyal boyfriend anyone could have. And that I didn't deserve him. Because it was the truth, Matt was way too good for me.

But I didn't say anything. Instead, I just stared at the driver in the mirror, then turned to look at the cab in front of us.

"Is it the secretary?" he continued. "It often is. Or maybe an old high school sweetheart who came to town? Those are always tough to beat. There's something about that first love that just won't leave you."

"Sounds like you speak from experience," I said dryly.

The cab driver chuckled. "Touché."

"Yeah, well, I've been told I'm pretty good at reading people."

"You some kind of psychologist or somethin'?" he asked.

"You might say so. Go right. They're going right."

"I've got this."

He turned, and I stared at the cab with Matt in it as it came to a halt in front of a Marriott. I handed the driver a bill and told him to stop further down the road.

"Good luck with your cheating boyfriend," he said. "For what it's worth, I'm sure she ain't half as pretty as you are."

I gave him a wry smile, then left the car and walked up toward the hotel, where Matt soon disappeared inside. I stood on the stairs outside for a little while, contemplating my plan, feeling myself get cold feet for a second. Would Matt believe me? Would he help me? Or was he here to take me down? Had he lost his confidence in me because of what I had done? It wasn't well-received among law-enforcement to take the law in your own hands, especially not a cop. Had he turned his back on me for doing what I did? Did he resent me for it?

There was only one way to find out.

Chapter 77

"DO YOU HAVE A SHOCK TOP, PLEASE?"

Matt sat on a stool with a heavy sigh. The bar in the hotel was pretty much empty except for a woman sitting at the other end of the counter, sipping a cocktail. She looked to be in her mid-thirties, slim, and with long blonde hair reaching down by her shoulders. She smiled gently at him, then saluted him as his beer landed in front of him. Matt responded with half a smile, making sure she knew he wasn't there to pick up ladies. It was the last thing on his mind right now. He really just needed a beer after a very, very long day. Her eyes told him she understood. She looked like she had a long day as well. He wondered if she was on a business trip. She didn't look like a tourist in her skirt and white buttoned-up shirt.

Matt looked away and took a sip of his beer. He closed his eyes as the liquid slid into his throat, then put the glass back down. Matt rubbed his forehead in agitation like he'd been doing all day.

How was he supposed to solve this? How was he going to help Eva Rae?

Carter had set his heart on taking her down; heck, he was willing to risk his entire career for it. Yet none of it made any sense to Matt. Was he just being blind? Was he unable to see it for what it was, just because he loved her?

You've known her your entire life, Matt. Get a grip.

Matt shook his head and sipped his beer again, thinking about the necklace. He had been through the file from the findings at Lori Moore's kitchen. The necklace had been found there, and he couldn't for the life of him figure out how it would end up there. He knew that necklace; heck, he remembered toying with it between his fingers while kissing her.

What he wouldn't give to be able to kiss her again, to feel those lips pressed against his, to smell her hair, to... to...

"A glass of Chardonnay, please."

Matt opened his eyes with a small gasp. The woman sitting on the stool next to him smiled gently and instantly melted his heart.

"Put it on his tab," she said addressed to the bartender while nodding in Matt's direction.

"Eva Rae?"

"The one and only," she said as the bartender slid the glass of white wine toward her. She grabbed it and drank.

"Oh, boy. I needed that."

"What the heck are you doing here?" Matt asked, suddenly overwhelmed with fear that someone would see them together. "The entire police force is looking for you. Your face has been on every screen in this town. If anyone sees you here, they'll..."

Eva Rae gave him a look that made him shut up. He bit his lip as her eyes pierced into his. He didn't know what to say. There was so much he wanted to tell her, but no words seemed sufficient. He had dreamt of seeing her again for so long, and there she was, right in front of him, looking even more gorgeous than ever. It seemed impossible. She was out of this world.

"You're being investigated," he said quite unromantically. "Not just for the petty stuff you did up north at the spas, like impersonating a health inspector and beating up the spa-owners, or even for the murder of Lori Moore or the three men at the harbor. But also, as someone involved in the three nerve gas attacks around town. This is serious, Eva Rae. This is getting really serious."

Chapter 78

I FELT like I was choking. I couldn't believe what I was hearing. Did they seriously think I had anything to do with the gas attacks? I stared at the man I loved, unable to speak a single word, unable to fathom what on Earth was going on.

"They found your necklace at Lori Moore's place," Matt continued. "They think you killed her because she wanted to reveal your plans since she defected from NYX. They think you're involved with NYX and Christopher Daniels, that… that you're the one pulling the strings."

My eyes grew wide, and I sipped more wine, then finished the glass and ordered a second one.

"And what do you think?" I asked when it arrived, and I could finally speak again. I waited for his response, scrutinizing his eyes, wondering if some part of him believed they were right, that I was capable of such a thing. He waited a little too long for my liking to give me his answer. The hesitation made me concerned.

"I think that it makes no sense, any of it," he said in almost a whisper. "But I don't know how to stop it. It's like lava coming toward you, and I can't prevent it from hitting you no matter how hard I try."

"You're darn right it makes no sense," I said with a snort.

"What were you doing at the estate?" he asked. "The NYX estate? They said you were there recently."

"I was hiding," I said and sipped my wine. "But then they wouldn't let me leave. They tried to force me to stay and locked me in. Sydney helped me escape. I thought I might find Olivia there, but she wasn't at the estate."

"We raided the place today," he said. "Took in everyone and interrogated them. They found your car, and it had traces of Sarin gas in it."

I wrinkled my forehead. "Why would there be Sarin gas in my car?"

He sighed and drank from his beer, his eyes avoiding mine. I didn't know what to make of him. He seemed confused, and it had me worried. I needed him to be on my side. No matter what happened, I needed him to know the truth. I placed a hand on his arm, and he looked up at me. I could tell he hadn't slept much lately. His eyes were red-rimmed, and he had deep furrows beneath them. This wasn't the healthy, always tanned and happy Matt that I knew so well. This had broken him.

"I am sorry," I said. "For dragging you into all this. It wasn't supposed to happen. I have made some bad choices along the way and gotten carried away emotionally, and I still haven't found my daughter. For a little while, I thought she might be at the NYX estate, but I couldn't find her there. Did they interrogate Christopher Daniels when they brought him in?"

Matt nodded heavily. "He's not talking. None of the cult members have said a word. Daniels doesn't even deny the accusations; he's just staring at us with a smug smile on his face. JTTF did the interrogation, but we watched it from the outside. You should have seen him, the way he thought it was all a joke. I want to punch him in that perfect face of his."

"That makes two of us," I said. "What about Sydney; was she brought in too?"

Matt nodded. "They want to use her to get to you. My partner Carter tried to work her all day. He is obsessed with getting you. But she has a good lawyer, and he will get her out tomorrow morning, just like the rest of the NYX members. They have some good lawyers and a lot of money. Sydney didn't say anything either, not even about NYX."

"Smart girl," I said. "The last thing she needs is them coming for her like they did to Lori Moore. There are some pretty powerful people in that cult. She could end up never working again, or worse."

Matt nodded and grew absent for a second, then looked at me again, affection in his eyes.

"I missed you, though," he said with a deep sigh. "I missed you a lot."

I swallowed and smiled back. "I was thinking about turning myself in. I need to tell my side of the story."

He nodded again but seemed hesitant. To my surprise, I realized that he didn't think it was a good idea. It was the right thing to do, in a perfect world where justice was served, but that wasn't our world, was it? By the look in his eyes, I sensed he didn't fully believe it was the right thing for me to do, yet he couldn't say so since it would go against everything he believed in, everything he stood for.

I sipped my wine again, a tear shaping in my eye, thinking about my poor Olivia. Was I ready to give up searching for her myself? Did I believe that she would be found if I left it to the police to look for her? The same police that believed I was a mass-murderer?

"I saw her, you know?" Matt said.

I almost choked on my white wine. "You saw Olivia? My Olivia?"

He nodded. His eyes weren't smiling, and he didn't seem happy to tell me, which scared me half to death.

"At the attack at the school. She was there. It was just for a brief moment, then she was gone, escaped somehow in the chaos." He grabbed my hand in his, then leaned over and whispered close to my ear. "I think she got away. She's alive, and she's out there somewhere."

I nodded, thinking about how I saw her on the footage from the chopper, but it felt good to have it confirmed. I wasn't just seeing things when I saw her on the surveillance footage from the train station either. She had been there, both times. But that also meant that my theory was correct. She was being used by unscrupulous people to perform these attacks along with other trafficked girls.

"They're using them for the attacks, right?" I said, hoping to get his confirmation.

Matt gave me a look. "You don't have it from me."

"Of course not."

"They haven't found any of the girls at the raid. They must be keeping them somewhere else, but who knows how long it might take to find them? By then, they'll probably be transported across the border and resold or maybe even killed."

I swallowed the rest of my wine while sensing the fear spreading like wildfire through my veins, engulfing everything on its way. He was right. If Olivia was still with these people, then they'd get rid of her soon, along with the others. If she wasn't and had actually escaped, then she was out there somewhere looking for me. No matter what, there was no time to waste. I knew what Matt was telling me to do, and I agreed.

Sometimes, you have to do the wrong things for the right reasons.

Chapter 79

HIS SOFT LIPS touching my skin made me shiver. I closed my eyes and moaned as he grew more insistent with each and every kiss. We had left the bar and gone to his hotel room, realizing this was our only chance, maybe for a long time, to be together. The thought was at once devastating and arousing. I just knew I needed to feel him close right now; I needed to have him.

"I missed the way you taste," he said between kisses. "I missed the way you smell, the way you look at me, even the way you breathe. I missed every part of you, Eva Rae."

I pulled him into a deep kiss, then wrapped my legs around him and pressed him closer. Neither of us wanted to think about the future in this instant, not even an hour from now. Still, it lurked in the back of our minds as he entered me. I felt tears roll down my cheeks as he pressed me back against the pillow.

We made love in silence, letting our desires overpower us and knock every thought of reality out of us.

Matt sank to the pillow next to me, moaning. His eyes were strained with sadness. I stroked his cheek, then kissed him again while he caught his breath. I forced a smile, but my tears revealed how I really felt.

I was terrified to the core. Scared that I was never going to see him again, that everything would go wrong after this and then we would never see each other again, and maybe I would never see my daughter again either.

It wasn't a result I was willing to live with. I had said this before, and I'd say it again. I was never going to give up looking for her. Ever. Not even if I had to continue my search from inside a prison cell. The people who had taken her were going to regret the hell that was being unleashed on them once I found them.

Matt mumbled something as he dozed off, and I realized he had once again told me he loved me.

I sat up in the bed, then looked at the clock. I couldn't stay the night. As soon as daylight came, it would be dangerous for me to try and leave the hotel.

I leaned over and kissed Matt on the lips, then whispered, "I love you too."

There, I had said it — the way I had wanted to for a long time. But then I realized Matt wasn't awake to hear it. He was in a deep, calm sleep, and I didn't want to wake him up. He needed his rest, and I wanted him to get a good night's sleep and for once not worry about me. At least not until he woke up and realized I wasn't there anymore.

As much as I hated to, I had to leave him once again. I felt another tear escape my eye, then wiped it away. I rose to my feet, found my clothes, and got dressed.

I stared at Matt from the edge of the bed, then leaned over, stroked his hair gently, and kissed him again. He mumbled my name, then smiled and turned to the side. I sniffled and chuckled, then smiled to myself, thinking about the hours we had spent together. I could still smell him on my skin, while leaving the room as silently as possible, closing the door carefully not to wake him up.

Chapter 80

I STOOD for a second by the door, a hand placed gently on it, the other holding my shoes and purse, while I let a tear escape my eye.

If only I could stay the night. If only I could make time stand still and stay in his arms forever.

I wiped the tear away with my sleeve, letting the images of us together in bed play like a movie in my mind, trying to savor the memory before I finally turned away and started to walk, my head slumped. I was so lost in my thoughts that I didn't even hear him approach me from behind. I walked down the carpeted hallway, then stopped to put my shoes back on.

"Well, well, well."

I jumped at the sound of his voice. I turned to see a small stubby man with sweaty patches on his light blue polo shirt. I immediately knew who he was. I had seen him with Matt in front of the Catholic church and coming out of my hotel.

It had to be Carter. Matt's partner.

"Eva Rae Thomas. We finally meet," he said and approached me. My eyes landed on the gun in his hand. Big drops of sweat lingered on his forehead, and I could hear his heavy breathing.

"I knew you two were involved. I sensed it," he almost snorted. "It was only a matter of time before you'd show up. And here you are."

"Please," I said. "Matt didn't…"

"Save it," he stopped me.

I felt my hands shaking as fear rushed through my body. The last thing I ever wanted was for Matt to get in trouble. First Sydney, now him? Was everyone that I loved going to have to pay for my decisions?

"Please…"

But he wouldn't listen. I could tell by the look in his eyes. He didn't care what I had to say. Instead, his lips pulled into a smile, and he raised the gun and fired.

Thank God for fast reflexes. As I heard the gun go off, I threw myself down. I dropped my purse on the floor. The shot whizzed over my head and ended up in the wall behind me. I screamed, got up on my feet, and jumped toward the emergency exit door in front of me. I pushed it open with all my weight as the gun was fired once again, this time aimed right at my back. Throwing myself out the door, the gun went off again, and the third shot hit me in the arm. I screamed, dropped my purse, and fell forward down the flight of stairs ahead of me, face first, the stabbing, throbbing pain in my arm making my entire torso shake. The door slammed shut behind me, and I scrambled to my feet while frantically staring at it, expecting it to open any second and him come out, shooting at me, this time to end me.

My purse had landed in the hallway, and I couldn't reach it. I felt the gun that I had strapped to my ankle and pulled it out so I could defend myself when he did come out after me.

I forced myself to move forward, even though the biting, burning pain in my arm made me want to give up. I somehow got myself down the next flight of stairs without my pursuer coming after me and, realizing this, I found the strength to get myself down one more. Seconds later, I was able to push open the door to the outside and, while leaving a trail of blood behind me, I staggered into the warm Miami night.

Chapter 81

MATT WOKE UP WITH A START. His eyes shot open, and he blinked to make sure he wasn't still dreaming. Had he heard right? Was that a shot being fired?

Hearing a scream, Matt jumped to his feet.

Eva Rae!

He bolted for the door, grabbed the handle, and pulled it open just in time to see Carter lift a gun and fire at Eva Rae. Eva Rae let out an ear-piercing scream and fell out the exit door. The door slammed shut, but Matt could hear her body as it fell down the stairs.

NO!

Carter was about to go after her and had his hand on the handle, when Matt leaped toward him, grabbed him around the neck, and pulled him back. Carter yelled in distress while Matt pulled him back and held him down, buying Eva Rae some valuable seconds to escape. Carter pushed the gun toward Matt's face and slammed it into his forehead. The pain made Matt lose his grip on Carter, and the small man jolted for the door, panting and agitated. He opened it, then ran down the stairs.

Please, be gone, Eva Rae; please, tell me you made it out.

Holding his breath, Matt waited. He listened anxiously and prayed that Carter wouldn't find her. Matt's eyes were fixated on the door in front of him, his hands shaking. He rose to his feet, then opened it and peeked out. It was eerily quiet out there, and all he could hear was his own ragged breath.

Where did they go?

Matt stood for a few seconds, feeling his knees go soft when he heard footsteps on the stairs below. He peeked down and spotted Carter coming back up, taking two steps at a time. He approached Matt on the plateau, sweat gushing from his face, his light blue shirt soaked. He spoke through gritted teeth.

"She got away. Because of you," he said, his voice growing louder and louder as he spoke like he was talking himself up, getting increasingly agitated the more he spoke. "Because of you, she got away. How do you explain that, *Detective*, huh? How are you planning on explaining what she was doing in your room, huh? Our main suspect in this town's biggest terrorism case, sleeping in your hotel room in the middle of our investigation. And then we add to it that you helped her escape? You know what that makes you? Do ya?"

Matt swallowed and stared at the angry little man in front of him. He knew it didn't matter what he said at this point. He knew how it looked. Still, he couldn't help but feel deep relief inside of him. Eva Rae had escaped. It was all that mattered at this point.

"That's right. You're now officially an accomplice," Carter continued and threw out his arms. "Congratulations."

Carter lifted the gun and placed it at Matt's forehead. He scrutinized him, his eyes oozing with anger.

"I knew there was something suspicious about you from the moment you set your feet in my police department. I have a brilliant nose for these things, you know. I'm glad I listened to my instincts and kept a close eye on you. Now, you're coming with me. I'm taking you in."

Chapter 82

THEY HAD BEATEN her up for running, and every fiber of her body was throbbing. She was back at the house with the rest of the girls but had been lying in a corner on the floor for most of the time since she got there, crying in pain.

Olivia looked around the room, and she realized that she didn't know any of the other girls anymore. She didn't know if the others had been killed or maybe sent away after the attack at the school, and she didn't allow herself to think about it. She hoped that they were arrested and maybe — *please let it be so* — sent back to their families.

Where are you, Mom? Why haven't you come for me yet? I need you, Mom. I need you more than ever.

Olivia smacked her lips and felt thirsty. She vaguely remembered someone helping her drink while she laid there, but she couldn't recall who it was. Deep down, she didn't want to know. If anyone had been kind to her, she was eternally grateful, but she didn't want to get to know any of the girls again. She knew too much to let herself get attached. The fact was, most of these girls would be killed in the next attack, and so would Olivia. It was only a matter of time.

Olivia curled herself into a ball and cried on the cold floor, her tears spilling on the tiles. She missed her family so much; it hurt her physically to think about. The guilt was eating her up. This was all her own fault. She deserved what happened to her. How could she have been so stupid as to meet with someone she barely knew? Why did she trust him? Because he said he could make her a model? How stupid was that? Her mother had warned her about this her entire life. After losing her own sister, she feared that her children would be kidnapped more than anything. Why hadn't Olivia listened? What made her think this guy was all right? That it wouldn't happen to her?

Olivia tried to imagine her siblings. Her sweet sister Christine and her annoying, yet so adorable, little brother, Alex. She pictured all three of them in the car, driving to the beach like they used to when she was younger. Back when her dad still lived with them, back when everything was all right, and life was worth living. But it was hard for her to picture them anymore. All the darkness and terror she had been through over the past months had altered the way she saw things. All her memories had turned gloomy.

"It's time to get up," a voice said.

Olivia felt a kick on her leg and lifted her head. She glanced at the man hovering above her, grinning from ear to ear.

"You. Get up now."

Fearing another beating, Olivia tried to push herself up using her arms, but the pain was terrible, and she fell back down. Seeing her struggle, the man laughed. He reached down and grabbed her by the collar, then pulled her to her feet. She gasped and felt like she was choking while the man grinned again.

"There. You're up. Now get in the line and follow the others. You have work to do."

Chapter 83

RYAN SCOTT WASN'T FEELING WELL. He hadn't been for a while now. Not since the day he had been on the Metrorail during the gas attack. Lately, he was beginning to realize that maybe he needed help. Perhaps he couldn't deal with this on his own after all.

He stood in his kitchen and stared at the rat that had been living with him for the past few days, gnawing its way through the garbage that was piling up in his condo that he didn't dare to take out. The rat was munching on an old pepperoni pizza slice, making eerie squeaking sounds.

Ryan swallowed and looked at his phone; his only means of contact with the outside world. There were seven new messages from his mother, but he didn't want to hear them. She was worried about him; he got that, but there really wasn't much she could do to help him. She kept telling him to go see a doctor, and he would like to do just that, but the problem was that it meant he'd have to leave the safety of his apartment, and he didn't dare to do that. He didn't have to take the train or bus; he could just grab a taxi, she had said. His parents would gladly pay.

Grab a taxi? Did she have any idea how many people were killed in traffic every day?

"You have to leave the condo someday. You can't stay in there forever," she had told him.

Why not? He had thought to himself. But that wasn't what he had said to her. He had indulged her and told her he would go and see a doctor. That was why she had been calling him over and over again. To ask him how it went, if he went. But he didn't, and he didn't want to have to tell her that. So, now, he had stopped answering his phone at all. Maybe she would go away, just like everyone else had.

In the beginning, he had watched the news all day long to see if there was any development in the search for the terrorists that nearly killed him. But it had ended up driving him nuts and filling him with even more fear, so he had shut the TV off completely and pulled out the plug. He had stopped going on social media or even the Internet. He didn't want to know about all the dangers that were out there. He just wanted to sit inside, on his couch, and be safe. He didn't want to talk to anyone or see anyone.

Ryan rubbed his neck agitatedly. He felt the panic as it rose inside him like a burning fire, just at the thought of taking out the trash. His heart began beating rapidly, and he felt short of breath. The same thing had happened every time he had tried — trash bag clutched in his hand — to open the door and step out. An overwhelming force had hit him as the panic spread into every fiber of his body, and he was unable to get any further than the threshold. His heart was beating so fast, it became unbearable, and all he could do was shut the door again and put the trash down.

Ryan sat on his couch, flies buzzing around his leftover food, then stared at the black TV screen. Outside his windows, he could hear sirens wailing as usual, and it reminded him of how dangerous the world was. Ryan sniffled, then glanced at the bottle of sleeping pills given to him by the doctor who had examined him after the attack. To make sure he managed to sleep. He had never taken any, not yet.

Ryan picked up the orange bottle. He popped the lid open and poured them all out into his hand, thinking this was the only way he would be able to make it outside ever again.

Ryan lifted his hand to swallow all the pills at once when a rapid knock on the door startled him.

Chapter 84

WHEN NO ONE ANSWERED, I knocked again. This time even harder.

"Ryan!" I yelled, slamming my fist into his door. "I know you're in there. You don't dare to leave the condo. Open up!"

"W-who is it?"

"It's Eva Rae Thomas," I said, leaning my forehead against the door. I was so exhausted from dragging my hurt body across town all night; I could barely find the energy to speak. But I had to. It was my only chance. Ryan was the only one in Miami that I knew and trusted not to turn me in.

"Go away," he said. "I don't want any visitors."

"I know you don't," I yelled, sweat pouring down my chest, my shoulder throbbing. It felt like I had a fever, but maybe it was just the pain. "But I'm not here for your sake. I'm here for my own. I need your help. Please, just open the door, will you? I'm not trying to trick you here, Ryan. This is an emergency."

"I'm sorry. Could you come again later?"

I clutched my fingers, feeling my legs go wobbly underneath me. The room started spinning, and I could no longer stay on my feet. Instead, I sank to the floor with a loud thud, grasping in thin air for something to hold onto, to stop the fall, while desperately thinking: *This is it! It ends here!*

I sank into a sea of stars for what felt like an eternity, and when I came to, the door had been opened, and a set of hands was dragging me across the floor. I was placed on the ground, and the door slammed shut behind me. I blinked my eyes and spotted Ryan, who was locking it safely, then breathing heavily, leaning his back against it. I saw the panic in his eyes and realized that grabbing me and pulling me back in had taken all the strength he could muster.

"Are you okay?" Ryan asked. "I heard you fall."

"I'll be all right," I said and felt my sore arm, then winced in pain. "I'm just a little lightheaded. Say, what is that stench? It's even worse than when I was here last."

Ryan ignored me and knelt next to me, looking at my bloody wound. "W-what happened?"

"I was shot," I said. "It's a long story."

He stared at the wound. It was a deep graze. The bullet had entered right above my elbow and gone through the flesh. It didn't feel like it had hit anything vital or splintered any bone. But then again, I was no doctor.

"You'll need that bandaged," he said, suddenly sounding very determined, the fear in his eyes dissipating. "Let me see what I can do. I used to be a lifeguard, and I am a trained paramedic."

My eyes grew wide. "Really?"

"Yes. It helped me earn money during summer break and put me through college." He rose to his feet, his eyes scanning the area. "I have a first aid kit here somewhere. Give me just a sec to find it. Wait here."

"Where would I go?" I asked with a shrug, then wrinkled my nose at the trash bags piling up in the corners.

Chapter 85

I WINCED in pain as Ryan wrapped the bandage around my wound. I had told him everything while he cleaned it. He had asked me to talk about something else, so I wouldn't think about the pain, and it just spilled right out of me. I guess I needed to get it off my chest, even though I wasn't sure he would believe me.

"So, you're telling me this NYX cult is behind the attack that almost killed me?" he said.

My arm felt warm and numb, but I knew this wasn't the end. More pain would come later. I had been shot before, so I was prepared.

I laid my head back on the couch with a nod. "That's what they think."

"And they've been using the young girls like your daughter to perform them?" he asked, startled.

I sighed. "I'm afraid so, yes."

"But they've been arrested now? And the girls?"

"A few of them were arrested during the attack at the school, but most escaped as far as I know. The thing is, most of them don't even speak English, so it's a mess, as you can imagine. Even finding out who they are and where they're from is going to take some time. Matt told me there was one woman, though, who had told the police everything. She was a member of the cult. She said they forced her to be in the attack. No one else has dared to speak up against the cult leader. One woman died after doing so. I just pray that they protect this woman properly, so she won't be killed like Lori Moore was. These cult people don't joke around."

I stared at Ryan, who looked at my bandage, then smiled. "There. You're as good as new. Well, almost. Now you must rest."

I smiled back. "Thank you. You're a lifesaver." I glanced toward his TV. "Do you mind if I watch the news while resting?"

He shook his head but seemed concerned. "No. No, of course not. Let me just plug it in."

Ryan rose to his feet, then walked to the TV and plugged it in the wall. He then handed me the remote. I turned it on, and Ryan sat down to keep me company. As expected, my face was all over the broadcast, and there were no limits to how dangerous they believed I was, especially after almost killing a detective at the hotel while escaping the night before.

"I didn't even pull out my gun," I grumbled like I could argue my way out of this with the TV.

We watched the next few segments that were also about me and my connections with the cult, and apparently a long-term friendship with the leader Christopher Daniels, and how it was believed that I was the one planning the attacks, the big mastermind behind it all. Because my daughter had been kidnapped and because my stepfather was a serial killer, I had gone rogue and lost it, was the explanation.

"She's extremely irrational and, frankly, we don't know what she might do next," said detective Carter in an interview, where he was wearing a sling on his arm.

I sat up straight on the couch and leaned forward in anger. "Look at this? I didn't even touch him! He shot at me while I tried to talk sense into him. Can you believe this guy?"

Ryan gave me an uncertain look, and I forced myself to calm down. I didn't know the kid very well, and for all I knew, he might not fully trust me or my story. The last thing I needed right now was for him to be suspicious or even afraid of me.

Next, they showed pictures of Christopher Daniels leaving the Miami-Dade Police Department with his lawyer, and suddenly, my blood was boiling again.

"They're letting him go? He's been released, that bastard? After what he did to those girls and to… to my daughter? I can't believe this; can you believe it?"

Ryan shook his head nervously. "He posted bail, they say."

"I still can't believe they'd let him even get bail with what he has done. It makes me so mad! Don't they know what he did to my daughter?"

I sat up, my fist clenched, and yelled at the TV through gritted teeth. "That means he's going to be out there instead of being interrogated about where my daughter is. God knows what he might be up to next, what his plans are. Olivia's life is in serious danger. If he finds her, he will kill her. I can't believe this."

I felt the gun in my ankle holster when touching it from the outside of my pants. Christopher Daniels, alias the Iron Fist, was on the loose once again, but so was I. He wouldn't be able to hurt my daughter anymore, not if I got to him first.

I took in a couple of deep breaths and controlled myself when the anchor showed up on the screen again. Under a severe expression, he presented a breaking news story about the arrest of someone who the police believed had been handing me inside information into the police investigation.

I held my breath as I watched this person be taken out of the police car and transported through the crowd of journalists, head bowed.

Then my heart dropped.

It was Matt.

Chapter 86

"COME ON, Detective Miller. You might as well tell us everything."

Carter looked at him from across the table. Next to him sat Agent Patrick Albertson from the FBI. Matt had never been on this side of the table in an interrogation room and had to admit he was beginning to understand why so many became aggressive when sitting there. They kept asking the same darn questions over and over again until they got what they wanted. But Matt couldn't give them that since he didn't have it.

"We just need to know where she's hiding," Patrick Albertson said. "We know you've been in contact with her."

He threw a stack of papers in front of Matt. "Phone records show anonymous calls in the middle of the night from different phones, burner phones. We assume they came from her. Here and here."

He pointed at the underlined numbers, but Matt didn't even want to look at them.

"I told you; I haven't seen her or spoken to her until she showed up last night. It was totally unexpected."

"Yet the two of you went to your room and had sex," Carter said. "Was that unexpected too?"

Matt swallowed. He thought about the intimacy they had shared and felt a warmth spread throughout his body. It had been intense. The fact that they didn't know when or if they'd ever see each other again had added to the intensity. He wasn't sad that it had happened or even that he had been caught. He was just sad that it was over, that he couldn't be with her longer. He was happy that he had managed to help her escape. Now, he just prayed that she would find Olivia before it was too late. No matter if she was still in the hands of those NYX people or if she had escaped and was walking the streets, she was in great danger.

"Didn't you?" Carter said.

"Yes, we had sex. We love each other; there. Is that what you want to hear? I love her. I love Eva Rae Thomas, and I know that she hasn't done any of what you accuse her of. All she wants is to find her daughter. That's it. Her daughter was in those attacks."

Carter burst into laughter. "But that's exactly it. Don't you see it? She's even using her own daughter in this. That's how unscrupulous she is. She's got you completely fooled; doesn't she? She comes here batting her eyelashes at you, and you just believe everything she tells you, don't you?"

"I'd believe her over you any day," Matt said, knowing that the smirk on his face wasn't doing him any favors. But in all fairness, he was just stating the truth.

Patrick Albertson gave him a look, then wrote on his notepad. "How much have you told her about our investigation?" he asked.

Matt exhaled. "I just told her that she was now being investigated as part of the terrorist group, that it was believed she killed Lori Moore and that we found the necklace, and that they found the traces of gas in her trunk. She said she wanted to turn herself in. She wanted to tell her side of the story, clear her name."

"But she didn't, did she?" Carter said. "She ran in the middle of the night after getting what she wanted from you. She fooled you again. Tricked you into telling her these things because she knew you couldn't say no to her. She's been using you, Miller."

Carter rose to his feet and gathered his papers. Patrick Albertson followed him to the door.

"But we're gathering lots of evidence against her now, and the fact is that the ground is burning underneath your little girlfriend," Carter said. "You better start talking soon, or she'll drag you right down with her, Detective."

Chapter 87

I WASN'T FEELING BETTER, nor was I able to rest. I couldn't sit still on that stupid couch when the man I loved was in trouble, and the man who caused it all was still on the loose. Christopher Daniels had caused so much suffering, and several lives were on the line now. Not just my daughter's, but also the other girls and that woman, Helen Wellington, who was the only former member who had stood up to him and told the truth. Christopher Daniels would come for her in one way or another like he had come for Lori Moore. I was certain of it and obsessed with the thought of stopping him.

But how? How would I find him? He would most certainly want to go into hiding now, and he had plenty of devoted very rich followers to help him do just that.

After turning off the TV in anger, I had borrowed Ryan's computer and flipped through news stories, reading about the case. It was all they wrote about, and the rest of the day, all I could do was flip through news sites, going through each and every article I could find, anger rising inside of me more and more as I realized the many lies that were being said.

Ryan was being sweet to me and made me chicken noodle soup from a can and made sure I was comfortable. I sensed that he was worried about having me there and maybe even a little scared of me, and so I wondered how long I would be able to stay. How long before he gave into that fear in him and called the police? On the other hand,

I got the feeling that he believed my story when I told it and that he genuinely wanted to help.

And there really wasn't anywhere else I could go right now. Also, Ryan was right. I needed rest to feel better, to regain my strength. I was stuck here. At least for now.

I sipped my water and opened an article from the *New York Times* dated a few days back. Luckily, Ryan was a member, so I could read the entire thing as it proved to be increasingly interesting. As I finished it, I Googled a name from the article and opened a few pages, then read through it, learning more and more about NYX.

I asked Ryan for a notepad and started to scribble a few things down, then frantically did another search and then another, taking a closer look at the NYX's members and who they were.

Day became evening, and Ryan served more soup and ate with me, his eyes continually lingering on my every move like he was scared I'd suddenly attack him.

I ignored him completely and stayed immersed in my research about NYX. I was hoping to find out if they had other places besides the estate in Miami where they might keep the girls they bought. A few hours later, Ryan announced that he was going to bed.

"Will you be okay on the couch?" he asked. "I'm sorry about the smell."

I lifted my glance from the screen, then smiled. "It's no problem. I'll be fine. And don't worry about the smell; I hardly notice anymore," I lied.

"Okay," he said and disappeared into his room.

Meanwhile, I had no intention of going to sleep. Instead, I stayed up all night, researching, and when the sun was about to rise, I suddenly felt better, good enough to get back on my feet. A gazillion thoughts still rushed through my mind, and I was frustrated that I still had no clue as to where those girls might be kept. I kept tapping on the computer when suddenly I stopped. I stared at a picture for a very long time, then went into Ryan's room.

"Wake up," I said.

He blinked and looked at me groggily. Outside the windows, the sun was beginning to rise, but it was still dark.

"Do you have any means of transportation? No, of course, you don't, or you wouldn't have taken the train to work on that morning. Does your neighbor have a car or anything we can borrow? It's urgent."

Ryan looked confused, then scratched his bed head. "My neighbor keeps his motorbike parked in my garage because he has his car in his."

"A bike, you say?" I answered. "You might want to show me where that is."

"I...I can't," he said and sat up in the bed.

"Why not?"

"I...I can't leave the apartment."

I walked out of his room, looked around, then spotted a set of keys hanging on a hook in the kitchen. I grabbed them and dangled them in the air. Ryan came up behind me, still looking sleepy, but now wearing pants and a shirt.

"I bet it's one of these; am I right? I'm guessing this one is for the garage, and this one is for the bike."

"Y-you can't do this," Ryan said and stepped forward. "He'll kill me."

I shrugged. "Well, better him than me, right?"

I held the keys tightly, then opened the front door.

"Stop," Ryan said and came after me.

I was out on the doormat now, and he was still standing inside, but one more step would take him out across the threshold. He stared at it, like crossing it meant apocalypse now.

"I don't have time for this," I said and shook my head. "There is someone I need to find. Now. My daughter's life is in danger. If you want to stop me, then you'll have to follow me."

With that, I turned around and rushed down the stairs. Ryan stayed behind and yelled for me to stop one more time, but I didn't have the time even to slow down.

I had reached the second set of stairs when I heard his tapping steps behind me.

Chapter 88

THE GARAGE DOOR squeaked eerily as it opened. Ryan turned on the light nervously. His hands were shaking, and he was breathing raggedly.

"H-here it is."

The Harley gleamed in the light from above it. I whistled and ran my finger across the fuel tank. She was a beauty. I couldn't blame the neighbor for being protective of her.

I wheeled the bike around and threw my leg over it, then revved it and let the noise echo in the parking garage underneath the building. I had been a bike rider in my younger days when everything was new and exciting with Chad.

"This will do just fine."

"You can't just take it," Ryan said. "What do I tell my neighbor?"

I shrugged and put on the helmet that was hanging from the handle. I snapped it shut, then gave him a look.

"Tell him we borrowed it."

"You can't do that."

"Yes, I can if you're with me," I said. "Come on."

Fear struck Ryan's eyes. Drops of sweat appeared on his upper lip. He shook his head.

"But… I… can't."

"Suit yourself," I said. "I'm going now."

"No!"

I stopped and looked at him.

He grunted nervously. "Okay. I'll come."

I smiled and revved the bike a few times. "Then what are you waiting for? Jump on but grab a helmet first."

Ryan found the other helmet and put it on, then whimpered lightly when he climbed onto the bike behind me before we rode out of the garage and into the dawning day. Ryan held onto me tightly from behind, and I could hear him moan loudly even above the noise coming from the bike below us.

What I didn't tell him was that I was very pleased to have him come along, since the police were looking for a single woman on foot and not a couple on a bike. The way I saw it, if we stayed clear of the roadblocks, we had an actual chance of making it through town unnoticed.

Chapter 89

OLIVIA FELT her pulse quickening as she approached the line in front of her. She stood close to a family of four and stared at the two children in their light summer clothes. In front of them, the line moved slowly toward the breakfast buffet.

They had given them new clothes and taken the girls there to spend the night, pretending to be several families on vacation. Not because of their generosity or because they wanted them to have a nice bed to sleep in for once. No, it was so they wouldn't stand out, so they would be able to get into the restaurant in the morning without anyone paying attention to them. After all, they looked just like the rest of the tourists and happy families in the hotel. The only difference was the bags of liquid gas that had been strapped to their stomachs, the same bags they were instructed to poke with forks as soon as they reached the buffet.

Two other girls had taken their seats in the restaurants by the exits and were waiting for their signal before they would do the same.

Olivia felt the bag under her loose white shirt with her finger. Once she poked a hole in it, she was going to die along with the people standing close to her. She knew this was to be her fate. They had told her so. She had been chosen to be one of those that didn't make it out. They had guards placed both inside and outside the hotel, ready to shoot her if she didn't do as told or if she tried to make contact with anyone.

There was no way she'd get out of this alive.

The little girl in front of her grabbed a fork and a plate from the pile and Olivia did the same, fighting to keep her hand from shaking so badly she risked dropping the plate on the floor and causing a spectacle. It was important that she didn't draw any attention to herself, were the instructions when she was sent down in the elevator with the three other girls. Olivia considered dropping the plate on purpose and maybe creating a diversion, but she didn't dare to. From the other end of the restaurant, a set of eyes followed her every move. A tall guy dressed in swim shorts and a Hawaiian shirt stared at her from behind the sunglasses, his hand clutched on the gun in his pocket. He was standing by the door, so he would be the first to get out once the gas was released.

Olivia exhaled nervously and held out the plate in front of her, while the girl next to her whined because she wanted to have a soda, but the buffet only had juice.

"You can have soda for lunch, okay?" her mother said.

"I don't wanna have soda for lunch. I want it now," the girl said and pulled her hand out of her mother's grip.

Olivia felt her heart race while thinking about her siblings and her own parents. She knew in this instant that she was never going to see any of them again, and it tormented her so deeply she felt tears pile up in her eyes. She wished that she'd at least get to say goodbye.

I miss you, Mom. I miss you so much. You would know what to do!

"Are you okay?" a man standing behind her suddenly asked.

Olivia gasped and bit her lip to stifle her crying. She glanced toward the guy by the door. His eyes were fixated on her, his hand on the gun.

"I'm fine," she said and looked up at him.

The man smiled comfortably. "Say, are you here alone?"

Olivia glanced briefly at the guard by the door again while contemplating telling the man the truth, just spilling it all, but once again, she didn't dare.

"No. I'm with my parents. They're over there," she said and nodded in the direction of a couple that sat at the other end of the restaurant.

"Ah, I see. You on vacation?"

She nodded as the line moved forward. She was supposed to poke the bag as soon as she reached the front of the line by the fruit. That way, she'd hit the densest area of people in the entire restaurant. The liquid would run out onto the floor, and she'd breathe in the gas, which would kill her slowly and painfully.

"Where from?" he asked as they took another step forward.

"I'm sorry; what?"

"Where are you visiting from?"

"Oh. Wisconsin."

"Wisconsin, huh? I'm from Texas."

"I hear it's nice there too," she said, her voice shaking.

But you'll never get to see it again if you don't run far away from me now. Run, you idiot, and take all the children with you.

"And hot," he said. "It's a different kind of hot than here, though."

"Because of the drier air," she said and took yet another step forward. There were about three steps left until she reached her target. She held the fork tightly in her sweaty hand. The two children in front of her were laughing, the girl holding her mother's hand tightly in hers again, having forgotten everything about the soda she wanted a few seconds ago. They were dressed in swimsuits underneath their thin shirts, ready to jump in the pool as soon as breakfast was devoured, while their parents were looking forward to spending an entire day just resting poolside while the kids played and had the time of their lives. They had probably been looking forward to this piece of heaven for months, maybe even years.

Olivia's eyes met those of the other girl that had come here with her, standing in the back of the line. She too was sweating heavily, and her eyes were struck with deep fear. She was supposed to die today as well, while the two other girls sitting at the tables by the exits would be able to make it out in time. They had already placed their bags on the floor and were ready to poke them as soon as it was time. Then they would leave while Olivia and the other girl in the line would never be able to make it out in time. They were too far from the doors, even if they threw the bags and ran.

The closer Olivia came to the fruit, the closer the man kept an eye on her, and the more strained his face got. The fork almost slipped out of Olivia's sweaty hand as she took another step forward, and now only stood a few feet away. She took in another deep breath as the line moved again, and she now stood right in front of the fruit.

She turned her head with a light gasp and looked at the man by the door. He nodded to let her know that it was time.

Olivia felt the fork in her hand and turned it a couple of times before she lifted it in the air.

Chapter 90

"OH, boy. I'm going to die!"

Ryan had his arms wrapped tightly around my waist while I zigzagged between cars through morning traffic. He was yelling and screaming behind me, but I chose to ignore him.

Cars honked at us, and someone flipped us off, but we had no time to waste on an idiot like him. As we came up toward a roadblock ahead, I turned around and went back. I found another way and raced through the smaller neighborhoods as fast as possible. At one point, I even drove off the road and over a hill to avoid a roadblock.

"Where are we going?" he yelled, his voice shivering as we came to a red light and I stopped for a few seconds.

"I told you; I'm going to find my daughter," I said. "And there is only one person who knows where she is."

"Do you know where this person is?"

"I have a hunch, yes."

"I'm risking my life on a hunch?" Ryan asked.

"You and me both, baby," I said and revved the machine as the light turned green again. "Hold on. This might get a little bumpy."

Ryan let out another shriek as I raced down a small street and soon reached downtown. I made a left turn and ran a red light when a patrol car caught my tail and put his siren on.

"Shoot."

Seeing this, I sped up, and he tried to follow, but I was way faster than him and able to zigzag between cars. Soon, he had called for backup, and three police cruisers were following us, racing across town toward Coconut Grove.

I could see the big, tall buildings as they rose in front of us and, soon, I raced the bike up in front of one of them. I threw the bike just as the patrol cars came up behind me, tires screeching. There was a lot of yelling, and Ryan screamed and stood with his hands over his head.

"Don't shoot. Don't shoot."

Guns were pointed at us, and the yelling continued.

"STOP, or we'll shoot! Hands where we can see them!"

I put my hands above my head while more patrol cars came driving up. Ryan whimpered and fell to his knees, while I stared at the entrance to the building, feeling my heart pound uncontrollably in my chest.

If they take you in now, it's over. You're so close, Eva Rae.

I sensed they were coming closer, guns pointed at me.

"I said down on your knees! Hands behind your head," someone yelled.

I contemplated this for a few seconds and was about to do as I was told; I really was. But then something came over me; I can't exactly explain what it was. A stubbornness, you might call it. Maybe stupidity. Whatever it was, it empowered me just enough to stop midway, then lower my hands and make a run for it.

I stormed toward the front entrance, while the police officers yelled behind me and a shot was fired. The doors slid open in front of me, and I threw myself into the lobby of the building.

Chapter 91

"MORE SALMON, SWEETIE?"

Helen shook her head. She had never liked salmon, but of course, her mother didn't know that.

Her mother's Botox-face tried to smile but was unsuccessful. It barely moved. She was sitting on the couch with the views over Biscayne Bay from everywhere you looked. It was a gorgeous place, and most people would love to be sitting where she was right now, but not Helen. She loathed this place more than anywhere in this world. She couldn't believe she had ended up back here again.

"It's just so good to have you back," her mother said and sipped her Champagne. It was still only eight in the morning but never too early for her mother to drink alcohol.

Helen's father shoveled in scrambled eggs and salmon while grumbling loudly.

"Don't you think, Jack?" her mother said. "That it is wonderful to have Helen back again? I'm just so glad that you finally were able to break free from that awful cult. And now we don't have to talk more about that. Just that we're happy that nightmare is finally over. Now, we can begin a new chapter."

Her mother moved a lock of hair from Helen's face, and she pulled away, annoyed, then sipped her coffee. Her sister Aubrey was standing by the window, looking out over the bay. She had barely spoken a word to Helen since she came back to them. Helen had disappointed them. She could tell by how they looked at her.

Helen's father drank from his cup, then put it down hard on the table, causing all the plates to jump. Helen's mother gasped, and they all looked at him.

"I just don't get how she could have been so stupid," he said with that low growl that had always frightened Helen so. He hadn't looked at her since she got back, and he wasn't looking at her now either. He still spoke about her like she wasn't even in the room.

"She gave them millions of our hard-earned money, for Christ's sake. Of the family's savings. Money I have worked to be able to give to her. Couldn't she see that it was a trap? How could anyone be so stupid?"

"Jack!" her mother exclaimed with a light snort. "You promised me. We need to put this behind us. Besides, I have read that this leader was very persuasive and charming. Lots of people fell for his schemes. Respectable people like our family. Helen is the victim here."

Her father grunted and rose to his feet, then began pacing. "But becoming a terrorist? Killing people? For what? Because she loved him? Because he was so attractive and charming, she couldn't say no to him? Explain this to me because I don't understand it. She did this willingly. She gave him money of her own free will; she took nerve gas into a high school intending to kill hundreds of children. They forced young kids, young girls that had been trafficked and held hostage by the cult to do these awful things. But you, Helen. You went to them. You chose to be in this cult. You were there because you wanted to be there. You could have walked out of it long ago before it got this far."

"She was brainwashed, Jack," her mother said. "The therapist told us so, remember?"

"The way I see it, you always have a choice," her sister said without turning around and looking at Helen.

Helen shook her head with a sniffle. "I couldn't get out of it," she said. "It was too late. I was in too deep. They would have locked me up if I refused to participate in this. That's what they do to people. One woman spent an entire year locked up, being abused by the leader. Haven't you read the stories that they have written, the interviews I have given where I tell everything?"

"Yes, we read those awful articles," her mother said, shaking her head. "I really wish you hadn't gone public with it that way. It is… terribly embarrassing."

NEVER EVER

Helen shook her head in disbelief. Here she thought she had done the right thing, telling the world about Christopher Daniels and the bastard he was, and still, her family resented her for it. She couldn't win with those people, could she?

It didn't matter what she did. It was simply never enough. *She* was never good enough.

Chapter 92

"WHERE ARE WE GOING?"

Somehow without me realizing it, Ryan had managed to follow me inside. He was pale as a ghost, staring at me while the commotion continued inside. The police had barricaded the exit with their cruisers and were running for the door.

My nostrils were flaring, my mind going in circles because of fear, but luckily, I was one of those people who thought best under pressure. I knew exactly where we were going.

"The elevator," I said and ran for it and pressed the button excessively. It dinged, and we entered just as four officers came through the sliding doors into the lobby. It took them one second to spot us inside the elevator.

"STOP!"

The doors weren't closing even though I kept slamming the button. Ryan whimpered next to me and, as the officers approached us, I knew the doors wouldn't close in time. I looked up at Ryan while the angry footsteps approached us, then said: "I'm sorry. I didn't want to have to do this."

"W-what do you mean?" he asked, holding his hands above his head. Meanwhile, I reached down to my ankle and pulled out my gun. The police yelled. One of them reached the elevator door and placed a hand in it so it couldn't close.

"I am sorry," I whispered, pulled out the gun, and placed it against Ryan's head.

"GUN!" one of the officers yelled, and I knew just what that word meant to them in a situation like this. Fear and adrenaline would rush through their minds while remembering all the colleagues they had lost and stories they had heard about situations escalating with a mad shooter.

This was serious now. The minute I pulled the gun, I had crossed a line. From now on, I knew they'd shoot me the second they got the chance.

"Step back, or he gets it," I said, pressing the gun against Ryan's temple. I was screaming like a madman, trying to sound convincing.

"I'm not joking here. Stand back, or I'll shoot!"

It worked. The officers took a few steps back, enough for the doors to close, and soon, the elevator was lifting us up. My heart rate was in a frenzy, and I could barely breathe. Ryan stood like he was frozen, his hands shaking, but not making a sound. I removed the gun, then bent forward to breathe better.

"That was close. I'm sorry, Ryan. That I had to do this to you. Are you okay?"

I looked up at him, and he breathed raggedly.

"You knew I wasn't going to shoot you, right?"

He finally nodded as the elevator reached its stop. "S-sure."

"Good because I wouldn't have. Not in a million years. I was only buying us some time. Now that they think I've kidnapped you, they'll have to call for the hostage taskforce. It'll take a while, and they'll stay away. Besides, once we are finally caught, they'll think you were a victim, not my accomplice, and you won't get in trouble. You're welcome, by the way."

We stopped by a door, and I took in a deep breath, then felt the Colt in my hand. This was it. It was time to face the music.

I knocked, and soon the door opened.

"You?" the person said, startled.

I nodded, making sure Christopher Daniels could see the gun in my hand. "Yes, me. You and I need to have a little chat."

Chapter 93

"HOW DID YOU FIND ME?" Christopher Daniels grumbled as he closed the door behind us. I made sure the gun was visible still as I sat down in a recliner by the window. Ryan looked nervously around, then stood by the window, staying a few steps away from both of us. Christopher Daniels sat down too, right across from me, folding his hands in his lap, looking at me with a smirk. He looked relaxed in his white loose linen clothes and, as usual, annoyingly handsome.

"Some punk took a picture of you entering this building and posted it on Instagram last night," I said. "I'm surprised to see that the place isn't already crawling with journalists, but the day is still young. They'll be here soon. It wasn't hard for me to find out that one of your inner circle cult members, Giselle Hovers, whom I had the pleasure of meeting while staying at the NYX estate, owned one of the top floor apartments here, and, of course, that was where you were staying."

He answered with a smile. "I always believed you were very bright. You could have made it far in NYX if you had cared to stay long enough for us to show you what we can offer."

"I know what you have to offer," I said. "And I am not interested."

He shrugged and leaned back. It bothered me that he didn't seem the least bit afraid of me or the gun in my hand. I had to control myself. I wanted to hurt this guy so terribly, but so far, he was the only one who could help me find my daughter.

NEVER EVER

"Suit yourself."

"I want my daughter back," I said.

"I'm sure you do," he answered.

I lifted the gun. "Where is she?"

He stretched out his hands. "I don't know."

"What do you mean you don't know? Don't mess with me," I said and rose to my feet. "I will hurt you and take great pleasure in doing so. Starting by shooting you in the right kneecap, then the left one, and moving my way up until you talk. The one in the crotch should make you scream. A lot."

He chuckled and leaned forward in the chair, hands clasped against one another.

"You can do all you want to me, but it won't help. I don't have your daughter. I never had her. Not her. Not any of those other girls that the police are accusing me of kidnapping."

I stared at him, my hands growing sweaty. "B-but... you used them. For the attacks. You're the Iron Fist."

He shook his head gently. "That's what everyone keeps telling me, but I am not him. I never was. I don't even know what an Iron Fist is. And I had nothing to do with those attacks."

"But... but the cult leader in Japan. You were inspired by him. You were just like him; you did what he did because you..."

He shook his head. "Never."

"You're bluffing. You do this. You mess with people's minds. You're the mad cult leader."

He sighed.

"That might be, but I would never do any of those things. I'm not a violent person. I believe in higher enlightenment. I believe you and I can reach a higher level of understanding ourselves, not by violence, but by reaching inside ourselves and stripping ourselves from our former nature. I believe in the releasing powers of the sexual act. Of submitting yourself to another human being, one who has obtained greater enlightenment than you."

I stared at him, unable to speak.

"B-but that can't be," I said. "If you're not behind this, then who is? And where is my daughter? No, it has to be you. You're just trying to trick me. Unless... Oh, dear Lord."

Could it be? No, it can't be... could it?

A huge piece of the puzzle suddenly fell into place, and I stared at

Christopher Daniels, then placed the gun to his head. "We're leaving, and you're coming with us."

"That might be a little difficult," Ryan said and glared out the window. "The place is surrounded by cops and reporters."

"I might have a solution for that," I said and gave Christopher Daniels elevator eyes.

Chapter 94

"GET OUT."

Matt did as he was told and got out of the patrol car. Carter grabbed him by the arm and pulled him up toward the condominium. Matt's hands were cuffed in front of him as he was being led to the scene. He didn't know exactly what was going on, only that it had to do with Eva Rae, and that terrified him.

"Your little lady has kidnapped someone and taken him into this building," Carter said as they walked up toward the many parked police cruisers and the group of officers waiting for them. Their nervous eyes were lingering on him. None of these officers would hesitate to shoot Eva Rae if they got the chance. That's how dangerous they believed she was. It was written all over their faces.

"What is this place?" Matt asked and looked up at the tall building. "Why did she choose this place?"

Carter sighed. "Her little friend, Christopher Daniels, is hiding from the press in one of the top condos. My guess is she came to pay him a visit. Maybe make sure he didn't talk to us and rat her out. Maybe she came to kill him. Who knows? The lady has gone nuts. Who knows what her next move is? But today, it ends. Today, we're taking her in, and you're going to help."

"There really isn't much I can do," Matt said, exhausted. He had been so worried about Eva Rae all night while pacing in his cell. He had seen the blood on the stairwell of the hotel and knew she was hurt.

Now, she was apparently trapped inside of that building and, by the looks of it, there was no way out. All exits were blocked by heavily armed cops. A Hostage Rescue Team had just arrived, and a SWAT team was on the way.

"The thing is," Carter said. "Our boss is really keen on getting her alive, so we need to at least try our best to do so. But you need to work with us here, Miller. You are her last resort. Either you talk her out of the building, with none of her hostages getting hurt, or we go in and take her down. It's up to you how this ends. Either way, we're getting her today. Do you understand what I'm saying?"

He did. But he just wasn't very sure that Eva Rae would listen to anything he had to say. When it came to getting her daughter back, she would stop at nothing. When it came down to choosing between Matt and her children, Matt knew he was her last priority. That was just the way she was wired.

"Now, the HRT is trying to establish contact and, as soon as they do, I need you to start talking to her. I'll give you one shot at getting her out of that building alive. If it doesn't work, then that's too bad. SWAT will go in on my orders."

Matt swallowed hard, then nodded to let Carter know he understood. He prepared himself for what he would say when an officer suddenly yelled.

"Someone is coming out!"

All the officers on the scene turned, guns pointing at the front door just as someone approached it. It was a man. He was wearing loose white clothes and walked with his head bowed.

"It's Christopher Daniels," Carter said. "Careful! He might be armed."

All the officers surrounding the building left their posts and ran to assist. Daniels walked out the sliding doors, then knelt on the ground, placing his hands behind his neck. Carter let go of Matt and ran to Daniels, along with the rest of the police force. They were yelling at the guy to stay down, not to move a muscle. As they slowly dared to come close enough, the man lifted his head and looked up at them. He spoke, his voice shivering.

"Don't shoot. Please, don't shoot me."

"It's not him," Carter yelled. "This is not Christopher Daniels."

Just as he realized this, Carter turned around. He then ran to the back of the building, yelling: "It's a diversion. It's a diversion!"

But he got there too late. As he reached the side of the building, the gate leading to the underground garage opened, and a Jaguar roared out, so close to Carter that he had to throw himself to the side not to get hit.

"STOP!" Carter yelled, then lifted his gun. Matt watched, holding his breath.

Step on it, Eva Rae. Floor that thing and get out of here!

Carter fired a shot at the car, but it was already too far away, and he missed. Soon, the black Jaguar was on the street, disappearing between the palm trees.

"That son of a gun!"

Carter cursed loudly, then stomped his foot like a child. He rushed to Matt and placed the gun to his head.

"Where are they going?"

Matt shrugged.

Carter gave Matt an angry look, then turned to address his officers.

"I'm not letting her get away. Not today, people. Track that Jaguar down. Get a chopper in the air if need be. She's not getting away this time. Not today, people. Do you hear me? Not today!"

Chapter 95

THE FORK SWIRLED through the air, spiraling down toward the bag underneath Olivia's shirt. But just as it was supposed to poke the bag like you'd pierce a microwavable bag of beans, Olivia turned her hand, and it missed.

Olivia couldn't breathe. She stared down at the fork in her hand. The children in front of her were still chatting, holding the hands of their parents, the restaurant still buzzing with happy voices.

I can't do it. I simply can't do it.

Olivia lifted her gaze, and she stared at the tall man with the sunglasses leaning against the door. He mouthed something that looked like a threat, his nostrils flaring aggressively. His hand on the gun in his pants moved, and she knew it was her last chance.

"Do it now," his lips said. "Or your family will die too. Not just you."

Olivia felt a ripple of fear rush through her body, and she could barely hold the fork between her fingers anymore. Her torso was shaking, her lips quivering, and soon she could no longer hold her tears back. They rolled down her cheeks as she — hands trembling — lifted the fork once again.

Just do it, Olivia. You'll die, no matter what. Poke a hole in the bag, take in a deep breath, and it'll be all over. The gas will make you pass out, and you won't feel death coming. Soon, you won't feel anything anymore.

Olivia took in a deep breath to steady her hand between sobs. The man behind her noticed her struggle.

"Say, are you okay?" he asked and put a hand on her shoulder.

That made her lose it completely. Olivia bent forward, crying.

"Hey... hey, are you okay?" the man continued nervously.

Olivia was sobbing now and didn't even see the tall man as he pulled out the gun and sprang forward.

"I... I can't do it," Olivia said and dropped the fork on the floor.

It's all over now.

The tall man approached her, and now she saw the gun. She readied herself for what was about to become her fate and decided to embrace it. It was out of her hands now. At least she wouldn't take anyone else with her when she went down. At least the kids in the line in front of her were safe.

Olivia stepped out of the line and staggered toward the tall man, who now held the gun up toward her. Seeing this made panic erupt in the restaurant, and it swept rapidly through the crowd. Someone screamed.

"GUN! He's got a gun!"

The tall man stood in front of her, blocking her way, gun pointed at her. Olivia stopped moving. She stared at the gun pointed at her, then closed her eyes, blocking out the world. Meanwhile, people ran for the exits, screaming. Olivia barely noticed them anymore. She was ready for this.

She was no longer afraid.

When the gun went off, she thought about her family and how she hoped they all knew how much she loved them.

Chapter 96

I WASN'T BREATHING. Everything inside of me had stopped. I stood in the middle of the restaurant at the Bayside Hotel, my gun clenched between my hands.

In front of me, a tall man in a Hawaiian shirt and sunglasses had his back turned to me. He was facing my daughter, gun lifted in his hand and pointed at her. On his back, the flamingoes on his shirt were being colored red as the blood gushed from his wound, where I had shot him.

He spurted, then tried to turn and see what had hit him, but he never made it that far. Instead — halfway turned — he dropped the gun from his hand and fell to the floor with a thud.

The restaurant had been emptied, and people had run outside. It was just us left.

Me and my daughter.

She still had her eyes closed, but soon opened them and blinked.

"M-mom?" Her voice grew shrill and loud as she repeated it, realizing I was truly there.

"Mom? Mo-om?"

I could hardly breathe, let alone speak, so instead of replying, I simply ran to her and grabbed her in my arms. I sobbed loudly as I felt her body close to mine. Our bodies shook violently as we held each other, crying. I kissed her face, stroked her hair, looked into her eyes, and still couldn't believe she was really there, that I had finally found her.

"H-how?" she finally said. "How did you know where I was?"

I sniffled and wiped my cheek with my arm. "I didn't. I came for someone else. I saw you and then the guy who was running for you, pointing his gun at you. I can't believe it's really you. I'm never letting you out of my sight again; you hear me?"

She chuckled, relieved. "Please, don't."

I felt something on her stomach and lifted her shirt to have a look. Olivia grew serious as I saw the bag attached to her. It was strapped around her waist. My heart stopped as I saw the green liquid inside of it.

"Careful," she whispered.

I turned and looked around us. Other bags just like it were placed on the floors. The green liquid was already leaking out.

"We need to get out of here," I said.

Christopher Daniels was standing behind me and helped me get the bag off of Olivia and leave it on the ground. We walked fast toward the exit of the restaurant, staying clear of the other bags. Luckily, the restaurant was in a big room, and we hadn't been close to any of the leaking bags. With some luck, we hadn't been exposed.

As we left the restaurant and closed the doors, I grabbed a couple of bottled waters, and we flushed our eyes with it, just in case. Outside, behind the sliding doors, we could hear sirens. The area was probably blocked off by now while the police tried to talk to the many people that had run outside. It would take a while for them to get the SWAT team ready, especially if they knew that gas had been released. They'd need to get hazmat suits. That bought us a little time.

"So, what do we do now?" Christopher Daniels asked.

I looked around me, then walked to the front desk in the lobby. I tapped on the computer and found the number I was looking for.

"The penthouse, of course. I should have guessed that. Now, how do we gain access to that?"

The doors opened, and a young bellboy came rushing out. He looked confused and probably had no idea what was going on. I smiled and lifted my gun.

"Hello there, young friend. You sure are a sight for sore eyes. How about we take a little ride in the elevator?"

Chapter 97

THE BELLBOY USED his keycard to get the elevator to the penthouse floor. As soon as it dinged and opened, we stepped out and let the boy go down again. The elevator opened straight into the penthouse apartment and, seconds later, we were standing in the living room of the owner of the hotel.

Jack Wellington was a big man, despite his seventy years of age. In his raging eyes, you could tell he wasn't someone who was used to being defied. And that was exactly what I was doing right now — defying him. I was standing in his living room, interrupting what seemed like a family brunch.

The man rose to his feet when he saw us. I had asked Christopher to stay behind me with Olivia.

"What in the…?"

His voice was hoarse and furious. I felt intimidated as he approached me with wrathful steps.

"Who are you people, and what are you doing in my home?" He paused when seeing me properly. "Wait. You're that woman. The one they're all searching for."

All eyes in the room were on me now. Jack Wellington's fell on Christopher behind me.

"And you… you… what are you doing here?" he spat. "You have some nerve to come here after all you've done to my family."

"I'm calling security," a small nervous-looking woman, who I could only assume was his wife, said. I remembered having seen pictures of both of them in magazines before, dressed for premieres or gallery openings.

"I wouldn't do that," I said and lifted the gun to stop her.

Mrs. Wellington put the phone down.

"What do you want?" Jack Wellington asked, addressed to Christopher. "More of my money? Huh? You haven't taken enough?"

Christopher shook his head. "I have never asked your daughter for any money. She came to me because she wanted my help; she was unhappy with her life, and I tried to help her, but… it went wrong."

"You're darn right it went wrong," Jack Wellington said.

"I might have done a lot of things wrong, but I never asked for a penny from your daughter."

"You're lying," Jack Wellington said. "I know your type. You're an embezzler; that's all you are. A maniac who thinks he can use our money to pay for his terrorist acts. But it's over, buddy. You're not getting one cent more from us."

"Christopher Daniels wasn't the man behind the attacks," I said. I turned my head and looked at Helen Wellington, sitting on a couch, her purse clutched between her hands. I turned the gun toward her.

"She was."

Mrs. Wellington huffed. Mr. Wellington grumbled. "Oh, you people are insane."

Christopher stepped forward. "Tell them, Helen. Clear your conscience and free your soul."

"Will you listen to him?" Jack Wellington snorted. "Trying to blame my daughter… for what? A terrorist attack? Will you look at her? She can barely even tie her own shoes."

Helen stood to her feet, her purse still in her hand, her eyes blazing.

"That's right, Daddy Dearest. I never could do anything, could I? But guess what? They're right. I did do something. Something no one would ever think I was capable of, least of all you. I killed all those people. In the Metrorail, in the church, at the school, and now here at your beloved hotel. I. Killed. Them. All."

Chapter 98

"I'D DO it all over again any day if I got the chance, Daddy Dear."

Helen stared at her father, who, for once in his life, had become speechless. "There. I finally have your attention, don't I?"

Helen turned to look at me. "How on Earth did you know?"

"It struck me when I read an interview about you in the *New York Times*," I said. "After your arrest, you told your story to every media outlet who would listen, didn't you? You spoke about NYX and said they had forced you to carry the gas into the school. You told the reporter in detail how they chose you among the members and that you had to go in with a bunch of trafficked girls that Christopher had bought online and that were dispensable. You spoke about NYX like you came straight from the house, but I never saw you there. And then there was something else that made me suspect you. I couldn't figure out why you were so open with the police and the press about the cult and what had been going on when every other member who was arrested stayed silent. But now I know why. You wanted them to go down. You wanted NYX to take the blame for the attacks. I wondered about these things while still thinking that Christopher was behind the attacks. It wasn't until I spoke to Christopher and asked about this that I fully understood what was going on. He told me what you had been through — about your past. And once he did, it all suddenly made sense."

"He was on the train, wasn't he?" Christopher said and stepped forward toward Helen. "Brian? Your ex-husband? He took the Metrorail every day to one of the courthouses where he worked, always getting out at Government Center."

"You wanted him hurt for what he did to you because he left you," I said. "He abandoned you when he realized you couldn't have children. And then he married someone else and had a family, leaving you all alone."

"You're right. I won't deny it," Helen said. "Daddy always thought I couldn't do anything, but I did this. Under the username the Iron Fist, I bought the girls in a chatroom on the Dark Web," she said. "I hired a guy to do it for me, someone who knew the Dark Web very well. It was so easy; you wouldn't believe it. A few others that had decided to leave NYX and I planned this together. We gathered a group of girls and kept them at my family's farm outside of town that my dad had put me in charge of, thinking I couldn't mess things up too badly all the way out there. He blamed me for the divorce, thinking I had ruined my marriage just like everything else. I used the girls at the chicken factory at night, breaking them until they obeyed my every word, making them my soldiers. No one would miss these girls who had already been trafficked across the country, some of them across half of the world, and they most certainly could never be traced back to me once their bodies showed up at the scene of the attacks. They were the perfect little soldiers."

My heart sank when hearing the brutal coldness to her voice when talking about these young girls, some of them just children. It was beyond cruel.

"It was because of the abuse; wasn't it?" I asked, my voice cracking slightly when thinking about Olivia in this woman's hands. "That you couldn't have children? You were abused when you were just a young child by a priest at the Catholic church your family attended and where you sang in the choir, at St. Mary's Cathedral, the second place you attacked. You were abused again and again, and no one would listen when you tried to tell them. Not even the nuns at the Catholic school you went to. And once it started showing, once it became evident that you were pregnant at the age of only fourteen, you were the one who was punished. It was reported to your father, and instead of punishing the priest, you were sent away to a place where they could perform an abortion, even though you were so far along that it was illegal."

"They killed my baby," she said, spitting. "They poked something up inside of me and murdered my child. Then they pulled out my baby. I saw him when they did it. I could have taken care of him. I wanted to, but my father wouldn't let me."

"And because of the procedure, you were unable to become pregnant again," I said. "They robbed you of that."

"There was scarring," the doctors told me later when Brian and I went to the fertility clinic, and they examined me. Brian became furious at me for having never told him about the abortion or the fact that I couldn't have children, and so he left. Our marriage was based on a lie, he said. I thought I was going to be alone for the rest of my life when Brian left me. I thought I'd never survive it."

"But then you met Christopher, and you fell in love all over again," I said, glancing at him standing by the window.

Chapter 99

THEN

HELEN STARED at the barren wall in front of her. She was sitting on her bed in the bedroom at the NYX house, a room that she shared with another girl. She had been there a year and a half now and had never felt so alive. Especially not back when she had been married to Brian.

"My God, I think I'm in love," she mumbled with a giggle into the empty room.

Just the very thought of Christopher Daniels and being with him filled her with butterflies of expectation.

The sex between them was intense. It wasn't often, only like once a month or so, but that was enough. She actually kind of liked having to wait for him to call on her to come to his room. She never knew when it would happen, and that made it all the more exciting. Everything about this man was so exhilarating; it made her blush just to think about it. She had no idea love could be this way. She had no idea life could be this way.

Helen smiled secretively. It amazed her how much better her life was now that she was at the NYX house and didn't have to deal with her family and their disappointment in her. Her father had given her the farm to take care of after the divorce, but she didn't have to actually be there to run it. It was just a way of keeping her busy; she knew that much. There were caretakers to handle the day-to-day stuff.

Helen stared at the stick in her hand. No one knew that she was taking the test; she had kept everything a secret. She had been disappointed so many times before in her life. But now, as she stared at the two lines, she could hardly contain herself.

Pregnant? It's really true? I am pregnant? But… but they said it was impossible? That it could never happen?

Stick still in her hand, Helen rose to her feet, almost bubbling over with excitement.

"Christopher is going to be so thrilled when he hears this. He's gonna be so happy. And then we can be together forever and ever. Oh, I can't wait to tell him."

Helen rushed out of her room, then hurried toward the stairs leading to Christopher's chambers on the top floor of the house. Normally, she wasn't allowed to go up there until she was called, but today was a special day. He would want to know right away.

Of course, he would.

Helen grabbed the railing and walked up the wooden stairs, butterflies fluttering in her stomach.

What shall we name the child? I know. Annie if it is a girl and Robert if it is a boy. I've always loved those names. Brian never liked those names, especially not Robert because it reminded him of a kid from his school who picked his nose in class and smelled bad. But screw him. I am calling my child — our child — Robert if it is a boy.

"Christopher?"

Helen reached the top of the stairs, then walked to the door. Behind it lay Christopher's private rooms. Not many were allowed up here. She felt another tickle in her stomach as she lifted her hand to knock. But no one answered. She tried again. Still, no answer. She then grabbed the handle and opened the door carefully.

"Christopher?"

She entered his reading quarters and office. This was where he wrote his books, where he came when he needed quiet.

He wasn't in there.

Could he be somewhere else in the house?

She was about to walk back out when she heard a noise coming from behind the next door, the one leading to the bedroom.

Ah, he's in there.

"Christopher?" she said, then walked to the door and pushed it open.

Helen stopped. In there, on the bed, she found Christopher, surrounded by several women. All naked.

"C-Christopher?" she said, perplexed. He lifted his head from between the breasts of a woman, and their eyes met across the room.

"Helen?"

She shook her head in disbelief. "But... I thought... I thought... you made me believe that I was someone special."

He approached her, reaching out his arms. His naked body suddenly repulsed her where it used to be so exhilarating.

"You *are* special, Helen. I have told you this over and over again. You are truly special. We all are."

He stood there, smiling like it was the most natural thing in the world that he was having sex with an entire group of women like it couldn't possibly hurt her in any way.

Helen took a step backward. As she did, Christopher spotted the stick in her hand, and his expression changed.

"No. No. No."

She nodded. "Yes, Christopher. We're having a child. Together."

He lifted his finger and walked closer. "No, we're not. I don't have children. I never wanted children, Helen. You must have it removed. Do you hear me? I can't have children. I simply won't."

Helen stared at the man she had loved so dearly until a few seconds ago. Suddenly, all she could see was her father's face as he told her she was going to have the baby removed, and she begged him to not do this to her. All she could see and hear were her own screams as she saw the dead baby be pulled out of her body. It overwhelmed her so violently that she started to shake.

Seeing this, Christopher stepped forward again. "Helen, it'll be okay. We'll find a solution for this, okay? It doesn't have to be like what happened last time. We can do it properly. There are ways. You're still not very far along. The baby is barely a baby yet. We can see a doctor and he'll..."

But Helen wasn't listening anymore. Tears streamed across her cheeks, and she stepped backward, shaking her head and crying heavily.

"Helen, let's talk about this..." he tried, but she was gone.

Helen turned around and ran out of the room, heart pounding in her chest, hearing nothing but the screams of her dead, unborn baby.

Chapter 100

"YOU WERE pregnant and wanted to keep the baby, but Christopher didn't," I said. "That's when it all came back, everything you had fought to keep down, tried to forget. It stared you directly in the face once again. The abuse, the people who didn't protect you when they should have, the forced abortion, and following infertility. Everything that had destroyed your life, you were reliving once again, and so you ran."

Helen was crying now. She was biting her lip, staring at Christopher, who shook his head.

"It wasn't my fault, Helen," he said. "You need to understand this. It was an accident. You fell down those stairs. You lost the baby, yes, you lost *our* baby, but it was an accident."

Helen swallowed hard. Her lip was quivering. "You killed our baby, Christopher. You killed him."

Christopher clasped his mouth, and I could tell he was fighting his tears. It was the first time I had seen genuine emotion in the man.

"I am sorry," he said. "I never got to tell you how sorry I am. I should have known this would break you. I knew your past. You had told me everything in our therapy sessions. I should have seen this coming. But you wouldn't talk to me. You left our group in anger, and I thought you needed your space — that it was for the best. I should have known it was you when the attacks occurred, especially when you hit the church and your old school. But I just never thought... it's no excuse, I know. I should have seen it. You did all these things to get back at those that had hurt you over the years. Your ex, the church and the priest, the school, and now... your family."

"By buying Sarin gas, which is also easily found on the Dark Web, on sites by chemists who earn a lot of money producing it and selling it, you made it look like the attacks in Japan back in 1995," I said. "Their leaders had just been executed recently, and their ways could be compared to those of NYX. It would easily be perceived that their leader, Christopher, was obsessed with the Japanese leader and wanted to be like him. To make sure the public understood, you told that about Christopher over and over again in the many interviews you did afterward. You described in detail how he talked about the Japanese leader Shoko Asahara constantly and how he even dressed like him and spoke of creating a utopian society. You ganged up with other former members of NYX, who were also angry or disappointed with Christopher, and wanted to hurt him. As it turned out, he had made a lot of enemies over the years. One of those you contacted was Lori Moore, who was very angry with NYX, but she didn't want to be a part of your plan, and she threatened to reveal it all, didn't she? So, you got rid of her and continued your plans with the others. Because they bore the brand when helping you perform the attacks, you made sure all suspicion turned in NYX's direction. Witnesses would see the burn marks, the brands, like Ryan Scott did in the Metrorail. You made it look like NYX was behind it, so you'd take Christopher down in the process. And then you planned an attack on your father's hotel, in the same place he lived, so that when you killed your family, it would look like it was just a part of the terrorist attack on the hotel. No one would ever suspect you, the daughter who had been a victim of NYX. They would think it was a way to get back at you because you had spoken up against NYX. With Christopher released from prison on bail, this morning was the perfect moment to strike. While the guests were eating their breakfast in peace and quiet, not suspecting to be exposed to a deathly gas."

Helen's parents turned their heads to look at her, mouths gaping. Her sister, Aubrey, came closer too.

"Is this true?" her father asked. "Tell me, Helen. Is this true?"

I walked up to Helen and grabbed her purse from her hand. She held onto it, but I pulled it out of her grip. I opened it and then showed its contents to her family. Inside was a clear bag with green liquid in it.

"Sarin gas," I said. "My guess is she was planning on appearing upset, then leaving this brunch prematurely and accidentally forgetting her purse, with the bag that had been punctured still inside of it. She'd then take the elevator down and use a back exit to get out of here. The police would arrive when it was too late and assume you had all died as a part of a terrorist attack, planned by NYX. Very clever."

Mrs. Wellington cupped her mouth. Her eyes lingered on her daughter. "I can't believe this. Helen? Please, tell me this isn't true?"

Chapter 101

JACK WELLINGTON SAT down in a chair, then hid his face between his hands. His wife stared at their daughter. She stood like she was frozen, like she was still waiting for her to say that it wasn't true.

"Don't you even have anything to say?" her mother asked, her voice cracking.

Helen Wellington's eyes lingered on me and the gun in my hand.

"It's over, Helen," I said.

I stared at the woman in front of me and didn't even notice her sister went for her purse. Not until it was too late, and she too had pulled out a gun. As I turned to look, it was pointed at my daughter, at Olivia's head. Aubrey's hand was shaking.

"I am sorry," she said. "For having to do this. But I can't let you destroy my family. Now, please lower your gun, or I will shoot."

"She's bluffing, Mom," Olivia said. "Don't do it."

I stared at my daughter, unable to believe her. There was no way I'd risk her life like that. Are you kidding me? I had just gotten her back.

I raised my hand with the gun in the air, then placed it on the ground and kicked it to Aubrey, who picked it up.

"Now what?" I asked. "You're gonna let your sister get away with this?"

"Actually," Helen said as she approached her sister and grabbed one of the guns. "My sister has been helping me all the way."

"Aubrey!" Mrs. Wellington exclaimed. "Why? I have never... I didn't raise you to..."

Aubrey took two steps forward. She lifted the arm that held the gun and shot her mother point-blank in the face.

Olivia screamed and turned her face away. I watched Mrs. Wellington jolt before she crumpled to the floor, her red blood gushing onto the white carpet below.

My heart pounded in my chest as Helen walked to her father and placed the gun on his forehead and pressed it against the skin until he was forced to look up at her.

"How does that feel, Daddy, huh? How does it feel that your fate is in someone else's hands? Huh? How does it feel to have someone completely ruin your entire life, everything you've dreamt about and worked for? Huh? How does it feel to be betrayed by your own flesh and blood? By the very ones that are supposed to care for you?"

He just stared at her, his steel-grey eyes overflowing with menace.

"Answer me!" Helen snorted. "How does it feel to be betrayed by your own daughter?"

Jack Wellington's eyes grew stale. He spoke with calmness.

"You weren't even worthy of my name. Not since the day you let that priest defile you. Since then, you were nothing but a dirty whore to me. A useless dirty who..."

With a loud scream, Helen fired the gun. Jack Wellington fell backward in the chair, while Helen fired another shot at his chest, then another, still while screaming.

"I HATE YOU. I HATE YOU. I HATE YOU!"

Aubrey came up behind her sister and pulled her into a hug.

"He isn't worth it, sis. He isn't worth it."

Helen sobbed and held her sister tight while my eyes met Christopher's. Knowing these sisters' level of anger and capability, especially toward men, I believed he would be next. Christopher knew it too. He turned around, then bolted for the elevator while the sisters were still hugging.

Chapter 102

HE ALMOST MADE IT. Almost. Christopher was by the door, and it was open when the sisters let go of one another, then cocked both of their guns and pointed them at him.

"Stop," Aubrey said.

Christopher paused for a second, but then realizing that they were at the other end of the living room, out of range, he continued into the elevator. He turned around and pushed the buttons, hard, frantically, while the sisters rushed toward him, soon getting close enough to shoot. I didn't know how well they shot, but I had a feeling it was something they had trained at since childhood, by the way they held the guns with confidence. It was customary for especially rich families in Florida to train their children in shooting guns. I myself had been trained by the man who I had believed was my father back then. At least once a month, he would take me to a shooting range, and we would spend the day there together.

Close the doors. Close the darn doors.

The doors began to move, and my heart raced while watching it. Olivia held onto me tightly while the sisters came closer and now both fired at Christopher. Three shots were fired before the elevator doors closed.

I held my breath.

Did he make it?

Seconds went by, while Aubrey pushed the button to get the

elevator to come back up. I scanned the apartment, searching for an emergency exit when the elevator dinged again, and the doors opened.

I probably shouldn't have, but I couldn't help myself. I stretched my neck to see, and then I saw it. I saw him. I saw Christopher lying inside the elevator, on the floor, in a pool of his own blood.

Oh, dear God.

Seeing this, Olivia turned her face away and hid in my arms. I held her tightly, trying to calm myself down.

In that second, the sisters turned to look at the two of us.

Chapter 103

THEY TIED US UP. Backs leaned against one another, Olivia and I were tied up with duct tape and placed on the floor. Then, Helen grabbed her purse and pulled out the plastic bag with the Sarin gas in it. My heart dropped as she placed it next to us.

"I am so sad not to be here to watch you die slowly because it would give me such deep joy," she said with a tilted head. "But we need to go down and talk to the police. We'll tell them how you came up here with the gas and then shot and killed my entire family. Then we'll tell them how Christopher backstabbed you and tried to kill you as well, then tied you up and released the gas, trying to kill us all. But, of course, my sister and I managed to escape and shot Christopher, then ran for the emergency exit, just in time for us not to be exposed to the gas. Unfortunately, we were the only ones to survive. Now, it might take us a while to tell the story properly since we are in such a deep state of shock, so you'll have to excuse us if it takes a little while before anyone comes up here. But you won't mind because, after about a few minutes of breathing this gas, you'll be so sick you'll hardly be able to speak anyway. Some people experience symptoms within as little as thirty seconds of having been exposed to it. Others take a few minutes. You'll probably die from respiratory paralysis pretty fast I'd assume when being this close to the contamination device. You know how they train for these types of events, how they prepare to approach a gas attack? They actually tell the first responders to resist the urge to rush to help. You wanna know why? Because if the patient is so incapacitated by the nerve agent, to the point where they are incapable of self-evacuation, it is highly likely they'll die despite any intervention the first responders might be able to provide. Isn't it nice? They'll simply leave you to die. Because there is nothing they can really do to prevent it. No one will come for you, Eva Rae Thomas. No one."

"You're sick," I said. "Do you know that? I'll come after you. I'll hunt you down and kill you. You hear me?"

I yelled at the top of my lungs, but it was too late. Helen stared at me, then took in a deep breath and held it, while lifting a small knife in the air and poking it through the plastic bag. I whimpered as I watched the hole grow, and the liquid inside of it start to move. For days, I had read about this type of gas and just what it did to the body. I knew this was definitely going to kill us both if I didn't act fast.

"Bastards!" I screamed as the two women rushed to the emergency exit at the other end of the room and left.

Chapter 104

"WHAT ARE we going to do, Mom? What do we do?"

The panic in my daughter's voice didn't help make me calmer. I was struggling with the duct tape while trying to not breathe in too deeply. Meanwhile, the liquid had reached the carpet now, and it was beginning to sting my eyes. So far, only a small amount of the gas had made it out of the hole. I didn't know how much of the liquid it took to kill us, and I wasn't planning on sticking around to find out.

I moved my hands back and forth, getting the tape loose, and soon pulled my hands out. I removed the tape from my feet then rushed to Olivia and started pulling at hers.

"How did you do that?" she asked. "How did you get your hands out?"

"When they tied me up, I made sure there was a good gap between my wrists, so they didn't fully touch," I said. "They didn't notice, luckily, since they were so busy talking. Once they left, it was easy to pull off since it was so loose. Here. Now, you're free too."

We sprang to our feet, and I pulled my daughter away from the gas. It was stinging my eyes severely now, and I felt like my throat was closing up. It had to be the worst feeling in the world, not to be able to breathe properly. Panic erupted in me as we rushed across the room.

"Mom," Olivia said. "I don't feel so good."

"I know, sweetie. We just need to get to the emergency exit. Hurry."

We tried to run, but it was hard when we couldn't breathe properly. I gasped for air and felt like my lungs were collapsing.

We reached the door to the emergency exit, then tried to open it, but it wouldn't budge.

"Mom? What's happening?" Olivia said. "Why won't it open?"

"They must have... blocked it somehow," I said and tried again, pushing it hard.

It didn't move.

"What do we do?" Olivia said.

"We'll try the elevator," I said and pulled her by the hand. We reached the elevator, where Christopher's dead body lay on the floor. I stepped in some of his blood and felt like I had to throw up. Olivia came inside with me, whimpering as she tried not to look at him. I pressed the button, but nothing happened.

"Mom?" Olivia said. "Why doesn't it do anything?"

I pressed again, then again and again. Nothing.

I stared into the apartment and realized there was no light on in any of the lamps. I couldn't hear the AC running either. I walked out and flipped a switch, but nothing happened.

"What's going on, Mom? Mom?" my daughter shrieked.

"They turned the power off. So, we couldn't get down in case we escaped somehow. They're smarter than I thought."

"But... but if the emergency exit is blocked and the elevator doesn't work, then what do we do?" Olivia said. "How do we get out of here before the gas kills us?"

Chapter 105

"WE'VE BEEN TOLD she's holding the entire Wellington family captive in the penthouse apartment," Carter said.

He looked at Matt, who was standing next to him. Matt held his cuffed hands in front of him. He folded his hands and mumbled a prayer under his breath. He was worried about Eva Rae more than anything.

"You still believe in her innocence? She's up there with him, with Christopher Daniels. The bellboy over there told us he helped them get up there, that Eva Rae Thomas put a gun to his head and forced him to take them up there. And you still want to defend her? I'm beginning to think that either you're very stupid or maybe very blinded by your love for her, or maybe you really are in it with her. But there is no way she's coming out of that building without us getting her. I have guards at every exit, and the entire area is surrounded. This time, we'll get her. I just know we will. Her reign of terror is over."

Matt swallowed hard and looked up toward the penthouse. He felt a pinch in his heart. How was this ever going to end well for her? Carter had told him that they believed Olivia was there too. The bellboy had said that a young girl was in the elevator with them, and when they showed him a picture of Olivia, he had said it looked like her, only she had shorter hair.

Matt breathed to calm himself down. At least Eva Rae had finally found her daughter. That provided Matt with some level of comfort. But would they make it out alive?

"Someone's coming out," a voice yelled.

Please, let it be Eva Rae; please, let it be Eva Rae.

Carter approached the entrance, escorting Matt with him. There was movement behind the sliding doors, and soon they opened. Two women came out, but it wasn't Eva Rae or Olivia.

Dang it.

"It's the Wellington sisters!" A reporter yelled, and they all threw themselves forward but were stopped by the police barrier they had put up. Officers rushed to the women. Both looked to be in great distress. Tears were rolling from their eyes.

"We need paramedics over here!" an officer yelled. "Fast!"

"It's was horrible," one of the sisters said. "She tried to kill us."

"Eva Rae Thomas did?" Carter asked when approaching them.

One of the sisters, who Matt recognized as Helen Wellington, lifted her head and nodded. "Her and Christopher Daniels. Christopher killed our parents, and then he killed her too."

"Eva Rae Thomas?" Matt asked, his pulse quickening.

Helen nodded. She struggled to get the words past her lips.

"Yes. And her daughter. Using nerve gas."

Matt didn't hear anything after that. He gasped for air and stepped backward, hearing only his own heartbeat.

Eva Rae is dead? She's dead?

He could barely breathe and felt dizzy. Carter was busy taking the sisters' statements, so he didn't notice him as he stepped out of the crowd to gather himself. He bent forward, squatting down, his cuffed hands held up in front of him and started to cry.

Carter came up behind him and placed a hand on his shoulder.

"It's time to go, buddy. I'm taking you back to the station. You're of no use to me anymore since Eva Rae is dead."

Matt nodded, still sobbing heavily, then rose to his feet. As he did, he threw a glance toward the top floor of the building in front of him. Up there, on the seventy-fifth floor, he could see something moving.

Was it someone waving?

No, it couldn't be.

Matt squinted his eyes. He always had hawk-like vision, but this was far away. Still, he couldn't help thinking that someone had opened the window and was waving.

Could he hear them screaming too?

"Wait a second," he said. He stepped forward, while Carter grabbed his shoulder.

"We need to go."

Matt stood still for a few seconds more, staring into the air, then turned to face Carter.

"I'm sorry," he said, "But I can't go right now."

Matt then lifted his knee and slammed it into Carter's crotch, causing him to bend over in deep pain.

Then, Matt turned around and made a run for it. It took a few seconds before Carter was able to speak and yell to his colleagues, and by the time he did, Matt was already approaching the sliding doors. They took off after him, but he was faster than them, and soon he stormed inside.

He knew they wouldn't follow him in, not when they knew there was gas inside of the building and, just as he thought, they stopped their pursuit at the doors.

Matt ran to the elevator, but nothing happened when he pressed the button. He found the exit sign, then ran down a hallway and soon reached the stairs.

Then, he started climbing.

The first steps went smooth and easy, and he took them two, sometimes three at a time, eager to get up to the penthouse before it was too late. He was certain it was Eva Rae he had seen in the window, waving at him. He might be mad, and it might end up killing him, going up there to the nerve gas without proper protection, but he had to do it. He simply had to.

As he reached the fortieth floor, he began slowing down, feeling his heart pumping in his chest, and as he reached the fiftieth floor, he had to stop and catch his breath before continuing.

It took forever to climb this many stairs, especially with no AC, and by the time he finally reached the seventy-fifth floor, he was completely drenched in sweat and out of breath. But it didn't matter. All that mattered was getting to her. Matt refused to believe she was dead. It simply couldn't be true.

He had to at least see it with his own eyes. Even if it meant he died while trying.

Matt reached the plateau and saw the door. He took in a couple of breaths, then approached it.

When he stood close to it, his blood froze to ice. The door had been blocked by several big, heavy boxes. The rest of them rested on a pallet against the wall next to it. It was obvious someone had just grabbed them to block it purposely.

Creating a deathtrap.

The thought made Matt's heart race even faster. This meant the two women had blocked the exit so no one else could follow them. No one else could make it out.

Matt raised his fists and hammered on the door with his cuffed hands.

"Eva Rae? Eva Rae? Are you in there?"

When no answer came, Matt started pulling the boxes to the side, frantically carrying them one at a time. It wasn't easy with his hands cuffed, and them being very heavy, but soon he had pushed them away. He grabbed for the handle, only to realize that there was none.

"Oh, dear God," he cried out in desperation. "The door only opens one way!"

Matt used both his fists to hammer on the door once more.

"Eva Rae! You need to open it from the inside. Come on, Eva Rae; come on!"

Matt slammed his fists against the door until his knuckles started to bleed. He cried and leaned against the door.

"Come on, Eva Rae. Push the door open."

He had almost given up hope when a small voice came from somewhere behind the door.

"M-Matt? Is that you?"

"Olivia?" he said, his voice shrill. "Olivia? Where's your mom?"

"She's passed out. She couldn't breathe and fell to the floor by the window. I'm not sure... I don't... my lungs are burning, Matt. It hurts. My eyes too."

"Olivia, I need you to push the door open. I've removed the boxes that blocked it, but you need to push it open from the inside. Can you do that for me?"

A heartbeat went by, and nothing happened. There was a fumbling behind the door, and then it clicked and slowly opened, but only a little. Matt put his fingers in the crack and pulled it all the way open. Olivia fell out in the hallway, her body shaking like she was having a seizure. Eva Rae lay utterly still on the floor by the window.

"My God," Matt exclaimed, then looked from one to the other. He stared at the stairs behind him, leading down. There were seventy-five floors. How was he supposed to carry two bodies down all those stairs? How was he supposed to make it in time? With both hands cuffed?

Matt turned to look at Eva Rae.

There was only one solution. He'd have to choose between them. He could only carry one at a time. The question was, should he take the woman he loved or her daughter?

Chances were only one of them would survive.

Chapter 106

MATT MADE it halfway before he tripped and dropped Olivia's lifeless body. He hit face-first into the ground and screamed with anger and frustration. Olivia's body slid across the floor.

He had chosen the daughter. Not that it was an easy choice, but he knew that Eva Rae would kill him if he took her over Olivia. She would want it this way, and he'd have to respect that.

Matt got up, grabbed Olivia by the arms, and tried to sling her back onto his shoulder. He made a grimace when his back hurt, then was about to take another step, when suddenly the lights in the hallway were turned back on. Matt gasped and looked up at the lamp above him.

The power is back on! That means the elevator is running again.

Matt found the door leading to the floor he was on, then carried Olivia inside and down the hallway. He found the elevator, then pushed the button, and soon it arrived. He gasped when seeing the dead body inside of it, but carried Olivia inside, then pushed the button to go down before running out of it and letting it leave without him. He knew that if he came downstairs with her, he'd get taken away and they would never look for Eva Rae. He had to get back up and take her down as well.

Before it was too late.

So, he did. He ran back up the many stairs, praying that the first responders would find Olivia and get her the help she needed. Turning the electricity on again meant they were inside the building. Matt guessed there were still many people trapped in their hotel rooms all over the building that they came to get out.

He had left Eva Rae on the plateau, so she wouldn't be exposed to any more of the gas, and she was still there as he came back. She was lying on her side, motionless, but she had a pulse when he felt for it.

He grabbed her by the waist and swung her above his shoulders, then — energized by fear of losing her, he started the climb back down again.

He made it two-thirds of the way down when he couldn't walk anymore. He fought to take another step, then another, before he felt like he couldn't walk anymore. His legs were getting wobbly beneath him, and he was getting dizzy.

You've got to make it, Matt. Just a few more steps.

At first, he thought he was just imagining things when he heard voices coming from below him, but he peeked down to see the first responders arriving wearing their hazmat suits, breathing heavily inside of them.

"Sir? Are you all right, sir? Have you been exposed to the gas?" the one who came up to him first asked.

Matt shook his head, breathing hard and tearing up. He was almost out of strength and hope. They had come at the right time. One more minute and he would have caved in.

"No, but she has. Please, help. This woman needs medical care right away."

THREE DAYS LATER

Chapter 107

"WHEN IT ALL comes down to it, you're in deep trouble."

I coughed behind the oxygen mask and fought to breathe. It was happening over and over again. My respiratory system had been damaged, and they didn't know how badly yet. But I was alive, and so was my daughter. I had been in the hospital for days, and they had given me a reversal agent to save my life. Now, Carter had come to visit and stood by my bed, telling me how much trouble I was in.

My arms were cuffed to the bed, so I had no way of actually doing it, but I wanted to punch the man in the face.

"But…" I said between heavy breaths. "But I told you that Helen and Aubrey Wellington…" I lost my breath and wheezed, then took in a couple of deep breaths through my oxygen mask.

"I know, I know. You stick to that story, but no one believes it. Detective Miller keeps saying the same thing, but frankly, it's a little too far out to be true, don't you think?"

I coughed again, then shook my head. "Not more far out than me being the great mastermind."

Carter shrugged. "Well, that's just too bad, isn't it? Because that's what I think. And I have the evidence to prove it."

I wheezed again before being able to speak. "You planted that evidence. Don't you think I know you did?"

Carter came closer, then leaned over me and spoke with a low voice. "Between you and me, yes, I did. I took the necklace from your hotel room when we searched it and placed it in Lori Moore's kitchen. I also used a cloth with the nerve gas that I took from the evidence room, sealed in a bag, and placed it in the trunk of your car. Just to help the case go a little smoother. But you'll never be able to prove it. It'll be your word against mine, and who do you think they'll believe? I'm guessing not the woman who is known as a fraud and who we have on surveillance video assaulting spa owners."

"Maybe you should try and guess again," a voice said coming from behind Carter.

A large woman stepped inside my room, gliding comfortably in her high heels and tight skirt.

"Oh, Detective Carter," I said. "Meet my former boss, FBI-director, Isabella Horne. She was in here earlier, and I had the chance to tell her the entire story. I told her I was certain I could get you to admit your guilt on tape, but she wasn't sure I could. You owe me five bucks, Isabella."

"I sure do," she said, then reached over and removed my phone from the table next to me.

"It's so simple these days," I said. "Can you believe how easy it is? Back in the day, we'd have to wear a wire and everything. It was a lot of trouble. But today, it's different. You can simply use your phone to record sensitive material without anyone knowing it."

"But... but..."

Matt came in behind Isabella, flanked by Chief Annie and a local officer from Miami. The officer removed my cuffs and placed them on Carter instead.

"See, the thing is," Chief Annie said, "it was actually the FBI who sent out Eva Rae on a mission, in cooperation with our department, to find the Iron Fist. He had long been under suspicion for the trafficking of girls in south Florida, and we saw no one better to do the job of finding him than Eva Rae."

"So, she was actually working for us all this time," Isabella said. "Undercover and top-secret, naturally, so we couldn't tell anyone — not even when you started to chase her. All we could do was to send Matt in to keep an eye on your investigation and make sure she wasn't harmed. But then we caught ourselves a corrupt cop along the way too, which isn't half bad. Helen Wellington and her sister have been taken into our custody now, and will not see daylight for a very, very long time. Lots of trials will follow in the coming years when the sisters and their helpers will have to answer for their actions. Finding the girls at the farm helped us a lot in putting the pieces together, and they will serve as excellent witnesses after they have been reunited with their families. We have even set up a group of investigators to look into NYX to see if there are others who will need to be prosecuted for what happened there before the leader was killed. So, all in all, a very successful mission. Meanwhile, you should probably prepare yourself to spend some time in the darkness as well. Nothing worse than a criminal cop, in my opinion, taking the law into his own hands."

Isabella nodded at the officer, who grabbed Carter and took him away. Chief Annie and Director Isabella Horne left as well, and Matt and I were alone. I asked Matt to come closer to me and wrapped my arms around him, then held him very tight.

"How are you feeling today?" he asked.

I smiled, relieved. "Better. Slowly getting there day by day. Now that we got Carter in custody, I have to say I feel a little like dancing. But not yet, though. My lungs aren't ready for that kind of activity. At least not yet."

"But are you maybe ready for a visit?" Matt asked.

Olivia stepped inside, and I couldn't help smiling through my tears. "Oh, my baby girl. Come here."

She walked up to me and threw her arms around my neck. I kissed her frantically and eventually she told me to stop.

"Never," I said. "I am never letting you out of my sight again; do you hear me?"

She leaned over and kissed my forehead. The doctors had told me she had been very lucky and that her lungs seemed fine. Her eyes were still bothered by the gas they had been exposed to, but it would get better in time.

As I looked at my beautiful daughter, I suddenly heard a set of voices coming up behind her. The sound made my heart run amok.

"Christine? Alex?"

"Mo-o-om! Alex won't stop talking about bunnies. It's all he ever talks about, and it is driving me nuts!" Christine exclaimed. "He's been reading everything on the Internet about them."

"Dad promised me we could get bunnies," Alex said with that glint in his eyes.

My mom and Chad came in with them. Chad held Alex by the shoulders. He shrugged while I hugged my mom.

"You look awful, dear," she said and corrected my hair like that would help. I chose to ignore her.

"You did what?" I asked Chad, suddenly thrown back to reality. "You promised them bunnies? And just who is supposed to take care of them?"

"I will," Alex said. "I love bunnies; they're so CUTE!"

"What can I say?" Chad said. "I felt bad for the kids. We didn't know when you'd be home, and I gave in. I was weak; forgive me."

I took in a deep breath of oxygen through the mask.

"I guess we're getting bunnies then."

"YEAH!" Alex exclaimed, then gave me a warm hug. I coughed again and had to take another couple of deep breaths with the oxygen when I realized someone else had arrived in the room too.

She was standing a little behind the others, looking shy. She was wearing a hat and sunglasses, even though we were indoors. Not to be recognized, I guessed, but someone had to tell her that wearing a hat and sunglasses only made people look at her even more.

"Sydney," I said with a sigh. I reached out my hands and grabbed hers in mine. "Thank you. For all your help. I couldn't have done this without you."

She shrugged. "What are sisters for, right? You could have told me you were on an FBI mission, though. Would have made me feel a whole lot better."

"It had to seem real," I said. "From now on, I'll tell you everything. I promise."

Sydney hugged me and held me tight, then whispered. "There was no mission, was there? It's something you have all come up with afterward, isn't it?"

I chuckled, then smiled. "On second thought, you don't need to know everything. There should be room for a little mystery between sisters."

I shared a glance with Matt, and he smiled. I then saw him look nervously at Chad. He was surrounded by our children, who seemed to be exhilarated to have their father back in their lives. I couldn't blame them, but I couldn't blame Matt either for feeling a little threatened by the presence of my ex.

I reached out my hand and grabbed Matt's in mine, then took a deep breath from the oxygen mask before I removed it and looked deeply into his eyes.

NEVER EVER

"Matt?"

"Yeah?"

"I love you," I said and touched his lips gently. "Gosh, how I love you."

THE END

Afterword

Hit The Road Jack (Jack Ryder Series Book 1)

EXCERPT

FOR A SPECIAL SNEAK peak of Willow Rose's Bestselling Mystery Novel **Hit the road Jack** turn to the next page.

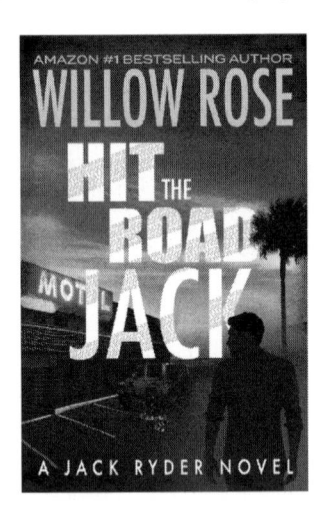

Prologue
DON'T COME BACK NO MORE

Prologue

MAY 2012

SHE HAS no idea who she is or where she is and cares to know neither. For some time, for what seems like forever, she has been in this daze. This haze, in complete darkness with nothing but the sounds. Sounds coming from outside her body, from outside her head. Sometimes, the sounds fade and there is only the darkness.

As time passes, she becomes aware that there are two realities. The one in her mind, filled with darkness and pain and then the one outside of her, where something or someone else is living, acting, smelling and…singing.

Yes, that's it. Someone is singing. Does she know the song?

…*What you say?*

The darkness is soon replaced by light. Still, her eyes are too heavy to open. Her consciousness returns slowly. Enough to start asking questions. Where is she? How did she end up here? A series of pictures of her at home come to her mind. She is waiting. What is she waiting for?

…*I guess if you said so.*

Him. She is waiting for him. She is checking her hair in the mirror every five minutes or so. Then correcting the make-up, looking at the clock again. Where is he? She looks out through the window and at the street and the many staring neighboring windows. A feeling of guilt hits her. Somehow, it seems wrong for this kind of thing to take place in broad daylight.

…*That's right!*

A car drives up. The anticipation. The butterflies in her stomach. The sound of the doorbell. She is straightening her dress and taking a last glance in the mirror. The next second, she is in his embrace. He is holding her so tight she closes her eyes and breathes him in until his lips cover hers and she swims away.

...*Whoa, Woman, oh woman, don't treat me so mean.*

His breath is pumping against her skin. She feels his hands on her breasts, under her skirt, coming closer, while he presses her up against the wall. She feels him in his hand. He is hard now, moaning in her ear.

"Where's your husband?" he whispers.

"Work," she moans back, feeling self-conscious. Why did he have to bring up her husband? The guilt is killing her. "The kids are in school."

"Good," he moans. "No one can ever know. Remember that. No one."

...*You're the meanest old woman that I've ever seen.*

He pushes himself inside of her and pumps. She lets herself get into the moment, but as soon as it is over, she finds herself regretting it...while he zips up the pants of his suit and kisses her gently on the lips, whispering, *same time next week*? She regrets having started it all. They are both married with children, and this is only an affair. Could never be anything else, even if she dreamt about it. The sex is great, but she wants more than just seeing him on her lunch break. But she can never tell him. She can never explain to him how much she hates this awkward moment that follows the sex.

"They're expecting me at the office...I have a meeting," he says, and puts his tie back on. "I'd better..."

...*Hit the road, Jack!*

She finally opens her eyes with a loud gasp. The bright light hurts her. Water is being splashed in her face. She can't breathe. The bathtub is slippery when she tries to get up. Her eyes lock with another set of eyes. The eyes of a man. He is staring at her with a twisted smile. She gasps again, suddenly remembering those dark chili eyes.

"*I guess if you said so...I'd have to pack my things and go*," he sings.

"You," she gasps. Breathing is hard for her. She feels like she is still choking. She is hyperventilating. Panicking.

The man smiles. On his neck crawls a snake. How does that old saying go again? *Red, black, yellow kills a fellow?* This one is all of that, all those colors. It stares at her while moving its tongue back and forth.

Prologue

The man is holding a washcloth in his hand. She looks down at her naked body. The smell of chlorine is strong and makes her eyes water.

"You tried to kill me," she says, while panting with anxiety.

I have to get home. Help me. I have to get home to my children! Oh, God. I can hear their voices! Am I going mad? I think I can hear them!

"I guess I didn't do a very good job, then," he answers. His chillingly calm voice is piercing through every bone in her body.

"I'll try again. *That's right!*"

Prologue
MAY 2012

SHE HAD NEVER BEEN MORE beautiful than in this exact moment. No woman ever had. So fragile, her skin so pale it almost looked bluish. The man who called himself the Snakecharmer stared at her body. It was still in the bathtub. He was still panting from the exertion, his hands shaking and hurting from strangling the girl. He felt so aroused in this moment, staring at the dead body. It was the most fascinating thing in the world. How the body simply ceased to function. And almost as fascinating was what followed next. The human decaying process. It wasn't something new. Fascination with death had occurred all throughout human history, characterized by obsessions with death and all things related to death. The Egyptians mummified their dead. He had always wished he could do the same. Keep his dead forever and ever. He remembered as a child how he would sometimes lie down in front of the mirror and try to lie completely still and look at himself, imagining he was looking at a dead body. He would capture cats and kill them and keep them in his room, just to watch what would happen to them. He wanted so badly to stop the decaying process, he wanted them to remain the same always and never leave.

 The Snakecharmer stared at the girl with fascination in his eyes. He caught his breath and calmed down again. He still felt the adrenalin rushing through his veins while he finished washing the girl. He washed away all the dirt, all the smells on her body. He reached down

Prologue

and cleaned her thoroughly between her legs. Scrubbed her to make sure he got all the dirt away, all the filth and impurities.

Then, he dried her with a towel before he pulled her onto the bathroom floor. His companions, his two pet Coral snakes, were sliding across her dead body. He grabbed one and let it slide across his arm while petting it. Then he knelt next to the girl and stroked her gently across her hair, making sure it wasn't in her face. Her blue eyes stared into the ceiling.

"Now, you'll never leave," he whispered.

With his cellphone, he took a picture of her naked body. That was his mummification. His way to always cherish the moment. To always remember. He never wanted to forget how beautiful she was.

He dried her with a towel. He brushed her brown hair with gentle strokes. He took yet another picture before he lifted her up and carried her into the bedroom, where he placed her in a chair, then sat in front of her and placed his head in her lap.

They would stay like this until she started to smell.

Part I
I GUESS IF YOU SAY SO

Chapter 1

JANUARY 2015

HE TOOK the dog out in the yard and shut the door carefully behind him, making sure he didn't make a sound to wake up his sleeping parents. It was Monday, but they had been very loud last night. The kitchen counter was still covered with empty bottles.

At first, Ben had waited patiently in the living room, watching a couple of shows on TV, waiting for his parents to wake up. When the clock passed nine, he knew he wouldn't make it to school that day either, and that was too bad because they had a fieldtrip to the zoo today and Ben had been looking forward to it. When they still hadn't shown up at ten o'clock, he decided the dog had to go out. The old Labrador kept sitting by the door and scraping on it. It had to go.

So, Ben took Bobby out in the backyard. He had to go with him. The yard ended at the canal, and Bobby had more than once jumped into the water. Ben had to keep an eye on him to make sure he didn't do it again. It had been such a mess last time, since the dog couldn't climb back up over the seawall on his own, so Ben's dad had to jump into the blurry water and carry the dog out.

The dog quickly gave in to nature and did his business. Ben had a plastic bag that he picked it up with and threw it in the trash can behind the house.

It was a beautiful day out. One of those clear days with a blue sky and not a cloud anywhere on the horizon. The wind was blowing out of the north and had been for two days, making the air drier. For once, Ben's shirt didn't stick to his body.

He threw the ball a few times for the dog to get some exercise. Ben could smell the ocean, even though he lived on the back side of the barrier island. When it was quiet, he could even hear it too. The waves had to be good. If he wasn't too sick from drinking last night, his dad might take him surfing.

Ben really hoped he would.

It had been months since his dad last took him to the beach. He never seemed to have time anymore. Sometimes, Ben would take his bike and ride down there by himself, but it was never as much fun as when the entire family went. They never seemed to do much together anymore. Ben wondered if it had anything to do with what happened to his baby sister a year ago. He never understood exactly what had happened. He just knew she didn't wake up one morning when their mother went to pick her up from her crib. Then his parents cried and cried for days and they had held a big funeral. But the crying hadn't stopped for a long time. Not until it was replaced with a lot of sleeping and his parents staying up all night, and all the empty bottles that Ben often cleaned up from the kitchen and put in the recycling bin.

Bobby brought back the ball and placed it at Ben's feet. He picked it up and threw it again. It landed close to the seawall. Luckily, it didn't fall in. Bobby ran to get it, then placed it at Ben's feet again, looking at him expectantly.

"Really? One more time, then we're done," he said, thinking he'd better get back inside and start cleaning up. He picked up the ball and threw it. The dog stormed after it again and disappeared for a second down the hill leading to the canal. Ben couldn't see him.

"Bobby?" he yelled. "Come on, boy. We need to get back inside."

He stared in the direction of the canal. He couldn't see the bottom of the yard. He had no idea if Bobby had jumped in the water again. His heart started to pound. He would have to wake up his dad if he did. He was the only one who could get Bobby out of the water.

Ben stood frozen for a few seconds until he heard the sound of Bobby's collar, and a second later spotted his black dog running towards him with his tongue hanging out of his mouth.

"Bobby!" Ben said. He bent down and petted his dog and best friend. "You scared me, buddy. You forgot the ball. Well, we'll have to get that later. Now, let's go back inside and see if Mom and Dad are awake."

Prologue

Ben grabbed the handle and opened the door. He let Bobby go in first.

"Mom?" he called.

But there was no answer. They were probably still asleep. Ben found some dog food in the cabinet and pulled the bag out. He spilled on the floor when he filled Bobby's tray. He had no idea how much the dog needed, so he made sure to give him enough, and poured till the bowl overflowed. Ben found a garbage bag under the sink and had removed some of the bottles, when Bobby suddenly started growling. The dog ran to the bottom of the stairs and barked. Ben found this to be strange. It was very unlike Bobby to act this way.

"What's the matter, boy? Are Mom and Dad awake?"

The dog kept barking and growling.

"Stop it!" Ben yelled, knowing how much his dad hated it when Bobby barked. "Bad dog."

But Bobby didn't stop. He moved closer and closer to the stairs and kept barking until the dog finally ran up the stairs.

"No! Bobby!" Ben yelled. "Come back down here!"

Ben stared up the stairs after the dog, wondering if he dared to go up there. His dad always got so mad if he went upstairs when they were sleeping. He wasn't allowed up there until they got out of bed. But, if he found Bobby up there, his dad would get really mad. Probably talk about getting rid of him again.

He's my best friend. Don't take my friend away.

"Bobby," he whispered. "Come back down here."

Ben's heart was racing in his chest. There wasn't a sound coming from upstairs. Ben held his breath, not knowing what to do. The last thing he wanted on a day like today was to make his dad angry. He expected his dad to start yelling any second now.

Oh no, what if he jumps into their bed? Dad is going to get so mad. He's gonna get real mad at Bobby.

"Bobby?" Ben whispered a little louder.

There was movement on the stairs, the black lab peeked his head out, then ran down the stairs.

"There you are," Ben said with relief. Bobby ran past him and sprang up on the couch.

"What do you have in your mouth? Not one of mom's shoes again."

It didn't look like it was big enough to be a shoe. Ben walked closer, thinking if it was a pair of Mommy's panties again, then the dog was dead. He reached down and grabbed the dog's mouth, then opened it and pulled out whatever it was. He looked down with a small shriek at what had come out of the dog's mouth. He felt nauseated, like the time when he had the stomach-bug and spent the entire night in the bathroom. Only this was worse.

It's a finger. A finger wearing Mommy's ring!

Chapter 2

JANUARY 2015

"HIT THE ROAD, Jack, and don't you come back no more no more no more."

The children's voices were screaming more than singing on the bus. I preferred *Wheels on the Bus*, but the kids thought it was oh so fun, since my name was Jack and I was actually driving the bus. I had volunteered to drive them to the Brevard Zoo for their field trip today. Two of the children, the pretty blonde twins in the back named Abigail and Austin, were mine. A boy and a girl. Just started Kindergarten six months ago. I could hardly believe how fast time passed. Everybody told me it would, but still. It was hard to believe.

I was thirty-five and a single dad of three children. My wife, Arianna, ran out on us four years ago…when the twins were almost two years old. It was too much, she told me. She couldn't cope with the children or me. She especially had a hard time taking care of Emily. Emily was my ex-partner's daughter. My ex-partner, Lisa, was shot on duty ten years ago during a chase in downtown Miami. The shooter was never captured, and it haunted me daily. I took Emily in after her mother died. What else could I have done? I felt guilty for what had happened to her mother. I was supposed to have protected my partner. Plus, the girl didn't know her father. Lisa never told anyone who he was; she didn't have any of her parents or siblings left, except for a homeless brother who was in no condition to take care of a child. So, I got custody and decided to give Emily the best life I could. She was six when I took her in, sixteen now, and at an age where it was hard for anyone to love you, besides your mom and dad. I tried hard to be both for her. Not always with much success. The fact was, I had no idea what it was like to be a black teenage girl.

Personally, I believed Arianna had depression after the birth of the twins, but she never let me close enough to talk about it. She cried for months after the twins were born, then one day out of the blue, she told me she had to go. That she couldn't stay or it would end up killing her. I cried and begged her to stay, but there was nothing I could do. She had made up her mind. She was going back upstate, and that was all I needed to know. I shouldn't look for her, she said.

"Are you coming back?" I asked, my voice breaking. I couldn't believe anyone would leave her own children.

"I don't know, Jack."

"But...The children? They need you? They need their mother?"

"I can't be the mother you want me to be, Jack. I'm just not cut out for it. I'm sorry."

Then she left. Just like that. I had no idea how to explain it to the kids, but somehow I did. As soon as they started asking questions, I told them their mother had left and that I believed she was coming back one day. Some, maybe a lot of people, including my mother, might have told me it was insane to tell them that she might be coming back, but that's what I did. I couldn't bear the thought of them growing up with the knowledge that their own mother didn't want them. I couldn't bear for Emily to know that she was part of the reason why Arianna had left us, left the twins motherless. I just couldn't. I had to leave them with some sort of hope. And maybe I needed to believe it too. I needed to believe that she hadn't just abandoned us...that she had some stuff she needed to work out and soon she would be back. At least for the twins. They needed their mother and asked for her often. It was getting harder and harder for me to believe she was coming back for them. But I still said she would.

And there they were.

On the back seat of the bus, singing along with their classmates, happier than most of them. Mother or no mother, I had provided a good life for them in our little town of Cocoa Beach. As a detective working for the Brevard County Sheriff's Office, working their homicide unit, I had lots of spare time and they had their grandparents

Prologue

close by. They received all the love in the world from me and their grandparents, who loved them to death (and let them get away with just about anything).

Some might think they were spoiled brats, but to me they were the love of my life, the light, the…the…

What the heck were they doing in the back?

I hit the brakes a little too hard at the red light. All the kids on the bus fell forwards. The teacher, Mrs. Allen, whined and held on to her purse.

"Abigail and Austin!" I thundered through the bus. "Stop that right now!"

The twins grinned and looked at one another, then continued to smear chocolate on each other's faces. Chocolate from those small boxes with Nutella and sticks you dipped in it. Boxes their grandmother had given them for snack, even though I told her it had to be healthy.

"Now!" I yelled.

"Sorry, Dad," they yelled in unison.

"Well…wipe that off or…"

I never made it any further before the phone in my pocket vibrated. I pulled it out and started driving again as the light turned green.

"Ryder. We need you. I spoke with Ron and he told me you would be assisting us. We desperately need your help."

It was the head of the Cocoa Beach Police Department. Weasel, we called her. I didn't know why. Maybe it had to do with the fact that her name was Weslie Seal. Maybe it was just because she kind of looked like a weasel because her body was long and slender, but her legs very short. Ron Harper was the county sheriff and my boss.

"Yes? When?"

"Now."

"But…I'm…"

"This is big. We need you now."

"If you say so. I'll get there as fast as I can," I said, and turned off towards the entrance to the zoo. The kids all screamed with joy when they saw the sign. Mrs. Allen shushed them.

"What, are you running a day-care now? Not that I have the time to care. Everything is upside down around here. We have a dead body. I'll text you the address. Meet you there."

. . .

END OF EXCERPT.

Order your copy today!

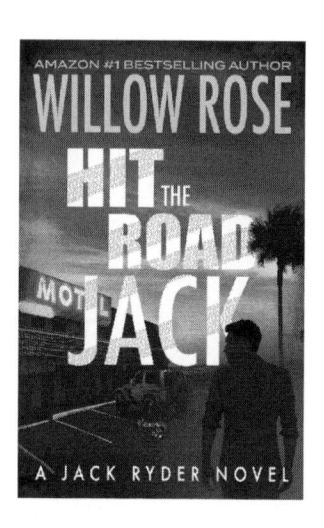

CLICK HERE TO ORDER

About the Author

Willow Rose is a multi-million-copy best-selling Author and an Amazon ALL-star Author of more than 60 novels. Her books are sold all over the world.

She writes Mystery, Thriller, Paranormal, Romance, Suspense, Horror, Supernatural thrillers, and Fantasy.

Willow's books are fast-paced, nail-biting pageturners with twists you won't see coming. That's why her fans call her The Queen of Scream.

Several of her books have reached the Kindle top 10 of ALL books in the US, UK, and Canada. She has sold more than three million books all over the world.

Willow lives on Florida's Space Coast with her husband and two daughters. When she is not writing or reading, you will find her surfing and watch the dolphins play in the waves of the Atlantic Ocean.

To be the first to hear about new releases and bargains—from Willow Rose—sign up below to be on the VIP List. (I promise not to share your email with anyone else, and I won't clutter your inbox.)

- SIGN UP TO BE ON THE VIP LIST HERE :
http://readerlinks.com/l/415254

Tired of too many emails? Text the word: "willowrose" to 31996 to sign up to Willow's VIP text List to get a text alert with news about New Releases, Giveaways, Bargains and Free books from Willow.

Follow Willow Rose on BookBub:
https://www.bookbub.com/authors/willow-rose

Connect with Willow online:

https://www.amazon.com/Willow-Rose/e/B004X2WHBQ
https://www.facebook.com/willowredrose/
https://twitter.com/madamwillowrose
http://www.goodreads.com/author/show/4804769.Willow_Rose
Http://www.willow-rose.net
madamewillowrose@gmail.com

facebook.com/willowredrose

twitter.com/madamwillowrose

instagram.com/madamewillowrose

Books by the Author

MYSTERY/THRILLER/HORROR NOVELS

- IN ONE FELL SWOOP
- UMBRELLA MAN
- BLACKBIRD FLY
- TO HELL IN A HANDBASKET
- EDWINA

MARY MILLS MYSTERY SERIES

- WHAT HURTS THE MOST
- YOU CAN RUN
- YOU CAN'T HIDE
- CAREFUL LITTLE EYES

EVA RAE THOMAS MYSTERY SERIES

- DON'T LIE TO ME
- WHAT YOU DID
- NEVER EVER
- SAY YOU LOVE ME

EMMA FROST SERIES

- ITSY BITSY SPIDER
- MISS DOLLY HAD A DOLLY
- RUN, RUN AS FAST AS YOU CAN
- CROSS YOUR HEART AND HOPE TO DIE
- PEEK-A-BOO I SEE YOU
- TWEEDLEDUM AND TWEEDLEDEE
- EASY AS ONE, TWO, THREE
- THERE'S NO PLACE LIKE HOME
- SLENDERMAN
- WHERE THE WILD ROSES GROW
- WALTZING MATHILDA

- Drip Drop Dead

JACK RYDER SERIES

- Hit the Road Jack
- Slip out the Back Jack
- The House that Jack Built
- Black Jack
- Girl Next Door
- Her Final Word
- Don't Tell

REBEKKA FRANCK SERIES

- One, Two…He is Coming for You
- Three, Four…Better Lock Your Door
- Five, Six…Grab your Crucifix
- Seven, Eight…Gonna Stay up Late
- Nine, Ten…Never Sleep Again
- Eleven, Twelve…Dig and Delve
- Thirteen, Fourteen…Little Boy Unseen
- Better Not Cry
- Ten Little Girls
- It Ends Here

HORROR SHORT-STORIES

- Mommy Dearest
- The Bird
- Better watch out
- Eenie, Meenie
- Rock-a-Bye Baby
- Nibble, Nibble, Crunch
- Humpty Dumpty
- Chain Letter

PARANORMAL SUSPENSE/ROMANCE NOVELS

- In Cold Blood
- The Surge
- Girl Divided

THE VAMPIRES OF SHADOW HILLS SERIES

- Flesh and Blood
- Blood and Fire
- Fire and Beauty
- Beauty and Beasts
- Beasts and Magic
- Magic and Witchcraft
- Witchcraft and War
- War and Order
- Order and Chaos
- Chaos and Courage

THE AFTERLIFE SERIES

- Beyond
- Serenity
- Endurance
- Courageous

THE WOLFBOY CHRONICLES

- A Gypsy Song
- I am WOLF

DAUGHTERS OF THE JAGUAR

- Savage
- Broken

Copyright Willow Rose 2019
Published by BUOY MEDIA LLC
All rights reserved.

No part of this book may be reproduced, scanned, or distributed in any printed or electronic form without permission from the author.

This is a work of fiction. Any resemblance of characters to actual persons, living or dead is purely coincidental. The Author holds exclusive rights to this work. Unauthorized duplication is prohibited.

Cover design by Juan Villar Padron,
https://www.juanjpadron.com

Special thanks to my editor Janell Parque
http://janellparque.blogspot.com/

To be the first to hear about new releases and bargains from Willow Rose, sign up below to be on the VIP List. (I promise not to share your email with anyone else, and I won't clutter your inbox.)

- Tap here to sign up to be on the VIP LIST -

Tired of too many emails? Text the word: "willowrose" to 31996 to sign up to Willow's VIP text List to get a text alert with news about New Releases, Giveaways, Bargains and Free books from Willow.

Follow Willow Rose on BookBub:

BB Follow me on BookBub

Connect with Willow online:
Facebook

Twitter
GoodReads
willow-rose.net
madamewillowrose@gmail.com

Contents

Copyright — iii

DON'T LIE TO ME

Prologue	5
Untitled	7
Untitled	9
Untitled	11
Chapter 1	14
Chapter 2	17
Chapter 3	20
Chapter 4	23
Chapter 5	26
Chapter 6	29
Chapter 7	32
Chapter 8	34
Chapter 9	36
Chapter 10	39
Chapter 11	42
Chapter 12	45
Chapter 13	47
Chapter 14	49
Chapter 15	54
Chapter 16	57
Chapter 17	59
Chapter 18	62
Chapter 19	65
Chapter 20	67
Chapter 21	69
Chapter 22	72
Chapter 23	75
Chapter 24	78

Chapter 25	80
Chapter 26	83
Chapter 27	86
Chapter 28	88
Chapter 29	90
Chapter 30	94
Chapter 31	96
Chapter 32	98
Chapter 33	100
Chapter 34	103
Chapter 35	105
Chapter 36	107
Chapter 37	109
Chapter 38	111
Chapter 39	113
Chapter 40	116
Chapter 41	119
Chapter 42	122
Chapter 43	125
Chapter 44	127
Chapter 45	129
Chapter 46	134
Chapter 47	136
Chapter 48	138
Chapter 49	140
Chapter 50	145
Chapter 51	148
Chapter 52	150
Chapter 53	154
Chapter 54	157
Chapter 55	161
Chapter 56	163
Chapter 57	166
Chapter 58	168
Chapter 59	170
Chapter 60	172
Chapter 61	175
Chapter 62	178
Chapter 63	180
Chapter 64	182

Chapter 65	185
Chapter 66	188
Chapter 67	192
Chapter 68	195
Chapter 69	198
Chapter 70	200
Chapter 71	202
Chapter 72	205
Chapter 73	207
Chapter 74	209
Chapter 75	211
Chapter 76	213
Chapter 77	216
Chapter 78	220
Chapter 79	222
Chapter 80	224
Chapter 81	226
Chapter 82	229
Chapter 83	232
Chapter 84	234
Chapter 85	238
Chapter 86	240
Chapter 87	242
Chapter 88	248
Chapter 89	250
Chapter 90	252
Chapter 91	254

WHAT YOU DID

Prologue	259
Chapter 1	263
Chapter 2	265
Chapter 3	267
Chapter 4	270
Chapter 5	277
Chapter 6	279
Chapter 7	282
Chapter 8	286

Chapter 9	288
Chapter 10	291
Chapter 11	293
Chapter 12	296
Chapter 13	299
Chapter 14	301
Chapter 15	305
Chapter 16	307
Chapter 17	309
Chapter 18	311
Chapter 19	313
Chapter 20	315
Chapter 21	317
Chapter 22	319
Chapter 23	321
Chapter 24	324
Chapter 25	327
Chapter 26	330
Chapter 27	333
Chapter 28	336
Chapter 29	338
Chapter 30	342
Chapter 31	344
Chapter 32	347
Chapter 33	349
Chapter 34	354
Chapter 35	358
Chapter 36	361
Chapter 37	365
Chapter 38	367
Chapter 39	369
Chapter 40	371
Chapter 41	376
Chapter 42	378
Chapter 43	381
Chapter 44	384
Chapter 45	387
Chapter 46	389
Chapter 47	391
Chapter 48	393

Chapter 49	396
Chapter 50	399
Chapter 51	402
Chapter 52	404
Chapter 53	406
Chapter 54	409
Chapter 55	412
Chapter 56	414
Chapter 57	416
Chapter 58	418
Chapter 59	420
Chapter 60	422
Chapter 61	426
Chapter 62	428
Chapter 63	430
Chapter 64	433
Chapter 65	435
Chapter 66	438
Chapter 67	440
Chapter 68	442
Chapter 69	445
Chapter 70	447
Chapter 71	449
Chapter 72	451
Chapter 73	453
Chapter 74	455
Chapter 75	457
Chapter 76	459
Chapter 77	465
Chapter 78	467
Chapter 79	469
Chapter 80	471
Chapter 81	473
Chapter 82	475
Chapter 83	479
Chapter 84	481
Chapter 85	483
Chapter 86	485
Chapter 87	487
Chapter 88	490

Chapter 89   492

NEVER EVER

Prologue	497
Chapter 1	499
Chapter 2	501
ONE MONTH LATER	503
Chapter 3	504
Chapter 4	506
Chapter 5	508
Chapter 6	511
Chapter 7	514
Chapter 8	516
Chapter 9	518
Chapter 10	520
Chapter 11	524
Chapter 12	526
Chapter 13	528
Chapter 14	531
Chapter 15	534
Chapter 16	536
Chapter 17	538
Chapter 18	541
Chapter 19	544
Chapter 20	546
Chapter 21	548
Chapter 22	551
Chapter 23	553
Chapter 24	555
Chapter 25	558
Chapter 26	560
Chapter 27	562
Chapter 28	565
Chapter 29	567
Chapter 30	571
Chapter 31	573
Chapter 32	575
Chapter 33	577

Chapter 34	580
Chapter 35	583
Chapter 36	585
Chapter 37	588
Chapter 38	591
Chapter 39	593
Chapter 40	596
Chapter 41	598
Chapter 42	600
Chapter 43	602
Chapter 44	605
Chapter 45	608
Chapter 46	611
Chapter 47	613
Chapter 48	615
Chapter 49	617
Chapter 50	619
Chapter 51	621
Chapter 52	624
Chapter 53	626
Chapter 54	628
Chapter 55	631
Chapter 56	633
Chapter 57	636
Chapter 58	639
Chapter 59	641
Chapter 60	643
Chapter 61	645
Chapter 62	647
Chapter 63	649
Chapter 64	651
Chapter 65	653
Chapter 66	656
Chapter 67	658
Chapter 68	660
Chapter 69	662
Chapter 70	664
Chapter 71	666
Chapter 72	669
Chapter 73	671

Chapter 74	673
Chapter 75	675
Chapter 76	678
Chapter 77	680
Chapter 78	682
Chapter 79	686
Chapter 80	688
Chapter 81	690
Chapter 82	692
Chapter 83	694
Chapter 84	696
Chapter 85	698
Chapter 86	701
Chapter 87	703
Chapter 88	706
Chapter 89	708
Chapter 90	711
Chapter 91	713
Chapter 92	716
Chapter 93	718
Chapter 94	721
Chapter 95	724
Chapter 96	726
Chapter 97	728
Chapter 98	730
Chapter 99	733
Chapter 100	736
Chapter 101	739
Chapter 102	741
Chapter 103	743
Chapter 104	745
Chapter 105	747
Chapter 106	752
THREE DAYS LATER	754
Chapter 107	755
Afterword	761
Hit The Road Jack (Jack Ryder Series Book 1)	762

Prologue

Prologue   765
Prologue   768

Part I

Chapter 1   773
Chapter 2   777

Order your copy today!

About the Author   783
Books by the Author   785
Copyright   789

Printed in Great Britain
by Amazon